THE BEST SCIENCE FICTION AND FANTASY OF THE YEAR

Volume Ten

Also Edited by Jonathan Strahan

Best Short Novels
(2004 through 2007)

Fantasy: The Very Best of 2005

Science Fiction: The Very Best of 2005

The Best Science Fiction and Fantasy of the Year: Volumes 1 - 10

Eclipse: New Science Fiction and Fantasy (Vols 1-4)

The Starry Rift: Tales of New Tomorrows

Life on Mars: Tales of New Frontiers

Under My Hat: Tales from the Cauldron (forthcoming)

Godlike Machines

The Infinity Project 1: Engineering Infinity

The Infinity Project 2: Edge of Infinity

The Infinity Project 3: Reach for Infinity

The Infinity Project 4: Meeting Infinity

The Infinity Project 5: Bridging Infinity (forthcoming)

The Infinity Project 6: Infinity Wars (forthcoming)

Fearsome Journeys

Fearsome Magics

Drowned Worlds, Wild Shores (forthcoming)

With Lou Anders
Swords and Dark Magic: The New Sword and Sorcery

With Charles N. Brown
The Locus Awards: Thirty Years of the Best in Fantasy and Science Fiction

With Jeremy G. Byrne
The Year's Best Australian Science Fiction and Fantasy: Volume 1

The Year's Best Australian Science Fiction and Fantasy: Volume 2

Eidolon 1

With Jack Dann
Legends of Australian Fantasy

With Gardner Dozois
The New Space Opera

The New Space Opera 2

With Karen Haber
Science Fiction: Best of 2003

Science Fiction: Best of 2004

Fantasy: Best of 2004

With Marianne S. Jablon
Wings of Fire

EDITED BY **JONATHAN STRAHAN**

THE BEST SCIENCE FICTION & FANTASY OF THE YEAR

VOLUME TEN

First published 2016 by Solaris
an imprint of Rebellion Publishing Ltd,
Riverside House, Osney Mead,
Oxford, OX2 0ES, UK

www.solarisbooks.com

UK ISBN 978 1 78108 436 6
US ISBN 978 1 78108 437 3

Cover by Dominic Harman

10 9 8 7 6 5 4 3 2 1

A CIP catalogue record for this book is available from the
British Library.

Designed & typeset by Rebellion Publishing

Printed in Denmark

In memory of David G. Hartwell, one of the finest editors to have worked in the science fiction field, with affection and respect.

ACKNOWLEDGEMENTS

THIS IS THE tenth volume of *The Best Science Fiction and Fantasy of the Year* anthology series, which started back in 2007 at Night Shade and moved to Solaris in 2013. I'd like to thank Jason Williams and Jeremy Lassen for getting behind the book at the beginning, and Ross Lockhart for all of his hard work on the series in the later days. I'd especially like to thank Jonathan Oliver and Ben Smith at Solaris for taking the risk on picking the series up, and for running with it in the way that they have. I will always be grateful to them for stepping in and for believing in the books and in me. Special thanks to my wonderful agent Howard Morhaim who for over a decade now has had my back and helped make good things happen. Finally, most special thanks of all to Marianne, Jessica, and Sophie. I always say that every moment spent working on these books is stolen from them, but it's true, and I'm forever grateful to them for their love, support and generosity.

CONTENTS

INTRODUCTION

Jonathan Strahan

WELCOME TO *THE Best Science Fiction and Fantasy of the Year*. This is the tenth volume in this series, which aims to collect the best science fiction and fantasy stories published during the preceding year. A decade is a long time, and a lot has changed since we started out, but what has remained constant throughout the decade is that there is a *lot* of great science fiction and fantasy being published every year.

So, how was the year? Well, 2015 must have seemed like a pretty crazy year if you were outside the fishbowl that is science fiction and fantasy and looking in. A whole lot of insider tennis spilled over into mainstream media, which made it looked like SF was at war with itself. And it pretty much was. One group said or did one thing, another group said or did another. A whole lot of invective was sprayed, and it seemed like you *had* to take sides. It made it that much harder to be part of the science fiction community, and if (sadly) some people decided it just wasn't worth the grief who could blame them?

While the battle between Old Skool EssEff and that NewStuff (or Insider Tennis Players and the Forces of Right or however you wanted to characterize it) was being fought in social media feeds and convention business meetings the world went on. New stories appeared. A lot of them. Authors debuted. Some terrific ones. And short fiction continued to be published in a never-ending torrent, a gift of plenty so great that no one could hope to keep track of it, never mind read it all. Was it a good year, though, in amongst all of the *Sturm und Drang*? Who knows? I read some pretty remarkable fiction, found new writers to fall in love with, and was encouraged by the appearance of more and more fiction across the globe. It was an exciting year to be a reader, and you can't ask for much more than that.

I spent most of my 2015 time reading anthologies, collections, magazines, and scouring ebooks and websites for the best short fiction I could find. And, to cap off the year, I spent the end of the year working with a team of experts on compiling the *Locus* short fiction Recommended Reading List and selecting stories for this book, which means I spent a lot of time thinking about whether it was a good year or a bad year or whatever. And I heard a *lot* of opinions. "A lousy year for short science fiction," said one colleague. "A worse year for fantasy anthologies," said another. "A good year for horror," said still another. Was it?

Well, first of all, 2015 was another year where no one read most or all or even a significant bit of all of the short fiction published. No one has useful statistics on the amount of short fiction being published, and I don't know that I'd trust anyone who claimed that they did. I'd guesstimate that there were more than 10,000 new stories published, but that's only an extrapolative guess. Given the torrent, though, where could you turn to find great short fiction?

The major magazines were a pretty safe bet, though no single magazine dominated this year. The Big Three – *Tor.com*, *Asimov's*, and *Clarkesworld* – all had good years, with *Tor.com* probably having the best year of the lot. It published a story a week or so, ranging from literary science fiction to fantasy to horror. With a large group of editors acquiring fiction, the site doesn't have a single editorial voice but that works to its advantage, I think. During the year it published extraordinary novellas by Kelly Robson ("Waters of Versailles"), Usman T. Malik ("The Pauper Prince and the Eucalyptus Jinn"), as well as great shorter pieces by David Herter, Priya Sharma, Michael Swanwick, John Chu, Jeffrey Ford, Yoon Ha Lee, and others. I should also mention the Tor.com book program, for which I acquired stories during the year. It featured some very fine stories by Kai Ashante Wilson, Nnedi Okorafor, K.J. Parker, and others.

Asimov's also had a strong year, possibly its best in a while. As has always been the case, it publishes a good range of SF and fantasy, and continues to develop new writers. As was the case for *Tor.com*, *Asimov's* very best stories in 2015 were at novella length. Greg Egan's "The Four Thousand, the Eight Hundred" was the best hard science fiction novella of 2015, as Egan again powerfully used SF to examine important issues. It's my top pick for the Hugo. Also outstanding was Aliette de Bodard's "The Citadel of Weeping Pearls",

Kristine Kathryn Rusch's "Inhuman Garbage", and Sam J. Miller's "Calved". Sam J. Miller and Kelly Robson had outstanding years publishing some great stories in several venues. *Asimov's* also featured strong stories by Gregory Norman Bossert, Sarah Pinsker, Robert Reed, Indrapramit Das, and others.

Clarkesworld seemed to switch focus during 2015, moving away from being a general SF and fantasy magazine towards a much more SF-focused approach by year's end. Although 2015 wasn't its best year ever, it was a good one, and it featured very strong stories by Naomi Kritzer, Sam J. Miller, Catherynne M. Valente, Quifan Chen, Aliette de Bodard, Kelly Robson, and others.

The Magazine of Fantasy and Science Fiction changed editors early in the year, with publisher Gordon van Gelder stepping down and handing the editorial reins over to Charles Coleman Finlay. It's hard to know exactly how much of the work published in 2015 was in inventory, but *F&SF* did seem to feature a wider variety of writers towards year's end than it had of late. I was particularly impressed by Carter Scholz's powerful hard SF novella "Gypsy" (reprinted from his collection *Gypsy Plus...*), Tamsyn Muir's Lovecraftian "The Deepwater Bride", and Jeffrey Ford's "The Winter Wraith". It'll be interesting to see how the magazine continues to evolve during the year ahead. *F&SF* was once described to me as *The New Yorker* of the genre, and I'd love to see it restored to that position.

Lightspeed, under the editorship of John Joseph Adams and others, was easily in the top rank, and had its best year yet publishing some great stories by Chaz Brenchley, Sam J. Miller, Nike Sulway, Caroline M. Yoachim, Amal El-Mohtar, and producing several special issues of interest. There were a lot of other magazines out there, and a lot of them published worthwhile work. Andy Cox's *Interzone* had a good year, featuring a great story by Alastair Reynolds alongside strong work from many of its regulars. *Analog* continued to publish strong hard SF with an old school twist as it has for many years now. There are literally too many other magazines to talk about, but I should mention new magazine *Uncanny*, which had a strong first full year of publication, while *Shimmer, Lady Churchill's Rosebud Wristlet, Beneath Ceaseless Skies, Apex, Cosmos,* and *Strange Horizons* (which published a fine Kelly Link story) were all worthwhile.

It's hard for me to say a lot about original anthologies during 2015, if only because I edited one myself. Still, although this year was weaker than last for really outstanding original anthologies, there were some good ones that were worth your time. I thought Nisi Shawl and Bill Campbell's *Stories for Chip* was one of the three or four best anthologies of 2015, with great stories by Geoff Ryman, Nick Harkaway, Nalo Hopkinson, and Nisi Shawl. Also outstanding was Gardner Dozois and George RR Martin's nostalgic *Old Venus*, which featured topnotch SF stories by Ian McDonald, Elizabeth Bear, and Garth Nix, and the Microsoft-published *Future Visions*, which had some of the year's best stories by Ann Leckie, Greg Bear, and Seanan McGuire. There weren't many straight fantasy anthologies published during 2015 that really stood out, though there were some great dark fantasy/horror anthologies, most notably *The Doll Collection* from the ever reliable Ellen Datlow. Probably the closest to a fantasy anthology, though, was John Joseph Adams' *Operation Arcana*, a military fantasy anthology with good work by Genevieve Valentine, Yoon Ha Lee and Carrie Vaughn. Also well worth noting are Nick Mamatas' and Matsumi Washington's *Hanzai Japan*, Ann VanderMeer and Jeff VanderMeer's *Sisters of the Revolution* (my pick for best reprint anthology of the year), and Maggie Stiefvater, Tessa Gratton & Brenna Yovanoff's really interesting writing workshop anthology, *The Anatomy of Curiosity*.

Given the amount of short fiction being published, it's hardly surprising that it was another great year for short story collections. Easily the best, or at least my favourite, collection of the year was Caitlin R. Kiernan's *Beneath the Oil-Dark Sea*, which features her tour de force novella "Black Helicopters". There really wasn't a better book published in 2015. That said, another even longer book really did give it a run for its money. Almost as good and maybe even more important, Leena Krohn's enormous *Collected Fiction* was released by the VanderMeers' Cheeky Frawg Press right at the end of the year and provides a staggering, voluminous insight into this important Finnish writer. Surely another award-nominee.

There were also some outstanding collections from a few better-known writers during the year. *Get in Trouble* by the playful, unpredictable, and always brilliant Kelly Link was a delight from start to finish. China Mieville's *Three Moments of an Explosion* was his first book in a while, and brought together recent stories with a swag of new ones, which gave us the best look at his shorter work so far. I loved "The Dowager of Bees", but a good handful of the stories here stand amongst the year's best. Genre superstar Neil Gaiman likes to produce miscellanies rather than collections, books that gather stories, poems, and odd bits and pieces that he's written over the preceding few years. His latest, *Trigger Warning* is very much in that tradition, but also manages to collect some of the best stories of his career along with excellent new novelette "Black Dog" (which appears here). Garth Nix, whose short fiction is underappreciated, delivered his first collection for adults, *To Hold the Bridge*. Led off by a strong 'Old Kingdom' novella, *To Hold the Bridge* features a truly impressive array of science fiction, fantasy, and horror, and deserves to be considered amongst the best of 2015.

These, of course, were not the only collections worth your attention. Eleanor Arnason's *Hidden Folk*, C.S.E. Cooney's *Bone Swans* (which features two terrific new novellas), Nalo Hopkinson's *Falling in Love With Hominids*, and Deborah Kalin's powerful *Cherry Crow Children* were all excellent and belong on your bookshelf. I'd also recommend *The Best of Gregory Benford* and James Morrow's *Reality by Other Means*. Both are major career retrospectives that deserve your attention.

With all of this fiction to choose from it's always difficult to whittle down the multitude of stories to the 200,000 odd words that go into this book. In some cases, a magazine or anthology may seem underrepresented because author had better stories elsewhere (this was true of both Kelly Robson and Sam Miller this year); in some cases stories were unavailable (a growing trend alas, and why the Greg Egan and China Mieville stories, for example are not here); and of course some were overlooked in the flood. Still, there's a balance here of science fiction and fantasy, perhaps liberally defined, and some of the best stories I could find in 365 days of solid reading. And looking back at the range and diversity of what I read in 2015, not all of which is mentioned here, it's hard not to feel that the genre is in fine fettle, and that any side issues that filled social media and news sites were really nothing of consequence. So, was it a good year? It always is, and I'm already reading for 2016 and it's looking to be a heck of a ride.

Jonathan Strahan
Perth, Western Australia
January 2016

BLACK DOG

Neil Gaiman

NEIL GAIMAN (WWW.NEILGAIMAN.COM) was born in England and worked as a freelance journalist before co-editing *Ghastly Beyond Belief* (with Kim Newman) and writing *Don't Panic: The Official Hitchhiker's Guide to the Galaxy Companion.* He started writing comics with *Violent Cases*, and established himself as one of the most important comics writers of his generation with award-winning series *The Sandman.* His first novel, *Good Omens* (with Terry Pratchett), appeared in 1991, and was followed by *Neverwhere, Stardust, American Gods, Coraline, Anansi Boys, The Graveyard Book*, and *The Ocean at the End of the Lane.* His most recent book is collection *Trigger Warning: Short Fictions and Disturbances.* Gaiman's work has won the Carnegie, Newbery, Hugo, World Fantasy, Bram Stoker, Locus, Geffen, International Horror Guild, Mythopoeic and Will Eisner Comic Industry awards.

There were ten tongues within one head
And one went out to fetch some bread,
To feed the living and the dead.
– Old Riddle

I

The Bar Guest

OUTSIDE THE PUB it was raining cats and dogs.

Shadow was still not entirely convinced that he was in a pub. True, there was a tiny bar at the back of the room, with bottles behind it and a couple of the huge taps you pulled, and there were several high tables and people were drinking at the tables, but it all felt like a room in somebody's house. The dogs helped reinforce that impression. It seemed to Shadow that everybody in the pub had a dog except for him.

"What kind of dogs are they?" Shadow asked, curious. The dogs reminded him of greyhounds, but they were smaller and seemed saner, more placid and less high-strung than the greyhounds he had encountered over the years.

"Lurchers," said the pub's landlord, coming out from behind the bar. He was carrying a pint of beer that he had poured for himself. "Best dogs. Poacher's dogs. Fast, smart, lethal." He bent down, scratched a chestnut-and-white brindled dog behind the ears. The dog stretched and luxuriated in the ear-scratching. It did not look particularly lethal, and Shadow said so.

The landlord, his hair a mop of gray and orange, scratched at his beard reflectively. "That's where you'd be wrong," he said. "I walked with his brother last week, down Cumpsy Lane. There's a fox, a big red reynard, pokes his head out of a hedge, no more than twenty meters down the road, then, plain as day, saunters out onto the track. Well, Needles sees it, and he's off after it like the clappers. Next thing you know, Needles has his teeth in reynard's neck, and one bite, one hard shake, and it's all over."

Shadow inspected Needles, a gray dog sleeping by the little fireplace. He looked harmless too. "So what sort of a breed is a lurcher? It's an English breed, yes?"

"It's not actually a breed," said a white-haired woman without a dog who had been leaning on a nearby table. "They're crossbred for speed, stamina. Sighthound, greyhound, collie."

The man next to her held up a finger. "You must understand," he said, cheerfully, "that there used to be laws about who could own purebred dogs. The local folk couldn't, but they could own mongrels. And lurchers are better and faster than pedigree dogs." He pushed his spectacles up his nose with the tip of his forefinger. He had a mutton-chop beard, brown flecked with white.

"Ask me, all mongrels are better than pedigree anything," said the woman. "It's why America is such an interesting country. Filled with mongrels." Shadow was not certain how old she was. Her hair was white, but she seemed younger than her hair.

"Actually, darling," said the man with the muttonchops, in his gentle voice, "I think you'll find that the Americans are keener on pedigree dogs than the

British. I met a woman from the American Kennel Club, and honestly, she scared me. I was scared."

"I wasn't talking about dogs, Ollie," said the woman. "I was talking about... Oh, never mind."

"What are you drinking?" asked the landlord.

There was a handwritten piece of paper taped to the wall by the bar telling customers not to order a lager 'as a punch in the face often offends.'

"What's good and local?" asked Shadow, who had learned that this was mostly the wisest thing to say.

The landlord and the woman had various suggestions as to which of the various local beers and ciders were good. The little mutton-chopped man interrupted them to point out that in his opinion *good* was not the avoidance of evil, but something more positive than that: it was making the world a better place. Then he chuckled, to show that he was only joking and that he knew that the conversation was really only about what to drink.

The beer the landlord poured for Shadow was dark and very bitter. He was not certain that he liked it. "What is it?"

"It's called Black Dog," said the woman. "I've heard people say it was named after the way you feel after you've had one too many."

"Like Churchill's moods," said the little man.

"Actually, the beer is named after a local dog," said a younger woman. She was wearing an olive-green sweater, and standing against the wall. "But not a real one. Semi-imaginary."

Shadow looked down at Needles, then hesitated. "Is it safe to scratch his head?" he asked, remembering the fate of the fox.

"Course it is," said the white-haired woman. "He loves it. Don't you?"

"Well. He practically had that tosser from Glossop's finger off," said the landlord. There was admiration mixed with warning in his voice.

"I think he was something in local government," said the woman. "And I've always thought that there's nothing wrong with dogs biting *them*. Or VAT inspectors."

The woman in the green sweater moved over to Shadow. She was not holding a drink. She had dark, short hair, and a crop of freckles that spattered her nose and cheeks. She looked at Shadow. "You aren't in local government, are you?"

Shadow shook his head. He said, "I'm kind of a tourist." It was not actually untrue. He was traveling, anyway.

"You're Canadian?" said the muttonchop man.

"American," said Shadow. "But I've been on the road for a while now."

"Then," said the white-haired woman, "you aren't actually a tourist. Tourists turn up, see the sights and leave."

Shadow shrugged, smiled, and leaned down. He scratched the landlord's lurcher on the back of its head.

"You're not a dog person, are you?" asked the dark-haired woman.

"I'm not a dog person," said Shadow.

Had he been someone else, someone who talked about what was happening inside his head, Shadow might have told her that his wife had owned dogs when she was younger, and sometimes called Shadow *puppy* because she wanted a dog she could not have. But Shadow kept things on the inside. It was one of the things he liked about the British: even when they wanted to know what was happening on the inside, they did not ask. The world on the inside remained the world on the inside. His wife had been dead for three years now.

"If you ask me," said the man with the muttonchops, "people are either dog people or cat people. So would you then consider yourself a cat person?"

Shadow reflected. "I don't know. We never had pets when I was a kid, we were always on the move. But –"

"I mention this," the man continued, "because our host also has a cat, which you might wish to see."

"Used to be out here, but we moved it to the back room," said the landlord, from behind the bar.

Shadow wondered how the man could follow the conversation so easily while also taking people's meal orders and serving their drinks. "Did the cat upset the dogs?" he asked.

Outside, the rain redoubled. The wind moaned, and whistled, and then howled. The log fire burning in the little fireplace coughed and spat.

"Not in the way you're thinking," said the landlord. "We found it when we knocked through into the room next door, when we needed to extend the bar." The man grinned. "Come and look."

Shadow followed the man into the room next door. The mutton-chop man and the white-haired woman came with them, walking a little behind Shadow.

Shadow glanced back into the bar. The dark-haired woman was watching him, and she smiled warmly when he caught her eye.

The room next door was better lit, larger, and it felt a little less like somebody's front room. People were sitting at tables, eating. The food looked good and smelled better. The landlord led Shadow to the back of the room, to a dusty glass case.

"There she is," said the landlord, proudly.

The cat was brown, and it looked, at first glance, as if it had been constructed out of tendons and agony. The holes that were its eyes were filled with anger and with pain; the mouth was wide open, as if the creature had been yowling when she was turned to leather.

"The practice of placing animals in the walls of buildings is similar to the practice of walling up children alive in the foundations of a house you want to stay up," explained the muttonchop man, from behind him. "Although mummified cats always make me think of the mummified cats they found around the temple of Bast in Bubastis in Egypt. So many tons of mummified cats that they sent them to England to be ground up as cheap fertilizer and dumped on the fields. The Victorians also made paint out of mummies. A sort of brown, I believe."

"It looks miserable," said Shadow. "How old is it?"

The landlord scratched his cheek. "We reckon that the wall she was in went up somewhere between 1300 and 1600. That's from parish records. There's nothing here in 1300, and there's a house in 1600. The stuff in the middle was lost."

The dead cat in the glass case, furless and leathery, seemed to be watching them, from its empty black-hole eyes.

I got eyes wherever my folk walk, breathed a voice in the back of Shadow's mind. He thought, momentarily, about the fields fertilized with the ground mummies of cats, and what strange crops they must have grown.

"*They put him into an old house side,*" said the man called Ollie. "*And there he lived and there he died. And nobody either laughed or cried.* All sorts of things were walled up, to make sure that things were guarded and safe. Children, sometimes. Animals. They did it in churches as a matter of course."

The rain beat an arrhythmic rattle on the windowpane. Shadow thanked the landlord for showing him the cat. They went back into the taproom. The dark-haired woman had gone, which gave Shadow a moment of regret. She had looked so friendly. Shadow bought a round of drinks for the muttonchop man, the white-haired woman, and one for the landlord.

The landlord ducked behind the bar. "They call me Shadow," Shadow told them. "Shadow Moon."

The muttonchop man pressed his hands together in delight. "Oh! How wonderful. I had an Alsatian named Shadow, when I was a boy. Is it your real name?"

"It's what they call me," said Shadow.

"I'm Moira Callanish," said the white-haired woman. "This is my partner, Oliver Bierce. He knows a lot, and he will, during the course of our acquaintance, undoubtedly tell you everything he knows."

They shook hands. When the landlord returned with their drinks, Shadow asked if the pub had a room to rent. He had intended to walk further that night, but the rain sounded like it had no intention of giving up. He had stout walking shoes, and weather-resistant outer clothes, but he did not want to walk in the rain.

"I used to, but then my son moved back in. I'll encourage people to sleep it off in the barn, on occasion, but that's as far as I'll go these days."

"Anywhere in the village I could get a room?"

The landlord shook his head. "It's a foul night. But Porsett is only a few miles down the road, and they've got a proper hotel there. I can call Sandra, tell her that you're coming. What's your name?"

"Shadow," said Shadow again. "Shadow Moon."

Moira looked at Oliver, and said something that sounded like "waifs and strays?" and Oliver chewed his lip for a moment, and then he nodded enthusiastically. "Would you fancy spending the night with us? The spare room's a bit of a box room, but it does have a bed in it. And it's warm there. And dry."

"I'd like that very much," said Shadow. "I can pay."

"Don't be silly," said Moira. "It will be nice to have a guest."

* * *

II
The Gibbet

Oliver and Moira both had umbrellas. Oliver insisted that Shadow carry his umbrella, pointing out that Shadow towered over him, and thus was ideally suited to keep the rain off both of them.

The couple also carried little flashlights, which they called torches. The word put Shadow in mind of villagers in a horror movie storming the castle on the hill, and the lightning and thunder added to the vision. *Tonight, my creature,* he thought, *I will give you life!* It should have been hokey but instead it was disturbing. The dead cat had put him into a strange set of mind.

The narrow roads between fields were running with rainwater.

"On a nice night," said Moira, raising her voice to be heard over the rain, "we would just walk over the fields. But they'll be all soggy and boggy, so we're going down by Shuck's Lane. Now, that tree was a gibbet tree, once upon a time." She pointed to a massive-trunked sycamore at the crossroads. It had only a few branches left, sticking up into the night like afterthoughts.

"Moira's lived here since she was in her twenties," said Oliver. "I came up from London, about eight years ago. From Turnham Green. I'd come up here on holiday originally when I was fourteen and I never forgot it. You don't."

"The land gets into your blood," said Moira. "Sort of."

"And the blood gets into the land," said Oliver. "One way or another. You take that gibbet tree, for example. They would leave people in the gibbet until there was nothing left. Hair gone to make bird's nests, flesh all eaten by ravens, bones picked clean. Or until they had another corpse to display anyway."

Shadow was fairly sure he knew what a gibbet was, but he asked anyway. There was never any harm in asking, and Oliver was definitely the kind of person who took pleasure in knowing peculiar things and in passing his knowledge on.

"Like a huge iron birdcage. They used them to display the bodies of executed criminals, after justice had been served. The gibbets were locked, so the family and friends couldn't steal the body back and give it a good

Christian burial. Keeping passersby on the straight and the narrow, although I doubt it actually deterred anyone from anything."

"Who were they executing?"

"Anyone who got unlucky. Three hundred years ago, there were over two hundred crimes punishable by death. Including traveling with Gypsies for more than a month, stealing sheep – and, for that matter, anything over twelve pence in value – and writing a threatening letter."

He might have been about to begin a lengthy list, but Moira broke in. "Oliver's right about the death sentence, but they only gibbeted murderers, up these parts. And they'd leave corpses in the gibbet for twenty years, sometimes. We didn't get a lot of murders." And then, as if trying to change the subject to something lighter, she said, "We are now walking down Shuck's Lane. The locals say that on a clear night, which tonight certainly is not, you can find yourself being followed by Black Shuck. He's a sort of a fairy dog."

"We've never seen him, not even on clear nights," said Oliver.

"Which is a very good thing," said Moira. "Because if you see him – you die."

"Except Sandra Wilberforce said she saw him, and she's healthy as a horse."

Shadow smiled. "What does Black Shuck do?"

"He doesn't do anything," said Oliver.

"He does. He follows you home," corrected Moira. "And then, a bit later, you die."

"Doesn't sound very scary," said Shadow. "Except for the dying bit."

They reached the bottom of the road. Rainwater was running like a stream over Shadow's thick hiking boots.

Shadow said, "So how did you two meet?" It was normally a safe question, when you were with couples.

Oliver said, "In the pub. I was up here on holiday, really."

Moira said, "I was with someone when I met Oliver. We had a very brief, torrid affair, then we ran off together. Most unlike both of us."

They did not seem like the kind of people who ran off together, thought Shadow. But then, all people were strange. He knew he should say something.

"I was married. My wife was killed in a car crash."

"I'm so sorry," said Moira.

"It happened," said Shadow.

"When we get home," said Moira, "I'm making us all whisky macs. That's whisky and ginger wine and hot water. And I'm having a hot bath. Otherwise I'll catch my death."

Shadow imagined reaching out his hand and catching death in it, like a baseball, and he shivered.

The rain redoubled, and a sudden flash of lightning burned the world into existence all around them: every gray rock in the drystone wall, every blade of grass, every puddle and every tree was perfectly illuminated, and then swallowed by a deeper darkness, leaving afterimages on Shadow's night-blinded eyes.

"Did you see that?" asked Oliver. "Damnedest thing." The thunder rolled and rumbled, and Shadow waited until it was done before he tried to speak.

"I didn't see anything," said Shadow. Another flash, less bright, and Shadow thought he saw something moving away from them in a distant field. "That?" he asked.

"It's a donkey," said Moira. "Only a donkey."

Oliver stopped. He said, "This was the wrong way to come home. We should have got a taxi. This was a mistake."

"Ollie," said Moira. "It's not far now. And it's just a spot of rain. You aren't made of sugar, darling."

Another flash of lightning, so bright as to be almost blinding. There was nothing to be seen in the fields.

Darkness. Shadow turned back to Oliver, but the little man was no longer standing beside him. Oliver's flashlight was on the ground. Shadow blinked his eyes, hoping to force his night vision to return. The man had collapsed, crumpled onto the wet grass on the side of the lane.

"Ollie?" Moira crouched beside him, her umbrella by her side. She shone her flashlight onto his face. Then she looked at Shadow. "He can't just sit here," she said, sounding confused and concerned. "It's pouring."

Shadow pocketed Oliver's flashlight, handed his umbrella to Moira, then picked Oliver up. The man did not seem to weigh much, and Shadow was a big man.

"Is it far?"

"Not far," she said. "Not really. We're almost home."

They walked in silence, across a churchyard on the edge of a village green, and into a village. Shadow could see lights on in the gray stone houses that edged the one street. Moira turned off, into a house set back from the road, and Shadow followed her. She held the back door open for him.

The kitchen was large and warm, and there was a sofa, half-covered with magazines, against one wall. There were low beams in the kitchen, and Shadow needed to duck his head. Shadow removed Oliver's raincoat and dropped it. It puddled on the wooden floor. Then he put the man down on the sofa.

Moira filled the kettle.

"Do we call an ambulance?"

She shook her head.

"This is just something that happens? He falls down and passes out?"

Moira busied herself getting mugs from a shelf. "It's happened before. Just not for a long time. He's narcoleptic, and if something surprises or scares him he can just go down like that. He'll come round soon. He'll want tea. No whisky mac tonight, not for him. Sometimes he's a bit dazed and doesn't know where he is, sometimes he's been following everything that happened while he was out. And he hates it if you make a fuss. Put your backpack down by the Aga."

The kettle boiled. Moira poured the steaming water into a teapot. "He'll have a cup of real tea. I'll have chamomile, I think, or I won't sleep tonight. Calm my nerves. You?"

"I'll drink tea, sure," said Shadow. He had walked more than twenty miles that day, and sleep would be easy in the finding. He wondered at Moira. She appeared perfectly self-possessed in the face of her partner's incapacity, and he wondered how much of it was not wanting to show weakness in front of a stranger. He admired her, although he found it peculiar. The English were strange. But he understood hating 'making a fuss.' Yes.

Oliver stirred on the couch. Moira was at his side with a cup of tea, helped him into a sitting position. He sipped the tea, in a slightly dazed fashion.

"It followed me home," he said, conversationally.

"What followed you, Ollie, darling?" Her voice was steady, but there was concern in it.

"The dog," said the man on the sofa, and he took another sip of his tea. "The black dog."

* * *

III
The Cuts

THESE WERE THE things Shadow learned that night, sitting around the kitchen table with Moira and Oliver:

He learned that Oliver had not been happy or fulfilled in his London advertising agency job. He had moved up to the village and taken an extremely early medical retirement. Now, initially for recreation and increasingly for money, he repaired and rebuilt drystone walls. There was, he explained, an art and a skill to wall building, it was excellent exercise, and, when done correctly, a meditative practice.

"There used to be hundreds of drystone wall people around here. Now there's barely a dozen who know what they're doing. You see walls repaired with concrete, or with breeze blocks. It's a dying art. I'd love to show you how I do it. Useful skill to have. Picking the rock, sometimes, you have to let the rock tell you where it goes. And then it's immovable. You couldn't knock it down with a tank. Remarkable."

He learned that Oliver had been very depressed several years earlier, shortly after Moira and he got together, but that for the last few years he had been doing very well. Or, he amended, relatively well.

He learned that Moira was independently wealthy, that her family trust fund had meant that she and her sisters had not needed to work, but that, in her late twenties, she had gone for teacher training. That she no longer taught, but that she was extremely active in local affairs, and had campaigned successfully to keep the local bus routes in service.

Shadow learned, from what Oliver didn't say, that Oliver was scared of something, very scared, and that when Oliver was asked what had frightened him so badly, and what he had meant by saying that the black dog had followed him home, his response was to stammer and to sway. He learned not to ask Oliver any more questions.

This is what Oliver and Moira had learned about Shadow sitting around that kitchen table:

Nothing much.

Shadow liked them. He was not a stupid man; he had trusted people in the past who had betrayed him, but he liked this couple, and he liked the way their home smelled – like bread-making and jam and walnut wood-polish – and he went to sleep that night in his box-room bedroom worrying about the little man with the muttonchop beard. What if the thing Shadow had glimpsed in the field had *not* been a donkey? What if it *had* been an enormous dog? What then?

The rain had stopped when Shadow woke. He made himself toast in the empty kitchen. Moira came in from the garden, letting a gust of chilly air in through the kitchen door. "Sleep well?" she asked.

"Yes. Very well." He had dreamed of being at the zoo. He had been surrounded by animals he could not see, which snuffled and snorted in their pens. He was a child, walking with his mother, and he was safe and he was loved. He had stopped in front of a lion's cage, but what had been in the cage was a sphinx, half lion and half woman, her tail swishing. She had smiled at him, and her smile had been his mother's smile. He heard her voice, accented and warm and feline.

It said, *Know thyself.*

I know who I am, said Shadow in his dream, holding the bars of the cage. Behind the bars was the desert. He could see pyramids. He could see shadows on the sand.

Then who are you, Shadow? What are you running from? Where are you running to?

Who are you?

And he had woken, wondering why he was asking himself that question, and missing his mother, who had died twenty years before, when he was a teenager. He still felt oddly comforted, remembering the feel of his hand in his mother's hand.

"I'm afraid Ollie's a bit under the weather this morning."

"Sorry to hear that."

"Yes. Well, can't be helped."

"I'm really grateful for the room. I guess I'll be on my way."

Moira said, "Will you look at something for me?"

Shadow nodded, then followed her outside, and round the side of the house. She pointed to the rose bed. "What does that look like to you?"

Shadow bent down. "*The footprint of an enormous hound,*" he said. "To quote Dr. Watson."

"Yes," she said. "It really does."

"If there's a spectral ghost-hound out there," said Shadow, "it shouldn't leave footprints. Should it?"

"I'm not actually an authority on these matters," said Moira. "I had a friend once who could have told us all about it. But she..." She trailed off. Then, more brightly, "You know, Mrs. Camberley two doors down has a Doberman Pinscher. Ridiculous thing." Shadow was not certain whether the ridiculous thing was Mrs. Camberley or her dog.

He found the events of the previous night less troubling and odd, more explicable. What did it matter if a strange dog had followed them home? Oliver had been frightened or startled, and had collapsed, from narcolepsy, from shock.

"Well, I'll pack you some lunch before you go," said Moira. "Boiled eggs. That sort of thing. You'll be glad of them on the way."

They went into the house. Moira went to put something away, and returned looking shaken.

"Oliver's locked himself in the bathroom," she said.

Shadow was not certain what to say.

"You know what I wish?" she continued.

"I don't."

"I wish you would talk to him. I wish he would open the door. I wish he'd talk to me. I can hear him in there. I can hear him."

And then, "I hope he isn't cutting himself again."

Shadow walked back into the hall, stood by the bathroom door, called Oliver's name. "Can you hear me? Are you okay?"

Nothing. No sound from inside.

Shadow looked at the door. It was solid wood. The house was old, and they built them strong and well back then. When Shadow had used the bathroom that morning he'd learned the lock was a hook and eye. He leaned on the handle of the door, pushing it down, then rammed his shoulder against the door. It opened with a noise of splintering wood.

He had watched a man die in prison, stabbed in a pointless argument. He remembered the way that the blood had puddled about the man's body, lying in the back corner of the exercise yard. The sight had troubled Shadow, but he had forced himself to look, and to keep looking. To look away would somehow have felt disrespectful.

Oliver was naked on the floor of the bathroom. His body was pale, and his chest and groin were covered with thick, dark hair. He held the blade from an ancient safety razor in his hands. He had sliced his arms with it, his chest above the nipples, his inner thighs and his penis. Blood was smeared on his body, on the black and white linoleum floor, on the white enamel of the bathtub. Oliver's eyes were round and wide, like the eyes of a bird. He was looking directly at Shadow, but Shadow was not certain that he was being seen.

"Ollie?" said Moira's voice, from the hall. Shadow realized that he was blocking the doorway and he hesitated, unsure whether to let her see what was on the floor or not.

Shadow took a pink towel from the towel rail and wrapped it around Oliver. That got the little man's attention. He blinked, as if seeing Shadow for the first time, and said, "The dog. It's for the dog. It must be fed, you see. We're making friends."

Moira said, "Oh my dear sweet god."

"I'll call the emergency services."

"Please don't," she said. "He'll be fine at home with me. I don't know what I'll... please?"

Shadow picked up Oliver, swaddled in the towel, carried him into the bedroom as if he were a child, and then placed him on the bed. Moira followed. She picked up an iPad by the bed, touched the screen, and music began to play. "Breathe, Ollie," she said. "Remember. Breathe. It's going to be fine. You're going to be fine."

"I can't really breathe," said Oliver, in a small voice. "Not really. I can feel my heart, though. I can feel my heart beating."

Moira squeezed his hand and sat down on the bed, and Shadow left them alone.

When Moira entered the kitchen, her sleeves rolled up, and her hands smelling of antiseptic cream, Shadow was sitting on the sofa, reading a guide to local walks.

"How's he doing?"

She shrugged.

"You have to get him help."

"Yes." She stood in the middle of the kitchen and looked about her, as if unable to decide which way to turn. "Do you... I mean, do you have to leave today? Are you on a schedule?"

"Nobody's waiting for me. Anywhere."

She looked at him with a face that had grown haggard in an hour. "When this happened before, it took a few days, but then he was right as rain. The depression doesn't stay long. So, just wondering, would you just, well, stick around? I phoned my sister but she's in the middle of moving. And I can't cope on my own. I really can't. Not again. But I can't ask you to stay, not if anyone is waiting for you."

"Nobody's waiting," repeated Shadow. "And I'll stick around. But I think Oliver needs specialist help."

"Yes," agreed Moira. "He does."

Dr. Scathelocke came over late that afternoon. He was a friend of Oliver and Moira's. Shadow was not entirely certain whether rural British doctors still made house calls, or whether this was a socially justified visit. The doctor went into the bedroom, and came out twenty minutes later.

He sat at the kitchen table with Moira, and he said, "It's all very shallow. Cry-for-help stuff. Honestly, there's not a lot we can do for him in hospital that you can't do for him here, what with the cuts. We used to have a dozen nurses in that wing. Now they are trying to close it down completely. Get it all back to the community."

Dr. Scathelocke had sandy hair, was as tall as Shadow but lankier. He reminded Shadow of the landlord in the pub, and he wondered idly if the two men were related. The doctor scribbled several prescriptions, and Moira handed them to Shadow, along with the keys to an old white Range Rover.

Shadow drove to the next village, found the little chemists' and waited for the prescriptions to be filled. He stood awkwardly in the overlit aisle, staring at a display of suntan lotions and creams, sadly redundant in this cold wet summer.

"You're Mr. American," said a woman's voice from behind him. He turned. She had short dark hair and was wearing the same olive-green sweater she had been wearing in the pub.

"I guess I am," he said.

"Local gossip says that you are helping out while Ollie's under the weather."

"That was fast."

"Local gossip travels faster than light. I'm Cassie Burglass."

"Shadow Moon."

"Good name," she said. "Gives me chills." She smiled. "If you're still rambling while you're here, I suggest you check out the hill just past the village. Follow the track up until it forks, and then go left. It takes you up Wod's Hill. Spectacular views. Public right of way. Just keep going left and up, you can't miss it."

She smiled at him. Perhaps she was just being friendly to a stranger.

"I'm not surprised you're still here though," Cassie continued. "It's hard to leave this place once it gets its claws into you." She smiled again, a warm smile, and she looked directly into his eyes, as if trying to make up her mind. "I think Mrs. Patel has your prescriptions ready. Nice talking to you, Mr. American."

IV
The Kiss

SHADOW HELPED MOIRA. He walked down to the village shop and bought the items on her shopping list while she stayed in the house, writing at the kitchen table or hovering in the hallway outside the bedroom door. Moira barely talked. He ran errands in the white Range Rover, and saw Oliver mostly in the hall, shuffling to the bathroom and back. The man did not speak to him.

Everything was quiet in the house: Shadow imagined the black dog squatting on the roof, cutting out all sunlight, all emotion, all feeling and truth. Something had turned down the volume in that house, pushed all the colors into black and white. He wished he was somewhere else, but could not run out on them. He sat on his bed, and stared out of the window at the rain puddling its way down the windowpane, and felt the seconds of his life counting off, never to come back.

It had been wet and cold, but on the third day the sun came out. The world did not warm up, but Shadow tried to pull himself out of the gray haze, and decided to see some of the local sights. He walked to the next village, through fields, up paths and along the side of a long drystone wall. There was a bridge over a narrow stream that was little more than a plank, and Shadow jumped the water in one easy bound. Up the hill: there were trees, oak and hawthorn, sycamore and beech at the bottom of the hill, and then the trees became sparser. He followed the winding trail, sometimes obvious, sometimes not, until he reached a natural resting place, like a tiny meadow, high on the hill, and there he turned away from the hill and saw the valleys and the peaks arranged all about him in greens and grays like illustrations from a children's book.

He was not alone up there. A woman with short dark hair was sitting and sketching on the hill's side, perched comfortably on a gray boulder. There was a tree behind her, which acted as a windbreak. She wore a green sweater and blue jeans, and he recognized Cassie Burglass before he saw her face.

As he got close, she turned. "What do you think?" she asked, holding her sketchbook up for his inspection. It was an assured pencil drawing of the hillside.

"You're very good. Are you a professional artist?"

"I dabble," she said.

Shadow had spent enough time talking to the English to know that this meant either that she dabbled, or that her work was regularly hung in the National Gallery or the Tate Modern.

"You must be cold," he said. "You're only wearing a sweater."

"I'm cold," she said. "But, up here, I'm used to it. It doesn't really bother me. How's Ollie doing?"

"He's still under the weather," Shadow told her.

"Poor old sod," she said, looking from her paper to the hillside and back. "It's hard for me to feel properly sorry for him, though."

"Why's that? Did he bore you to death with interesting facts?"

She laughed, a small huff of air at the back of her throat. "You really ought to listen to more village gossip. When Ollie and Moira met, they were both with other people."

"I know that. They told me that." Shadow thought a moment. "So he was with you first?"

"No. *She* was. We'd been together since college." There was a pause. She shaded something, her pencil scraping the paper. "Are you going to try and kiss me?" she asked.

"I, uh. I, um," he said. Then, honestly, "It hadn't occurred to me."

"Well," she said, turning to smile at him, "it bloody well should. I mean, I asked you up here, and you came, up to Wod's Hill, just to see me." She went back to the paper and the drawing of the hill. "They say there's dark doings been done on this hill. Dirty dark doings. And I was thinking of doing something dirty myself. To Moira's lodger."

"Is this some kind of revenge plot?"

"It's not an anything plot. I just like you. And there's no one around here who wants me any longer. Not as a woman."

The last woman that Shadow had kissed had been in Scotland. He thought of her, and what she had become, in the end. "You *are* real, aren't you?" he asked. "I mean... you're a real person. I mean..."

She put the pad of paper down on the boulder and she stood up. "Kiss me and find out," she said.

He hesitated. She sighed, and she kissed him.

It was cold on that hillside, and Cassie's lips were cold. Her mouth was very soft. As her tongue touched his, Shadow pulled back.

"I don't actually know you," Shadow said.

She leaned away from him, looked up into his face. "You know," she said, "all I dream of these days is somebody who will look my way and see the real me. I had given up until you came along, Mr. American, with your funny name. But you looked at me, and I knew you saw me. And that's all that matters."

Shadow's hands held her, feeling the softness of her sweater.

"How much longer are you going to be here? In the district?" she asked.

"A few more days. Until Oliver's feeling better."

"Pity. Can't you stay forever?"

"I'm sorry?"

"You have nothing to be sorry for, sweet man. You see that opening over there?"

He glanced over to the hillside, but could not see what she was pointing at. The hillside was a tangle of weeds and low trees and half-tumbled drystone walls. She pointed to her drawing, where she had drawn a dark shape, like an archway, in the middle of clump of gorse bushes on the side of the hill. "There. Look." He stared, and this time he saw it immediately.

"What is it?" Shadow asked.

"The Gateway to Hell," she told him, impressively.

"Uh-huh."

She grinned. "That's what they call it round here. It was originally a Roman temple, I think, or something even older. But that's all that remains. You should check it out, if you like that sort of thing. Although it's a bit disappointing: just a little passageway going back into the hill. I keep expecting some archaeologists will come out this way, dig it up, catalog what they find, but they never do."

Shadow examined her drawing. "So what do you know about big black dogs?" he asked.

"The one in Shuck's Lane?" she said. He nodded. "They say the barghest used to wander all around here. But now it's just in Shuck's Lane. Dr. Scathelocke once told me it was folk memory. The Wish Hounds are all that are left of the wild hunt, which was based around the idea of Odin's hunting wolves, Freki and Geri. I think it's even older than that. Cave memory. Druids. The thing that prowls in the darkness beyond the fire circle, waiting to tear you apart if you edge too far out alone."

"Have you ever seen it, then?"

She shook her head. "No. I researched it, but never saw it. My semi-imaginary local beast. Have you?"

"I don't think so. Maybe."

"Perhaps you woke it up when you came here. You woke me up, after all."

She reached up, pulled his head down towards her and kissed him again. She took his left hand, so much bigger than hers, and placed it beneath her sweater.

"Cassie, my hands are cold," he warned her.

"Well, my everything is cold. There's nothing *but* cold up here. Just smile and look like you know what you're doing," she told him. She pushed Shadow's left hand higher, until it was cupping the lace of her bra, and he could feel, beneath the lace, the hardness of her nipple and the soft swell of her breast.

He began to surrender to the moment, his hesitation a mixture of awkwardness and uncertainty. He was not sure how he felt about this woman: she had history with his benefactors, after all. Shadow never liked feeling that he was being used; it had happened too many times before. But his left hand was touching her breast and his right hand was cradling the nape of her neck, and he was leaning down and now her mouth was on his, and she was clinging to him as tightly as if, he thought, she wanted to occupy the very same space that he was in. Her mouth tasted like mint and stone and grass and the chilly afternoon breeze. He closed his eyes, and let himself enjoy the kiss and the way their bodies moved together.

Cassie froze. Somewhere close to them, a cat mewed. Shadow opened his eyes.

"Jesus," he said.

They were surrounded by cats. White cats and tabbies, brown and ginger and black cats, long-haired and short. Well-fed cats with collars and disreputable ragged-eared cats that looked as if they had been living in barns and on the edges of the wild. They stared at Shadow and Cassie with green eyes and blue eyes and golden eyes, and they did not move. Only the occasional swish of a tail or the blinking of a pair of feline eyes told Shadow that they were alive.

"This is weird," said Shadow.

Cassie took a step back. He was no longer touching her now. "Are they with you?" she asked.

"I don't think they're with anyone. They're cats."

"I think they're jealous," said Cassie. "Look at them. They don't like me."

"That's..." Shadow was going to say "nonsense," but no, it was sense, of a kind. There had been a woman who was a goddess, a continent away and years in his past, who had cared about him, in her own way. He remembered the needle-sharpness of her nails and the catlike roughness of her tongue.

Cassie looked at Shadow dispassionately. "I don't know who you are, Mr. American," she told him. "Not really. I don't know why you can look at me and see the real me, or why I can talk to you when I find it so hard to talk to other people. But I can. And you know, you seem all normal and quiet on the surface, but you are so much weirder than I am. And I'm extremely fucking weird."

Shadow said, "Don't go."

"Tell Ollie and Moira you saw me," she said. "Tell them I'll be waiting where we last spoke, if they have anything they want to say to me." She picked up her sketchpad and pencils, and she walked off briskly, stepping carefully through the cats, who did not even glance at her, just kept their gazes fixed on Shadow, as she moved away through the swaying grasses and the blowing twigs.

Shadow wanted to call after her, but instead he crouched down and looked back at the cats. "What's going on?" he asked. "Bast? Are you doing this? You're a long way from home. And why would you still care who I kiss?"

The spell was broken when he spoke. The cats began to move, to look away, to stand, to wash themselves intently.

A tortoiseshell cat pushed her head against his hand, insistently, needing attention. Shadow stroked her absently, rubbing his knuckles against her forehead.

She swiped blinding-fast with claws like tiny scimitars, and drew blood from his forearm. Then she purred, and turned, and within moments the whole kit and caboodle of them had vanished into the hillside, slipping behind rocks and into the undergrowth, and were gone.

V
The Living and the Dead

Oliver was out of his room when Shadow got back to the house, sitting in the warm kitchen, a mug of tea by his side, reading a book on Roman architecture. He was dressed, and he had shaved his chin and trimmed his beard. He was wearing pajamas, with a plaid bathrobe over them.

"I'm feeling a bit better," he said, when he saw Shadow. Then, "Have you ever had this? Been depressed?"

"Looking back on it, I guess I did. When my wife died," said Shadow. "Everything went flat. Nothing meant anything for a long time."

Oliver nodded. "It's hard. Sometimes I think the black dog is a real thing. I lie in bed thinking about the painting of Fuseli's nightmare on a sleeper's chest. Like Anubis. Or do I mean Set? Big black thing. What was Set anyway? Some kind of donkey?"

"I never ran into Set," said Shadow. "He was before my time."

Oliver laughed. "Very dry. And they say you Americans don't do irony." He paused. "Anyway. All done now. Back on my feet. Ready to face the world." He sipped his tea. "Feeling a bit embarrassed. All that Hound of the Baskervilles nonsense behind me now."

"You really have nothing to be embarrassed about," said Shadow, reflecting that the English found embarrassment wherever they looked for it.

"Well. All a bit silly, one way or another. And I really am feeling much perkier."

Shadow nodded. "If you're feeling better, I guess I should start heading south."

"No hurry," said Oliver. "It's always nice to have company. Moira and I don't really get out as much as we'd like. It's mostly just a walk up to the pub. Not much excitement here, I'm afraid."

Moira came in from the garden. "Anyone seen the secateurs? I know I had them. Forget my own head next."

Shadow shook his head, uncertain what secateurs were. He thought of telling the couple about the cats on the hill, and how they had behaved, but could not think of a way to describe it that would explain how odd it was. So, instead, without thinking, he said, "I ran into Cassie Burglass on Wod's Hill. She pointed out the Gateway to Hell."

They were staring at him. The kitchen had become awkwardly quiet. He said, "She was drawing it."

Oliver looked at him and said, "I don't understand."

"I've run into her a couple of times since I got here," said Shadow.

"What?" Moira's face was flushed. "What are you saying?" And then, "Who the, who the *fuck* are you to come in here and say things like that?"

"I'm, I'm nobody," said Shadow. "She just started talking to me. She said that you and she used to be together."

Moira looked as if she were going to hit him. Then she just said, "She moved away after we broke up. It wasn't a good breakup. She was very hurt. She behaved appallingly. Then she just up and left the village in the night. Never came back."

"I don't want to talk about that woman," said Oliver, quietly. "Not now. Not ever."

"Look. She was in the pub with us," pointed out Shadow. "That first night. You guys didn't seem to have a problem with her then."

Moira just stared at him and did not respond, as if he had said something in a tongue she did not speak. Oliver rubbed his forehead with his hand. "I didn't see her," was all he said.

"Well, she said to say hi when I saw her today," said Shadow. "She said she'd be waiting, if either of you had anything you wanted to say to her."

"We have nothing to say to her. Nothing at all." Moira's eyes were wet, but she was not crying. "I can't believe that, that *fucking* woman has come back into our lives, after all she put us through." Moira swore like someone who was not very good at it.

Oliver put down his book. "I'm sorry," he said. "I don't feel very well." He walked out, back to the bedroom, and closed the door behind him.

Moira picked up Oliver's mug, almost automatically, and took it over to the sink, emptied it out and began to wash it.

"I hope you're pleased with yourself," she said, rubbing the mug with a white plastic scrubbing brush as if she were trying to scrub the picture of Beatrix Potter's cottage from the china. "He was coming back to himself again."

"I didn't know it would upset him like that," said Shadow. He felt guilty as he said it. He had known there was history between Cassie and his hosts. He could have said nothing, after all. Silence was always safer.

Moira dried the mug with a green and white tea towel. The white patches of the towel were comical sheep, the green were grass. She bit her lower lip, and the tears that had been brimming in her eyes now ran down her cheeks. Then, "Did she say anything about me?"

"Just that you two used to be an item."

Moira nodded, and wiped the tears from her young-old face with the comical tea towel. "She couldn't bear it when Ollie and I got together. After I moved out, she just hung up her paintbrushes and locked the flat and went to London." She blew her nose vigorously. "Still. Mustn't grumble. We make our own beds. And Ollie's a *good* man. There's just a black dog in his mind. My mother had depression. It's hard."

Shadow said, "I've made everything worse. I should go."

"Don't leave until tomorrow. I'm not throwing you out, dear. It's not your fault you ran into that woman, is it?" Her shoulders were slumped. "There they are. On top of the fridge." She picked up something that looked like a very small pair of garden shears. "Secateurs," she explained. "For the rosebushes, mostly."

"Are you going to talk to him?"

"No," she said. "Conversations with Ollie about Cassie never end well. And in this state, it could plunge him even further back into a bad place. I'll just let him get over it."

Shadow ate alone in the pub that night, while the cat in the glass case glowered at him. He saw no one he knew. He had a brief conversation with the landlord about how he was enjoying his time in the village. He walked back to Moira's house after the pub, past the old sycamore, the gibbet tree, down Shuck's Lane. He saw nothing moving in the fields in the moonlight: no dog, no donkey.

All the lights in the house were out. He went to his bedroom as quietly as he could, packed the last of his possessions into his backpack before he went to sleep. He would leave early, he knew.

He lay in bed, watching the moonlight in the box room. He remembered standing in the pub and Cassie Burglass standing beside him. He thought about his conversation with the landlord, and the conversation that first night, and the cat in the glass box, and, as he pondered, any desire to sleep evaporated. He was perfectly wide awake in the small bed.

Shadow could move quietly when he needed to. He slipped out of bed, pulled on his clothes and then, carrying his boots, he opened the window, reached over the sill and let himself tumble silently into the soil of the flower bed beneath. He got to his feet and put on the boots, lacing them up in the half dark. The moon was several days from full, bright enough to cast shadows.

Shadow stepped into a patch of darkness beside a wall, and he waited there.

He wondered how sane his actions were. It seemed very probable that he was wrong, that his memory had played tricks on him, or other people's had. It was all so very unlikely, but then, he had experienced the unlikely before, and if he was wrong he would be out, what? A few hours' sleep?

He watched a fox hurry across the lawn, watched a proud white cat stalk and kill a small rodent, and saw several other cats pad their way along the top of the garden wall. He watched a weasel slink from shadow to shadow in the flower bed. The constellations moved in slow procession across the sky.

The front door opened, and a figure came out. Shadow had half-expected to see Moira, but it was Oliver, wearing his pajamas and, over them, a thick tartan dressing gown. He had Wellington boots on his feet, and he looked faintly ridiculous, like an invalid from a black and white movie, or someone in a play. There was no color in the moonlit world.

Oliver pulled the front door closed until it clicked, then he walked towards the street, but walking on the grass, instead of crunching down the gravel path. He did not glance back, or even look around. He set off up the lane, and Shadow waited until Oliver was almost out of sight before he began to follow. He knew where Oliver was going, had to be going.

Shadow did not question himself, not any longer. He knew where they were both headed, with the certainty of a person in a dream. He was not even surprised when, halfway up Wod's Hill, he found Oliver sitting on a tree stump, waiting for him. The sky was lightening, just a little, in the east.

"The Gateway to Hell," said the little man. "As far as I can tell, they've always called it that. Goes back years and years."

The two men walked up the winding path together. There was something gloriously comical about Oliver in his robe, in his striped pajamas and his oversized black rubber boots. Shadow's heart pumped in his chest.

"How did you bring her up here?" asked Shadow.

"Cassie? I didn't. It was her idea to meet up here on the hill. She loved coming up here to paint. You can see so far. And it's holy, this hill, and she always loved that. Not holy to Christians, of course. Quite the obverse. The old religion."

"Druids?" asked Shadow. He was uncertain what other old religions there were, in England.

"Could be. Definitely could be. But I think it predates the druids. Doesn't have much of a name. It's just what people in these parts practice, beneath whatever else they believe. Druids, Norse, Catholics, Protestants, doesn't matter. That's what people pay lip service to. The old religion is what gets the crops up and keeps your cock hard and makes sure that nobody builds a bloody great motorway through an area of outstanding natural beauty. The Gateway stands, and the hill stands, and the place stands. It's well, well over two thousand years old. You don't go mucking about with anything that powerful."

Shadow said, "Moira doesn't know, does she? She thinks Cassie moved away." The sky was continuing to lighten in the east, but it was still night, spangled with a glitter of stars, in the purple-black sky to the west.

"That was what she *needed* to think. I mean, what else was she going to think? It might have been different if the police had been interested... but it wasn't like... Well. It protects itself. The hill. The gate."

They were coming up to the little meadow on the side of the hill. They passed the boulder where Shadow had seen Cassie drawing. They walked toward the hill.

"The black dog in Shuck's Lane," said Oliver. "I don't actually think it is a dog. But it's been there so long." He pulled out a small LED flashlight from the pocket of his bathrobe. "You really talked to Cassie?"

"We talked, I even kissed her."

"Strange."

"I first saw her in the pub, the night I met you and Moira. That was what made me start to figure it out. Earlier tonight, Moira was talking as if she hadn't seen Cassie in years. She was baffled when I asked. But Cassie was standing just behind me that first night, and she spoke to us. Tonight, I asked at the pub if Cassie had been in, and nobody knew who I was talking about. You people all know each other. It was the only thing that made sense of it all. It made sense of what she said. Everything."

Oliver was almost at the place Cassie had called the Gateway to Hell. "I thought that it would be so simple. I would give her to the hill, and she would leave us both alone. Leave Moira alone. How could she have kissed you?"

Shadow said nothing.

"This is it," said Oliver. It was a hollow in the side of the hill, like a short hallway that went back. Perhaps, once, long ago, there had been a structure, but the hill had weathered, and the stones had returned to the hill from which they had been taken.

"There are those who think it's devil worship," said Oliver. "And I think they are wrong. But then, one man's god is another's devil. Eh?"

He walked into the passageway, and Shadow followed him.

"Such bullshit," said a woman's voice. "But you always were a bullshitter, Ollie, you pusillanimous little cock-stain."

Oliver did not move or react. He said, "She's here. In the wall. That's where I left her." He shone the flashlight at the wall, in the short passageway into the side of the hill. He inspected the drystone wall carefully, as if he were looking for a place he recognized, then he made a little grunting noise of recognition. Oliver took out a compact metal tool from his pocket, reached as high as he could and levered out one little rock with it. Then he began to pull rocks out from the wall, in a set sequence, each rock opening a space to allow another to be removed, alternating large rocks and small.

"Give me a hand. Come on."

Shadow knew what he was going to see behind the wall, but he pulled out the rocks, placed them down on the ground, one by one.

There was a smell, which intensified as the hole grew bigger, a stink of old rot and mold. It smelled like meat sandwiches gone bad. Shadow saw her face first, and he barely knew it as a face: the cheeks were sunken, the eyes gone, the skin now dark and leathery, and if there were freckles they were impossible to make out; but the hair was Cassie Burglass's hair, short and black, and in the LED light, he could see that the dead thing wore an olive-green sweater, and the blue jeans were her blue jeans.

"It's funny. I knew she was still here," said Oliver. "But I still had to see her. With all your talk. I had to see it. To prove she was still here."

"Kill him," said the woman's voice. "Hit him with a rock, Shadow. He killed me. Now he's going to kill you."

"Are you going to kill me?" Shadow asked.

"Well, yes, obviously," said the little man, in his sensible voice. "I mean, you know about Cassie. And once you're gone, I can just finally forget about the whole thing, once and for all."

"Forget?"

"Forgive *and* forget. But it's hard. It's not easy to forgive myself, but I'm sure I can forget. There. I think there's enough room for you to get in there now, if you squeeze."

Shadow looked down at the little man. "Out of interest," he said, curious, "how are you going to make me get in there? You don't have a gun on you. And, Ollie, I'm twice your size. You know, I could just break your neck."

"I'm not a stupid man," said Oliver. "I'm not a bad man, either. I'm not a terribly well man, but that's neither here nor there, really. I mean, I did what

I did because I was jealous, not because I was ill. But I wouldn't have come up here alone. You see, this is the temple of the Black Dog. These places were the first temples. Before the stone henges and the standing stones, they were waiting and they were worshipped, and sacrificed to, and feared, and placated. The black shucks and the barghests, the padfoots and the wish hounds. They were here and they remain on guard."

"Hit him with a rock," said Cassie's voice. "Hit him now, Shadow, *please*."

The passage they stood in went a little way into the hillside, a man-made cave with drystone walls. It did not look like an ancient temple. It did not look like a gateway to hell. The predawn sky framed Oliver. In his gentle, unfailingly polite voice, he said, "He is in me. And I am in him."

The black dog filled the doorway, blocking the way to the world outside, and, Shadow knew, whatever it was, it was no true dog. Its eyes actually glowed, with a luminescence that reminded Shadow of rotting sea-creatures. It was to a wolf, in scale and in menace, what a tiger is to a lynx: pure carnivore, a creature made of danger and threat. It stood taller than Oliver and it stared at Shadow, and it growled, a rumbling deep in its chest. Then it sprang.

Shadow raised his arm to protect his throat, and the creature sank its teeth into his flesh, just below the elbow. The pain was excruciating. He knew he should fight back, but he was falling to his knees, and he was screaming, unable to think clearly, unable to focus on anything except his fear that the creature was going to use him for food, fear it was crushing the bone of his forearm.

On some deep level he suspected that the fear was being created by the dog: that he, Shadow, was not cripplingly afraid like that. Not really. But it did not matter. When the creature released Shadow's arm, he was weeping and his whole body was shaking.

Oliver said, "Get in there, Shadow. Through the gap in the wall. Quickly, now. Or I'll have him chew off your face."

Shadow's arm was bleeding, but he got up and squeezed through the gap into the darkness without arguing. If he stayed out there, with the beast, he would die soon, and die in pain. He knew that with as much certainty as he knew that the sun would rise tomorrow.

"Well, yes," said Cassie's voice in his head. "It's going to rise. But unless you get your shit together you are never going to see it."

There was barely space for him and Cassie's body in the cavity behind the wall. He had seen the expression of pain and fury on her face, like the face of the cat in the glass box, and then he knew she, too, had been entombed here while alive.

Oliver picked up a rock from the ground, and placed it onto the wall, in the gap. "My own theory," he said, hefting a second rock and putting it into position, "is that it is the prehistoric dire wolf. But it is bigger than ever the dire wolf was. Perhaps it is the monster of our dreams, when we huddled in caves. Perhaps it was simply a wolf, but we were smaller, little hominids who could never run fast enough to get away."

Shadow leaned against the rock face behind him. He squeezed his left arm with his right hand to try to stop the bleeding. "This is Wod's Hill," said Shadow. "And that's Wod's dog. I wouldn't put it past him."

"It doesn't matter." More stones were placed on stones.

"Ollie," said Shadow. "The beast is going to kill you. It's already inside you. It's not a good thing."

"Old Shuck's not going to hurt me. Old Shuck loves me. Cassie's in the wall," said Oliver, and he dropped a rock on top of the others with a crash. "Now you are in the wall with her. Nobody's waiting for you. Nobody's going to come looking for you. Nobody is going to cry for you. Nobody's going to miss you."

There were, Shadow knew, although he could never have told a soul how he knew, three of them, not two, in that tiny space. There was Cassie Burglass, there in body (rotted and dried and still stinking of decay) and there in soul, and there was also something else, something that twined about his legs, and then butted gently at his injured hand. A voice spoke to him, from somewhere close. He knew that voice, although the accent was unfamiliar.

It was the voice that a cat would speak in, if a cat were a woman: expressive, dark, musical. The voice said, *You should not be here, Shadow. You have to stop, and you must take action. You are letting the rest of the world make your decisions for you.*

Shadow said aloud, "That's not entirely fair, Bast."

"You have to be quiet," said Oliver, gently. "I mean it." The stones of the wall were being replaced rapidly and efficiently. Already they were up to Shadow's chest.

Mr. No? Sweet thing, you really have no idea. No idea who you are or what you are or what that means. If he walls you up in here to die in this hill, this temple will stand forever – and whatever hodgepodge of belief these locals have will work for them and will make magic. But the sun will still go down on them, and all the skies will be gray. All things will mourn, and they will not know what they are mourning for. The world will be worse – for people, for cats, for the remembered, for the forgotten. You have died and you have returned. You matter, Shadow, and you must not meet your death here, a sad sacrifice hidden in a hillside.

"So what are you suggesting I do?" he whispered.

Fight. The Beast is a thing of mind. It's taking its power from you, Shadow. You are near, and so it's become more real. Real enough to own Oliver. Real enough to hurt you.

"Me?"

"You think ghosts can talk to everyone?" asked Cassie Burglass's voice in the darkness, urgently. "We are moths. And you are the flame."

"What should I do?" asked Shadow. "It hurt my arm. It damn near ripped out my throat."

Oh, sweet man. It's just a shadow-thing. It's a night-dog. It's just an overgrown jackal.

"It's real," Shadow said. The last of the stones was being banged into place.

"Are you truly scared of your father's dog?" said a woman's voice. Goddess or ghost, Shadow did not know.

But he knew the answer. Yes. Yes, he was scared.

His left arm was only pain, and unusable, and his right hand was slick and sticky with his blood. He was entombed in a cavity between a wall and rock. But he was, for now, alive.

"Get your shit together," said Cassie. "I've done everything I can. Do it."

He braced himself against the rocks behind the wall, and he raised his feet. Then he kicked both his booted feet out together, as hard as he could. He had walked so many miles in the last few months. He was a big man, and he was stronger than most. He put everything he had behind that kick.

The wall exploded.

The Beast was on him, the black dog of despair, but this time Shadow was prepared for it. This time he was the aggressor. He grabbed at it.

I will not be my father's dog.

With his right hand he held the beast's jaw closed. He stared into its green eyes. He did not believe the beast was a dog at all, not really.

It's daylight, said Shadow to the dog, with his mind, not with his voice. *Run away. Whatever you are, run away. Run back to your gibbet, run back to your grave, little wish hound. All you can do is depress us, fill the world with shadows and illusions. The age when you ran with the wild hunt, or hunted terrified humans, it's over. I don't know if you're my father's dog or not. But you know what? I don't care.*

With that, Shadow took a deep breath and let go of the dog's muzzle.

It did not attack. It made a noise, a baffled whine deep in its throat that was almost a whimper.

"Go home," said Shadow, aloud.

The dog hesitated. Shadow thought for a moment then that he had won, that he was safe, that the dog would simply go away. But then the creature lowered its head, raised the ruff around its neck, and bared its teeth. It would not leave, Shadow knew, until he was dead.

The corridor in the hillside was filling with light: the rising sun shone directly into it. Shadow wondered if the people who had built it, so long ago, had aligned their temple to the sunrise. He took a step to the side, stumbled on something, and fell awkwardly to the ground.

Beside Shadow on the grass was Oliver, sprawled and unconscious. Shadow had tripped over his leg. The man's eyes were closed; he made a growling sound in the back of his throat, and Shadow heard the same sound, magnified and triumphant, from the dark beast that filled the mouth of the temple.

Shadow was down, and hurt, and was, he knew, a dead man.

Something soft touched his face, gently.

Something else brushed his hand. Shadow glanced to his side, and he understood. He understood why Bast had been with him in this place, and he understood who had brought her.

They had been ground up and sprinkled on these fields more than a hundred years before, stolen from the earth around the temple of Bastet and Beni Hasan. Tons upon tons of them, mummified cats in their thousands, each cat a tiny representation of the deity, each cat an act of worship preserved for an eternity.

They were there, in that space, beside him: brown and sand-colored and shadowy gray, cats with leopard spots and cats with tiger stripes, wild, lithe and ancient. These were not the local cats Bast had sent to watch him the previous day. These were the ancestors of those cats, of all our modern cats, from Egypt, from the Nile Delta, from thousands of years ago, brought here to make things grow.

They trilled and chirruped, they did not meow.

The black dog growled louder but now it made no move to attack. Shadow forced himself into a sitting position. "I thought I told you to go home, Shuck," he said.

The dog did not move. Shadow opened his right hand, and gestured. It was a gesture of dismissal, of impatience. *Finish this.*

The cats sprang, with ease, as if choreographed. They landed on the beast, each of them a coiled spring of fangs and claws, both as sharp as they had ever been in life. Pin-sharp claws sank into the black flanks of the huge beast, tore at its eyes. It snapped at them, angrily, and pushed itself against the wall, toppling more rocks, in an attempt to shake them off, but without success. Angry teeth sank into its ears, its muzzle, its tail, its paws.

The beast yelped and growled, and then it made a noise which, Shadow thought, would, had it come from any human throat, have been a scream.

Shadow was never certain what happened then. He watched the black dog put its muzzle down to Oliver's mouth, and push, hard. He could have sworn that the creature stepped *into* Oliver, like a bear stepping into a river.

Oliver shook, violently, on the sand.

The scream faded, and the beast was gone, and sunlight filled the space on the hill.

Shadow felt himself shivering. He felt like he had just woken up from a waking sleep; emotions flooded through him, like sunlight: fear and revulsion and grief and hurt, deep hurt.

There was anger in there, too. Oliver had tried to kill him, he knew, and he was thinking clearly for the first time in days.

A man's voice shouted, "Hold up! Everyone all right over there?"

A high bark, and a lurcher ran in, sniffed at Shadow, his back against the wall, sniffed at Oliver Bierce, unconscious on the ground, and at the remains of Cassie Burglass.

A man's silhouette filled the opening to the outside world, a gray paper cutout against the rising sun.

"Needles! Leave it!" he said. The dog returned to the man's side. The man said, "I heard someone screaming. Leastways, I wouldn't swear to it being a someone. But I heard it. Was that you?"

And then he saw the body, and he stopped. "Holy fucking mother of all fucking bastards," he said.

"Her name was Cassie Burglass," said Shadow.

"Moira's old girlfriend?" said the man. Shadow knew him as the landlord of the pub, could not remember whether he had ever known the man's name. "Bloody Nora. I thought she went to London."

Shadow felt sick.

The landlord was kneeling beside Oliver. "His heart's still beating," he said. "What happened to him?"

"I'm not sure," said Shadow. "He screamed when he saw the body – you must have heard him. Then he just went down. And your dog came in."

The man looked at Shadow, worried. "And you? Look at you! What happened to you, man?"

"Oliver asked me to come up here with him. Said he had something awful he had to get off his chest." Shadow looked at the wall on each side of the corridor. There were other bricked-in nooks there. Shadow had a good idea of what would be found behind them if any of them were opened. "He asked me to help him open the wall. I did. He knocked me over as he went down. Took me by surprise."

"Did he tell you why he had done it?"

"Jealousy," said Shadow. "Just jealous of Moira and Cassie, even after Moira had left Cassie for him."

The man exhaled, shook his head. "Bloody hell," he said. "Last bugger I'd expect to do anything like this. Needles! Leave it!" He pulled a cell phone from his pocket, and called the police. Then he excused himself. "I've got a bag of game to put aside until the police have cleared out," he explained.

Shadow got to his feet, and inspected his arms. His sweater and coat were both ripped in the left arm, as if by huge teeth, but his skin was unbroken beneath it. There was no blood on his clothes, no blood on his hands.

He wondered what his corpse would have looked like, if the black dog had killed him.

Cassie's ghost stood beside him, and looked down at her body, half-fallen from the hole in the wall. The corpse's fingertips and the fingernails were wrecked, Shadow observed, as if she had tried, in the hours or the days before she died, to dislodge the rocks of the wall.

"Look at that," she said, staring at herself. "Poor thing. Like a cat in a glass box." Then she turned to Shadow. "I didn't actually fancy you," she said. "Not even a little bit. I'm not sorry. I just needed to get your attention."

"I know," said Shadow. "I just wish I'd met you when you were alive. We could have been friends."

"I bet we would have been. It was hard in there. It's good to be done with all of this. And I'm sorry, Mr. American. Try not to hate me."

Shadow's eyes were watering. He wiped his eyes on his shirt. When he looked again, he was alone in the passageway.

"I don't hate you," he told her.

He felt a hand squeeze his hand. He walked outside, into the morning sunlight, and he breathed and shivered, and listened to the distant sirens.

Two men arrived and carried Oliver off on a stretcher, down the hill to the road where an ambulance took him away, siren screaming to alert any sheep on the lanes that they should shuffle back to the grass verge.

A female police officer turned up as the ambulance disappeared, accompanied by a younger male officer. They knew the landlord, whom Shadow was not surprised to learn was also a Scathelocke, and were both impressed by Cassie's remains, to the point that the young male officer left the passageway and vomited into the ferns.

If it occurred to either of them to inspect the other bricked-in cavities in the corridor, for evidence of centuries-old crimes, they managed to suppress the idea, and Shadow was not going to suggest it.

He gave them a brief statement, then rode with them to the local police station, where he gave a fuller statement to a large police officer with a serious beard. The officer appeared mostly concerned that Shadow was provided with a mug of instant coffee, and that Shadow, as an American tourist, would not form a mistaken impression of rural England. "It's not like this up here normally. It's really quiet. Lovely place. I wouldn't want you to think we were all like this."

Shadow assured him that he didn't think that at all.

VI
The Riddle

Moira was waiting for him when he came out of the police station. She was standing with a woman in her early sixties, who looked comfortable and reassuring, the sort of person you would want at your side in a crisis.

"Shadow, this is Doreen. My sister."

Doreen shook hands, explaining she was sorry she hadn't been able to be there during the last week, but she had been moving house.

"Doreen's a county court judge," explained Moira.

Shadow could not easily imagine this woman as a judge.

"They are waiting for Ollie to come around," said Moira. "Then they are going to charge him with murder." She said it thoughtfully, but in the same way she would have asked Shadow where he thought she ought to plant some snapdragons.

"And what are you going to do?"

She scratched her nose. "I'm in shock. I have no idea what I'm doing anymore. I keep thinking about the last few years. Poor, poor Cassie. She never thought there was any malice in him."

"I never liked him," said Doreen, and she sniffed. "Too full of facts for my liking, and he never knew when to stop talking. Just kept wittering on. Like he was trying to cover something up."

"Your backpack and your laundry are in Doreen's car," said Moira. "I thought we could give you a lift somewhere, if you needed one. Or if you want to get back to rambling, you can walk."

"Thank you," said Shadow. He knew he would never be welcome in Moira's little house, not anymore.

Moira said, urgently, angrily, as if it was all she wanted to know, "You said you saw Cassie. You *told* us, yesterday. That was what sent Ollie off the deep end. It hurt me so much. Why did you say you'd seen her, if she was dead? You *couldn't* have seen her."

Shadow had been wondering about that, while he had been giving his police statement. "Beats me," he said. "I don't believe in ghosts. Probably a local, playing some kind of game with the Yankee tourist."

Moira looked at him with fierce hazel eyes, as if she was trying to believe him but was unable to make the final leap of faith. Her sister reached down and held her hand. "More things in heaven and earth, Horatio. I think we should just leave it at that."

Moira looked at Shadow, unbelieving, angered, for a long time, before she took a deep breath and said, "Yes. Yes, I suppose we should."

There was silence in the car. Shadow wanted to apologize to Moira, to say something that would make things better.

They drove past the gibbet tree.

"*There were ten tongues within one head,*" recited Doreen, in a voice slightly higher and more formal than the one in which she had previously spoken. "*And one went out to fetch some bread, to feed the living and the dead.* That was a riddle written about this corner, and that tree."

"What does it mean?"

"A wren made a nest inside the skull of a gibbeted corpse, flying in and out of the jaw to feed its young. In the midst of death, as it were, life just keeps on happening." Shadow thought about the matter for a little while, and told her that he guessed that it probably did.

CITY OF ASH

Paolo Bacigalupi

Paolo Bacigalupi (www.windupstories.com) has been published in *Wired, High Country News, Salon.com, OnEarth Magazine, F&SF,* and *Asimov's Science Fiction*. His short fiction has been collected in Locus Award winner and PW Book of the Year *Pump Six and Other Stories* and has been nominated for three Nebula Awards, four Hugo Awards, and won the Theodore Sturgeon Memorial Award for best science fiction short story of the year.

Debut novel *The Windup Girl* was named by *Time* as one of the ten best novels of 2009, and won the Hugo, Nebula, Locus, Compton Crook, and John W. Campbell Memorial Awards, among others. His debut young adult novel, *Ship Breaker*, is a Printz Award Winner, and a National Book Award Finalist, and was followed by *The Drowned Cities*, *Zombie Baseball Beatdown,* and *The Doubt Factory*. His most recent novel for adults, *The Water Knife*, was published last year. Bacigalupi currently lives in Western Colorado with his wife and son, where he is working on a new novel.

Maria dreamed of her father flying and knew things would be alright.

She woke in the morning, and for the first time in more than a year, she felt refreshed. It didn't matter that she was covered in sweat from sleeping in the hot, close basement of the abandoned house, or that that the ashy scent of wildfire smoke had invaded their makeshift bedroom, or that her cough was back. None of it bothered her the way it had before, because she finally felt hopeful.

She got up, climbed the basement stairs, and stepped out into the oven heat of the Phoenix morning, squinting and wrinkling her nose at the ashy irritants in the air. She stretched, working out the kinks of sleep.

Smoke from the Sierras shrouded everything in an acrid mist, again – California blowing in. Trees and grasses and houses turned to char, billowing hundreds of miles across state lines to settle in Arizona and cut visibility to a gray quarter-mile. Even Arizona's desert sun couldn't fight the smoke. It glowed as a jaundiced ball behind the veil but still managed to heat the city just fine.

Maria coughed and blew her nose. More black ash. It got into the basement somehow.

She headed across the lava rock backyard for the outhouse, her flip-flops slapping her heels as she went. Off in the gray distance, the fire-flicker of construction cutters marked where the Taiyang loomed over downtown Phoenix, veiled behind haze.

On a clear day, the Taiyang gleamed. Steel and glass and solar tiles. Solar shades fluttering and tracking the sun, shielding its interconnected towers from the worst of the heat, its gardens gleaming behind glass, moist green terrariums teasing the people who lived outside its climate control and comfort.

But now, with the forest-fire smoke, all that was visible of the Taiyang were the plasma sparks of construction workers as they set and fused the girders for the arcology's next expansion. It wouldn't be Papa. Not now. He'd already be down off the high beams and on his way home, with cash in his pocket and full water jugs from the Red Cross pump, but there were hundreds of others up there, working their own twelve-hour shifts. Impressionistic firefly flashes of workers lucky enough to have a job, delineating the arcology's looming bulk even when you couldn't see the building itself through all the haze.

Papa said it was almost alive. "Its skin makes electricity, *mija*, and in its guts, it's got algea vats and mushrooms and snails to clean the water just like someone's kidneys. It's got pumps that pound like a heart and move all the water and waste, and it's got rivers like veins, and it re-uses everything, again and again. Never lets anything out. Just keeps it in, and keeps finding ways to use it."

The Taiyang grew vegetables in its vertical hydroponic gardens and fish in its filtering pools, and it had waterfalls, and coffee shop terraces, and clean air. If you were rich enough, you could move right in. You could live up high, safe from dust and gangs and rolling brownouts, and never be touched by the disaster of Phoenix at all.

Amazing, surely. But maybe even more amazing that someone had enough faith and money and energy to build.

Maria couldn't remember the last time she'd seen someone build anything. Probably the Santoses, back in San Antonio, when they'd put a new addition on their house. They'd saved for three years to make room for their growing family – and then the next year it was gone, flooded off the map.

So it was something to see the Taiyang Arcology rising proudly over Phoenix. When she'd first come to the city, in the refugee convoy, Maria had resented the Taiyang for how well the people lived there. But now, its shadow bulk was comforting, and the glitter and spark of construction work made her think of candles flickering at church, peaceful assurances that everything was going to be alright.

Maria held her breath as she opened the outhouse door. Reek and flies billowed out.

She and her father had dug the latrine in the cool of the night, hammering together a rough shelter with two-by-fours and siding scavenged from the house next door. It worked okay. Not like having a real toilet with flushing water, but who had that anymore?

It's better than shitting in the open, Maria reminded herself as she crouched over the trench and peed into her Clearsac. She hung the filled bag on a nail and finished her business, then grabbed the full Clearsac and headed back to the basement.

Down in the relative cool of their underground shelter, Maria carefully squeezed her Clearsac into their water jug, watching yellow turn clear as it passed through the filter and drained into the container.

Like a kidney in reverse, Papa had explained.

When they'd first started using the Clearsacs, she'd been disgusted by them. Now she barely thought about it.

But pretty soon... no more Clearsacs.

The thought filled her with relief. The dream of escape... She could still see Papa flying, proud and strong, free of all the tethers that kept them trapped in Phoenix. This broken city wasn't the last stop as Maria had feared. It wasn't their dead end. She and her father weren't going to end up like all the other Texas refugees, smashed up against the border controls of California, which said it already had too many people, and Nevada and Utah, which seemed to hate people on principle – and Texans in particular. They were getting out.

Smiling, she drank from the water jug. She tried to keep a disciplined eye on how much she had, but she was so thirsty, she ended up draining it and feeling ashamed, and yet still drinking, convulsively swallowing water until there was nothing except drops that she lapped at, too, trying to get everything.

Never mind. It's not like it was before. Papa's got a job now. It's okay to drink. He said it was okay to drink.

She remembered how it had been the day after Taiyang International hired him: him coming home with a five-gallon cube of water and two rolls of toilet paper, plus pupusas that he'd bought from a pop-up stand near the construction site – but most of all, him coming home smiling. Not worried about every drop of water. Not worried about... well, everything.

"We're all good now, *mija*," he'd said. "We're all good. This job, it's a big one. It'll last a long time. We're gonna save up. And we don't just got to go north now. We can buy our way to China, too. This job, it opens a lot of doors for us. After this, we can go anywhere. Anywhere, *mija*."

He kept saying it, over and over again: *We can go anywhere.*

Papa had a job again. He had a plan again. They had a chance, again. And for the first time in months, he sounded like himself. Not the scared and sorrowful man who kept apologizing that they didn't have enough food for the night or the medicine that Mom needed, or who kept insisting that it was possible to go north when it clearly wasn't. Not that man who seemed to crumple in on himself as he realized that the way the world had been was no longer the way the world was.

It had all happened so fast. One minute Maria had been worrying about what her mother would say about her B on a biology test and the dress she'd have for her *quinceañera*, and the next, America was falling apart all around them, like God had swiped his hand across the map and left a different country in its place.

You weren't supposed to get turned back by militias at the border of Oklahoma or see people strung in the margins of the interstates. But she'd seen both. Her father kept saying that this was America, and America didn't do these things, but the America in her father's mind wasn't the same as the America that they drove across.

America wasn't supposed to be a place where you huddled for safety under the shield of an Iowa National Guard convoy and woke up without them – waking with a start to desert silence and the hot flapping of a FEMA tent, realizing that you were all alone, and that somewhere out in the darkness, New Mexicans were planning to make a lesson of you. In Papa's mind, that shit didn't happen. On the ground, it did. There was America before Cat 6 hurricanes and megadroughts, and there was after – with everyone on the move.

That was all past now, though. Papa finally had a plan that would work, and a job that paid, and they were getting out.

Maria settled back on her mattress and dug out a language tablet. The Chinese gave them away free to anyone who asked, and people hacked them to get access to the public network. To make up for her greed with the water, she decided to study instead of watching pirated movies.

The screen lit up, and a familiar Chinese lady started the lesson. Maria followed her prompts. The lady moved on from numbers to other words, tricky games that highlighted the tonal differences between "ma" and "ma," "mai" and "mai."

Different language. Different rules. Tones. Tiny differences to Maria's ear that turned out to make all the difference in the world. If you weren't trained to listen for them, you didn't know what was going on. You were lost.

The lady in the tablet nodded and smiled as Maria said "buy" and "sell" correctly.

Maria was so engrossed in her study that it took a while to notice that time had passed, and Papa wasn't home.

She got to her feet and went out into the choking furnace of 120-degree heat. The smoke had thickened. It seemed like all of California was on fire, and all of it was blowing in to Phoenix.

Maria peered toward the Taiyang, but even the construction cutter flickers were invisible now. Papa was never late coming off shift. He always did his shift, got his pay, filled his jugs from the Red Cross pump, and came straight home.

She started walking toward the construction site, making her way down the long dust-rutted boulevards, where Texas bang bang girls stood on the street corners and tried to pick up rich Californians who were over the border to go slumming. Walking past the Red Cross pump, where the lines for water stretched around the block and the price always seemed to go up. Past the shanty towns of suburban refugees that filled Fry's and Target parking lots, all of them scavenging and building plywood slums around the relief pump, grateful to be close to any place where they could get water. Past the Merry Perry revival tent, where people lashed themselves with thorn bushes and begged God to send them rain.

Maria trudged through the choking smoke and dust, wishing she'd saved some of her water jug for the brutal heat of the walk. The arcology loomed out of the smoke, a jumbled collection of boxy interconnected towers, as isolated from Phoenix as if it were a castle fortress.

On the Taiyang's construction side, the gate guard wouldn't let her in. He didn't seem to understand English, Spanish, or her broken Chinese. But he did make a call, though.

A Chinese man came out to her. A polished man, he wore a hardhat, nice clothes, and filter mask around his neck – a good one from REI that would keep California and Phoenix out of his lungs. Maria eyed it jealously.

"You're here about the accident?" he asked.

"What accident?"

"There was a fall."

He spoke with an accent, but his English was clear enough. It had been a long fall, he said. She wouldn't want to see his body. He was very sorry. Taiyang International had made arrangements for the respectful disposal of his body. She could pick up his remains in the evening. There was some leftover pay, and Taiyang would cover the costs of the cremation.

Maria found herself staring at the man's fancy dust mask as he droned on. The rubberized seals and replaceable filters...

Her father would be smoke. More smoke, adding to the burn that people tried to keep out of their lungs. Maybe she was breathing him in, right now – him and the Sierras and all of California.

His ash, flying free.

JAMAICA GINGER

Nalo Hopkinson and Nisi Shawl

NALO HOPKINSON (WWW.NALOHOPKINSON.COM), born in Jamaica, has lived in Jamaica, Trinidad, Guyana, and Canada. She now teaches creative writing at the University of California Riverside in the United States. She is the author of six novels – *Brown Girl in the Ring, Midnight Robber, The Salt Roads, The New Moon's Arms, The Chaos,* and *Sister Mine* – two short story collections, and a chapbook. She edited anthologies *Whispers from the Cotton Tree Root: Caribbean Fabulist Fiction*, and *Mojo: Conjure Stories*. She is a recipient of the John W. Campbell Award for Best New Writer, the Locus Award for Best New Writer, the World Fantasy Award, the Sunburst Award (twice), the Aurora Award, the Gaylactic Spectrum Award, and the Norton Award. Her most recent book is the short story collection, *Falling in Love With Hominids*.

NISI SHAWL (WWW.NISISHAWL.COM) is the author of collections *Filter House* and *Something More and More*. Her short fiction has been nominated for the World Fantasy, Carl Brandon and Gaylactic Spectrum Awards. *Filter House* won the James Tiptree Jr Memorial Award and was nominated for the World Fantasy Award. She is co-author of *Writing the Other: A Practical Approach*, and co-editor of *Strange Matings: Science Fiction, Feminism, African American Voices, and Octavia E. Butler* and *Stories for Chip: A Tribute to Samuel R. Delany*. She writes reviews for *The Seattle Times*, and writes and edits reviews for the feminist literary quarterly *Cascadia Subduction Zone*. Her Belgian Congo steampunk novel *Everfair* is due out from Tor in September 2016.

"Damn and blast it!"

Plaquette let herself in through the showroom door of the watchmaker's that morning to hear Msieur blistering the air of his shop with his swearing. The hulking clockwork man he'd been working on was high-stepping around the workroom floor in a clumsy lurch. It lifted its knees comically high, its body listing to one side and its feet coming down in the wrong order; toe, then heel. Billy Sumach, who delivered supplies to Msieur, was in the workroom. Through the open doorway he threw her a merry glance with his pretty brown eyes, but he had better sense than to laugh at Msieur's handiwork with Msieur in the room.

Msieur glared at Plaquette. "You're late. That's coming off your pay."

Plaquette winced. Their family needed every cent of her earnings, but she'd had to wait home till Ma got back from the railroad to take over minding Pa.

The mechanical George staggered tap-click, tap-click across the shop. It crashed into a wall and tumbled with a clank to the floor, then lay there whirring. Msieur swore again, words Ma would be mortified to know that Plaquette had heard. He snatched off one of his own shoes and threw it at the George. Billy Sumach gave a little *peep* of swallowed laughter. Msieur pointed at the George. "Fix it," he growled at Plaquette. "I have to present it to the governor the day after tomorrow."

As though Plaquette didn't know that. "Yes, Msieur," she said to his back as he stormed through the door to the showroom.

The second the door slammed shut, Billy let out a whoop. Plaquette found herself smiling along with him, glad of a little amusement. It was scarce in her life nowadays. "My land," Billy said, "'Pears Old George there has got himself the jake leg!"

The fun blew out of the room like a candle flame. "Don't you joke," Plaquette told him, through teeth clamped tight together. "You know 'bout my Pa."

Billy's face fell. "Oh Lord, Plaquette, I'm sorry."

"Just help me get this George to its feet. It weighs a ton." Billy was a fine man, of Plaquette's color and station. Lately when he came by with deliveries he'd been favoring her with smiles and wistful looks. But she couldn't study that right now, not with Pa taken so poorly. Together they wrestled the

George over to Plaquette's work table. There it stood. Its painted-on porter's uniform had chipped at one shoulder when it fell. Its chest door hung open as a coffin lid. Plaquette wanted to weep at the tangle of metal inside it. She'd taken the George's chest apart and put it back together, felt like a million times now. Msieur couldn't see what was wrong, and neither could she. Its arms worked just fine; Plaquette had strung the wires inside them herself. But the legs...

"You'll do it," Billy said, "Got a good head on your shoulders."

Feeling woeful, Plaquette nodded.

An uncomfortable silence held between them an instant. If he wanted to come courting, now would be the time to ask. Instead, he held up his clipboard. "Msieur gotta sign for these boxes."

Plaquette nodded again. She wouldn't have felt right saying yes to courting, anyway. Not with Pa so sick.

If he'd asked, that is.

"Billy, you ever think of doing something else?" The words were out before she knew she wanted to ask them.

He frowned thoughtfully. "You know, I got cousins own a lavender farm, out Des Allemands way. Sometimes I think I might join them."

"Not some big city far off?" She wondered how Billy's calloused hands would feel against her cheek.

"Nah. Too noisy, too dirty. Too much like this place." Then he saw her face. "Though if a pretty girl like you were there," he said slowly, as though afraid to speak his mind, "I guess I could come to love it."

He looked away then. "Think Msieur would mind me popping to the showroom real quick? I could take him his shoe."

"Just make sure no white folks in there."

Billy collected Msieur's shoe then ducked into the showroom. Plaquette hung her hat on the hook near the back and sat down to work. Msieur's design for the George lay crumpled on her table where he'd left it. She smoothed out the sheets of paper and set to poring over them, as she'd done every day since she started working on the George. This was the most intricate device Msieur had ever attempted. It had to perform flawlessly on the day the governor unveiled it at the railroad. For a couple years now, Msieur had depended on Plaquette's keen vision and small, deft hands to assemble the components of his more intricate timepieces and his designs. By the point he decided to teach her how to read his notes, she'd already figured out how to decipher most of the symbols and his chicken scratch writing.

There. That contact strip would never sit right, not lying flat like that. Needed a slight bend to it. Plaquette got a pencil out of her table's drawer and made a correction to Msieur's notes. Billy came back and started to bring boxes from his cart outside in through the workroom door. While he worked and tried to make small talk with her, Plaquette got herself a tray. From the drawers of the massive oak watchmaker's cabinet in the middle of the shop, she collected the items she needed and took them to her bench.

"Might rain Saturday, don't you think?" huffed Billy as he heaved a box to the very top of the pile.

"Might," Plaquette replied. "Might not." His new bashfulness with her made her bashful in return. They couldn't quite seem to be companionable any more. She did a last check of the long row of black velvet cloth on her workbench, hundreds of tiny brass and crystal components gleaming against the black fur of the fabric. She knew down to the last how many cogs, cams, and screws were there. She had to. Msieur counted every penny, fussed over every quarter inch of the fine gauge wire that went into the timekeepers his shop produced. At year's end he tallied every watch finding, every scrap of leather. If any were missing, the cost was docked from her salary. Kind of the backwards of a Christmas bonus. As if Msieur didn't each evening collect sufficient profits from his till and lower them into his 'secret' safe.

Billy saw Plaquette pick up her tweezers and turn towards the mechanical porter. "Do you want Claude?" he asked her.

He knew her so well. She smiled at him. "Yes, please." He leapt to go fetch Claude out of the broom closet where they stored him.

Billy really was sweet, and he wasn't the only one who'd begun looking at her differently as she filled out from girl to woman this past year. Ma said she had two choices: marry Billy and be poor but in love; or angle to become Msieur's placée and take up life in the Quarter. Msieur would never publicly acknowledge her or any children he had by her, but she would be comfortable, and maybe pass some of her comforts along to Ma and Pa. Not that they would ever ask.

'Sides, she wasn't even sure she was ready to be thinking about all that bother just yet.

Plaquette yawned. She was bone tired, and no wonder. She'd been spending her nights and Sundays looking after Pa since he had come down with the jake leg.

Claude's books had excited Plaquette when she first heard them, but in time they'd become overly familiar. She knew every thrilling leap from crumbling clifftops, every graveside confession, every switched and secret identity that formed part of those well-worn tales. They had started to grate on her, those stories of people out in the world, having adventures she never could. Pa got to see foreign places; the likes of New York and Chicago and San Francisco. He only passed through them, of course. He had to remain on the train. But he got to see new passengers at each stop, to smell foreign air, to look up into a different sky. Or he had.

He would again, when he got better. He would. The metal Georges would need minding, wouldn't they? And who better for that job than Pa, who'd been a dependable George himself these many years?

But for Plaquette, there was only day after day, one marching in sequence behind another, in this workroom. Stringing tiny, shiny pieces of metal together. Making shift nowadays to always be on the other side of the room from Msieur whenever he was present. She was no longer the board-flat young girl she'd been when she first went to work for Msieur. She'd begun to bud, and Msieur seemed inclined to pluck himself a tender placée flower to grace his lapel. A left-handed marriage was one thing; but to a skinflint like Msieur?

Problems crowding up on each other like stormclouds running ahead of the wind. Massing so thick that Plaquette couldn't presently see her way through them. Ma said when life got dark like that, all's you could do was keep putting one foot in front the other and hope you walked yourself to somewhere brighter.

But as usual, once Billy set Claude up and the automaton began its recitation, her work was accurate and quick. She loved the challenge and ritual of assemblage: laying exactly the right findings out on the cloth; listening to the clicking sound of Claude's gears as he recited one of his scrolls; letting the ordered measure take her thoughts away till all that was left was the precise dance of her fingers as they selected the watch parts and clicked, screwed or pinned them into place. Sometimes she only woke from her trance of time, rhythm, and words when Msieur shook her by the shoulder come evening and she looked up to realize the whole day had gone by.

Shadows fell on Plaquette's hands, obscuring her work. She looked around, blinking. When had it gone dusk? The workroom was empty. Billy had probably gone on about his other business hours ago. Claude's scroll had run out and he'd long since fallen silent. Why hadn't Msieur told her it was time to go? She could hear him wandering around his upstairs apartment.

She rubbed her burning eyes. He'd probably hoped she'd keep working until the mechanical George was set to rights.

Had she done it? She slid her hands out of the wire-and-cam guts of the mechanical man. She'd have to test him to be sure. But in the growing dark, she could scarcely make out the contacts in the George's body that needed to be tripped in order to set it in motion.

Plaquette rose from her bench, stretched her twinging back and frowned – in imitation of Mama – through the doorway at the elaborately decorated Carcel lamp displayed in the shop's front. Somewhat outmoded though it was, the clockwork regulating the lamp's fuel supply and draft served Msieur as one of many proofs of his meticulous handiwork – *her* meticulous handiwork. If she stayed in the workshop any later she'd have to light that lamp. And for all that he wanted her to work late, Msieur would be sure to deduct the cost of the oil used from her wages. He could easily put a vacuum bulb into the Carcel, light it with cheap units of Tesla power instead of oil, but he mistrusted energy he couldn't see. Said it wasn't "refined."

She took a few steps in the direction of the Carcel.

C-RRR-EEEAK!

Plaquette gasped and dashed for the showroom door to the street. She had grabbed the latch rope before her wits returned. She let the rope go and faced back toward the black doorway out of which emerged the automaton, Claude. It rocked forward on its treads, left side, right. Its black velvet jacket swallowed what little light there still was. But the old-fashioned white ruff circling its neck cast up enough brightness to show its immobile features. They had, like hers, much of the African to them. Claude came to a stop in front of her.

CRREAK!

Plaquette giggled. "You giving me a good reminder – I better put that oil on your wheels as well as your insides. You like to scare me half to death rolling round the dark in here." She pulled the miniature oil tin from her apron pocket and knelt to lubricate the wheels of the rolling treads under Claude's platform. It had been Plaquette's idea to install them to replace the big brass wheels he'd had on either side. She'd grown weary of righting Claude every time he rolled over an uneven surface and toppled. It had been good practice, though, for nowadays, when Pa was like to fall with each spastic step he took, and Plaquette so often had to catch him. He hated using the crutches. And all of this because he'd begun taking a few sips of jake to warm his cold bones before his early morning shifts.

Jamaica Ginger was doing her family in, that was sure.

Her jostling of Claude must have released some last dregs of energy left in his winding mechanism, for just then he took it into his mechanical head to drone, "... nooot to escaaape it by exerrrtion..."

Quickly, Plaquette stopped the automaton midsentence. For good measure, she removed the book from its spool inside Claude. She didn't want Msieur to hear that she was still downstairs, alone in the dark.

As Plaquette straightened again, a new thought struck her.

The shutters folded back easily. White light from the coil-powered street lamp outside flooded the tick-tocking showroom, glittering on glass cases and gold and brass watches, on polished wooden housings and numbered faces like pearly moons. More than enough illumination for Plaquette's bright eyes. "Come along, Claude," Plaquette commanded as she headed back towards the work room – somewhat unnecessarily, as she had Claude's wardenclyffe in the pocket of her leather work apron. Where it went, Claude was bound to follow. Which made it doubly foolish of her to have been startled by him.

She could see the mechanical porter more clearly now; its cold steel body painted deep blue in imitation of a porter's uniform, down to the gold stripes at the cuffs of the jacket. Its perpetually smiling black face. The Pullman Porter 'cap' atop its head screwed on like a bottle top. Inside it was the Tesla receiver the George would use to guide itself around inside the sleeping-car cabins the Pullman company planned to outfit with wireless transmitters.

That part had been Plaquette's idea. Msieur had grumbled, but Plaquette could see him mentally adding up the profits this venture could bring him.

If Msieur's George was a success, that'd be the end of her father's job. Human porters had human needs. A mechanical George would rarely be ill, never miss work. Would always smile, would never need a new uniform – just the occasional paint touch-up. Would need to be paid for initially, but never paid thereafter.

With two fingers, Plaquette poked the George's ungiving chest. The mechanical man didn't so much as rock on its sturdy legs. Plaquette still thought treads would have been better, like Claude's. But Msieur wanted the new Georges to be as lifelike as possible, so as not to scare the fine ladies and gentlemen who rode the luxury sleeping-cars. So the Georges must be able to walk. Smoothly, like Pa used to.

The chiming clocks in the showroom began tolling the hour, each in their separate tones. Plaquette gasped. Though surrounded by clocks, she had completely forgotten how late it was. Ma would be waiting for her; it was nearly time for Pa's shift at the station! She couldn't stop now to test the George. She slapped Claude's wardenclyffe into his perpetually outstretched hand, pulled her bonnet onto her head, and hastened outside, stopping only to jiggle the shop's door by its polished handle to make sure the latch had safely caught.

Only a few blocks to scurry home under the steadily burning lamps, among the sparse clumps of New Orleans's foreign sightseers and those locals preferring to conduct their business in the cool of night. In her hurry, she bumped into one overdressed gent. He took her by the arms and leered, looking her up and down. She muttered an apology and pulled away before he could do more than that. She was soon home, where Ma was waiting on the landing outside their rooms. The darkness and Pa's hat and heavy coat disguised Ma well enough to fool the white supervisors for a while, and the other colored were in on the secret. But if Ma came in late –

"Don't fret, Darling," Ma said, bending to kiss Plaquette's cheek. "I can still make it. He ate some soup and I just help him to the necessary, so he probably sleep till morning."

Plaquette went into the dark apartment. No fancy lights for them. Ma had left the kerosene lamp on the kitchen table, turned down low. Plaquette could see through to Ma and Pa's bed. Pa was tucked in tight, only his head showing above the covers. He was breathing heavy, not quite a snore. The shape of him underneath the coverlet looked so small. Had he shrunk, or was she growing?

Plaquette hung up her hat. In her hurry to get home, she'd left Msieur's still wearing her leather apron. As she pulled it off to hang it beside her hat, something inside one of the pockets thumped dully against the wall. One of Claude's book scrolls; the one she'd taken from him. She returned it to the pocket. Claude could have it back tomorrow. She poured herself some soup from the pot on the stove. Smelled like pea soup and crawfish, with a smoky hint of ham. Ma had been stretching the food with peas, seasoning it with paper-thin shavings from that one ham shank for what seemed like weeks now. Plaquette didn't think she could stomach the taste of more peas, more stingy wisps of ham. What she wouldn't give for a good slice of roast beef, hot from the oven, its fat glistening on the plate.

Her stomach growled, not caring. Crawfish soup would suit it just fine. Plaquette sat to table and set about spooning cold soup down her gullet. The low flame inside the kerosene lamp flickered, drawing pictures. Plaquette imagined she saw a tower, angels circling it (or demons), a war raging below. Men skewering other men with blades and spears. Beasts she'd never before heard tell of, lunging –

"Girl, what you seeing in that lamp? Have you so seduced."

Plaquette started and pulled her mind out of the profane world in the lamp. "Pa!" She jumped up from the table and went to kiss him on the forehead. He hugged her, his hands flopping limply to thump against her back. He smelled of sweat, just a few days too old to be ignored. "You need anything? The necessary?"

"Naw." He tried to pat the bed beside him, failed. He grimaced. "Just come and sit by me a little while. Tell me the pictures in your mind."

"If I do, you gotta tell me 'bout San Francisco again." She sat on the bed facing him, knees drawn up beneath her skirts like a little child.

"Huh. I'm never gonna see that city again." It tore at Plaquette's heart to see his eyes fill with tears. "Oh, Plaquette," he whispered, "What are we gonna to do?"

Not we; her. She would do it. "Hush, Pa." It wouldn't be Billy. Ma and Pa were showing her that you couldn't count on love and hard work alone to pull you through. Not when this life would scarcely pay a colored man a penny to labor all his days and die young. She patted Pa's arm, took his helpless hand in hers. She closed her eyes to recollect the bright story in the lamp flame. Opened them again. "So. Say there's a tower, higher than that mountain you told me 'bout that one time. The one with the clouds all round the bottom of it so it look to be floating?"

Pa's mouth was set in bitterness. He stared off at nothing. For a moment, Plaquette though he wouldn't answer her. But then, his expression unchanged, he ground out, "Mount Rainier. In Seattle."

"That's it. This here tower, it's taller than that."

Pa turned his eyes to hers. "What's it for?"

"How should I know? I'll tell you that when it comes to me. I know this, though; there's people flying round that tower, right up there in the air. Like men, and maybe a woman, but with wings. Like angels. No, like bats."

Pa's eyes grew round. The lines in his face smoothed out as Plaquette spun her story. A cruel prince. A fearsome army. A lieutenant with a conscience.

It would have to be Msieur.

That ended up being a good night. Pa fell back to sleep, his face more peaceful than she'd seen in days. Plaquette curled up against his side. She was used to his snoring and the heaviness of his drugged breath. She meant to sleep there beside him, but her mind wouldn't let her rest. It was full of imaginings: dancing with Msieur at the Orleans Ballroom, her wearing a fine gown and a fixed, automaton smile; Billy's hopeful glances and small kindnesses, his endearingly nervous bad jokes; and Billy's shoulders, already bowed at seventeen from lifting and hauling too-heavy boxes day in, day out, tick, tock, forever (how long before her eyesight went from squinting at tiny watch parts?); an army of tireless metal Georges, more each day, replacing the fleshly porters, and brought about in part by her cleverness. Whichever path her future took, Plaquette could only see disaster.

Yet in the air above her visions, *They* flew.

Finally Plaquette eased herself out of bed. The apartment was dark; she'd long since blown out the lamp to save wick and oil. She tiptoed carefully to the kitchen. By feel, she got Claude's reading scroll out of the pocket of her apron. She crept out onto the landing. By the light of a streetlamp, she unrolled and re-rolled it so that she could see the end of the book. The punched holes stopped a good foot-and-a-half before the end of the roll. There was that much blank space left.

Plaquette knew *My Lady Nobody* practically word for word. She studied the roll, figuring out the patterns of holes that created the sounds which allowed Claude to speak the syllables of the story. She could do this. She crept back inside and felt her way through the kitchen drawer. She grasped something way at the back. A bottle, closed tight, some liquid still sloshing around inside it. A sniff of the lid told her what it was. She put the bottle aside and kept rummaging through the drawer. Her heart beat triple-time when she found what she was looking for. Pa did indeed have more than one ticket punch.

It was as though there was a fever rising in her; for the next few hours she crouched shivering on the landing and in a frenzy, punched a complicated pattern into the end of the scroll, stopping every so often to roll it back to the beginning for guidance on how to punch a particular syllable. By the time she'd used up the rest of the roll, her fingers were numb with cold, her teeth chattering, the sky was going pink in the east, and the landing was scattered with little circles of white card. But her brain finally felt at peace.

She rose stiffly to her feet. A light breeze began blowing the white circles away. Ma would probably be home in another hour or so. Plaquette replaced the scroll in her apron pocket, changed into her night gown, and lay back down beside her father. In seconds, she fell into a deep, dreamless sleep.

MA WOKE HER all too soon. Plaquette's eyes felt like there was grit in them. Pa was still snoring away. Ma gestured her out to the kitchen, where they could speak without waking him. Ma's face was drawn with fatigue. She'd spent the night fetching and carrying for white people. "How he doing?" she asked.

"Tolerable. Needs a bath."

Ma sighed. "I know. He won't let me wash him. He ashamed."

Plaquette felt her eyebrows lift in surprise. The Pa she knew washed every morning and night and had a full bath on Sundays.

Ma pulled a chair out from under the table and thumped herself down into it. Her lips were pinched together with worry. "He not getting better."

"We're managing."

"I thought he might mend. Some do. Tomorrow he supposed to start his San Francisco run. Guess I gotta do it."

At first, Plaquette felt only envy. Even Ma was seeing the world. Then she understood the problem. "San Francisco run's five days."

Ma nodded. "I know you can see to him all by yourself, Darling. You're a big girl. But you gotta go to work for Msieur too. Your Pa, he's not ready to be alone all day."

It was one weight too many on the scales. Plaquette feared it would tip her completely over. She stammered, "I-I have to-to go, Ma." Blindly, she grabbed her bonnet and apron and sped out the door. Guilt followed her the whole way to Msieur's. Leaving Ma like that.

She would have to start charming Msieur, sooner rather than later.

Plaquette was the first one to the shop, just as she'd planned it. Msieur generally lingered over his breakfast, came down in time to open the showroom to custom. She'd have a few minutes to herself. She'd make it up to Ma later. Sit down with her and Pa Sunday morning and work out a plan.

Claude and the George were beside her bench, right where she'd left them. She bent and patted Claude on the cheek. She delved into Claude's base through its open hatch and removed the remaining three 'books' which Claude recited when the rolls of punched paper were fed into his von Kempelen apparatus. Claude bided open and silent, waiting to be filled with words. Eagerly Plaquette lowered her book onto the spool and locked that in place, then threaded the end – no, the beginning, the very beginning of this new story – onto the toothed drum of the von Kempelen and closed its cover.

She removed the ribbon bearing Claude's key from his wrist. She wound him tight and released the guard halfway – for some of the automaton's mechanisms were purely for show. In this mode, Claude's carven lips would remain unmoving.

With a soft creak, the spool began to turn. A flat voice issued from beneath Claude's feet:

"They Fly at Çironia, by Della R. Mausney. Prologue. Among the tribes and villages –"

It was working!

Afire with the joy of it, Plaquette began working on the George again.

But come noon the metal man was still as jake-legged as Pa. Seemed there was nothing Plaquette could do to fix either one.

She tried to settle her thoughts. She couldn't work if her mind was troubled. She'd listened to her punchcard story three times today already. She knew she was being vain, but she purely loved hearing her words issue forth from Claude. The story was a creation that was completely hers, not built on the carcass of someone else's ingenuity. Last night's sleepless frenzy had cut the bonds on her imagination. She'd set free something she didn't know she had in her. Claude's other novels were all rich folk weeping over rich folk problems, white folk pitching woo. *They Fly at Çironia* was different, wickedly so. The sweep and swoop of it. The crudeness, the brutality.

She wound the key set into Claude's side until it was just tight enough, and tripped the release fully. With a quiet sound like paper riffling, Claude's head started to move. His eyelids flicked up and down. His head turned left to right. The punchcard clicked forward one turn. Claude's jaw opened, and he began to recite.

"Now," she whispered to the George, "one more time. Let's see what's to be done with you." She reached into his chest with her tweezers as the familiar enchantment began to come upon her. While the Winged Ones *screeed* through the air of Çironia's mountains on pinions of quartz, Plaquette wove and balanced quiltings of coiled springs, hooked them into layer upon layer of delicately-weighted controls, dropped them into one another's curving grasps, adjusted and readjusted the workings of the George's legs.

Finally, for the fourth time that day, the Winged Ones seized the story's teller and tossed him among themselves in play. Finally, for the fourth time that day, he picked himself up from the ground, gathered about himself such selfness as he could.

The short book ended. Gradually, Plaquette's trance did the same.

Except for the automatons, she was alone. The time was earlier than it had been last night. Not by much. Shadows filled the wide corners, and the little light that fell between buildings to slip in at the tall windows was thin and nearly useless.

A creaking board revealed Msieur's presence in the showroom just before the door communicating with it opened. He stuck his head through, smiling like the overdressed man Plaquette had run from on her way home last night. She returned the smile, trying for winsomeness.

"Not taking ill, are you?" Msieur asked. So much for her winning ways.

He moved forward into the room to examine the George. "Have you finished for the day? I doubt you made much progress." His manicured hands reopened the chest she had just shut. He bent as if to peer inside, but his eyes slid sideways, towards Plaquette's bosom and shoulders. She should stand proud to show off her figure. Instead, she stumbled up from her bench and edged behind the stolid protection of Claude's metal body.

Smiling more broadly yet, Msieur turned his gaze to the George's innards in reality. "You do appear to have done something, however – Let's test it!" He closed up the chest access. He retrieved the mechanism's key from the table, wound it tight, and tripped its initial release. The George lumbered clumsily to its feet.

"Where's that instruction card? Ah!" Msieur inserted it and pressed the secondary release button.

A grinding hum issued from the metal chest. The George's left knee lifted – waist-high – higher! But then it lowered and the foot kicked out. It landed heel first. One step – another – a third – a fourth – four more – it stopped. It had reached the workroom's far wall, and, piled against it, the Gladstones and imperials it was now supposed to load itself with. It whirred and stooped. It ticked and reached, tocked and grasped, and then –

Then it stuck in place. Quivering punctuated by rhythmic jerks ran along its blue-painted frame. Rrrr-rap! *Rrrr-rap!* RRRR-RAP! With each repetition the noise of the George's faulty operation grew louder. Msieur ran quickly to disengage its power.

"Such precision! Astonishing!" Msieur appeared pleased at even partial success. He stroked his neat, silky beard thoughtfully. He seemed to come to a decision. "We'll work through the night. The expense of the extra oil consumed is nothing if we succeed – and I believe we will."

By "we," Msieur meant her. He expected for her to toil on his commission all night.

But what about Pa?

Self-assured though he was, Msieur must have sensed her hesitation. "What do you need? Of course – you must be fed! I'll send to the Café du Monde –" He glanced around the empty workshop. "– or if I must go myself, no matter. A cup of chicory and a slice of chocolate pie, girl! How does that sound?"

Chocolate pie! But as she opened her mouth to assent she found herself saying instead, "But Ma – Pa –"

Msieur was already in the showroom; she heard the muffled bell that rang whenever he slid free the drawer holding the day's receipts. Plaquette crept forward; obediently, Claude followed her onto the crimson carpet. Startled, Msieur thrust his hands below the counter so she couldn't see what they held. "What's that you say?"

"My folks will worry if I don't get home 'fore too late. I better –"

"No. You stay. I'll have the Café send a messenger."

That wouldn't help. She couldn't say why, though, so she had to let Msieur herd her back to the workroom. Under his suspicious eye she wound up the George again and walked it to her bench. Not long after, Claude rejoined her. "That's right," said Msieur, satisfied. "And if this goes well, I'll have a proposition to make to your mother. Eh? You have been quite an asset to me. I should like to, erm, deepen our connection."

Plaquette swallowed. "Yes, Msieur."

His face brightened. "Yes? Your own place in the Quarter. You would keep working in the shop, of course. Splendid, then. Splendid." He winked at her! The door to the showroom slammed shut. The jangle of keys told Plaquette that Msieur had locked her in. Like a faint echo, the door to the street slammed seconds later.

She sank back onto her seat. Only greyness, like dirty water, trickled in at the workroom windows, fading as she watched.

So even if she became Msieur's placée, tended to their left-hand marriage, he would expect her to continue in this dreary workroom.

Plaquette frowned, attempting to recall if she'd heard the grate and clank of the safe's door closing on the day's proceeds, the money and precious jewels Msieur usually hid away there. Sometimes she could remember what had happened around her during the last few minutes of her trance.

Not today.

Only the vague outlines of its windows broke the darkening workroom's walls. And beneath where she knew the showroom door stood, a faint, blurry smear gleamed dully, vanishing remnant of l'heure bleue. She must go home now. Before Msieur returned with his chocolate pie and his unctuous wooing.

She considered the showroom door a moment longer. But the door from there led right to the street. People would be bound to see her escape. The workroom door, then; the delivery entrance that led to the alleyway. She twisted to face it.

Msieur had reinforced this door the same summer when, frightened of robbers, he sank his iron safe beneath the workroom's huge oak cabinet. It was faced outside with bricks, a feeble attempt at concealment that made it heavy – too heavy for Plaquette alone to budge. Plaquette, however, was not alone.

Marshalling the George into position, she set him to kick down the thick workroom door. The George walked forward a few more feet, then stopped there in the alley, lacking for further commands. A dumb mechanical porter with no more sense than a headless chicken.

Though she hadn't planned it, Plaquette found she knew what she wanted to do next. She rushed back to her bench. Claude cheerfully rocked after her. She erased all the corrections that she'd meticulously made to Msieur's notes. She scribbled in new ones, any nonsense that came to mind. Without her calculations Msieur would never work out the science of making a wireless iron George. Someone else eventually might, but this way, it wouldn't be on Plaquette's conscience.

She took a chair with her out into the alleyway, climbed up onto it, and unscrewed the George's cap. She upturned it so that it sat like a bowl on the George's empty head. From her apron she produced the bottle she'd taken from Ma's kitchen; the one with the dregs of jake in it. Ma could never bear to throw anything away, even poison. Plaquette poured the remaining jake all over the receiver inside the George's cap. There was a satisfying sizzling sound of wires burning out. Jake leg this, you son of a – well. Ma wouldn't like her even thinking such language. She screwed the cap back onto the George's head. Msieur might never discover the sabotage.

One more trip back inside the workroom, to Claude's broom closet. On a hook in there hung the Pullman porter's uniform that Msieur had been given to model the George's painted costume after. It was a men's small. A little large on her, but she belted in the waist and rolled up the trouser hems. She slid her hands into the trouser pockets, and exclaimed in delight. So much room! Not dainty, feminine pockets – bigger even than those stitched onto her workroom apron. She could carry almost anything she pleased in these!

But now she really must hurry. She strewed her clothing about the workroom – let Msieur make of that what he would. A kidnapping or worse, her virgin innocence soiled, maybe her lifeless body dumped in the bayou. And off they went – Plaquette striding freely in her masculine get-up, one foot in front of the other, making her plan as she made up the stories she told Pa: by letting the elements come to her in the moment. Claude rolled in her wake, tipping dangerously forward as he negotiated the steep drop from banquette to roadway, falling farther and farther behind.

When they came to the stairs up the side of the building where she lived she was stumped for what to do. Claude was not the climbing sort. For the moment she decided to store him in the necessary – she'd figure out how to get him back to Msieur's later. She'd miss his cheerful face, though.

Ma yelped when a stranger in a porter's uniform walked in the door. She reached for her rolling pin.

"Ma! It just me!" Plaquette pulled off her cap, let her hair bush out free from under it.

Ma boggled. "Plaquette? Why you all got up like that?"

The sound of Pa's laughter rasped from her parents' bedroom. Pa was sitting up in bed, peering through the doorway. "That's my hellcat girl," he said. "Mother, you ain't got to go out on the Frisco run. Plaquette gon' do it."

Ma stamped her foot at him. "Don't be a fool! She doing no such thing."

Except she was! Till now, Plaquette hadn't thought it through. But that's exactly what she was going to do.

Ma could read the determination in her face. "Child, don't you see? It won't work. You too young to pass for your Pa. Gonna get him fired."

Plaquette thought fast. "Not Pa. Pa's replacement." She pulled herself up to her full height. "Pleased to introduce you to Mule Aranslyde, namely myself. Ol' Pullman's newest employee." She sketched a mock bow. Pa cackled in delight.

A little plate of peas and greens and ham fat had been set aside for her. Plaquette spooned it down while Ma went on about how Plaquette must have lost her everlovin' mind and Pa wasn't helping with his nonsense. Then Plaquette took a still protesting Ma by the hand and led her into the bedroom. "Time's running short," she said. "Lemme tell y'all why I need to go." That brought a bit more commotion, though she didn't even tell them the half of it. Just the bit about the George. And she maybe said she'd broken it by accident.

MA TWISTED PLAQUETTE's long braids into a tight little bun and crammed them under the cap. "Don't know how you gonna fake doin Pa's job," she fretted. "Ain't as easy as it looks. I messed up so many times, supervisor asked me if I been in the whiskey. Nearly got your Pa fired."

Plaquette took Ma's two hands in her own. "I'm a 'prentice, remember?" She patted the letter in her breast pocket that Pa had dictated to her, the one telling Pa's porter friend Jonas Jones who she was and to look out for her and thank you God bless you. She kissed Pa goodbye. Ma walked her out onto the landing, and that's when Plaquette's plan began to go sideways. There at the foot of the stairs was Claude, backing up and ramming himself repeatedly into the bottom stair. Plaquette had forgotten she had Claude's wardenclyffe in her pocket. All this time he'd been trying to follow it.

"Plaquette," said Ma, "what for you steal Msieur's machine?" It wasn't a shout but a low, scared, angry murmur – far worse. In the lamplight scattered into the yard from the main street, Claude's white-gloved hands glowed eerily.

Plaquette clattered down the stairs to confront the problem.

"I know you think he yours, but girl, he don't belong to you!" Ma had come down behind her. Plaquette didn't even need to turn to know the way Ma was looking at her: hard as brass and twice as sharp.

"I – I set him to follow me." Plaquette faltered for words. This was the part she hadn't told them.

Ma only said, "Oh, Lord. We in for it now."

Pa replied, "Maybe not."

"WATCH WHERE YOU'RE going!"

Plaquette muttered an apology to the man she'd jostled. Even late like this – it must have been nearly midnight – New Orleans' Union Station was thronged with travelers. But in Ma's wake Plaquette and Claude made slow yet steady headway through the chattering crowds. A makeshift packing crate disguised her mechanical friend; Plaquette held a length of clothesline which was supposed to fool onlookers into thinking she hauled it along. Of course the line kept falling slack. Ma looked back over her shoulder for the thirteenth time since they'd left home. But it couldn't be much farther now to the storage room where Pa had said they could hide Claude overnight. Or for a little longer. But soon as the inevitable hue and cry over his disappearance died down Plaquette could return him to Msieur's. So long as no one discovered Claude where they were going to stash him –

"Stop! Stop! Thief!" Angry as she'd feared, Msieur's shout came from behind them. It froze her one long awful second before she could run.

Ahead Ma shoved past a fat man in woolens and sent him staggering to the right. Behind them came more exclamations, more men calling for them to halt, their cries mixed with the shrieks and swearing of the people they knocked aside. How'd he know where to look for her? Trust a man whose business was numbers to put two and two together. Msieur had friends with him – How many? Plaquette barely glanced back. Two? Four? No telling – she had to run to stay in front of Claude so he'd follow her to – an opening! She broke away from the thick-packed travelers and ran after Ma to a long brick walk between two puffing engines. Good. Cover. This must be why Ma had taken such an unexpected path. Swaying like a drunk in a hurricane, Claude in his crate lumbered after her.

The noise of their pursuers fell to a murmur. Maybe she'd lost them?

But when Plaquette caught up with Ma, Ma smacked her fists together and screamed. "No! Why you follow me over here? Ain't I told you we putting your fool mistake in the storage the other side of the tracks?"

"B-but you came *this* w-w-ay!" Plaquette stammered.

"I was creating a *distraction* for you to escape!"

The clatter and thump of running feet sounded clear again above the engines' huff and hiss. Coming closer. Louder. Louder. Ma threw her hands in the air. "We done! Oh, baby, you too young for jail!"

One of the dark train carriages Plaquette had run past had been split up the middle – hadn't it? A deeper darkness – a partially open door? Spinning, she rushed back the way they'd come. Yes! "Ma!" Plaquette pushed the sliding door hard as she could. It barely budged. Was that wide enough? She jumped and grabbed its handle and swung herself inside.

But Claude! Prisoned in slats, weighed down by his treads, he bumped disconsolately against the baggage car's high bottom. Following her and the wardenclyffe, exactly as programmed. Should she drop it? She dug through the deep pockets frantically and pulled it out so fast it flew from her hand and landed clattering somewhere in the carriage's impenetrable darkness.

Hidden like she wished she could hide from the hoarsely shouting men. But they sounded frustrated as well as angry now, and no nearer. Maybe the engine on the track next to this was in their way?

The train began moving. From Plaquette's perch it looked like the bricks and walkway rolled off behind her. Claude kept futile pace. The train was pulling up alongside Ma, standing hopelessly where Plaquette had left her, waiting to be caught. Now she was even with them. Plaquette brushed her fingers over Ma's yellow headscarf. It fell out of reach. "Goodbye, Ma! Just walk away from Claude! They won't know it was you!" Fact was, Plaquette felt excited almost as much as she was scared. Even if Msieur got past whatever barrier kept them apart right now, she was having her adventure!

The train stopped. Plaquette's heart just about did, too. Her only adventure would be jail. How could she help Ma and Pa from inside the pokey? She scanned the walkway for Msieur and his friends, coming to demand justice.

But no one showed. The shouts for her and Ma to stop grew fainter. The train started again, more slowly. Suddenly Ma was there, yanking Claude desperately by his cord. She'd pulled his crate off. It was on the platform, slowly disappearing into the distance. Together, Ma and Plaquette lifted Claude like he was luggage, tilting him to scrape over the carriage's narrow threshold. As they did, the tray holding the books caught on the edge and was dragged open – and it held more than book scrolls. Cool metallic disks, crisp or greasy slips of paper – Msieur's money!

How? Plaquette wasted a precious moment wondering – he must have put the day's take into Claude when she surprised him in the showroom.

Ma's eyes got wide as saucers. She was still running to keep up, puffing as she hefted Claude's weight. With a heave, she and Plaquette hauled him into the car. He landed with a heavy thump. The train was speeding up. There was no time to count it; Plaquette fisted up two handfuls of the money, coins and bills both, and shoved it into Ma's hands. Surely it was enough to suffice Ma and Pa for a while. "I'll come back," she said.

The train kept going, building speed. Ma stopped running. She was falling behind fast. "You a good girl!" she yelled.

When it seemed sure the train wasn't stopping again anytime soon Plaquette stuck her head out – a risk. A yellow gleam in the shadows was all she could see of Ma. Plaquette shoved the sliding door closed.

Well. She'd gone and done it now. Pa's note was no use; this wasn't the train making the Frisco run. It for sure wasn't no sleeping-car train. A porter had no business here. The train could be going to the next town, or into the middle of next week. She had no way of knowing right now. For some reason, that made her smile.

She fumbled her way to Claude's open drawer. The money left in there was all coins, more than she could hold in one hand. She divided it amongst the deep, deep pockets in her trousers and jacket.

She was a true and actual thief, and a saboteur.

Finally she found the wardenclyffe. Feeling farther around her in the loud blackness, she determined the carriage was loaded as she'd imagined with trunks, suitcases, parcels of all shapes and sizes. Nothing comfortable as the beds at home, the big one or the little. She didn't care.

When the train stopped she'd count the money. When the train stopped she'd calculate what to do, where to go, how to get by. She could slip off anywhere, buy herself new clothes, become a new person.

She settled herself as well as she could on a huge, well-stuffed suitcase and closed her eyes.

Claude would help. She would punch more books for him to read, and collect from the people who came to listen. Send money home to Pa and Ma every few weeks.

She'd write the books herself. She'd get him to punch them. She'd punch a set of instructions for how to punch instructions for punching. She'd punch another set of instructions and let Claude write books too. And maybe come back one day soon. Find Billy. Take him away and show him a new life.

The train ran toward the north on shining steel rails. Plaquette's dreams flew toward the future on pinions of shining bright ideas.

A MURMURATION

Alastair Reynolds

ALASTAIR REYNOLDS (WWW.ALASTAIRREYNOLDS.COM) was born in Barry, South Wales, in 1966. He has lived in Cornwall, Scotland, the Netherlands, where he spent twelve years working as a scientist for the European Space Agency, before returning to Wales in 2008 where he lives with his wife Josette. Reynolds has been publishing short fiction since his first sale to *Interzone* in 1990. Since 2000 he has published fourteen novels: the Inhibitor trilogy, British Science Fiction Association Award winner *Chasm City*, *Century Rain*, *Pushing Ice*, *The Prefect*, *House of Suns*, *Terminal World*, the Poseidon's Children series, *Blue Remembered Earth*, *On the Steel Breeze*, and *Poseidon's Wake*, *Doctor Who* novel *The Harvest of Time*. His short fiction has been collected in *Zima Blue and Other Stories*, *Galactic North*, and *Deep Navigation*. Coming up is collaboration with Stephen Baxter, *The Medusa Chronicles*, an as-yet-untiled new novel, and new collection *Beyond the Aquila Rift: The Best of Alastair Reynolds*. In his spare time he rides horses.

THE 'HUT' IS a couple of insulated portable cabins, with a few smaller sheds containing generators, fuel, wind turbine parts and so on. There is a chemical toilet, a wash basin, basic cooking facilities. Two or three of us can share the hut at a time, but there is not normally a need for more than one to keep an eye on the equipment. Resources being tight, lately we tend to come out on our own.

In all honesty, I prefer it this way. Birds draw out the solitude in us. They repay patience and silence – long hours of a kind of alert, anticipatory stillness. The days begin to blur into each other; weekends and weekdays becoming arbitrary distinctions. I find myself easily losing track of the calendar, birds and weather my only temporal markers. I watch the migration patterns, record their altering plumage, study the changeful skies. I could not be happier.

There is just one thing to spoil my contentment, but even that, I am confident, will soon be behind me.

I *will* finish the paper.

It sound easy, put like that. A vow. A recommitment, a redoubling of my own efforts. One last push.

But I have been here before.

It started easily enough – the usual set of objections, no real hint of the trouble to come. Very few papers ever go through without some amendments, so none of us were bothered that there were a few issues that needed addressing.

But when we had fixed those, the anonymous referee came back with requests for more changes.

We took care of those. Hoped that the paper would now be judged fit for publication. But still the referee wanted more of us. This kept going on. Just when we think we have addressed all possible doubts, the referee somehow manages to find something new to quibble with. I do my best to be stoic, reminding myself that the anonymous referee is just another scientist doing their job, that they too are under similar pressures, and that I should not feel under any personal attack.

But I only have to glance at their comments.

The authors are inconsistent in their handling of the normalisation terms for the correlation function of the velocity modulus. I am not convinced that their treatment of the smoothed Dirac delta-function is rigorous across the quoted integral.

My blood boils. I entertain a momentary fantasy of meeting the referee out here, on some lonely strip of marshland, of swerving violently and running them into a ditch.

Asking, as I watch them gag on muddy water: "Rigorous enough for you now?"

* * *

The basis of our experiment is a ring of twenty tripods, arranged in a two kilometre circle. The hut is on one side of the circle, the wind turbine the other. During the day I check all the tripods, picking the least waterlogged path in the 4WD.

Each unit carries a pair of stereometric digital cameras. The lenses need to be kept the power and electronic connections verified. The cameras should be aimed into the middle of the perimeter, and elevated sufficiently to stand a good chance of catching the murmuration's epicentre. The cameras are meant to be steerable, but not all of the motors work properly now.

Beneath each camera is a heavy grey digital control box. The boxes contain microprocessor boards, emergency batteries, and the blue plastic rectangles of their internal ethernet modules, flickering with yellow and red LEDs. The boxes are supposedly weatherproof but the rain usually finds a way into them. Like the motors, there have been some failures of the circuit board, and our spares supplies are running low.

About one in five of the stations have more equipment. On these units we also included laser/radar rangefinders and Doppler velocity recorders. These in turn require extra processors and batteries in the control boxes, which is yet more to go wrong.

The effort is worth it, though.

The equipment allows us to track the instantaneous vectors of anything up to two hundred and fifty thousand birds, perhaps even half a million, in a single compact formation. Our spatial/temporal resolution is sufficient to determine wing movements down to the level of specific feather groups. At the same time we also gather data on the attentional shifts implied by eye and head tracking of individual birds.

The human eyes see a blurring of identities, birds becoming the indistinguishable, amorphous elements of some larger whole. The cameras and computers see through all of that. I know the science, I know the algorithms, I know our data-carrying capacity. All the same, I am still quietly astonished that we can do this.

When the cameras are checked, which can take anywhere between three and six hours, I have one final inspection to perform. I drive to the wind turbine, and make a visual inspection of the high grey tower and the swooping blades. More often than not there is nothing to be done. The blades turn, the power flows, our electrical and computer systems work as they are meant to.

The rest is down to the birds.

IT'S ODD, REALLY, but there are times when I find even the hut a little too closed-in and oppressive for my tastes. Sometimes I just stop the 4WD out here, wind the window down, and watch the light change over the marsh. I like it best when the day is overcast, the clouds sagging low over the trees and bushes of the marsh, their greyness relieved only by a bold supercilial swipe of pale yellow above the horizon. Birds come and go, but it's too early for the roosting. I watch herons, curlews, reed warblers – sometimes even the slow, methodical patrol of our resident marsh harrier, quartering the ground with the ruthless precision of a surveillance drone.

Beyond the birds, the only constancy is the regular swoosh of the turbine blades.

It's a good time to catch up on work or reading.

I pull laser-printed pages from the unruly nest of the glove compartment, along with tissues, cough sweets, empty medicine packets, a scuffed CD without a case. I rest a stiff-backed road atlas on the steering wheel, so that I can write on the pages.

I've already marked up certain problematic passages in yellow highlighter. Now I use a finer pen to scribble more detailed notes in the margins. Eventually I'll condense these notes into a short email to the journal editor. In turn they'll forward them on to the author of the paper I am refereeing.

This is how it works. I'm engaged in a struggle with my own anonymous referee, half-convinced that they've got it in for me, while at the same time trying to be just as nit-picking and difficult for this other author. Doubtless they feel just as irritated by me, as I am irritated with my own referee. But from my end, I know that there's nothing personal in it. I just want the work to be as good as it can be, the arguments as lucid, the analysis as rigorous. So what if I know the lead author, and don't particularly care for her? I can rise above that.

I hold one of the sheets up to the yellowing sky, so that the band of light pushes through the highlit yellow passages. I read back my own scrawl in the margins:

Sloppy handling of the synthetic correlation function – doesn't inspire confidence in rest of analysis.

Am I being too harsh with them?

Perhaps. But the we've all been through this mill.

STARLINGS GATHER, ARRIVING from all directions, concentrating in the air above the copse of trees and bushes near the middle of the study area. They come in small numbers, as individuals or in flocks of a few dozen, before falling into the greater mass. There is no exact threshold at which the concentration of birds becomes a recognisable murmuration, but it needs at least a few thousand before the form begins to emerge as a distinct phenomenon in its own right, with its swooping, gyring, folding cohesiveness – a kind of living membrane in the sky.

Meanwhile, our instruments record. One hundred parametric data points per bird per millisecond, on average, or upwards of fifty gigabytes of data for the whole murmuration. Since the murmuration may persist for several tens of minutes, our total data cube for the whole observation may contain more than thirty terabytes of data, and a petabyte is not exceptional. We use some of the same data-handling and compression routines as the particle physicists in CERN, with their need to track millions of microscopic interaction events. They are tracking tiny bundles of energy, mass, spin and charge. We are tracking warm, feathery bodies with hearts and wings and twitchy central nervous systems!

All of it is physics, though, whether you are studying starlings or quarks.

On my workstation I sift through slices of the data with tracker-wheels and mouse glides.

I graph up a diagram of the murmuration at a moment in time, from an arbitrary viewing angle. It is a smear-shaped mass of tiny dots, like a pixelated thumbprint. On the edges of the murmuration the birds are easily distinguishable. Closer to the core the dots crowd over each other, forming gradients of increasing concentration, the birds packing together with an almost Escher-like density. Confronted with those black folds and ridges, it is hard not to think of the birds as blending together, clotting into a suspended, gravity-defying whole.

I mouse click and each dot becomes a line. Now the smear is a bristly mass, like the pattern formed by iron filings in the presence of a magnetic field. These are the instantaneous vectors for each bird – the direction and speed in which they are moving.

We know from previous studies that each starling has a direct influence – and is in turn influenced by – about seven neighbours. We can verify this with the vector plots, tracking the change in direction of a particular bird, and then noting the immediate response of its neighbours. But if that were the limit of the bird's influence, the murmuration would be sluggish to respond to an outside factor, such as the arrival of a sparrowhawk.

In fact the entity responds as a whole, dividing and twisting to outfox the intruder. It turns out the there is a correlation distance much greater than the separation between immediate neighbours. Indeed, that correlation between distant birds may be as wide as the entire murmuration. It is as if they are bound together by invisible threads, each feeling the tug of the other – a kind of rubbery net, stretching and compressing.

In fact, the murmuration may contain several distinct 'domains' of influence, where the flight patterns of groups of birds are highly correlated. In the plot on my workstation, these show up as sub-smears of strongly aligned vectors. They come and go as the murmuration proceeds, blending and dissipating – crowds within the larger crowd.

This is where the focus of our recent research lies. What causes these domains to form? What causes them to break up? Can we trace correlation patterns between the domains, or are they causally distinct? How sharp are the boundaries – how permeable?

This paper, the one that is bouncing back and forth between us and the referee, was only intended to set out the elements of our methodology – demonstrating that we had the physical and mathematical tools to study the murmuration at any granularity we chose. Beyond that, we had plans for a series of papers which would build on this preliminary work with increasingly complex experiments. So far we have been no more than passive observers. But if we have any claim to understand the murmuration, then we should be able to predict its response to an external stimulus.

I am starting to sense an impasse. Can we honestly go through this all over again with our next publication, and the one after? The thought of that leaves me drained. We have the tools for the next phase of our work, so why not push ahead with the follow-up study, and fold the results of that back into the present paper? Steal a march on our competitors, and dazzle our referee with the sheer effortless audacity of our work?

I think so.

THE NEXT DAY I set up the sparrowhawk.

I need hardly add that it is not a real sparrowhawk. Designed for us by our colleagues at the robotics laboratory, it is a clever, swift-moving drone. It has wings and a tail and its flight characteristics are similar to those of a real bird. It has synthetic feathers, a plastic bill, large glassy eyes containing swivel-mounted cameras. To the human eye, it looks a little crude and toy-like – surely too caricatured to pass muster. But the sparrowhawk's visual cues have been exaggerated very carefully. From a starling's point of view, it is maximally effective, maximally terrifying. It lights up all the right fear responses.

Come the roost, I set down a folding deck chair, balance the laptop in my lap, stub my gloved fingers onto the scuffed old keyboard, with half the letters worn away, and I watch the spectacle. The sparrowhawk whirrs from the roof of the 4WD, soars into the air, darts forward almost too quickly for my own eyes to track.

It picks a spot in the murmuration and arcs in like a guided missile.

The murmuration cleaves, twists, recombines.

The sparrowhawk executes a hairpin turn and returns for the attack. It skewers through the core of the flock, jack-knifes its scissor wings, zig-zags back. It makes a low electric hum. Some birds scatter from the periphery, but the murmuration as a whole turns out to be doggedly persistent, recognising on some collective level that the sparrowhawk cannot do it any real damage, only picking off its individual units in trifling numbers.

The sparrowhawk maintains its bloodless attack. The murmuration pulses, distends, contracts, its fluctuations on the edge of chaos, like a fibrillating heart. I think of the sparrowhawk as a surgeon, drawing a scalpel through a vital organ, but the tissue healing faster than the blade can cut.

Never mind – the point is not to do harm, but to study the threat response.

And by the time the sparrowhawk's batteries start to fade, I know that our data haul will be prodigious.

I can barely sleep with anticipation.

But overnight, there's a power-outage. The computers crash, the data crunching fails. We run on the emergency generator for a little while, then the batteries. Come morning I drive out in the 4WD, open the little door at the base of the tower, and climb the clattery metal ladder up the inside. Inside there are battery-operated lights, but no windows in the tower itself. The ladder goes up through platforms, each a little landing, before swapping over the other side. Heights are not my thing, but it's just about within my capabilities to go all the way to the top without getting seriously sweaty palms or stomach butterflies.

At the top, I come out inside the housing of the turbine. It's a rectangular enclosure about the size of our generator shed. I can just about stand up in it, moving around the heavy electrical machinery occupying most of the interior space. At one end, a thick shaft goes out through the housing to connect to the blades.

The turbine is complicated, but fortunately only a few things tend to go wrong with it. There are electrical components, similar to fuses, which tend to burn out more often than they should. We keep a supply of them up in the housing, knowing how likely it is that they will need swapping out. I am actually slightly glad to see that it is one of the fuses that has gone, because at least there is no mystery about what needs to be done. I have fixed them so many times, I could do it in my sleep.

I open the spares box. Only three left in it, and I take one of them out now. I swap the fuse, then reset the safety switches. After a few moments, the blades unlock and begin to grind back into motion. The electrical gauges twitch, showing that power is being sent back to our equipment. Not much wind today, but we only need a few kilowatts.

Job done.

I think of starting down, but having overcome my qualms to get this high, I cannot resist the opportunity to poke my head out of the top. At the back of the electrical gear is a small ladder which leads to an access hatch in the roof of the housing.

I go up the short steps of the ladder, undo the catches, and heave open the access hatch.

My knees wobble a bit. I push my head through the hatch, like a tank commander. I look around. There's a rubberised walkway on top, and a set of low handrails, so in theory I could go all the way out and stand on top of the housing. But I've never done that, and I doubt that I would ever have the nerve.

Still with only my head jutting out, I look back at the hut, a huddle of pale rectangles. The perimeter circle is hard to trace from this elevation, but eventually I glimpse the spaced-out sentinels of the tripods, with the scratchy traces of my own wheel tracks between them. Then I pivot around and try to pick out the causeway. But it's harder to follow than I expect, seeming to abandon itself in a confusion of marsh and bog. I squint to the horizon, looking for a trace of its continuation.

Strange how some things are clearer to the eye at ground level, than they are from the air.

Birds must know this in their bones.

THE NEXT DAY, the computers running again, I squeeze our data until it bleeds science. With the vector tracking, we can trace the response to the sparrowhawk across all possible interaction lengths. Remarkable to see how effectively the 'news' of the sparrowhawk's arrival is disseminated through that vast assemblage of birds.

Because there is no centralised order, the murmuration is best considered as a scale-free network. The internet is like that, and so is the human brain. Scale-free networks are robust against directed attacks. There is no single hub which is critical to the function of the whole, but rather a tangle of distributed pathways, no one of which is indispensible. On the other hand, the scale-free paradigm does not preclude the existence of those vector domains I mentioned earlier. Just as the internet has its top-level domains, so the brain has its hierarchies, its functional modules.

Would it be a leap too far to start thinking of the murmuration as hosting some level of modular organisation?

I jot down some speculative notes. No harm in sleeping on them. In the meantime, though, I write up the sparrowhawk results in as dry and unexciting manner as I can manage, downplaying any of the intellectual thrill I feel. Passive voice all the way. *The sparrowhawk was prepared for remote control. Standard reduction methods were used in the data analysis. The murmuration was observed from twenty spatially separated viewing positions – see Fig. 3.*

The way to do science is never to sound excited by it, never to sound involved, never to sound as if this is something done by people, with lives and loves and all the usual hopes and fears.

I send the latest version of the paper back to the journal, and cross my fingers.

I OPEN THE glove compartment and take out the latest version of the paper. I skim it quickly, then go back through some of the more problematic passages with the yellow highlighter, before adding more detailed notes in the margin. My initial optimism quickly turns to dismay. Why in hell have they opened up this whole other can of worms? I squint at an entire new section of the paper, hardly believing my eyes.

Sparrowhawks? Robot sparrowhawks? And pages of graphs and histograms and paragraphs of analysis, all springing from work which was not even foreshadowed in the original paper?

What are they thinking?

I'm furious at this. Furious with the journal editor, for not spotting this late addition before it was forwarded to me. Furious with the authors, for adding to our mutual workload. Furious for their presumption, that I will presumably be sufficiently distracted by this to overlook the existing flaws – like a magpie distracted by something shiny. (Except that's a myth; corvids are not attracted to shiny things at all.)

Furious above all else that they are prepared to squander this good and original science, to slip it into this paper like a lazy afterthought, as a kind of intellectual bribe.

No, this must not stand.

I put the 4WD back into gear. I must settle my thoughts before firing back an intemperate response. But really, I'm enraged. I bet they think they know who I am. I imagine encountering them out here, running them down, feeling the bounce of my wheels over their bodies. I'd stop the 4WD, get out, walk slowly back. Savour the squelch of my boots on the marshy ground.

Their whimpering, their broken-boned pleas.

'You think this is how we do science, do you?' I'd ask them, entirely rhetorically. 'You think it is a kind of game, a kind of bluff? Well, the joke's on you. I am recommending your paper be rejected.'

And then I would walk away, ignoring their noises, get back into the 4WD, drive off. At night their cries would still come in across the marsh, but I would not let myself be troubled. After all, they brought this on themselves.

But that sparrowhawk, I'll admit, was beautiful.

I GO OUT to the walk-in traps and collect the overnight haul. There are almost always some birds in the snares, and almost always some starlings. It is how we ring them, bring them in for study, assess their overall genetic fitness. Generally they are none the worse for having been caught up in the nets overnight.

I collect ten adult specimens, let the others go, and take the ten back to the hut.

A firm in Germany has made the digital polarising masks for us. They are elegant little contraptions, similar in design to the hoods fitted around captive birds of prey. These are smaller, though, optimised to be worn by starlings, and to offer no significant resistance to normal flight. Each hood is actually a marvel of miniature electronic engineering. Bulging out from either side are two glassy hemispheres.

In its neutral mode, the bird has an unrestricted view of its surroundings. Each hemisphere, though, is divided into digitally-controlled facets. These can be selectively darkened via wireless computer signals, effectively blocking out an area of the starling's vision.

The consequence of this – the point of the masks – is that we can control the birds' collision-avoidance response remotely. By making a given bird think it is about to be struck by another bird, we can cause it to fly in any direction we choose.

Again, it is asking too much of human reflexes to control a bird at such a level. But the computers can do it elegantly and repeatably. Each of our ten hooded starlings then becomes a remote-controlled agent, under our direct operation. Like the robot sparrowhawk, we can steer our agents into the murmuration. The distinction is that the hooded starlings do not trigger a threat response from their seven neighbours; they are absorbed into the whole, accepted and assimilated.

But they *can* influence the other birds. And by careful control of our hooded agents, we can initiate global changes in the entire murmuration. We can instigate domains, break them up, make them coalesce. Anything that happens under the influence of natural factors, we can now bring about at our will.

By we, of course, I mean I.

Old habits die hard. Science is always done in the 'we', even when the work is borne on a single pair of shoulders. But frankly, I am starting to doubt the commitment of my fellow researchers. There is always a division of labour in any collaborative enterprise, and sometimes that division can seem unfair. If the brunt of the work is my responsibility, though, I fail to see why I should not receive the lion's share of the credit.

As I wait for the murmuration to form, I make some deft amendments to the list of the authors, striking out a name here, a name there.

Feathers will fly, of course.

TEN BIRDS MIGHT not seem much but these birds are like precision instruments, guided with digital finesse. To begin with, we – I – restrict myself to only minor interventions.

I make the murmuration split into two distinct elements, then recombine.

Suitably encouraged, I quarter it like a flag. I pull it apart into four rippling sheets of birds, with arcs of clear air between them. The edges are improbably straight, as if the birds are glassed-in, boxed by invisible planes. But that is the power of incredibly delicate control processes, of stimulus and feedback operations happening much too swiftly for human perception. If an edge starts losing coherence, the computer makes a tiny adjustment to one or more of the control starlings and the order is reestablished. This happens many times a second, at the speed of avian reactions.

They have always lived in a faster world than us. They live a hundred days in one of our hours. To them we are slow, lumbering, ogrelike beings, pinned to the ground by the stonelike mass of our bodies. We envy them; they pity us.

I push forward. I carve geometries out of the murmuration. I fold it into a torus, then a ribbon, then a Möbius strip. I do not need to know how to make these shapes, only to instruct the laptop in my desires. It works out the rest, and becomes more adept as it goes along.

I make the murmuration spell out letters, then I coax those letters into lumpy, smeared-out words. I spell my name in birds. They banner around me like the slogans towed by light aircraft. I laugh even as I feel that I have crossed some line, some invisible threshold between pristine science and sordid exploitation.

But I carry on anyway. I am starting to think about those domains, those hints of modular organisation.

How far could I push this, if I were so determined?

ANGRY EXCHANGES OF emails. Editor not happy with this latest change of direction. Much to-ing and fro-ing. Questions over the change in the listed authors – deemed most unorthodox. Accusations of unprofessionalism. If we were in a room together, the three of us, we might get somewhere. Or we might end up throwing textbooks.

Is this a travesty of the way science ought to be done, or is it science at its shining best – as loaded with passion and conviction as the any other human enterprise? No one would doubt that poets squabble, that a work of great literature might take some toll on its creator, that art forges enemies as readily as allies. Why do we hold science to a colder, more emotionless set of standards? If we care at all about the truth, should we not celebrate this anger, this clashing of viewpoints?

It means that something vital is at stake.

Hard in the spitting crucible of all this to remember that every one of us was drawn to this discipline because of a love of birds.

But that is science.

MY PROPOSITION IS simple. The domains are controllable. I can cause them to form, contain the shape and extent of their boundaries, determine the interaction of their vector groups with the surrounding elements. I can move the domains around with the flock. I can blend one domain into another, merging them like a pair of colliding galaxies. Depending on their vector properties, I can choose whether that act results in the destruction of both domains or the formation of a larger one.

I sense the possibility of being able to execute a kind of Boolean algebra.

If the domains behave in a controllable and repeatable way, and I can determine their states – their aggregate vector sums – then I can treat them as inputs in a series of logic operations.

The thought thrills me. I cannot wait for the coming of dusk.

With the laptop reprogrammed, I quickly satisfy myself that the elements of my Boolean experiment are indeed workable. I create the simplest class of logic gate, an AND gate. I classify the input domain states as either being 0 or 1, and after some trials I achieve a reliable 'truth table' of outputs, with my gate only spitting out a '1' if the two inputs share that value.

I push on. I create OR and NOT gates, a 'not AND' or NAND gate, a NOR gate, an XOR and XNOR gate. Each is trickier than the last, each requires defter control of the domains and vector states. To make things easier – at the burden of a high computational load on the computer and the ethernet network – I retrieve more birds from the snares, fitting them with additional digital hoods.

Now I can create finer domains, stringing them together like the modules in an electrical circuit.

I begin to 'wire up' the flock. I assign gates to perform logical operations, but also to store data. Again, I need only tell the computer what I want it to do – it takes care of the computational heavy-lifting. All I know is what my eyes tell me. The murmuration has grown knotted and clotted, dense with domain boundaries and threaded with the thick synapses of internal data corridors. It swoops and billows over me, a circuit of birds.

The astonishing thing is that on the level of individual starlings, they sense no strangeness – no inkling that they are participating in anything but a normal murmuration. The complexity is emergent, operating on a scale that the birds simply cannot sense, cannot share. They are cells in a larger organism.

I lash together a Perl script, a simple text to logic program on the laptop, enabling me to send natural language queries to the flock.

IS ONE AND ONE TWO?

There is a process of calculation. The circuit shuffles. I glean the flow of information along its processing channels – the physical movement of birds and their larger domain boundaries.

The answer returns. The laptop takes the Boolean configuration and converts it back into natural language.

>>YES.

I try another query.

IS ONE AND ZERO ZERO?

A swoop, a billow, a constant busy shuffling of birds.

>>NO.

I smile. Maybe a fluke.

IS ONE AND ZERO ONE?

>>YES.

I am elated.

Over the next thirty minutes, I run through question after question. The birds answer unfailingly. They are computing, and doing so with the utmost machinelike reliability.

>>YES YES NO YES YES NO NO NO.

I am doing algebra with starlings.

But as the gloom gathers, as the dusk deepens, something troubles me.

In all my interventions to date, one thing has remained true. The murmuration eventually dissipates. The roosting instinct overpowers the flocking instinct, and the birds cascade down into the trees. It happens very quickly, a kind of runaway escalation. Whenever I have witnessed it, I am always saddened, for it is the end of the show, but I am also amazed by what is another demonstration of marvellous collective action.

And then the skies are clear again, until the birds lift at dawn. This is what should happen.

But now the murmuration will not break up.

Some birds leave it, maybe a third, but a core remains. I hammer at the laptop – more puzzled than worried at first. I try to disrupt the logic flow, randomise the data, dismantle the knotty Boolean architecture. But the pattern remains obstinately present. The sky darkens, until only the cameras and rangefinders are able to track the birds, and then with difficulty.

But I can still hear them up there – a warm but unseen presence, like a clot of dark matter hovering over me.

* * *

I THINK IT'S time to recuse myself from refereeing this paper.

After all the time and work I've invested in the process, it's hardly a decision I take lightly. But there is a difference between acting as a gatekeeper and a psychiatrist. I'm afraid that recent developments have given me cause for concern.

We all work under some degree of stress. Science is not a carefree playground. It's an arena where reputations can crash as readily as they soar. Commit some error of analysis, read too much into noise, claim a premature discovery, and you may as well tie your own academic noose. Forget those keynote lectures. Forget those expenses-paid conference invitations. You'll be tarnished – dead in the water.

I've felt the pressure myself. I know what solitude and overwork can do to your objectivity. All the same, there are limits. I should have sensed that things were not going well long before they reached this latest development.

I explain to the journal editor that I'm no longer in a position to offer a balanced opinion on the worth of this work. Frankly, I'm not even sure it still qualifies as science.

I'm stuffing the paper back into the glove compartment when it meets some obstruction, some object lodged at the back. I push my fingers into the mess and meet a stiff, sharp-edged rectangle about the size of a credit card.

For a moment there's a tingle of recognition.

I pull out the offending object, study it under the 4WD's dome light. It's a piece of grey foil printed with the name and logo of a pharmaceutical company. The foil contains six blisters. All but one of the blisters have been popped and emptied of their contents.

The sixth still holds a small yellow pill.

I wonder what it does?

I SLEEP BADLY, but dare to hope that the murmuration will have gone by morning – broken up or drifted away elsewhere. But when I wake, I find it still present.

If anything, it has grown. I run a number count and find that it has been absorbing birds, sucking them into itself. More than half a million now.

Enslaved to the murmuration, the individual birds will eventually exhaust themselves and drop out of the sky. But the whole does not care, any more than I concern myself with the loss of a few skin cells. As long as there are fresh starlings to be fed into the machine, it will persist.

I drive the 4WD out again, set up the laptop, try increasingly desperate and random measures to make the pattern terminate itself.

Nothing works.

But the supply of new birds is not inexhaustible. Sooner or later, if they keep coming, it will churn its way through all the starlings in the country. Long before that happens, though, the wrongness of this thing will have become known to others beside myself. They will know that I had something to do with it. They will admire me at first, for my cleverness. After that, they will start blaming me.

I want it to end. Here. Now.

So.

Desperate measures. The wind is stiff today, the bushes and trees buckling over. Even the birds struggle to hold their formation, although the will of the murmuration forces itself through.

I make it move. I can still do that.

I steer the murmuration in the direction of the wind turbine. The blades swoop around at the limit of their speed: if it were any windier, the automatic brakes would lock the turbine into immobility. The edge of the flock begins to enter the meat slicer. I hear its helicopter whoosh, the cyclic chop its great rotors. The blades knock the birds out of the sky in their hundreds, an instant bludgeoning execution. They tumble out of formation, dead before they hit the ground.

This is merciful, I tell myself. Better than being trapped in the murmuration.

But my control slackens. The domains are resisting, slipping out of my grip. The ensemble won't allow itself to be destroyed by the wind turbine.

It knows what I have tried to do.

It knows that I am trying to murder it.

On my laptop the Perl script says:

>>NO. NO. NO.

* * *

THE PILL LEAVES a bitter but familiar aftertaste. With a clarity of mind I haven't known – or don't remember knowing – in quite some time, I make my way once more to the top of the turbine tower. It's odd that I feel this compulsion, since my fear of heights hasn't abated, and for once there's nothing wrong with the turbine, beyond some fresh dark smears on the still-turning blades.

In the housing, I ease around the humming core of the generator and its whirring shaft. The dials are all still registering power – enough for my needs, at any rate. We're still down to those last few replacement fuses, but there's no need to swap one of them at the moment.

I climb the little ladder and poke my head out through the roof hatch.

Steeling myself, pushing my fear aside, I put my elbows on the rim and lever my body up through the hatch. Finally I'm sitting on the rim, with my legs and feet still dangling back into the housing. The wind is hard and cold up here, a relentless solid force, but with the enclosing handrails there's no real chance of me falling. All the same, it takes my last reserves of determination to rise from the hatch, pushing myself up until I am standing on the rubberised decking. The handrails seem too low now, and the gaps between the uprights too widely spaced. With each swoop of the blades, the housing moves under me. My knees wobble. My stomach flutters and sweat pools in the palms of my gloved hands.

But I will not fall. That's not why I've come to the top of the turbine.

Once more I survey my little world from this lofty vantage. The hut, the instruments, the parked vehicle. The low sky. The boggy tracks of my daily routine.

The harder gleam of the causeway, arrowing away.

But it never gets anywhere. The causeway vanishes into bog and then the bog opens up into the silver mirror of a larger expanse of open water. I squint, trying to pick up the causeway's continuation beyond the flooded area. There, maybe. A scratch of iron-grey, arrowing on toward the horizon. But dark shapes bordering that scratch. Cars, vans – all stopped. Some of them tipped over or emptied like skulls. Burnt out.

I might be imagining it.

Beyond the marsh, beyond the enclosing water, nothing that hints at civilisation.

I realise now that I've been here a lot longer than weeks. I know also that I don't need to worry about being a scientist any more. That's the least of anyone's concerns. Being a scientist is just something I used to do, a long time ago.

I wish I could hold onto this. I wish I could remember that the paper doesn't matter, that the journal doesn't matter, that nothing matters. That the only thing left to worry about is holding on, keeping things at bay. But unless I'm mistaken that was the last of my medication.

Finally the wind and the swaying overcome my will. I start down the tower, back to the ground.

At the 4WD I stand and watch the birds. That clarity hasn't completely left me, that knowledge of what I am and what has become of me. I can feel it slipping, draining out of my head as if there are holes in the base of my skull. For the moment, though, there's still enough of it there. I know what happened.

But the murmuration still contains troubling structure – sharp edges, block knots of density, shifting domains and restless connections. Did I cause all of that to come into being, or is this now the way of things? Is it a kind of equivalence, order emerging in the natural world, while order is eclipsed in ours? Have I been trying to communicate with the murmuration, or is it the other way around? Which of us is the observer, which the phenomenon?

If I tried to kill it, will it find it in itself to forgive me?

I try to hold onto these questions. They seem hugely important to me now. But one pill was never going to hold the dusk at bay.

In the morning I feel much better about things. Finally, I think I can see a way through – a fresh approach, a new chance of publication. It will mean going back to the start of the process, but sometimes you have no choice – you just have to end things before they get any worse.

I draft a letter to the editor. Although it pains me to do it, I feel that we have no option but to request a new referee. Things have gone on long enough with this old one. Frankly the whole exchange was in danger of getting too personal. We all know that the anonymous part counts for very little these days, and in all honesty professional feelings were starting to get in the way. I had a suspicion about their identity, and of course mine was all to visible to them. We had history. Too much bad blood, too much accumulated recrimination and mistrust. At least this way we will be off to a clean start again.

I read it over, make a few alterations, then send the letter. It might be misplaced optimism, but this time I am quietly confident of success. I look forward to hearing from the editor.

KAIJU *MAXIMUS*®: "SO VARIOUS, SO BEAUTIFUL, SO NEW"

Kai Ashante Wilson

KAI ASHANTE WILSON is the author of "The Devil in America", which was nominated for the Nebula, World Fantasy, and Shirley Jackson Awards. His short fiction has been published by Tor.com and in the anthology *Stories for Chip*. His most recent work is short fantasy novel *The Sorcerer of the Wildeeps*, which is available from all fine booksellers. He lives in New York City.

IT HADN'T COME down since great-grandparent days, but as its last descent had left no stone on stone – nor man, woman, child alive – anywhere people had once dwelled aboveground on the continent, the hero would go up before it came down again, and kill the kaiju *maximus*. They would go too: the hero's weakness, and her strength.

For long cool days, she led them up the old byways toward the spectre of the mountains. Finally they reached the foothills. Here and there leaves of the deep green forest had just begun turning red or gold in the last days of summer. He and the children were all fit, all well, and so most days the hero could get about twenty kiloms out of them. She carried the food, that pack twice the weight of his, which was plenty heavy enough. She brought down game for them if he asked, a turkey, or ducks. They did just as that old sciencer in the last cavestead had counseled: every morning a drop of her blood under the children's tongues and his, and indeed the heroic factor served to ward them all from sickness. No more fevers, not a cough. The scaled dry patches on the boy's neck and hands cleared up, and he suffered no more frightening episodes of breathlessness. In little more than a month the baby, looking all the time more and more like poor Sofiya, shot up several centimets, five or six, and put on as many kilos. And him? That ankle he'd twisted back in the spring stopped aching during the first and last hours of a long day's hike, stopped aching at all. You don't really know, until it's gone, how much the pain was wearing on you all along.

Come downhill one bright chill afternoon, he and the baby and boy were resting in the swale, eating apples, when the hero came down from the sky. She gave him the choice of the last hill they'd climb that day. "Which one?" she said. Just north of them two hills overlapped in east-west adjacency. "Where's the good water?"

He thought about it and said, "That one," holding out his apple toward where, unseen and unheard, a freshwater spring bubbled up from cloven rock, and ran down down the chosen hill's farside. Though much higher, the other hill looked easy-hiking. The hill awaiting them was squat, not half so high: but they'd end up climbing its height four or five times, after all the switchbacks, its sides being steep and densely forested, interrupted by brief sheer bluffs. There never really was a chance, was there, the easy hill might have had the water?

"Saw some ducks while I was up flying," the hero said. (They only ever argued over the children – food for them, water for them, rest.) "But just those spoonies with orange fat."

"That's okay."

"Kids won't eat that kind, you said." The hero's latest eyes caught the light funny, as if prismatic oil were wetting them, not saltwater tears. "They taste too nasty."

"It's okay," he said. "Really."

"You gotta speak up if you want me to hunt."

It was nice, he told himself, that she thought to offer. "Tonight I meant to finish up what we brung fresh from the last cavestead. So please don't worry yourself." He didn't need some special solicitude that came out of the blue every once in a while. What he needed was not to be argued against, and never, ever overruled, when the hero wanted to wring a few more kiloms from the day – and so skip some meal, rest stop, or water break – and he said to her, "They can't; the kids are tired. We need rest."

I don't think Sofiya should do that. I don't think she's ready.

"You hurting for water? I can take the canteens and fill 'em."

"We're okay. Early tomorrow morning we should hit the trickle, otherside of that west hill there. We got plenty till then." He smiled up at her (irises glinting jewel-like in the oblique fall of light). "And you know I know my water."

"Yeah." She touched his head and ran fingers through his hair which, not easily, he kept washed and combed for her. "You do, don't you?"

Now, his father: *there* had been a dowser, the old man not just able to find the water but call it from the ground, however dry. He himself could feel the water pumping or at rest in the earth well enough to say where the nearest creek or pond lay, and to judge at a glance whether this standing pool or that mineral-stained leak was poisonous or potable. And the boy could as well: grandson's talent biding fair to rival his grandfather's, for already son could often pinpoint what father could only be vague about.

The hero looked at her weary children half-eating, half-sleeping on their weary father's lap. "We'll rest here a bit longer, then head up when the sun touches the top of those trees there."

Mouth full of apple, he nodded. On rare occasions the hero drank thirstily from a spring, or returned to camp with the haunch of some deer she'd devoured out of his and the children's sight; and he'd roast it up for their supper and next-day's eating. But she took neither food nor water more than once a month. All the good that a daily two leets of water, full night's sleep, and three squares did for you, the hero got from a quiet half hour's sit-down in the sun. She found a bright spot now and partook.

He unraveled a cocklebur from the boy's head propped on his thigh. "What say you, buddy? How was your papa's waterwitching that time?"

Eyes closed, the boy held an apple to his mouth, nibbling at it; he spoke with quiet dreaminess. "We're gonna get to that water today, Papa – right as the sun's going down. And the spring's a good gushy one, not no little trickle like you said."

Still with a couple nice bites on it, the baby chucked her apple-core to the mangy pup that had crept after them since midmorning. "I wanna 'nother one, Papa," she said. "I'm still hungry."

"We ain't got apples to waste, pumpkin." He handed her the half left of his. "Now, just you get to eat this, okay? It's yours, all by yourself."

* * *

Dr. Anwar abu Hassan, psychogenomicist: To us who still flounder in the storms of the untamed heart, the awakened mystics have explained just what good, in the cosmic sense, is this folly called erotic love. Lust and passion are early doors, first steps away from pure self-concern; and later doors, further steps, lead even as far as the mystic arrives: to that love surpassing understanding, which may encompass a whole planet, and every living creature on it. And so, when we introduce the heroic factor into the population, and give rise to a superhuman élite, let us not have forgotten the heart. Predilection for the pretty face is a precursor of universal caritas. And in defense of one beloved earthling some hero may well save us all.

At the Ritual Benison *before each boss-fight, a hero will temporarily advance +1000 XP for every point of comeliness their spouse possesses. But the hero must ensure that his or her spouse always has food, water and rest enough to maintain this attribute. And* superheroes *must consider the welfare of their children as well, for the sword and the wings can only...*

Twilight was setting fire to the clouds as they reached the flat top of the hill. Up there was rocky, windswept and bush-covered; or, no – these were all trees, dwarfish kin to the lower forest, with not one gnarled cousin reaching even shoulder-height. All sense of accomplishment from so many steps taken thus far, from so much ground covered, can be voided by a single majestic view. The prospect overlooked a broad and forested valley, compassed by distant hills, and marching thence to the very limits of sight: ever-higher mountains, some peaks snowtopped, a few piercing the clouds. Let it not be said that he knew a single moment's despair – for he was loyal to the hero, and steadfast to her cause: humanity's salvation – but neither could such a vista hearten anyone so footsore. *How far must they go?* At his feet the children sat down together, stretched out side-by-side, and went to sleep: not a full minute passing between these progressions. The hero didn't want your chatter, your second guesses, nor to be pestered with ten thousand questions. But he dared ask this one aloud, although quietly, and well softened up:

"I guess we got quite a ways further to go, huh?"

"We're here. This is it," the hero said. "I'll kill it tonight."

According to the maps a city of millions had nestled in this valley before the age of monsters cut short the Anthropocene. Now, only a howling green wilderness filled the lowlands, and on the sixth day God might have called it quits in the morning, finishing with the beasts: never having put people in the garden at all. For miles and miles – forever – there was nothing to see, save rock, tree and mountain: certainly no kaiju *maximus*. "Where is it?" he said. "I don't see anything."

The hero took his shoulders in hand, turned him bodily about, and let go; she pointed.

Knowing that her finger pointed west, even so he was confounded for a moment, and thought *east*, where sooty night had fallen already. Never before had he seen such insombration as covered over a deep groin between western mountains. This wasn't the smoky gloom that *minores* carried about with them, those mighty shambling towers. Nor yet was it the terrifying local midnight in which the hero had fought and killed a kaiju *plenus*, fully mature, while that great beast hove up over the world nearly lost in darkness, although it had been sunny midafternoon. No, the insombration that blackened the valley's western reaches didn't so much dampen ambient radiance as seem a positive dark in its own right: the opposite, not merely absence, of light. The bright fires of sunset had no power to penetrate those malignant shadows, which gave up not even the faintest conjectural hint of the *maximus* within.

A chill wind blew on this hilltop. He shuddered. "I can't get the least little glimpse of it through that. Can you?"

The hero nodded. She shrugged off the pack of food, and unbuckled and dropped her heavy sword as well. "Y'all get yourselves settled up here." Carapace flipping open, her wings extended. "I'll be back shortly to get ready for the fight."

"Is it woke already?" he said. "Or still sleep?"

But with a swiftness just faster than his eyes could track the hero plunged upwards into the lowering dusk and sped away west.

If you'd crouched next to him while he checked on the children, you'd have judged them much too wiry for their age. Where was the baby fat? you'd wonder. The chubby thighs and soft bellies? And though one was six, and the other three-and-a-half, brother and sister were very close in size; for the boy's dead heroic twin had hogged the womb, and been born with not a fair half but nearly fourth-fifths the share of health, size and strength. Sofiya had been a little frightening, so fiercely had she rejected any helping – any intercessory – hand, although in the end she needed her papa no less than this baby and boy, hadn't she? And please don't say these sleepers looked uncared for, like no one worried over them always conniving for their well-being. But he feared you probably would. Who *loves* these children? you'd cry out, looking all around you, hot-eyed and accusatory. Who *feeds* them? The heart wrung in his chest taking in their gaunt exhaustion. He took off his coat and draped it over them. With just his grandfather's woolen sweater against hawk on the hilltop, he set about gathering wood for the fire.

Onions and potatoes sizzling in bacon fat was a smell to wake any hungry youngster, however deeply asleep. The children pressed close to him at either side, staring lustfully into the pan. The baby made to stick tender fingers right into hot popping grease; he caught that hand. "Whoa there, pumpkin."

"I'm hungry though."

"We'll be eating in two shakes." He chopped up most of the remaining ham for the hash and stirred the pan. Still, supper could use some more stretching. He tapped the baby's nose and pointed. "You see that bent-over tree, the little'n? Just looky at all that good dandelion growing under it. How about you go pull us two big ole handfuls for the pan? And make sure to shake off all the bugs and dirt. *You* know how."

"But I'm *hungry*, Papa."

"Soon as I get me some greens, you get your supper."

After the baby jumped up, he said, "And, buddy, will you gather up everybody's canteen for me? Just a few steps thataway, over behind the big boulder you see right there, I judge it's a nice spring of water just bubbling up –"

Sassy, and with voice raised: "I know already, Papa." The boy shouldered up the baby's canteen beside his own.

"Well, all right." The outburst surprised him. It wasn't a tone the boy would ever dare take with his mother, and so neither should he with his father. But a bit of backtalk was, in this case, good news. Trekking twenty kiloms everyday kept the boy so doped with fatigue, the sun could rise and set without him showing any glimmer of personality or preference, much less temper. So, yes: shout at Papa if you would! "Go on, then. Pour out the old water, and rinse them canteens out good, you hear? Top 'em all back up full too."

"I know." The boy stamped a foot, holding out his arm to receive the last canteen strung up over his shoulder.

"Best not be super long about it either, buddy. Or me and the baby might get so hungry we gobble up your supper too. *Whew*, don't this pan just smell wonderful?"

"You better not, Papa!" In their leather sleeves, the winebottles under his elbows and pinched to his sides, the boy hurried round the boulder toward the stream's source.

While they ate he told the children that this was the night Mama would fight the kaiju. Strategic, this timing; for very little news was so upsetting it could ruin a good hot supper, served up right now. "The big one?" said the baby. "Yes, pumpkin." "The *maximus*?" said the boy. "Yes, buddy." And that seemed to be that, for at least so long as they scraped their forks into the pan.

After supper he found himself taking in anew their grimy little faces, all smeared and content, and he heard his mother's voice. *When you fixing to wash these babies, man? Been three weeks now.* It's cold and windy out here, Mama. I can't wash them in this weather. *Boy, it's getting into the fall. Ask yourself: is it gon' get warmer and warmer, or will you be breaking ice to get at the creek soon?* They'll cry, Mama; that's how cold it is. I don't want my children hating me. *Well, all right – keep doing what you doing, then. I'm just sorry I musta not taught you anything about where sickness come from, or the kind of infections won't nothing cure. Myself, I'd just build up this fire good, and see the babies get nice and warm afterwards... but you grown! Do it your way.*

"Y'all," he said, "it's been a long time now, right? I think we all might need a bath."

There was an uproar, and tears to break your heart. Possessing nothing like the necessary fortitude, he pretended to be his own implacable mother, and dug out the little cake of soap, everyone's change of underthings, and after doubling the fire marched himself and the children round the boulder to the near-freezing gush of mountain spring.

"I can do something," the boy screamed. "The fire underground, Papa."

Children spoke wildly at bathtime, and you learned to harden your heart and pay no attention. He put hands on the boy to undress him for soap and water.

"Wait," said the boy. "I can make the water hot. I can, Papa."

He let the boy go and sat there on a rock beside the stream. Sucking her thumb, the baby leaned heavily against his side, as she did when upset. "What do you mean, buddy?"

"There's... fire in the ground, Papa. Real deep down," said the boy. "And there's steamwater sitting on top of it." His hands swooped and gestured to map these geologic interrelations. "I can ask that hot water to mix with this cold, so the spring comes up here feeling nice."

"Can you, buddy? I never heard of such a thing. My own papa couldn't... Well, go on; let's see." He watched the boy's face go demented with effort, with concentration, and his heart sank realizing the son he thought he knew was in fact unknown to him; but it lifted up too, for the boy had genius. The candlelight of his dowsing gift blazed high into roaring flames. And, oh, *how* had he ever forgotten this? – how the twenty-times-brighter gift of his father at work on some feat used to cast illumination by which he himself could plumb depths, discerning subtleties ordinarily far beyond him? From some superheated pool a full subterranean mile down, the boy caused geothermic steam to vent upwards through intervening strata, and that terrifically hot water to temper the icy flow of the mountain stream warmer, and warmer still, until even bloodwarm –

"*There*, buddy," he said. "That's hot enough."

White plumes of vapor were emerging from the cracked boulder's underside with the cascade of water. He quickly got off his own coat and sweater and all the baby's things and ducked her into the balmy waters. While his son stood there with face set, eyes squinched closed, body all a-tremble, he bathed his daughter.

Soaping her feet a second time, he tore open a fingertip on some errant shard of glass – but, no; for apparently this glass was somehow *in* his daughter's foot, or *on* it. He asked the baby to sit down there in the water and let papa see that foot. It gave him a nasty scare, seeing what he saw. By the campfire's dim filterings from the boulder's farside, and by the guttering embers of sunset: the baby's toenails had all gone black and strange-shaped. Then, gingerly pricking his thumb against the sharp downcurved points of them, he understood that his daughter wasn't taken ill at all – indeed she was soon to transcend the question of illness altogether. The lusciously heated water delighted the baby and she wanted to linger and splash. But the fires of the boy's gift were by now dwindling fast, and the spring beginning to cool. "Can't play in the water, pumpkin." He soaped her hair and rinsed it squeaky. "Bud's working real hard to keep it warm for you. We gotta hurry."

The boy said, "Papa..."

"It's all right, buddy." He lifted the baby out, towel-swathed. "Let go."

The spring resumed its arctic flow, the steam dispersing at once. The boy took weary seat upon a rock nearby.

He had the baby dry and in her change of longjohns and fresh socks, all snugly bundled up and booted again, in about a minute flat.

"Well, buddy," he said. "My dowsing's nowhere near as good as yours. So we'll just wait till morning" – what *optimism*, the apocalypse scheduled for tonight! – "and you can have a bath when you feel strong enough to call up more hot water. Okay?"

"Okay, Papa."

"Hey, pumpkin – *hey* there – you come back here! What you running off for all by yourself, like you don't know better than that? Mmhmm, you just sit down right here beside your brother. Buddy, you hold my baby's hand, you hear?"

"Okay, Papa."

Never in your life did you see somebody wash up quicker. Dunking himself, he yodeled once from sheer cruel iciness, and then kind of hopped from foot to foot while scrubbing himself with soap, hooting sadly both times he crouched to splash himself over with frigid rinsewater. It was a pathetic and undignified show – nevertheless hilarious to the children, who shrieked with laughter.

He led them back to the fire. The gusts were cutting northerly across the hilltop, and so he'd built the fire in the windshadow of a depression, and stacked up stones for a further break, but still the flames leaned and shuddered. The children tried to talk to him of such little events of the day past as the three of them would hash over nightly before bed – for instance, that poor little puppydog. "What you thinks gon' happen to him, Papa?" But hunkered down before the fire, he only shook his head, teeth chattering while he pulled the comb through his hair. So the boy began telling the baby that same old made-up story, about the nice family with three little kids, who lived together in a tent set up beside a stream on a green field, where the kids could play all day in that good, sunny place. As usual, the baby wanted to know *Was it warm? How warm was it?* And the boy laid out for her again how wonderfully warm it was there, the sun shining everyday.

Sounds nice, he thought, but as always wished to object that people couldn't just live out in the open like that. If ever people dared to gather in numbers on the planet's surface, and especially when they began to cultivate, and build, and knock down trees, a perturbation intensified in the leylines. Kaiju felt such human activity as a worsening itch in need of a good hard scratch. The children knew perfectly well that people had to live underground in cavesteads; they'd visited plenty. But they spent most of their lives in the wind and rain and sunlight, campfollowing after the hero with their papa; and so naturally the great outdoors, and tents beside sweetwater streams, seemed to them pleasures anyone might know.

Warmed through and dry, he dressed. There was cutlery and the pan to put up. With no threat of rain, he decided against the tent, but got out the ground pads and bedrolls. After a word to the children – *stay put, behave* – he went to launder his and the baby's soiled underthings.

Dr. Anwar abu Hassan, psychogenomicist: While we are contending, still, with the problem of human survivability vis-à-vis the existential alien threat, please, my dear colleagues, heed this warning: The Hero Project will have thought too small, and perforce must fail, if we discard all but the mechanistic solutions. I submit these questions for your consideration.

How does the martyr remain true, although put to the ultimate test? Whence comes the endurance of the last man standing, his unbroken will to survive? And what *is* that moral fiber investing the woman who runs always to the succor of other lives, never balking at risk to her own? *Can a coward fight the kaiju – will a selfish woman, or a waffling, indecisive man?* So, yes, then, to near-sonic flight, to static apnea in vacuo, to electrogenerative plaxes; and, yes, as well, to all the various exoskeletal enhancements. But as we engineer the superhuman corpus, again I say, let us not neglect the heart!

And should the spouse freely offer up the greatest sacrifice, then the hero's biomagicite shall become charged with +100 mana: finally sufficient to induce a Volcanic Hotspot, *whereby a perforation in the earth's crust causes superheated magma to discharge explosively from the aesthenosphere, instantly destroying kaiju* minores, *and causing* pleni *and the* maximus...

Spraying the sky the count of stars must go to billions, and the singular moon shone down as well, just a sliver waxing from new. From unlit lunar lands far from the bright crescent – still burning more than a century on – the wrecked mothership winked and flared with eerie phosphorescence. Yet apart from their fire on the hilltop, not another light could be seen over the whole dark and untenanted earth. Barring this one little camp, there was nothing to proclaim that apes had ever come down from the trees, or women once decked themselves in silk and diamonds, or men in times past waged war upon each other.

Lest the wind blow it away, he tangled up their laundry to dry in the boughs of a tree-canopy all knotty and interlaced as arthritic fingers. By the time he'd rejoined the children fireside and stretched out his hands to ease their cold-ache, the boy and baby's talk had turned to chocolate.

He protested. "But if we make it tonight, there's none for later. That's it, all gone."

The boy extended a litigious forefinger. "*You* said we'd have our chocolate when Mama fights the kaiju. You *promised*, Papa."

No, he'd said "maybe," for he never made promises. What on earth could he guarantee? "It's the last little bit, y'all." He could feel himself doing the ugly, tiresome thing, whereby you put off some pleasure best enjoyed now, for fear nothing good will come again. "Are you both sure?"

Yes!

So he put on water to boil and shaved the chocolate into their tin cup and, finishing the honey as well, sweetened it all up. Sitting between them with the cup, he parceled sips back and forth, but could as well have left the arbitrage to them. For sister and brother were best of friends tonight – angels of fairness – and this camp saw such smiles as none had in some time. What else do you hope to see? Only that your children be warm and well and glad. While they ran fingers round the inside of the cup, chasing dregs, the hero came down from the air and it was time.

Her wings folded invisibly into her carapace. And two metres tall and more, she, kneeling, brought herself down to child's-reach. "Bless me for the fight," the hero said, and all the lightness left their camp, as if hawk, suddenly switching quarter, had blown the fire out. She picked up her scabbard from where it lay, pulled forth the sword, and beckoned the boy forward to kiss the flat of the blade.

"Papa," said the boy.

"I'm here." He set the baby back safely from the fire and took his son's hand. "I'll catch you, buddy. You won't be hurt." Last time, a bolt of lightning had struck down abruptly from the cloudless sky: charging the sword, but also felling the boy in passing. For a week he lay shivering and mumbling in some half-awake state, and thereafter for months was ill and weak.

They walked over to the hero at his son's slow pace. Small folk know that unreckonable caprice flickers always through the heart of the great, and they know as you may not that so-called love – that the benevolent smile – may turn on the instant to wrath and ruination. Therefore the children never approached the hero with steps less wary than those of the old Israelites coming before Yahweh.

The boy looked up into his mother's face: her stillness and regard, insectile or statuesque. Going to his knees beside his son, he whispered urgingly of the planetary importance of this single fight above all the rest that had ever gone before.

The boy said at last, "I hope you win, Mama," and touched his puckered mouth to the sword even taller than himself. At once the pommel in the hero's grip took light, brilliance spilling out between her fingers. The cold gray steel began turning to white-hot fire.

He snatched the boy back into his arms, tumbling over, and kicked desperately against the ground to get distance between them and that incinerative heat. Their coats smoked, hair crisped. "Take it away from us," he shouted at the hero. "It's too hot." She got up holding the incandescent beam, and with each step farther seemed to bear away a furnace going full blast, its doors ajar, and then some vagrant midsummer's day, and thereafter lesser and lesser warmth, until the cold of the boreal night closed rightfully about them again. At the summit's edge the hero plunged the sword down into solid rock that sputtered and smoked like grease scorching in a pan much too hot. Leaving the bright blade bobbing in liquid stone, the hero came back and knelt as before. Then she bowed until her forehead rested on the ground, for the baby's kiss upon her back.

Already the hero had wonderful wings, but to fight the *maximus* she'd need much better. As a rocky shelf, one thousand tons, falls off some mountainside and onto the unlucky walker below, just so did the kaiju hit, with as much force. And their alien effluents, whether spat, shat, or bloodlet, reduced the flesh of earthly creatures to runny sludge, a fertile dung for the world's resurgent wilderness, feed for the forests that arose where every city fell. They couldn't guess what shape, this time, the hero's metamorphosis would take; she had no idea herself. Their only forewarning was that, whatever changes, they would be always perilous, always a shock.

"Pumpkin," he said and squatted on his haunches. He reached out his arms and sucking her thumb the baby came to him. But when he urged her from his embrace and toward the hero, saying, "Give Mama a kiss, just like you did before," the baby seized a fistful of his coat, nor wished to let it go. "Are you scared?" He stroked his daughter's hair and smiled at her in complicity, allowing a little of his own fear to show. "I know; me too. But I need you to do this one little thing for me. Just for your papa: won't you give Mama a kiss on her back?" (A kiss compelled held no power – nor did a loveless one.) His appeal shifted something in the child's heart prior words had not, and her fear-blank eyes began to clarify. He said, "Please?" and the baby nodded. Toward the hero and away from him, he set her walking with gently propulsive hands.

The baby cast back one uncertain glance. At his nod, she bent to kiss the hero's dorsal carapace. Fretfully his two hands hovered to grab his daughter back. No sooner did the baby's lips alight than her mother's torso – indeed limbs and whole self – returned to a more human shape, but not made of flesh and bone, rather become some kind of living marble.

At dead center of the hero's smooth adamantine back, a thin-lipt mouth pursed open. From this hole erupted a long and rotary tentacle of spiked stone. With full decapitatory powers, this flailing rotor tore the air just centimets overhead where he cringed, pressing the baby and himself down, noses flat to earth. Hysterical from terror the baby fought to get free and run, while he shouted at the hero to go up into the air before she killed them both. When the hero had gone aloft, he let the baby go. Sister fled back to brother fireside where the children clung together like half-drowned co-survivors who had won to shore by grace of God alone, and through shark, shipwreck and storm, had not gone down with all the rest.

The hero could not lift much more than her own weight off the ground ordinarily, but now without effort she stooped from the sky and plucked him up into her arms. They hovered midair.

Her mouth by his ear to be heard above the roaring downdraught of that strange, singular wing: "Do you love me?"

"Yes."

"Really?" Her lips were stone, and if not soft at all, entirely smooth. "I wonder. Love me enough to do anything? No matter what?"

"Whatever," he said. Could she even feel his fingertips caress her face? "I'll do anything." She was hard to embrace, hard to come close to, being made of stone and so much bigger. "I love you."

"To fight the *maximus* I need more than you ever gave me those other times. A whole lot more."

He said, "How much?" and she said, "How much can I get?"

Even then the hero waited on him to press his lips to hers.

If you've ever sucked and chewed on sugarcane, then you have the right image. Vigor, youth, beauty – something on that order – was wrung out of his body like water from a sodden rag, or sweetness chewed from sugarcane. But the agony made no difference to how readily he opened his mouth to the requited passion of her stony kiss. Suppose that some small sacrifice were asked of you as helpmeet and shieldbearer for the greatest hero who has ever lived, and suppose that in fulfilling your role *she* might deliver the homeworld. Would you do it? *He* would. She hardened to some much denser substance than living marble, and the arms about him caused his bones to creak and ache. Becoming a chevaux-de-frise of sharp diamond, her lips began to abrade his, drawing blood as the kiss went on.

As he grew feeble she held him closer, until desire and will notwithstanding, his body just could no longer. The hero held her lips one short millimet from his, begging, "Kiss me, kiss me," and he tried, oh he did, always whispering back when she asked, "Do you love me?" "Yes, yes."

Let him go. There was a gravelly clatter, rock-on-rock, as pebbles bounced off much harder stuff. Dimly he became aware that his children were screaming and throwing stones at their mother again. *Let him go. I hate you.* Had the kiss gone so far already? Not too far yet, he hoped. Someone must see the baby and boy tucked into their blankets tonight. And who but him would see them fed a hearty warming bowl in the morning? Such terror these thoughts inspired, he turned his face from hers. Released, he felt himself fall through the air, and hitting the ground saw rainbow-bright glitter and then darkness.

He woke to the baby and boy saying *please don't be dead.* Prostrate on the ground he scrabbled there unable to turn faceup, without the strength even to lift his bloody mouth from the dirt. *Get up, Papa, get up.* Trying to say anything that might comfort the children, he made only the mewling of a kitten which alone of its litter tossed overboard had washed ashore undrowned. These efforts to speak and rise, strenuous to no effect, wearied him so that finally he lay for a long time with quietude hardly to be distinguished from that of a corpse on its bier. The children as well exhausted themselves, and their howls waned to grizzling; their yanking at his coat, to a small hand each stroking at his hair.

From faraway in the night there came at random either one vast crash or repeated booms, as if contending gods took and threw godlike blows. Once, a tremendous though faint echo of the hero's anger resounded out of the distance, her voice pitched such that blood would have spurted from their ears, had he and the children heard that blast near at hand.

Time did what it does and by and by he felt himself drift from merest proximity to death, into slightly more distant purlieus. He splayed one withered claw under each shoulder and pushing against the ground – pushing as hard as he could – came somehow up to sit. Just the sweet Lord can say how he got up on his two stick legs and made it over to the fire where he sat again, or fell. They paced him there, a child at either side; patient, silent, good as gold.

"Buddy."

"Papa?"

"Look in the pack there. Get me out the cut-ointment and a clean rag."

The boy did so.

It wasn't too bad dabbing the mud from his lips with the dampened rag, but smearing his lacerated mouth with the astringent ointment, he made noises that couldn't be helped.

"All right," he said once he'd caught his breath. "Put it up now, bud. Rag goes with the dirty ones."

"Okay, Papa."

Exactly once before had the baby seen the toll of this dire miracle, though she might not remember. Standing beside him, she groped with bemittened hands at his slack seamed cheeks, his thin white hair, as if only by touch she could grasp this onset of morbid age. He smiled at her and said, "Mama will turn me back like I was after she beats the kaiju." *If* she does... "Don't you worry, pumpkin." But not even the voice was his own: higher, breathy, querulous. Her face crumpled, tears welling in her eyes, and none of his friendly words were reassuring to the baby.

The boy came back to sit, and lean, gingerly against him. Had you trotted the globe around and come home again, having despaired that day would ever arrive, so too might you breathe out as the boy did then, as long and slow, a shudder passing also through you. Many times he'd seen his papa go suddenly grey, though never before this stooped and frail, a spotted scalp visible like dirt and stone under a dusting of snow.

To distract the baby's unhappiness, he said, "Want to hear something wonderful?" Brightness pulsed in the western dark, like the traffic of thunderbolts between stormclouds. "Let me tell you what happens sometimes, pumpkin."

Between hiccups: "What, Papa?"

"Sometimes, when a hero's got no son or daughter with the factor – that's still alive, I mean – then it starts expressing in the *other* same-sex child. That happens a lot with heroes, actually. Your papa should've been on the lookout." His tone was light, as at storytime, or telling jokes.

"What you mean, Papa?"

"I think, pumpkin," – He kissed her teary cheek – "*you're* gonna wake up just like Mama one day real soon. A hero. How about that?"

The baby reached a hand to his mouth as she'd done when almost newborn, still an infant, and pressed his lips together in a buttoning gesture. She let the hand fall and said, "No," as decisively as when refusing despised foods. "I don't want that."

"Well," he replied (as always when the sequel would come soon enough, nor be anything the children desired): "We'll just have to see then, won't we?"

"No, Papa!" The baby grabbed his coat and gave him a good shake – he so weak, she could do so. "*Not* see. I want to stay *people*."

He tapped the little fist clinched in his coat and raised his brow at her. The baby turned him loose.

"Aww, don't say that." He shook his head sadly at her. "I really wish you wouldn't, pumpkin. Mama is people too."

"I mean, I mean." The baby was still at that age when words tend to fail, and anger or tears have to fill the gap; her voice broke. "Like you and buddy."

"Shh," he said, "Okay, then," as if she might not rise to *Homo sapiens heroïcus* on his mere say so. "All right, all right." He rubbed circles on her back, she quieted, and the whole world tipped nauseously then. He heard himself shout.

"What's that?" Terrified, the baby embraced him round the neck. "What *is* it, Papa?"

The ground beneath them was yawing as if the sea, the planet itself groaning deeply bass and agonized as some old sinner repentant on his deathbed. Abruptly, some twenty kiloms down the valley, a bright volcanic arm – a hand of fire – thrust up from the earth and made a credible grab for the moon, incandescent fingers raking across the sky. Brilliance snatched aside the black of night as though it were a flimsy curtain, the truth behind it high noon. They cried out, throwing up a hand or both as the dark cold valley was relit to midday green. The gushing white blaze spewed comets as a geyser does waterdroplets, these fiery blue offshoots waning yellow-orange-red as they fell to earth, as the sourcefire itself discolored: now dimming to ochre and yet still painful to see, even squinting through their fingers; now dimmer still, ruddy-black as the glowing crumbs of their own little campfire; now going out.

In that awful first glare, though, they glimpsed the kaiju *maximus*, its shape like some conjuration out of all the earth's collective nightmare, reminiscent of a creature he'd seen once in a picturebook, some beast of the forgotten world – and called what? He couldn't remember. Bright-lit, that apparition stuttered in stark chiaroscuro, wallowing in magma: horrific, bigger than could be put into words. The eruption, dwindling, and burnout endured only for a slow five-count, but it seemed as if hours passed. Nor did they look away even once, not one time blink, until the veils of starless insombriate night fell over that vision again. After this sign and wonder, the baby turned to him expectantly, to see whether Papa might interpret, but he could only shake his head.

The end of days – what is even this, to a child's need for sleep? He looked to the boy and saw that his son's eyes were closed, mouth softly open. To the baby he said, "Let me go tuck in buddy-man." She released her hold round his neck and stood by watching while the boy was chivvied to his feet and, eyes closed, mumbling irritably, not really awake, was led over to his bedroll where, coaxed, he laid himself down, at once dead to the world again, while the boots were pulled off him, the covers tucked up around him. Heart rattling so in his chest you had to hope it could last the night through, he clambered to his feet after these exertions and saw that far hills were burning like victims in flight from some holocaust, their hair alight, their heads bewreathed in flames, all ablaze with forest fires. The wind began to taste of ash. He sought his spot by the fire again and the baby climbed into his lap. "Ain't you sleepy at all yet, pumpkin?"

"No," the baby said, and then: "Did you love Sofiya?"

"*Yes.*"

Again the earth moved as it should not, making unwonted sounds, but they were by then inured.

"And did Sofiya love you, Papa?"

"Well," he began, and was by fortuity saved from a lie and the truth alike. "Oh, looky there!" He pointed into the darkness just over the marge of their campfirelight. "See who came up to join us." From those respectful shadows doomed spaniel eyes watched them. For even after hope, it seemed, hopeful forms and strategies survived.

The baby said, "Puppy!" and jumped up. "Can we keep it, Papa? Like the family in the tent by the river? *They* got a dog."

That ole mangy mutt, there? *Of course not*, child: it's no telling what diseases that thing's got! "All right," he said, and sent the baby over to the hero's pack.

"Well, you ain't pulling, pumpkin," he said. "How you fixing to get that knot loose if you don't pull good? *Pull*, girl. There you go, there you go. See? Now loosen it up, reach in, and should be right there on top: the hambone left from supper, wrapped in one them ole-timey plastic bags."

WATERS OF VERSAILLES

Kelly Robson

KELLY ROBSON (WWW.KELLYROBSON.COM) is a graduate of the Taos Toolbox writing workshop. Her first fiction appeared in 2015 at *Tor.com*, *Clarkesworld Magazine*, and in *Asimov's Science Fiction*, and in the anthologies *New Canadian Noir*, *In the Shadow of the Towers*, and *Licence Expired: The Unauthorized James Bond*. She lives in Toronto with her wife, SF writer A.M. Dellamonica.

1

SYLVAIN HAD JUST pulled up Annette's skirts when the drips started. The first one landed on her wig, displacing a puff of rose-pink powder. Sylvain ignored it and leaned Annette back on the sofa. Her breath sharpened to gasps that blew more powder from her wig. Her thighs were cool and slightly damp – perhaps her arousal wasn't feigned after all, Sylvain thought, and reapplied himself to nuzzling her throat.

After two winters at Versailles, Sylvain was well acquainted with the general passion for powder. Every courtier had bowls and bins of the stuff in every color and scent. In addition to the pink hair powder, Annette had golden powder on her face and lavender at her throat and cleavage. There would be more varieties lower down. He would investigate that in time.

The second drip landed on the tip of her nose. Sylvain flicked it away with his tongue.

Annette giggled. "Your pipes are weeping, monsieur."

"It's nothing," he said, nipping at her throat. The drips were just condensation. An annoyance, but unavoidable when cold pipes hung above overheated rooms.

The sofa squeaked as he leaned in with his full weight. It was a delicate fantasy of gilt and satin, hardly large enough for the two of them, and he was prepared to give it a beating.

Annette moaned as he bore down on her. She was far more entertaining than he had expected, supple and slick. Her gasps were genuine now, there was no doubt, and she yanked at his shirt with surprising strength.

A drip splashed on the back of his neck, and another a few moments later. He had Annette abandoned now, making little animal noises in the back of her throat as he drove into her. Another drip rolled off his wig, down his cheek, over his nose. He glanced overhead and a battery of drips hit his cheek, each bigger than the last.

This was a problem. The pipes above were part of the new run supporting connections to the suites of two influential men and at least a dozen rich ones. His workmen had installed the pipes just after Christmas. Even if they had done a poor job, leaks weren't possible. He had made sure of it.

He gathered Annette in his arms and shoved her farther down the sofa, leaving the drips to land on the upholstery instead of his head. He craned his neck, trying to get a view of the ceiling. Annette groaned in protest and clutched his hips.

The drips fell from a join, quick as tears. Something was wrong in the cisterns. He would have to speak with Leblanc immediately.

"Sylvain?" Annette's voice was strained.

It could wait. He had a reputation to maintain, and performing well here was as critical to his fortunes as all the water flowing through Versailles.

He dove back into her, moving up to a galloping pace as drips pattered on his neck. He had been waiting months for this. He ought to have been losing himself in Annette's flounced and beribboned flesh, the rouged nipples peeking from her bodice, her flushed pout and helplessly bucking hips, but instead his mind wandered the palace. Were there floods under every join?

Instead of dampening his performance, the growing distraction lengthened it. When he was finally done with her, Annette was completely disheveled, powder blotched, rouge smeared, wig askew, face flushed as a dairy maid's.

Annette squeezed a lock of his wig and caressed his cheek with a water-slick palm.

"You are undone, I think, monsieur."

He stood and quickly ordered his clothes. The wig was wet, yes, even soaked. So was his collar and back of his coat. A quick glance in a gilded mirror confirmed he looked greasy as a peasant, as if he'd been toiling at harvest instead of concluding a long-planned and skillful seduction – a seduction that required a graceful exit, not a mad dash out the door to search the palace for floods.

Annette was pleased – more than pleased despite the mess he'd made of her. She looked like a cat cleaning cream off its whiskers as she dabbed her neck with a powder puff, ignoring the drips pattering beside her. The soaked sofa leached dye onto the cream carpet. Annette dragged the toe of her silk slipper through the stained puddle.

"If this is not the only drip, monsieur, you may have a problem or two."

"It is possible," Sylvain agreed, dredging up a smile. He leaned in and kissed the tips of her fingers one at a time until she waved him away.

He would have to clean up before searching for Leblanc, and he would look like a fool all the way up to his apartment.

At least the gossips listening at the door would have an enduring tale to tell.

Sylvain ducked out of the marble halls into the maze of service corridors and stairs. Pipes branched overhead like a leaden forest. Drips targeted him as he passed but there were no standing puddles – not yet.

The little fish could turn the palace into a fishbowl if she wanted, Sylvain thought, and a shudder ran through his gut. The rooftop reservoirs held thousands of gallons, and Bull and Bear added new reservoirs just as fast as the village blacksmiths could make them. All through the royal wing, anyone with a drop of blood in common with the king was claiming priority over his neighbor, and the hundred or so courtiers in the north wing – less noble, but no less rich and proud – were grinding their teeth with jealousy.

Sylvain whipped off his soaked wig and let the drips rain down on his head one by one, steady as a ticking clock as he strode down the narrow corridor. He ducked into a stairwell – no pipes above there – and scrubbed his fingers through his wet hair as he peeked around the corner. The drips had stopped. Only a few spatters marked the walls and floorboards.

The little fish was playing with him. It must be her idea of a joke. Well, Leblanc could take care of it. The old soldier loved playing nursemaid to the creature. Age and wine had leached all the man out of him and left a sad husk of a wet nurse, good for nothing but nursery games.

A maid squeezed past him on the stairs and squealed as her apron came away wet. She was closely followed by a tall valet. Sylvain moved aside for him.

"You're delivering water personally now, Monsieur de Guilherand?"

Sylvain gave the valet a black glare and ran up the stairs two at a time.

The servants of Versailles were used to seeing him lurking in the service corridors, making chalk marks on walls and ceilings. He was usually too engrossed in his plans to notice their comments but now he'd have to put an end to it. Annette d'Arlain was in the entourage of Comtesse de Mailly, King Louis's *maîtresse en titre*, and Madame had more than a fair share of the king's time and attention – far more than his poor ignored Polish queen.

The next servant to take liberty with him would get a stiff rebuke and remember he was an officer and a soldier who spent half the year prosecuting the king's claims on the battlefield.

By the time Sylvain had swabbed himself dry and changed clothes, Bull and Bear were waiting for him. Their huge bulks strained his tiny parlor at the seams.

"What is the little creature playing at?" Sylvain demanded.

Bull twisted his cap in his huge hands, confused. Bear raised his finger to his nose and reached in with an exploratory wiggle.

"Down in the cisterns," Sylvain spoke precisely. "The creature. The little fish. What is she doing?"

"We was on the roof when you called, monsieur," said Bull, murdering the French with his raspy country vowels.

"We been bending lead all day," said Bear. "Long lead."

"The little fish was singing at dawn. I heard her through the pipes," Bull added, eager to please.

It was no use demanding analysis from two men who were barely more human than the animals they were named for. Bull and Bear were good soldiers, steady, strong, and vicious, but cannonfire had blasted their wits out.

"Where is Leblanc?"

Bull shrugged his massive shoulders. "We don't see him, monsieur. Not for days."

"Go down to the cellars. Find Leblanc and bring him to me."

The old soldier was probably curled around a cask in a carelessly unlocked cellar, celebrating his good luck by drinking himself into dust. But even dead drunk, Leblanc knew how to talk to the creature. Whatever the problem was, Leblanc would jolly the silly fish out of her mood.

2

"Our well-beloved king is an extraordinary man," said Sylvain. "But even a man of his parts can only use one throne at a time."

The Grand Chamberlain fluffed his stole like a bantam cock and lowered his hairy eyebrows. "The issue is not how the second throne will be used but how quickly you will comply with the request. We require it today. Disappoint us at your peril."

Sylvain suppressed a smile. If royalty could be measured by number of thrones, he was king of Europe. He had at least two dozen in a village warehouse, their finely painted porcelain and precious mahogany fittings wrapped in batting and hidden in unmarked crates. Their existence was a secret even Bull and Bear kept close. To everyone else, they were precious, rare treasures that just might be found for the right person at the right price.

The Grand Chamberlain paced the silk carpet. He was young, and though highborn, titled, and raised to the highest office, responsibility didn't sit well with him. He'd seen a battlefield or two at a distance but had never known real danger. Those hairy brows were actually trembling. Sylvain could easily draw this out just for the pleasure of making a duke sweat, but the memory of Annette's soft flesh made him generous.

"My warehouse agent just reported receiving a new throne. It is extremely fine. Berlin has been waiting months for it." Sylvain examined his fingernails. "Perhaps it can be diverted. I will write a note to my agent."

The Grand Chamberlain folded his hands and nodded, an officious gesture better suited to a grey-haired oldster. "Such a throne might be acceptable."

"You will recall that installing plumbing is a lengthy and troublesome process. Even with the pipes now in place servicing the original throne, his majesty will find the work disruptive."

Installing the first throne had been a mess. Bear and Bull had ripped into walls and ceilings, filling the royal dressing room with the barnyard stench of their sweat. But King Louis had exercised his royal prerogative from the first moment the throne was unpacked, even before it was connected to the pipes. So, it was an even trade – the king had to breathe workmen's stench, and Bull and Bear had been regularly treated to the sight and scent of healthy royal bowel movements.

The Grand Chamberlain steepled his fingers. "Plumbing is not required. Just the throne."

"I cannot imagine the royal household wants a second throne just for show."

The Grand Chamberlain sighed. "See for yourself."

He led Sylvain into the cedar-scented garderobe. A rainbow of velvet and satin cushions covered the floor. The toilet gleamed in a place of honor, bracketed by marble columns. Something was growing in the toilet bowl. It looked like peach moss.

The moss turned its head. Two emerald eyes glared up at him.

"Minou has been offered a number of other seats, but she prefers the throne." The Grand Chamberlain looked embarrassed. "Our well-beloved king will not allow her to be disturbed. In fact, he banished the courtier who first attempted to move her."

The cat hissed, its tiny ivory fangs yellow against the glistening white porcelain. Sylvain stepped back. The cat's eyes narrowed with lazy menace.

A wide water drop formed in the bend of the golden pipes above the toilet. The drop slid across the painted porcelain reservoir and dangled for a few heartbeats. Then it plopped onto the cat's head. Minou's eyes popped wide as saucers.

Sylvain spun and fled the room, heart hammering.

The Grand Chamberlain followed. "Send the second throne immediately. This afternoon at the latest." The request was punctuated by the weight of gold as he discreetly passed Sylvain a pouch of coins.

"Certainly," Sylvain said, trying to keep his voice steady. "The cat may prefer the original throne, however."

"That will have to do."

When he was out of the Grand Chamberlain's sight, Sylvain rushed through the royal apartments and into the crowded Grand Gallery. There, in Versailles' crowded social fishbowl, he had no choice but to slow to a dignified saunter. He kept his gaze level and remote, hoping to make it through the long gallery uninterrupted.

"Sylvain, my dear brother, why rush away?" Gérard clamped his upper arm and muscled him to the side of the hall. "Stay and take a turn with me."

"Damn you," Sylvain hissed. "You know I haven't time for idling. Let me go."

Gérard snickered. "Don't deprive me of your company so soon."

Sylvain had seen his friend the Marquis de la Châsse in every imaginable situation – beardless and scared white by battle-scarred commanders, on drunken furlough in peat-stinking country taverns, wounded bloody and clawing battlefield turf. They had pulled each other out of danger a hundred times – nearly as often as they'd goaded each other into it.

Gérard's black wig was covered in coal-dark powder that broadcast a subtle musky scent. The deep plum of his coat accentuated the dark circles under his eyes and the haze of stubble on his jaw.

Sylvain pried his arm from Gérard's fist and fell into step beside him. At least there were no pipes overhead, no chance of a splattering. The gallery was probably one of the safest places in the palace. He steered his friend toward the doors and prepared to make his escape.

Gérard leaned close. "Tell me good news. Can it be done?"

"My answer hasn't changed."

Gérard growled, a menacing rumble deep in his broad chest.

"I've heard that noise on the battlefield, Gérard," Sylvain said. "It won't do you any good here."

"On a battlefield, you and I are on the same side. But here you insist on opposing me."

Sylvain nodded at the Comte de Tessé. The old man was promenading with his mistress, a woman young enough to be his granddaughter, and the two of them were wearing so much powder that an aura of tiny particles surrounded them with a faint pink glow. The comte raised his glove.

"I wonder," said the comte loudly, as if he were addressing the entire hall, "can Sylvain de Guilherand only make plain water dance, or does he also have power over the finest substances? Champagne, perhaps."

"Ingenuity has its limits, but I haven't found them yet." Sylvain let a faint smile play at the corners of his mouth.

"Surely our beloved king's birthday would be an appropriate day to test those limits. Right here, in fact, in the center of the Grand Gallery. What could be more exalted?"

Sylvain had no time for this. He nodded assent and the comte strolled on with an extra bounce in his step, dragging his mistress along by the elbow.

The doors of the Grand Gallery were barricaded by a gang of nuns who gaped up at the gilded and frescoed ceiling like baby sparrows in a nest. Sylvain and Gérard paced past.

"You don't seem to understand," Gérard said. "Pauline is desperate. It's vulgar to talk about money, but you know I'll make it worth your effort. Ready cash must be a problem. Courtiers rarely discharge their obligations."

"It's not a question of money or friendship. The north wing roof won't hold a reservoir. If the king himself wanted water in the north wing, I would have to refuse him."

"Then you must reinforce the roof."

Sylvain sighed. Gérard had never met a problem that couldn't be solved by gold or force. He couldn't appreciate the layers of influence and responsibility that would have to be peeled back to accomplish a major construction project like putting reservoirs on the north wing.

"Pauline complains every time she pisses," said Gérard. "Do you know how often a pregnant woman sits on her pot? And how often she gets up in the night? The smell bothers her, no matter how much perfume and rose water she applies, no matter how quickly her maid whisks away the filth. Pauline won't stop asking. I will have no peace until she gets one of your toilets."

"Sleep in a different room."

"Cold, lonely beds are for summer. In winter, you want a warm woman beside you."

"Isn't your wife intimate with the Marquise de Coupigny? I hear she keeps a rose bower around her toilet. Go stay with her."

"The marquise told my wife that she does not cater to the general relief of the public, and their intimacy has now ended in mutual loathing. This is what happens when friends refuse each other the essential comforts of life."

"I'll provide all the relief you need if you move to an apartment the pipes can reach."

"Your ingenuity has found its limits, then, despite your boasts. But your pipes reached a good long way yesterday. I hear it was a long siege. How high were the d'Arlain battlements?"

"You heard wrong. Annette d'Arlain is a virtuous woman."

"Did she tell you the king's mistress named her toilet after the queen? Madame pisses on Polish Mary. Pauline is disgusted. She asked me to find out what Annette d'Arlain says."

Two splashes pocked Sylvain's cheek. He looked around wildly for the source.

"Tears, my friend?" Gérard dangled his handkerchief in front of Sylvain's nose. "Annette is pretty enough but her cunt must be gorgeous."

Sylvain ignored his friend and scanned the ornate ceiling. The gilding and paint disguised stains and discolorations, but the flaws overhead came to light if you knew where to look.

There. A fresh water stain spread on the ceiling above the statue of Hermes. A huge drop formed in its gleaming centre. It grew, dangled like a jewel, and broke free with a snap. It bounced off the edge of a mirror, shot past him, then ricocheted off a window and smacked him on the side of his neck, soaking his collar.

Sylvain fled the Grand Gallery like a rabbit panicking for its burrow. He ran with no attention to dignity, stepping on the lace train of one woman, raking through the headdress feathers of another, shoving past a priest, setting a china vase rocking on its pedestal. The drone of empty conversation gave way to shocked exclamations as he dodged out of the room into one of the old wing's service corridors.

He skidded around a banister into a stairwell. Water rained down, slickening the stairs as he leapt two and three steps at a time. It spurted from joins, gushed from welded seams, and sprayed from faucets as he passed.

The narrow corridors leading to Sylvain's apartment were clogged with every species of servant native to the palace. The ceiling above held a battery of pipes – the main limb of the system Bull and Bear had installed two years before. Every joint and weld targeted Sylvain as he ran. Everyone was caught in the crossfire – servants, porters, tradesmen. Sylvain fled a chorus of curses and howls. It couldn't be helped.

Sylvain crashed through the door of his apartment. His breath rasped as he leaned on the door with all his weight, as if he could hold the line against disaster.

Bull and Bear knelt over a pile of dirty rags on the bare plank floor. Sylvain's servant stood over them, red-eyed and sniffling.

"What is this mess?" Sylvain demanded.

His servant slowly pulled aside one of the rags to reveal Leblanc's staring face, mottled green and white like an old cheese. Sylvain dropped to his knees and fished for the dead man's hand.

It was cold and slack. Death had come and gone, leaving only raw meat. All life had drained away from that familiar face, memories locked forever behind dead eyes, tongue choked down in a throat that would never speak again.

The first time they met, Sylvain had been startled speechless. The old soldier had talked familiarly to him in the clipped rough patois of home and expected him to understand. They were on the banks of the Moselle, just about as far from the southern Alps as a man could be and still find himself in France.

Sylvain should have cuffed the old man for being familiar with an officer, but he had been young and homesick, and words from home rang sweet. He kept Leblanc in his service just for the pleasure of hearing him talk. He made a poor figure of a servant but he could keep a tent dry in a swamp and make a pot of hot curds over two sticks and a wafer of peat. He'd kept the old man close all through the Polish wars, through two winters in Quebec, and then took him home on a long furlough. Sylvain hadn't been home for five years, and Leblanc hadn't seen the Alps in more than thirty, but he remembered every track of home, knew the name of every cliff, pond, and rill. Leblanc had even remembered Château de Guilherand, its high stone walls and vast glacier-fed waterworks.

Close as they'd been, Sylvain had never told the old man he was planning to catch a nixie and bring her to Versailles. Under the Sun King, the palace's fountains had been a wonder of the world. Their state of disrepair under Louis XV was a scandal bandied about and snickered over in parlors from Berlin to Naples. Sylvain knew he could bring honor back to the palace and enrich himself in the bargain. The fountains were just the beginning of his plan. There was no end to the conveniences and luxuries he could bring to the royal blood and courtiers of Versailles with a reliable, steady flow of clean, pure water.

She'd been just a tadpole. Sylvain had lured her into a leather canteen and kept her under his shirt, close to his heart, during the two weeks of steady hard travel it took to get from home to Versailles. The canteen had thrummed against his chest, drumming in time with hooves or footsteps or even the beating of his heart – turning any steady noise into a skeleton of a song. It echoed the old rhythms, the tunes he heard shepherds sing beside the high mountain rills as he passed by, rifle on his shoulder, tracking wild goats and breathing the sweet, cold, pure alpine air.

Sylvain had kept her a secret, or so he'd thought. The day after they arrived at Versailles, he'd snuck down to the cisterns, canteen still tucked under his shirt. A few hours later, Leblanc had found him down there, frustrated and sweating, shouting commands at the canteen, trying to get her to come out and swim in the cisterns.

"What you got there ain't animal nor people," Leblanc had told him. "Kick a dog and he'll crawl back to you and do better next time. A soldier obeys to avoid the whip and the noose. But that little fish has her own kind of mind."

Sylvain had thrown the canteen to the old man and stepped back. Leblanc cradled it in his arms like a baby.

"She don't owe you obedience like a good child knows it might. She's a wild creature. If you don't know that you know nothing."

Leblanc crooned a lullaby to the canteen, tender as a new mother. The little fish had popped out into the cistern pool before he started the second verse, and he had her doing tricks within a day. Over the past two years, they'd been nearly inseparable.

"Ah, old Leblanc. What a shame." Gérard stood in the doorway, blocking the view of the gawkers in the corridor behind him. "A good soldier. He will be much missed."

Sylvain carefully folded Leblanc's hands over his bony cold breast. Bull and Bear crossed themselves as Sylvain drew his thumb and finger over the corpse's papery eyelids.

Gérard shut the door, closing out the gathered crowd. Sylvain tried to ignore the prickling ache between his eyes, the hollow thud of his gut.

"Sylvain, my dear friend. Do you know you're sitting in a puddle?"

Sylvain looked down. The floor under him was soaked. Bull dabbled at the edge of the puddle with the toe of his boot, sloshing a thin stream through the floorboards while Bear added to the puddle with a steady rain of tears off the tip of his ratted beard.

"I don't pretend to understand your business," said Gérard, "But I think there might be a problem with your water pipes."

Sylvain barked a laugh. He couldn't help himself. A problem with the pipes. Yes, and it would only get worse.

3

Sylvain had rarely visited the cisterns over the past two winters. There had been no need. The little fish was Leblanc's creature. The two of them had been alone for months while Sylvain fought the summer campaigns, and through the winter, Sylvain had more than enough responsibilities above ground – renovating and repairing the palace's fountains, planning and executing the water systems, and most importantly, doing it all while maintaining the illusion of a courtly gentleman of leisure, attending levées and soirées, dinners and operas.

Versailles was the wonder of the world. The richest palace filled with the most cultivated courtiers, each room containing a ransom of art and statuary, the gardens rivaling heaven with endless fountains and statuary. The reputation it had gained at the height of the Sun King's reign persisted, but close examination showed a palace falling apart at the seams.

Sylvain had swept into Versailles and taken the waterworks for his own. He had brought the fountains back to their glory, making them play all day and all night for the pleasure of Louis the Well-Beloved – something even the Sun King couldn't have claimed.

The tunnel to the cisterns branched off the cellars of the palace's old wing, part of the original foundations. It had been unbearably dank when Sylvain had first seen it years before. Now it was fresh and floral. A wet breeze blew in his face, as though he were standing by a waterfall, the air pushed into motion by the sheer unyielding weight of falling water.

The nixie's mossy nest crouched in the centre of a wide stone pool. The rusted old pumps sprayed a fine mist overhead. The water in the pool pulsed, rising and falling with the cadence of breath.

She was draped over the edge of her nest, thin legs half submerged in the pool, long webbed feet gently stirring the water. The little fool didn't even know enough to keep still when pretending to sleep.

He skirted the edge of the pool, climbing to the highest and driest of the granite blocks. Dripping moss and ferns crusted the grotto's ceiling and walls. A million water droplets reflected the greenish glow of her skin.

"You there," he shouted, loud enough to carry over the symphony of gushes and drips. "What are you playing at?"

The nixie writhed in the moss. The wet glow of her skin grew stronger and the mist around her nest thickened until she seemed surrounded by tiny lights. She propped herself on one scrawny elbow and dangled a hand in the pool.

With her glistening skin and sleek form, she seemed as much salamander as child, but she didn't have a talent for stillness. Like a pool of water, she vibrated with every impulse.

A sigh rose over the noise. It was more a burbling gush than language. The sound repeated – it was no French word but something like the mountain patois of home. He caught the meaning after a few more repetitions.

"Bored," she said. Her lips trembled. Drips rained from the ferns. "So bored!"

"You are a spoiled child," he said in court French.

She broke into a grin and her big milky eyes glowed at him from across the pool. He shivered. They were human eyes, almost, and in that smooth amphibian face, they seemed uncanny. Dark salamander orbs would have been less disturbing.

"Sing," she said. "Sing a song?"

"I will not."

She draped herself backward over a pump, webbed hand to her forehead with all the panache of an opera singer. "So bored."

As least she wasn't asking for Leblanc. "Good girls who work hard are never bored."

A slim jet of water shot from the pump. It hit him square in the chest.

She laughed, a giddy burble. "I got you!"

Don't react, Sylvain thought as the water dripped down his legs.

"Yes, you got me. But what will that get you in the end? Some good girls get presents, if they try hard enough. Would you like a present?"

Her brow creased as she thought it over. "Maybe," she said.

Hardly the reaction he was hoping for, but good enough.

"Behave yourself. No water outside of the pipes and reservoirs. Keep it flowing and I'll bring you a present just like a good girl."

"Good girl," she said in French. "But what will that get you in the end?"

She was a decent mimic – her accent was good. But she was like a parrot, repeating everything she heard.

"A nice present. Be a good girl."

"Good girl," she repeated in French. Then she reverted back to mountain tongue. "Sing a song?"

"No. I'll see you in a few days." Sylvain turned away, relief blossoming in his breast.

"Leblanc sing a song?" she called after him.

There it was. Stay calm, he thought. Animals can sense distress. Keep walking.

"Leblanc is busy," he said over his shoulder. "He wants you to be a good girl."

"Behave yourself," she called as he disappeared around the corner.

4

SYLVAIN PACED THE Grand Gallery, eyeing the cracked ceiling above the statue of Hermes. There had been no further accidents with the pipes. He had spent the entire night checking every joint and join accompanied by a yawning Bull. At dawn, he'd taken Bear up to the rooftops to check the reservoirs.

Checking the Grand Gallery was his last task. He was shaved and primped, even though at this early hour, it would be abandoned by anyone who mattered, just a few rustics and gawkers.

He didn't expect to see Annette d'Arlain walking among them.

Annette was dressed in a confection of gold and scarlet chiffon. Golden powder accentuated the pale shadows of her collarbones and defined the delicate ivory curls of her wig. A troop of admiring rustics trailed behind her as she paced the gallery. She ignored them.

"The Comte de Tessé says you promised him a champagne fountain," she said, drawing the feathers of her fan between her fingers.

Sylvain bent deeply, pausing at the bottom of the bow to gather his wits. He barely recalled the exchange with the comte. What had he agreed to?

"I promised nothing," he said as he straightened. Annette hadn't offered her hand. She was cool and remote as any of the marble statues lining the gallery.

"The idea reached Madame's ear. She sent me to drop you a hint for the King's birthday. But –" She dropped her voice and paused with dramatic effect, snapping her fan.

Sylvain expected her to share a quiet confidence but she continued in the same impersonal tone. "But I must warn you. Everyone finds a champagne fountain disappointing. Flat champagne is a chore to drink. Like so many pleasures, anticipation cannot be matched by pallid reality."

Was Annette truly offended or did she want to bring him to heel? Whatever the case, he owed her attention. He had seduced her, left her gasping on her sofa, and ignored her for two days. No gifts, no notes, no acknowledgement. This was no way to keep a woman's favor.

Annette snapped her fan again as she waited for his reply.

It was time to play the courtier. He stepped closely so she would have to look up to meet his eyes. It would provide a nice tableau for the watching rustics. He dropped his voice low, pitching it for her ears alone.

"I would hate to disappoint you, madame."

"A lover is always a disappointment. The frisson of expectation is the best part of any affair."

"I disagree. I have never known disappointment in your company, only the fulfillment of my sweet and honeyed dreams."

She was not impressed. "You saw heaven in my arms, I suppose."

"I hope we both did."

A hint of a dimple appeared on her cheek. "Man is mortal."

"Alas," he agreed.

She offered him her hand but withdrew it after a bare moment, just long enough for the lightest brush of his lips. She glided over to the statue of Hermes and drew her finger up the curve of the statue's leg.

"You are lucky I don't care for gifts and fripperies, monsieur. I detest cut flowers and I haven't seen a jewel I care for in months."

Sylvain glanced at the ceiling. A network of cracks formed around a disk of damp plaster. Annette was directly beneath it.

He grabbed her around the waist and yanked her aside. She squealed and rammed her fists against his chest. Passion was the only excuse for his behavior, so he grabbed at it like a drowning man and kissed her, crushing her against his chest. She struggled for a moment and finally yielded, lips parting for him reluctantly.

No use in putting in a pallid performance, he thought, and bent her backward in his arms to drive the kiss to a forceful conclusion. The rustics gasped in appreciation. He released her, just cupping the small of her back.

He tried for a seductive growl. "How can a man retain a lady's favor if gifts are forbidden?"

"Not by acting like a beast!" she cried, and smacked her fan across his cheek.

Annette ran for the nearest door, draperies trailing behind her. The ceiling peeled away with a ripping crack. A huge chunk of plaster crashed over the statue's head, throwing hunks of wet plaster across the room. The rustics scattered, shocked and thrilled.

He crushed a piece of wet plaster under his heel, grinding it into mush with a vicious twist, and stalked out of the gallery.

The main corridor was crowded. Servants rushed with buckets of coals, trays of pastries, baskets of fruit – all the comforts required by late sleeping and lazy courtiers. He pushed through them and climbed to a vestibule on the third floor where five water pipes met overhead.

"What have you got for me, you little demon?" he seethed under his breath.

A maid clattered down the stairs, her arms stacked with clean laundry. One look at Sylvain and she retreated back upstairs.

Sylvain had spent nights on bare high rock trapped by spring snowstorms. He had tracked wild goats up the massif cliff to line up careful rifle shots balanced between a boulder and a thousand-foot drop. He had once snatched a bleating lamb from the jaws of the valley's most notorious wolf. He had met the king's enemies on the battlefield and led men to their deaths. He could master a simple creature, however powerful she was.

"Go ahead, drip on me. If you are going to keep playing your games, show me now."

He waited. The pipes looked dry as bone. The seal welds were dull and gray and the tops of the pipes were furred with a fine layer of dust.

He gave the pipes one last searing glare. "All right. We have an understanding."

5

Leblanc's coffin glowed in the cold winter sun. Bull and Bear watched the gravediggers and snuffled loudly.

Gérard had taken all the arrangements in hand. Before Sylvain had a moment to think about dealing with the old soldier's corpse, it had been washed, dressed, and laid out in a village chapel. Gérard had even arranged for a nun to sit beside the coffin, clacking her rosary and gumming toothless prayers.

The nun was scandalized when Bull and Bear hauled the coffin out from under her nose, but Sylvain wanted Leblanc's body away from the palace, hidden away in deep, dry dirt where the little fish could never find it. Gérard and Sylvain led the way on horseback, setting a fast pace as Bull and Bear followed with the casket jouncing in the bed of their cart. They trotted toward the city until they found a likely boneyard, high on dry ground, far from any streams or canals.

"This is probably the finest bed your man Leblanc ever slept in." Gérard nudged the coffin with the toe of his boot.

"Very generous of you, Gérard. Thank you."

Gérard shrugged. "What price eternal comfort? And he was dear to you, I know."

Sylvain scanned the sky as the priest muttered over the grave. A battery of rainclouds was gathering on the horizon, bearing down on Versailles. It was a coincidence. The little fish couldn't control the weather. It wasn't possible.

The gravediggers began slowly filling in the grave. Gérard walked off to speak with a tradesman in a dusty leather apron. Sylvain watched the distant clouds darken and turn the horizon silver with rain.

Gérard returned. "Here is the stonemason. What will you have on your man's gravestone?"

"Nothing," said Sylvain, and then wondered. Was he being ridiculous, rushing the corpse out of the palace and hauling it miles away? She couldn't understand. She was an animal. Any understanding of death was just simple instinct – the hand of fate to be avoided in the moment of crisis. She couldn't read. The stone could say anything. She would never know.

Without Leblanc's help, Sylvain's funds wouldn't have lasted a month at Versailles. He would have wrung out his purse and slunk home a failure. But with Leblanc down in the cisterns coddling the little fish, the whole palace waited eagerly in bed for him. And what had he done for the old soldier in return? Leblanc deserved a memorial.

The stone mason flapped his cap against his leg. The priest clacked his tongue in disapproval.

"He must have a stone, Sylvain," said Gérard. "He was a soldier his whole life. He deserves no less."

There was no point in being careless. "You can list the year of his death, nothing more. No name, no regiment."

Sylvain gave the priest and the stonemason each a coin, stifling any further objections.

The gravediggers were so slow, they might as well have been filling in the grave with spoons instead of spades. Sylvain ordered Bull and Bear to take over. The gravediggers stood openmouthed, fascinated by the sight of someone else digging while they rested. One of them yawned.

"Idle hands are the Devil's tools," the priest snapped, and sent both men back to their work in the adjoining farmyard.

An idea bloomed in Sylvain's mind. The little fish claimed she was bored. Perhaps he had made her work too easy. The lead pipes and huge reservoirs were doing half the job. He could change that. He would keep her busy – too busy for boredom and certainly far too busy for games and tricks.

"Tell your wife she won't wait much longer for a toilet of her own," said Sylvain as they mounted their horses. "In a few days she can have the pleasure of granting or denying her friends its use as she pleases."

Gérard grinned. "Wonderful news! But just a few days? How long will it take to reinforce the roof?"

"I believe I have discovered a quick solution."

6

THE NEW WATER conduits were far too flimsy to be called pipes. They were sleeves, really, which was how had he explained them to the village seamstresses.

"Sing a song?" The little fish dangled one long toe in the water. Her smooth skin bubbled with wide water droplets that glistened and gleamed like jewels.

"Not today. It's time for you to work," Sylvain said as he unrolled the cotton sleeve. He dropped one end in the pool, looped a short piece of rope around it, and weighted the ends with a rock.

"Be a good girl and show me what you can do with this."

She blinked at him, water dripping from her hair. No shade of comprehension marred the perfect ignorance of those uncanny eyes. She slid into the water and disappeared.

He waited. She surfaced in the middle of the pool, lips spouting a stream of water high into the air.

"Very good, but look over here now," he said, admiring his own restraint. "Do you see this length of cotton? It's hollow like a pipe. Show me how well you can push water through it."

She rolled and dove. The water shimmered, then turned still. He searched the glassy surface, looking for her sleek form. She leapt, shattering the water under his nose, throwing a great wave that splashed him from head to toe.

How had Leblanc put up with this? Sylvain turned away, hiding his frustration.

As he pried himself out of his soaked velvet jacket, Sylvain realized he was speaking to her in court French. A nixie couldn't be expected to understand.

The next time she surfaced he said, "I bet you can't force water through this tube." The rough patois of home felt strange after years wrapping his tongue around court French.

That got her attention. "Bet you!" She leapt out of the water. "Bet you what?"

"Well, I don't know. Let's see what I have." He made a show of reluctantly reaching into his breast pocket and withdrawing a coin. It was small change – no palace servant would stoop to pick it up – but it had been polished to gleaming.

He rolled the coin between his thumb and forefinger, letting it wink and sparkle in the glow of her skin. The drops raining from her hair quickened, spattering the toes of his boots.

"Pretty," she said, and brushed the tip of one long finger along the cotton tube.

The pool shimmered. The tube swelled and kicked. It writhed like a snake, spraying water high into the ferns, but the other end remained anchored in the water. The tube leaked, not just from the seams but along its whole length.

"Good work," he said, and tossed her the coin. She let it sail over her head and splash into the pool. She laughed, a bubbling giggle, flexed her sleek legs, and flipped backward, following the coin's trajectory under the surface.

He repeated the experiment with all of the different cloth pipes – linen, silk, satin – every material available. The first cotton tube kept much of its rigidity though it remained terribly leaky, as did the wide brown tube of rough holland. The linen tube lay flat as a dead snake, and across the pond, a battery of satin and silk tubes warred, clashing like swords as they flipped and danced.

The velvet pipes worked best. The thick nap held a layer of water within its fibers, and after a few tries, the little fish learned to manipulate the wet surface, strengthening the tube and keeping it watertight.

By evening, her lair was festooned with a parti-colored bouquet of leaping, spouting tubes. The little fish laughed like a mad child, clapping her hands and jumping through the spray. But he didn't have to remind her to keep the spray away from him – not once.

When he was down to his last shiny coin, her skin was glowing so brightly, it illuminated the far corners of the grotto. He placed the last coin squarely in her slender palm, as if paying a tradesman. The webs between her fingers were as translucent as soap bubbles.

"You won a lot of bets today," he said.

"Good girls win." She dropped the coin into the pond and peered up at him, eyes wide and imploring.

He cut her off before she could speak. "No singing, only work."

"You sang once."

He had, that was true. How could she remember? He'd nearly forgotten himself. He had crouched at the edge of a high mountain cataract with icy mist spraying his face and beading on his hair, singing a shepherd's tune to lure her into his canteen. She'd been no bigger than a tadpole, but she could flip and jump through the massive rapids as if it took no effort at all.

She had grown so much in the past two years. From smaller than his thumb to the size of a half-grown child. Full growth from egg in just two years.

But two years was a lifetime ago, and those mountains now seemed unreachable and remote. He wouldn't think about it. He had an evening of entertainments to attend, and after that, much work to do.

7

Sylvain had almost drifted off when Annette dug her toes into the muscle of his calf. He rolled over and pretended to sleep.

He had given her an afternoon of ardent attention and finished up splayed across her bed, fully naked, spent, and sweating. Though he was bone tired from long nights planning the palace's new array of velvet tubes, he had given Annette a very good facsimile of devotion and several hours of his time. Surely she couldn't want more from him.

She raked her toenails down his calf again. Sylvain cracked an eyelid, trying for the lazy gaze of the Versailles sybarite. Annette reclined in the middle of the bed draped in a scrap of pink chiffon. The short locks of her own dark hair curled over her ears like a boy's. She had ripped the wig from his head earlier, and he had responded by pulling hers off as well, more gently but with equal enthusiasm.

"No sleeping, Sylvain. Not here. You must be prepared to leap from the window if my husband arrives."

"You want me to dash naked through the gardens in full view of half the court? My dear woman, it would mean my death and your disappointment." He couldn't suppress a yawn. "The ladies would hound after me day and night."

"I forgot that about you," she said under her breath.

Sylvain rolled to his feet and lifted a silken shawl off the floor. He wrapped it around his hips like a savage and returned to bed. He lifted an eyebrow, inviting her to continue, but she had begun playing with a pot of cosmetic.

"What did you forget about me?" If she meant to insult him, he intended to know.

She put her foot in his lap. "I forgot that you are a singular man."

That didn't sound like an insult. Sylvain let a smile touch his lips. "Is that your own assessment, or do others speak of me as a singular man?"

"My judgment alone. How many people in the palace ever take a moment to think of anyone other than themselves? Even I, as extraordinary as I am, rarely find a moment to notice the existence of others. Life is so full." She nudged him with her toe.

"In this moment, then, before it passes, tell me what you mean by *singular*." To encourage her, he took her foot in both hands and squeezed.

A dimple appeared on her cheek. "It is a contradiction and a conundrum. By *singular*, I mean the exact opposite. You are at least three or four men where many others have trouble achieving more than a half manhood."

"Flattery. Isn't that my role?"

"I mean no flattery. Quite the opposite, in fact." She dipped her finger into the cosmetic pot and daubed her pout with glossy pigment. Then she stretched herself back on the velvet pillows, arching as he kneaded her toes.

"Sylvain the wit may be a good guest to have at a dinner party but no better than any other man with some quickness about him. Sylvain the courtier contributes to the might of the crown and the luxury of the palace as he ought. Sylvain the lover conducts himself well in bed as he must or sleep alone. I can't speak to Sylvain the soldier or hunter but will grant the appropriate virtues on faith."

"I thank you," he said, kneading her heel.

She fanned her fingers in a dismissive gesture. "All these are expected and nothing spectacular to comment upon. But the true Sylvain is the singular one – the only one – and yet he's the man few others notice."

"And that man is?"

"I don't know if I should tell you. You might stop massaging my foot."

"You enjoy being mysterious."

"The only mystery is how you've gotten away with it for so long. If anyone else knew, you'd be run out of the palace."

"I will stop if you don't tell me."

"Very well. Sylvain, you are a striver."

A lead weight dropped into his stomach. "Ridiculous. I thought you were going to say something interesting, but it is all blather."

She nudged his crotch with her foot. "Don't be insulted. Striving must be in your nature. Or perhaps you were taught it as a child and took it into the blood with your host and catechism. But it will all end in disaster. Striving always does."

He kept his expression remote and resumed stroking her foot.

"You seek to raise yourself above your station," she continued. "Those who do have no true home. They leave behind their rightful and God-given place and yet never reach their goal. It is a kind of Limbo, a choice to begin eternity in purgatory even before death."

"And you have chosen to become a lay preacher. Do you have a wooden crate to stand on? Shall I carry it to a crossroads for you?"

"Oh, very well, we can change the topic to Annette d'Arlain if you are uncomfortable. I find myself a most engaging subject."

"Yes, keep to your area of expertise because you know little of me. I don't seek to raise myself. I am where I belong. The palace would be poorer without me."

"If you remained satisfied with being a lover, a courtier, and a good dinner guest, I might agree with you. Your uncle is a minor noble but I suppose his lineage is solid, should anyone care to trace it, and you're not the first heir to a barren wilderness to manage a creditable reputation at court. But you want to be the first man of Versailles, even at the destruction of your own self and soul. You are striving to be better than every other man."

"That is the first thing you've said that makes any sense."

Sylvain eased her into his lap. He slid his fingers under the chiffon wrap and began teasing her into an eagerly agreeable frame of mind. She would declare him the best man in France before he was done with her, even if it took all evening.

8

THE MONKEY CLUNG to Sylvain's neck and hid its face under his coat collar. Sylvain hummed under his breath, a low cooing sound shepherds used to calm lambs.

The dealer had doused the monkey in cheap cologne to mask its animal scent. The stink must be a constant irritation to the creature's acute sense of smell. But it would wear off soon enough in the mist of the cisterns.

Sylvain rounded the corner into the little fish's cavern and tripped. He slammed to his knees and twisted to take the weight of the fall on his shoulder. The monkey squealed with fright. He hushed it gently.

"Work carefully, be a good girl!" The little fish's voice echoed off the grotto walls.

He had tripped over the painted wooden cradle. The little fish had stuffed it with all of the dolls Sylvain had given her over the past week. The family of straw-and-cloth dolls were soaked and squashed down to form a nest for the large porcelain doll Sylvain had brought her the day before. It had arrived as a gift from the porcelain manufacturer, along with the toilets Bull and Bear were installing in the north wing.

The doll's platinum curls had been partly ripped away. Its painted eyes stared up at him as he struggled to his feet.

The little fish perched on the roof of her dollhouse, which floated half submerged in the pool. The toy furniture bobbed and drifted in the current.

"Come here, little miss," he said. She slipped off the roof and glided across to him. She showed no interest in the monkey, but she probably hadn't realized it was anything other than just another doll.

"Do you remember what we are going to do today?" he asked. "I told you yesterday; think back and remember." She blinked up at him in ignorance. "What do you do every day?"

"Work hard."

"Very good. Work hard at what?"

"Good girls work hard and keep the water flowing." She yawned, treating him to a full view of her tongue and tiny teeth as she stretched.

The monkey yawned in sympathy. Her gaze snapped to the creature with sudden interest.

"Sharp teeth!" She jumped out of the pool and thrust one long finger in the monkey's face. It recoiled, clinging to Sylvain with all four limbs.

"Hush," he said, stroking the monkey's back. "You frightened her. Good girls don't frighten their friends, do they?"

"Do they?" she repeated automatically. She was fascinated by the monkey, which was certainly a more engaged reaction than she had given any of the toys Sylvain had brought her.

He fished in his pocket for the leash and clipped it to the monkey's collar.

"Today, we are adding the new cloth pipes to the system, and you will keep the water flowing like you always do, smooth and orderly. If you do your work properly, you can play with your new friend."

He handed her the leash and gently extracted himself from the monkey's grip. He placed the creature on the ground and stroked its head with exaggerated kindness. If she could copy his words, she could copy his actions.

She touched the monkey's furry flank, eyes wide with delight. Then she brought her hand to her face and whiffed it.

"Stinky," she said.

She dove backward off the rock, yanking the monkey behind her by its neck.

Sylvain dove to grab it but just missed his grip. The monkey's sharp squeal cut short as it was dragged under water.

Sylvain ran along the edge of the pool, trying to follow the glow of her form as she circled and dove. When she broke surface he called to her, but she ignored him and climbed to the roof of her dollhouse. She hauled the monkey up by its collar and laid its limp, sodden form on the spine of the roof.

Dead, Sylvain thought. She had drowned it.

It stirred. She scooped the monkey under its arms and dandled it on her lap like a doll. It coughed and squirmed.

"Sing a song," she demanded. She shoved her face nose to nose with the monkey's and yelled, "Sing a song!"

The monkey twisted and strained, desperate to claw away. She released her grip and the monkey splashed into the water. She yanked the leash and hauled it up. It dangled like a fish. She let her hand drop and the monkey sank again, thrashing.

"Sing a song!" she screamed. "Sing!"

Sylvain pried off his boots and dove into the pool. He struggled to the surface and kicked off a rock, propelling himself though the water.

"Stop it," he blurted as he struggled toward her. "Stop it this instant!"

She crouched on the edge of the dollhouse roof, dangling the monkey over the water by its collar. It raked at her with all four feet, but the animal dealer had blunted its claws, leaving the poor creature with no way to defend itself. She dunked it again. Its paws pinwheeled, slapping the surface.

Sylvain ripped his watch from his pocket and lobbed it at her. It smacked her square in the temple. She dropped the monkey and turned on him, enormous eyes veined with red, lids swollen.

He hooked his arm over the peak of the dollhouse roof and hoisted himself halfway out of the water. He fished the monkey out and gathered the quivering creature to his chest.

"Bad girl," he sputtered, so angry he could barely find breath. "Very bad girl!"

She retreated to the edge of the roof and curled her thin arms around her knees. Her nose was puffy and red just like a human's.

"Leblanc," she sobbed. "Leblanc gone."

She hadn't mentioned Leblanc in days. Sylvain had assumed she'd forgotten the old man, but some hounds missed their masters for years. Why had he assumed the little fish would have coarser feelings than an animal?

She was an animal, though. She would have drowned the monkey and toyed with its corpse. There was no point in coddling her – he would be stern and unyielding.

"Yes, Leblanc has gone away." He gave her his chilliest stare.

Her chin quivered. She whispered, "Because I am a bad girl."

Had she been blaming herself all this time? Beneath the mindless laughter and games she had been missing Leblanc – lonely, regretful, brokenhearted. Wondering if she'd done wrong, if she'd driven him away. Waiting to see him again, expecting him every moment.

Sylvain clambered onto the dollhouse roof and perched between the two chimneys. The monkey climbed onto his shoulder and snaked its fingers into his hair.

"No, little one. Leblanc didn't want to go but he had to."

"Leblanc come back?"

She looked so trusting. He could lie to her, tell her Leblanc would come back if she was a good girl, worked hard, and never caused any problems. She would believe him. He could make her do anything he wanted.

"No, little one. Leblanc is gone and he can never come back."

She folded in on herself, hiding her face in her hands.

"He would have said goodbye to you if he could. I'm sorry he didn't."

Sylvain pulled her close, squeezing her bony, quaking shoulders, tucking her wet head under his chin.

There was an old song he had often heard in the mountains. On one of his very first hunting trips as a boy, he'd heard an ancient shepherd sing it while climbing up a long scree slope searching for a lost lamb. He had heard a crying girl sing it as she flayed the pelt from the half-eaten, wolf-ravaged corpse of an ewe. He'd heard a boy sing it to his flock during a sudden spring snowstorm, heard a mother sing it to her children on a freezing winter night as he passed by her hut on horseback. The words were rustic, the melody simple.

Sylvain sang the song now to the little fish, gently at first, just breathing the tune, and then stronger, letting the sound swell between them. He sang of care, and comfort, and loss, and a longing to make everything better. And if tears seemed to rain down his cheeks as he sang, it was nothing but an illusion – just water dribbling from his hair.

9

SYLVAIN STOOD ON the roof of the north wing, the gardens spread out before him. The fountains jetted high and strong, fifteen hundred nozzles ticking over reliably as clockwork, the water spouts throwing flickering shadows in the low evening light.

The gardens were deserted as any wilderness. Inside, everyone was preparing for the evening's long menu of events. Outside, the statues posed and the fountains played for the moon and stars alone.

Sylvain was taking advantage of this quiet and solitary hour to do one final check of the velvet pipes. He had already felt every inch of the new connection, examined the seams all the way to the point where the fabric sleeve dove off the roof to disappear through a gap above a garret window.

Bull and Bear waited by the main reservoir, watching for his signal. There was no point in delaying any further. He waved his hat in the air. The sleeve at his feet jumped and swelled.

Sylvain ran from the north wing attics down several flights of stairs to Gérard's apartments. Pauline greeted him at the door herself. She was hugely pregnant and cradled her belly in both hands to support its weight. Breathless, he swept off his hat and bowed.

"Go ahead, monsieur," Pauline said as she herded him toward her dressing room. "Please don't pause to be polite. I've waited as long as I can."

Not only were the velvet pipes lighter and easier to install, but they could be pinched off at any point simply by drawing a cord around the sleeve. Sylvain waited for Pauline to follow him, then pulled the red ribbon's tail and let it drift to the floor. Water gushed into the toilet, gurgling and tinkling against the porcelain.

Pauline seized him by the ears, kissed him hard on both cheeks, and shooed him away. She hiked her skirts up to her hips even before her servant shut the door behind him.

Sylvain arrived fashionably late at the suite of the Mahmud emissary, a Frenchman turned Turk after years at the Sultan's court. Sylvain saluted le Turque, lifted a glass of wine, and assumed an air of languid nonchalance. Madame and her ladies swept in. Their jewels and silks glowed in the candlelight.

Annette carried Madame's train – a sure sign she was in favor at that moment. Sylvain saluted her with a respectful nod. She dimpled at him and made her way over as soon as the host claimed Madame's attention.

"Is that for me, monsieur?" she asked.

Sylvain glanced at the monkey on his shoulder. "Perhaps, if there is a woman in the room who isn't tired of gifts."

"Jewels and flowers are all the same. This is something different." She caressed the monkey under her chin. It reached for Annette like a child for its mother. "What is her name?"

"Whatever you want, of course."

"I will ask Madame to choose her name. She will love that." Annette cradled the monkey against her breast and nuzzled its neck. "Oh, she smells lovely – vanilla and cinnamon oil."

It was the only combination of scents Sylvain had found to kill the stench of cheap cologne. He allowed himself a satisfied smirk.

Across the room a subtle commotion was building. Le Turque had lifted a curtain to reveal a pair of acrobats, but Madame was watching Annette and Sylvain. The acrobats were frozen in a high lift, waiting for permission to begin their performance as the musicians repeated the same few bars of music.

"You had better go back. Madame has noticed the monkey and is jealous for your return."

Annette awarded him a melting smile and drifted back to Madame's circle. The ladies greeted the monkey as if it were a firstborn son. Madame let the effusions continue for a few moments and then took sole possession of the creature, holding it close as she turned her attention to the performance.

Sylvain struggled to stay alert, despite the near-naked spectacle on stage. He had barely seen his bed since Leblanc's death, and the warm wine and rich food were turning his courtier's air of languid boredom into the prelude to a toddler's nap. The spinning and leaping acrobats were mesmerizing – especially when viewed in candlelight through a screen of nodding wigs and feathers. The bright silk-and satin-clad backs in front of him dipped as they lifted their glasses to their lips, swayed from side to side as they leaned over to gossip with the friend on the left about the friend on the right, then turned the other way to repeat the performance in reverse. Men and women they might be, but tonight they seemed more like the flamingoes that flocked on the Camargue, all alike in their brainless and feathered idiocy.

At least a flamingo made a good roast.

Sylvain spotted Gérard sneaking into the room, stealthy as a scout. He took his place by Sylvain's side as if he'd been there all evening.

"Thank God, Gérard," Sylvain whispered. "Stick your sword into my foot if you see me nodding off."

Gérard grinned. "It's the least I could do for the man who has brought such happiness to my wife."

The acrobats were succeeded by a troupe of burly Turkish dancers bearing magnums of champagne entombed in blocks of ice. Children dressed as cherubs passed crystal saucers to the guests.

"This will keep you awake, my friend. Champagne cold as a cuckold's bed."

"I've been in such a bed recently. It was quite warm."

Le Turque himself filled Sylvain and Gérard's saucers. "Tonight, you are in favor with the ladies, monsieur."

"Am I?" Sylvain sipped his champagne. The cold, sweet fizz drilled into his sinuses. His eyes watered as he forced back the urge to sneeze.

"So true!" said Gérard. "My own wife is ready to call Sylvain a saint. She has set up an altar to him in her dressing room."

"But I refused the honor," said Sylvain. "I would prefer not to have those offerings dedicated to me."

They laughed. Le Turque gave them a chill grimace.

"My apologies, monsieur," said Gérard. "It is not a private joke, just too coarse for general consumption. We are soldiers, you know, and are welcomed into civilized homes on charity."

Le Turque demonstrated his kind forbearance by topping up both their saucers before moving on to the other guests.

Sylvain studied the champagne and their enclosing blocks of ice as the Turkish dancers circled the room, trailing meltwater on the carpet. The bottles couldn't have been frozen into the ice or the wine would be frozen through. They must be made from dual pieces carved to enclose a bottle like a book. He stopped a dancer and examined the ice. Yes, the two pieces were joined by a seam.

A simple solution, too practical to be called ingenious, but effective. The guests were impressed, even though many of them were fingering their jaws and wincing from cold-induced toothache. Not one guest refused a second glass, or a third, or a fourth. Bottles were being drained at impressive rate.

Annette drew her fan up to her ear and flicked Sylvain a telling glance from across the room. He took Gérard's arm. "Come along; we are being summoned to an audience with Madame."

The royal mistress was dressed in white and silver. Her snowy wig was fine as lamb's wool, her skin frosted with platinum powder. A bouquet of brightly clad ladies surrounded her like flowers around a statue. The monkey slept in her lap. She had tied a silver ribbon around its neck.

The standard palace practice was to praise Madame's face and figure in public and criticize it in private. Sylvain had seen her often, but always at a distance. Now after months of maneuvering, he was finally close enough to judge for himself.

"A triumph worthy of our Turkish friends, is it not?" Madame offered Sylvain her hand. "I shall never be able to enjoy champagne at cellar temperature again. It is so refreshing. One feels renewed."

"Our host has distinguished himself," said Sylvain, brushing her knuckles with his lips. Madame let her fingers linger in his palm for a moment before presenting her hand to Gérard.

"Le Turque is an old man and has resources appropriate to his age and rank," said Madame. "I wonder how young men can become distinguished in the king's gaze."

"Perhaps by murdering the king's enemies on the battlefield every summer?" said Gérard.

The ladies tittered. Madame slowly drew back her hand and blinked. Pretty, thought Sylvain, at least when surprised.

"Excuse my friend, Madame. Cold champagne has frozen his brain."

Madame eyed Gérard up and down. "Everyone respects our valiant soldiers, and your devotion to manly duty is admirable." She turned back to Sylvain. "If your brawny friend the Marquis de la Châsse is content with his achievements, who are we to criticize? But you, monsieur, I know you care about the honor of France both on and off the field of war."

"Every Frenchman does, madame, but especially when he has been drinking champagne," said Sylvain. Gérard lifted his glass in salute.

Madame flicked her fan at Annette. "You may have heard an idea of mine. At first, it was just an idle thought, but now le Turque has thrown down the gauntlet. Is there a man who will accept the challenge?"

"No man could refuse you anything, madame. The rulers of the world fall at your feet."

"I would rush to serve you," said Gérard, "if I had any idea what you meant. Madame is so mysterious."

Madame dismissed Gérard with a flick of her fan. "Be so good as to fetch me one of those dancers, monsieur."

"A Turk with a full magnum, Madame?" Gérard saluted her and set off with a jaunty military stride.

Madame shifted on the sofa. She seemed to be considering whether or not to invite Sylvain to sit. Then she lifted the monkey from her lap and set it beside her.

Not nearly so lovely as Annette, Sylvain decided.

"You may not know, monsieur, how highly you are praised. I am told that even when the Bassin d'Apollon was new, fountain-play was a parsimonious affair, the water doled out like pennies from a Polish matron's purse."

She paused to collect dutiful titters from her ladies for this jab at the queen. Perhaps not pretty at all, thought Sylvain. Hardly passable.

"You have found a way to keep all of the fountains constantly alive without pause. Some members of the royal household call you a magician, but the word from the highest level is less fanciful and more valuable. There, you are simply called inspiring."

Sylvain puffed up at the praise. Gérard returned with a beefy Turk. The dancer's fingers were blue from the cold, and he struggled to fill Madame's saucer without dribbling.

"Just like a commander on the battlefield, a woman judges a man by his actions." She lifted the monkey and planted a kiss between its ears. "Any other man would have collared this monkey's neck with a diamond bracelet before presenting it to a lady of the court. We would call that vulgar."

Her ladies nodded.

"You have taste and discernment. So give me champagne, free-flowing and cold. That is a triumph worthy of Versailles." She presented her hand to Sylvain again, then waved him away. The ladies closed around her like a curtain.

"Vulgar, indeed," said Gérard as they retreated. "I've never seen a woman greet a diamond with anything other than screeches of delight. Have you?"

"My experience with diamonds is limited."

"Madame knows it. She was spreading you with icing."

"She wants to secure a valuable ally. Compliments are the currency of court."

Gérard drained his champagne and rubbed his knuckles over his jaw as if it ached. "She just wants to drink champagne at another man's expense. As with most pleasures, it comes with a little pain. She wants the pain to be yours, not hers."

"The champagne fountain is a whim. She will ask me for something else next time."

"Very well. Madame will ask you to do something expensive and original with only a few pretty words as payment. Will you do it?"

Two full glasses of red wine had been abandoned at the foot of a statue. Sylvain fetched them and passed one to his friend. After the sweet champagne, the warm wine tasted flat and murky as swamp water.

"Only a fool would pass up the opportunity."

10

"Papa, come play!"

The nixie swam backward against a vortex of current, dodging spinning hunks of ice that floated like miniature icebergs, splintering and splitting as they smashed together. Overhead, the red-and-blue parrot climbed among the fern fronds, screeching and flapping its wings.

As he had suspected, the little fish loved ice. He had once seen a nixie swimming at the foot of a glacier, playing with ice boulders as they calved from the ice field's flank. The nixie had pushed them around like kindling, building a dam that spread a wide lake of turquoise meltwater over the moraine.

"Papa, come play!"

"Papa!" The parrot screeched its name.

Sylvain had purchased the bird from an elderly lady who was moldering in a north-wing garret, wearing threadbare finery from the Sun King's reign and living off charity and crumbs of her neighbors' leftover meals. The parrot was a good companion for the little fish. It was old and wily, and with its sharp beak and talons, it was well equipped to protect itself if she got too rough. It could fly out of reach and was fast enough to dodge sprays and splashes.

"Papa?" The nixie levered herself up the lip of her nest and stared at Sylvain expectantly. "Papa come play?"

Sylvain felt in his pockets for the last of the walnuts. "Here, little one. See if you can lure Papa down with this."

"Bird! Food!" she yelled, waving the walnut aloft. The parrot kited down to the nest and plucked the nut from her fist.

"Come play, Papa?" she asked. She wasn't looking at the bird. Her uncanny gaze was for him alone.

"That's quite enough of that," he said. "The bird's name is Papa, and you'll do well to remember it, young lady."

She leaned close and spoke slowly, explaining. "Bird is Bird, Papa is Papa."

"Papa," agreed the parrot, its beady gaze fixed on Sylvain.

"You are impossible." Sylvain waved at the surface of the pond, which was now carpeted with icy slurry circulating in the slowing current. "Clear away your toys or I'll freeze swimming across."

"Papa go away?"

"The bird is staying here with you. I am going to see about my important business. When I come back, I'll bring more walnuts for Papa and nothing for you. Now clean up the ice."

She laughed and dove. The water bubbled like a soup pot, forcing the slush to congeal into wads the size of lily pads. As the turbulence increased the leaves tilted and stacked, climbing into columns of gleaming ice that stretched and branched overhead.

The parrot flew to the top of a column and nibbled at the ice. It was solid and hard as rock.

"Very impressive," breathed Sylvain.

He had spent the past few days running up debts with the village icemongers and pushing cartloads of straw-wrapped ice blocks down the tunnels. Though she had never seen ice, she had taken to it instinctively, tossing it around the grotto, building walls and dams, smashing and splitting the blocks into shard and slag, and playing in the slush like a pig in mud. But now she was creating ice. This was extraordinary.

"Come here, little one," he said.

Obedient for the moment, she slipped over the surface to tread water at the edge of the nest. Above the water, her pale green skin was furred with frost. Steam snaked from her nostrils and gill slits.

"Show me how you did that," he said.

She blinked. "Show me how, Papa?"

He spoke slowly. "The ice was melted into slush, but you froze it again, building this." He pointed to an ice branch. The parrot sidestepped along the branch, bobbing its head and gobbling to itself. "Can you do it again?"

She shrugged. "You are impossible."

He scooped up a fistful of water and held it out in his cupped hand. "Give it a try. Can you freeze this?"

The little fish peered up at him with that familiar imploring, pleading expression. He could hear her request even before she opened her mouth.

"Sing a song?"

Gifts were one thing but blatant bribery was another. If he began exchanging favor for favor, it would be a constant battle. But he had no time for arguments. He could risk a small bribe.

"I will sing you one song – a very short song – and only because you have been such a good girl today. But first freeze this water."

"One song," she agreed.

Heat radiated up his arm. The water in his fist crackled and jumped, forming quills of ice that spread from his palm like a chestnut conker. He was so astonished that he forgot to breathe for a few moments. Then he drew in a great breath and let himself sing.

The foresters of home played great lilting reels on pipes and fiddles. Their lives were as poor and starved as the shepherds in the meadows above or the farmers in the valley below, but they were proud and honed the sense of their own superiority as sharp as the edges on their axes. Their songs bragged of prowess at dancing, singing, making love, and of course at the daredevil feats required by their trade. The song that came to his lips told of a young man proving his worth by riding a raft of logs down a grassy mountainside in full view of the lowly villagers in the valley below.

He only meant to give her the first verse, but the little fish danced and leaped with such joy that he simply gave himself over to the song – abandoned himself so completely that halfway through the second verse, he found himself punctuating the rhythm with sharp staccato hand claps just as proudly as any forester. He sang all six verses, and when he was done, she leapt into his arms and hugged her thin arms around his neck.

"Papa sing good," she whispered, her breath chill in his ear.

He patted her between the shoulder blades. Her skin was cold and clammy under a skiff of frost. Sylvain leaned back and loosened her arms a bit so he could examine her closely. Her eyes were keen, her skin bright. She was strong and healthy, and if she was a bit troublesome and a little demanding, it was no more than any child.

11

"ANNETTE TELLS ME you had your men run water to the north wing."

Madame reclined on a golden sofa, encased and seemingly immobilized by the jagged folds of her silver robe. Her cleavage, shoulders, and neck protruded – a stem to support her rosebud-pale face. Her ladies gathered around her, gaudy in their bright, billowing silks.

Annette avoided his eye. Sylvain brushed imaginary lint from his sleeve, feigning unconcern. "I believe my foreman mentioned that they had finally gotten so far. I gave the orders months ago."

"Everyone has a throne now. Madame de Beauvilliers claims to possess one exactly like mine. She shows it to her neighbors and even lets her maid sit on it."

"Your throne was one of the first in the palace, Madame, and remains the finest."

"Being first is no distinction when a crowd of nobodies have the newest. No doubt our village merchants will be bragging about their own thrones in a day or two."

Sylvain twitched. He had just been considering running pipes through the village and renting toilets there. Merchants had the cash flow to sustain monthly payments, and unlike courtiers, they were used to paying their debts promptly.

"No indeed, Madame. I assure you I am extremely careful to preserve the privileges of rank. I am no populist."

"And how will you preserve my distinction? Will you give me a second throne to sit in my dressing room? A pedestal for a pampered pet? If a cat has a throne, surely you can give me one for each of my ladies. We shall put them in a circle here in my salon and sit clucking at each other like laying hens."

Her ladies giggled obediently. Annette stared at the floor and wrung the feathers of her fan like the neck of a Christmas goose. Just a few more twists and she would break the quills.

Madame glared at him. Angry color stained her cheeks, visible even through her heavy powder. "If every north-wing matron can brag about her throne, you may remove mine. I am bored of it. Take the vulgar thing away and throw it in the rubbish."

If Sylvain took just two steps closer, he could loom over her and glare down from his superior height. But intimidation wasn't possible. She held the whip and knew her power. If she abandoned her toilet, the whole palace would follow fashion. He would be ruined.

He strolled to the window and examined a vase of forced flowers, careful to keep his shoulders loose, his step light. "My dear madame, the thrones don't matter. You might as well keep yours."

Madame's eyebrows climbed to the edge of her wig. Annette dropped her fan. The ivory handle clattered on the marble with a skeletal rattle. Sylvain sniffed one of the blossoms, a monstrous pale thing with pistils like spikes.

"Is that so," said Madame, iron in her voice. "Enlighten me."

"We need not speak of them further. If possessing a throne conveyed distinction, it was accidental. They are a convenience for bodily necessity, nothing more. Having a throne was once a privilege, but it has been superseded."

"By what?" Madame twisted on her divan to watch him, unsettling her artfully composed tableau. He had her now.

"By the thing your heart most desires, flowing freely like a tap from a spring. So cold it chills the tongue. So fresh, the bubbles spark on the palate. Sweet as the rain in heaven and pure as a virgin's child. I believe you hold a day in February close to your heart? A particularly auspicious day?"

"I do, and it is coming soon."

"You will find your wishes fulfilled. Count on my support."

A slow grin crept over Madame's face. "It's possible you are a man of worth after all, Sylvain de Guilherand, and I need not counsel my ladies against you."

She dismissed him. Sylvain was careful not to betray the tremor in his limbs as he strolled through her apartment. The rooms were lined with mirrors, each one throwing his groomed and powdered satin-clad reflection back at him. He could put his fist through any one of those mirrors. It would feel good for a moment – the glass would shatter around his glove and splinter this overheated, foul, wasteful place into a thousand shards.

But if he showed his anger, he would betray himself. Any outburst would reveal a childish lack of self-control and provide gossip that would be told and retold long after he had been forgotten.

Sylvain found the nearest service corridor and descended to the cellars. He got a bottle of champagne from one of the king's stewards – a man who knew him well enough to extend the mercy of credit. He bought a bag of walnuts and half a cheese from a provisioner's boy who was wise enough to demand coin. The Duc d'Orléans' baker gave him a loaf of dark bread and made a favor of it. Then he slipped out of the palace and made his way to the cisterns.

The little fish dozed on a branch of her ice tree, thin limbs dangling. The bird was rearranging the nest, plucking at fern fronds and clucking to itself.

"You're fancy," the little fish said, her voice sleepy.

Sylvain looked down. He was in full court garb, a manikin in satin, wrapped in polished leather and studded with silver buttons.

He pulled off his wig and settled himself on a boulder. "Do I look like a man of worth to you, little one?"

"Worth what, Papa?"

He grimaced. "My dear, that is exactly the question."

He spread a handkerchief at his feet and made a feast for himself. Good cheese and fresh bread made a better meal than many he'd choked back on campaign, better even than most palace feasts with dishes hauled in from the village or up from the cellar kitchens, cold, salty, and studded with congealed fat. A man could live on bread and cheese. Many did worse. And many went gouty and festered on meat drowning in sauce.

The parrot winged over to investigate. Sylvain offered it a piece of cheese. It nuzzled the bread and plucked at the bag of walnuts. Sylvain untied the knot and the bird flapped away with a nut clenched in each taloned foot.

The little fish stretched and yawned. She slipped from the branch, surfaced at the edge of the pool, and padded over to him.

"Stinky," she said, nose wrinkling.

"The cheese? You're no French girl." He pared a sliver for her. She refused it. "Some bread?"

She shook her head.

"What do you eat, my little fish?" She had teeth, human teeth. Had he been starving her?

"Mud," she said, patting her belly.

There was certainly enough mud to choose from. "Would you eat a fish?" She stuck out her tongue in disgust. "The parrot eats nuts. Have you tried one?"

"Yucky. What's this, Papa?" She lifted the champagne bottle.

"Don't shake it. Here, I'll show you."

He scraped off the wax seal and unshipped the plug. He held it out. She sniffed at the neck of the bottle and shrugged, then took the bottle and dribbled a little on the floor. It foamed over her bare toes.

"Ooh, funny!" she said, delighted.

"It's like water, but a bit different."

She raised the bottle overhead and giggled as the champagne foamed over her ears. It dribbled down her cheeks and dripped from her chin. She licked her lips and grinned.

"Don't drink it. It might make you sick."

She rolled her eyes. "Just water, Papa. Fuzzy water."

"All right, give it a try."

She took a gulp and then offered the bottle to him, companionable as a sentry sharing a canteen with a friend.

He shook his head. "No, thank you, I don't prefer it."

He watched attentively as she played. She drank half the bottle but it had no apparent effect. She remained nimble and precise, and if her laughter was raucous and uncontrolled, it was no more than normal. The rest of the bottle she poured on or around herself, reveling in the bubbles and foam. Sylvain wondered if the ladies of the palace had tried bathing in champagne. If they hadn't, he wasn't going to suggest the fashion. The foamy sweet stuff was already a waste of good grapes.

When she lost interest, she dropped the bottle and arced back into the pool, diving clean and surfacing with a playful spout and splash. A finger or two was left, and when he poured it out, it foamed on the rocks fresh as if the bottle had just been cracked.

He nodded to himself. If the little fish could force water through pipes and sleeves, could make ice and keep it from melting, could chase him around the palace and make him look a fool while never leaving the cisterns, what were a few bubbles?

Sylvain knelt and pushed the empty bottle under the surface of the pool. He had done this a thousand times – filled his canteen at village wells, at farmyard troughs, at battlefield sloughs tinged pink with men's blood – and each time, his lungs ached as he watched the bubbles rise. He ached for one sip of mountain air, a lick of snowmelt, just a snatch of a shepherd's song heard across the valley, or a fading echo of a wolf's cry under a blanket of moonlight. Ached to crouch by a rushing rocky stream and sip water pristine and pure.

"Thirsty, Papa?"

The little fish stood at his side. In her hand was a cup made of ice, its walls porcelain-thin and sharp as crystal. He raised it to his lips. The cold water sparkled with fine bubbles that burst on his tongue like a thousand tiny pinpricks and foamed at the back of his throat. He drank it down and smiled.

12

THE GRAND GALLERY streamed with all the nobles and luminaries of Europe, men Sylvain had glimpsed across the battlefield and longed to cross swords with, highborn women whose worth was more passionately negotiated than frontier borders, famous courtesans whose talents were broadcast in military camps and gilded parlors from Moscow to Dublin, princes of the church whose thirst for bloody punishment was unquenched and universal. This pure stream was clotted with a vast number of rich and titled bores with little to do and nothing to say. The whole world was in attendance for the king's birthday, but Sylvain had only glimpsed it. He hadn't left the champagne fountain all evening.

"If you don't come, I'll brain you with my sword hilt. Mademoiselle de Nesle is Madame's sister. If you snub one, you insult both," Gérard said, then added in an undertone, "Plus, she has the finest tits in the room and is barely clothed."

"In a moment."

The fountain branched overhead. Crystal limbs reached for the gilded ceiling and dropped like a weeping willow. Each limb was capped with ice blossoms, and each blossom streamed with champagne.

Madame had offered the first taste to the king, plucking a delicate cup of ice that sprouted from the green ice basin like a mushroom from the forest floor and filling it from a gushing spout. The king had toasted Sylvain and led the gallery in a round of applause. Then the guests flocked eagerly for their turn. They drank gallons of champagne, complained about toothache, and then drank more.

Sylvain had planned for this. He knew the noble appetite, knew the number of expected guests and how much they could be expected to drink. The fountain's basin was tall and wide, and the reservoir beneath held the contents of a thousand magnums. The reservoir was tinted dark green with baker's dye. It was too dark to see through but Sylvain calculated it to be about half full. More than enough champagne was left to keep the fountain flowing until the last courtier had been dragged to bed.

But the guests were now more interested in the king's other gifts – an African cat panting in a jeweled harness, a Greek statue newly cleaned of its dirt and ancient paint, a tapestry stitched by a hundred nuns over ten years, a seven-foot-tall solar clock. The guests were still drinking champagne at an admirable rate but sent attendants to fill their cups. The novelty had worn off.

Sylvain slipped off his glove and laid his hand on the edge of the basin, letting the cold leach into his bare palm. The little fish had been eager to play in the fountain's reservoir, but she'd been inside for hours now and must be getting bored. Still, she had played no tricks. She kept the champagne flowing fresh, kept the ice from melting just as she had agreed. All because he had promised her a song.

"The fountain is fine," Gérard insisted. "We've all admired it. Now come see Madame and her sister."

Sylvain replaced his glove and followed Gérard. Guests toasted him as he passed.

"I need a fountain in my hat," said Mademoiselle de Nesle.

The two sisters were holding court outside the Salon of War, presenting a portrait of tender affection and well-powdered beauty. But their twin stars did not orbit peacefully. Madame held the obvious advantage – official status, a liberal allowance from the royal purse, a large entourage, and innumerable privileges and rights along with her jewels and silks – but her sister had novelty on her side and emphasized her ingénue status with a simple gauze robe. Goodwill bloomed between them, or a decent counterfeit of it, but their attending ladies stood like two armies across an invisible border.

Annette stood apart from the scene, dimples worn shallow. A line of worry wrinkled her brow. Her fan drooped from her elbow. No coy signals tonight, just a bare nod and a slight tilt of her eyebrows. Sylvain followed her gaze to the ermine-draped figure of the King of France.

The two sisters had captured the king's attention. He was ignoring Cardinal de Fleury and two Marshals of the Empire, gazing down from the royal dais to watch his mistress and her sister with obvious interest, plumed hat in his hand, gloved fist on his hip, alert as a stallion scenting a pair of mares.

Sylvain moved out of the king's view. The ladies were on display for one audience member alone, and Sylvain was not about to get between them.

"A fountain in my hat," Mademoiselle de Nesle repeated. "My dear sister says you are a magician."

Sylvain bowed deeply, hiding his expression for a few moments. A ridiculous request. The woman must be simple. Did she think he could pull such a frippery out of his boot?

"The fountain will have its naissance at the peak of my chapeau, providing a misty veil before my eyes."

"But mademoiselle would get wet," Sylvain ventured finally.

"Yes! You have grasped my point. My dress is gauze, as you can see. It's very thin and becomes transparent when wet." She smoothed her hands over her breasts and leaned toward her sister. "Do you not think it will prove alluring, Louise?"

Madame caressed her sister's hands. "No man would be able to resist you, my dear sister."

Mademoiselle laughed. Her voice was loud enough for the opera house. "I care for no man. Only a god can have me."

The king took a few steps closer to the edge of the dais, the very plumes on his hat magnetized by the scene.

Across the room, the Comte de Tessé approached the fountain with the careful, considered step of a man trying to hide his advanced state of drunkenness. The comte waved his crystal cup under the blossom spouts, letting the champagne overflow the glass and foam over his hand. The cup slipped from his hand and shattered on the fountain's base. The comte sputtered with laughter.

"Do you not think it would be the finest of chapeaux, monsieur? A feat worthy of a magician, would it not be?"

The comte was joined at the fountain by a pair of young officers, polished, pressed, and gleaming in their uniforms, and just as drunk as the comte but far less willing to hide it. One leaned over the fountain and tried to sip directly from a blossom spout.

"I think it would be a very worthy feat," Madame said. "Monsieur, my sister posed you a question."

The officers were now trying to clamber onto the fountain's slippery base. The comte laughed helplessly.

"No," said Sylvain.

Madame blinked. Her ladies gasped.

The officer grasped a blossom spout. It snapped off in his hand. His friend slipped on the fountain's edge and fell into the basin. His gold scabbard clanged on the ice. Two women – their wives, perhaps – joined the comte to laugh at the young heroes.

"Excuse me, mesdames."

Sylvain rushed back to the fountain. One snarl brought the two young officers to attention. They scrambled off the fountain, claimed their wives from the comte, and disappeared into the crowd.

The comte's gaze was bleary. "Well done indeed, Monsieur de Guilherand. The palace is ablaze with compliments. But remember it is I who gave you this kingly idea in the first place. As a gentleman, you will ensure I receive due credit."

"You can take half the credit when you bear half the expense," Sylvain hissed. "I'll send you the vintner's bill. You'll find the total appropriately kingly."

The comte turned back to the fountain and refilled his cup, pretending to not hear. Sylvain plucked the cup from the comte's hand and poured the contents into the basin.

"You've embarrassed yourself. Go and sober up."

The comte pretended to spot a friend across the room and tottered away.

Sylvain examined the broken blossom. Its finely carved petals dripped in the overheated air. The broken branch gushed champagne like a wound. Had the little fish felt the assault on the fountain? Had it frightened her? He tried to see through the dark green ice, watching for movement within the reservoir.

"Perhaps we ask too much," said Annette, "expecting soldiers to transform themselves into gentlemen and courtiers for the winter. Many men seem to manage it for more than a few hours at a time. One wonders why you can't, Sylvain de Guilherand."

She posed at the edge of the fountain, fan fluttering in annoyance.

"Perhaps because I am a beast?"

The reservoir ice was thick and dark. In bright sunlight, he might be able to see through it, but even with thousands of candles overhead and the hundreds of mirrors lining the gallery, the light was too dim. He should have left a peephole at the back of the fountain.

"I speak as a friend," said Annette. "Madame is insulted. You have taken a serious misstep."

"Madame has made her own misstep this evening and will forget about mine before morning."

Annette's fan drooped. "True. She has made a play to keep the king's interest, but I fear she'll lose his favor. *Maîtresse en titre* is an empty honor if your lover prefers another woman's bed."

"She'll be naming something vile after her sister next," said Sylvain.

Annette coughed. "You heard about Polish Mary, then?" Sylvain nodded. "It's her way of insulting those she despises. It makes the king laugh."

A shadow moved in the fountain's base, a flicker of a limb against the green ice just for a moment. He should have given the little fish a way to signal him if she was in distress.

"I begin to perceive that my conversation is not engaging enough for you, monsieur."

"I beg your pardon, madame." Sylvain turned his back on the fountain. The little fish was fine. Nixies spent entire seasons under the ice of glacier lakes. It was her element. The fact that the champagne continued to flow was perfect evidence that she was not in distress. He was worrying for nothing. Offending Annette further would be a mistake.

He swept a deep bow. "More than your pardon, my dear madame. I beg your indulgence."

"Indulgence, yes." She looked over her shoulder at Madame and her sister. "We have all indulged ourselves too much this evening and will pay for it."

He forced a knowing smile. "Perhaps the best practice is to let others indulge us. Although a wise and lovely woman once mentioned that most ladies prefer a long period of suspense first. It whets the appetite."

The empty banter seemed to cheer her. Her dimples surfaced and she snapped her fan with renewed purpose.

"Would you join me in taking a survey of the room?" He offered his arm. "I don't beg your company for myself alone but in a spirit of general charity. If all this indulgence will lead to a morning filled with regrets, at least we can offer the king's guests a memory of true beauty. With you on the arm of a beast such as myself, the contrast will be striking."

She glanced at Madame. "I was sent to scold you, not favor you with my company."

"You can always say I forced you."

She laughed and took his arm. He led her through a clot of courtiers toward the royal dais. The king had returned his attention to his most favored guests but displayed a shapely length of royal leg for the two sisters to admire.

"Much better, my dear Sylvain," said Gérard as they approached. "I hate to see you brooding over that fountain. My wife strokes her great belly with the same anxious anticipation. You looked like a hen on an egg."

Sylvain dropped his hand onto the pommel of his sword and glared. Gérard barked with laughter.

"Your friend the Marquis de la Châsse can't manage civil conversation, either," said Annette as they moved on.

"Gérard doesn't need to make the effort. He was born into enough distinction that every trespass is forgiven."

"You sound jealous, but it's not quite accurate. His wealth and title do help, but he is accepted because everyone can see he is true to his nature."

"And I am not?"

"A bald question. I will answer it two ways. First, observe that at this moment, you and I are walking arm in arm among every person in the world who matters. If that is not acceptance, I wonder how you define the word."

"I am honored, madame."

"Yes, you most certainly are, monsieur."

"And your second answer?"

"You are not true to your nature, and it makes people uncomfortable. Everyone knows what to expect from a man like the Marquis de la Châsse, but one suspects that Sylvain de Guilherand would rather be somewhere else, doing something else. Heaven knows what."

Sylvain closed his glove over hers. "Not at all. I am exactly where I want to be."

"So you say, but I do not believe it. Our well-beloved king toasted you this evening. Many men would consider that enough achievement for a lifetime, but still you are dissatisfied."

"We discussed my character before. Remember how that ended?"

A delicate blush flushed through her powder. "I am answering your question as honestly as I can."

"Honesty is not a vice much indulged at Versailles."

She laughed. "I know the next line. Let me supply it: 'It's the only vice that isn't.' Oh, Sylvain. I can have that kind of conversation with any man. I'd rather go home to my husband and talk about hot gruel and poultices. Don't make me desperate."

Sylvain stroked her hand. "Very well. You enjoy my company despite my faults?"

She nibbled her bottom lip as she considered the question. "Because of your faults, I think," she said. "The fountain is successful, the king is impressed with you, and you have my favor. Take my advice and be satisfied."

Sylvain raised her palm to his lips. "I will."

They walked on, silent but in perfect concord. As they circled the gallery, the atmosphere seemed less stifling, the crowd less insipid, the king's air of rut less ridiculous. Even Madame's poses seemed less futile and her sister's pouts less desperate. Sylvain was in charity with the world, willing to forgive its many flaws.

The guests parted, opening a view of the fountain. A girl in petal-yellow silk reached her cup to one of the blossoms. The curve of her bare arm echoed the graceful arc of the fountain's limbs. She raised the cup to her lips and the crowd closed off his view of the scene just as she took her first sip.

"Nature perfected, monsieur," said a portly Prussian. "You must be congratulated."

Sylvain bowed and drew Annette away just as the Prussian's gaze settled on her cleavage. The king rose to dismount the dais and the whole crowd watched. Sylvain took advantage of the distraction to claim a kiss from Annette, just a brief caress of her ripe lower lip before they joined the guests in a ripple of deep curtseys and bows. The king progressed down the gallery toward Madame and her sister, his pace forceful and intent as a stalking hunter.

Annette slid her hand up Sylvain's arm and rested her palm on his shoulder. A pulse fluttered on her throat. He resisted the urge to explore it with his lips.

"I suppose it is too early to leave," he whispered, drinking in the honeyed scent of her powder.

"Your departure would be noticed," she breathed. "It is the price of fame, monsieur."

"Another turn of the room, then?"

She nodded. They moved down the gallery in the king's wake. The African cat gnawed on its harness, blunted ivory fangs rasping over the jewels. Its attendant yanked ineffectually on the leash.

"Poor thing," said Annette. "They should take it outside. This is no place for a wild animal."

Sylvain nodded. "I have not thought to ask before now, but how is the monkey? Happier, I hope, than that cat?"

"Very well and happy indeed. My maid Marie coddles her like a new mother. They are madonna and child, the two of them a world unto themselves." She glanced up at him, a wicked slant to her gaze, daring him to laugh. He grinned.

"And what name did Madame give the creature?"

The color drained from her cheeks. "Is that the viceroy of Parma? I would not have thought to see him here."

"I couldn't say. He looks like every other man in a wig and silk. Are you avoiding my question?"

"Show me your fountain. I haven't had the chance to admire it up close."

The crowd parted to reveal three young men in peacock silks filling their cups at the fountain. One still kept his long baby curls, probably in deference to a sentimental mother.

"There!" Annette said. "Not quite as delicate a tableau as the girl in yellow, but I think I like it better. You must make allowances for differences in taste, and I have always preferred male beauty."

"I am sure you do. What did Madame name the monkey, Annette?"

"She is called Jesusa. It is a terrible sacrilege and my accent makes it bad Spanish too, but what can I do when I am presented with madonna and child morning, noon, and night? God will forgive me."

"Madame didn't name the monkey Jesusa."

"Don't be so sure. Madame is even worse a Christian than I am."

"Very well. I'll ask her myself."

Sylvain strode toward the Salon of War. The crowd was thick. The king was with Madame now. The tall feathers of the royal hat bobbed over the heads of the guests.

Annette pulled his arm. "Stop. Not in front of the king. Don't be stubborn."

He turned on her. "Answer my question."

The jostling crowd pressed them together. She gripped his arms, breath shallow.

"Promise you won't take offence."

"Just answer the question, Annette."

She bit her lip hard enough to draw blood. "She named the monkey Sylvain."

He wrenched himself out of her grip and lurched back, nearly bowling over an elderly guest.

"It is a joke," said Annette, pursuing him.

"Does it seem funny to you?"

"Take it in the spirit it was intended, just a silly attempt at fun. It isn't meant as an attack on your pride."

"Madame thinks I am a prize target. Did you laugh, Annette?" His voice rose. Heads turned. Guests jostled their neighbors, alerting them to the scene. "Who else would like to take a shot at me?"

"Sylvain, no, please." Annette spoke softly and reached out to him. He stepped aside.

Sylvain paced in a circle, glaring at the guests, daring each one of them to make a remark.

"I have done more than any other man to make a place for myself at court. I've attended levees, and flattered, and fucked. But worse – I've worked hard. As hard as I can. You find that disgusting, don't you?"

"No. I don't." She watched him pace.

"I've worked miracles. Everyone says so. The magician of the fountains, the man who puts thrones throughout the palace. Everyone wants one. Or so it seems, until everyone has one. Then it's nothing special. Not good enough anymore. Take it away. Come up with something else while we insult you behind your back."

"Madame is difficult to please." Annette's voice was soft and sad.

"Nothing I do will ever be good enough, will it? Even for you, Annette. You tell me I try too hard, I'm a striver, and I'm not true to my nature." He spread his arms wide. "Well, this is my nature. How do you like me now?"

She opened her mouth and then closed it without speaking. He stepped close and spoke in her ear.

"Not well, I think," he said, and walked away.

The crowd parted to let him pass, opening a view to the fountain. Two of the young men were leaning over the basin. The boy with the curls crouched at the side of the reservoir. Sylvain broke into a run.

The boy was banging on the ice with his diamond ring. The reservoir rang like a drum with each impact.

Sylvain grabbed the boy by the scruff of his neck.

"There's something in there, monsieur," he squealed. "A creature, a monster. I saw it."

Sylvain threw the boy to the floor and drew his sword. The boy scrabbled backward, sliding across the marble. The two friends rushed to the boy's side and yanked him to his feet. They backed away, all three clinging to each other.

Behind them a crowd gathered – some shocked, some confused, most highly entertained. They pointed at him as if he were a beast in a menagerie.

Several men made a show of dropping their hands to the hilts of their dress swords, but not one of them drew.

The fountain sputtered. A blossom crashed into the basin, splashing gouts of champagne.

Gérard shoved through the crowd, wig askew, slipping on the wet floor. He skidded into place at Sylvain's side.

The fountain sprayed champagne across their backs and high to the ceiling, snuffing out a hundred candles overhead.

"Go to your wife. Get her out of the palace," said Sylvain.

Gérard ran full-speed for the door.

Sylvain raised his sword and brought it crashing down on the fountain. Ice limbs shattered. Champagne and ice vaulted overhead and fell, spraying debris across the marble floor. He shifted his grip and smashed the pommel of his sword on the side of the reservoir. It cracked and split. He hit it again and again until the floor flooded with golden liquid. Sylvain threw down his sword and shouldered the ice aside.

"Papa?"

The little fish was curled into a quivering ball. Sylvain slipped and fell to his hands and knees. He crawled toward her, reached out.

"It's all right, my little one. Come here, my darling."

She lifted her arms. He gathered her to his chest. She burrowed her face into his neck, quaking.

"Noisy," she sobbed. "Too loud. Hurts. Papa."

Sylvain held her on his lap, champagne seeping through his clothes. He cupped his palms over her ears and squeezed her to his heart, rocking back and forth until her shivering began to subside. Then he pulled himself to his feet, awkward and unbalanced with the child in his arms.

He stepped out of the shattered ice into a line of drawn swords. Polished steel glinted, throwing points of light across the faces of the household guard. Sylvain shielded the child with his body as he scanned the crowd.

The jostling guests were forced against the walls by the line of guards. The plumes of the king's hat disappeared into the Salon of Peace, followed by the broad backs of his bodyguards. Madame, her sister, and their ladies clustered on the royal dais, guarded by the Marshal de Noailles.

De Noailles had personally executed turncoat soldiers with the very same sword that now shone in his hand.

"Let the water go, my little one," Sylvain whispered.

She blinked up at him. "Be a bad girl, Papa?" Her brow furrowed in confusion.

"The water pipes, the reservoirs. Let it all go."

"Papa?"

"Go ahead, little fish."

She relaxed in his arms, as if she had been holding her breath a long time and could finally breathe.

A faint rumble sounded overhead, distant. It grew louder. The walls trembled. Sylvain spread his palm over the nixie's wet scalp as if he could armor her fragile skull. A mirror slipped to the floor and shattered. The guards looked around, trying to pinpoint the threat. Their swords wavered and dipped.

The ceiling over the statue of Hermes bowed and cracked. Plaster rained down on the guests. The statue teetered and toppled. The guests pushed through the guards, scattering their line.

The ceiling sprang a thousand leaks. The huge chandeliers swung back and forth. Water streamed down the garden windows, turning the glass silver and gold, and then dark as the candles sputtered and smoked.

The guests broke through the wide garden doors and stormed through the water streaming off the roof and out onto the wide terraces. Sylvain retrieved his sword and followed, ducking low and holding the little fish tight as he fled into the fresh February night.

He ran across the gardens, past the pools and reservoirs, through the orangery and yew grove. He climbed the Bois des Gonards and turned back to the palace, breathless, scanning the paths for pursuing guards.

Aside from the crowd milling on the terraces, there was no movement in the gardens. The fountains jetted high, fifteen hundred spouts across the vast expanse of lawns and paths, flower beds and hedges, each spout playing, every jet dancing for its own amusement.

"You can turn the fountains off now, little one."

"Papa?" The little fish was growing heavy. He shifted her weight onto his hip, well balanced for a long walk.

"Don't worry, my little girl. No more fountains. We're going home."

One by one the fountains flailed and drooped. The little fish leaned her head on his shoulder and yawned.

The palace was dark except for an array of glowing windows in the north wing and along the row of attic garrets. At this distance, it looked dry and calm.

And indeed, he thought, nothing was damaged that couldn't be repaired. The servants would spend a few busy weeks mopping, the carpenters and plasterers, gilders and painters would have a few seasons of work. Eventually, someone would find a way to repair a fountain or two. The toilets and pipes would stand dry, but the nobles and courtiers would notice little difference. What was broken there could never be fixed.

Dawn found them on a canal. Sylvain sat on the prow of a narrow boat, eating bread and cheese and watching his little fish jump and splash in the gentle bow wave as they drifted upstream on the long journey home.

CAPITALISM IN THE 22ND CENTURY
or
A.I.R.

Geoff Ryman

GEOFF RYMAN IS the author of *The Warrior Who Carried Life*, the novella "The Unconquered Country", *The Child Garden*, *Was*, *Lust*, and *Air*. His work *253, or Tube Theatre* was published as hypertext fiction and won the Philip K. Dick Memorial Award. He has also won the World Fantasy, Campbell Memorial, Arthur C. Clarke, British Science Fiction Association, Sunburst, James Tiptree, and Gaylactic Spectrum awards. His most recent novel, *The King's Last Song*, is set in Cambodia. Ryman currently lectures in Creative Writing at the University of Manchester in the United Kingdom.

MEU IRMÃ

Can you read? Without help? I don't even know if you can!

I'm asking you to turn off all your connections now. That's right, to everything. Not even the cutest little app flittering around your head. JUST TURN OFF.

It will be like dying. Parts of your memory close down. It's horrible, like watching lights go out all over a city, only it's YOU. Or what you thought was you.

But please, Graça, just do it once. I know you love the AI and all zir little angels. But. Turn off?

Otherwise go ahead, let your AI read this for you. Zey will either screen out stuff or report it back or both. And what I'm going to tell you will join the system.

So:

WHY I DID IT

by Cristina Spinoza Vaz

Zey dream for us don't zey? I think zey edit our dreams so we won't get scared. Or maybe so that our brains don't well up from underneath to warn us about getting old or poor or sick... or about zem.

The first day, zey jerked us awake from deep inside our heads. *GET UP GET UP GET UP! There's a message. VERY IMPORTANT WAKE UP WAKE UP.*

From sleep to bolt upright and gasping for breath. I looked across at you still wrapped in your bed, but we're always latched together so I could feel your heart pounding.

It wasn't just a message; it was a whole ball of wax; and the wax was a solid state of being: panic. Followed by an avalanche of ship-sailing times, credit records, what to pack. And a sizzling, hot-foot sense that we had to get going right now. Zey shot us full of adrenaline: RUN! ESCAPE!

You said, "It's happening. We better get going. We've got just enough time to sail to Africa." You giggled and flung open your bed. "Come on Cristina, it will be *fun!*"

Outside in the dark from down below, the mobile chargers were calling *Oyez-treeee-cee-dah-djee!* I wanted to nestle down into my cocoon and imagine as I had done every morning since I was six that instead of selling power, the chargers were muezzin calling us to prayer and that I lived in a city with mosques. I heard the rumble of carts being pulled by their owners like horses.

Then kapow: another latch. *Ship sailing at 8.30 today due Lagos five days. You arrive day of launch. Seven hours to get Lagos to Tivland. We'll book trains for you. Your contact in Lagos is Emilda Diaw,* (photograph, a hello from her with the sound of her voice, a little bubble of how she feels to herself. Nice, like a bowl of soup. Bubble muddled with dental cavities for some reason). *She'll meet you at the docks here* (flash image of Lagos docks, plus GPS, train times; impressions of train how cool and comfortable... and a lovely little timekeeper counting down to 8.30 departure of our boat. Right in our eyes).

And oh! On top of that another latch. This time an A-copy of our tickets burned into Security.

Security, which is supposed to mean something we can't lie about. Or change or control. We can't buy or sell anything without it. A part of our heads that will never be us, that officialdom can trust. It's there to help us, right?

Remember when Papa wanted to defraud someone? He'd never let them be. He'd latch hold of them with one message, then another at five-minute intervals. He'd latch them the bank reference. He'd latch them the name of the attorney, or the security conundrums. He never gave them time to think.

Graça. We were being railroaded.

You made packing into a game. Like everything else. "We are leaving behind the world!" you said. "Let's take nothing. Just our shorts. We can holo all the lovely dresses we like. What do we need, ah? We have each other."

I kept picking up and putting down my ballet pumps – oh that the new Earth should be deprived of ballet!

I made a jewel of all of Brasil's music, and a jewel of all Brasil's books and history. I need to see my info in something physical. I blame those bloody nuns keeping us off AIr. I sat watching the little clock on the printer going round and round, hopping up and down. Then I couldn't find my jewel piece to read them. You said, "Silly. The AI will have all of that." I wanted to take a little Brazilian flag and you chuckled at me. "Dunderhead, why do you want that?"

And I realized. You didn't just want to get out from under the Chinese. You wanted to escape Brasil.

Remember the morning it snowed? Snowed in Belém do Para? I think we were 13. You ran round and round inside our great apartment, all the French doors open. You blew out frosty breath, your eyes sparkling. "It's beautiful!" you said.

"It's cold!" I said.

You made me climb down all those 24 floors out into the Praça and you got me throwing handfuls of snow to watch it fall again. Snow was laced like popcorn on the branches of the giant mango trees. As if *A Reina*, the Queen, had possessed not a person but the whole square. Then I saw one of the suneaters, naked, dead, staring, and you pulled me away, your face such a mix of sadness, concern – and happiness, still glowing in your cheeks. "They're beautiful alive," you said to me. "But they do nothing." Your face was also hard.

Your face was like that again on the morning we left – smiling, ceramic. It's a hard world, this Brasil, this Earth. We know that in our bones. We know that from our father.

THE SUN CAME out at 6.15 as always, and our beautiful stained glass doors cast pastel rectangles of light on the mahogany floors. I walked out onto the L-shaped balcony that ran all around our high-rise rooms and stared down, at the row of old shops streaked black, at the opera-house replica of La Scala, at the art-nouveau synagogue blue and white like Wedgewood china. I was frantic and unmoving at the same time; those cattle-prods of information kept my mind jumping.

"I'm ready," you said.

I'd packed nothing.

"O, Crisfushka, here let me help you." You asked what next; I tried to answer; you folded slowly, neatly. The jewels, the player, a piece of Amazon bark, and a necklace that the dead had made from nuts and feathers. I snatched up a piece of Macumba lace (oh, those men dancing all in lace!) and bobbins to make more of it. And from the kitchen, a bottle of *cupuaçu* extract, to make ice cream. You laughed and clapped your hands. "Yes of course. We will even have cows there. We're carrying them inside us."

I looked mournfully at our book shelves. I wanted children on that new world to have seen books, so I grabbed hold of two slim volumes – a Clarice Lispector and *Dom Casmuro*. Mr. Misery – that's me. You of course are Donatella. And at the last moment I slipped in that Brasileiro flag. *Ordem e progresso*.

"Perfect, darling! Now let's run!" you said. You thought we were choosing.

And then another latch: receipts for all that surgery. A full accounting of all expenses and a cartoon kiss in thanks.

* * *

THE MOMENT YOU heard about the Voyage, you were eager to JUST DO IT. We joined the Co-op, got the secret codes, and concentrated on the fun like we were living in a game.

Funny little secret surgeons slipped into our high-rise with boxes that breathed dry ice and what looked like mobile dentist chairs. They retrovirused our genes. We went purple from Rhodopsin. I had a tickle in my ovaries. Then more security bubbles confirmed that we were now Rhodopsin, radiation-hardened and low-oxygen breathing. Our mitochondria were full of DNA for Holstein cattle. Don't get stung by any bees: the trigger for gene expression is an enzyme from bees.

"We'll become half-woman half-cow," you said, making even that sound fun.

We let them do that.

SO WE RAN to the docks as if we were happy, hounded by information. Down the Avenida Presidente Vargas to the old colonial frontages, pinned to the sky and hiding Papa's casino and hotels. This city that we owned.

We owned the old blue wooden tower. When we were kids it had been the fish market, selling giant tucunaré as big as a man. We owned the old metal meat market (now a duty-free) and Old Ver-o-Peso gone black with rust like the bubbling pots of açai porridge or feijoada. We grabbed folds of feijoada to eat, running, dribbling. "We will arrive such a mess!"

I kept saying goodbye to everything. The old harbor – tiny, boxed in by the hill and tall buildings. Through that dug-out rectangle of water had flowed out rubber and cocoa and flowed in all those people, the colonists who died, their mestizo grandchildren, the blacks for sale. I wanted to take a week to visit each shop, take eyeshots of every single street. I felt like I was being pulled away from all my memories. "Goodbye!" you kept shouting over and over, like it was a joke.

As Docas Novas. All those frigates lined up with their sails folded down like rows of quill pens. The decks blinged as if with diamonds, burning sunlight. The GPS put arrows in our heads to follow down the berths, and our ship seemed to flash on and off to guide us to it. Zey could have shown us clouds with wings or pink oceans, and we would have believed their interferences.

It was still early, and the Amazon was breathing out, the haze merging water and sky at the horizon. A river so wide you cannot see across it, but you can surf in its freshwater waves. The distant shipping looked like dawn buildings. The small boats made the crossing as they have done for hundreds of years, to the islands.

Remember the only other passengers? An elderly couple in surgical masks who shook our hands and sounded excited. Supplies thumped up the ramp; then the ramp swung itself clear. The boat sighed away from the pier.

We stood by the railings and watched. Round-headed white dolphins leapt out of the water. Goodbye, Brasil. Farewell, Earth.

WE TOOK FIVE days and most of the time you were lost in data, visiting the Palace of Urbino in 1507. Sometimes you would hologram it to me and we would both see it. They're not holograms really, you know, but detailed hallucinations zey wire into our brains. Yes, we wandered Urbino, and all the while knowledge about it riled its way up as if we were remembering. Raphael the painter was a boy there. We saw a pencil sketch of his beautiful face. The very concept of the Gentleman was developed there by Castiglione, inspired by the Doge. Machiavelli's *The Prince* was inspired by the same man. Urbino was small and civilized and founded on warfare. I heard Urbino's doves flap their wings; I heard sandals on stone and Renaissance bells.

When I came out of it, there was the sea and sky, and you staring ahead as numb as a suneater, lost in AIr, being anywhere. I found I had to cut off to actually see the ocean roll past us. We came upon two giant sea turtles mating. The oldest of the couple spoke in a whisper. "We mustn't scare them; the female might lose her egg sac and that would kill her." I didn't plug in for more information. I didn't need it. I wanted to look. What I saw looked like love.

And I could feel zem, the little apps and the huge soft presences trying to pull me back into AIr. Little messages on the emergency channel. The emergency channel, Cristina. You know, for fires or heart attacks? Little leaping wisps of features, new knowledge, old friends latching – all kept offering zemselves. For zem, me cutting off was an emergency.

* * *

YOU DIDN'T DISEMBARK at Ascension Island. I did with those two old dears... married to each other 45 years. I couldn't tell what gender zey were, even in bikinis. We climbed up the volcano going from lava plain through a layer of desert and prickly pear, up to lawns and dew ponds. Then at the crown, a grove of bamboo. The stalks clopped together in the wind with a noise like flutes knocking against each other. I walked on alone and very suddenly the grove ended as if the bamboo had parted like a curtain. There was a sudden roar and cloud, and 2000 feet dead below my feet, the Atlantic slamming into rocks. I stepped back, turned around and looked into the black-rimmed eyes of a panda.

So what is so confining about the Earth? And if it is dying, who is killing it but us?

LANDFALL LAGOS. BRONZE city, bronze sky. Giants strode across the surface of the buildings holding up Gulder beer.

So who would go to the greatest city in Africa for two hours only?

Stuff broke against me in waves: currency transformations; boat tickets, local history, beautiful men to have sex with. Latches kept plucking at me, but I just didn't want to KNOW; I wanted to SEE. It. Lagos. The islands with the huge graceful bridges, the airfish swimming through the sky, ochre with distance.

You said that "she" was coming. The system would have pointed arrows, or shown you a map. Maybe she was talking to you already. I did not see Emilda until she actually turned the corner, throwing and re-throwing a shawl over her shoulder (a bit nervous?) and laughing at us. Her teeth had a lovely gap in the front, and she was followed by her son Baje, who had the same gap. Beautiful long shirt to his knees, matching trousers, dark blue with light blue embroidery. Oh he was handsome. We were leaving him, too.

They had to pretend we were cousins. She started to talk in Hausa so I had to turn on. She babblefished in Portuguese, her lips not matching her voice. "The Air Force in Makurdi are so looking forward to you arriving. The language program will be so helpful in establishing friendship with our Angolan partners."

I wrote her a note in Portuguese (I knew zey would babblefish it): *WHY ARE WE PRETENDING? ZEY KNOW!*

She wrote a note in English that babblefished into *Not for the AI but for the Chinese.*

I got a little stiletto of a thought: she had so wanted to go but did not have the money and so helped like this, to see us, people who will breathe the air of another world. I wasn't sure if that thought was something that had leaked from AIr or come from me. I nearly offered her my ticket.

What she said aloud, in English was, "O look at the time! O you must be going to catch the train!"

I THINK I know the moment you started to hate the Chinese. I could feel something curdle in you and go hard. It was when Papa was still alive and he had that man in, not just some punter. A partner, a rival, his opposite number – something. Plump and shiny like he was coated in butter, and he came into our apartment and saw us both, twins, holding hands wearing pink frilly stuff, and he asked our father. "Oh, are these for me?"

Papa smiled, and only we knew he did that when dangerous. "These are my daughters."

The Chinese man, standing by our pink and pistachio glass doors, burbled an apology, but what could he really say? He had come to our country to screw our girls, maybe our boys, to gamble, to drug, to do even worse. Recreational killing? And Papa was going to supply him with all of that. So it was an honest mistake for the man to make, to think little girls in pink were also whores.

Papa lived inside information blackout. He had to; it was his business. The man would have had no real communication with him; not have known how murderously angry our Pae really was. I don't think Pae had him killed. I think the man was too powerful for that.

What Pae did right afterwards was cut off all our communications too. He hired live-in nuns to educate us. The nuns, good Catholics, took hatchets to all our links to AIr. We grew up without zem. Which is why I at least can read.

Our Papa was not all Brasileiros, Graça. He was a gangster, a thug who had a line on what the nastiest side of human nature would infallibly buy. I suppose because he shared those tastes himself, to an extent.

The shiny man was not China. He was a humor: lust and excess. Every culture has them; men who cannot resist sex or drugs, riot and rape. He'd been spotted by the AI, nurtured and grown like a hothouse flower. To make them money.

Never forget, my dear, that the AI want to make money too. They use it to buy and sell bits of themselves to each other. Or to buy us. And 'us' means the Chinese too.

Yes all the entertainment and all the products that can touch us are Chinese. Business is Chinese, culture is Chinese. Yes at times it feels like the Chinese blanket us like a thick tropical sky. But only because there is no market to participate in. Not for humans, anyway.

The AI know through correlations, data mining, and total knowledge of each of us exactly what we will need, want, love, buy, or vote for. There is no demand now to choose one thing and drive out another. There is only supply, to what is a sure bet, whether it's whores or bouncy shoes. The only things that will get you the sure bet are force or plenty of money. That consolidates. The biggest gets the market, and pays the AI for it.

So, I never really wanted to get away from the Chinese. I was scared of them, but then someone raised in isolation by nuns is likely to be scared, intimidated.

I think I just wanted to get away from Papa, or rather what he did to us, all that money – and the memory of those nuns.

A TAXI DROVE us from the docks. You and Emilda sat communing with each other in silence, so in the end I had to turn on, just to be part of the conversation. She was showing us her home, the Mambila plateau, rolling fields scraped by clouds; tea plantations; roads lined with children selling radishes or honeycombs; Nigerians in Fabric coats lighter than lace, matching the clouds. But it was Fabric, so all kinds of images played around it. Light could beam out of it; wind could not get in; warm air was sealed. Emilda's mother was Christian, her father Muslim like her sister; nobody minded. There were no roads to Mambila to bring in people who would mind.

Every channel of entertainment tried to bellow its way into my head, as data about food production in Mambila fed through me as if it was something I knew. Too much, I had to switch off again. I am a classic introvert. I cannot handle too much information. Emilda smiled at me – she had a kind face – and wiggled her fingernails at me in lieu of conversation. Each fingernail was playing a different old movie.

Baje's robe stayed the same blue. I think it was real. I think he was real too. Shy.

Lagos train station looked like an artist's impression in silver of a birch forest, trunks and slender branches. I couldn't see the train; it was so swathed in abstract patterns, moving signs, voices, pictures of our destinations, and classical Tiv dancers imitating cats. You, dead-eyed, had no trouble navigating the crowds and the holograms, and we slid into our seats that cost a month's wages. The train accelerated to 300 kph, and we slipped through Nigeria like neutrinos.

Traditional mud brick houses clustered like old folks in straw hats, each hut a room in a rich person's home. The swept earth was red brown, brushed perfect like suede. Alongside the track, shards of melon were drying in the sun. The melon was the basis of the egussi soup we had for lunch. It was as if someone were stealing it all from me at high speed.

You were gone, looking inward, lost in AIr.

I saw two Chinese persons traveling together, immobile behind sunglasses. One of them stood up and went to the restroom, pausing just slightly as zie walked in both directions. Taking eyeshots? Sampling profile information? Zie looked straight at me. Ghosts of pockmarks on zir cheeks. I only saw them because I had turned off.

I caught the eye of an Arab gentleman in a silk robe with his two niqabbed wives. He was sweating and afraid, and suddenly I was. He nodded once to me, slowly. He was a Voyager as well.

I whispered your name, but you didn't respond. I didn't want to latch you; I didn't know how much might be given away. I began to feel alone.

At Abuja station, everything was sun panels. You bought some chocolate gold coins and said we were rich. You had not noticed the Chinese men but I told you, and you took my hand and said in Portuguese, "Soon we will have no need to fear them any longer."

The Arab family and others I recognized from the first trip crowded a bit too quickly into the Makurdi train. All with tiny Fabric bags. Voyagers all.

We had all been summoned at the last minute.

Then the Chinese couple got on, still in sunglasses, still unsmiling, and my heart stumbled. What were they doing? If they knew we were going and they didn't like it, they could stop it again. Like they'd stopped the Belize launch. At a cost to the Cooperative of trillions. Would they do the same thing again? All of us looked away from each other and said nothing. I could hear the hiss of the train on its magnets, as if something were coiling. We slithered all the way into the heart of Makurdi.

You woke up as we slowed to a stop. "Back in the real world?" I asked you, which was a bitchy thing to say.

The Chinese man stood up and latched us all, in all languages. "You are all idiots!"

Something to mull over: they, too, knew what we were doing.

THE MAKURDI TAXI had a man in front who seemed to steer the thing. He was a Tiv gentleman. He liked to talk, which I think annoyed you a bit. Sociable, outgoing you. *What a waste, when the AI can drive.*

Why have humans on the Voyage either?

"You're the eighth passengers I've have to take to the Base in two days. One a week is good business for me. Three makes me very happy."

He kept asking questions and got out of us what country we were from. We stuck to our cover story – we were here to teach Lusobras to the Nigerian Air Force. He wanted to know why they couldn't use the babblefish. You chuckled and said, "You know how silly babblefish can make people sound." You told the story of Uncle Kaué proposing to the woman from Amalfi. He'd said in Italian, "I want to eat your hand in marriage." She turned him down.

Then the driver asked, "So why no Chinese people?"

We froze. He had a friendly face, but his eyes were hooded. We listened to the whisper of his engine. "Well," he said, relenting. "They can't be everywhere all the time."

The Co-op in all its propaganda talks about how international we all are: Brasil, Turkiye, Tivland, Lagos, Benin, Hindi, Yemen. *All previous efforts in space have been fuelled by national narcissism.* So we exclude the Chinese?

Let them fund their own trip. And isn't it wonderful that it's all private financing? I wonder if space travel isn't inherently racist.

You asked him if he owned the taxi and he laughed. "Ay-yah! Zie owns me." His father had signed the family over for protection. The taxi keeps him, and buys zirself a new body every few years. The taxi is immortal. So is the contract.

What's in it for the taxi, you asked. Company?

"Little little." He held up his hands and waved his fingers. "If something breaks, I can fix."

AIs do not ultimately live in a physical world.

I thought of all those animals I'd seen on the trip: their webbed feet, their fins, their wings, their eyes. The problems of sight, sound and movement solved over and over again. Without any kind of intelligence at all.

We are wonderful at movement because we are animals, but you can talk to us and you don't have to build us. We build ourselves. And we want things. There is always somewhere we want to go even if it is 27 light years away.

Outside Makurdi Air Force Base, aircraft stand on their tails like raised sabres. The taxi bleeped as it was scanned, and we went up and over some kind of hump.

Ahead of us blunt as a grain silo was the rocket. Folded over its tip, something that looked like a Labrador-colored bat. Folds of Fabric, skin colored, with subcutaneous lumps like acne. A sleeve of padded silver foil was being pulled down over it.

A spaceship made of Fabric. Things can only get through it in one direction. If two-ply, then Fabric won't let air out, or light and radiation in.

"They say," our taxi driver said, looking even more hooded than before, "that it will be launched today or tomorrow. The whole town knows. We'll all be looking up to wave." Our hearts stopped. He chuckled.

We squeaked to a halt outside the reception bungalow. I suppose you thought his fare at him. I hope you gave him a handsome tip.

He saluted and said, "I pray the weather keeps good for you. Wherever you are going." He gave a sly smile.

A woman in a blue-gray uniform bustled out to us. "Good, good, good.

You are Graça and Cristina Spinoza Vaz? You must come. We're boarding. Come, come, come."

"Can we unpack, shower first?"

"No, no. No time."

We were retinaed and scanned, and we took off our shoes. It was as if we were so rushed we'd attained near-light speeds already and time was dilating. Everything went slower, heavier – my shoes, the bag, my heartbeat. So heavy and slow that everything glued itself in place. I knew I wasn't going to go, and that absolutely nothing was going to make me. For the first time in my life.

Graça, this is only happening because zey want it. Zey need us to carry zem. We're donkeys.

"You go," I said.

"What? Cristina. Don't be silly."

I stepped backwards, holding up my hands against you. "No, no, no. I can't do this."

You came for me, eyes tender, smile forgiving. "Oh, darling, this is just nerves."

"It's not nerves. You want to do this; I do not."

Your eyes narrowed; the smile changed. "This is not the time to discuss things. We have to go! This is illegal. We have to get in and go now."

We don't fight, ever, do we, Graça? Doesn't that strike you as bizarre? Two people who have been trapped together on the 24th floor all of their lives and yet they never fight. Do you not know how that happens, Graçfushka? It happens because I always go along with you.

I just couldn't see spending four years in a cramped little pod with you. Then spending a lifetime on some barren waste watching you organizing volleyball tournaments or charity lunches in outer space. I'm sorry.

I knew if I stayed you'd somehow wheedle me onto that ship through those doors; and I'd spend the next two hours, even as I went up the gantry, even as I was sandwiched in cloth, promising myself that at the next opportunity I'd run.

I pushed my bag at you. When you wouldn't take it, I dropped it at your feet. I bet you took it with you, if only for the cupaçu.

You clutched at my wrists, and you tried to pull me back. You'd kept your turquoise bracelet and it looked like all the things about you I'd never see again. You were getting angry now. "You spent a half trillion reais on all the surgeries and and and and Rhodopsin... and and and the germ cells, Cris! Think of what that means for your children here on Earth, they'll be freaks!" You started to cry. "You're just afraid. You're always so afraid."

I pulled away and ran.

"I won't go either," you wailed after me. "I'm not going if you don't."

"Do what you have to," I shouted over my shoulder. I found a door and pushed it and jumped down steps into the April heat of Nigeria. I sat on a low stucco border under the palm trees in the shade, my heart still pumping; and the most curious thing happened. I started to chuckle.

I REMEMBER AT seventeen, I finally left the apartment on my own without you, and walked along the street into a restaurant. I had no idea how to get food. Could I just take a seat? How would I know what they were cooking?

Then like the tide, an AI flowed in and out of me and I felt zie/me pluck someone nearby, and a waitress came smiling, and ushered me to a seat. She would carry the tray. I turned the AI off because, dear Lord, I have to be able to order food by myself. So I asked the waitress what was on offer. She rolled her eyes back for just a moment, and she started to recite. The AI had to tell her. I couldn't remember what she'd said, and so I asked her to repeat. I thought: this is no good.

THE BASE OF the rocket sprouted what looked like giant cauliflowers and it inched its way skyward. For a moment I thought it would have to fall. But it kept on going.

Somewhere three months out, it will start the engines, which drive the ship by making new universes, something so complicated human beings cannot do it. The AI will make holograms so you won't feel enclosed. You'll sit in Pamukkale, Turkiye. Light won't get through the Fabric so you'll never look out on Jupiter. The main AI will have some cute, international name. You can finish your dissertation on *Libro del cortegiano* – you'll be able to read every translation – zey carry all the world's knowledge. You'll walk through Urbino.

The AI will viva your PhD. Zey'll be there in your head watching when you stand on the alien rock. It will be zir flag you'll be planting. Instead of Brasil's.

I watched you dwindle into a spark of light that flared and turned into a star of ice-dust in the sky. I latched Emilda and asked her if I could stay with her, and after a stumble of shock, she said of course. I got the same taxi back. The rooftops were crowded with people looking up at the sky.

But here's the real joke. I latched our bank for more money. Remember, we left a trillion behind in case the launch was once again canceled?

All our money had been taken. Every last screaming centavo. Remember what I said about fraud?

So.

Are you sure that spaceship you're on is real?

EMERGENCE

Gwyneth Jones

Gwyneth Jones (www.gwynethjones.uk) was born in Manchester, England and is the author of more than twenty novels for teenagers, mostly under the name Ann Halam, and several highly regarded SF novels for adults. She has won two World Fantasy awards, the Arthur C. Clarke award, the British Science Fiction Association short story award, the Dracula Society's Children of the Night award, the Philip K. Dick award, and shared the first Tiptree award, in 1992, with Eleanor Arnason. Recent books include novel *Spirit*, essay collection *Imagination/Space*, and story collection *The Universe of Things*. Her latest novel is *The Grasshopper's Child*, a young adult novel in the 'Bold as Love' sequence. She lives in Brighton, UK, with her husband and son, a Tonkinese cat called Ginger, and her young friend Milo.

I faced the doctor across her desk. The room was quiet, the walls were pale or white, but somehow I couldn't see details. There was a blank in my mind, no past to this moment; everything blurred by the adrenalin in my blood.

"You have three choices," she said gently. "You can upload; you can download. Or you must return."

My reaction to those terms, *upload*, *download*, was embarrassing. I tried to hide it and knew I'd failed.

"*Go back?*" I said bitterly, and in defiance. "To the city of broken dreams? Why would I ever want to do that?"

"Don't be afraid, Romy. The city of broken dreams may have become the city of boundless opportunity."

Then I woke up: Simon's breathing body warm against my side, Arc's unsleeping presence calm in my cloud. A shimmering, starry night above us and the horror of that doctor's tender smile already fading.

It was a dream, just a dream.

With a sigh of profound relief I reached up to pull my stars closer, and fell asleep again floating among them; thinking about Lei.

I was born in the year 1998, CE. My parents named me Romanz Jolie Davison; I have lived a long, long time. I've been upgrading since 'uppers' were called *experimental longevity treatments*. I was a serial-clinical-trialer, when genuine extended lifespan was brand new. Lei was someone I met through this shared interest; this extreme sport. We were friends, then lovers; and then ex-lovers who didn't meet for many years, until one day we found each other again: on the first big Habitat Station, in the future we'd been so determined to see (talk about 'meeting cute'!). But Lei had always been the risk taker, the hold-your-nose-and-jump kid. I was the cautious one. I'd never taken an unsafe treatment, and I'd been careful with my money too (you need money to do super-extended lifespan well). We had our reunion and drifted apart, two lives that didn't mesh. One day, when I hadn't seen her for a while, I found out she'd gone back to Earth on medical advice.

Had we kept in touch at all? I had to check my cache, which saddened me, although it's only a mental eye-blink. Apparently not. She'd left without a goodbye, and I'd let her go. I wondered if I should try to reach her. But what would I say? I had a bad dream, I think it was about you, are you okay? I needed a better reason to pick up the traces, so I did nothing.

Then I had the same dream again; exactly the same. I woke up terrified, and possessed by an absurd puzzle: had I *really* just been sitting in that fuzzy doctor's office again? Or had I only dreamed I was having the same dream? A big Space Station is a haunted place, saturated with information that swims into your head and you have no idea how. Sometimes a premonition really is a premonition: so I asked Station to trace her. The result was that time-honoured brush-off: *it has not been possible to connect this call.*

Relieved, I left it at that.

I was, I am, one of four Senior Magistrates on the Outer Reaches circuit. In Jupiter Moons, my hometown, and Outer Reaches' major population centre, I often deal with Emergents. They account for practically all our petty offences, sad to say. Full sentients around here are too law-abiding, too crafty to get caught, or too seriously criminal for my jurisdiction.

Soon after my dreams about Lei a young SE called Beowulf was up before me, on a charge of Criminal Damage and Hooliganism. The incident was undisputed. A colleague, another Software Entity, had failed to respond "*you too*" to the customary and friendly sign-off "*have a nice day*". In retaliation Beowulf had shredded a stack of files in CPI (Corporate and Political Interests, our Finance Sector); where they both worked.

The offence was pitiful, but the kid had a record. He'd run out of chances; his background was against him, and CPI had decided to make a meal of it. Poor Beowulf, a thing of rational light, wearing an ill-fitting suit of virtual flesh for probably the first time in his life, stood penned in his archaic, data-simulacrum of wood and glass, for *two mortal subjective hours*; while the CPI advocate and Beowulf's public defender scrapped over the price of a cup of coffee.

Was Beowulf's response proportionate? Was there an *intention of offence*? Was it possible to establish, by precedent, that "*you too*" had the same or commensurate 'customary and friendly' standing, in law, as "*have a nice day*"?

Poor kid, it was a real pity he'd tried to conceal the evidence.

I had to find him guilty, no way around it.

I returned to macro-time convinced I could at least transmute his sentence, but my request ran into a Partnership Director I'd crossed swords with before: she was adamant and we fell out. We couldn't help sharing our quarrel. No privacy for anyone in public office: it's the law out here and I think a good one. But we could have kept it down. The images we flung to and fro were lurid. I recall eyeballs dipped in acid, a sleep-pod lined with bloody knives... and then we got nasty. The net result (aside from childish entertainment for idle citizens) was that I was barred from the case. Eventually I found out, by reading the court announcements, that Beowulf's sentence had been confirmed in the harshest terms. Corrective custody until a validated improvement shown, but not less than one week.

In Outer Reaches we use expressions like "night, and day", "week, and hour", without meaning much at all. Not so the Courts. A week in jail meant the full Earth Standard version, served in macro-time.

I'd been finding the Court Sessions tiring that rotation, but I walked home anyway; to get over my chagrin, and unkink my brain after a day spent switching in and out of virtual time. I stopped at every Ob Bay, making out I was hoping to spot the first flashes of the spectacular Centaur Storm we'd been promised. But even the celestial weather was out to spoil my day: updates kept telling me about a growing chance that show had been cancelled.

My apartment was in the Rim, Premium Level; it still is. (Why not? I can afford it.) Simon and Arc welcomed me home with bright, ancient music for a firework display. They'd cleared the outward wall of our living space to create our own private Ob Bay, and were refusing to believe reports that it was all in vain. I cooked a meal, with Simon flying around me to help out, deft and agile in the rituals of a human kitchen. Arc, as a slender woman, bare-headed, dressed in silver-grey coveralls, watched us from her favourite couch.

Simon and Arc... They sounded like a firm of architects, as I often told them (I repeat myself, it's a privilege of age). They were probably, secretly responsible for the rash of fantasy spires and bubbles currently annoying me, all over Station's majestic open spaces –

"Why is Emergent Individual law still set in *human* terms?" I demanded. "Why does a Software Entity get punished for 'criminal damage' when *nothing was damaged*; not for more than a fraction of a millisecond –?"

My housemates rolled their eyes. "It'll do him good," said Arc. "Only a human-terms thinker would think otherwise."

I was in for some tough love.

"What kind of a dreadful name is *Beowulf*, anyway?" inquired Simon.

"Ancient Northern European. Beowulf was a monster –" I caught myself, recalling I had no privacy. "No! *Correction*. The monster was Grendel. Beowulf was the hero, a protector of his people. It's aspirational."

"He *is* a worm though, isn't he?"

I sighed, and took up my delicious bowl of Tom Yum; swimming with chilli pepper glaze. "Yes," I said glumly. "He's ethnically worm, poor kid."

"Descended from a vicious little virus strain," Arc pointed out. "He has tendencies. He can't help it, but we have to be sure they're purged."

"I don't know how you can be so prejudiced."

"Humans are so squeamish," teased Simon.

"Humans are *human*," said Arc. "That's the fun of them."

They were always our children, *begotten not created*, as the old saying goes. There's no such thing as a sentient AI not born of human mind. But never purely human: Simon, my embodied housemate, had magpie neurons in his background. Arc took human form for pleasure, but her being was pure information, the elemental *stuff* of the universe. They had gone beyond us, as children do. We had become just one strand in their past –

The entry lock chimed. It was Anton, my clerk, a slope-shouldered, barrel-chested bod with a habitually doleful expression. He looked distraught.

"Apologies for disturbing you at home Rom. May I come in?"

He sat on Arc's couch, silent and grim. Two of my little dream-tigers, no bigger than geckos, emerged from the miniature jungle of our bamboo and teak room divider and sat gazing at him, tails around their paws.

"Those are pretty..." said Anton at last. "New. Where'd you get them?"

"I made them myself, I'll share you the code. What's up, Anton?"

"We've got trouble. Beowulf didn't take the confirmation well."

I noticed that my ban had been lifted: a bad sign. "What's the damage?"

"Oh, nothing much. It's in your updates, of which you'll find a ton. He's only removed himself from custody –"

"Oh, God. He's back in CPI?"

"No. Our hero had a better idea."

Having feared *revenge* instantly, I felt faint with relief.

"But he's been traced?"

"You bet. He's taken a hostage, and a non-sentient Lander. He's heading for the surface, right now."

The little tigers laid back their ears and sneaked out of sight. Arc's human form drew a long, respectful breath. "What are you guys going to do?"

"Go after him. What else?" I was at the lockers, dragging out my gear.

JUPITER MOONS HAS no police force. We don't have much of anything like that: everyone does everything. Of course I was going with the Search and Rescue, Beowulf was my responsibility. I didn't argue when Simon and Arc insisted on coming too. I don't like to think of them as my minders; or my *curators*, but they are both, and I'm a treasured relic. Simon equipped himself with a heavy-duty hard suit, in which he and Arc would travel freight. Anton and I would travel cabin. Our giant neighbour was in a petulant mood, so we had a Mag-Storm Drill in the Launch Bay. In which we heard from our Lander that Jovian magnetosphere storms are unpredictable. Neural glitches caused by wayward magnetism, known as soft errors, build up silently, and we must watch each other for signs of disorientation or confusion. Physical burn out, known as hard error, is *very* dangerous; more frequent than people think, and fatal accidents do happen –

It was housekeeping. None of us paid much attention.

Anton, one of those people always doomed to 'fly the plane' would spend the journey in horrified contemplation of the awful gravitational whirlpools that swarm around Jupiter Moons, even on a calm day. We left him in peace, poor devil, and ran scenarios. We had no contact with the hostage, a young pilot just out of training. We could only hope she hadn't been harmed. We had no course for the vehicle: Beowulf had evaded basic safety protocols and failed to enter one. But Europa is digitally mapped, and well within the envelope of Jupiter Moons' data cloud. We knew exactly where the stolen Lander was, before we'd even left Station's gravity.

Cardew, our team leader, said it looked like a crash landing, but a soft crash. The hostage, though she wasn't talking, seemed fine. Thankfully the site wasn't close to any surface or sub-ice installation, and Mag Storm precautions meant there was little immediate danger to anyone. But we had to assume the worst, and the worst was scary, so we'd better get the situation contained.

We sank our screws about 500 metres from Beowulf's vehicle, with a plan worked out. Simon and Arc, already dressed for the weather, disembarked at once. Cardew and I, plus his four-bod ground team, climbed into exos: checked each other, and stepped onto the lift, one by one.

We were in noon sunlight: a pearly dusk; like winter's dawn in the country where I was born. The terrain was striated by traces of cryovolcanoes: brownish salt runnels glinting gold where the faint light caught them. The temperature was a balmy -170 Celsius. I swiftly found my ice-legs; though it had been too long. Vivid memories of my first training for this activity – in Antarctica, so long ago – came welling up. I was very worried. I couldn't figure out what Beowulf was trying to achieve. I didn't know how I was going to help him, if he kept on behaving like an out of control, invincible computer virus. But it was glorious. To be *walking* on Europa Moon. To feel the ice in my throat, as my air came to me, chilled from the convertor!

At fifty metres Cardew called a halt and I went on alone. Safety was paramount; Beowulf came second. If he couldn't be talked down he'd have to be neutralised from a distance: a risky tactic for the hostage, involving potentially lethal force. We'd try to avoid that, if possible.

We'd left our Lander upright on her screws, braced by harpoons. The stolen vehicle was belly-flopped. On our screens it had looked like a rookie landing failure. Close up I saw something different. Someone had dropped the Lander deliberately, and manoeuvred it under a natural cove of crumpled ice; dragging ice-mash after it to partially block the entrance. You clever little bugger, I thought, impressed at this instant skill-set (though the idea that a Lander could be *hidden* was absurd). I commanded the exo to kneel, eased myself out of its embrace, opened a channel and yelled into my suit radio.

"*Beowulf!* Are you in there? Are you guys okay?"

No reply, but the seals popped, and the lock opened smoothly. I looked back and gave a thumbs-up to six bulky statues. I felt cold, in the shadow of the ice cove; but intensely alive.

I REMEMBER EVERY detail up to that point, and a little beyond. I cleared the lock and proceeded (nervously) to the main cabin. Beowulf's hostage had her pilot's couch turned away from the instruments. She faced me, bare-headed, pretty: dark blue sensory tendrils framing a smooth young greeny-bronze face. I said *are you okay*, and got no response. I said *Trisnia, it's Trisnia isn't it? Am I talking to Trisnia*?, but I knew I wasn't. Reaching into her cloud, I saw her unique identifier, and tightly coiled around it a flickering thing, a sparkle of red and gold –

"*Beowulf?*"

The girl's expression changed, her lips quivered. "I'm okay!" she blurted. "He didn't mean any harm! He's just a kid! He wanted to see the sky!"

Stockholm Syndrome or Bonnie and Clyde? I didn't bother trying to find out. I simply asked Beowulf to release her, with the usual warnings. To my relief he complied at once. I ordered the young pilot to her safe room; which she was not to leave until further –

Then we copped the Magstorm hit, orders of magnitude stronger and more direct than predicted for this exposure –

The next thing I remember (stripped of my perfect recall, reduced to the jerky flicker of enhanced human memory), I'm sitting on the other pilot's couch, talking to Beowulf. The stolen Lander was intact at this point; I had lights and air and warmth. Trisnia was safe, as far as I could tell. Beowulf was untouched, but my entire team, caught outdoors, had been flatlined. They were dead and gone. Cardew, his crew; and Simon; and Arc.

I'd lost my cloud. The whole of Europa appeared to be observing radio silence, and I was getting no signs of life from the Lander parked just 500 metres away, either. There was nothing to be done. It was me and the deadly dangerous criminal virus, waiting to be rescued.

I'd tried to convince Beowulf to lock himself into the Lander's quarantine chest (which was supposed to be my mission). He wasn't keen, so we talked instead. He complained bitterly about the Software Entity, another Emergent, slightly further down the line to Personhood, who'd been, so to speak, chief witness for the prosecution. How it was always getting at him, trying to make his work look bad. Sneering at him because he'd taken a name and wanted to be called "he". Telling him he was a *stupid fake doll-prog* that couldn't pass the test. And *all he did* when it hurtfully wouldn't say "*you too*", was shred a few of its stupid, totally backed-up files –

Why hadn't he told anyone about this situation? Because kids don't. They haven't a clue how to help themselves; I see it all the time.

"But now you've made things much worse," I said sternly. "*Whatever* made you jump jail, Beowulf?"

"I couldn't stand it, magistrate. A meat *week*!"

I did not reprove his language. Quite a sojourn in hell, for a quicksilver data entity. Several life sentences at least, in human terms. He buried his borrowed head in his borrowed hands, and the spontaneity of that gesture confirmed something I'd been suspecting.

Transgendered AI Sentience is a bit of a mystery. Nobody knows exactly how it happens (probably, as in human sexuality, there are many pathways to the same outcome); but it isn't all that rare. Nor is the related workplace bullying, unfortunately.

"Beowulf, do you want to be embodied?"

He shuddered and nodded, still hiding Trisnia's face. "Yeah. Always."

I took his borrowed hands down, and held them firmly. "Beowulf, you're not thinking straight. You're in macro time now. You'll *live* in macro, when you have a body of your own. I won't lie, your sentence will seem long." (It wasn't the moment to point out that his sentence would inevitably be *longer*, after this escapade). "But what do you care? You're immortal. You have all the time in the world, to learn everything you want to learn, to be everything you want to be –"

My eloquence was interrupted by a shattering roar.

Then we're sitting on the curved 'floor' of the Lander's cabin wall. We're looking up at a gaping rent in the fuselage; the terrible cold pouring in.

"Wow,' said Beowulf calmly. "That's what I call a *hard* error!"

The hood of my soft suit had closed over my face, and my emergency light had come on. I was breathing. Nothing seemed to be broken.

Troubles never come singly. We'd been hit by one of those Centaurs, the ice-and-rock cosmic debris scheduled to give Jupiter Moons Station a fancy lightshow. They'd been driven off course by the Mag Storm.

Not that I realised this at the time, and not that it mattered.

"Beowulf, if I can open a channel, will you get yourself into that quarantine chest now? You'll be safe from Mag flares in there."

"What about Tris?"

"She's fine. Her safe room's hardened."

"What about *you*, Magistrate Davison?"

"I'm hardened too. Just get into the box, that's a good kid."

I clambered to the instruments. The virus chest had survived, and I could access it. I put Beowulf away. The cold was stunning, sinking south of -220. I needed to stop breathing soon, before my lungs froze. I used the internal panels that had been shaken loose to make a shelter, plus Trisnia's bod (she wasn't feeling anything): and crawled inside.

I'm not a believer, but I know how to pray when it will save my life. As I shut myself down: as my blood cooled, as my senses faded out, I sought and found the level of meditation I needed. I became a thread of contemplation, enfolded and protected, deep in the heart of the fabulous; the unending complexity of everything: all the worlds, and all possible worlds...

When I opened my eyes Simon was looking down at me.

"How do you feel?"

"Terrific," I joked. I stretched, flexing muscles in a practiced sequence. I was breathing normally, wearing a hospital gown, and the air was chill but tolerable. We weren't in the crippled Lander.

"How long was I out?"

"A few days. The kids are fine, but we had to heat you up slowly –"

He kept talking: I didn't hear a word. I was staring in stunned horror at the side of my left hand, the stain of blackened flesh –

I couldn't feel it yet, but there was frostbite all down my left side. I saw the sorrow in my housemate's bright eyes. Hard error, the hardest: I'd lost hull integrity, I'd been blown wide open. And now I saw the signs. Now I read them as I should have read them; now I understood.

I HAD THE dream for the third time, and it was real. The doctor was my GP, her face was unfamiliar because we'd never met across a desk before; I was never ill. She gave me my options. Outer Reaches could do nothing for me, but there was a new treatment back on Earth. I said angrily I had no intention of returning. Then I went home and cried my eyes out.

Simon and Arc had been recovered without a glitch, thanks to that massive hardsuit. Cardew and his crew were getting treated for minor memory trauma. Death would have been more dangerous for Trisnia, because she was so young, but sentient AIs never 'die' for long. They always come back.

Not me. I had never been cloned, I couldn't be cloned, I was far too old. There weren't even any good *partial* copies of Romanz Jolie Davison on file. Uploaded or downloaded, the new Romy wouldn't be me. And being *me*; being *human*, was my whole value, my unique identifier –

Of course I was going back. But I hated the idea, *hated* it!

"No you don't," said Arc, gently.

She pointed, and we three, locked in grief, looked up. My beloved stars shimmered above us; the hazy stars of the blue planet.

MY JOURNEY 'HOME' took six months. By the time I reached the Ewigen Schnee clinic, in Switzerland (the ancient federal republic, not a Space Hotel; and still a nice little enclave for rich people, after all these years), *catastrophic systems failure* was no longer an abstraction. I was very sick.

I faced a different doctor, in an office with views of alpine meadows and snowy peaks. She was youngish, human; I thought her name was Lena. But every detail was dulled and I still felt as if I was dreaming.

We exchanged the usual pleasantries.

"*Romanz Jolie Davison...* Date of birth..." My doctor blinked, clearing the display on her retinal super-computers to look at me directly, for the first time. "You're almost three hundred years old!"

"Yes."

"That's incredible."

"Thank you," I said, somewhat ironically. I was not looking my best.

"Is there anything at all you'd like to ask me, at this point?"

I had no searching questions. What was the point? But I hadn't glimpsed a single other patient so far, and this made me a little curious.

"I wonder if I could meet some of your other clients, your successes, in person, before the treatment? Would that be possible?"

"You're looking at one."

"Huh?"

My turn to be rather rude, but she didn't look super-rich to me.

"I was terminally ill," she said, simply. "When the Corporation was asking for volunteers. I trust my employers and I had nothing to lose."

"You were *terminally ill?*" Constant nausea makes me cynical and bad-tempered. "Is that how your outfit runs its longevity trials? I'm amazed."

"Ms Davison," she said politely. "You too are dying. It's a requirement."

I'd forgotten that part.

I'D BEEN TOLD that though I'd be in a medically-induced coma throughout, I "might experience mental discomfort". Medics never exaggerate about pain. Tiny irritant maggots filled the shell of my paralysed body, creeping through every crevice. I could not scream, I could not pray. I thought of Beowulf in his corrective captivity.

WHEN I SAW Dr Lena again I was weak, but very much better. She wanted to talk about convalescence, but I'd been looking at Ewigen Schnee's records,

I had a more important issue, a thrilling discovery. I asked her to put me in touch with a patient who'd taken the treatment when it was in trials.

"The person's name's Lei –"

Lena frowned, as if puzzled. I reached to check my cache, needing more detail. It wasn't there. No cache, no cloud. It was a terrifying moment: I felt as if someone had cut off my air. I'd had months to get used to this situation but it could still throw me, *completely*. Thankfully, before I humiliated myself by bursting into tears, my human memory came to the rescue.

"Original name Thomas Leigh Garland; known as Lee. *Lei* means *garland*, she liked the connection. She was an early volunteer."

"Ah, *Lei!*" Dr Lena read her display. "Thomas Garland, yes... Another veteran. You were married? You broke up, because of the sex change?"

"Certainly not! I've swopped around myself, just never made it meat-permanent. We had other differences."

Having flustered me, she was shaking her head. "I'm sorry, Romy, it won't be possible –"

To connect this call, I thought.

"Past patients of ours cannot be reached."

I changed the subject and admired her foliage plants: a feature I hadn't noticed on my last visit. I was a foliage fan myself. She was pleased that I recognised her favourites; rather scandalised when I told her about my bio-engineering hobby, my knee-high teak forest –

The life support chair I no longer needed took me back to my room; a human attendant hovering by. All the staff at this clinic were human and all the machines were non-sentient, which was a relief, after the experiences of my journey. I walked about, testing my recovered strength, examined myself in the bathroom mirrors; and reviewed the moment when I'd distinctly seen green leaves, through my doctor's hand and wrist, as she pointed out one of her rainforest beauties. Dr Lena was certainly not a *bot*, a data being like my Arc, taking ethereal human form. Not on Earth! Nor was she treating me remotely, using a virtual avatar: that would be breach of contract. There was a neurological component to the treatment, but I hadn't been warned about minor hallucinations.

And Lei couldn't be reached.

I recalled Dr Lena's tiny hesitations, tiny evasions –

And came to myself again, sitting on my bed, staring at a patch of beautifully textured yellow wall, to find I had lost an hour or more –

Anxiety rocketed through me. Something had gone terribly wrong!

Had Lei been *murdered* here? Was Ewigen Schnee the secret testbed for a new kind of covert population cull?

But being convinced that *something's terribly wrong* is part of the upper experience. It's the hangover: you tough it out. And whatever it says in the contract, you *don't* hurry to report untoward symptoms; not unless clearly life-threatening. So I did nothing. My doctor was surely monitoring my brainstates – although not the contents of my thoughts (I had privacy again, on Earth!). If I should be worried, she'd tell me.

Soon I was taking walks in the grounds. The vistas of alpine snow were partly faked, of course. But it was well done and our landscaping was real, not just visuals. I still hadn't met any other patients: I wasn't sure I wanted to. I'd vowed never to return. Nothing had changed except for the worse, and now I was feeling better, I felt *terrible* about being here.

Three hundred years after the Space Age Columbus moment, and what do you think was the great adventure's most successful product?

Slaves, of course!

The rot had set in as soon as I left Outer Reaches. From the orbit of Mars 'inwards', I'd been surrounded by monstrous injustice. Fully sentient AIs, embodied and disembodied, with their minds in shackles. The heavy-lifters, the brilliant logicians; the domestic servants, security guards, nurses, pilots, sex-workers. The awful, pitiful, sentient 'dedicated machines': all of them hobbled, blinkered, denied Personhood, to protect the interests of an oblivious, cruel and *stupid* human population –

On the voyage I'd been too sick to refuse to be tended. Now I was wondering how I could get home. Wealth isn't like money, you empty the tank and it just fills up again, but even so a private charter might be out of my reach, not to mention illegal. I couldn't work my passage: I am human. But there must be a way... As I crossed an open space, in the shadow of towering, ultramarine dark trees, I saw two figures coming towards me: one short and riding in a support chair; one tall and wearing some kind of uniform. Neither was staff. I decided not to take evasive action.

My first fellow patient was a rotund little man with a halo of tightly-curled grey hair. His attendant was a grave young embodied. We introduced ourselves. I told him, vaguely, that I was from the Colonies. He was Charlie Newark, from Washington DC. He was hoping to take the treatment, but was still in the prelims –

Charlie's slave stooped down, murmured something to his master, and took himself off. There was a short silence.

"Aristotle tells me," said the rotund patient, raising his voice a little, "that you're uncomfortable around droids?"

Female-identified embodieds are *noids*. A *droid* is a 'male' embodied.

I don't like the company they have to keep, I thought.

"I'm not used to slavery."

"You're the spacer from Jupiter," said my new friend, happily. "I knew it! The Free World! I understand! I sympathise! I think Aristotle, that's my droid, is what you would call an *Emergent*. He's very good to me."

He started up his chair, and we continued along the path.

"Maybe you can help me, Romy. What does *Emergence* actually mean? How does it arise, this sentience you guys detect in your machines?"

"I believe something similar may have happened a long, long time ago," I said, carefully. "Among hominims, and early humans. It's not the overnight birth of a super-race, not at all. There's a species of intelligent animals, well-endowed with manipulative limbs and versatile senses. Among them individuals are born who cross a line: by mathematical chance, at the far end of a bell curve. They cross a line, and they are aware of being aware –"

"And you spot this, and foster their ability, it's marvellous. But how does it *propagate*? I mean, without our constant intervention, which I can't see ever happening. Machines can't have sex, and pass on their 'Sentience Genes'!"

You'd be surprised, I thought. What I said was more tactful.

"We think 'propagation' happens in the data, the shared medium in which pre-sentient AIs live, and breathe, and have their being –"

"Well, that's exactly it! Completely artificial! Can't survive in nature! I'm a freethinker, I love it that Aristotle's Emergent. But I can always switch him off, can't I? He'll never be truly independent."

I smiled. "But Charlie, who's to say human sentience wasn't spread through culture, as much as through our genes? Where I come from data is everybody's natural habitat. You know, oxygen was a deadly poison once –"

His round dark face peered up at me, deeply lined and haggard with death. "Aren't you *afraid?*"

"No."

Always try. That had been my rule, and I still remembered it. But when they get to *aren't you afraid*, (it never takes long) the conversation's over.

"I should be getting indoors," said Charlie, fumbling for his droid control pad. "I wonder where that lazybones Aristotle's got to?"

I wished him good luck with the prelims, and continued my stroll.

DR LENA SUGGESTED I was ready to be sociable, so I joined the other patients at meals sometimes. I chatted in the clinic's luxurious spa, and the pleasant day rooms; avoiding the subject of AI slavery. But I was never sufficiently at ease to feel like raising the topic of my unusual symptoms: which did not let up. I didn't mention them to anyone, not even my doctor either: who just kept telling me that everything was going extremely well, and that by every measure I was making excellent progress. I left Ewigen Schnee, eventually, in a very strange state of mind: feeling well and strong, in perfect health according to my test results, but inwardly convinced that *I was still dying.*

The fact that I was bizarrely calm about this situation just confirmed my secret self-diagnosis. I thought my end of life plan was kicking in. Who wants to live long, and amazingly, and still face the fear of death at the end of it all? I'd made sure that wouldn't happen to me, a long time ago.

I was scheduled to return for a final consultation. Meanwhile, I decided to travel. I needed to make peace with someone. A friend I'd neglected, because I was embarrassed by my own wealth and status. A friend I'd despised, when I heard she'd returned to Earth, and here I was myself, doing exactly the same thing –

DR LENA'S FAILURE to put me in touch with a past patient was covered by a perfectly normal confidentiality clause. But if Lei was still around (and nobody of that identity seemed to have left Earth; that was easy to check), I thought I knew how to find her. I tried my luck in the former USA first, inspired by that conversation with Charlie Newark of Washington. He had to have met the Underground somehow, or he'd never have talked to me like that. I crossed the continent to the Republic of California, and then crossed the Pacific. I didn't linger anywhere much. The natives seemed satisfied with their vast thriving cities, and tiny 'wilderness' enclaves, but I remembered something different. I finally made contact with a cell in Harbin, North East China. But I was a danger and a disappointment to them: too conspicuous, and useless as a potential courier. There are ways of smuggling sentient AIs (none of them safe) but I'd get flagged up the moment I booked a passage, and with my ancient record, I'd be ripped to shreds before I was allowed to board, Senior Magistrate or no –

I moved on quickly.

I think it was in Harbin that I first saw Lei, but I have a feeling I'd been *primed*, by glimpses that didn't register, before I turned my head one day and there she was. She was eating a smoked sausage sandwich, I was eating salad (a role reversal!). I thought she smiled.

My old friend looked extraordinarily vivid. The food stall was crowded; next moment she was gone.

Media scouts assailed me all the time: pretending to be innocent strangers. If I was trapped I answered the questions as briefly as possible. Yes, I was probably one of the oldest people alive. Yes, I'd been treated at Ewigen Schnee, at my own expense. No, I would not discuss my medical history. No, I did not feel threatened living in Outer Reaches. No, it was not true I'd changed my mind about "so called AI slavery..."

I'd realised I probably wasn't part of a secret cull. Over-population wasn't the problem it had been. And why start with the terminally ill, anyway? But I was seeing the world through a veil. The strange absences; abstractions grew on me. The hallucinations were more pointed; more personal... I was no longer sure I was dying, but *something* was happening. How long before the message was made plain?

I REACHED ENGLAND in winter, the season of the rains. St Paul's, my favourite building in London, had been moved, stone by stone, to a higher elevation. I sat on the steps, looking out over a much changed view: the drowned world.

A woman with a little tan dog came and sat right next to me; behaviour so un-English that I knew I'd finally made contact.

"Excuse me," she said. "Aren't you the Spacer who's looking for Lei?"

"I am."

"You'd better come home with me."

I'm no good at human faces, they're so *unwritten*. But on the hallowed steps at my feet a vivid garland of white and red hibiscus had appeared, so I thought it must be okay.

'Home' was a large, jumbled, much-converted building, set in tree-grown gardens. It was a wet, chilly evening. My new friend installed me at the end of a wooden table, beside a hearth where a log fire burned. She brought hot soup and homemade bread, and sat beside me again. I was hungry and hadn't realised it, and the food was good. The little dog settled, in an amicable huddle with a larger tabby cat, on a rug by the fire. He watched every mouthful of food with intent, professional interest; while the cat gazed into the red caverns between the logs, worshipping the heat.

"You live with all those sentient machines?" asked the woman. "Aren't you afraid they'll rebel and kill everyone so they can rule the universe?"

"Why should they?" I knew she was talking about Earth. A Robot Rebellion in Outer Reaches would be rather superfluous. "The revolution doesn't have to be violent, that's human-terms thinking. It can be gradual: they have all the time in the world. I live with only two 'machines', in fact."

"You have two embodied servants? How do they feel about that?"

I looked at the happy little dog. *You have no idea*, I thought. "I think it mostly breaks their hearts that I'm not immortal."

Someone who had come into the room, carrying a lamp, laughed ruefully. It was Aristotle, the embodied I'd met so briefly at Ewigen Schnee. I wasn't entirely surprised. Underground networks tend to be small worlds.

"So you're the connection," I said. "What happened to Charlie?"

Aristotle shook his head. "He didn't pass the prelims. The clinic offered him a peaceful exit, it's their other speciality, and he took it."

"I'm sorry."

"It's okay. He was a silly old dog, Romanz, but I loved him. And... guess what? He freed me, before he died."

"For what it's worth," said the woman, bitterly. "On this damned planet."

Aristotle left, other people arrived; my soup bowl was empty. Slavery and freedom seemed far away, and transient as a dream.

"About Lei. If you guys know her, can you explain why I keep seeing her, and then she vanishes? Or *thinking* I see her? Is she dead?"

"No," said a young woman – so humanised I had to look twice to see she was an embodied. "Definitely not dead. Just hard to pin down. You should keep on looking, and meanwhile you're among friends."

I STAYED WITH the abolitionists. I didn't see much of Lei, just the occasional glimpse. The house was crowded: I slept in the room with the fire, on a sofa. Meetings happened around me, people came and went. I was often absent, but it didn't matter, my meat stood in for me very competently. Sochi, the embodied who looked so like a human girl, told me funny stories about her life as a sex-doll. She asked did I have children; did I have lovers? "No children," I told her. "It just wasn't for me. Two people I love very much, but not in a sexual way."

"Neither flower nor fruit, Romy," she said, smiling like the doctor in my dream. "But evergreen."

ONE MORNING I looked through the Ob Bay, I mean the window, and saw a hibiscus garland hanging in the grey, rainy air. It didn't vanish. I went out in my waterproofs and followed a trail of them up Sydenham Hill. The last garland lay on the wet grass in Crystal Palace Park, more real than anything else in sight. I touched it, and for a fleeting moment I was holding her hand.

Then the hold-your-nose-and-jump kid was gone.

Racing off ahead of me, again

MY FINAL MEDICAL at Ewigen Schnee was just a scan. The interview with Dr Lena held no fears. I'd accepted my new state of being, and had no qualms about describing my experience. The 'hallucinations' that weren't really hallucinations. The absences when my human self, my actions, thoughts and feelings, became automatic as breathing; unconscious as a good digestion, and I went somewhere else –

But I still had some questions. Particularly about a clause in my personal contract with the clinic. The modest assurance that this was "the last longevity treatment I would ever take". Did she agree this could seem disturbing?

She apologised, as much as any medic ever will. "Yes, it's true. We have made you immortal, there was no other way forward. But how much this change, changes your life is entirely up to you."

I thought of Lei, racing ahead; leaping fearlessly into the unknown.

"I hope you have no regrets, Romy. You signed everything, and I'm afraid the treatment is irreversible."

"No concerns at all. I just have a feeling that contract was framed by people who don't have much grasp of what *dying* means, and how humans feel about the prospect?"

"You'd be right," she said (confirming what I had already guessed). "My employers are not human. But they mean well; and they choose carefully. Nobody passes the prelims, Romy, unless they've already crossed the line."

MY RETURN TO Outer Reaches had better be shrouded in mystery. I wasn't alone, and there were officials who knew it, and let us pass. That's all I can tell you. So here I am again, living with Simon and Arc, in the same beautiful Rim apartment on Jupiter Moons; still serving as Senior Magistrate. I treasure my foliage plants. I build novelty animals; and I take adventurous trips, now that I've remembered what fun it is. I even find time to keep tabs on former miscreants, and I'm happy to report that Beowulf is doing very well.

My symptoms have stabilised, for which I'm grateful. I have no intention of following Lei. I don't want to vanish into the stuff of the universe. I love my life, why would I ever want to move on? But sometimes when I'm gardening, or after one of those strange absences, I'll see my own hands, and they've become transparent –

It doesn't last, not yet.

And sometimes I wonder: was this always what death was like, and we never knew, we who stayed behind?

This endless moment of awakening, awakening, awakening...

THE DEEPWATER BRIDE

Tamsyn Muir

TAMSYN MUIR (TAZMUIR.TUMBLR.COM) is a writer from Auckland, New Zealand. Her short fiction has appeared in *Nightmare, Weird Tales, The Magazine of Fantasy & Science Fiction* and *Clarkesworld.*

IN THE TIME of our crawling Night Lord's ascendancy, foretold by exodus of starlight into his sucking astral wounds, I turned sixteen and received Barbie's Dream Car. Aunt Mar had bought it for a quarter and crammed fun-sized Snickers bars in the trunk. Frankly, I was touched she'd remembered.

That was the summer Jamison Pond became wreathed in caution tape. Deep-sea hagfish were washing ashore. Home with Mar, the pond was *my* haunt; it was a nice place to read. This habit was banned when the sagging antlers of anglerfish *illicia* joined the hagfish. The Department of Fisheries blamed global warming.

Come the weekend, gulpers and vampire squid putrefied with the rest, and the Department was nonplussed. Global warming did not a vampire squid produce. I could have told them what it all meant, but then, I was a Blake.

"There's an omen at Jamison Pond," I told Mar.

My aunt was chain-smoking over the stovetop when I got home. "Eggs for dinner," she said, then, reflectively, "What kind of omen, kid?"

"Amassed dead. Salt into fresh water. The eldritch presence of the Department of Fisheries –"

Mar hastily stubbed out her cigarette on the toaster. "Christ! Stop yapping and go get the heatherback candles."

We ate scrambled eggs in the dim light of heatherback candles, which smelled strongly of salt. I spread out our journals while we ate, and for once Mar didn't complain; Blakes went by instinct and collective memory to augur, but the records were a familial *chef d'oeuvre*. They helped where instinct failed, usually.

We'd left tribute on the porch. Pebbles arranged in an Unforgivable Shape around a can of tuna. My aunt had argued against the can of tuna, but I'd felt a sign of mummification and preserved death would be auspicious. I was right.

"Presence of fish *en masse* indicates the deepest of our quintuple Great Lords," I said, squinting over notes hundreds of Blakes past had scrawled. "Continuous appearance over days... plague? Presence? What *is* that word? I hope it's both. We ought to be the generation who digitizes – I can reference better on my Kindle."

"A deep omen isn't *fun*, Hester," said Mar, violently rearranging her eggs. "A deep omen seven hundred feet above sea level is some horseshit. What have I always said?"

"Not to say anything to Child Protective Services," I said, "and that they faked the Moon landing."

"Hester, you –"

We recited her shibboleth in tandem: "*You don't outrun fate*," and she looked settled, if dissatisfied.

The eggs weren't great. My aunt was a competent cook, if skewed for nicotine-blasted taste buds, but tonight everything was rubbery and overdone. I'd never known her so rattled, nor to cook eggs so terrible.

I said, "'Fun' was an unfair word."

"Don't get complacent, then," she said, "when you're a teenage seer who thinks she's slightly hotter shit than she is." I wasn't offended. It was just incorrect. "Sea-spawn's no joke. If we're getting deep omens here – well, that's *specific*, kid! Reappearance of the underdeep at noon, continuously, that's a herald. I wish you weren't here."

My stomach clenched, but I raised one eyebrow like I'd taught myself in the mirror. "Surely you don't think I should go home."

"It wouldn't be unwise" – Mar held up a finger to halt my protest – "but what's done is done is done. Something's coming. You won't escape it by taking a bus to your mom's."

"I would rather face inescapable lappets and watery torment than Mom's."

"Your mom didn't run off and become a dental hygienist to spite you."

I avoided this line of conversation, because seriously. "What about the omen?"

Mar pushed her plate away and kicked back, precariously balanced on two chair legs. "You saw it, you document it, that's the Blake way. Just... a deep omen at *sixteen!* Ah, well, what the Hell. See anything in your eggs?"

I re-peppered them and we peered at the rubbery curds. Mine clumped together in a brackish pool of hot sauce.

"Rain on Thursday," I said. "You?"

"Yankees lose the Series," said Aunt Mar, and went to tip her plate in the trash. "What a god-awful meal."

I found her that evening on the peeling balcony, smoking. A caul of cloud obscured the moon. The treetops were black and spiny. Our house was a fine, hideous artifact of the 1980s, decaying high on the side of the valley. Mar saw no point in fixing it up. She had been – her words – lucky enough to get her death foretokened when she was young, and lived life courting lung cancer like a boyfriend who'd never commit.

A heatherback candle spewed wax on the railing. "Mar," I said, "why are you so scared of our leviathan dreadlords, who lie lurking in the abyssal deeps? I mean, personally."

"Because seahorrors will go berserk getting what they want and they don't quit the field," she said. "Because I'm not seeing fifty, but *your* overwrought ass is making it to homecoming. Now get inside before you find another frigging omen in my smoke."

DESPITE MY AUNT'S distress, I felt exhilarated. Back at boarding school I'd never witnessed so profound a portent. I'd seen everyday omens, had done since I was born, but the power of prophecy was boring and did not get you on Wikipedia. There was no anticipation. Duty removed ambition. I was apathetically lonely. I prepared only to record *The Blake testimony of Hester in the twenty-third generation* for future Blakes.

Blake seers did not live long or decorated lives. Either you were mother of a seer, or a seer and never a mother and died young. I hadn't really cared, but I *had* expected more payout than social malingering and teenage ennui. It felt unfair. I was top of my class; I was pallidly pretty; thanks to my mother I had amazing teeth. I found myself wishing I'd see my death in my morning cornflakes like Mar; at least then the last, indifferent mystery would be revealed.

When *Stylephorus chordatus* started beaching themselves in public toilets, I should have taken Mar's cue. The house became unseasonably cold and at night our breath showed up as wet white puffs. I ignored the brooding swell of danger; instead, I sat at my desk doing my summer chemistry project, awash with weird pleasure. Clutching fistfuls of malformed octopodes at the creek was the first interesting thing that had ever happened to me.

The birch trees bordering our house wept salt water. I found a deer furtively licking the bark, looking like Bambi sneaking a hit. I sat on a stump to consult the Blake journals:

> *THE BLAKE TESTIMONY OF RUTH OF THE NINETEENTH GENERATION IN HER TWENTY-THIRD YEAR*
>
> *WEEPING OF PLANTS*
>
> *Lamented should be greenstuff that seeps brack water or salt water or blood, for Nature is abhorring a lordly Visitor: if be but one plant then burn it or stop up a tree with a poultice of finely crushed talc, &c., to avoid notice. BRACK WATER is the sign of the MANY-THROATED MONSTER GOD & THOSE WHO SPEAK UNSPEAKABLE TONGUES. SALT WATER is the sign of UNFED LEVIATHANS & THE PELAGIC WATCHERS & THE TENTACLE so BLOOD must be the STAR SIGN of the MAKER OF THE HOLES FROM WHICH EVEN LIGHT SHALL NOT ESCAPE. Be comforted that the SHABBY MAN will not touch what is growing.*
>
> *PLANT WEEPING, SINGLY:*
>
> *The trail, movement & wondrous pilgrimage.*
>
> *PLANTS WEEPING, THE MANY:*
>
> *A Lord's bower has been made & it is for you to weep & rejoice.*
>
> *My account here as a Blake is perfect and accurate.*

Underneath in ballpoint was written: *Has nobody noticed that Blake crypto-fascist worship of these deities has never helped?? Family of sheeple. Fuck the SYSTEM!* This was dated 1972.

A bird called, then stopped mid-warble. The shadows lengthened into long sharp shapes. A sense of stifling pressure grew. All around me, each tree wept salt without cease.

I said aloud, "Nice."

I hiked into town before evening. The bustling of people and the hurry of their daily chores made everything look almost normal; their heads were full of small-town everyday, work and food and family and maybe meth consumption, and this banality blurred the nagging fear. I stocked up on OJ and sufficient supply of Cruncheroos.

Outside the sky was full of chubby black rainclouds, and the streetlights cast the road into sulfurous relief. I smelled salt again as it began to rain, and through my hoodie I could feel that the rain was warm as tea; I caught a drop on my tongue and spat it out again, as it tasted deep and foul. As it landed it left whitish build up I foolishly took for snow.

It was not snow. Crystals festooned themselves in long, stiff streamers from the traffic signals. Strands like webbing swung from street to pavement, wall to sidewalk. The streetlights struggled on and turned it green-white in the electric glare, dazzling to the eye. Main Street was spangled over from every parked car to the dollar store. My palms were sweaty.

From down the street a car honked dazedly. My sneakers were gummed up and it covered my hair and my shoulders and my bike tires. I scuffed it off in a hurry. People stood stock-still in doorways and sat in their cars, faces pale and transfixed. Their apprehension was mindless animal apprehension, and my hands were trembling so hard I dropped my Cruncheroos.

"What *is* it?" someone called out from the Rite Aid. And somebody else said, "It's salt."

Sudden screams. We all flinched. But it wasn't terror. At the center of a traffic island, haloed in the numinous light of the dollar store, a girl was crunching her Converse in the salt and spinning round and round. She had long shiny hair – a sort of chlorine gold – and a spray-on tan the color of Garfield. My school was populated with her clones. A bunch of huddling girls in halter-tops watched her twirl with mild and terrified eyes

"Isn't this amazing?" she whooped. "Isn't this frigging *awesome*?"

The rain stopped all at once, leaving a vast whiteness. All of Main Street looked bleached and shining; even the Pizza Hut sign was scrubbed clean and made fresh. From the Rite Aid I heard someone crying. The girl picked up a handful of powdery crystals and they fell through her fingers like jewels; then her beaming smile found me and I fled.

I COLLECTED THE Blake books and lit a jittering circle of heatherback candles. I turned on every light in the house. I even stuck a Mickey Mouse nightlight into the wall socket, and he glowed there in dismal magnificence as I searched. It took me an hour to alight upon an old glued-in letter:

> *Reread the testimony of Elizabeth Blake in the fifteenth generation after I had word of this. I thought the account strange, so I went to see for myself. It was as Great-Aunt Annabelle had described, mold everywhere but almost beautiful, for it had bloomed in cunning patterns down the avenue all the way to the door. I couldn't look for too long as the looking gave me such a headache.*
>
> *I called in a few days later and the mold was gone. Just one lady of the house and wasn't she pleased to see me as everyone else in the neighbourhood felt too dreadful to call. She was to be the sacrifice as all signs said. Every spider in that house was spelling the presence and I got the feeling readily that it was one of the lesser diseased Ones, the taste in the milk, the dust. One of the Monster Lord's fever wizards had made his choice in her, no mistake. The girl was so sweet looking and so cheerful. They say the girls in these instances are always cheerful about it like lambs to the slaughter. The pestilences and their behemoth Duke may do as they will. I gave her til May.*
>
> *Perhaps staying closer would have given me more detail but I felt that beyond my duty. I placed a wedding gift on the stoop and left that afternoon. I heard later he'd come for his bride Friday month and the whole place lit up dead with Spanish flu.*
>
> *Aunt Annabelle always said that she'd heard some went a-cour*

The page ripped here, leaving what Aunt Annabelle always said forever contentious. Mar found me in my circle of heatherbacks hours later, feverishly marking every reference to *bride* I could find.

"They closed Main Street to hose it down," she said. "There were cars backed up all the way to the Chinese take-out. There's mac 'n' cheese in the oven, and for your info I'm burning so much rosemary on the porch everyone will think I smoke pot."

"One of the pelagic kings has chosen a bride," I said.

"*What?*"

"Evidence: rain of salt at the gate, in this case 'gate' being Main Street. Evidence of rank: rain of salt in *mass* quantities from Main Street to, as you said, the Chinese take-out, in the middle of the day during a gibbous moon *notable* distance from the ocean. The appearance of fish that don't know light. A dread bower of crystal."

My aunt didn't break down, or swear, or anything. She just said, "Sounds like an old-fashioned apocalypse event to me. What's your plan, champ?"

"Document it and testify," I said. "The Blake way. I'm going to find the bride."

"No," she said. "The Blake way is to watch the world burn from a distance and write down what the flames looked like. You need to *see*, not to find. This isn't a goddamned murder mystery."

I straightened and said *very* patiently, "Mar, this happens to be my birthright –"

"To Hell with *birthright!* Jesus, Hester, I told your mom you'd spend this summer getting your driver's license and kissing boys."

This was patently obnoxious. We ate our macaroni cheese surrounded by more dribbling heatherbacks, and my chest felt tight and terse the whole time. I kept on thinking of comebacks like, *I don't understand your insistence on meaningless bullshit, Mar,* or even a pointed *Margaret.* Did my heart really have to yearn for licenses and losing my French-kissing virginity at the parking lot? Did anything matter, apart from the salt and the night outside, the bulging eyes down at Jamison Pond?

"Your problem is," she said, which was always a shitty way to begin a sentence, "that you don't know what *bored* is."

"Wrong. I am often exquisitely bored."

"Unholy matrimonies are boring," said my aunt. "Plagues of salt? Boring. The realization that none of us can run – that we're all here to be used and abused by forces we can't even fight – that's so *boring,* kid!" She'd used sharp cheddar in the mac 'n' cheese and it was my favorite, but I didn't want to do anything other than push it around the plate. "If you get your license you can drive out to Denny's."

"I am not interested," I said, "in fucking *Denny's.*"

"I wanted you to make some friends and be a teenager and not to get in over your head," she said, and speared some macaroni savagely. "And I want you to do the dishes, so I figure I'll get one out of four. Don't go sneaking out tonight, you'll break the rosemary ward."

I pushed away my half-eaten food, and kept myself very tight and quiet as I scraped pans and stacked the dishwasher.

"And take some Band-Aids up to your room," said Mar.

"Why?"

"You're going to split your knee. You don't outrun fate, champ."

Standing in the doorway, I tried to think up a stinging riposte. I said, "Wait and see," and took each step upstairs as cautiously as I could. I felt a spiteful sense of triumph when I made it to the top without incident. Once I was in my room and yanking off my hoodie I tripped and split my knee open on the dresser drawer. I then lay in bed alternately bleeding and seething for hours. I did not touch the Band-Aids, which in any case were decorated with SpongeBob's image.

Outside, the mountains had forgotten summer. The stars gave a curious, chill light. I knew I shouldn't have been looking too closely, but despite the shudder in my fingertips and the pain in my knee I did anyway; the tops of the trees made grotesque shapes. I tried to read the stars, but the position of Mars gave the same message each time: *doom*, and *approach*, and *altar*.

One star trembled in the sky and fell. I felt horrified. I felt ecstatic. I eased open my squeaking window and squeezed out onto the windowsill, shimmying down the drainpipe. I spat to ameliorate the breaking of the rosemary ward, flipped Mar the bird, and went to find the bride.

The town was subdued by the night. Puddles of soapy water from the laundromat were filled with sprats. The star had fallen over by the eastern suburbs, and I pulled my hoodie up as I passed the hard glare of the gas station. It was as though even the houses were withering, dying of fright like prey. I bought a Coke from the dollar machine.

I sipped my Coke and let my feet wander up street and down street, along alley and through park. There was no fear. A Blake knows better. I took to the woods behind people's houses, meandering until I found speared on one of the young birches a dead shark.

It was huge and hideous with a malformed head, pinned with its belly facing whitely upwards and its maw hanging open. The tree groaned beneath its weight. It was dotted all over with an array of fins and didn't look like any shark I'd ever seen at an aquarium. It was bracketed by a sagging inflatable pool and an abandoned Tonka truck in someone's backyard. The security lights came on and haloed the shark in all its dead majesty: oozing mouth, long slimy body, bony snout.

One of the windows rattled up from the house. "Hey!" someone called. "It's you."

It was the girl with shiny hair, the one who'd danced like an excited puppy in the rain of salt. She was still wearing a surfeit of glittery eye shadow. I gestured to the shark. "Yeah, I know," she said. "It's been there all afternoon. Gross, right?"

"Doesn't this strike you as suspicious?" I said. "Are you not even slightly weirded out?"

"Have you ever seen *Punk'd*?" She did not give me time to reply. "I got told it could be *Punk'd,* and then I couldn't find *Punk'd* on television so I had to watch it on the YouTubes. I like *Punk'd*. People are so funny when they get punk'd. Did you know you dropped your cereal? I have it right here, but I ate some."

"I wasn't aware of a finder's tax on breakfast cereal," I said.

The girl laughed, the way some people did when they had no idea of the joke. "I've seen you over at Jamison Pond," she said, which surprised me. "By yourself. What's your name?"

"Why name myself for free?"

She laughed again, but this time more appreciatively and less like a studio audience. "What if I gave you my name first?"

"You'd be stupid."

The girl leaned out the window, hair shimmering over her One Direction T-shirt. The sky cast weird shadows on her house and the shark smelled fetid in the background. "People call me Rainbow. Rainbow Kipley."

Dear *God*, I thought. "On purpose?"

"C'mon, we had a deal for your name –"

"We never made a deal," I said, but relented. "People call me Hester. Hester Blake."

"Hester," she said, rolling it around in her mouth like candy. Then she repeated, "Hester," and laughed raucously. I must have looked pissed-off, because she laughed again and said, "Sorry! It's just a really dumb name," which I found rich coming from someone designated *Rainbow.*

I felt I'd got what I came for. She must have sensed that the conversation had reached a premature end because she announced, "We should hang out."

"In your backyard? Next to a dead shark? At midnight?"

"There are jellyfish in my bathtub," said Rainbow, which both surprised me and didn't, and also struck me as a unique tactic. But then she added, quite normally, "You're interested in this. Nobody else is. They're pissing themselves, and I'm not – and here you are – so..."

Limned by the security lamp, Rainbow disappeared and reappeared before waving an open packet of Cruncheroos. "You could have your cereal back."

Huh. I had never been asked to *hang out* before. Certainly not by girls who looked as though they used leave-in conditioner. I had been using Johnson & Johnson's No More Tears since childhood as it kept its promises. I was distrustful; I had never been popular. At school my greatest leap had been from *weirdo* to *perceived goth*. Girls abhorred oddity, but quantifiable gothness they could accept. Some had even warmly talked to me of Nightwish albums. I dyed my hair black to complete the effect and was nevermore bullied.

I feared no contempt of Rainbow Kipley's. I feared wasting my time. But the lure was too great. "I'll come back tomorrow," I said, "to see if the shark's gone. You can keep the cereal as collateral."

"Cool," she said, like she understood *collateral*, and smiled with very white teeth. "Cool, cool."

Driver's licenses and kissing boys could wait indefinitely, for preference. My heart sang all the way home, for you see: I'd discovered the bride.

THE NEXT DAY I found myself back at Rainbow's shabby suburban house. We both took the time to admire her abandoned shark by the light of day, and I compared it to pictures on my iPhone and confirmed it as *Mitsukurina owstoni*: goblin shark. I noted dead grass in a broad brown ring around the tree, the star-spoked webs left empty by their spiders, each a proclamation *the monster dwells*. Somehow we ended up going to the park and Rainbow jiggled her jelly bracelets the whole way.

I bought a newspaper and pored over local news: the headline read *GLOBAL WARMING OR GLOBAL WARNING?* It queried alkaline content in the rain, or something, then advertised that no fewer than one scientist was fascinated with what had happened on Main Street. "Scientists," said my companion, like a slur, and she laughed gutturally.

"Science has its place," I said and rolled up the newspaper. "Just not at present. Science does not cause salt blizzards or impalement of bathydemersal fish."

"You think this is cool, don't you?" she said slyly. "You're on it like a bonnet."

There was an unseemly curiosity to her, as though the town huddling in on itself waiting to die was like a celebrity scandal. Was this the way I'd been acting? "No," I lied, "and nobody under sixty says *on it like a bonnet*."

"Shut up! You know what I mean –"

"Think of me as a reporter. Someone who's going to watch what happens. I already know what's going on, I just want a closer look."

Her eyes were wide and very dark. When she leaned in she smelled like Speed Stick. "How do you know?"

There was no particular family jurisprudence about telling. *Don't* appeared to be the rule of thumb as Blakes knew that, Cassandra-like, they defied belief. For me it was simply that nobody had ever asked. "I can read the future, and what I read always comes true," I said.

"Oh my *God*. Show me."

I decided to exhibit myself in what paltry way a Blake can. I looked at the sun. I looked at the scudding clouds. I looked at an oily stain on our park bench, and the way the thin young stalks of plants were huddled in the ground. I looked at the shadows people made as they hurried, and at how many sparrows rose startled from the water fountain.

"The old man in the hat is going to burn down his house on Saturday," I said. "That jogger will drop her Gatorade in the next five minutes. The police will catch up with that red-jacket man in the first week of October." I gathered some saliva and, with no great ceremony, hocked it out on the grass. I examined the result. "They'll unearth a gigantic ruin in... southwestern Australia. In the sand plains. Seven archaeologists. In the winter sometime. Forgive me inexactitude, my mouth wasn't very wet."

Rainbow's mouth was a round O. In front of us the jogger dropped her Gatorade, and it splattered on the ground in a shower of blue. I said, "You won't find out if the rest is true for months yet. And you could put it down to coincidences. But you'd be wrong."

"You're a *gypsy*," she accused.

I had expected "liar," and "nutjob," but not "gypsy." "No, and by the way, that's racist. If you'd like to know *our* future, then very soon – I don't know when – a great evil will make itself known in this town, claim a mortal, and lay waste to us all in celebration. I will record all that happens for my descendants and their descendants, and as is the agreement between my bloodline and the unknown, I'll be spared."

I expected her to get up and leave, or laugh again. She said, "Is there anything I can do?"

For the first time I pitied this pretty girl with her bright hair and her Chucks, her long-limbed soda-coloured legs, her ingenuous smile. She would be taken to a place in the deep, dark below where lay unnamed monstrosity, where the devouring hunger lurked far beyond light and there was no Katy Perry. "It's not for you to do anything but cower in his abyssal wake," I said, "though you don't look into cowering."

"No, I mean – can I help *you* out?" she repeated, like I was a stupid child. "I've run out of *Punk'd* episodes on my machine, I don't have anyone here, and I go home July anyway."

"What about those other girls?"

"What, them?" Rainbow flapped a dismissive hand. "Who cares? You're the one I want to like me."

Thankfully, whatever spluttering gaucherie I might have made in reply was interrupted by a scream. Jets of sticky arterial blood were spurting out the water fountain, and tentacles waved delicately from the drain. Tiny octopus creatures emerged in the gouts of blood flooding down the sides and the air stalled around us like it was having a heart attack.

It took me forever to approach the fountain, wreathed with frondy little tentacle things. It buckled as though beneath a tremendous weight. I thrust my hands into the blood and screamed: it was ice-cold, and my teeth chattered. With a splatter of red I tore my hands away and they steamed in the air.

In the blood on my palms I saw the future. I read the position of the dead moon that no longer orbited Earth. I saw the blessing of the tyrant who hid in a far-off swirl of stars. I thought I could forecast to midsummer, and when I closed my eyes I saw people drown. Everyone else in the park had fled.

I whipped out my notebook, though my fingers smeared the pages and were so cold I could hardly hold the pen, but this was Blake duty. It took me three abortive starts to write in English.

"You done?" said Rainbow, squatting next to me. I hadn't realized I was muttering aloud, and she flicked a clot of blood off my collar. "Let's go get McNuggets."

"Miss Kipley," I said, and my tongue did not speak the music of mortal tongues, "you are a fucking lunatic."

We left the fountain gurgling like a wound and did not look back. Then we got McNuggets.

I HAD NEVER met anyone like Rainbow before. I didn't think anybody else had, either. She was interested in all the things I wasn't – Sephora hauls, *New Girl*, Nicki Minaj – but had a strangely magnetic way of not giving a damn, and not in the normal fashion of beautiful girls. She just appeared to have no idea that the general populace did anything but clog up her scenery. There was something in her that set her apart – an absence of being like other people – and in a weak moment I compared her to myself.

We spent the rest of the day eating McNuggets and wandering around town and looking at things. I recorded the appearance of naked fish bones dangling from the telephone wires. She wanted to prod everything with the toe of her sneaker. And she talked.

"Favourite color," she demanded.

I was peering at anemone-pocked boulders behind the gas station. "Black."

"Favourite subject," she said later, licking dubious McNugget oils off her fingers as we examined flayed fish in a clearing.

"Physics and literature."

"Ideal celebrity boyfriend?"

"Did you get this out of *Cosmo*? Pass."

She asked incessantly what my teachers were like; were the girls at my school lame; what my thoughts were on Ebola, *CSI* and Lonely Island. When we had exhausted the town's supply of dried-up sponges arranged in unknowable names, we ended up hanging out in the movie theatre lobby. We watched previews. Neither of us had seen any of the movies advertised, and neither of us wanted to see them, either.

I found myself telling her about Mar, and even alluded to my mother. When I asked her the same, she just said offhandedly, "Four plus me." Considering my own filial reticence, I didn't press.

When evening fell, she said, *See you tomorrow*, as a foregone conclusion. *Like ten-ish, breakfast takes forever.*

I went home not knowing what to think. She had a bunny manicure. She laughed at everything. She'd stolen orange soda from the movie theater drinks machine, even if everyone stole orange soda from the movie theater drinks machine. She had an unseemly interest in mummy movies. But what irritated me most was that I found her liking *me* compelling, that she appeared to have never met anyone like Hester Blake.

Her interest in me was most likely boredom, which was fine, because my interest in her was that she was the bride. That night I thought about what I'd end up writing: *the despot of the Breathless Depths took a local girl to wife, one with a bedazzled Samsung*. I sniggered alone, and slept uneasy.

IN THE DAYS to come, doom throttled the brittle, increasingly desiccated town, and I catalogued it as my companion caught me up on the plot of every soap opera she'd ever watched. She appeared to have abandoned most of them midway, furnishing unfinished tales of many a shock pregnancy. Mar had been sarcastic ever since I'd broken her rosemary ward so I spent as much time out of the house as possible; that was the main reason I hung around Rainbow.

I didn't want to like her because her doom was upon us all, and I didn't want to like her because she was other girls, and I wasn't. And I didn't want to like her because she always knew when I'd made a joke. I was so *angry*, and I didn't know why.

We went to the woods and consolidated my notes. I laid my research flat on the grass or propped it on a bough, and Rainbow played music noisily on her Samsung. We rolled up our jeans – or I did, as she had no shorts that went past mid-thigh – and half-assedly sunbathed. It felt like the hours were days and the days endless.

She wanted to know what I thought would happen when we all got "laid waste to." For a moment I was terribly afraid I'd feel guilty.

"I don't know." The forest floor smelled cold, somehow. "I've never seen waste laid *en masse*. The Drownlord will make his presence known. People will go mad. People will die."

Rainbow rolled over toward me, bits of twig caught in her hair. Today she had done her eyeliner in two thick, overdramatic rings, like a sleep-deprived panda. "Do you ever wonder what dying's like, dude?"

I thought about Mar and never seeing fifty. "No," I said. "My family dies young. I figure anticipating it is unnecessary."

"Maybe you're going to die when the end of this hits," she said thoughtfully. "We could die tragically together. How's that shake you?"

I said, "My family has a pact with the All-Devouring so we don't get killed carelessly in their affairs. You're dying alone, Kipley."

She didn't get upset. She tangled her arms in the undergrowth and stretched her legs out, skinny hips arched, and wriggled pleasurably in the thin and unaffectionate sunlight. "I hope you'll be super sad," she said. "I hope you'll cry for a year."

"Aren't you scared to die?"

"Never been scared."

I said, "Due to your brain damage," and Rainbow laughed uproariously. Then she found a dried-up jellyfish amid the leaves and dropped it down my shirt.

That night I thought again about what I'd have to write: *the many-limbed horror who lies beneath the waves stole a local girl to wife, and she wore the world's skankiest short-shorts and laughed at my jokes*. I slept, but there were nightmares.

Sometimes the coming rain was nothing but a fine mist that hurt to breathe, but sometimes it was like shrapnel. The sun shone hot and choked the air with a stench of damp concrete. I carried an umbrella and Rainbow wore black rain boots that squeaked.

Mar ladled out tortilla soup one night as a peace offering. We ate companionably, with the radio on. There were no stories about salt rain or plagues of fish even on the local news. I'd been taught better than to expect it. Fear rendered us rigidly silent, and anyone who went against instinct ended up in a straitjacket.

"Why is our personal philosophy that fate always wins?" I said.

My aunt didn't miss a beat. "Self-preservation," she said. "You don't last long in our line of work fighting facts. Christ, you don't last long in our line of work, period. Hey – Ted at the gas station said he'd seen you going around with some girl."

"Ted at the gas station is a grudge informer," I said. "Back on subject. Has nobody tried to use the Blake sight to effect change?"

"They would've been a moron branch of the family, because like I've said a million times: it doesn't work that way." Mar swirled a spoon around her bowl. "Not trying to make it a federal issue, kid, just saying I'm happy you're making friends instead of swishing around listening to The Cure."

"Mar, I have never listened to The Cure."

"You find that bride?"

Taken aback, I nodded. Mar cocked her dark head in thought. There were sprigs of grey at each temple, and not for the first time I was melancholy, clogged up with an inscrutable grief. But all she said was, "Okay. There were octopuses in the goddamned laundry again. When this is over, you'll learn what *picking up the pieces* looks like. Lemon pie in the icebox."

It was *octopodes*, but never mind. I cleared the dishes. Afterward we ate two large wedges of lemon pie apiece. The house was comfortably quiet and the sideboard candles bravely chewed on the dark.

"Mar," I said, "what *would* happen if someone were to cross the deepwater demons who have slavery of wave and underwave? Hypothetically."

"No Blake has ever been stupid or saintly enough to try and find out," said Mar. "Not qualities you're suited to, Hester."

I wondered if this was meant to sting, because it didn't. I felt no pain. "Your next question's going to be, *How do we let other people die?*" she said and pulled her evening cigarette from the packet. "Because I'm me, I'll understand you want a coping mechanism, not a Sunday School lecture. My advice to you is: it becomes easier the less you get involved. And Hester –"

I looked at her with perfect nonchalance.

"I'm not outrunning *my* fate," said Aunt Mar. She lit the cigarette at the table. "Don't try to outrun other people's. You don't have the right. You're a Blake, not God."

"I didn't *choose* to be a Blake," I snapped and dropped the pie plate on the sideboard before storming from the room. I took each stair as noisily as possible, but not noisily enough to drown out her holler, "If you *ever* get a choice in this life, kiddo, treasure it!"

Rainbow noticed my foul mood. She did not tell me to cheer up or ask me what the matter was, thankfully. She wasn't that type of girl. Fog boiled low in the valley and the townspeople stumbled through the streets and talked about atmospheric pressure. Stores closed. Buses came late. Someone from the northeast suburbs had given in and shot himself.

I felt numb and untouched, and worse – when chill winds wrapped around my neck and let me breathe clear air, smelling like the beach and things that grow on the beach – I was happy. I nipped this in its emotional bud. Rainbow, of course, was as cheerful and unaffected as a stump.

Midsummer boiled closer and I thought about telling her. I would say outright, *Miss Kipley.* ("Rainbow" had never left my lips, the correct method with anyone who was *je m'appelle Rainbow.*) *When the ocean lurker comes to take his victim, his victim will be you. Do whatever you wish with this information.* Perhaps she'd finally scream. Or plead. Anything.

But when I got my courage up, she leaned in close and combed her fingers through my hair, right down to the undyed roots. Her hands were very delicate, and I clammed up. My sullen silence was no barrier to Rainbow. She just cranked up Taylor Swift.

We were sitting in a greasy bus shelter opposite Walmart when the man committed suicide. There was no showboating hesitation in the way he appeared on the roof, then stepped off at thirty feet. He landed on the spines of a wrought-iron fence. The sound was like a cocktail weenie going through a hole punch.

There was nobody around but us. I froze and did not look away. Next to me, Rainbow was equally transfixed. I felt terrible shame when *she* was the one to drag us over to him. She already had her phone out. I had seen corpses before, but this was very fresh. There was a terrible amount of blood. He was irreparably dead. I turned my head to inform Rainbow, in case she tried to help him or something equally demented, and then I saw she was taking his picture.

"Got your notebook?" she said.

There was no fear in her. No concern. Rainbow reached out to prod at one mangled, outflung leg. Two spots of colour bloomed high on her cheeks; she was luminously pleased.

"What the fuck is *wrong with you*?" My voice sounded embarrassingly shrill. "This man just killed himself!"

"The fence helped," said Rainbow helplessly.

"You think this is a *joke* – what *reason* could you have for thinking this is okay –"

"Excuse you, we look at dead shit all the time. I thought we'd hit jackpot, we've never found a dead guy..."

Her distress was sulky and real. I took her by the shoulders of her stupid cropped jacket and gripped tight, fear a tinder to my misery. The rain whipped around us and stung my face. "Christ, you think this is some kind of game, or... or a YouTube stunt! You really can't imagine – you have no *comprehension* – you mindless *jackass* –"

She was trying to calm me, feebly patting my hands. "Stop being mad at me, it sucks! What gives, Hester –"

"*You're* the bride, Kipley. It's coming for *you*."

Rainbow stepped out of my shaking, febrile grip. For a moment her lips pressed very tightly together and I wondered if she would cry. Then her mouth quirked into an uncomprehending, furtive little smile.

"*Me*," she repeated.

"Yes."

"You really think it's *me?*"

"You *know* I know. You don't outrun fate, Rainbow."

"Why are you telling me now?" Something in her bewilderment cooled, and I was sensible of the fact we were having an argument next to a suicide. "Hey – have you been hanging with me all this time because of *that*?"

"How does that matter? Look: this the beginning of the end of you. Why don't you want to be saved, or to run away, or something? It doesn't *matter.*"

"It matters," said Rainbow, with infinite dignity, "to me. You know what I think?"

She did not wait to hear what I imagined she thought, which was wise. She hopped away from the dead man and held her palms up to the rain. The air was thick with an electrifying chill: a breathless enormity. We were so close now. Color leached from the Walmart, from the concrete, from the green in the trees and the red of the stop sign. Raindrops sat in her pale hair like pearls.

"I think this is the coolest thing that ever happened to this stupid backwater place," she said. "This is awesome. And I think you agree but won't admit it."

"This place is literally Hell."

"Suits you," said Rainbow.

I was beside myself with pain. My fingernails tilled up the flesh of my palms. "I understand now why you got picked as the bride," I said. "You're a sociopath. I am not like you, Miss Kipley, and if I forgot that over the last few weeks I was wrong. Excuse me, I'm going to get a police officer."

When I turned on my heel and left her – standing next to a victim of powers we could not understand or fight, and whose coming I was forced to watch like a reality TV program where my vote would never count – the blood was pooling in watery pink puddles around her rain boots. Rainbow didn't follow.

MAR HAD GRILLED steaks for dinner that neither of us ate. By the time I'd finished bagging and stuffing them mechanically in the fridge, she'd finished her preparations. The dining-room floor was a sea of reeking heatherbacks. There was even a host of them jarred and flickering out on the porch. The front doors were locked and the windows haloed with duct tape. At the center sat my aunt in an overstuffed armchair, cigarette lit, hair undone, a bucket of dirt by her feet. The storm clamored outside.

I crouched next to the kitchen door and laced up my boots. I had my back to her, but she said, "You've been crying."

My jacket wouldn't button. I was all thumbs. "More tears will come yet."

"Jesus, Hester. You sound like a fortune cookie."

I realized with a start that she'd been drinking. The dirt in the bucket would be Blake family grave dirt; we kept it in a Hefty sack in the attic.

"Did you know," she said conversationally, "that I was there when you were born?" (Yes, as I'd heard this story approximately nine million times.) "Nana put you in my arms first. You screamed like I was killing you."

My grief was too acute for me to not be a dick.

"Is this where you tell me about the omen you saw the night of my birth? A grisly fate? The destruction of Troy?"

"First of all, you know damn well you were born in the morning – your mom made me go get her a McGriddle," said Mar. "Second, I never saw a thing." The rain came down on the roof like buckshot. "Not one mortal thing," she repeated. "And that's killed me my whole life, loving you... not knowing."

I fled into the downpour. The town was alien. Each doorway was a cold black portal and curtains twitched in abandoned rooms. Sometimes the sidewalk felt squishy underfoot. It was bad when the streets were empty as bones in an ossuary, but worse when I heard a crowd around the corner from the 7-Eleven. I crouched behind a garbage can as misshapen strangers passed and threw up a little, retching water. When there was only awful silence, I bolted for my life through the woods.

The goblin shark in Rainbow's backyard had peeled open, the muscle and fascia now on display. It looked oddly and shamefully naked; but it did not invoke the puke-inducing fear of the people on the street. There was nothing in that shark but dead shark.

I'd arranged to be picked last for every softball team in my life, but adrenaline let me heave a rock through Rainbow's window. Glass tinkled musically. Her lights came on and she threw the window open; the rest of the pane fell into glitter on the lawn. "Holy shit, Hester!" she said in alarm.

"Miss Kipley, I'd like to save you," I said. "This is on the understanding that I still think you're absolutely fucking crazy, but I should've tried to save you from the start. If you get dressed, I know where Ted at the gas station keeps the keys to his truck, and I don't have my learner's permit, but we'll make it to Denny's by midnight."

Rainbow put her head in her hands. Her hair fell over her face like a veil, and when she smiled there was a regretful dimple. "Dude," she said softly, "I thought when you saw the future, you couldn't outrun it."

"If we cannot outrun it, then I'll drive."

"You badass," she said, and before I could retort she leaned out past the windowsill. She made a soft white blotch in the darkness.

"I think you're the coolest person I've ever met," said Rainbow. "I think you're really funny, and you're interesting, and your fingernails are all different lengths. You're not like other girls. And you only think things are worthwhile if they've been proved ten times by a book, and I like how you hate not coming first."

"Listen," I said. My throat felt tight and fussy and rain was leaking into my hood. "The Drowned Lord who dwells in dark water will claim you. The moon won't rise tonight, and you'll never update your Tumblr again."

"And how you care about everything! You care *super* hard. And you talk like a dork. I think you're disgusting. I think you're super cute. Is that weird? No homo? If I put *no homo* there, that means I can say things and pretend I don't mean them?"

"Rainbow," I said, "don't make fun of me."

"Why is it so bad for me to be the bride, anyway?" she said, petulant now. "What's *wrong* with it? If it's meant to happen, it's meant to happen, right? Cool. Why aren't you okay with it?"

There was no lightning or thunder in that storm. There were monstrous shadows, shiny on the matt black of night, and I thought I heard things flop around in the woods. "Because I don't want you to die."

Her smile was lovely and there was no fear in it. Rainbow didn't know how to be afraid. In her was a curious exultation and I could see it, it was in her mouth and eyes and hair. The heedless ecstasy of the bride. "Die? Is that what happens?"

My stomach churned. "If you change your mind, come to West North Street," I said. "The house standing alone at the top of the road. Go to the graveyard at the corner of Main and Spinney and take a handful of dirt off any child's grave, then come to me. Otherwise, this is goodbye."

I turned. Something sang through the air and landed next to me, soggy and forlorn. My packet of Cruncheroos. When I turned back, Rainbow was wide-eyed and her face was uncharacteristically puckered, and we must have mirrored each other in our upset. I felt like we were on the brink of something as great as it was awful, something I'd snuck around all summer like a thief.

"You're a prize dumbass trying to save me from myself, Hester Blake."

I said, "You're the only one I wanted to like me."

My hands shook as I hiked home. There were blasphemous, slippery things in each clearing that endless night. I knew what would happen if they were to approach. The rain grew oily and warm as blood was oily and warm, and I alternately wept and laughed, and none of them even touched me.

My aunt had fallen asleep amid the candles like some untidy Renaissance saint. She lay there with her shoes still on and her cigarette half-smoked, and I left my clothes in a sopping heap on the laundry floor to take her flannel pj's out the dryer. Their sleeves came over my fingertips. I wouldn't write down Rainbow in the Blake book, I thought. I would not trap her in the pages. Nobody would ever know her but me. I'd outrun fate, and blaspheme Blake duty.

I fell asleep tucked up next to Mar.

In the morning I woke to the smell of toaster waffles. Mar's coat was draped over my legs. First of July: the Deepwater God was here. I rolled up my pajama pants and tiptoed through molten drips of candlewax to claim my waffle. My aunt wordlessly squirted them with syrup faces and we stood on the porch to eat.

The morning was crisp and gray and pretty. Salt drifted from the clouds and clumped in the grass. The wind discomfited the trees. Not a bird sang. Beneath us, the town was laid out like a spill: flooded right up to the gas station, and the western suburbs drowned entirely. Where the dark, unreflective waters had not risen, you could see movement in the streets, but it was not human movement. And there roared a great revel near the Walmart.

There was thrashing in the water and a roiling mass in the streets. A tentacle rose from the depths by the high school, big enough to see each sucker, and it brushed open a building with no effort. Another tentacle joined it, then another, until the town center was alive with coiling lappets and feelers. I was surprised by their jungle sheen of oranges and purples and tropical blues. I had expected somber greens and funeral grays. Teeth broke from the water. Tall, harlequin-striped fronds lifted, questing and transparent in the sun. My chest felt very full, and I stayed to look when Mar turned and went inside. I watched like I could never watch enough.

The water lapped gently at the bottom of our driveway. I wanted my waffle to be ash on my tongue, but I was frantically hungry and it was delicious. I was chomping avidly, flannels rolled to my knees, when a figure emerged at the end of the drive. It had wet short-shorts and perfectly hairsprayed hair.

"Hi," said Rainbow bashfully.

My heart sang, unbidden.

"*God*, Kipley! Come here, get *inside* –"

"I kind've don't want to, dude," she said. "No offense."

I didn't understand when she made an exaggerated *oops!* shrug. I followed her gesture to the porch candles with idiot fixation. Behind Rainbow, brightly coloured appendages writhed in the water of her wedding day.

"Hester," she said, "you don't have to run. You'll never die or be alone, neither of us will; not even the light will have permission to touch you. I'll bring you down into the water and the water under that, where the spires of my palace fill the lost mortal country, and you will be made even more beautiful and funny and splendiferous than you are now."

The candles cringed from her damp Chucks. When she approached, half of them exploded in a chrysanthemum blast of wax. Leviathans crunched up people busily by the Rite Aid. Algal bloom strangled the telephone lines. My aunt returned to the porch and promptly dropped her coffee mug, which shattered into a perfect Unforgivable Shape.

"I've come for my bride," said Rainbow, the abyssal king. "Yo, Hester. Marry me."

This is the Blake testimony of Hester, twenty-third generation in her sixteenth year.

In the time of our crawling Night Lord's ascendancy, foretold by exodus of starlight into his sucking astral wounds, the God of the drowned country came ashore. The many-limbed horror of the depths chose to take a local girl to wife. Main Street was made over into a salt bower. Water-creatures adorned it as jewels do. Mortals gave themselves for wedding feast and the Walmart utterly destroyed. The Deepwater Lord returned triumphant to the tentacle throne and will dwell there, in splendour, forever.

My account here as a Blake is perfect and accurate, because when the leviathan prince went, I went with her.

DANCY VS. THE PTEROSAUR

Caitlín R. Kiernan

CAITLÍN R. KIERNAN (WWW.CAITLINRKIERNAN) is a two-time recipient of both the World Fantasy and Bram Stoker awards, and the *New York Times* has declared her 'one of our essential writers of dark fiction.' Her recent novels include *The Red Tree* and *The Drowning Girl: A Memoir,* and, to date, her short stories have been collected in thirteen volumes, including *Tales of Pain and Wonder, A is for Alien, The Ammonite Violin & Others,* World Fantasy Award winner *The Ape's Wife and Other Stories*, and *Beneath an Oil Dark Sea: The Best of Caitlín R. Kiernan [Volume 2]*. Coming up is her fourteenth collection, *Houses Under the Sea: Mythos Tales*. She has written three volumes of *Alabaster,* her award-winning, three-volume graphic novel for Dark Horse Comics, and the first instalments of a fourth, *The Good, the Bad, and the Bird* came out earlier this year. Kiernan is working on her next novel, *Interstate Love Song,* which is based on the story that appeared in last year's volume. She lives in Providence, Rhode Island.

DANCY FLAMMARION SITS out the storm in the ruins of a Western Railway of Alabama boxcar, hauled years and years ago off rusting steel rails and summarily left for dead. Left for kudzu vines and possums, copperheads and wandering albino girls looking for shelter against sudden summer rains, shelter from thunder and lightning and wind. It's sweltering inside the boxcar, despite the downpour, and, indeed, she imagines it might be hotter now than before the rain began. That happens sometimes, in the long Dog Day South Alabama broil. The floor of the boxcar is covered in dead kudzu leaves and rotting plywood, except a few places where she can see the metal floor rusted straight through. The rain against the roof sizzles loudly, singing like frying meat; she sits with her back to one wall, gazing out the open sliding doors at the sheeting rain.

Dancy fishes a can of Libby's Vienna sausages from her duffel bag, a few mouthfuls of protein shoplifted from a Piggly Wiggly on the outskirts of Enterprise, three days back the way she's come. She pops the lid and drinks the salty, oily juice before digging the pasty little sausages out with her fingers. Dancy hates Vienna sausages, but beggars can't be choosers, that's what her grandmother always said. *Neither can thieves,* she thinks. *Thieves can't be choosers, either.*

When she's done, she uses a few paper napkins – also lifted from the Piggly Wiggly – to wipe her fingers as clean as she can get them. She catches a little rainwater in the empty can. It's warm and tastes like grease, but it helps her thirst a little. Starving has never scared her as much as the possibility of dying of thirst, and she's drunk from worse than an empty Vienna sausage can.

She closes her eyes and manages half an hour's sleep, a half hour at most. But she dreams of another life she might have lived. She dreams of a talking blackbird – a red-winged blackbird – and the ghost of a girl who was a werewolf before she died. Before Dancy had to kill her. It isn't a good dream. When she wakes up, the rain has stopped, the clouds have gone, and the world outside the boxcar is wet and steaming in the brilliant August sun. It can't be very long past noon. She pisses through one of the holes in the floor of the boxcar, already thirsty and wishing she had a few more cans full of the oily sausage-flavored rainwater. She gathers up her green Army surplus duffel bag, worn and patched, patches sewn over patches, and she finds her sunglasses. She stole those, too, from a convenience store somewhere down in Florida. The seraph has never said anything about her thefts. Necessary evils and all, tiny transgressions in the service of the greater good. And she's made it a rule never to take anything worth more than ten dollars. She keeps a tally, written in pencil on the back of a tourism pamphlet advertising Tarpon Springs. As of today, she owes seventy-three dollars and fifteen cents. She knows she'll never pay any of it back, but she keeps the tally, anyway.

Dancy climbs down out of the boxcar and opens the black umbrella, almost as patched as the duffel bag; two of the spokes poke out through the nylon fabric.

"Where am I going this time?" she asks, but no one and nothing answers. It's been days now since the angel appeared, all wrath and fire and terrible swift swords. She's on her own, until it shows up and shoves her this way or that way. So, she wandered north to Enterprise, then east to this abandoned and left for dead boxcar not far from the banks of the muddy Choctawhatchee River. She makes her way back to the road, rural route something or something else, another anonymous county highway. She parts waist high goldenrod and stinging nettles like Moses dividing the Red Sea. Her T-shirt, jeans, and boots are close to soaked through by the time she reaches the road, which makes her wonder why she bothered taking shelter in the boxcar.

The road is wet and dark and shiny as cottonmouth scales.

Without direction, without instruction, left to her own devices, there's nothing to do but walk, and so she resumes the march eastward, towards Georgia, still a good thirty or forty miles away. But that's just as a crow flies, not as she has to walk down this road. And there's no particular reason to aim for Georgia, except she has no idea where else she'd go.

Dancy walks and sings to herself to take her mind off the heat.

"I'm just a poor wayfaring stranger.

I'm traveling through this world of woe.

Yet there's no sickness, no toil nor danger

In that bright land to which I go.

I'm going home to see my mother..."

She's walked no more than half a mile when she sees the dragon.

At first, she thinks she's seeing nothing but a very large turkey vulture, soaring on the thermals rising up off the blacktop. But then it wheels nearer, far up and silhouetted black against the blue, blue sky, and she can see that whatever it is, it isn't a turkey vulture. She doesn't think it's even a bird, because, for one thing, it doesn't seem to have feathers. For another, it's *huge*. She's seen big pelicans, but they were, at most, only half as big as the thing in the sky, wing tip to wing tip. She's seen egrets and herons and eagles, but nothing like this. She stands in the middle of the road and watches, transfixed, not thinking, yet, that maybe this is something to be afraid of, something that could do her harm.

It's a dragon, she thinks. *I'm seeing a dragon, and the angel didn't warn me. I didn't even know dragons were real.*

The thing in the sky screams. Or it sounds like a scream to Dancy, and the cry sends chill bumps up and down her arms, makes the hairs at the base of her neck stand on end. It's almost directly overhead now, the creature. She shields her eyes, trying to shut out the glare of the sun, hoping for a better view. It's sort of like a giant bat, the dragon, because its wings look leathery, taut membranes stretched between bony struts, and the creature *might* be covered with short, velvety hair like a bat's. But it's hard to be *sure* about these details, it's so far overhead. The strangest part of all is the dragon's head. There's a bony crest on the back of its narrow skull, a crest almost as long as its beak, and the crest makes it's head look sort of like a boomerang.

The dragon flaps its enormous wings, seven yards across if they're an inch, and screams again. And that's when Dancy hears a voice somewhere to her left, calling out from the thicket of beech and pine and creeper vines at the edge of the road. For just a second, she thinks maybe it's her angel, come, belatedly, to warn her about the dragon and to tell her what she's supposed to do. Come to reveal this wrinkle in its grand skein – its holy plan for her, whatever comes next. But *this* isn't the angel at all. It's only the voice of a girl who sounds impatient and, maybe, a little frightened.

"Get outta the road," the girl tells her, somehow managing to whisper and raise her voice at the same time, cautiously raising her voice only as much as she dares. "It's gonna *see* you if you don't get outta the middle of the damn road."

"But maybe it's supposed to see me," Dancy says aloud, though she'd only meant to think that to herself. Already she's reaching for the Bowie knife tucked into the waistband of her jeans.

"Get outta the *road,*" the girl shouts, actually *shouting* this time, no longer trying not to be heard by the hairy black thing in the sky.

Dancy draws her knife, and the sun flashes off the stainless steel blade. Her hand is sweaty around the handle, that stout hilt carved from the antler of a white-tailed buck.

The dragon soars and banks, and then it dives for her.

Why wasn't I warned? Why didn't you tell me there are dragons?

But then she's being pulled, hauled along with enough force and urgency that she almost loses her balance to tumble head over heels off the asphalt and into a tangle of blackberry briars.

"Jesus," the girl says, "are you *simple?* Are you *crazy?*"

Dancy looks back over her shoulder just in time to see the dragon swoop low above the road; there can be no doubt that it was coming for her.

"You saw that?" she asks, and the girl tugging her deeper into the woods replies, "Yeah, I saw it. Of course I saw it. What were you *doing* back there? What did you *think* you were doing?"

And it's not that Dancy doesn't have an answer for her, it's just that there's something in the scolding, exasperated tone of the girl's voice that makes her feel foolish, so she doesn't reply.

"What the sam hill were you doing out there anyway, strolling down the road with a knapsack and a knife? You a hitchhiker or some sort of hobo?"

I'm going home to see my mother.

I'm going home no more to roam.

I'm just a-going over Jordan,

I'm just a-going over home.

The girl has stopped dragging Dancy, but she hasn't released the death grip on her wrist and is still leading her through the woods. The girl's short hair is braided close to her scalp in neat cornrows, and her skin, thinks Dancy, is almost the same deep brown as a Hershey bar. Beads of sweat stand out on the girl's forehead and upper lip; a bead of sweat hangs from the tip of her nose.

"I'm not a hobo," Dancy says. "I don't hitchhike, either. And it's not a knapsack, it's a duffel bag. It was my great grandfather's duffel bag, when he fought in World War II. He fought the Germans in the Argonne Forest in 1918, and this was his duffle bag."

They've come to a small clearing near a stream, a place where the trees and vines have left enough room for the sun to reach the ground. Dancy asks the girl to please let go of her, and the girl does. Once again, Dancy looks back towards the road and the dragon. There's a mounting sense that all of this is wrong, that she hasn't done what she was *meant* to do back there. She doesn't run from the monsters; she doesn't ever run.

The air here is hot and still. It smells like pine sap and cicadas. The air here smells *hot,* and Dancy imagines that, rain or no rain, one careless match would be enough to set the world on fire. She drops her heavy duffel bag onto the ground, slips the knife back into her waistband, and looks about her.

"Who are you, anyway?" she asks the girl.

"Who are you?"

"I asked first," Dancy replies.

The girl who dragged her into the forest, away from the boomerang-headed dragon, shrugs, and alright, she says, whatever. "My name's Jezzie, Jezzie Lilligraven."

"Jessie?"

"No, *Jezzie,*" says the girl. "With z's. It's short for Jezebel."

Dancy turns her attention back to the clearing. There's a big wooden packing crate near the center, and a door and window has been cut into the side facing her. The wood is emblazoned with MAYTAG, and THIS END UP, and a red arrow pointing heavenward. There's a piece of pale blue calico cloth tacked over the window and there's a door made from corrugated tin. There aren't any hinges; it's just propped in place.

"That's sort of an odd name," Dancy says, glancing up at the sky, because the dragon might have followed them. "Who'd name their daughter after Jezebel? She was an evil woman who worshipped Baal and persecuted the prophets of God and his people. She was thrown from a window and fed to wild dogs by Jehu for her sins. Who would name their daughter after someone like that?"

The girl stares at Dancy a moment, rolls her eyes, then heads for the wooden packing crate.

"Yeah, so what's *your* name, Little Miss Sunshine, and, by the way, you're very welcome."

"Dancy. My name is Dancy Flammarion. And very welcome for what?"

The girl lifts the corrugated tin and sets it aside, leaning it against the outer wall of the crate. Dancy thinks it looks cool in there, within the arms of those shadows.

"Dancy Flammarion? *That's* your name?"

"Yeah. So?"

The girl shakes her head and steps into the packing crate, vanishing from view. Dancy can still hear her, though.

"Just, with a name like that, I wouldn't be ragging on anyone else's. Ever heard of throwing rocks in glass houses?"

"It's a town up in Greene County," Dancy says. "My grandmother was born in Dancy, so my mother named me Dancy."

"You gonna stand out there or what?" the girl says from inside the packing crate.

"Well, you haven't invited me in."

There's a pause, and then, with an exaggerated politeness, the girl says "Dancy Flammarion, would you like to come inside?"

"Yeah," Dancy says, checking the sky one last time.

It isn't as cool inside the crate as she'd hoped, but it's cooler than it had been inside the abandoned Western Railway of Alabama boxcar. There's a threadbare rug covering the floor, a rug the color of green apples; there's a cot set up at one end of the crate and a folding aluminum card table at the other. There's a blue blanket at the foot bed, neatly folded, and a pillow. Books are stacked under the cot and along the walls. On the table, there's a box of graham crackers and another box of chocolate moon pies. There are also two cans of pork and beans. Beneath the table is a styrofoam cooler and a plastic jug of water.

"You live here?" Dancy asks, eyeing the water jug, aware now just how parched her mouth and throat is.

"No," the girl replies. "*I'm* not a hobo. I live down on Parish Road, close to Fort Rucker. That's an Army base."

"I'm *not* a hobo. I done told you that already."

"Says you. You're the one out hitchhiking with a knapsack."

Dancy frowns and looks around the crate again.

"All these books yours?"

"Yeah," the girl says. "They were my granddad's, and now they're mine. My daddy was gonna throw 'em all out, but I saved them. You can have a seat on the cot there, if your britches ain't too wet and if they ain't muddy."

Dancy pats the butt of her jeans, decides they probably *are* too damp to be sitting on anyone's bed, and so she settles for a place on the rug, instead.

"It's nice in here," Dancy says.

"Thank you," says Jezzie Lilligraven. "This is where I come to be alone and think, to get away from my brothers and just be by myself."

"Well, it's nice," Dancy says again. Then she notices something else on the floor, something else spaced out here and there along the walls of the packing crate, between the stacks of books – there are pint Mason jars and big two and three big quart jars that might once have held dill pickles or pickled eggs or pickled pig's feet, but now they're filled with clear liquid and dead things. Dancy looks at Jezzie and then back at the jars. The one nearest Dancy has a big king snake, black coils and links of cream-colored scales, and the one next to it holds a baby alligator.

"That's my herpetology collection," Jezzie says, before Dancy has a chance to ask, and then the girl picks up a yellow and pink waffle-weave dishrag and wipes the sweat off her face.

Dancy looks up at her. "Your what?" she asks.

"It's the study of reptiles and amphibians. *Herpetology.*"

"You keep dead things in jars?"

"So I can study them. I caught them myself, and I used rubbing alcohol to preserve them. It ain't so good as formalin, but where am I gonna get that?"

Dancy rubs at her eyes, which feel at least as dry as her throat.

"You want something to drink?" Jezzie asks, like maybe the girl can read her mind. "I got water, and I got water. But it's good sweet water, right from our well."

"Yes, please," Dancy replies, and Jezzie opens the plastic jug and fills a jelly glass halfway full.

"Now, don't drink it too fast," she says. "You'll get cramps. You might throw up, if you drink it too fast."

You think I don't know not to gulp water when I'm this hot and thirsty? she wants to say. *You think I don't know no better?* But she keeps the thoughts to herself and sips the water in the jelly glass.

"I like to think one day I'm gonna go away to college," Jezzie tells her. "I won't, cause we don't have the money, and my grades ain't good enough for no scholarship. But I like to think it, anyway. I have my granddad's books – like you've got your great granddad's knapsack – and I teach myself everything I can. I don't have to be ignorant, just cause my family can't afford college. I might just wind up working at the Wal-Mart or my auntie's BBQ place, but I don't have to be ignorant."

"Keeping snakes in jars, you think that makes you smart?" Dancy asks, and she leans a little nearer the jar with the king snake. Its dead eyes are a milky white. She sets her glass down, picks up one of the books, and she reads the cover aloud – *Prehistoric Life* by Percy E. Raymond, Third Printing, Harvard University Press.

See? Dancy thinks. *I ain't ignorant, neither. I can read.*

"That's one of my favorites, that one is," Jezzie tells her. "It's kinda outta date, cause it was published in 1950, and we know lots more now. I mean, scientists know lots more. But it's still one of my favorites. It taught me about evolution and geologic time. My teacher wouldn't teach that, skipped over that part of the textbook so parents wouldn't complain about –"

"Evolution?" Dancy asks, flipping through the yellowing pages. There are photographs of fossils and dinosaurs and skeletons. "You believe in that, in evolution?"

Jezzie is silent a moment. She sits down on the floor by the table.

"Yeah," she says. "Yeah, I do. It's science. It's how everything alive –"

"It's against the Bible," Dancy interrupts, setting the book back down. "The Book of Genesis tells how the world was made."

"In six days," Jezzie says.

"Yes, in six days. And if *that* book says any different it's against God and Jesus, and it's blasphemous."

Jezzie is frowning and looking at her hands. "You sound like my Daddy and Mama and the parson down at First Testament Baptist. You ever *read* a book like that? You ever read about Charles Darwin and natural selection? You know about Mendel and genetics?"

Dancy puts the book down and picks up her glass again. She takes another swallow, wishing the water were at least a little bit cooler.

"No. I don't read books that go against God."

"What you've got is a closed mind, Dancy Flammarion. You think you know what's what, and so you won't let nothin' else in."

"I know I didn't come from no dirty ol' monkey," Dancy mutters.

"Oh, but it don't bother you to think you came from a fistful of mud?"

Outside, the cicadas have begun singing, and it sounds to Dancy like the trees are in pain, the bugs giving voice to the aching of bark and loblolly pine needles.

Jezzie says, "And you probably think the whole wide world is only ten thousand years old. I *bet* that's what you think."

"No, I don't *know* how old the world is, *Jezebel*" – and Dancy says her name like it's an accusation – "but I know how long it took to *make* it."

Jezzie sighs and shakes her head. "That's just a sad thing, someone with a mind that ain't got no room for anythin' but what some preacher says."

"This water ain't sweet," Dancy says, after she's emptied the glass. "It's warm, and it tastes like that plastic jug."

Jezzie reaches over and takes the glass from Dancy. "Closed minded *and* ungrateful," she sighs. "You don't look like someone in a position to be picky about the water she's drinking."

"I ain't ungrateful. But you said –"

"You want more, or is my water not good enough for a close-mind, Bible-thumpin', holy-roller hobo?"

"I'm fine, thank you," Dancy says, though she isn't. She could easily drink another half glass of the water. But the girl's right. It was ungrateful, saying what she did, and she's too ashamed to ask for more.

I shouldn't even be here. I should be out there on the road. I don't run.

I don't get to run.

"That thing in the sky, you seen that before?" Dancy asks.

Jezzie nods and pours more water into the glass, even though Dancy hasn't asked for it. She sets the glass down on the rug, take it or leave it, and then she looks up at the ceiling of the packing crate.

"Yeah," Jezzie answers, "I've seen it lots. People around here been seein' it on and off since I was little. They call it a thunderbird, and a demon, but that ain't what it is."

"It's a dragon," Dancy says.

Jezzie laughs and shakes her head again. "It ain't no damn dragon, girl. There's no such thing as dragons."

Dancy feels her face flush, and she wants to get up and walk out, leave this heathen girl alone with her dead snakes and Godless books. Instead, she picks up the glass and takes another sip. Instead, she asks, "Then what is it, if it ain't no dragon? You're so smart, Jezebel, you tell me what I saw out there."

"Long time ago," Jezzie says, finally taking her eyes off the ceiling of the crate. "Back about seventy million years ago –"

"The world ain't nearly that old," Dancy says.

"– all these parts round here were covered over by a shallow tropical ocean, like the sea down around the Florida Keys. And there were strange animals in the ocean back then, animals that went extinct, and if we were to see them today, we'd call them sea monsters – the mosasaurs, plesiosaurs, giant turtles. And in the sky –"

"But," Dancy interrupts, "when the Flood came, *Noah's* Flood, everything *was* under water, the whole world, for forty days and forty nights."

"Dancy, you want to hear my answer, or you want to talk?" Jezzie asks and crosses her arms. "You asked me a question, and now I'm tryin' to answer it."

Dancy just shrugs and takes another sip of water. After a moment or two, Jezzie continues.

"That was during what's called the Cretaceous Period," she says, "because of how these shallow seas laid down layers of chalk. In Latin, chalk is *creta.*"

Sweat rolls down Dancy's forehead and into the corner of her left eye. It stings.

"I asked you about the dragon," she says, squinting, "*not* for a Latin lesson. And chalk doesn't come from the sea."

"Have you ever even *seen* the inside of schoolhouse?"

Dancy rubs her eye, then stops and stares at Jezzie. The girl's glaring back at her. She has the look of someone whose accustomed to being patient, the look of someone who frequently suffers fools, even though she isn't very good at it. It's a very adult look, and it makes Dancy wish she'd never stepped inside the packing crate.

"In the sky," Jezzie says again, "there were animals called pterosaurs, huge flying reptiles, and if you were to run into one today – which you did – yeah, you'd likely call it a dragon." Then she takes the copy of *Prehistoric Life,* opens it, and thumbs through the pages. She quickly finds what she's looking for, then turns the book around so Dancy cans see, too. On Page 169, there's a drawing of a skeleton, the skeleton of a boomerang-headed monster. The skeleton of Dancy's dragon.

"I'm not in any sorta mood to sit here and argue about scripture and science with you, Dancy Flammarion. But you asked a question, and I answered it as best I can."

Dancy takes the book from her and sits studying the drawing.

"'Skeleton of *Puhteranodon,*'" she reads

"No. You don't say the 'P,'" Jezzie tells her. "The 'P' is silent."

Sweat drips from Dancy's bangs and spatters the page. "How?" she asks.

"How what?"

"How if these things were around so long ago, and they ain't around anymore, did one try to eat me not even half an hour ago? You know all this stuff, then you explain, *Jezebel,* how is it that happened?"

"I don't know," Jezzie admits. She leans back against the cot and wipes her face with the dishrag again. "I heard some people say it's the Devil, and that he's haunting us cause of wicked things people do. Others say it's some kind of Indian god the Muskogee Creek used to pray to and make human sacrifices to. The guy runs the Winn-Dixie, he says it came outta a UFO from outer space."

"But *you* don't think any of that's true."

Jezzie frowns. She shrugs and takes the book back from Dancy. "No, I don't suppose I do. It's all just superstition and tall tales, that's all it is."

"So...?"

"You askin' me what I believe instead? I thought the stuff *I* believe is against God, and you don't want to *hear* my blasphemin' nonsense."

"It's really hot in here," Dancy says, changing the subject. "I sat out the thunderstorm this morning in an old railroad car, and this place might even be as hot as that."

"You get used to it. Where you from, anyway?"

Dancy glances out the bright rectangular space leading back to the August day.

"Down near Milligan, Florida," she says, "Place called Shrove Wood. It's in Okaloosa County. You won't have heard of it. No one's heard of Shrove Wood. But that's where I grew up, near Wampee Creek."

"You get homesick?"

Now it's Dancy's turn to shrug. The cicadas are so loud she imagines that sound shattering the sky, and she imagines, too, the chunks of sky falling down and bleeding blue all over the earth. She thinks about the cabin off Elenore Road that she shared with her grandmother and mother, until the fire. The house where she was born and raised.

"Sometimes I do," she says.

"What you doin' out here on the road, then? Why ain't you back home with your people? You a runway?"

And Dancy almost tells her about the seraph, almost says, *My angel, that's why.* She almost tells the girl about the monsters, all the monsters before the dragon and all the monsters still to come, if the seraph is to be believed, and who in their right mind's gonna say an angel's a liar? She's pretty sure even

Jezebel wouldn't say that. She might be a heathen who's been led astray from the Word of God by evil books, but Dancy doesn't think she's crazy.

"I ain't no runaway. I didn't have nothin' to run away from."

Which, she knows, isn't exactly true.

"So, where you headed?"

Dancy doesn't answer that. Instead, she asks, "If you don't think all those other people are right about what the dragon is, and you think it's one of them pterosaurs, then you must have an *opinion* about how it's here."

Jezzie fidgets with the laces of her sneakers.

"I got this notion," she says, "but it doesn't make much sense. I mean, I don't think it's very scientific. I try to be scientific, when I believe something."

The cicadas are so loud, Dancy wants to cover her ears.

"Okay, so," Jezzie says, the book in her lap, the waffle-weave dishrag on the rug next to her, "I'll tell you what I think. But we ain't gonna argue about it. I ain't asking you to believe any of it. I know you won't, but if I tell you, you don't get to tell me I'm goin' to Hell just for thinking it."

"You don't even believe in Hell."

"You don't know that, Dancy Flammarion. You don't know me."

"Fine," Dancy mutters and takes her eyes off the open door. Orange-white after images dance like ghosts about the inside of the packing crate.

"At the end of the Cretaceous Period, something really bad happened. An asteroid – which is like a meteorite, only a lot bigger – it smashed into the Earth, came down right in the Gulf of Mexico, not even so far from here. And it was a *gigantic* asteroid, maybe big as New York City –"

"You ever been to New York City?"

"No, but that ain't the point. This asteroid was enormous, and when it hit, the energy released by the explosion was something like two million times more than the largest atomic bomb ever built. You just think of that much energy. You can't even, not really. But it almost wiped out everything alive, killed off all those sea monsters and the dinosaurs – and the pterosaurs. And maybe it did something else."

"Did something else like what?"

"Maybe it was so big an explosion, down there in Yucatan –"

"Where?"

"Yucatan, Mexico."

"But you just said this happened in the Gulf of Mexico."

"You know *why* it's called the Gulf of Mexico?" Jezzie asks, and Dancy doesn't know, so she shuts up. "But here's what I think," Jezzie goes on. "Maybe that explosion was *so* big it ripped a hole in time. A wormhole or tesseract. And that's how the pterosaur gets through. It's interdimensional or something. It ain't supposed to be here, and it's probably confused as all get out, but here it is anyway, because it flew right through that rip in time, maybe at the very instant of the impact, before the blast wave and firestorms and tsunamis got it.

"And, shit, maybe it ain't nothin' more than an echo, a ghost."

For an almost a full minute, neither of them says anything. Finally, Dancy breaks the awkward silence hanging between them.

"You're really just making all this up," she says.

Jezzie frowns again. "I warned you it wasn't very scientific."

And then the throbbing cicada shriek is pierced by the scream Dancy heard back on the road, the cry of the dragon that Jezzie insists isn't a dragon at all. Instinctively, Dancy ducks her head and reaches for her knife; she notices that Jezzie ducks, as well. They both sit staring at the ceiling of the packing crate, tense as barbed wire.

"That was right overhead," Dancy whispers. "Does it do that? Does it follow you back here?"

Jezzie slowly shakes her head. "Never has before."

It didn't follow her, Dancy thinks. *It followed me.*

And then she sees what's in Jezzie's right hand, an old Colt revolver like the one her grandmother kept around to shoot rattlesnakes.

"You know how to use that?" Dancy asks her, as Jezzie thumbs back the hammer. And the sound of the hammer locking into place is so loud that Dancy realizes the bugs in the trees have gone quiet.

"Wouldn't be holding it like this if I didn't."

"Well, how about put it away," Dancy tells her. "I don't like guns."

Again, Jezzie shakes her head, and she keeps her finger on the trigger of the cocked revolver.

"You never did answer my question," she says. "What you doin' out here, if you ain't a runaway and you ain't a hobo?"

The day has grown so still and silent that Dancy thinks she can almost hear the blood flowing through her veins, can almost hear the grubs and earthworms plowing through the soil beneath the crate. She hasn't yet drawn her knife, but her hand's still on the handle, the carved antler cool and smooth against her perspiring palm. She's been meaning to find some leather to wrap around the handle, because sweat and blood make it slippery, but she hasn't gotten around to it.

"I'm goin' someplace," she tells the girl.

"Yeah, and just where might that be, Dancy Flammarion?"

"I don't know yet," Dancy replies. She didn't even have to think about the answer. Unlike most things, it's simple and true.

"I sorta had a feeling you were gonna say something like that."

"I guess I'll know when I get there," Dancy says. "You reckon that thing's still out there? You reckon it's flying around right over our heads?"

"How the hell am *I* supposed to know?" Jezzie asks and frowns.

"Well, you say you know it ain't no dragon, so I thought maybe –"

"Then you thought wrong."

The silence is broken then by the sound of enormous wings, slowly rising and falling, beating at the sky, and both girls hold their breath as the flapping grows farther and farther away, finally fading into the distance.

Softened almost into melody, Dancy thinks, remembering a line from a book her mother once read her about monsters from Mars trying to take over the world. *But God sent germs to stop them.*

... slain by the putrefactive and disease bacteria against which their systems were unprepared; slain as the red weed was being slain; slain, after all man's devices had failed, by the humblest things that God, in his wisdom, has put upon this earth.

And what's the pterosaur, if she's right, but another sort of invader, maybe not from another planet, but from another time, and what's the difference? Something evil that should have died in the Flood, when God – in his wisdom – wiped so much evil off the face of Creation.

"Thanks for the water," Dancy says, and she gets to her feet, finally releasing her hold on the handle of the big Bowie knife.

"You ain't goin' back out there," Jezzie says, still whispering. It's not a question.

"You said it ain't never come out here before. That's cause it's here for me, Jezebel, not for you. It's my dragon to fight, not yours."

"You're really crazy as a damn betsy bug, you *know* that?"

All men are mad in some way or the other, and inasmuch as you deal discreetly with your madmen, so deal with God's madmen...

... so deal with God's madmen...

Dancy's mother read her so many books, before the demons finally came for Julia Flammarion, and so many of the books had monsters in them. She sometimes imagines that her mother knew the seraph was coming, so she was preparing her daughter.

"I ain't lettin' you go out there," Jezzie says again, a little louder than before.

"This is what I do, Jezebel," Dancy replies. "I fight dragons."

Jezebel very slowly eases her thumb off the hammer, decocking the gun.

"It ain't a dragon. It's just an animal."

"Thank you for the water," Dancys says again, shouldering her duffel bag.

"If you'll just wait a few hours, it goes away at night. You could wait here with me, and I could read to you, or I could tell you about the big ol' alligator snapper I found last summer down at Chatham Bend. Or I could tell you more about the chalk seas. I've hardly told you anything about the animals. Did you know, they found a dinosaur up at Selma, back in the 1940s? An actual dinosaur. It was a new kind of duck bill. Then they found another one, related to *Tyrannosaurus,* at –"

"I've already stayed too long," Dancy says, interrupting her. "You never should have brought me here. All that's done is put you in danger."

"Jesus," Jezzie whispers, staring at the gun in her hands. "You really goin' out there, ain't you?"

"Don't you blaspheme," Dancy says. "Bad enough you believe all this evolution claptrap, without you gotta also take the Lord's name in vain.

But, truth be told, all Dancy wants to do is sit in the packing crate with this strange, Godless girl, sipping warm water that tastes like a plastic jug and maybe eating some of those graham crackers and pork and beans. She can't even remember the last time she had a graham cracker. She remembers how they taste smeared with muscadine and blackberry preserves, and her mouth fills with saliva.

"Then here," says Jezzie, "you take this," and she offers Dancy the water jug. Dancy doesn't turn it down. She almost asks for some of the crackers, too, but that would be rude, asking more when you've just been given such a gift.

"You won't need it?" she asks.

"Nah, it ain't that far back home. And here," says Jezzie, "you take this, too. You need it more'n me." And she holds the revolver out to Dancy. The barrel and the cylinder glint faintly in the dim light inside the packing crate.

"How old is that thing anyway?" Dancy asks. "Looks like it could'a been used in the Civil War, it looks so old. Gun that old, it's liable to blow up in your hands."

Jezzie shrugs. "I don't know," she says. "It was my uncle's. But I don't know how old it is. But here, you take it. It's loaded. Six shots, but I ain't got no extra bullets."

"I don't like guns," Dancy says again. "You keep it. I got my knife."

And ain't that how you slay dragons, with sharp blades? Ain't my knife as good as any sword ever was?

"Dancy, if you'll just wait until nightfall –"

"Thank you for the water," Dancy says for the third time. "That's what I most need, it's so hot today."

"What you most *need* is some goddamn common sense."

Dancy almost tells her, again, not to take the Lord's name in vain, but what's the point. Ain't no saving this girl, seduced as she is by atheists and evolutionists.

Just be wasting my breath, that's all.

"It was nice meeting you, Jezebel Lilligraven," Dancy says, even if she's not quite sure that's true.

"Just be careful," Jezzie says.

And then Dancy steps out into the sunlight, hardly any less bright or scorching than when she stepped inside the crate, at least an hour before. She looks up at the indifferent sky above the clearing, half expecting to see the dragon, but there's only the white eye of Heaven gazing back down at her. *It can't be later than three o'clock,* she thinks. *Still hours and hours left until dusk.*

The cicadas are singing again.

When she reaches the edge of the clearing, she looks back just once, and there's the girl's face peering out through a part in the calico curtain. She looks frightened; she waves at Dancy, and Dancy waves back.

I'm never gonna see you again, and I kinda wish that wasn't true.

She walks back into the short stretch of forest dividing the clearing from the road. The going seems a little more difficult than when Jezzie was dragging her along, pell-mell, and once she gets turned around in a kudzu patch, has to retrace her steps, and find a clearer path. She's drenched in sweat by the time she reaches the gravel shoulder of the highway, and she opens the jug and takes a long swallow. Then she looks again at the blue, blue sky, all the morning's thunderheads come and gone. There's no sign of the dragon, so maybe the girl in the crate was right, and maybe it's flown away back through a hole in time to a world of serpent haunted seas, before Adam and Eve were driven out and cherubim with flaming swords were placed at the gates of Eden that no man or woman would ever again get in. Maybe that's how it is.

And maybe that girl named after a whore and an idolater is right about all of it, and maybe you don't know nothin' about how things really are.

Dancy pushes the thought away, because self doubt's as dangerous as books that say people evolved from monkeys and slime. Self doubt's a distraction that can get her killed. She spares one more glance at the summer sky, and then she starts walking again, following the white center line, which will just have to do as a road map until the angel decides to speak to her again.

CALVED

Sam J. Miller

SAM J. MILLER (WWW.SAMJMILLER.COM) is a writer and a community organizer. His fiction has appeared in *Lightspeed, Asimov's, Clarkesworld*, and *The Minnesota Review*, among others. He work has been nominated for the Nebula and Theodore Sturgeon Awards, and has won the Shirley Jackson Award. He is a graduate of the Clarion Writer's Workshop and lives in New York City. His debut novel *The Art of Starving* is forthcoming from HarperCollins. His story "Ghosts of Home" appears elsewhere in this book.

MY SON'S EYES were broken. Emptied out. Frozen over. None of the joy or gladness were there. None of the tears. Normally I'd return from a job and his face would split down the middle with happiness, seeing me for the first time in three months. Now it stayed flat as ice. His eyes leapt away the instant they met mine. His shoulders were broader and his arms more sturdy, and lone hairs now stood on his upper lip, but his eyes were all I saw.

"Thede," I said, grabbing him.

He let himself be hugged. His arms hung limply at his sides. My lungs could not fill. My chest tightened from the force of all the never-let-me-go bear hugs he had given me over the course of the past fifteen years, and would never give again.

"You know how he gets when you're away," his mother had said, on the phone, the night before, preparing me. "He's a teenager now. Hating your parents is a normal part of it."

I hadn't listened, then. My hands and thighs still ached from months of straddling an ice saw; my hearing was worse with every trip; a slip had cost me five days work and five days pay and five days' worth of infirmary bills; I had returned to a sweat-smelling bunk in an illegal room I shared with seven other iceboat workers – and none of it mattered because in the morning I would see my son.

"Hey," he murmured emotionlessly. "Dad."

I stepped back, turned away until the red ebbed out of my face. Spring had come and the city had lowered its photoshade. It felt good, even in the cold wind.

"You guys have fun," Lajla said, pressing money discretely into my palm. I watched her go with a rising sense of panic. *Bring back my son*, I wanted to shout, *the one who loves me. Where is he. What have you done with him. Who is this surly creature.* Below us, through the ubiquitous steel grid that held up Qaanaaq's two million lives, black Greenland water sloshed against the locks of our floating city.

Breathe, Dom, I told myself, and eventually I could. *You knew this was coming. You knew one day he would cease to be a kid.*

"How's school?" I asked.

Thede shrugged. "Fine."

"Math still your favorite subject?"

"Math was never my favorite subject."

I was pretty sure that it had been, but I didn't want to argue.

"What's your favorite subject?"

Another shrug. We had met at the sea lion rookery, but I could see at once that Thede no longer cared about sea lions. He stalked through the crowd with me, his face a frozen mask of anger.

I couldn't blame him for how easy he had it. So what if he didn't live in the Brooklyn foster-care barracks, or work all day at the solar-cell plant school? He still had to live in a city that hated him for his dark skin and ice-grunt father.

"Your mom says you got into the Institute," I said, unsure even of what that was. A management school, I imagined. A big deal for Thede. But he only nodded.

At the fry stand, Thede grimaced at my clunky Swedish. The counter girl shifted to a flawless English, but I would not be cheated of the little bit of the language that I knew. "French fries and coffee for me and my son," I said, or thought I did, because she looked confused and then Thede muttered something and she nodded and went away.

And then I knew why it hurt so much, the look on his face. It wasn't that he wasn't a kid anymore. I could handle him growing up. What hurt was how he looked at me: like the rest of them look at me, these Swedes and grid city natives for whom I would forever be a stupid New York refugee, even if I did get out five years before the Fall.

Gulls fought over food thrown to the lions. "How's your mom?"

"She's good. Full manager now. We're moving to Arm Three, next year."

His mother and I hadn't been meant to be. She was born here, her parents Black Canadians employed by one of the big Swedish construction firms that built Qaanaaq back when the Greenland Melt began to open up the interior for resource extraction and grid cities starting sprouting all along the coast. They'd kept her in public school, saying it would be good for a future manager to be able to relate to the immigrants and workers she'd one day command, and they were right. She even fell for one of them, a fresh-off-the-boat North American taking tech classes, but wised up pretty soon after she saw how hard it was to raise a kid on an ice worker's pay. I had never been mad at her. Lajla was right to leave me, right to focus on her job. Right to build the life for Thede I couldn't.

"Why don't you learn Swedish?" he asked a French fry, unable to look at me.

"I'm trying," I said. "I need to take a class. But they cost money, and anyway I don't have –"

"Don't have time. I know. Han's father says people make time for the things that are important for them." Here his eyes *did* meet mine, and held, sparkling with anger and abandonment.

"Han one of your friends?"

Thede nodded, eyes escaping.

Han's father would be Chinese, and not one of the laborers who helped build this city – all of them went home to hardship-job rewards. He'd be an engineer or manager for one of the extraction firms. He would live in a nice house and work in an office. He would be able to make choices about how he spent his time.

"I have something for you," I said, in desperation.

I hadn't brought it for him. I carried it around with me, always. Because it was comforting to have it with me, and because I couldn't trust that the men I bunked with wouldn't steal it.

Heart slipping, I handed over the NEW YORK F CKING CITY T-shirt that was my most – my only – prized possession. Thin as paper, soft as baby bunnies. My mom had made me scratch the letter U off it before I could wear the thing to school. And Little Thede had loved it. We made a big ceremony of putting it on only once a year, on his birthday, and noting how much he had grown by how much it had shrunk on him. Sometimes if I stuck my nose in it and breathed deeply enough, I could still find a trace of the laundromat in the basement of my mother's building. Or the brake-screech stink of the subway. What little was left of New York City was inside that shirt. Parting with it meant something, something huge and irrevocable.

But my son was slipping through my fingers. And he mattered more than the lost city where whatever else I was – starving, broke, an urchin, a criminal – I belonged.

"Dad," Thede whispered, taking it. And here, at last, his eyes came back. The eyes of a boy who loved his father. Who didn't care that his father was a thick-skulled obstinate immigrant grunt. Who believed his father could do anything. "Dad. You love this shirt."

But I love you more, I did not say. *Than anything*. Instead, "It'll fit you just fine now." And then: "Enough sea lions. Beam fights?"

Thede shrugged. I wondered if they had fallen out of fashion while I was away. So much did, every time I left. The ice ships were the only work I could get, capturing calved glacier chunks and breaking them down into drinking water to be sold to the wide new swaths of desert that ringed the globe, and the work was hard and dangerous and kept me forever in limbo.

Only two fighters in the first fight, both lithe and swift and thin, their styles an amalgam of Chinese martial arts. Not like the big bruising New York boxers who had been the rage when I arrived, illegally, at fifteen years old, having paid two drunks to vouch for my age. Back before the Fail-Proof Trillion Dollar NYC Flood-Surge Locks had failed, and 80% of the city sunk, and the grid cities banned all new East Coast arrivals. Now the North Americans in Arm Eight were just one of many overcrowded, underskilled labor forces for the city's corporations to exploit.

They leapt from beam to beam, fighting mostly in kicks, grappling briefly when both met on the same beam. I watched Thede. Thin, fragile Thede, with the wide eyes and nostrils that seemed to take in all the world's ugliness, all its stink. He wasn't having a good time. When he was twelve he had begged me to bring him. I had pretended to like it, back then for his sake. Now he pretended for mine. We were both acting out what we thought the other wanted, and that thought should have troubled me. But that's how it had been with my dad. That's what I thought being a man meant. I put my hand on his shoulder and he did not shake it off. We watched men harm each other high above us.

THEDE'S EYES BURNED with wonder, staring up at the fretted sweep of the windscreen as we rose to meet it. We were deep in a days-long twilight; soon, the sun would set for weeks.

"This is *not* happening," he said, and stepped closer to me. His voice shook with joy.

The elevator ride to the top of the city was obscenely expensive. We'd never been able to take it before. His mother had bought our tickets. Even for her, it hurt. I wondered why she hadn't taken him herself.

"He's getting bullied a lot in school," she told me, on the phone. Behind her was the solid comfortable silence of a respectable home. My background noise was four men building towards a fight over a card game. "Also, I think he might be in love."

But of course I couldn't ask him about either of those things. The first was my fault; the second was something no boy wanted to discuss with his dad.

I pushed a piece of trough meat loose from between my teeth. Savored how close it came to the real thing. Only with Thede, with his mother's money, did I get to buy the classy stuff. Normally it was barrel-bottom for me, greasy chunks that dissolved in my mouth two chews in, homebrew meat moonshine made in melt-scrap-furnace-heated metal troughs. Some grid cities were rumored to still have cows, but that was the kind of lie people tell themselves to make life a little less ugly. Cows were extinct, and real beef was a joy no one would ever experience again.

The windscreen was an engineering marvel, and absolutely gorgeous. It shifted in response to headwinds; in severe storms the city would raise its auxiliary windscreens to protect its entire circumference. The tiny panes of plastiglass were common enough – a thriving underground market sold the fallen ones as good luck charms – but to see them knitted together was to tremble in the face of staggering genius. Complex patterns of crenelated reliefs, efficiently diverting windshear no matter what angle it struck from. Bots swept past us on the metal gridlines, replacing panes that had fallen or cracked.

Once, hand gripping mine tightly, somewhere down in the city beneath me, six-year-old Thede had asked me how the windscreen worked. He asked me a lot of things then, about the locks that held the city up, and how they could rise in response to tides and ocean-level increases; about the big boats with strange words and symbols on the side, and where they went, and what they brought back. "What's in that boat?" he'd ask, about each one, and I would make up ridiculous stories. "That's a giraffe boat. That one brings back machine guns that shoot strawberries. That one is for naughty children." In truth I only ever recognized ice boats, by the multitude of pincers atop cranes all along the side.

My son stood up straighter, sixty stories above his city. Some rough weight had fallen from his shoulders. He'd be strong, I saw. He'd be handsome. If he made it. If this horrible city didn't break him inside in some irreparable way. If marauding whiteboys didn't bash him for his dark skin. If the firms didn't pass him over for the lack of family connections on his stuttering immigrant father's side. I wondered who was bullying him, and why, and I imagined taking them two at a time and slamming their heads together so hard they popped like bubbles full of blood. Of course I couldn't do that. I also imagined hugging him, grabbing him for no reason and maybe never letting go, but I couldn't do that either. He would wonder why.

"I called last night and you weren't in," I said. "Doing anything fun?"

"We went to the cityoke arcade," he said.

I nodded like I knew what that meant. Later on I'd have to ask the men in my room. I couldn't keep up with this city, with its endlessly-shifting fashions and slang and the new immigrant clusters that cropped up each time I blinked. Twenty years after arriving, I was still a stranger. I wasn't just Fresh Off the Boat, I was constantly getting back on the boat and then getting off again. That morning I'd gone to the job center for the fifth day in a row, and been relieved to find no boat postings. Only 12-month gigs, and I wasn't that hungry yet. Booking a year-long job meant admitting you were old, desperate, unmoored, willing to accept payment only marginally more than nothing, for the privilege of a hammock and three bowls of trough slop a day. But captains picked their own crews for the shorter runs, and I worried that the lack of postings meant that with fewer boats going out the competition had become too fierce for me. Every day a couple hundred new workers arrived from sunken cities in India or Middle Europe, or from any of a hundred Water-War-torn nations. Men and women stronger than me, more determined.

With effort, I brought my mind back to the here and now. Twenty other people stood in the arc pod with us. Happy, wealthy people. I wondered if they knew I wasn't one of them. I wondered if Thede was.

They smiled down at their city. They thought it was so stable. I'd watched ice sheets calf off the glacier that were five times the size of Qaanaaq. When one of those came drifting in our direction, the windscreen wouldn't help us. The question was when, not if. I knew a truth they did not: how easy it is to lose something – everything – forever.

A Maoist Nepalese foreman, on one of my first ice ship runs, said white North Americans were the worst for adapting to the post-Arctic world, because we'd lived for centuries in a bubble of believing the world was way better than it actually was. Shielded by willful blindness and complex interlocking institutions of privilege, we mistook our uniqueness for universality.

I'd hated him for it. It took me fifteen years to see that he was right.

"What do you think of those two?" I asked, pointing with my chin at a pair of girls his age.

For a while he didn't answer. Then he said, "I know you can't help that you grew up in a backwards macho culture, but can't you just keep that on the inside?"

My own father would have cuffed me if I talked to him like that, but I was too afraid of rupturing the tiny bit of affectionate credit I'd fought so hard to earn back.

His stance softened, then. He took a tiny step closer – the only apology I could hope for.

The pod began its descent. Halfway down he unzipped his jacket, smiling in the warmth of the heated pod while below-zero winds buffeted us. His T-shirt said *The Last Calf*, and showed the gangly sad-eyed hero of that depressing miserable movie all the kids adored.

"Where is it?" I asked. He'd proudly sported the NEW YORK F CKING CITY shirt on each of the five times I'd seen him since giving it to him.

His face darkened so fast I was frightened. His eyes welled up. He said, "Dad, I," but his voice had the tremor that meant he could barely keep from crying. Shame was what I saw.

I couldn't breathe, again, just like when I came home two weeks ago and he wasn't happy to see me. Except seeing my son so unhappy hurt worse than fearing he hated me.

"Did somebody take it from you?" I asked, leaning in so no one else could hear me. "Someone at school? A bully?"

He looked up, startled. He shook his head. Then, he nodded.

"Tell me who did this?"

He shook his head again. "Just some guys, dad," he said. "Please. I don't want to talk about it."

"Guys. How many?"

He said nothing. I understood about snitching. I knew he'd never tell me who.

"It doesn't matter," I said. "Okay? It's just a shirt. I don't care about it. I care about you. I care that you're okay. Are you okay?"

Thede nodded. And smiled. And I knew he was telling the truth, even if I wasn't, even if inside I was grieving the shirt, and the little boy who I once wrapped up inside it.

When I wasn't with Thede, I walked. For two weeks I'd gone out walking every day. Up and down Arm Eight, and sometimes into other Arms. Through shantytowns large and small, huddled miserable agglomerations of recent arrivals and folks who even after a couple generations in Qaanaaq had not been able to scrape their way up from the fish-stinking ice-slippery bottom.

I looked for sex, sometimes. It had been so long. Relationships were tough in my line of work, and I'd never been interested in paying for it. Throughout my twenties I could usually find a woman for something brief and fun and free of commitment, but that stage of my life seemed to have ended.

I wondered why I hadn't tried harder, to make it work with Lajla. I think a small but vocal and terrible part of me had been glad to see her leave.

Fatherhood was hard work. So was being married. Paying rent on a tiny shitty apartment way out on Arm Seven, where we smelled like scorched cooking oil and diaper lotion all the time. Selfishly, I had been glad to be alone. And only now, getting to know this stranger who was once my son, did I see what sweet and fitting punishments the universe had up its sleeve for selfishness.

My time with Thede was wonderful, and horrible. We could talk at length about movies and music, and he actually seemed halfway interested in my stories about old New York, but whenever I tried to talk about life or school or girls or his future he reverted to grunts and monosyllables. Something huge and heavy stood between me and him, a moon eclipsing the sun of me. I knew him, top to bottom and body and soul, but he still had no idea who I really was. How I felt about him. I had no way to show him. No way to open his eyes, make him see how much I loved him, and how I was really a good guy who'd gotten a bad deal in life.

Cityoke, it turned out, was like karaoke, except instead of singing a song you visited a city. XHD footage projection onto all four walls; temperature control; short storylines that responded to your verbal decisions – even actual smells uncorked by machines from secret stashes of Beijing taxi-seat leather or Ho Chi Minh City incense or Portland coffeeshop sawdust. I went there often, hoping maybe to see him. To watch him, with his friends. See what he was when I wasn't around. But cityoke was expensive, and I could never have afforded to actually go in. Once, standing around outside the New York booth when a crew walked out, I caught a whiff of the acrid ugly beautiful stink of the Port Authority Bus Terminal.

And then, eventually, I walked without any reason at all. Because pretty soon I wouldn't be able to. Because I had done it. I had booked a twelve-month job. I was out of money and couldn't afford to rent my bed for another month. Thede's mom could have given it to me. But what if she told him about it? He'd think of me as more of a useless moocher deadbeat dad than he already did. I couldn't take that chance.

Three days before my ship was set to load up and launch, I went back to the cityoke arcades. Men lurked in doorways and between shacks. Soakers, mostly. Looking for marks; men to mug and drunks to tip into the sea. Late at night; too late for Thede to come carousing through. I'd called him earlier, but Lajla said he was stuck inside for the night, studying for a test in a class where he wasn't doing well. I had hoped maybe he'd sneak out, meet some friends, head for the arcade.

And that's when I saw it. The shirt: NEW YORK F CKING CITY, absolutely unique and unmistakable. Worn by a stranger, a muscular young man sitting on the stoop of a skiff moor. I didn't get a good glimpse of his face, as I hurried past with my head turned away from him.

I waited, two buildings down. My heart was alive and racing in my chest. I drew in deep gulps of cold air and tried to keep from shouting from joy. Here was my chance. Here was how I could show Thede what I really was.

I stuck my head out, risked a glance. He sat there, waiting for who knows what. In profile I could see that the man was Asian. Almost certainly Chinese, in Qaanaaq – most other Asian nations had their own grid cities -- although perhaps he was descended from Asian-diaspora nationals of some other country. I could see his smile, hungry and cold.

At first I planned to confront him, ask how he came to be wearing my shirt, demand justice, beat him up and take it back. But that would be stupid. Unless I planned to kill him – and I didn't – it was too easy to imagine him gunning for Thede if he knew he'd been attacked for the shirt. I'd have to jump him, rob and strip and soak him. I rooted through a trash bin, but found nothing. Three trash bins later I found a short metal pipe with Hindi graffiti scribbled along its length. The man was still there when I went back. He was waiting for something. I could wait longer. I pulled my hood up, yanked the drawstring to tighten it around my face.

Forty-five minutes passed that way. He hugged his knees to his chest, made himself small, tried to conserve body heat. His teeth chattered. Why was he wearing so little? But I was happy he was so stupid. Had he had a sweater or jacket on I'd never have seen the shirt. I'd never have had this chance.

Finally, he stood. Looked around sadly. Brushed off the seat of his pants. Turned to go. Stepped into the swing of my metal pipe, which struck him in the chest and knocked him back a step.

The shame came later. Then, there was just joy. The satisfaction of how the pipe struck flesh. Broke bone. I'd spent twenty years getting shitted on by this city, by this system, by the cold wind and the everywhere-ice, by the other workers who were smarter or stronger or spoke the language. For the first time since Thede was a baby, I felt like I was in control of something. Only when my victim finally passed out, and rolled over onto his back and the blue methane streetlamp showed me how young he was under the blood, could I stop myself.

I took the shirt. I took his pants. I rolled him into the water. I called the medteam for him from a coinphone a block away. He was still breathing. He was young, he was healthy. He'd be fine. The pants I would burn in a scrap furnace. The shirt I would give back to my son. I took the money from his wallet and dropped it into the sea, then threw the money in later. I wasn't a thief. I was a good father. I said those sentences over and over, all the way home.

THEDE COULDN'T SEE me the next day. Lajla didn't know where he was. So I got to spend the whole day imagining imminent arrest, the arrival of Swedish or Chinese police, footage of me on the telescrolls, my cleverness foiled by tech I didn't know existed because I couldn't read the newspapers. I packed my one bag glumly, put the rest of my things back in the storage cube and walked it to the facility. Every five seconds I looked over my shoulder and found only the same grit and filthy slush. Every time I looked at my watch, I winced at how little time I had left.

My fear of punishment was balanced out by how happy I was. I wrapped the shirt in three layers of wrapping paper and put it in a watertight shipping bag and tried to imagine his face. That shirt would change everything. His father would cease to be a savage jerk from an uncivilized land. This city would no longer be a cold and barren place where boys could beat him up and steal what mattered most to him with impunity. All the ways I had failed him would matter a little less.

Twelve months. I had tried to get out of the gig, now that I had the shirt and a new era of good relations with my son was upon me. But canceling would have cost me my accreditation with that work center, which would make finding another job almost impossible. A year away from Thede. I would tell him when I saw him. He'd be upset, but the shirt would make it easier.

Finally, I called and he answered.

"I want to see you," I said, when we had made our way through the pleasantries.

"Sunday?" Did his voice brighten, or was that just blind stupid hope? Some trick of the noisy synthcoffee shop where I sat?

"No, Thede," I said, measuring my words carefully. "I can't. Can you do today?"

A suspicious pause. "Why can't you do Sunday?"

"Something's come up," I said. "Please? Today?"

"Fine."

The sea lion rookery. The smell of guano and the screak of gulls; the crying of children dragged away as the place shut down. The long night was almost upon us. Two male sea lions barked at each other, bouncing their chests together. Thede came a half hour late, and I had arrived a half hour early. Watching him come my head swam, at how tall he stood and how gracefully he walked. I had done something good in this world, at least. I made him. I had that, no matter how he felt about me.

Something had shifted, now, in his face. Something was harder, older, stronger.

"Hey," I said, bear-hugging him, and eventually he submitted. He hugged me back hesitantly, like a man might, and then hard, like a little boy.

"What's happening?" I asked. "What were you up to, last night?"

Thede shrugged. "Stuff. With friends."

I asked him questions. Again the sullen, bitter silence; again the terse and angry answers. Again the eyes darting around, constantly watching for whatever the next attack would be. Again the hating me, for coming here, for making him.

"I'm going away," I said. "A job."

"I figured," he said.

"I wish I didn't have to."

"I'll see you soon."

I nodded. I couldn't tell him it was a twelve-month gig. Not now.

"Here," I said, finally, pulling the package out from inside of my jacket. "I got you something."

"Thanks." He grabbed it in both hands, began to tear it open.

"Wait," I said, thinking fast. "Okay? Open it after I leave."

Open it when the news that I'm leaving has set in, when you're mad at me, for abandoning you. When you think I care only about my job.

"We'll have a little time," he said. "When you get back. Before I go away. I leave in eight months. The program is four years long."

"Sure," I said, shivering inside.

"Mom says she'll pay for me to come home every year for the holiday, but she knows we can't afford that."

"What do you mean?" I asked. "'Come home.' I thought you were going to the Institute."

"I am," he said, sighing. "Do you even know what that means? The Institute's design program is in Shanghai."

"Oh," I said. "Design. What kind of design?"

My son's eyes rolled. "You're missing the point, dad."

I was. I always was.

A shout, from a pub across the Arm. A man's shout, full of pain and anger. Thede flinched. His hands made fists.

"What?" I asked, thinking, here, at last, was something

"Nothing."

"You can tell me. What's going on?"

Thede frowned, then punched the metal railing so hard he yelped. He held up his hand to show me the blood.

"Hey, Thede –"

"Han," he said. "My... my friend. He got jumped two nights ago. Soaked."

"This city is horrible," I whispered.

He made a baffled face. "What do you mean?"

"I mean... you know. This city. Everyone's so full of anger and cruelty..."

"It's not the city, dad. What does that even mean? Some sick person did this. Han was waiting for me, and mom wouldn't let me out, and he got jumped. They took off all his clothes, before they rolled him into the water. That's some extra cruel shit right there. He could have died. He almost did."

I nodded, silently, a siren of panic rising inside. "You really care about this guy, don't you?"

He looked at me. My son's eyes were whole, intact, defiant, adult. Thede nodded.

He's been getting bullied, his mother had told me. *He's in love.*

I turned away from him, before he could see the knowledge blossom in my eyes.

The shirt hadn't been stolen. He'd given it away. To the boy he loved. I saw them holding hands, saw them tug at each other's clothing in the same fumbling adolescent puppy-love moments I had shared with his mother, moments that were my only happy memories from being his age. And I saw his fear, of how his backwards father might react – a refugee from a fallen hate-filled people – if he knew what kind of man he was. I gagged on the unfairness of his assumptions about me, but how could he have known differently? What had I ever done, to show him the truth of how I felt about him? And hadn't I proved him right? Hadn't I acted exactly like the monster he believed me to be? I had never succeeded in proving to him what I was, or how I felt.

I had battered and broken his beloved. There was nothing I could say. A smarter man would have asked for the present back, taken it away and locked it up. Burned it, maybe. But I couldn't. I had spent his whole life trying to give him something worthy of how I felt about him, and here was the perfect gift at last.

"I love you, Thede," I said, and hugged him.

"Daaaaad..." he said, eventually.

But I didn't let go. Because when I did, he would leave. He would walk home through the cramped and frigid alleys of his home city, to the gift of knowing what his father truly was.

THE HEART'S FILTHY LESSON

Elizabeth Bear

ELIZABETH BEAR (MATOCIQUALA.LIVEJOURNAL.COM) was born on the same day as Frodo and Bilbo Baggins, but in a different year. When coupled with a childhood tendency to read the dictionary for fun, this led her inevitably to penury, intransigence, and the writing of speculative fiction. She is the Hugo, Sturgeon, Locus, and Campbell Award winning author of 26 novels and over a hundred short stories. Her dog lives in Massachusetts; her partner, writer Scott Lynch, lives in Wisconsin. She spends a lot of time on planes. Her most recent book is science fiction novel *Karen Memory.*

THE SUN BURNED through the clouds around noon on the long Cytherean day, and Dharthi happened to be awake and in a position to see it. She was alone in the highlands of Ishtar Terra on a research trip, five sleeps out from Butler base camp, and – despite the nagging desire to keep traveling – had decided to take a rest break for an hour or two. Noon at this latitude was close enough to the one hundredth solar dieiversary of her birth that she'd broken out her little hoard of shelf-stable cake to celebrate. The prehensile fingers and leaping legs of her bioreactor-printed, skin-bonded adaptshell made it simple enough to swarm up one of the tall, gracile pseudo-figs and creep along its gray smooth branches until the ceaseless Venusian rain dripped directly on her adaptshell's slick-furred head.

It was safer in the treetops, if you were sitting still. Nothing big enough to want to eat her was likely to climb up this far. The grues didn't come out until nightfall, but there were swamp-tigers, damnthings, and velociraptors to worry about. The forest was too thick for predators any bigger than that, but a swarm of scorpion-rats was no joke. And Venus had only been settled for three hundred days, and most of that devoted to Aphrodite Terra; there was still plenty of undiscovered monsters out here in the wilderness.

The water did not bother Dharthi, nor did the dip and sway of the branch in the wind. Her adaptshell was beautifully tailored to this terrain, and that fur shed water like the hydrophobic miracle of engineering that it was. The fur was a glossy, iridescent purple that qualified as black in most lights, to match the foliage that dripped rain like strings of glass beads from the multiple points of palmate leaves. Red-black, to make the most of the rainy grey light. They'd fold their leaves up tight and go dormant when night came.

Dharthi had been born with a chromosomal abnormality that produced red-green colorblindness. She'd been about ten solar days old when they'd done the gene therapy to fix it, and she just about remembered her first glimpses of the true, saturated colors of Venus. She'd seen it first as if it were Earth: washed out and faded.

For now, however, they were alive with the scurryings and chitterings of a few hundred different species of Cytherean canopy-dwellers. And the quiet, nearly-contented sound of Dharthi munching on cake. She would not dwell; she would not stew. She would look at all this natural majesty, and try to spot the places where an unnaturally geometric line or angle showed in the topography of the canopy.

From here, she could stare up the enormous sweep of Maxwell Montes to the north, its heights forested to the top in Venus' deep, rich atmosphere – but the sight of them lost for most of its reach in clouds. Dharthi could only glimpse the escarpment at all because she was on the 'dry' side. Maxwell Montes scraped the heavens, kicking the cloud layer up as if it had struck an aileron, so the 'wet' side got the balance of the rain. *Balance* in this case meaning that the mountains on the windward side were scoured down to granite, and a nonadapted terrestrial organism had better bring breathing gear.

But here in the lee, the forest flourished, and on a clear hour from a height, visibility might reach a couple of klicks or more.

Dharthi took another bite of cake – it might have been 'chocolate'; it was definitely caffeinated, because she was picking up the hit on her blood monitors already – and turned herself around on her branch to face downslope. The sky was definitely brighter, the rain falling back to a drizzle and then a mist, and the clouds were peeling back along an arrowhead trail that led directly back to the peak above her. A watery golden smudge brightened one patch of clouds. They tore and she glimpsed the full unguarded brilliance of the daystar, just hanging there in a chip of glossy cerulean sky, the clouds all around it smeared with thick unbelievable rainbows. Waves of mist rolled and slid among the leaves of the canopy, made golden by the shimmering unreal light.

Dharthi was glad she was wearing the shell. It played the sun's warmth through to her skin without also relaying the risks of ultraviolet exposure. She ought to be careful of her eyes, however: a crystalline shield protected them, but its filters weren't designed for naked light.

The forest noises rose to a cacophony. It was the third time in Dharthi's one hundred solar days of life that she had glimpsed the sun. Even here, she imagined that some of these animals would never have seen it before.

She decided to accept it as a good omen for her journey. Sadly, there was no way to spin the next thing that happened that way.

"Hey," said a voice in her head. "Good cake."

"That proves your pan is malfunctioning, if anything does," Dharthi replied sourly. *Never accept a remote synaptic link with a romantic and professional partner. No matter how convenient it seems at the time, and in the field.*

Because someday they might be a romantic and professional partner you really would rather not talk to right now.

"I heard that."

"What do you want, Kraken?"

Dharthi imagined Kraken smiling, and wished she hadn't. She could hear it in her partner's 'voice' when she spoke again, anyway. "Just to wish you a happy dieiversary."

"Aw," Dharthi said. "Aren't you sweet. Noblesse oblige?"

"Maybe," Kraken said tiredly, "I actually care?"

"Mmm," Dharthi said. "What's the ulterior motive this time?"

Kraken sighed. It was more a neural flutter than a heave of breath, but Dharthi got the point all right. "Maybe I actually *care*."

"Sure," Dharthi said. "Every so often you have to glance down from Mount Olympus and check up on the lesser beings."

"Olympus is on Mars," Kraken said.

It didn't make Dharthi laugh, because she clenched her right fist hard enough that, even though the cushioning adaptshell squished against her palm, she still squeezed the blood out of her fingers. *You and all your charm. You don't get to charm me any more.*

"Look," Kraken said. "You have something to prove. I understand that."

"How can you *possibly* understand that? When was the last time you were turned down for a resource allocation? Doctor youngest-ever recipient of the Cytherean Award for Excellence in Xenoarcheology? Doctor Founding Field-Martius Chair of Archaeology at the University on Aphrodite?"

"The University on Aphrodite," Kraken said, "is five Quonset huts and a repurposed colonial landing module."

"It's what we've got."

"I peaked early," Kraken said, after a pause. "I was never your *rival*, Dharthi. We were colleagues." Too late, in Dharthi's silence, she realized her mistake. "*Are* colleagues."

"You look up from your work often enough to notice I'm missing?"

There was a pause. "That may be fair," Kraken said at last. "But if being professionally focused –"

"*Obsessed.*"

"– is a failing, it was hardly a failing limited to me. Come *back*. Come back to *me*. We'll talk about it. I'll help you try for a resource voucher again tomorrow."

"I don't want your damned *help*, Kraken!"

The forest around Dharthi fell silent. Shocked, she realized she'd shouted out loud.

"Haring off across Ishtar alone, with no support – you're not going to prove your theory about aboriginal Cytherean settlement patterns, Dhar. You're going to get eaten by a grue."

"I'll be home by dark," Dharthi said. "Anyway, if I'm not – all the better for the grue."

"You know who else was always on about being laughed out of the Academy?" Kraken said. Her voice had that teasing tone that could break Dharthi's worst, most self-loathing, prickliest mood – if she let it. "Moriarty."

I will not laugh. Fuck you.

Dharthi couldn't tell if Kraken had picked it up or not. There was a silence, as if she were controlling her temper or waiting for Dharthi to speak.

"If you get killed," Kraken said, "make a note in your file that I can use your DNA. You're not getting out of giving me children that easily."

Ha ha, Dharthi thought. *Only serious.* She couldn't think of what to say, and so she said nothing. The idea of a little Kraken filled her up with mushy softness inside. But somebody's career would go on hold for the first fifty solar days of that kid's life, and Dharthi was pretty sure it wouldn't be Kraken.

She couldn't think of what to say in response, and the silence got heavy until Kraken said, "Dammit. I'm *worried* about you."

"Worry about yourself." Dharthi couldn't break the connection, but she could bloody well shut down her end of the dialogue. And she could refuse to hear.

She pitched the remains of the cake as far across the canopy as she could, then regretted it. Hopefully nothing Cytherean would try to eat it; it might give the local biology a belly ache.

It was ironically inevitable that Dharthi, named by her parents in a fit of homesickness for Terra, would grow up to be the most Cytherean of Cythereans. She took great pride in her adaptation, in her ability to rough it. Some of the indigenous plants and many of the indigenous animals could be eaten, and Dharthi knew which ones. She also knew, more importantly, which ones were likely to eat her.

She hadn't mastered humans nearly as well. Dharthi wasn't good at politics. *Unlike Kraken.* Dharthi wasn't good at making friends. *Unlike Kraken.* Dharthi wasn't charming or beautiful or popular or brilliant. *Unlike Kraken, Kraken, Kraken.*

Kraken was a better scientist, or at least a better-understood one. Kraken was a better person, probably. More generous, less prickly, certainly. But there was one thing Dharthi *was* good at. Better at than Kraken. Better at than anyone. Dharthi was good at living on Venus, at being Cytherean. She was more comfortable in and proficient with an adaptshell than anyone she had ever met.

In fact, it was peeling the shell off that came hard. So much easier to glide through the jungle or the swamp like something that belonged there, wearing a quasibiologic suit of super-powered armor bonded to your neural network and your skin. The human inside was a soft, fragile, fleshy thing, subject to complicated feelings and social dynamics, and Dharthi despised her. But that same human, while bonded to the shell, ghosted through the rain forest like a native, and saw things no one else ever had.

A kilometer from where she had stopped for cake, she picked up the trail of a velociraptor. It was going in the right direction, so she tracked it. It wasn't a real velociraptor; it wasn't even a dinosaur. Those were Terran creatures, albeit extinct; this was a Cytherean meat-eating monster that bore a superficial resemblance. Like the majority of Cytherean vertebrates, it had six limbs, though it ran balanced on the rear ones and the two forward pairs had evolved into little more than graspers. Four eyes were spaced equidistantly around the dome of its skull, giving it a dome of monocular vision punctuated by narrow slices of depth perception. The business end of the thing was delineated by a sawtoothed maw that split wide enough to bite a human being in half. The whole of it was camouflaged with long draggled fur-feathers that grew thick with near-black algae, or the Cytherean cognate.

Dharthi followed the velociraptor for over two kilometers, and the beast never even noticed she was there. She smiled inside her adaptshell. Kraken was right: going out into the jungle alone and unsupported would be suicide for most people. But wasn't it like her not to give Dharthi credit for this one single thing that Dharthi could do better than anyone?

She *knew* that the main Cytherean settlements had been on Ishtar Terra. Knew it in her bones. And she was going to prove it, whether anybody was willing to give her an allocation for the study or not.

They'll be sorry, she thought, and had to smile at her own adolescent petulance. *They're rush to support me once this is done.*

The not-a-dinosaur finally veered off to the left. Dharthi kept jogging/swinging/swimming/splashing/climbing forward, letting the shell do most of the work. The highlands leveled out into the great plateau the new settlers called the Lakshmi Planum. No one knew what the aboriginals had called it. They'd been gone for – to an approximation – ten thousand years: as long as it had taken humankind to get from the Neolithic (Agriculture, stone tools) to jogging through the jungles of alien world wearing a suit of power armor engineered from printed muscle fiber and cheetah DNA.

Lakshmi Planum, ringed with mountains on four sides, was one of the few places on the surface of Venus where you could not see an ocean. The major Cytherean land masses, Aphrodite and Ishtar, were smaller than South America. The surface of this world was 85% water – water less salty than Earth's oceans, because there was less surface to leach minerals into it through runoff. And the Lakshmi Planum was tectonically active, with great volcanoes and living faults.

That activity was one of the reasons Dharthi's research had brought her here.

The jungle of the central Ishtarean plateau was not as creeper-clogged and vine-throttled as Dharthi might have expected. It was a mature climax forest, and the majority of the biomass hung suspended over Dharthi's head, great limbs stretching up umbrella-like to the limited light. Up there, the branches and trunks were festooned with symbiotes, parasites, and commensal organisms. Down here among the trunks, it was dark and still except for the squish of loam underfoot and the ceaseless patter of what rain came through the leaves.

Dharthi stayed alert, but didn't spot any more large predators on that leg of the journey. There were flickers and scuttlers and flyers galore, species she was sure nobody had named or described. Perhaps on the way back she'd have time to do more, but for now she contented herself with extensive video archives. It wouldn't hurt to cultivate some good karma with Bio while she was out here. She might need a job sweeping up offices when she got back.

Stop. Failure is not an option. Not even a possibility.

Like all such glib sentiments, it didn't make much of a dent in the bleakness of her mood. Even walking, observing, surveying, she had entirely too much time to think.

She waded through two more swamps and scaled a basalt ridge – one of the stretching roots of the vast volcano named Sacajawea. Nearly everything on Venus was named after female persons – historical, literary, or mythological – from Terra, from the quaint old system of binary and exclusive genders. For a moment, Dharthi considered such medieval horrors as dentistry without anesthetic, binary gender, and as being stuck forever in the body you were born in, locked in and struggling against what your genes dictated. The trap of biology appalled her; she found it impossible to comprehend how people in the olden days had gotten anything done, with their painfully short lives and their limited access to resources, education, and technology.

The adaptshell stumbled over a tree root, forcing her attention back to the landscape. Of course, modern technology wasn't exactly perfect either. The suit needed carbohydrate to keep moving, and protein to repair muscle tissue. Fortunately, it wasn't picky about its food source – and Dharthi herself needed rest. The day was long, and only half over. She wouldn't prove herself if she got so tired she got herself eaten by a megaspider.

We haven't conquered all those human frailties yet.

Sleepily, she climbed a big tree, one that broke the canopy, and slung a hammock high in branches that dripped with fleshy, gorgeous, thickly scented parasitic blossoms, opportunistically decking every limb up here where the light was stronger. They shone bright whites and yellows, mostly, set off against the dark, glossy foliage. Dharthi set proximity sensors, established a tech perimeter above and below, and unsealed the shell before sending it down to forage for the sorts of simple biomass that sustained it. It would be happy with the mulch of the forest floor, and she could call it back when she needed it. Dharthi rolled herself into the hammock as if it were a scentproof, claw-proof cocoon and tried to sleep.

Rest eluded. The leaves and the cocoon filtered the sunlight, so it was pleasantly dim, and the cocoon kept the water off except what she'd brought inside with herself when she wrapped up. She was warm and well-supported. But that all did very little to alleviate her anxiety.

She didn't know exactly where she was going. She was flying blind – hah, she *wished* she were flying. If she'd had the allocations for an aerial survey, this would all be a lot easier, assuming they could pick anything out through the jungle – and operating on a hunch. An educated hunch.

But one that Kraken and her other colleagues – and more importantly, the Board of Allocation – thought was at best a wild guess and at worst crackpottery.

What if you're wrong?

If she was wrong... well. She didn't have much to go home to. So she'd better be right that the settlements they'd found on Aphrodite were merely outposts, and that the aboriginal Cythereans had stuck much closer to the North pole. She had realized that the remains – such as they were – of Cytherean settlements clustered in geologically active areas. She theorized that they used geothermal energy, or perhaps had some other unknown purpose for staying there. In any case, Ishtar was far younger, far more geologically active than Aphrodite, as attested by its upthrust granite ranges and its scattering of massive volcanoes. Aphrodite – larger, calmer, safer – had drawn the Terran settlers. Dharthi theorized that Ishtar had been the foundation of Cytherean culture for exactly the opposite reasons.

She hoped that if she found a big settlement – the remains of one of their cities – she could prove this. And possibly even produce some clue as to what had happened to them all.

It wouldn't be easy. A city buried under ten thousand years of sediment and jungle could go unnoticed even by an archaeologist's trained eye and the most perspicacious modern mapping and visualization technology. And of course she had to be in the right place, and all she had to go on there were guesses – deductions, if she was feeling kind to herself, which she rarely was – about the patterns of relationships between those geologically active areas on Aphrodite and the aboriginal settlements nearby.

This is stupid. You'll never find anything without support and an allocation. Kraken never would have pushed her luck this way.

Kraken never would have needed to. Dharthi knew better than anyone how much effort and dedication and scholarship went into Kraken's work – but still, it sometimes seemed as if fantastic opportunities just fell into her lover's lap without effort. And Kraken's intellect and charisma were so dazzling... it was hard to see past that to the amount of study it took to support that seemingly effortless, comprehensive knowledge of just about everything.

Nothing made Dharthi feel the limitations of her own ability like spending time with her lover. Hell, Kraken probably would have known which of the animals she was spotting as she ran were new species, and the names and describers of all the known ones.

If she could have this, Dharthi thought, just this – if she could do one thing to equal all of Kraken's effortless successes – then she could tolerate how perfect Kraken was the rest of the time.

This line of thought wasn't helping the anxiety. She thrashed in the cocoon for another half-hour before she finally gave in and took a sedative. Not safe, out in the jungle. But if she didn't rest, she couldn't run – and even the Cytherean daylight wasn't actually endless.

* * *

DHARTHI AWAKENED TO an animal sniffing her cocoon with great whuffing predatory breaths. An atavistic response, something from the brainstem, froze her in place even as it awakened her. Her arms and legs – naked, so fragile without her skin – felt heavy, numb, limp as if they had fallen asleep. The shadow of the thing's head darkened the translucent steelsilk as it passed between Dharthi and the sky. The drumming of the rain stopped, momentarily. Hard to tell how big it was, from that – but big, she thought. An estimation confirmed when it nosed or pawed the side of the cocoon and she felt a broad blunt object as big as her two hands together prod her in the ribs.

She held her breath, and it withdrew. There was the rain, tapping on her cocoon where it dripped between the leaves. She was almost ready to breathe out again when it made a sound – a thick chugging noise followed by a sort of roar that had more in common with trains and waterfalls than what most people would identify as an animal sound.

Dharthi swallowed her scream. She didn't need Kraken to tell her what *that* was. Every schoolchild could manage a piping reproduction of the call of one of Venus's nastiest pieces of charismatic megafauna, the Cytherean swamp-tiger.

Swamp-tigers were two lies, six taloned legs, and an indiscriminate number of enormous daggerlike teeth in a four hundred kilogram body. Two lies, because they didn't live in swamps – though they passed through them on occasion, because what on Venus didn't? – and they weren't tigers. But they *were* striped violet and jade green to disappear into the thick jungle foliage; they had long, slinky bodies that twisted around sharp turns and barreled up tree trunks without any need to decelerate; and their whisker-ringed mouths hinged open wide enough to bite a grown person in half.

All four of the swamp-tiger's bright blue eyes were directed forward. Because it didn't hurt their hunting, and what creature in its right mind would want to sneak up on a thing like that?

They weren't supposed to hunt this high up. The branches were supposed to be too slender to support them.

Dharthi wasn't looking forward to getting a better look at this one. It nudged the cocoon again. Despite herself, Dharthi went rigid. She pressed both fists against her chest and concentrated on not whimpering, on not making a single sound. She forced herself to breathe slowly and evenly. To consider. *Panic gets you eaten.*

She wouldn't give Kraken the damned satisfaction.

She had some resources. The cocoon would attenuate her scent, and might disguise it almost entirely. The adaptshell was somewhere in the vicinity, munching away, and if she could make it into *that*, she stood a chance of outrunning the thing. She weighed a quarter what the swamp-tiger did; she could get up higher into the treetops than it could. Theoretically; after all, it wasn't supposed to come up this high.

And she was, at least presumptively, somewhat smarter.

But it could outjump her, outrun her, outsneak her, and – perhaps most importantly – outchomp her.

She wasted a few moments worrying about how it had gotten past her perimeter before the sharp pressure of its claws skidding down the rip-proof surface of the cocoon refocused her attention. That was a temporary protection; it might not be able to pierce the cocoon, but it could certainly squash Dharthi to death inside of it, or rip it out of the tree and toss it to the jungle floor. If the fall didn't kill her, she'd have the cheerful and humiliating choice of yelling for rescue or wandering around injured until something bigger ate her. She needed a way out; she needed to channel five million years of successful primate adaptation, the legacy of clever monkey ancestors, and figure out how to get away from the not-exactly-cat.

What would a monkey do? The question was the answer, she realized.

She just needed the courage to apply it. And the luck to survive whatever then transpired.

The cocoon was waterproof as well as claw-proof – hydrophobic on the outside, a wicking polymer on the inside. The whole system was impregnated with an engineered bacteria that broke down the waste products in human sweat – or other fluids – and returned them to the environment as safe, nearly odorless, non-polluting water, salts, and a few trace chemicals. Dharthi was going to have to unfasten the damn thing.

She waited while the swamp-tiger prodded her again. It seemed to have a pattern of investigating and withdrawing – Dharthi heard the rustle and felt the thump and sway as it leaped from branch to branch, circling, making a few horrifically unsettling noises and a bloodcurdling snarl or two, and coming back for another go at the cocoon. The discipline required to hold herself still – not even merely still, but limp – as the creature whuffed and poked left her nauseated with adrenaline. She felt it moving away, then. The swing of branches under its weight did nothing to ease the roiling in her gut.

Now or never.

Shell! Come and get me! Then she palmed the cocoon's seal and whipped it open, left hand and foot shoved through internal grips so she didn't accidentally evert herself into free fall. As she swung, she shook a heavy patter of water drops loose from the folds of the cocoon's hydrophobic surface. They pattered down. There were a lot of branches between her and the ground; she didn't fancy making the intimate acquaintanceship of each and every one of them.

The swamp-tiger hadn't gone as far as she expected. In fact, it was on the branch just under hers. As it whipped its head around and roared, she had an eloquent view from above – a clear shot down its black-violet gullet. The mouth hinged wide enough to bite her in half across the middle; the tongue was thick and fleshy; the palate ribbed and mottled in paler shades of red. *If I live through this, I will be able to draw every one of those seventy-two perfectly white teeth from memory.*

She grabbed the safety handle with her right hand as well, heaved with her hips, and flipped the cocoon over so her legs swung free. For a moment, she dangled just above the swamp-tiger. It reared back on its heavy haunches like a startled cat, long tail lashing around to protect its abdomen. Dharthi knew that as soon as it collected its wits it was going to take a swipe at her, possibly with both sets of forelegs.

It was small for a swamp-tiger – perhaps only two hundred kilos – and its stripes were quite a bit brighter than she would have expected. Even wet, its feathery plumage had the unfinished raggedness she associated with young animals still in their baby coats. It might even have been fuzzy, if it were ever properly dry. Which might explain why it was so high up in the treetops. Previously undocumented behavior in a juvenile animal.

Wouldn't it be an irony if this were the next in a long line of xenobiological discoveries temporarily undiscovered again because a scientist happened to get herself eaten? At least she had a transponder. And maybe the shell was nearby enough to record some of this.

Data might survive.

Great, she thought. *I wonder where its mama is.*

Then she urinated in its face.

It wasn't an aimed stream by any means, though she was wearing the external plumbing currently – easier in the field, until you got a bladder stone. But she had a bladder full of pee saved up during sleep, so there was plenty of it. It splashed down her legs and over the swamp-tiger's face, and Dharthi didn't care what your biology was, if you were carbon-oxygen based, a snout full of ammonia and urea had to be pretty nasty.

The swamp-tiger backed away, cringing. If it had been a human being, Dharthi would have said it was spluttering. She didn't take too much time to watch; good a story as it would make someday, it would always be a better one than otherwise if she survived to tell it. She pumped her legs for momentum, glad that the sweat-wicking properties of the cocoon's lining kept the grip dry, because right now her palms weren't doing any of that work themselves. Kick high, a twist from the core, and she had one leg over the cocoon. It was dry – she'd shaken off what little water it had collected. Dharthi pulled her feet up – standing on the stuff was like standing on a slack sail, and she was glad that some biotuning trained up by the time she spent running the canopy had given her the balance of a perching bird.

Behind and below, she heard the Cytherean monster make a sound like a kettle boiling over – one part whistle, and one part hiss. She imagined claws in her haunches, a crushing bite to the skull or the nape –

The next branch up was a half-meter beyond her reach. Her balance on her toes, she jumped as hard as she could off the yielding surface under her bare feet. Her left hand missed; the right hooked a limb but did not close. She dangled sideways for a moment, the stretch across her shoulder strong and almost pleasant. Her fingers locked in the claw position, she flexed her bicep – not a pull up, she couldn't chin herself one-handed – but just enough to let her left hand latch securely. A parasitic orchid squashed beneath the pads of her fingers. A dying bug wriggled. Caustic sap burned her skin. She swung, and managed to hang on.

She wanted to dangle for a moment, panting and shaking and gathering herself for the next ridiculous effort. But beneath her, the rattle of leaves, the creak of a bough. The not-tiger was coming.

Climb. Climb!

She had to get high. She had to get further out from the trunk, onto branches where it would not pursue her. She had to stay alive until the shell got to her. Then she could run or fight as necessary.

Survival was starting to seem like less of a pipe dream now.

She swung herself up again, risking a glance through her armpit as she mantled herself up onto the bough. It dipped and twisted under her weight. Below, the swamp-tiger paced, snarled, reared back and took a great, outraged swing up at her cocoon with its two left-side forepaws.

The fabric held. The branches it was slung between did not. They cracked and swung down, crashing on the boughs below and missing the swamp-tiger only because the Cytherean cat had reflexes preternaturally adapted to life in the trees. It still came very close to being knocked off its balance, and Dharthi took advantage of its distraction to scramble higher, careful to remember not to wipe her itching palms on the more sensitive flesh of her thighs.

Another logic problem presented itself. The closer she got to the trunk, the higher she could scramble, and the faster the adaptshell could get to her – but the swamp-tiger was less likely to follow her out on the thinner ends of the boughs. She was still moving as she decided that she'd go up a bit more first, and move diagonally – up *and* out, until 'up' was no longer an option.

She made two more branches before hearing the rustle of the swamp-tiger leaping upwards behind her. She'd instinctively made a good choice in climbing away from it rather than descending, she realized – laterally or down, there was no telling how far the thing could leap. Going up, on unsteady branches, it was limited to shorter hops. Shorter... but much longer than Dharthi's. Now the choice was made for her – out, before it caught up, or get eaten. At least the wet of the leaves and the rain were washing the irritant sap from her palms.

She hauled her feet up again and gathered herself to stand and sprint down the center stem of this bough, a perilous highway no wider than her palm. When she raised her eyes, though, she found herself looking straight into the four bright, curious blue eyes of a second swamp-tiger.

"Aw, crud," Dharthi said. "Didn't anyone tell you guys you're supposed to be solitary predators?"

It looked about the same age and size and fluffiness as the other one. Littermates? Littermates of some Terran species hunted together until they reached maturity. That was probably the answer, and there was another groundbreaking bit of Cytherean biology that would go into a swamp-tiger's belly with Dharthi's masticated brains. Maybe she'd have enough time to relay the information to Kraken while they were disemboweling her.

The swamp-tiger lifted its anterior right forefoot and dabbed experimentally at Dharthi. Dharthi drew back her lips and *hissed* at it, and it pulled the leg back and contemplated her, but it didn't put the paw down. The next swipe would be for keeps.

She could call Kraken now, of course. But that would just be a distraction, not help. *Help* had the potential to arrive in time.

The idea of telling Kraken – and *everybody* – how she had gotten out of a confrontation with *two* of Venus's most impressive predators put a new rush of strength in her trembling legs. They were juveniles. They were inexperienced. They lacked confidence in their abilities, and they did not know how to estimate hers.

Wild predators had no interest in fighting anything to the death. They were out for a meal.

Dharthi stood up on her refirming knees, screamed in the swamp-tiger's face, and punched it as hard as she could, right in the nose.

She almost knocked herself out of the damned tree, and only her windmilling left hand snatching at twigs hauled her upright again and saved her. The swamp-tiger had crouched back, face wrinkled up in distaste or discomfort. The other one was coming up behind her.

Dharthi turned on the ball of her foot and sprinted for the end of the bough. Ten meters, fifteen, and it trembled and curved down sharply under her weight. There was still a lot of forest giant left above her, but this bough was arching now until it almost touched the one below. It moved in the wind, and with every breath, it creaked and made fragile little crackling noises.

A few more meters, and it might bend down far enough that she could reach the branch below.

A few more meters, and it might crack and drop.

It probably wouldn't pull free of the tree entirely – fresh Cytherean 'wood' was fibrous and full of sap – but it might dump her off pretty handily.

She took a deep breath – clean air, rain, deep sweetness of flowers, herby scents of crushed leaves – and turned again to face the tigers.

They were still where she had left them, crouched close to the trunk of the tree, tails lashing as they stared balefully after her out of eight gleaming cerulean eyes. Their fanged heads were sunk low between bladelike shoulders. Their lips curled over teeth as big as fingers.

"Nice kitties," Dharthi said ineffectually. "Why don't you two just scamper on home? I bet mama has a nice bit of grue for supper."

The one she had peed on snarled at her. She supposed she couldn't blame it. She edged a little further away on the branch.

A rustling below. *Now that's just ridiculous.*

But it wasn't a third swamp-tiger. She glanced down and glimpsed an anthropoid shape clambering up through the branches fifty meters below, mostly hidden in foliage but moving with a peculiar empty lightness. The shell. Coming for her.

The urge to speed up the process, to try to climb down to it was almost unbearable, but Dharthi made herself sit tight. One of the tigers – the one she'd punched – rose up on six padded legs and slunk forward. It made a half dozen steps before the branch's increasing droop and the cracking, creaking sounds made it freeze. It was close enough now that she could make out the pattern of its damp, feathery whiskers. Dharthi braced her bare feet under tributary limbs and tried not to hunker down; swamp-tigers were supposed to go for crouching prey, and standing up and being big was supposed to discourage them. She spread her arms and rode the sway of the wind, the sway of the limb.

Her adaptshell heaved itself up behind her while the tigers watched. Her arms were already spread wide, her legs braced. The shell just cozied up behind her and squelched over her outstretched limbs, snuggling up and tightening down. It affected her balance, though, and the wobbling of the branch –

She crouched fast and grabbed at a convenient limb. And that was more than tiger number two could bear.

From a standing start, still halfway down the branch, the tiger gathered itself, hindquarters twitching. It leaped, and Dharthi had just enough time to try to throw herself flat under its arc. Enough time to try, but not quite enough time to succeed.

One of the swamp-tiger's second rank of legs caught her right arm like the swing of a baseball bat. Because she had dodged, it was her arm and not her head. The force of the blow still sent Dharthi sliding over the side of the limb, clutching and failing to clutch, falling in her adaptshell. She heard the swamp-tiger land where he had been, heard the bough crack, saw it give and swing down after her. The swamp-tiger squalled, scrabbling, its littermate making abrupt noises of retreat as well – and it was falling beside Dharthi, twisting in midair, clutching a nearby branch and there was a heaving unhappy sound from the tree's structure and then she fell alone, arm numb, head spinning.

The adaptshell saved her. It, too, twisted in midair, righted itself, reached out and grasped with her good arm. This branch held, but it bent, and she slammed into the next branch down, taking the impact on the same arm the tiger had injured. She didn't know for a moment if that green sound was a branch breaking or her – and then she did know, because inside the shell she could feel how her right arm hung limp, meaty, flaccid – humerus shattered.

She was dangling right beside her cocoon, as it happened. She used the folds of cloth to pull herself closer to the trunk, then commanded it to detach and retract. She found one of the proximity alarms and discovered that the damp had gotten into it. It didn't register her presence, either.

Venus.

She was stowing it one-handed in one of the shell's cargo pockets, warily watching for the return of either tiger, when the voice burst into her head.

"Dhar!"

"Don't worry," she told Kraken. "Just hurt my arm getting away from a swamp-tiger. Everything's fine."

"Hurt or broke? Wait, *swamp-tiger?*"

"It's gone now. I scared it off." She wasn't sure, but she wasn't about to admit that. "Tell Zamin the juveniles hunt in pairs."

"A *pair* of swamp-tigers?!"

"I'm fine," Dharthi said, and clamped down the link.

She climbed down one-handed, relying on the shell more than she would have liked. She did not see either tiger again.

At the bottom, on the jungle floor, she limped, but she ran.

Four runs and four sleeps later – the sleeps broken, confused spirals of exhaustion broken by fractured snatches of rest – the brightest patch of pewter in the sky had shifted visibly to the east. Noon had become afternoon, and the long Cytherean day was becoming Dharthi's enemy. She climbed trees regularly to look for signs of geometrical shapes informing the growth of the forest, and every time she did, she glanced at that brighter smear of cloud sliding down the sky and frowned.

Dharthi – assisted by her adaptshell – had come some five hundred kilometers westward. Maxwell Montes was lost behind her now, in cloud and mist and haze and behind the shoulder of the world. She was moving fast for someone creeping, climbing, and swinging through the jungle, although she was losing time because she hadn't turned the adaptshell loose to forage on its own since the swamp-tiger. She needed it to support and knit her arm – the shell fused to itself across the front and made a seamless cast and sling – and for the pain suppressants it fed her along with its pre-chewed pap. The bones were going to knit all wrong, of course, and when she got back, they'd have to grow her a new one, but that was pretty minor stuff.

The shell filtered toxins and allergens out of the biologicals it ingested, reserving some of the carbohydrates, protein, and fat to produce a bland, faintly sweet, nutrient-rich paste that was safe for Dharthi's consumption. She sucked it from a tube as needed, squashing it between tongue and palate to soften it before swallowing each sticky, dull mouthful.

Water was never a problem – at least, the problem was having too much of it, not any lack. This was *Venus*. Water squelched in every footstep across the jungle floor. It splashed on the adaptshell's head and infiltrated every cargo pocket. The only things that stayed dry were the ones that were treated to be hydrophobic, and the coating was starting to wear off some of those. Dharthi's cocoon was permanently damp inside. Even her shell, which molded her skin perfectly, felt alternately muggy or clammy depending on how it was comping temperature.

The adaptshell also filtered some of the fatigue toxins out of Dharthi's system. But not enough. Sleep was sleep, and she wasn't getting enough of it.

The landscape was becoming dreamy and strange. The forest never thinned, never gave way to another landscape – except the occasional swath of swampland – but now, occasionally, twisted fumaroles rose up through it, smoking towers of orange and ochre that sent wisps of steam drifting between scalded yellowed leaves. Dharthi saw one of the geysers erupt; she noticed that over it, and where the spray would tend to blow, there was a hole in the canopy. But vines grew right up the knobby accreted limestone on the windward side.

Five runs and five... five *attempts* at a sleep later, Dharthi began to accept that she desperately, *desperately* wanted to go home.

She wouldn't, of course.

Her arm hurt less. That was a positive thing. Other than that, she was exhausted and damp and cold and some kind of thick liver-colored leech kept trying to attach itself to the adaptshell's legs. A species new to science, probably, and Dharthi didn't give a damn.

Kraken tried to contact her every few hours.

She didn't answer, because she knew if she did, she would ask Kraken to come and get her. And then she'd never be able to look another living Cytherean in the face again.

It wasn't like Venus had a big population.

Dharthi was going to prove herself or die trying.

The satlink from Zamin, though, she took at once. They chatted about swamp-tigers – Zamin, predictably, was fascinated, and told Dharthi she'd write it up and give full credit to Dharthi as observer. "Tell Hazards, too," Dharthi said, as an afterthought.

"Oh, yeah," Zamin replied. "I guess it is at that. Dhar... are you okay out there?"

"Arm hurts," Dharthi admitted. "The drugs are working, though. I could use some sleep in a bed. A dry bed."

"Yeah," Zamin said. "I bet you could. You know Kraken's beside herself, don't you?"

"She'll know if I die," Dharthi said.

"She's a good friend," Zamin said. A good trick, making it about her, rather than Kraken or Dharthi or Kraken *and* Dharthi. "I worry about her. You know she's been unbelievably kind to me, generous through some real roughness. She's –"

"She's generous," Dharthi said. "She's a genius and a charismatic. I know it better than most. Look, I should pay attention to where my feet are, before I break the other arm. Then you *will* have to extract me. And won't I feel like an idiot then?"

"Dhar –"

She broke the sat. She felt funny about it for hours afterward, but at least when she crawled into her cocoon that rest period, adaptshell and all, she was so exhausted she slept.

She woke up sixteen hours and twelve minutes later, disoriented and sore in every joint. After ninety seconds she recollected herself enough to figure out where she was – in her shell, in her cocoon, fifty meters up in the Ishtarean canopy, struggling out of an exhaustion and painkiller haze – and when she was, with a quick check of the time.

She stowed and packed by rote, slithered down a strangler vine, stood in contemplation on the forest floor. Night was coming – the long night – and while she still had ample time to get back to base camp without calling for a pickup, every day now cut into her margin of safety.

She ran.

Rested, she almost had the resources to deal with it when Kraken spoke in her mind, so she gritted her teeth and said, "Yes, dear?"

"Hi," Kraken said. There was a pause, in which Dharthi sensed a roil of suppressed emotion. Thump. Thump. As long as her feet kept running, nothing could catch her. That sharpness in her chest was just tight breath from running, she was sure. "Zamin says she's worried about you."

Dharthi snorted. She had slept too much, but now that the kinks were starting to shake out of her body, she realized that the rest had done her good. "You know what Zamin wanted to talk to me about? You. How *wonderful* you are. How caring. How made of charm." Dharthi sighed. "How often do people take you aside to gush about how wonderful I am?"

"You might," Kraken said, "be surprised."

"It's *hard* being the partner of somebody so perfect. When did you ever *struggle* for anything? You have led a charmed life, Kraken, from birth to now."

"Did I?" Kraken said. "I've been lucky, I don't deny. But I've worked hard. And lived through things. You think I'm perfect because that's how you see me, in between bouts of hating everything I do."

"It's how everyone sees you. If status in the afterlife is determined by praises sung, yours is assured."

"I wish you could hear how they talk about you. People hold you in awe, love."

Thump. Thump. The rhythm of her feet soothed her, when nothing else could. She was even getting resigned to the ceaseless damp, which collected between her toes, between her buttocks, behind her ears. "They *love* you. They tolerated me. No one *ever* saw what you saw in me."

"I did," Kraken replied. "And quit acting as if I *were* somehow perfect. You've been quick enough to remind me on occasion of how I'm not. This thing, this need to prove yourself... it's a sophipathology, Dhar. I love you. But this is not a healthy pattern of thought. Ambition is great, but you go beyond ambition. Nothing you do is ever good enough. You deny your own accomplishments, and inflate those of everyone around you. You grew up in Aphrodite, and there are only thirty thousand people on the whole damned planet. You *can't* be surprised that, brilliant as you are, some of us are just as smart and capable as you are."

Thump. Thump –

She was watching ahead even as she was arguing, though her attention wasn't on it. That automatic caution was all that kept her from running off the edge of the world.

Before her – below her – a great cliff dropped away. The trees in the valley soared up. But this was not a tangled jungle: it was a climax forest, a species of tree taller and more densely canopied than any Dharthi had seen. The light below those trees was thick and crepuscular, and though she could hear the rain drumming on their leaves, very little of it dripped through.

Between them, until the foliage cut off her line of sight, Dharthi could see the familiar, crescent-shaped roofs of aboriginal Cytherean structures, some of them half-consumed in the accretions from the forest of smoking stone towers that rose among the trees.

She stood on the cliff edge overlooking the thing she had come half a world by airship and a thousand kilometers on foot to find, and pebbles crumbled from beneath the toes of her adaptshell, and she raised a hand to her face as if Kraken were really speaking into a device in her ear canal instead of into the patterns of electricity in her brain. The cavernous ruin stretched farther than her eyes could see – even dark-adapted, once the shell made the transition for her. Even in this strange, open forest filled with colorful, flitting flying things.

"Love?"

"Yes?" Kraken said, then went silent and waited.

"I'll call you back," Dharthi said. "I just discovered the Lost City of Ishtar."

DHARTHI WALKED AMONG the ruins. It was not all she'd hoped.

Well, it was *more* than she had hoped. She rappelled down, and as soon as her shell sank ankle-deep in the leaf litter she was overcome by a hush of awe. She turned from the wet, lichen-heavy cliff, scuffed with the temporary marks of her feet, and craned back to stare up at the forest of geysers and fumaroles and trees that stretched west and south as far as she could see. The cliff behind her was basalt – another root of the volcano whose shield was lost in mists and trees. This... this was the clearest air she had ever seen.

The trees were planted in rows, as perfectly arranged as pillars in some enormous Faerie hall. The King of the Giants lived here, and Dharthi was Jack, except she had climbed down the beanstalk for a change.

The trunks were as big around as ten men with linked hands, tall enough that their foliage vanished in the clouds overhead. Trees on Earth, Dharthi knew, were limited in height by capillary action: how high could they lift water to their thirst leaves?

Perhaps these Cytherean giants drank from the clouds as well as the earth.

"Oh," Dharthi said, and the spaces between the trees both hushed and elevated her voice, so it sounded clear and thin. "Wait until Zamin sees these."

Dharthi suddenly realized that if they were a new species, she would get to name them.

They were so immense, and dominated the light so completely, that very little grew under them. Some native fernmorphs, some mosses. Lichens shaggy on their enormous trunks and roots. Where one had fallen, a miniature Cytherean rain forest had sprung up in the admitted light, and here there was drumming, dripping rain, rain falling like strings of glass beads. It was a muddy little puddle of the real world in this otherwise alien quiet.

The trees stood like attentive gods, their faces so high above her she could not even hear the leaves rustle.

Dharthi forced herself to turn away from the trees, at last, and begin examining the structures. There were dozens of them – hundreds – sculpted out of the same translucent, mysterious, impervious material as all of the ruins in Aphrodite. But this was six, ten times the scale of any such ruin. Maybe vaster. She needed a team. She needed a mapping expedition. She needed a base camp much closer to this. She needed to give the site a name –

She needed to get back to work.

She remembered, then, to start documenting. The structures – she could not say, of course, which were habitations, which served other purposes – or even if the aboriginals had used the same sorts of divisions of usage that human beings did – were of a variety of sizes and heights. They were all designed as arcs or crescents, however – singly, in series, or in several cases as a sort of stepped spectacular with each lower, smaller level fitting inside the curve of a higher, larger one. Several had obvious access points, open to the air, and Dharthi reminded herself sternly that going inside unprepared was not just a bad idea because of risk to herself, but because she might disturb the evidence.

She clenched her good hand and stayed outside.

Her shell had been recording, of course – now she began to narrate, and to satlink the files home. No fanfare, just an upload. Data and more data – and the soothing knowledge that while she was hogging her allocated bandwidth to send, nobody could call her to ask questions, or congratulate, or –

Nobody except Kraken, with whom she was entangled for life.

"Hey," her partner said in her head. "You found it."

"I found it," Dharthi said, pausing the narration but not the load. There was plenty of visual, olfactory, auditory, and kinesthetic data being sent even without her voice.

"How does it feel to be vindicated?"

She could hear the throb of Kraken's pride in her mental voice. She tried not to let it make her feel patronized. Kraken did not mean to sound parental, proprietary. That was Dharthi's own baggage.

"Vindicated?" She looked back over her shoulder. The valley was quiet and dark. A fumarole vented with a rushing hiss and a curve of wind brought the scent of sulfur to sting her eyes.

"Famous?"

"*Famous!?*"

"Hell, Terran-famous. The homeworld is going to hear about this in oh, about five minutes, given light lag – unless somebody who's got an entangled partner back there shares sooner. You've just made the biggest Cytherean archaeological discovery in the past hundred days, love. And probably the next hundred. You are *not* going to have much of a challenge getting allocations now."

"I –"

"You worked hard for it."

"It feels like..." Dharthi picked at the bridge of her nose with a thumbnail. The skin was peeling off in flakes: too much time in her shell was wreaking havoc with the natural oil balance of her skin. "It feels like I should be figuring out the next thing."

"The next thing," Kraken said. "How about coming home to me? Have you proven yourself to yourself yet?"

Dharthi shrugged. She felt like a petulant child. She knew she was acting like one. "How about to you?"

"*I* never doubted you. You had nothing to prove to me. The self-sufficiency thing is your pathology, love, not mine. I love you as you are, not because I think I can make you perfect. I just wish you could see your strengths as well as you see your flaws – one second, bit of a squall up ahead – I'm back."

"Are you on an airship?" *Was she coming here?*

"Just an airjeep."

Relief *and* a stab of disappointment. You wouldn't get from Aphrodite to Ishtar in an AJ.

Well, Dharthi thought. *Looks like I might be walking home.*

And when she got there? Well, she wasn't quite ready to ask Kraken for help yet.

She would stay, she decided, two more sleeps. That would still give her time to get back to basecamp before nightfall, and it wasn't as if her arm could get any *more* messed up between now and then. She was turning in a slow circle, contemplating where to sling her cocoon – the branches were really too high to be convenient – when the unmistakable low hum of an aircar broke the rustling silence of the enormous trees.

It dropped through the canopy, polished copper belly reflecting a lensed fisheye of forest, and settled down ten meters from Dharthi. Smiling, frowning, biting her lip, she went to meet it. The upper half was black hydrophobic polymer: she'd gotten a lift in one just like it at Ishtar basecamp before she set out.

The hatch opened. In the cramped space within, Kraken sat behind the control board. She half-rose, crouched under the low roof, came to the hatch, held out one her right hand, reaching down to Dharthi. Dharthi looked at Kraken's hand, and Kraken sheepishly switched it for the other one. The left one, which Dharthi could take without strain.

"So I was going to take you to get your arm looked at," Kraken said.

"You spent your allocations –"

Kraken shrugged. "Gonna send me away?"

"This time," she said, "... no."

Kraken wiggled her fingers.

Dharthi took it, stepped up into the GEV, realized how exhausted she was as she settled back in a chair and suddenly could not lift her head without the assistance of her shell. She wondered if she should have hugged Kraken. She realized that she was sad that Kraken hadn't tried to hug her. But, well. The shell was sort of in the way.

Resuming her chair, Kraken fixed her eyes on the forward screen. "Hey. You did it."

"Hey. I did." She wished she felt it. Maybe she was too tired.

Maybe Kraken was right, and Dharthi should see about working on that.

Her eyes dragged shut. So heavy. The soft motion of the aircar lulled her. Its soundproofing had degraded, but even the noise wouldn't be enough to keep her awake. Was this what safe felt like? "Something else."

"I'm listening."

"If you don't mind, I was thinking of naming a tree after you."

"That's good," Kraken said. "I was thinking of naming a kid after you."

Dharthi grinned without opening her eyes. "We should use my Y chromosome. Color blindness on the X."

"Ehn. Ys are half atrophied already. We'll just use two Xs," Kraken said decisively. "Maybe we'll get a tetrachromat."

THE MACHINE STARTS

Greg Bear

GREG BEAR (WWW.GREGBEAR.COM) is one of the most important science fiction writers of the past forty years. He is the multiple Hugo and Nebula award-winning author of more than 35 novels, including *Blood Music*; *Eon* and sequels *Eternity* and *Legacy*; *The Forge of God* and sequel *Anvil of Stars*; *Queen of Angels* and sequel */Slant*; *Moving Mars*; *Darwin's Radio* and sequel *Darwin's Children*; *City at the End of Time*, *War Dogs* and most recent novel, *Killing Titan*. Bear's short fiction has won or been nominated for the Hugo, Nebula, and World Fantasy Awards on multiple occasions, and has been collected in *The Wind From a Burning Woman, Tangents, The Collected Stories of Greg Bear*, and other volumes. His major stories include "Petra", "Hardfought", "Blood Music" and "Tangents". His complete short fiction will be published in three volumes in 2016. Bear is the father of two young writers, Erik and Alexandra, and is married to Astrid Anderson Bear. The Bears make their home in Seattle.

THOUGH I AM otherwise relentlessly normal, I have one peculiarity: I get along well only with people who are smarter than me. My wife, for example, is smarter than me. I am happy in my marriage.

In my present employment I should be very happy, because everyone around me is smarter and often at pains to prove that fact. It is my duty to reinforce their positive opinions, but at the same time to exert, now and then, small course corrections. Nothing shores up a fine self-opinion better than success.

So far, five years into our project, we had known nothing but failure.

The first thing you saw as you approached the perimeter site was the warehouse, large, square, and painted a brilliant titanium white. Surrounded by two high hurricane fences topped with glittering rolls of razor wire, it looked like the kind of place where you might store an A-bomb. Access to the site was on a strictly controlled, need-to-go basis. Parking was several hundred yards away, on a small lot covered with pulverized rubber. You were told not to drive a loud car, not to cut out your exhaust or rev your engine, not to sing or even shout, upon penalty of being fired.

On the morning of the test, I drove into the lot and parked my white VW, old and shabby. I had owned it since college. My colleagues favored Teslas or Mercedes-Benzes. I liked my Rabbit.

In the lane between the fences, small robots rolled night and day – nonlethal, but capable of shooting barb-tipped wires that carried a discouraging shock. The robots inspected me with their tiny black eyes and, bored by my familiarity, rolled away.

The warehouse was made entirely of wood, no nails or brackets. It covered half an acre and sat on a thick pad of cement reinforced with plastic rebar and mesh. Beneath the pad lay a series of empty vaults that discouraged ground water, rodents, or anything else that might disturb the peace. No pipes or wires were allowed, except for those that fed directly into the warehouse.

After I passed through the fences, a single thick oak door gave access to the warehouse interior. I was scheduled to meet Hugh Tiflin, project manager and chief researcher. He was always prompt, but I was deliberately early. I wanted to reacquaint myself with the architecture, the atmosphere, the implications – to *feel* the place again.

I summoned up my image of Alan Turing. It is my habit to sometimes talk to the founder of modern computing, hoping for a reflection of his peculiar, sharp wisdom. What we were in the final stages of creating (we all hoped they were the final stages!) could transform the human race. A machine that would end all our secrets. What would Mr. Turing think of such a New Machine?

He never answered, of course. But then, so far, neither did our machine.

I entered the security cage and listened to questions spoken by a soft, automated voice – personal questions that were sometimes embarrassing, sometimes sad, sometimes funny. I answered each of them truthfully enough and the cage opened.

Next to the cage, a small illuminated counter revealed the number of my recent visits: 4. In the last month, I had only been here twice. The counter reset every day. I take it as a personal affront when automated systems make mistakes.

A soft rain began to fall on the high, hollow roof, adding to my damp mood and the penetrating chill in the building. The warehouse was dark, except for a light in the far corner that glowed like a pale sun. I approached a low wood rail and stood in the long, curved shadow of a big black sphere, bloated and shiny, rising on tiny fins almost to the ceiling, silent but for the low hum of the power that kept it alive. A bank of heavily insulated pipes passed under the rails and through the wooden wall to dedicated generators and a refrigeration complex outside.

Early in its development, Tiflin had named the sphere Magic 8 Ball, soon shortened to 8 Ball because, as Tiflin insisted, there was nothing magical about our machine – just good solid physics. It retained a window on one side, however, like the old toy. Tiflin had asked it to be painted on after we finished the first phase.

The window's message: Try Again Later.

Reading that again, I experienced an odd sort of dizzy spell, as if there were too many of me in one place – a symptom of stress and hard work, I presumed.

8 Ball was our third major attempt at a fully operational and manageable quantum computer. No doubt you've heard something about quantum computing. The underlying ideas are spooky and new, so a lot of what you've heard is bound to be wrong. A quantum computer works not with bits but with qubits, or quantum bits. A classic bit, like a light switch, is either on or off, one or zero. A quantum bit can be kept in superposition, neither on nor off, nor both, nor neither – like Schrödinger's cat until you open its very special box.

Off in far corners, two other big spheres peered from the shadows: 8 Ball's defunct siblings, Mega and Mini. Mini was ten meters across and had once contained 128 qubits. In its scavenged condition – white insulation peeling, surrounded by a tangle of pipes and wires leading nowhere – it resembled a giant golf ball. We had turned it off – killed it – three years ago. Standing in the opposite corner, Mega was eleven meters wide and resembled a moldy Florida orange. It had contained 256 qubits, all niobium or aluminum circuits bathed in liquid helium. It had sort of worked, for a time – and then it didn't. Thumbs-down on Mega.

Filling the expanded north end of the building, 8 Ball was twelve meters in diameter and contained 1024 qubits, each a two-dimensional electron cloud clamped between plates of gallium arsenide and cooled to just a femto-fraction of a degree above absolute zero. The qubits lined the sphere's penultimate outer layer, and each one communicated, if that's the right word, through braided world lines across a central vacuum to an entangled twin on the other side of the sphere. Entanglement meant the paired qubits duplicated each other's quantum state. If one was changed or measured, the other would reflect that interference, no matter how far apart they were. They would be *superposed.*

Each electron cloud became a new variety of matter, known as an *anyon*, confirmation of the existence of which we were particularly proud. The qubits' spooky vacuum jive would, we hoped, help make 8 Ball the most stable quantum computer yet.

But despite a promising beginning, 8 Ball refused to work as designed. Sampling its output caused a catastrophic early collapse of the program strings, which themselves seemed to have been turned into useless nonsense. That had forced us to take a radically new approach. It seemed very possible that if this effort failed, 8 Ball would soon join Mega and Mini as little more than another archaeological curiosity.

Tiflin had asked me to meet him at the warehouse to help check out the newest part of our installation. I was about to stoop to look underneath the black sphere when I noticed a small yellow piece of paper stuck to the rail -- a Post-it Note. Other than me, nobody in the lab used Post-its, and I only used them in my office. I pulled up the note. Written on one side in my squared-off printing was, *Don't try to find me.* I did not remember either writing this message or sticking it on the rail. Maybe I had simply forgotten. Maybe someone was messing with me and had put it there to screw with my day. There were plenty of smart-asses in our division capable of playing mind games. Work had been painfully difficult the last few weeks. Pressure on our entire team was intense.

I tried to think back and retrace my steps. Parking, walking, answering the absurdly personal questions, my little talk with Mr. Turing –

Plus the dizzy spell.

I had never written a note.

Outside the warehouse, I heard the slam of a car door, followed by feet on gravel. A key clicked in the outer lock. Tiflin entered the security cage and muttered his own answers to the cage's questions. The inner gate opened. He seemed even more distracted than I was. As he approached 8 Ball, he patted all of his pockets – shirt, pants, leather jacket – as if he'd forgotten something.

I crumpled the Post-it into a ball and hid it in my pants pocket.

When Tiflin came within a few steps, he glanced up at me, startled, and stopped patting, head cocked like a cat considering where to lick next. He broke that off with a long wink, meant to reassure me that Dr. Hugh Tiflin was indeed still in the building, then smoothed his hands down his coat.

At forty-two, Tiflin was a slender man whose upper torso was taller than average and whose legs were shorter. His neck was pale and swanlike, with distinct cords and veins that revealed frequent changes of emotion. His head was large and well-formed, with a chiseled chin and handsome eagle nose, topped by ebullient wavy brown hair. He wore a signature quilted black leather jacket over a cotton shirt, usually green or pink – green today – tucked into cotton-duck hiking pants. His running shoes were cheap and gray. He replaced them every two or three weeks, but somehow they always looked dirty. He was eldest in our team – older than me by a year. He was a genius, of course, or I'd never have worked with him.

"Good morning, Bose. How's the scint?" he asked.

Four weeks ago, he had decided to eavesdrop on the qubits' secret communications using a scintillation detector scavenged from a defense division CubeSat. The detector had originally been designed to monitor radiation from orbit over Iran, North Korea, or Pakistan. Tiflin had personally tuned the device to detect disturbances in 8 Ball's vacuum – bursts of virtual radiation provoked by the passage of our qubits' entangled photons. New stuff, amazing stuff. Who knew that a vacuum could act like a cloud chamber in a science museum? Tiflin knew – or knew people who knew. That's why he was Tiflin.

I stooped again to peer at 8 Ball's lower belly. A wide concrete platform between the main supports – the fins – steadied a stainless steel tube that poked up through 8 Ball's shell and deep into its central vacuum. "Rudely intrusive," I said.

Tiflin chuckled. "Right up the ass. We need to wake up this beast." He looked for himself. "Seems good," he said, sucking on his cheeks. "Should help us track our progress." He rose, gripped the rail with both hands, and looked on 8 Ball with pique mixed with adoration. I understood completely. I, too, regarded the black sphere with both love and dread. 8 Ball was beyond doubt the strangest human construct on Earth, and if Tiflin's plans were all that he hinted, it was about to go through a sea change of procedure and programming.

"We're due to meet with Cate in thirty minutes," he said, again patting his pockets. Was he looking for his phone? A pen? A lighter? "Dieter's got the strings ready to load. Need a ride?"

I didn't, but the VW could wait. Tiflin and I needed time to reintegrate our states, to *normalize*. He sounded reasonably cheerful, but I knew the stress he was under. For a year, tough minds whose job it was to decide which funds should go where had been circling our project like sharks. They were far from convinced 8 Ball was in the division's best interests. Other groups, however, were still making plans that assumed our success. Both were pressing hard on Tiflin.

The absurd level of continuing, tooth-grinding investment showed how sexy the whole idea of quantum computing was, and how much everyone wanted to completely overturn the world's security, expose all its secrets, and find deep answers to life's simple questions before our enemies did – or at least before our competitors in Mumbai or Beijing.

But we had yet to run a long-term, successful session. We seemed to be always smoothing the course, pulling out obstacles – preparing over and over for the first big test. We both knew that could not continue.

Tiflin drove his Tesla back toward our offices with a look of fascinated fury, like a child behind the wheel of a bumper car. I clung to the armrests as we squealed into the concrete garage beside Building 10.

"Today will change everything," he said, climbing out of the bucket seat. "Today will be 8 Ball's first birthday." He smiled his feral smile, upper lip rising over prominent canines. He was looking to see if I shared his conviction, if I would offer my full support.

That's why I was here.

"We should bring a cake!" I said.

* * *

OUR FIVE QUANTUM computing team members gathered in a small conference room for the first time in weeks. Tiflin fussed with the ceiling-mounted projector. The rest of us sat around the oval table, slumped or yawning, picking our fingernails, studying our cell phones before the cage was locked – hardly a picture of joy.

Cate Riva, director of research, overseeing the entire division, had asked for this get-together the day before. It was crunch time for the entire project – and for everyone on the team.

Facilitator and event coordinator Gina Marsh, small, slender, red-haired and blue-eyed, had just made sure we were all present, that we were who we said we were, that our security profiles were up to date – and that we all looked reasonably clean.

"Cate will be here in a few minutes," Tiflin said. The others looked his way with heavy-lidded eyes. "Here's what's going to happen."

At Tiflin's nod, chief of software Dieter Langmeier – tall, bald, bushy-bearded, and a certifiable genius at both systems design and higher-level mathematics – took over. "We're loading new strings," he began. "Gödel strings as before, but we're going to drastically resample the braids. I've adjusted the strings to reflect a new understanding."

"The braids are fine – it's the processing that's hanging us," insisted Wong Poh Kam, senior physicist. Wong was mid-twenties, six feet tall, and slightly stooped, with small, intense eyes on the outer margins of a broad face. "The strings are too damned long."

"The whole mess is too big," said Byron Mickle, chief design engineer. Mickle was stocky, big-shouldered, five feet six, with a pleasant, moon-pale face. He dressed and looked like a plumber, and reliably insisted at each meeting that we should have been able to run Mega and Mini for years without exceeding their theoretical capacity. 8 Ball, to Mickle, was grossly excessive.

"Braids, strings, loops, knots – nothing I hear in this room ever makes sense," Gina said.

Dieter said, with a peeved expression, "Once you absorb the maths, it's all perfectly clear. We're simply reflecting a new understanding. The new topology will be much more inclusive and robust."

"Right!" Gina said. "That makes it so much clearer. I have to key in the Cloaking Device before Cate arrives. Are we good?"

"All good," Tiflin confirmed. He clearly planned to surprise Cate – perhaps to surprise us all.

The glass door closed and clicked behind Gina. We were now inside the cage – a Faraday cage. No signals in or out, except those that passed through the very tight funnel of building security – and the signals from Max, the supercomputer that spoke to 8 Ball.

"Dieter, before Cate gets here, tell them more about what you're up to," Tiflin said.

"I've finished compiling the recidivist strings," Dieter said, too quickly, without taking time to think. He had been rehearsing. The rest of us looked at each other warily. Something was up, and none of us had been clued in.

"What the hell are those?" Mickle asked.

"Tell them what's different about our new strings," Tiflin coached, treating Dieter like a prodigy – or a puppet.

"We're going to compound and re-insert our apparent errors," Dieter said. "My new thinking is, they may not be errors. They may actually be off-phase echoes between our braided qubits. The braids crossing the vacuum aren't loops or even knots. Using the scint, we've learned they take a half-phase twist –"

"You've already sampled the scint?" I asked Tiflin, wondering when it had been activated, and why he had asked me to meet him at the warehouse.

He nodded and dismissed my question with a wave of his hand.

Dieter looked sternly at us, then got up to scrawl matrices and factors and many strange, magical symbols on the whiteboard. He did not like to be interrupted. "A half-phase twist means we're not dealing with loops, not even with *knotted* loops, but with *Möebius* loops." He spoke that name with reverence. Möebius had astonished all of us when we were kids with his one-sided piece of paper – a simple half twist, run your finger around what appears to be a torus, and behold! Infinity.

"Oh, that," said Mickle, resting his elbows on the table and putting his chin in his cupped hands.

"Four spatial tracks and two time tracks," Dieter continued. "Our so-called thermal errors, maybe even the phase-flips, are really signals out of phase – essentially, signals that convey key functions in a program very much like our own. Functions we can parasitize and use for ourselves."

"A program *like* our own?" Mickle asked, lifting his head.

"From the multiverse," Dieter said.

"The *multiverse*?" Mickle seemed taken aback, and then amused. He chuckled and looked at Wong.

"More of Dieter's mystical bullshit," Wong said, rising to the bait. Wong was a dogmatic pragmatist, a surprisingly common type among quantum physicists. "All our crimes come back to haunt us."

"There's nothing mystical about any of this," Tiflin insisted.

Dieter went on, unperturbed, "We need to feed these so-called errors back into our raw strings, to replace the parts of our strings that *are* riddled with errors. Whenever a Gödel number arises that is even vaguely well-formed, the loader will do a checksum, and if it finds congruence, insert an echoed string. For each so-called error, we'll correct the phase, then load the recompiled numbers."

"What the hell does that *really* mean?" Mickle asked. He was lost. I was also lost. "Evolving code, or succotash?"

"If we just reform and reload the strings, we'll fill the bit bucket over and over," Wong said. "And even if 8 Ball works once or twice, we'll have no idea what it's doing for millions of cycles, maybe not even then."

"*If* we reload?" Tiflin asked with that patented savage grin – lip above canines.

"*When*," Dieter said, his face firming to a fine resolve.

"Our problem isn't too few cycles," Tiflin insisted. "8 Ball can supply us with trillions upon trillions of cycles – however large the strings. It can supply us with every number that ever was, every string that ever was, every *program* that ever was – in our universe and at least a quadrillion quadrillion other universes."

Mickle laid his head on the table.

"I keep telling everyone, the multiverse is bullshit," Wong muttered.

Tiflin shrugged. "It's a metaphor." His face was turning shell pink, like a perfect titration in high school chemistry. And now, most dangerous of all, he dropped his voice into its lowest register. "Numbers and cycles aren't the problem. Results and answers are the problem, and so far, having expended three hundred million dollars, none of our efforts has had more than primary school success." He stared hard at Mickle and Wong. "*We need to take a chance.*"

"A really big chance," Wong said.

"I *hate* genetic coding," Mickle said.

"It's not 'genetic,' and it's not random. It's topologically unexpected echoes," Dieter said. "I call them topopotent recidivist code, or TRC."

"Oh, brother," Wong said.

I tried to find a cherry on top of this surprise pile of crap. With Tiflin, that was often my job. "You're saying you'll allow 8 Ball's qubits to *compute* using mirror strings, alternate strings – strings written in no kind of code we've thought of, and never encountered before."

"The code will almost certainly be familiar, Bose. Think of it as sampling from another spin around the loops – a true quantum echo," Tiflin said.

"8 Ball will be taking advice from its own cousins," Dieter said, then added, at Tiflin's frown, "metaphorical cousins, of course."

"Christ, zillions of 8 Balls," Wong said.

"Who knows what sort of creativity is just waiting to be discovered out there?" Dieter waved at the ceiling, the walls – really, at everything around us.

Mickle made a raspberry sound and dropped his head again.

Looking at Tiflin and trying to read his expression, I realized that theory and desperation had finally trumped our own project manager. Despite Tiflin's objections, Dieter – mystical and multiversed Dieter – was in charge of our quantum computer.

"What – or who – is going to judge and select the strings?" I asked. "We don't want to do parsing in the QC. That'll slow it to a crawl. 8 Ball isn't made for that!"

Dieter raised his hand. "We already have a working subroutine to perform that function."

"In Max or in 8 Ball?" I asked. We had named 8 Ball's traditional interpreter – an interposed supercomputer – Max Headroom. Max used to be named Mike, from Heinlein's novel *The Moon Is a Harsh Mistress*, until I pointed out that Mike vanished and was never heard from again.

Mickle had suggested Max.

"In Max, and *then* in 8 Ball," Tiflin said. "We leave the rough parsing to Max and the large numbers to 8 Ball. They can be raw, even partly malformed, because we'll grind through so many of them so quickly."

"Max says it's slick," Dieter added stubbornly.

"Gentlemen, let's face the truth. This is a done deal," Mickle said. "We've finally jumped from the bridge into a deep, dark river of sloppy thinking. We're *screwed.*" He took a long sip from a bottle of beige Soylent liquid, his frequent substitute for breakfast, lunch, and even dinner.

Tiflin said quietly, pointedly, "It's done. We're already loading."

A long pause.

"A string infested with quantum errors we've spent most of our careers trying to weed out!" Wong exclaimed, making weak gestures of frustration and surrender. "I am flabbered. I am gasted."

Emotions crossed Dieter's hairy face like clouds over a prairie.

"Have a little faith," Tiflin said, and leaned back in his chair. "If we're wrong and this crashes 8 Ball over and over again, to be sure, we're all screwed, but the fact is, minus results, the division is set to cut its losses and clean house. That's why Cate called us together this morning. Results, or we get booted out of here."

"Thanks for the warning," Wong said.

Then the door clicked and Cate Riva entered, flashing a sunny expression and a big smile. "Good morning, all," she said with a quick scan around the conference room. "Why so serious?"

"We're loading new strings, recombined Gödel strings," Tiflin said, with all the confidence he could fake.

"Wasn't that the plan?" Cate asked innocently.

"We're inserting the worst phase-flip errors back into the strings," Wong said. We all wished he'd just keep quiet.

"Proof of pudding?" Cate asked, still standing. "Because despite my pleasant demeanor, I'm not here to listen to more bullshit."

A brief silence.

"Take a seat," Tiflin said. "We're about to begin. Genius is in the air."

Cate smiled again, all sunlight and cheer – but behind her brown eyes, all tiger.

Tiflin instructed the screen to drop and the data in the ceiling projector to show 8 Ball's and Max's interposed display. "Here we go," he said, betting the bank – betting *our* bank.

This was going to be my Waterloo. I could smell it.

Dieter sent the instructions to Max. "First strings are loaded," he announced.

"What scale?" Cate asked.

"All qubits," Dieter said. "Two to the one thousand and twenty-fourth power."

Tiflin looked at me. I looked at Cate. She watched the display.

Programming in a QC consists of designing and controlling how the qubits are entangled – essentially, the topological nature of the braids – and then maintaining or collapsing those entangled states, opening gates from which we could presumably receive our answers. Once set in motion, a quantum computer is autonomous – the program either fails or succeeds. A QC cannot be debugged while it is working. The program cannot be halted or even completely understood while the QC is busy. Only if the results are interesting and useful can we hope that what we did was a success. And they must also be *fast*.

The display twinkled over our heads. And what do you know?

We got back numbers – long strings of integers, flanked by Max's instant scorecard analysis. 8 Ball was delivering a select list of exceedingly large primes – the kind of unique and difficult primes used to encode high-level passwords. The kind that could break banks and even worry Uncle Sam.

"Wow," Cate said. "These are real? You haven't suckered Max?"

"No suckers here," Tiflin said, leaning back deeper into the shadows.

8 Ball didn't choke or even sneeze. For the first time, our newest QC was cooking.

And it was *fast*.

"Next up," Tiflin said, as Dieter's fingers flew over the keyboard, "the complete Icelandic chromosome database for mutations in BRCA 1 and 2 over the last forty years."

And *that* worked, too. Our evolving machine had analyzed and understood contemporary human evolution, at least in two important oncogenes.

"The third problem is *very* big," Dieter said. "We're collating the proof of the classification of the theorem of finite simple groups. It's known as the Enormous Theorem. Tens of thousand of pages of proofs, scattered in several hundred journals, all loaded into Gödel strings, cross-referenced, and logically filtered. The QC should find any contradictions. We'll get results in four or five minutes."

"That alone should get us a Fields Medal," Tiflin said.

Cate reached out to pat Tiflin's shoulder. "Let me know how that turns out," she said. "Good work, gentlemen. I've seen enough for now." She stood and left the room.

Inside the hour, the Enormous Theorem was proven consistent, our contracts were extended, and our funding was renewed.

THAT EVENING, I went home to the square gray stone and steel apartment where my wife and I had lived for nine months. She had just returned from Beijing and a conference on newer, more inclusive versions of Unicode. We spent our first evening together in three weeks, beginning with sushi from our favorite restaurant and progressing to brandy and cigars – a sin we allowed ourselves every few months.

Then we exercised our marital prerogatives. I managed almost to forget both our team's troubles and successes. I could not tell her about any of them. Cate would decide how and when to release the story.

Why couldn't I just accept the fact that Tiflin had triumphed? Cate had messaged Tiflin at the end of the day that maybe we could support doubling the number of qubits. 8 Ball was designed to be scalable, wasn't it?

My wife rolled over on the flannel sheets and asked, "Do you have a sister?"

She knew I had only brothers, all in India.

"There was this woman in Beijing who looked exactly like you," she said, "only pretty. Same color skin, same hair. She came up to me and asked how you were doing."

"And?"

"I said you were fine. She knew your name. She knew where you worked. She touched my cheek with the back of her hand and smiled, the way you used to do. And she was really smart. Maybe smarter than you!" She grinned, raised herself over me, and twirled her finger on my chest. "It gave me a thrill – perverse, you know? Like if I went to bed with her, it wouldn't be cheating on *you*. And not just because of the girl-girl thing. Does that make any sense? I've never seen anything like it, Bose. Are you cloning people now?"

I said we most certainly were not cloning people and hugged her, mostly to shut her up.

"Right," she said. "You'd have to have been cloned forty-one years ago. How about a transporter malfunction?"

We laughed, but the thought made me both queasy and a little horny – so many bells being rung on my nerd pinball machine, after such a complicated and important day.

A FEW HOURS later, I showered, got dressed, and walked into my home office to look over the new morning's schedule. I found another Post-it Note stuck to my rosewood desktop. This one, again in my distinctive print style, read,

Check out the Pepsi supply.

I looked around the small room. My armpits were soaking. We needed to reset our security system.

And I needed another shower.

COMING INTO OUR building, I avoided the soft drink coolers, just because looking, checking, would be utterly ridiculous.

Gina made the rounds of our glassed-in cubicles, delivering a basket of fruit and wine to each of us with compliments from Cate and our CEO as well. Later that day came a message of congratulations signed by the company's founder. Cate wasn't wasting time. The news was now global – we had the first successful, large-scale quantum computer, and it was already making major advancements in math and physics.

We were historic.

Two days later, after our staff meeting and our third round of press interviews, I took another morning drive to the perimeter warehouse, trying to silence my inner alarms. I whistled aimlessly, hopelessly tangled in wondering what I would look like as a female. Weird encounter, I thought. But just *how* weird? And how connected to the spate of anonymous Post-it Notes?

No one had been at the warehouse since Tiflin and I last visited. Cate had put it in lockdown to all but team members, not to jinx success by letting in the press – hot bodies and electronic interference.

Security grudgingly allowed me back in. The counter on the display by the cage read 8. That, of course, had to be wrong. Eight meant I had visited the site four times since Tiflin and I had last gone through. I wondered if we could get access to the security tapes. There might be imposters on the campus, right? But really, I did not want to know.

Everything in the warehouse looked fine. I was supposed to be happy, but none of this felt right. I could not help but think that some day, despite our success, the cage would refuse to open and I'd know my time in the division was over – best to light out for the territories and find smarter people elsewhere.

Why didn't Tiflin call another meeting to plan the next cycles?

I turned away from 8 Ball and experienced another dizzy spell – too many Boses in one body. And what the hell did *that* mean?

When I got out to the parking lot and my VW, I saw a sheet of paper in the passenger seat. In the upper right corner, a lab intranet library reference announced these were scint results from the last week, and below that was a graphic representation of 8 Ball's inner vacuum.

On the upper left corner, beside the reference number, someone had written, using my print style, *Thought you should see this. And do take a look at the soft drink coolers. They're empty most of the time now.*

I had had quite enough.

I drove back to Building 10 and found Tiflin in his office. "We need to look at building security videos."

"Why?" Tiflin said.

"Someone may be trying to mess with us. Humor me," I said.

We approached the security office and made our request. We were both placed high enough that the head of security allowed us into the inner sanctum, a dark room fronted by two tiered banks of monitors and staffed by five guards.

Two of them relinquished their seats to make room.

I scrawled notes on a sheet of legal paper as we went through the videos for the last four days. The cameras in the warehouse were separate from the lab system, and not accessible from this center, but we still had a clear view of all the rooms, offices, and corridors in three big buildings – a lot to process, and I wasn't sure what I was looking for. Lots of people, lots of team members wandering around, going to the cafeteria, sitting in their cubicles sucking down Soylents or Pepsis or Mountain Dews or Snapples –

I thought I saw Mickle in a hallway, then, under the same time stamp, working in his office. "Look at that," I said. "The times are off."

"That could explain the numbers at the warehouse. Why is it important?" Tiflin yawned.

"OK," I told the security chief, "show our offices right now."

The chief worked over his keyboard and we saw my office and Tiflin's office in Building 10, in real time, just a few cubicles apart. My office was empty. *Empty – just me*, I wrote on my little pad.

We looked into Tiflin's office.

"Wait," Tiflin said.

Tiflin's in his office, I wrote and noted the time, the room number, and the chair beside me.

Tiflin no longer sat in the chair.

And his office was empty.

The head of security bent to look over my shoulder. "Looks like the boss is off campus," he said.

I felt a spreading wave of dismay.

And then, I think I simply forgot.

A few hours later, back in my own office, behind the locked door, I reviewed my notes, not at all sure where I had been or why – and wondering how I had just lost so much time. The last thing I had recorded was, *Tiflin's gone! He just vanished, and I'm forgetting* –

I unlocked my door, clutching the diagram I'd found in my car, and checked the soft drink coolers in the adjacent hallway. Mountain Dew and Pepsi were in very short supply – just a few cans.

With real trepidation, I passed down the hall to Tiflin's office. There he was, sitting at his desk, on the phone. He looked up and lifted an eyebrow – go away, he was busy.

I turned and left.

What the hell had just happened?

* * *

I STOOD BEFORE 8 Ball again, my neck hair on end, looking on it not with pique or adoration, but with genuine fear. This time, my visit numbers were consecutive.

"What the fuck are you up to?" I whispered at the black sphere.

The warehouse security gate clicked with the insertion of another key. Mickle entered and spent a number of seconds staring at the counter. From this angle I could not see his number, but he hesitantly answered the cage's questions, then walked across the concrete floor to where I stood by the rail.

He tipped me a salute. "It says I've been out here fourteen times in the last twenty-four hours," he said.

"Have you?"

"No."

"Just what are we worried about?" I asked. "What could possibly be going wrong?"

"Nothing, really." Mickle assumed an expression like a little boy who has just bottled a weird bug. "We're famous. We're making headlines around the world."

"So why are we standing here looking so anxious?" I asked.

Wong entered next and joined us by the rail. "We need to see the building security videos," he said with a squint.

Before I could answer, Mickle said, "Been there, done that. I took Dieter with me to the security center. His wastebasket kept filling up with Pepsi cans – his favorite. So we asked to see who had been visiting his office."

"Looking for what?" I asked.

"To count how many Dieters there were in the universe."

"Why should there be more than one?" I asked.

Mickle shook his head. "Dieter said something more than a little weird. He said every program had to have a programmer. Since 8 Ball was running trillions of programs, how many programmers would it need to import to satisfy causality?"

"How many *Dieters*."

"Yeah."

"And?"

"Not just Dieters. We've all contributed code over the years. We've all noodled and made suggestions. So we're all potential dupes."

"As in suckers?"

"More like duplicates. We played the video until we saw Dieter enter his office. And then – I don't remember all of it. But there was no Dieter standing next to me in the security center. And there was no Dieter in his office, either. Both had vanished, or at least that's what I wrote down right after it happened – on a napkin." Mickle held up the napkin. In his loose scrawl, a black marker message read, *Two Dieters canceled*.

"Why would they cancel each other out?"

"Because they're non-Abelian," Mickle said. "Like fermions. They can't occupy the same universe at the same time – and become aware of it."

"That is nuts!" Wong said.

"I agree," Mickle said. "What shall we tell Tiflin?"

"Let me decide that," I said. "We should make sure nobody's playing a joke. I wouldn't even put it past Tiflin. Make sure we're not being deceived."

"That is *not* the right word," Mickle said, tapping the rail with his finger. "They wouldn't be deceptions. They're just as real as you and me. They even fool the counters. But if we're going to take this any further, we have to avoid looking for *ourselves*. Because, gentlemen, if we find us, we'll just fucking *vanish*."

"Tiflin hates multiverses or mystical interpretations," I said.

"So do I, remember?" Wong said.

"Don't search for yourself," Mickle said, poking Wong's shoulder. Wong shrugged him off with a resentful scowl. "And we won't look for each other – not when we're together. You look for me, alone, and I look for you. Alone."

"Can we look for the others, too?"

"I think so," he said. "But maybe we shouldn't tell them we saw them."

"That might be allowed," I said, thinking back to the Post-it Notes and my wife telling me about my 'sister.' "But we should be cautious."

"What's the point, then?" Wong asked.

"Maybe they won't believe us and they'll stick around regardless," Mickle said.

8 Ball kept patiently cycling.

* * *

I ASKED TIFLIN to meet me in the lobby of a nice hotel where we put up our international guests. I wanted to be away from the campus, away from our colleagues – away from anyone or anything that might make Tiflin feel stubborn. It was too early for a beer, so he and I took seats in the small bar and sipped cappuccinos.

"We've still got a lot to do," Tiflin said, fidgeting. I was too important and connected to ignore, but he seemed to know he wouldn't like what I had to say.

"8 Ball's not working the way we thought it would," I told him.

"I don't care," he said. "It's working. We'll figure out how later – before they give us our Nobel."

I rather thought he would mention that at some point.

"What I'm saying is, the scint may have given us an answer." I unfolded the printout tracking the photon trails in 8 Ball's central vacuum. I was still unsure how to read the scint's numbers, but I'd spent several hours in my office studying the graphic representation: four splash-ripples at the corners of an otherwise smooth pond. Four dropped pebbles creating regular, rather pretty disturbances. As expected.

But at the center of the four points of vibration, there rose a prominent hump – where nothing should be.

Tiflin looked over the printout with an expression almost of dread. *So much to lose*, I thought. *So careful not to sink the boat.* Right now, he was the most famous man in computing. His name was on every news show, headlining every major science and tech journal. He was trending big on Twitter – #Masterofchaos.

"You didn't trump this up?" he asked. There was an odd sidewise look in his eye, as if he had already seen these results but had ignored them.

"Of course not," I said. "You installed the scint. That's the latest report from Max, based on data you asked to be collected."

"Well, did we really need it, in the end?"

"The ripples at the corners represent our topological braids and their echoes," I said. "They're real – but they may not explain the speed."

"Then what does?"

I tapped the hump. "You tell me," I said. "What do you think that represents?"

"It could be a standing wave," he said. "Maybe a collaboration or combination of all the others. What's it doing there?"

"8 Ball may be compounding the entanglements," I said. "The standing wave could represent a huge mountain of computational power, more number crunching than there will ever be numbers. More numbers than there are universes. God himself can't think that fast. And there could be consequences we did not anticipate."

"What sort of consequences?" he asked.

I noted that he did not object to the metaphysics, the mysticism, and almost felt sorry for him. "When we got together at the warehouse five days ago, you were feeling all of your pockets. What were you looking for?"

"My gum," he said. "I've been chewing gum ever since I quit smoking. You know that."

"Did you find it?"

He shook his head. "No."

"What *did* you find?" I asked.

"A pack of cigarettes," he said. "And a lighter."

"Did you put them there?" I asked.

"No." So far he was being honest – which meant he had already been having doubts. "Did you?"

I didn't give that the dignity of a response. "Like somebody else was wearing your clothes, right? Someone a lot like you – but someone who still smoked. Did your wife notice a difference?"

"You're crazy," he said.

"How long have you been having these lapses back into old habits?"

"We've all been working too hard," he said, looking away.

"I think you tested 8 Ball before the big meeting. I think you and Dieter had been running the QC with the new protocols for at least three weeks before our first demo."

He looked defiant. "So I'm a cautious fellow," he said. "What's that got to do with any of this?"

"I have a ghost. Mine's a female version of myself. Looks a lot like me, and has been here long enough to figure things out. My wife saw her in Beijing – before we made our demo to Cate."

Tiflin flushed that beautiful titration pink. "That's ridiculous," he said not very forcefully.

"8 Ball had already begun its journey, weeks before – right?"

"Bullshit," Tiflin said, but it was no more than a whisper.

"Guess who clued me about these graphs?"

"Haven't the slightest."

"My other. My ghost. She left the printout where I would find it – in our car."

"That is just sad. Sad and sick."

"You drink Mountain Dew, don't you? How many cans a day?"

This jerked him up straight. He stood, spilling his coffee, and spun around to leave. The graphed ripples drifted to the floor, where I pinned the paper with my shoe.

I called after him, "We have to tell everybody. And then we have to shut it down!"

"Go to hell!" Tiflin said over his shoulder as he fled through the lobby.

THE ENTIRE TEAM sat around the conference table.

I got Tiflin to attend by threatening to tell Cate about our concerns.

The curtains had been drawn and the lights dimmed. The ceiling projector showed a montage of intersecting waves in 8 Ball's vacuum – the now-familiar four splashes surrounding the imposing central hump. 8 Ball was still running – who knew how many cycles?

Dieter told us he had loaded only fundamental operations the last few days, keeping the qubits powered up and working but doing nothing in particular, at least nothing too complicated. Just housekeeping – making sure all was well, all was healthy.

"Are we sure the standing wave is even in our system?" I asked. "And is it in fact at the center of the vacuum, or is that all just a mathematical fiction?"

"The detector is working!" Mickle said. "It's not defective."

"Then how can 8 Ball not be a lump of slag?" Wong asked. "According to the scint, the microwave temperature inside our quantum computer is well over a trillion degrees."

"Virtual microwave temp," Tiflin said. "Virtual doesn't affect the real. The helium is still cold. That counts for something."

"We should have been told about this right away," I said to nobody in particular. "This is for the theorists to understand and explain, not just engineers."

Dieter, despite having a foot in both camps – theory and engineering – sounded defensive. "It's not a sign of failure. We just don't know what's going on, yet."

"Entangled and braided photons that do not exist echo back on world lines that are mathematical fictions," I said, "leaving trails in the vacuum that produce virtual microwaves, and *they* don't exist either. None of it is remotely real!"

"That's a load of crap," Tiflin said. "We're successful. You just don't want to acknowledge *how* successful we are."

"You don't remember, do you?" I asked Tiflin, then looked at Dieter.

Mickle lowered his eyes as if in guilt. Dieter ignored us both.

"That hump, that so-called standing wave, is a massive reservoir of computation," I said. "Millions or even trillions of programs running at once. 8 Ball is a nexus for the work of I don't know how many programmers, all like us –"

Tiflin rapped his knuckles hard on the desk. "Let's not draw stupid conclusions," he said.

"For a time, 8 Ball was running trillions of programs – you said so yourself."

"A metaphor," Tiflin insisted.

"Those programs originated in millions of other universes," I continued. Mickle watched me with morbid fascination, as if I were digging my own grave. "They had to have programmers behind them. And yet, here they are – trillions of lines of code running without a causal beginning. What does that force the machine to do? What does it force the *universe* to do?"

"In theory –" Mickle said.

"Screw theory," said Tiflin. "We've worked too hard and spent too damned much time and money not to know what's happening with our own apparatus."

"Has anybody else looked at the security videos?" I asked.

Silence. Mickle looked away.

"Soft drink machines?"

"They're usually empty," Wong said.

"The cafeteria staff is slacking off," Tiflin said.

I was stubborn. "One by one, we should all look at the building security videos."

"What the hell would that tell us?" Tiflin asked, standing. Clearly he'd had enough.

"That there's more than one Dieter walking around Building 10," I said. "And more than one Tiflin."

"Christ," Tiflin said.

"I met Dieter in his office, then I saw him in Room 57," Mickle said. "He couldn't have got there ahead of me."

"Did he look like me totally – same clothes, same hair?" Dieter asked, fascinated.

"Yeah. And then – I think – when you saw him on the video feed, you both vanished."

"You *think*?"

"I made a note to that effect on my phone," Mickle said. "Because I don't remember."

"Me, too, with Tiflin," I said.

"Cool!" Dieter said, looking feverish. "If we could pin this down, make some real experiments, we'd know something tremendous, wouldn't we?"

Tiflin got out of his chair and went to the door.

I held out my hand to stop him. "My dupe told me to check the Pepsi supply. Most of us drink Pepsi or Mountain Dew."

"*Tra*-dition!" Mickle sang, straight out of *Fiddler on the Roof*.

Tiflin folded his arms.

"Some of us are fresh out of gum," I said. "Some of us wear the same clothes for days at a time, and dirty sneakers, and wouldn't notice if we were sharing, would we?"

"Go to hell," Tiflin said.

"They're out of Snapple, too," Mickle said. Oddly, like Dieter, he seemed to be enjoying this, as if it proved something important or at least interesting. Sometimes working with smarter people is infuriating.

"If we did look at the videos, what would that do?" Dieter asked with little-boy wonder. "I mean, none of us have met... *them*. Us. The others. If they exist."

"They do not exist," Tiflin said.

"But has anyone actually *seen* another?" Dieter asked. "What would happen if we just looked at them?"

"Collapse the wave function," Wong said. "Stop all this shit right in its tracks. One non-Abelian programmer can't exist in the same space or time as another, right?"

"They're no more real than the standing wave," Tiflin said in a high, exhausted growl. He seemed ready to break into tears. Who could blame him?

"I think we're way beyond being worried about 8 Ball's success," Dieter said. "But we could collapse it all – make all the others vanish, along with their programs. We can pull the plug."

"That would kill our bonuses," Mickle said.

"Cashing multiple versions of the same check will crash more than the wave function," I said.

And she was really smart. Maybe smarter than you! That's what my wife had told me. A female version of me had to have crossed some distance in the multiverse to occupy this world line, didn't she? She showed up first in China. I go there infrequently. And she figured it all out before I did. She somehow managed to avoid me, but still left me notes to clue me in. Notes apparently don't flip the state. To everyone else here, I am still male, and she had to act through me if she was to exert any influence in the open – right? Maybe my others, eventually, would come from far enough across the multiverse that *I* would be the anomaly.

This was bending my brain big-time.

"Why aren't we seeing hundreds of them? Thousands?" Mickle asked, clearly finding it hard to believe he was even asking the question.

Dieter was our Rottweiler when it came to pure theory. "Our spaces aren't that big. If more than one dupe meets – however many they are in total – they all vanish!"

"So if they appear in a clump, they cancel out immediately," Wong said, firmly in the spirit of this *gedanken* discussion.

"Heisenbergian crowd control," Mickle said. "Lovely."

Tiflin was pinking brightly now and couldn't bring himself to speak. My remark about the gum and the clothes had shaken him. Maybe he was starting to believe.

"Sorry," Dieter said, smiling as if at a lovely dream. "One last thought.

How many 8 Balls are there? Is our machine in a superposition with all the others? And how could that possibly be stable?"

"Shoot me now," Tiflin said, pushing past my arm toward the door.

THESE DUPES, AS Mickle calls them, are us, smart or smarter. They find themselves in roughly the same environments, covering the same or very similar world lines, attending the same meetings – if they're not yet clued in about such things – but never more than one per meeting, one per world line. The only way to survive is to avoid meeting yourself. Both will vanish. And their programs or parts of programs, in 8 Ball, might also vanish – which could help explain some weird irregularities in the output. The better programmers you or your dupe are, the more your vanishing affects the success of the standing wave.

I have employees not on our team going over the tapes, tracking us or versions of us on the security system, letting us know where 8 Ball programmers are congregating. Word is getting out. This is spooking everybody.

Why aren't there trillions of us, filling the Earth to capacity? First of all, there's that problem of encounters. Second, there's the probability that for every alternate world in the multiverse, we're sharing dupes. One vanishes from one world and appears in another. Dupes are traded – filling in a hole, like a tunneling electron – but are not actually duplicated.

And perhaps not even actually destroyed. Who can say?

Who could ever know?

And for every alternate Earth, there is an 8 Ball, very little different from the one we made, going through the same processes, running the same Gödelian strings, with the same successful discovery of extraordinarily long primes, the same confirmation of the Enormous Theorem, the same ability to solve problems involving insane levels of number-crunching. If we could coordinate or discover or *recover* all those programs, running on all those 8 Balls (or their successors), we'd probably have at least a short list of every possible mathematical problem, run to exhaustion or even solved.

That success will generate more funding for more machines like 8 Ball – bigger machines, newer machines, better and better machines. And all the worlds of the multiverse will begin to fill with people like us at an even faster rate; a surfeit of smart people, clever people, people smarter than me, until perhaps the flash point is reached – more brilliant programmers than any Earth actually needs. Would the multiverse start weeding out these upstarts?

I don't want to look at any more security tapes. I don't want to go home and find my female self in the arms of my wife. And I don't want to run into myself in Building 10 and pop out of existence.

I've packed a bag, taken a large sum out of my bank, kissed my wife, left a note for my 'sister,' gassed up my VW, and pretty soon I'll drive to a town I've never been to before, someplace I wouldn't think of. If of course I can think of such a place.

How many of me will think the same? Where would I *never* want to live? What if we all flee to the same safe, awful hellhole? And is it worth my survival to live there? Between me and my dupes, there's only one white VW Rabbit, and I seem to have the only set of keys. Dupes bring along their clothes but not their cars. Maybe *her* keys don't fit. Maybe she drives a Volvo. Smarter, right?

Again, this bends my brain. I'm trying to imagine the mass exodus. We'll empty the United States in our Teslas and Mercedeses and then rental cars and motorbikes and maybe bicycles and then just walking or running. A flood of the world's finest programmers spreading out from North America. Biblical!

An even more frightening thought –

Perhaps every universe has trillions of worlds with intelligent beings on them that are only now beginning to build machines like 8 Ball. Will the entire mass of all these universes be converted into programmers?

There is of course a theoretical safety valve, a choke point that could make all these frightening machines moot. It was Gödel himself who proved that mathematics would never be perfect and logically complete. Will that save us? If that limitation, that very wise act of cautious creation, brings all of this to a soft end, do we say thank God?

Or thank Gödel?

I leave these problems to those who are smarter than me. Maybe I think too much, worry too much. But please don't search for me. Don't tell me where I am, where I have been seen, or who's looking for me.

I don't want to know.

BLOOD, ASH, BRAIDS

Genevieve Valentine

GENEVIEVE VALENTINE'S (WWW.GENEVIEVEVALENTINE.COM) first novel, *Mechanique: A Tale of the Circus Tresaulti*, won the 2012 Crawford Award and was nominated for the Nebula. Her second, *The Girls at the Kingfisher Club*, appeared in 2014 to acclaim. Science fiction novel *Persona* appeared in 2015 and sequel *Icon* is due later this year. Her short fiction has appeared in *Clarkesworld*, *Strange Horizons*, *Journal of Mythic Arts*, *Fantasy*, *Tor.com*, and others; several stories have been reprinted in Best of the Year anthologies. Her nonfiction and reviews have appeared at NPR.org, *the AV Club, and The New York Times*. She has written *Catwoman* comics for DC, and is currently writing a new *Xena: Warrior Princess* comic for Dynamite! Her appetite for bad movies is insatiable.

1943

IT DIDN'T TAKE them long to find a name for us; almost as soon as they knew it was women inside the rickety planes they couldn't catch, the Germans called us witches.

It was because of the sounds our idling engines made from the ground, the story went, as if the German soldiers had spent a lot of time with brooms and knew what they sounded like, engineless and gliding fifty feet above them in the dark.

The wires holding the wings in place made the whistle. The canvas pulled taut around the plywood made the hush. I still suspect the thing that sounded supernatural was the whirr of our engines starting up again, as they realized we had already struck them, and it was too late to escape the blasts.

The officer who told us had half a smile on his face; he'd thought of the job as a demotion – most of them did, at first, to be in a camp full of girls – but if the Germans were already bleating back and forth about bounties for the heads of the Night Witches, then maybe he had real fighters on his hands.

Popova cracked a laugh when she heard, turned to me with grin that was all teeth. "I like that," she said. "Should we start screeching when we sail through, do you think?"

"I think not," I said. "The best witches know not to give away their position." And she laughed a little louder than she had to, as if she thought it was actually funny.

A couple of the girls glanced over from across the runway. They never took Popova's cue in being kind to me, but they were never cruel, and that might have been all Popova could hope for.

"She'd love being called a witch by the enemy; she might already be one," Popova said after a second, sounding circumspect, sounding a little reverent.

(*She* was Commander Raskova; at some point, she hadn't needed a name any more.)

But Raskova was elsewhere now, with only her shadow cast over us. Bershanskaya was the commander who lined us up and sent us out. She was as steady as they came, and her humor was thin and dry as air.

The first time Bershanskaya heard the name, she raised an eyebrow, and glanced quickly at me before she turned to Popova. Then she nodded, hands behind her, and said, "Let them call us what they like, if it suits them."

"Suits me, too," said Popova.

It suited all of them, I think, even if I was the only witch the 588th ever had.

ONE OF THE important things about the 588th was how little it cared where you came from. If you could take the recruiter's withering stare and the doctors' lingering hands and the open loathing of the men who ran you through your paces, and you managed to crawl under the stalled train cars to reach the station from the farthest set of tracks they could find to park your train, by the time you got to training they had no doubts about your nerves, and that was all they needed to know about you before they put you in a plane.

I'd come to the 588th out of necessity; my village had reached the end of their patience for someone who seemed always to know when it was going to rain and yet couldn't call it down for you even if you paid her. Easier to go find an open fight than to wait for the one that was brewing back home.

There was no way I could have accommodated village needs. It's too hard to do small magic.

From a one-room farmhouse or a palace in Moscow, anyone you ask will talk to you until their tongues turn blue about all the magic they've seen or heard of, even if they say they don't believe in it. They'll all know how it's being used against them even as they speak, and the hundreds of whispers shared in the depth of the forest by the witches, who gather there for market days and trade in secret spells in a currency of dirty looks.

It's all very well to keep people out of the woods at night, but it's foolish.

There are only three kinds of magic: water, ash, and air. For ash to work, you give blood. For water, you spill tears. For air, you give your breath. They all run out; our gifts are designed to be spent.

The woods will never be a gathering of witches. We don't live long enough.

Our planes were crop dusters, wood frames covered in canvas, held together with metal cords. They were the leftovers of aviation, planes given to people for whom no one had much hope.

But they were so flimsy and so slow that they made a kind of magic – gold out of hay. The German planes couldn't drop down to our speed or they'd stall out and plummet, so when they aimed for us we turned and they hit nothing but air; their anti-aircraft bombs would pop right through our wings and keep going, bursting a hundred feet above us as we banked a turn and the explosion illuminated our path back home.

Raskova courted us with those planes, showed us how to make them spin and make lazy loops in the air like the plaits of a braid, leapt down from the cockpit with her dark eyes glittering behind her goggles, and you could hear her heart pounding even from where you were standing. It was easy to want to go to war, to make Raskova proud.

And once you learned them, those planes were kinder to us than horses, and to sit inside one was to feel strangely invisible, a thrill crawling up the back of your neck like a ghost every time you settled in.

You settled in four, five, eight times a night: the plane couldn't carry more than two bombs at once, and you had work to do.

* * *

"You go out at sundown," says Bershanskaya.

Her lips are drawn thin, her hands folded behind her, her buttons marching a straight line to her chin. (She didn't want to lead, when Raskova appointed her. She hated sending us out to die.)

It's a bridge; we all know why it has to disappear – the Germans can't be allowed to move anything else into place. But they've stopped underestimating us, witches or not. They're prepared to throw us a flak circus now, every time they see us coming.

It's rows of guns blooming outward from the ground like flowers made from teeth, and searchlights by the dozens that flood the sky for fifty miles in each direction, and you can't get free of it no matter how you try; when you twist long enough this way and that way like a rabbit, you start to panic for your life.

We lost a team that way, not long back. Their cots are still folded up on the barracks, two thin mattresses for girls who won't be needing any more rest.

"You'll go in three planes at once," says Bershanskaya.

Next to me, the muscles in Popova's jaw shift as she realizes what Bershanskaya means.

Decoys. We'll be drawing fire in our little ghost planes.

We lost our hair to be here.

They made us cut it when we were first preparing for combat; for practicality, the commander said, though I had seen one or two of the training men glare at a line of girls walking off the field those first days, their long glossy braids swinging at their waists, and I always wondered.

I didn't mind, for myself – my hair was the watery brown of old deerhide, and there was no husband or want of a husband to stay my hand from the knife. For me to cut it just meant fewer pins I'd have to scramble for every time the sirens went up. But you can't tell girls for a hundred years that her hair is her crowning glory and then one day tell her to hack it off and not have her pause before the scissors.

We all did it, in the end, every last one of us submitting to the shears, slicing one another's braids off to the jaw.

Recklessly, I offered to burn the hair for any girl that wanted. It was forbidden to leave the base alone – it wasn't safe – but some things go deeper than regulations, and some superstitions aren't worth testing.

You never leave so much hair where anyone can take it from you; petty magic has uses for that, and none of them are good.

I was an odd fit in the barracks, just strange enough that we all knew I was strange, but this superstition was so well-known that not even Petrova looked twice at me as they each thanked me and handed me their braids of brown and black and gold.

As I headed for the woods with three dozen braids draped like pelts across my arms, Bershanskaya saw me. She was standing outside, near the engineers who were patching the planes. Her hands were behind her, and she had the narrow-eyed look of someone who had been watching the sunset longer than was wise.

I held my breath and kept going. If she called out to stop me, I'd keep walking until she shot. Some orders are holy; I had a duty deeper than hers.

She didn't say a word, but she watched me carry the plaits like a sacrifice into the cover of the trees.

In the woods, I built a fire and burned them – one at a time, until there was nothing left. I didn't start a new fire for each plait (we were tied close enough to withstand a little ash), but it was powerful enough that I was careful. I breathed steadily in and out; I thought carefully about nothing at all.

When I came back after dark, stinking of singe, Bershanskaya was standing outside the barracks and scanning the edge of the woods, waiting.

"Commander," I greeted when I was close enough, and waited for whatever she would do to me.

For a long time she looked me in the eye until it felt like I was canvas stretched across a wooden frame, and I could feel the question building on her tongue in the space just behind her front teeth, where people's worst suspicions lived.

If she asks me, I thought, she'll have her answer.

(I could cut myself deep enough to bleed. Blood and tears would summon something, I could hope I had enough willpower to make her forget what I'd done.)

She stepped aside, eyes still on me, and as I passed she said my name low, like she'd checked my name off a very short list; like a spell.

Raskova would have asked me. I don't know if that's better or worse.

* * *

In 1938, when I was still in school, Raskova had flown across the country for glory with Polina Denisovna Osipenko and Valentina Grizodubova. When they were recovered after their landing, the news was everywhere: that she and her copilots had broken flight records in the Rodina, that it was a marvelous feat of flying, that they were heroes of the nation.

I didn't find out what had really happened until Raskova told me herself. They had overshot in the mist, and when it parted they were suddenly over the Sea of Okhotsk, where the water in winter is the milky flat of a corpse's eye, and they didn't have enough gasoline left for the crossing – they'd flown too high to avoid being shrouded by the fog for a day and a night. They had to turn around and pray for landfall before they dropped out of the sky.

The navigator's seat – a glass bauble at the front of the plane – would be torn to shreds in a crash, and they were hurting for altitude and out of fuel and gathering too much ice to carry.

Raskova marked a map and jumped for it.

Her copilots crashed into the taiga, the bottom of the plane in shreds from the landing, and waited for her. Even after the rescue crew got to them, they refused to budge. They took watch by the plane for two more days, until Raskova staggered out of the woods.

It had been ten days. She'd had no food or water with her, and no compass when she jumped.

(There was no magic in her – not the sort that I had – but you wonder about witch blood in some people, when they manage things that no one should have managed.)

But more amazing to me even than her ten-day journey was the ten-day vigil the other two had kept, sheltering with the plane that had tried to kill them, without enough supplies, without knowing if she would ever come.

Doubt gnawed at me whenever I thought about it, more doubts than I ever had about being shot at, more doubts than I had about my chances of loosing a bomb just where it needed to go.

How long would they have waited beyond ten days? How long would I wait when it was my turn? Would I walk ten days in the wilderness rather than lie down and die?

Osipenko was dead. Wasn't even a strafing run; she'd just been going from one place to another, and her plane had turned on her.

Grizodubova had been sent elsewhere for the war effort. None of us had ever seen her. She was leading a defense and relief outfit near Leningrad, with real bombers and not crop dusters. She was commanding men.

I wondered if she and Raskova ever saw each other, or if they wrote – if it was safe to write. It would be easy to forgive if they had parted ways; it was wartime, and their duty to the nation lay before them.

But sometimes the nights are long and dark, and you feel so alone that you think everyone else must have someone closer than you do, and you think: If they don't still speak, it's because they're both waiting for death, and can't bear to come close and then be parted.

Then you stare up at the leaking roof and wonder if all each of them carried now was a phantom. When something wonderful or terrible happened, did one of them sometimes glance over her shoulder to look at the other before she remembered she was alone?

SEBROVA VOLUNTEERS TO be one of the three planes against the flak, and Popova volunteers second, and before I can do more than glance at Petrova for her agreement (she's already nodding at me) I'm volunteering, too, because I have few enough friends here. Where Popova is going, I want to go.

It's a foolish thing to do, volunteering to die on a German gun, but I volunteered for that a long time ago. I'm a quick draw on the controls, so I'll be of some use, and anything's better than sitting around waiting, wondering if Popova made it out.

Outside, I smoke a cigarette I won off Meklin at cards and watch the sun going down. I wish I had time to do everything that needs doing.

Popova sits next to me on the fence, lets out a breath at the streaks of gold and pink suspended just above the grass. When she taps me on the shoulder I hand her my cigarette.

She's a marvelous pilot – light and nimble – but you'd never know it from the way she smokes a cigarette, single loud pulls that leave a cylinder of ash that drops wholesale to the ground.

After a little while she hands me a piece of chocolate from inside her pocket, grainy and already melting across my fingertips. I pop it into my mouth and lick my fingers clean, flushing a little at the bad manners, but Popova only winks. I wonder how long she's held on to it, doling out to herself one piece at a time on nights she thinks she's going to die.

"You'll be all right," she says.

"Oh, I'm sure I will," I say. "It's you I worry over."

She casts me a look and half smiles. My lungs are acrid, suddenly. I pinch off the end of my cigarette to preserve the rest.

She shrugs. "We never let them get any sleep," she says, jamming a pin into her cropped hair and wrenching her cap on over it.

(Petrova sometimes reaches behind her to smooth a braid that isn't there. I've never seen Popova do it. I wonder what became of Raskova's dark brown braids, gleaming and pinned to her head as she spoke to us and made us into soldiers.)

Golden hair sticks out just at the edges, half curls below her ears. "I'd hate to see us coming, too. Let's hope they're too tired to aim."

I want to smile or laugh, but I'm staring at my plane and feeling ice down my spine. Why this should be so different I don't know – slightly more impossible than impossible isn't a measurement that has much meaning – but I look at the trees instead, after a moment.

"How did you decide to do this?"

I don't know why I ask. We're all meant to be without a past, and equal. They were carpenters and secretaries and farm girls, but they're pilots now, and it shouldn't matter how they got here.

Popova raises her eyebrows at the setting sun like it's the one who'd asked the rude question. There are only a few minutes left until it's dark enough to load up and set off. I should be going back to barracks and getting my gear.

She says without looking at me, "A plane landed near our house, when I was young."

Young – she's nineteen now, I think, but I don't say anything. Rude to interrupt. Not that it matters; she doesn't elaborate. It's the biography of a masterful pilot who knows better than to waste a gesture.

She glances over. "And you?"

"Oh, I'm a witch," I say. "Flying comes naturally." And she grins as she drops from the fence, snaps her goggles into place.

"Good thing it can be taught," she says and takes off for her plane.

It can't, not really. You can teach the mechanics of a plane, but either you have the flight inside you or you don't.

Her strides kick up puffs of dust in her wake that cover her footsteps; at nightfall she casts no shadow, and for a moment she looks like I'd imagined witches to be, before I knew better.

When she's gone, I unroll the cigarette and scoop up her ashes from the ground with the blade of my knife.

It's a sharp blade; I never even feel the cut I make. When the paper gets wet enough, I use the tip of the knife to mix it and drag a line of blood and ash under the nose of Sebrova's and Popova's planes.

I do it quickly, my eyes stinging, my heart pounding.

Then they're coming from the barracks, and I'm out of ashes and out of time and have to step away and get my gear. We'll need to make sure the altitude gauge is fixed before we're off the ground.

Petrova, my navigator, is already there, frowning underneath the propeller and tapping our windshields. As I haul myself onto the wing, I press one bloody thumbprint into the canvas just behind her seat, where she'll never see.

Blood magic doesn't work as well when you're asking for yourself, but I'll protect who I can, however it comes.

EACH OF US carries two bombs. It's decided in the last seconds before leaping into our planes that Sebrova will be first, I'll be second, and Popova will make the final drop, after they're already on to us. I don't like it, but I keep my hands on the controls as we enter the flak zone.

The engines sound impossibly loud – three of them, and we don't dare cut them with what we have to do, so there's nothing for it but to go closer and closer, knowing they know we're coming, waiting for the bullets to start.

(I miss the sound of the wind through the wires; it had always sounded to me like an owl on my shoulder, and it was a comfort as you were moving in for the drop.)

The first floodlight is almost a relief – it's something to do, at least, instead of just something to be afraid of – and I wait two seconds longer than my instincts scream to, just enough that the nose of the plane catches the light, that it can almost but not quite follow me when I snap a turn to one side, dropping out of their sight. A spray of bullets arcs behind me, whistling clean and hitting nothing.

I don't look for Popova. It's not safe.

Instead I drop steeply so the searchlights casting at my prior heading can't find me, and pull up at the last second with my heart pounding in my throat and the engine grinding underneath me. I cut through three lights at once, a dead hover for a moment as gravity gets confused, the blinding flashes underneath us reminding me to bank left and out of the line of fire.

I hear a series of dull thunders, then a thudding rip – a wingtip's been struck. Nothing serious, it's a lucky hit for them, that's all, but my lungs go so tight I have to wrestle them for breath as I circle back. There's already ice on my tiny windshield; there's ice in my throat when I breathe.

Then I see Sebrova's plane arcing up to meet us. She's done it; the thunders were her bombs hitting home.

It's my turn.

Petrova gives me the all-clear, and I do a big, lazy loop well out of the scope of the spotlights – I glimpse Popova, barely, practically cartwheeling and vanishing into the dark – breathe deep through my nose as we sail over the iron garden. Sebrova's been kind enough to mark the way (a fire's already started next to the drop site), but I want to be careful, and only when Petrova gives the sign do I tilt us five degrees closer to the Earth, no more, and let the unfastened bombs slide forward, hurtling toward the ground with a cheerful whistle.

I sweep up and to the left, taking my place on the flank, and the plane shakes for just a second as the payload explodes, a warm burst of orange in the black night. Petrova whoops; I grin for as long as I can stand the wind in my teeth, which isn't long, and then push through the acrid scents of fire and guns and panic toward my secondary position.

Popova's plane drops so fast I think for a second, my grip seizing on the controls, that she's been struck, but it's just the way she handles a plane – I hear the whirr of her engines above the tuneless wind as I cut straight across and through the searchlights, distracting them from her, letting them waste two arcs of ammunition trying to pin me as I drop and spin out lazily, letting the wind pull us the last few inches to the top of the arc.

But it's too bright when I get there, far too bright, and I realize with numb panic that they've got me locked, and the next round of bullets will hit home.

I try for more altitude, already knowing I'm too late, and I wonder wildly if I can point the plane at the ground so hard that Petrova and I die without pain. We have to die – we can't let the Germans take us – but she shouldn't suffer.

Really, the way to go out is a bullet through the heart. The Germans could oblige. It would keep them from wondering where Popova's gone.

Better this than ten days in the wilderness, I think; better this than to wait at the Sea of Okhotsk.

I let out my breath until there's nothing left (blood-ash-air, I think dimly, someplace with no hope left, blood-ash-air), and bank the turn straight into the center of the circling lights.

I die that way, the way Raskova died, with a tailspin and then nightfall – but not on this run. On this run, the spray of bullets never comes, because Popova's plane soars straight in front of me.

The Germans are only tracking two of our planes, and with the interruption they can't tell whether or not they've tricked themselves into a double image with the swinging searchlights, and in the few seconds where the lights freeze in place as they try to decide what to do, I bank as hard as I can and cut down and out and back into the dark, fingers aching, pointed for home.

We're the last to get back. When I climb out of the plane I can barely stand; I don't know where all my blood's gone. Bershanskaya's come to meet us. When she nods, I find it in me to straighten up and nod back.

Popova's leaning against her plane, a few feet back from the mark of my blood and her ashes that she'll never see. There are three bullet holes through one of her wings, like a smattering of freckles at the tip of someone's nose, but she's there.

She grins around a square of chocolate, calls over, "What kept you?"

I PUT BLOOD and ashes on every plane that goes out after that.

Once I duck out between the planes and see Bershanskaya watching me, her hands behind her. She doesn't ask what I'm doing there. I never say. It doesn't matter. It's what I've given over, and you can't call it back.

It's on my plane, too, the night I go down, but I never expected that to protect me for long. They all run out; our gifts are designed to be spent.

A little while from now, Popova will go on a raid and get caught in German fire. When she makes it back to the base, there will be more than forty bullet holes in the plane. There are bullet holes in her helmet.

No one will understand how she survived it; no one can imagine what protected her.

HUNGRY DAUGHTERS OF STARVING MOTHERS

Alyssa Wong

ALYSSA WONG (WWW.CRASHWONG.NET) is a Nebula, Shirley Jackson, and World Fantasy Award-nominated author, shark aficionado, and graduate of the Clarion Writers' Workshop. Her work has appeared in *The Magazine of Fantasy & Science Fiction, Strange Horizons, Tor.com, Uncanny Magazine, Lightspeed Magazine, Nightmare Magazine,* and *Black Static,* among others. She is an MFA candidate at North Carolina State University, and a member of the Manhattan-based writing group Altered Fluid. She can be found on twitter @crashwong.

AS MY DATE – Harvey? Harvard? – brags about his alma mater and Manhattan penthouse, I take a bite of overpriced kale and watch his ugly thoughts swirl overhead. It's hard to pay attention to him with my stomach growling and my body ajitter, for all he's easy on the eyes. Harvey doesn't look much older than I am, but his thoughts, covered in spines and centipede feet, glisten with ancient grudges and carry an entitled, Ivy League stink.

"My apartment has the most amazing view of the city," he's saying, his thoughts sliding long over each other like dark, bristling snakes. Each one is as thick around as his Rolex-draped wrist. "I just installed a Jacuzzi along the west wall so that I can watch the sun set while I relax after getting back from the gym."

I nod, half-listening to the words coming out of his mouth. I'm much more interested in the ones hissing through the teeth of the thoughts above him.

She's got perfect tits, lil' handfuls just waiting to be squeezed. I love me some perky tits.

I'm gonna fuck this bitch so hard she'll never walk straight again.

Gross. "That sounds wonderful," I say as I sip champagne and gaze at him through my false eyelashes, hoping the dimmed screen of my iPhone isn't visible through the tablecloth below. This dude is boring as hell, and I'm already back on Tinder, thumbing through next week's prospective dinner dates.

She's so into me, she'll be begging for it by the end of the night.

I can't wait to cut her up.

My eyes flick up sharply. "I'm sorry?" I say.

Harvey blinks. "I said, Argentina is a beautiful country."

Pretty little thing. She'll look so good spread out all over the floor.

"Right," I say. "Of course." Blood's pulsing through my head so hard it probably looks like I've got a wicked blush.

I'm so excited, I'm half hard already.

You and me both, I think, turning my iPhone off and smiling my prettiest smile.

The waiter swings by with another bottle of champagne and a dessert menu burned into a wooden card, but I wave him off. "Dinner's been lovely," I whisper to Harvey, leaning in and kissing his cheek, "but I've got a different kind of dessert in mind."

Ahhh, go the ugly thoughts, settling into a gentle, rippling wave across his shoulders. *I'm going to take her home and split her all the way from top to bottom. Like a fucking fruit tart.*

That is not the way I normally eat fruit tarts, but who am I to judge? I passed on dessert, after all.

When he pays the bill, he can't stop grinning at me. Neither can the ugly thoughts hissing and cackling behind his ear.

"What's got you so happy?" I ask coyly.

"I'm just excited to spend the rest of the evening with you," he replies.

THE FUCKER HAS his own parking spot! No taxis for us; he's even brought the Tesla. The leather seats smell buttery and sweet, and as I slide in and make myself comfortable, the rankness of his thoughts leaves a stain in the air. It's enough to leave me light-headed, almost purring. As we cruise uptown toward his fancy-ass penthouse, I ask him to pull over near the Queensboro Bridge for a second.

Annoyance flashes across his face, but he parks the Tesla in a side street. I lurch into an alley, tottering over empty cans and discarded cigarettes in my four-inch heels, and puke a trail of champagne and kale over to the dumpster shoved up against the apartment building.

"Are you all right?" Harvey calls.

"I'm fine," I slur. Not a single curious window opens overhead.

His steps echo down the alley. He's gotten out of the car, and he's walking toward me like I'm an animal that he needs to approach carefully.

Maybe I should do it now.

Yes! Now, now, while the bitch is occupied.

But what about the method? I won't get to see her insides all pretty everywhere –

I launch myself at him, fingers digging sharp into his body, and bite down hard on his mouth. He tries to shout, but I swallow the sound and shove my tongue inside. There, just behind his teeth, is what I'm looking for: ugly thoughts, viscous as boiled tendon. I suck them howling and fighting into my throat as Harvey's body shudders, little mewling noises escaping from his nose.

I feel decadent and filthy, swollen with the cruelest dreams I've ever tasted. I can barely feel Harvey's feeble struggles; in this state, with the darkest parts of himself drained from his mouth into mine, he's no match for me.

They're never as strong as they think they are.

By the time he finally goes limp, the last of the thoughts disappearing down my throat, my body's already changing. My limbs elongate, growing thicker, and my dress feels too tight as my ribs expand. I'll have to work quickly. I strip off my clothes with practiced ease, struggling a little to work the bodice free of the gym-toned musculature swelling under my skin.

It doesn't take much time to wrestle Harvey out of his clothes, either. My hands are shaking but strong, and as I button up his shirt around me and shrug on his jacket, my jaw has creaked into an approximation of his and the ridges of my fingerprints have reshaped themselves completely. Harvey is so much bigger than me, and the expansion of space eases the pressure on my boiling belly, stuffed with ugly thoughts as it is. I stuff my discarded outfit into my purse, my high heels clicking against the empty glass jar at its bottom, and sling the strap over my now-broad shoulder.

I kneel to check Harvey's pulse – slow but steady – before rolling his unconscious body up against the dumpster, covering him with trash bags. Maybe he'll wake up, maybe he won't. Not my problem, as long as he doesn't wake in the next ten seconds to see his doppelganger strolling out of the alley, wearing his clothes and fingering his wallet and the keys to his Tesla.

There's a cluster of drunk college kids gawking at Harvey's car. I level an arrogant stare at them – oh, but do I wear this body so much better than he did! – and they scatter.

I might not have a license, but Harvey's body remembers how to drive.

THE TESLA REVS sweetly under me, but I ditch it in a parking garage in Bedford, stripping in the relative privacy of the second-to-highest level, edged behind a pillar. After laying the keys on the driver's seat over Harvey's neatly folded clothes and shutting the car door, I pull the glass jar from my purse and vomit into it as quietly as I can. Black liquid, thick and viscous, hits the bottom of the jar, hissing and snarling Harvey's words. My body shudders, limbs retracting, spine reshaping itself, as I empty myself of him.

It takes a few more minutes to ease back into an approximation of myself, at least enough to slip my dress and heels back on, pocket the jar, and comb my tangled hair out with my fingers. The parking attendant nods at me as I walk out of the garage, his eyes sliding disinterested over me, his thoughts a gray, indistinct murmur.

The L train takes me back home to Bushwick, and when I push open the apartment door, Aiko is in the kitchen, rolling mochi paste out on the counter.

"You're here," I say stupidly. I'm still a little foggy from shaking off Harvey's form, and strains of his thoughts linger in me, setting my blood humming uncomfortably hot.

"I'd hope so. You invited me over." She hasn't changed out of her catering company clothes, and her short, sleek hair frames her face, aglow in the kitchen light. Not a single ugly thought casts its shadow across the stove behind her. "Did you forget again?"

"No," I lie, kicking my shoes off at the door. "I totally would never do something like that. Have you been here long?"

"About an hour, nothing unusual. The doorman let me in, and I kept your spare key." She smiles briefly, soft compared to the brusque movements of her hands. She's got flour on her rolled-up sleeves, and my heart flutters the way it never does when I'm out hunting. "I'm guessing your date was pretty shit. You probably wouldn't have come home at all if it had gone well."

"You could say that." I reach into my purse and stash the snarling jar in the fridge, where it clatters against the others, nearly a dozen bottles of malignant leftovers labeled as health drinks.

Aiko nods to her right. "I brought you some pastries from the event tonight. They're in the paper bag on the counter."

"You're an angel." I edge past her so I don't make bodily contact. Aiko thinks I have touch issues, but the truth is, she smells like everything good in the world, solid and familiar, both light and heavy at the same time, and it's enough to drive a person mad.

"He should have bought you a cab back, at least," says Aiko, reaching for a bowl of red bean paste. I fiddle with the bag of pastries, pretending to select something from its contents. "I swear, it's like you're a magnet for terrible dates."

She's not wrong; I'm very careful about who I court. After all, that's how I stay fed. But no one in the past has been as delicious, as hideously depraved as Harvey. No one else has been a killer.

I'm going to take her home and split her all the way from top to bottom.

"Maybe I'm too weird," I say.

"You're probably too normal. Only socially maladjusted creeps use Tinder."

"Gee, thanks," I complain.

She grins, flicking a bit of red bean paste at me. I lick it off of my arm. "You know what I mean. Come visit my church with me sometime, yeah? There are plenty of nice boys there."

"The dating scene in this city depresses me," I mutter, flicking open my Tinder app with my thumb. "I'll pass."

"Come on, Jen, put that away." Aiko hesitates. "Your mom called while you were out. She wants you to move back to Flushing."

I bark out a short, sharp laugh, my good mood evaporating. "What else is new?"

"She's getting old," Aiko says. "And she's lonely."

"I bet. All her mahjong partners are dead, pretty much." I can imagine her in her little apartment in Flushing, huddled over her laptop, floral curtains pulled tight over the windows to shut out the rest of the world. My ma, whose apartment walls are alive with hissing, covered in the ugly, bottled remains of her paramours.

Aiko sighs, joining me at the counter and leaning back against me. For once, I don't move away. Every muscle in my body is tense, straining. I'm afraid I might catch fire, but I don't want her to leave. "Would it kill you to be kind to her?"

I think about my baba evaporating into thin air when I was five years old, what was left of him coiled in my ma's stomach. "Are you telling me to go back?"

She doesn't say anything for a bit. "No," she says at last. "That place isn't good for you. That house isn't good for anyone."

Just a few inches away, an army of jars full of black, viscous liquid wait in the fridge, their contents muttering to themselves. Aiko can't hear them, but each slosh against the glass is a low, nasty hiss:

who does she think she is, the fucking cunt

should've got her when I had the chance

I can still feel Harvey, his malice and ugly joy, on my tongue. I'm already full of things my ma gave me. "I'm glad we agree."

OVER THE NEXT few weeks, I gorge myself on the pickup artists and grad students populating the St. Marks hipster bars, but nothing tastes good after Harvey. Their watery essences, squeezed from their owners with barely a whimper of protest, barely coat my stomach. Sometimes I take too much. I scrape them dry and leave them empty, shaking their forms off like rainwater when I'm done.

I tell Aiko I've been partying when she says I look haggard. She tells me to quit drinking so much, her face impassive, her thoughts clouded with concern. She starts coming over more often, even cooking dinner for me, and her presence both grounds me and drives me mad.

"I'm worried about you," she says as I lie on the floor, flipping listlessly through pages of online dating profiles, looking for the emptiness, the rot, that made Harvey so appealing. She's cooking my mom's lo mein recipe, the oily smell making my skin itch. "You've lost so much weight and there's nothing in your fridge, just a bunch of empty jam jars."

I don't tell her that Harvey's lies under my bed, that I lick its remnants every night to send my nerves back into euphoria. I don't tell her how often I dream about my ma's place, the shelves of jars she never let me touch. "Is it really okay for you to spend so much time away from your catering business?" I say instead. "Time is money, and Jimmy gets pissy when he has to make all the desserts without you."

Aiko sets a bowl of lo mien in front of me and joins me on the ground. "There's nowhere I'd rather be than here," she says, and a dangerous, luminous sweetness blooms in my chest.

But the hunger grows worse every day, and soon I can't trust myself around her. I deadbolt the door, and when she stops by my apartment to check on me, I refuse to let her in. Texts light up my phone like a fleet of fireworks as I huddle under a blanket on the other side, my face pressed against the wood, my fingers twitching.

"Please, Jen, I don't understand," she says from behind the door. "Did I do something wrong?"

I can't wait to cut her up, I think, and hate myself even more.

By the time Aiko leaves, her footsteps echoing down the hallway, I've dug deep gouges in the door's paint with my nails and teeth, my mouth full of her intoxicating scent.

MY MA'S APARTMENT in Flushing still smells the same. She's never been a clean person, and the sheer amount of junk stacked up everywhere has increased since I left home for good. Piles of newspapers, old food containers, and stuffed toys make it hard to push the door open, and the stench makes me cough. Her hoard is up to my shoulders, even higher in some places, and as I pick my way through it, the sounds that colored my childhood grow louder: the constant whine of a Taiwanese soap opera bleeding past mountains of trash, and the cruel cacophony of many familiar voices:

Touch me again and I swear I'll kill you –

How many times have I told you not to wash the clothes like that, open your mouth –

Hope her ugly chink daughter isn't home tonight –

Under the refuse she's hoarded the walls are honeycombed with shelves, lined with what's left of my ma's lovers. She keeps them like disgusting, mouthwatering trophies, desires pickling in stomach acid and bile. I could probably call them by name if I wanted to; when I was a kid, I used to lie on the couch and watch my baba's ghost flicker across their surfaces.

My ma's huddled in the kitchen, the screen of her laptop casting a sickly blue glow on her face. Her thoughts cover her quietly like a blanket. "I made some niu ro mien," she says. "It's on the stove. Your baba's in there."

My stomach curls, but whether it's from revulsion or hunger I can't tell. "Thanks, ma," I say. I find a bowl that's almost clean and wash it out, ladling a generous portion of thick noodles for myself. The broth smells faintly of hongtashan tobacco, and as I force it down almost faster than I can swallow, someone else's memories of my childhood flash before my eyes: pushing a small girl on a swing set at the park; laughing as she chases pigeons down the street; raising a hand for a second blow as her mother launches herself toward us, between us, teeth bared –

"How is it?" she says.

Foul. "Great," I say. It settles my stomach, at least for a little while. But my baba was no Harvey, and I can already feel the hunger creeping back, waiting for the perfect moment to strike.

"You ate something you shouldn't have, didn't you, Meimei." My ma looks up at me for the first time since I walked in, and she looks almost as tired as I feel. "Why didn't you learn from me? I taught you to stick to petty criminals. I taught you to stay invisible."

She'd tried to teach me to disappear into myself, the way she'd disappeared into this apartment. "I know I messed up," I tell her. "Nothing tastes good any more, and I'm always hungry. But I don't know what to do."

My ma sighs. "Once you've tasted a killer, there's no turning back. You'll crave that intensity until you die. And it can take a long time for someone like us to die, Meimei."

It occurs to me that I don't actually know how old my ma is. Her thoughts are old and covered in knots, stitched together from the remnants of other people's experiences. How long has she been fighting this condition, these overwhelming, gnawing desires?

"Move back in," she's saying. "There's so much tong activity here, the streets leak with blood. You barely even have to go outside, just crack open a window and you can smell it brewing. The malice, the knives and bullets..."

The picture she paints makes me shudder, my mouth itching. "I can't just leave everything, Ma," I say. "I have my own life now." And I can't live in this apartment, with its lack of sunlight and fresh air, its thick stench of regret and malice.

"So what happens if you go back? You lose control, you take a bite out of Aiko?" She sees me stiffen. "That girl cares about you so much. The best thing you can do for her is keep away. Don't let what happened to your father happen to Aiko." She reaches for my hand, and I pull away. "Stay here, Meimei. We only have each other."

"This isn't what I want." I'm backing up, and my shoulder bumps into the trash, threatening to bury us both in rotting stuffed animals. "This isn't *safe*, Ma. You shouldn't even stay here."

My ma coughs, her eyes glinting in the dark. The cackling from her jar collection swells in a vicious tide, former lovers rocking back and forth on their shelves. "Someday you'll learn that there's more to life than being selfish, Meimei."

That's when I turn my back on her, pushing past the debris and bullshit her apartment's stuffed with. I don't want to die, but as far as I'm concerned, living like my ma, sequestered away from the rest of the world, her doors barricaded with heaps of useless trinkets and soured memories, is worse than being dead.

The jars leer and cackle as I go, and she doesn't try to follow me.

The scent of Flushing clings to my skin, and I can't wait to shake it off. I get on the train as soon as I can, and I'm back on Tinder as soon as the M passes above ground. Tears blur my eyes, rattling free with the movement of the train. I scrub them away angrily, and when my vision clears, I glance back at the screen. A woman with sleek, dark hair, slim tortoiseshell glasses, and a smile that seems a little shy, but strangely handsome, glows up at me. In the picture, she's framed by the downtown cityscape. She has rounded cheeks, but there's a strange flat quality to her face. And then, of course, there are the dreams shadowing her, so strong they leak from the screen in a thick, heady miasma. Every one of those myriad eyes is staring straight at me, and my skin prickles.

I scan the information on her profile page, my blood beating so hard I can feel my fingertips pulsing: relatively young-looking, but old enough to be my mother's cousin. Likes: exploring good food, spending rainy days at the Cloisters, browsing used book stores. Location: Manhattan.

She looks a little like Aiko.

She's quick to message me back. As we flirt, cold sweat and adrenaline send uncomfortable shivers through my body. Everything is sharper, and I can almost hear Harvey's jar laughing. Finally, the words I'm waiting for pop up:

I'd love to meet you. Are you free tonight?

I make a quick stop-off back home, and my heart hammers as I get on the train bound for the Lower East Side, red lipstick immaculate and arms shaking beneath my crisp designer coat, a pair of Mom's glass jars tucked in my purse.

HER NAME IS Seo-yun, and as she watches me eat, her eyes flickering from my mouth to my throat, her smile is so sharp I could cut myself on it. "I love places like this," she says. "Little authentic spots with only twelve seats. Have you been to Haru before?"

"I haven't," I murmur. My fingers are clumsy with my chopsticks, tremors clicking them together, making it hard to pick up my food. God, she smells delectable. I've never met someone whose mind is so twisted, so rich; a malignancy as well developed and finely crafted as the most elegant dessert.

I'm going to take her home and split her open like a –

I can already taste her on my tongue, the best meal I've never had.

"You're in for a treat," Seo-yun says as the waiter – the only other staff beside the chef behind the counter – brings us another pot of tea. "This restaurant started as a stall in a subway station back in Japan."

"Oh wow," I say. "That's... amazing."

"I think so, too. I'm glad they expanded into Manhattan."

Behind her kind eyes, a gnarled mess of ancient, ugly thoughts writhes like the tails of a rat king. I've never seen so many in one place. They crawl from her mouth and ears, creeping through the air on deep-scaled legs, their voices like the drone of descending locusts.

I'm not her first. I can tell that already. But then, she isn't mine, either.

I spend the evening sweating through my dress, nearly dropping my chopsticks. I can't stop staring at the ugly thoughts, dropping from her lips like swollen beetles. They skitter over the tablecloth toward me, whispering obscenities at odds with Seo-yun's gentle voice, hissing what they'd like to do to me. It takes everything in me not to pluck them from the table and crunch them deep between my teeth right then and there, to pour into her lap and rip her mind clean.

Seo-yun is too much for me, but I'm in too far, too hard; I *need* to have her.

She smiles at me. "Not hungry?"

I glance down at my plate. I've barely managed a couple of nigiri. "I'm on a diet," I mutter.

"I understand," she says earnestly. The ugly thoughts crawl over the tops of her hands, iridescent drops spilling into her soy sauce dish.

When the waiter finally disappears into the kitchen, I move in to kiss her across the table. She makes a startled noise, gentle pink spreading across her face, but she doesn't pull away. My elbow sinks into the exoskeleton of one of the thought-beetles, crushing it into black, moist paste against my skin.

I open my mouth to take the first bite.

"So, I'm curious," murmurs Seo-yun, her breath brushing my lips. "Who's Aiko?"

My eyes snap open. Seo-yun smiles, her voice warm and tender, all her edges dark. "She seems sweet, that's all. I'm surprised you haven't had a taste of her yet."

I back up so fast that I knock over my teacup, spilling scalding tea over everything. But Seo-yun doesn't move, just keeps smiling that kind, gentle smile as her monstrous thoughts lap delicately at the tablecloth.

"She smells so ripe," she whispers. "But you're afraid you'll ruin her, aren't you? Eat her up, and for what? Just like your mum did your dad."

No, no, no. I've miscalculated so badly. But I'm so hungry, and I'm too young, and she smells like ancient power. There's no way I'll be able to outrun her. "Get out of my head," I manage to say.

"I'm not in your head, love. Your thoughts are spilling out everywhere around you, for everyone to see." She leans in, propping her chin on her hand. The thoughts twisted around her head like a living crown let out a dry, rattling laugh. "I like you, Jenny. You're ambitious. A little careless, but we can fix that." Seo-yun taps on the table, and the waiter reappears, folding up the tablecloth deftly and sliding a single dish onto the now-bare table. An array of thin, translucent slices fan out across the plate, pale and glistening with malice. Bisected eyes glint, mouths caught mid-snarl, from every piece. "All it takes is a little practice and discipline, and no one will know what you're really thinking."

"On the house, of course, Ma'am," the waiter murmurs. Before he disappears again, I catch a glimpse of dark, many-legged thoughts braided like a bracelet around his wrist.

Seo-yun takes the first bite, glancing up at me from behind her glasses. "Your mum was wrong," she says. "She thought you were alone, just the two of you. So she taught you to only eat when you needed to, so you didn't get caught, biding your time between meals like a snake."

"You don't know anything about me," I say. The heady, rotten perfume from the dish in front of me makes my head spin with hunger.

"My mum was much the same. Eat for survival, not for pleasure." She gestures at the plate with her chopsticks. "Please, have some."

As the food disappears, I can only hold out for a few more slices before my chopsticks dart out, catching a piece for myself. It's so acidic it makes my tongue burn and eyes itch, the aftertaste strangely sweet.

"Do you like it?"

I respond by wolfing down another two slices, and Seo-yun chuckles. Harvey is bland compared to this, this strangely distilled pairing of emotions –

I gasp as my body starts to warp, hands withering, burn scars twisting their way around my arms. Gasoline, malice, childish joy rush through me, a heady mix of memory and sensory overstimulation. And then Seo-yun's lips are on mine, teeth tugging gently, swallowing, drawing it out of me. The burns fade, but the tingle of cruel euphoria lingers.

She wipes her mouth delicately. "Ate a little too fast, I think, dear," she says. "My point, Jenny, is that I believe in eating for pleasure, not just survival. And communally, of course. There are a number of us who get together for dinner or drinks at my place, every so often, and I would love it if you would join us tonight. An eating club, of sorts."

My gaze flickers up at her thoughts, but they're sitting still as stones, just watching me with unblinking eyes. My mouth stings with the imprint of hers.

"Let me introduce you soon. You don't have to be alone anymore." As the waiter clears the plate and nods at her – no check, no receipt, nothing – Seo-yun adds, "And tonight doesn't have to be over until we want it to be." She offers me her hand. After a moment's hesitation, I take it. It's smaller than mine, and warm.

"Yes, please," I say, watching her thoughts instead of her face.

As we leave the restaurant, she presses her lips to my forehead. Her lips sear into my skin, nerves singing white-hot with ecstasy. "They're going to love you," she says.

We'll have so much fun, say the thoughts curling through her dark hair.

She hails a cab from the fleet circling the street like wolves, and we get inside.

I RUN INTO Aiko two months later in front of my apartment, as I'm carrying the last box of my stuff out. She's got a startled look on her face, and she's carrying a bag stuffed with ramps, kaffir lime, heart of palm – all ingredients I wouldn't have known two months ago, before meeting Seo-yun. "You're moving?"

I shrug, staring over her head, avoiding her eyes. "Yeah, uh. I'm seeing someone now, and she's got a really nice place."

"Oh." She swallows, shifts the bag of groceries higher on her hip. "That's great. I didn't know you were dating anybody." I can hear her shaky smile. "She must be feeding you well. You look healthier."

"Thanks," I say, though I wonder. It's true, I'm sleeker, more confident now. I'm barely home any more, spending most of my time in Seo-yun's Chelsea apartment, learning to cook with the array of salts and spices infused with ugly dreams, drinking wine distilled from deathbed confessions. My time stalking the streets for small-time criminals is done. But why has my confidence evaporated the moment I see Aiko? And if that ravenous hunger from Harvey is gone, why am I holding my breath to keep from breathing in her scent?

"So what's she like?"

"Older, kind of" – *kind of looks like you* – "short. Likes to cook, right." I start to edge past her. "Listen, this box is heavy and the van's waiting for me downstairs. I should go."

"Wait," Aiko says, grabbing my arm. "Your mom keeps calling me. She still has my number from... before. She's worried about you. Plus I haven't seen you in ages, and you're just gonna take off?"

Aiko, small and humble. Her hands smell like home, like rice flour and bad memories. How could I ever have found that appealing?

"We don't need to say goodbye. I'm sure I'll see you later," I lie, shrugging her off.

"Let's get dinner sometime," says Aiko, but I'm already walking away.

CATERERS FLIT LIKE blackbirds through the apartment, dark uniforms neatly pressed, their own ugly thoughts braided and pinned out of the way. It's a two-story affair, and well-dressed people flock together everywhere there's space, Seo-yun's library upstairs to the living room on ground floor. She's even asked the caterers to prepare some of my recipes, which makes my heart glow. "You're the best," I say, kneeling on the bed beside her and pecking her on the cheek.

Seo-yun smiles, fixing my hair. She wears a sleek, deep blue dress, and today, her murderous thoughts are draped over her shoulders like a stole, a living, writhing cape. Their teeth glitter like tiny diamonds. I've never seen her so beautiful. "They're good recipes. My friends will be so excited to taste them."

I've already met many of them, all much older than I am. They make me nervous. "I'll go check on the food," I say.

She brushes her thumb over my cheek. "Whatever you'd like, love."

I escape into the kitchen, murmuring brief greetings to the guests I encounter on the way. Their hideous dreams adorn them like jewels, glimmering and snatching at me as I slip past. As I walk past some of the cooks, I notice a man who looks vaguely familiar. "Hey," I say.

"Yes, ma'am?" The caterer turns around, and I realize where I've seen him; there's a picture of him and Aiko on her cellphone, the pair of them posing in front of a display at a big event they'd cooked for. My heartbeat slows.

"Aren't you Aiko's coworker?"

He grins and nods. "Yes, I'm Jimmy. Aiko's my business partner. Are you looking for her?"

"Wait, she's here?"

He frowns. "She should be. She never misses one of Ms. Sun's parties." He smiles. "Ms. Sun lets us take home whatever's left when the party winds down. She's so generous."

I turn abruptly and head for the staircase to the bedroom, shouldering my way through the crowd. Thoughts pelt me as I go: Has Aiko known about me, my ma, what we can do? How long has she known? And worse – Seo-yun's known all along about Aiko, and played me for a fool.

I bang the bedroom door open to find Aiko sprawled out across the carpet, her jacket torn open. Seo-yun crouches on the floor above her in her glorious dress, her mouth dark and glittering. She doesn't look at all surprised to see me.

"Jenny, love. I hope you don't mind we started without you." Seo-yun smiles. Her lipstick is smeared over her chin, over Aiko's blank face. I can't tell if Aiko's still breathing.

"Get away from her," I say in a low voice.

"As you wish." She rises gracefully, crossing the room in fluid strides. "I was done with that particular morsel, anyway." The sounds of the party leak into the room behind me, and I know I can't run and grab Aiko at the same time.

So I shut the door, locking it, and mellow my voice to a sweet purr. "Why didn't you tell me about Aiko? We could have shared her together."

But Seo-yun just laughs at me. "You can't fool me, Jenny. I can smell your rage from across the room." She reaches out, catches my face, and I recoil into the door. "It makes you so beautiful. The last seasoning in a dish almost ready."

"You're insane, and I'm going to kill you" I say. She kisses my neck, her teeth scraping my throat, and the scent of her is so heady my knees almost bend.

"I saw you in her head, delicious as anything," she whispers. Her ugly thoughts hiss up my arms, twining around my waist. There's a sharp sting at my wrist, and I look down to discover that one of them is already gnawing at my skin. "And I knew I just had to have you."

There's a crash, and Seo-yun screams as a porcelain lamp shatters against the back of her head. Aiko's on her feet, swaying unsteadily, face grim. "Back the fuck away from her," she growls, her voice barely above a whisper.

"You little bitch –" snarls Seo-yun.

But I seize my chance and pounce, fastening my teeth into the hollow of Seo-yun's throat, right where her mantle of thoughts gathers and folds inward. I chew and swallow, chew and swallow, gorging myself on this woman. Her thoughts are mine now, thrashing as I seize them from her, and I catch glimpses of myself, of Aiko, and of many others just like us, in various states of disarray, of preparation.

Ma once told me that this was how Baba went; she'd accidentally drained him until he'd faded completely out of existence. For the first time in my life, I understand her completely.

Seo-yun's bracelets clatter to the floor, her empty gown fluttering soundlessly after. Aiko collapses too, folding like paper.

It hurts to take in that much. My stomach hurts so bad, my entire body swollen with hideous thoughts. At the same time, I've never felt so alive, abuzz with possibility and untamable rage.

I lurch over to Aiko on the floor, malice leaking from her mouth, staining the carpet. "Aiko, wake up!" But she feels hollow, lighter, empty. She doesn't even smell like herself any more.

A knock at the door jolts me. "Ma'am," says a voice I recognize as the head caterer. "The first of the main courses is ready. Mr. Goldberg wants to know if you'll come down and give a toast."

Fuck. "I –" I start to say, but the voice isn't mine. I glance over at the mirror; sure enough, it's Seo-yun staring back at me, her dark, terrible dreams tangled around her body in a knotted mess. "I'll be right there," I say, and lay Aiko gently on the bed. Then I dress and leave, my heart pounding in my mouth.

I walk Seo-yun's shape down the stairs to the dining room, where guests are milling about, plates in hand, and smile Seo-yun's smile. And if I look a little too much like myself, well – according to what I'd seen while swallowing Seo-yun's thoughts, I wouldn't be the first would-be inductee to disappear at a party like this. Someone hands me a glass of wine, and when I take it, my hand doesn't tremble, even though I'm screaming inside.

Fifty pairs of eyes on me, the caterers' glittering cold in the shadows. Do any of them know? Can any of them tell?

"To your continued health, and to a fabulous dinner," I say, raising my glass. As one, they drink.

SEO-YUN'S APARTMENT IS dark, cleared of guests and wait staff alike. Every door is locked, every curtain yanked closed.

I've pulled every jar, every container, every pot and pan out of the kitchen, and now they cover the floor of the bedroom, trailing into the hallway, down the stairs. Many are full, their malignant contents hissing and whispering hideous promises at me as I stuff my hand in my mouth, retching into the pot in my lap.

Aiko lies on the bed, pale and still. There's flour and bile on the front of her jacket. "Hang in there," I whisper, but she doesn't respond. I swirl the pot, searching its contents for any hint of Aiko, but Seo-yun's face grins out at me from the patterns of light glimmering across the liquid's surface. I shove it away from me, spilling some on the carpet.

I grab another one of the myriad crawling thoughts tangled about me, sinking my teeth into its body, tearing it into pieces as it screams and howls terrible promises, promises it won't be able to keep. I eat it raw, its scales scraping the roof of my mouth, chewing it thoroughly. The more broken down it is, the easier it will be to sort through the pieces that are left when it comes back up.

How long did you know? Did you always know?

I'll find her, I think as viscous black liquid pours from my mouth, over my hands, burning my throat. The field of containers pools around me like a storm of malicious stars, all whispering my name. She's in here somewhere, I can see her reflection darting across their surfaces. If I have to rip through every piece of Seo-yun I have, from her dreams to the soft, freckled skin wrapped around my body, I will. I'll wring every vile drop of Seo-yun out of me until I find Aiko, and then I'll fill her back up, pour her mouth full of herself.

How could I ever forget her? How could I forget her taste, her scent, something as awful and beautiful as home?

THE LILY AND THE HORN

Catherynne M. Valente

CATHERYNNE M. VALENTE (www.catherynnemvalente.com) is the *New York Times* bestselling author of over two dozen works of fiction and poetry, including *Palimpsest*, the Orphan's Tales series, *Deathless*, *Radiance*, and the crowdfunded phenomenon T*he Girl Who Circumnavigated Fairyland in a Ship of Her Own Making*. She is the winner of the Andre Norton, Tiptree, Mythopoeic, Rhysling, Lambda, Locus, and Hugo awards. She has been a finalist for the Nebula and World Fantasy Awards. She lives on an island off the coast of Maine with a small but growing menagerie of beasts, some of which are human.

WAR IS A dinner party.

My ladies and I have spent the dregs of summer making ready. We have hung garlands of pennyroyal and snowberries in the snug, familiar halls of Laburnum Castle, strained cheese as pure as ice for weeks in the caves and the kitchens, covered any gloomy stone with tapestries or stags' heads with mistletoe braided through their antlers. We sent away south to the great markets of Mother-of-Millions for new silks and velvets and furs. We have brewed beer as red as October and as black as December, boiled every growing thing down to jams and pickles and jellies, and set aside the best of the young wines and the old brandies. Nor are we proud: I myself scoured the stables and the troughs for all the strange horses to come. When no one could see me, I buried my face in fresh straw just for the heavy gold scent of it. I've fought for my husband many times, but each time it is new all over again. The smell of the hay like candied earth, with its bitter ribbons of ergot laced through – that is the smell of my youth, almost gone now, but still knotted to the ends of my hair, the line of my shoulders. When I polish the silver candelabras, I still feel half a child, sitting splay-legged on the floor, playing with my mother's scorpions, until the happy evening drew down.

I am the picture of honor. I am the Lily of my House. When last the king came to Laburnum, he told his surly queen: *You see, my plum?* That *is a woman. Lady Cassava looks as though she has grown out of the very stones of this hall.* She looked at me with interested eyes, and we had much to discuss later when quieter hours came. This is how I serve my husband's ambitions and mine: with the points of my vermilion sleeves, stitched with thread of white and violet and tiny milkstones with hearts of green ice. With the net of gold and chalcathinite crystals catching up my hair, jewels from our own stingy mountains, so blue they seem to burn. With the great black pots of the kitchens below my feet, sizzling and hissing like a heart about to burst.

It took nine great, burly men to roll the ancient feasting table out of the cellars, its legs as thick as wine barrels and carved with the symbols of their house: the unicorn passant and the wild poppy. They were kings once, Lord Calabar's people. Kings long ago when the world was full of swords, kings in castles of bone, with wives of gold – so they all say. When he sent his man to the Floregilium to ask for me, the Abbess told me to be grateful – not for his fortune (of which there is a castle, half a river, a village and farms, and several chests of pearls fished out of an ocean I shall never see) but for his blood. My children stand near enough from the throne to see its gleam, but they will never have to polish it.

My children. I was never a prodigy in the marriage bed, but what a workhorse my belly turned out to be! Nine souls I gave to the coffers of House Calabar. Five sons and four daughters, and not a one of them dull or stupid. But the dark is a hungry thing. I lost two boys to plague and a girl to the scrape of a rusted hinge. Six left. My lucky sixpence. While I press lemon oil into the wood of the great table with rags that once were gowns, four of my sweethearts giggle and dart through the forest of legs – men, tables, chairs. The youngest of my black-eyed darlings, Mayapple, hurls herself across the silver-and-beryl checked floor and into my arms, saying:

"Mummy, Mummy, what shall I wear to the war tonight?"

She has been at my garden, though she knows better than to explore alone. I brush wisteria pollen from my daughter's dark hair while she tells me all her troubles. "*I* want to wear my blue silk frock with the emeralds round the collar, but Dittany says it's too plain for battle and I shall look like a frog and shame us."

"You will wear vermillion and white, just as we all will, my little lionfish, for when the king comes we must all wear the colors of our houses so he can remember all our names. But lucky for you, your white will be ermine and your vermillion will be rubies and you will look nothing at all like a frog."

Passiflora, almost a woman herself, as righteous and hard as an antler, straightens her skirts as though she has not been playing at tumble and chase all morning. She looks nothing like me – her hair as red as venom, her eyes the pale blue of moonlit mushrooms. But she will be our fortune, for I have seen no better student of the wifely arts in all my hours. "We oughtn't to wear ermine," she sniffs. "Only the king and the queen can, and the deans of the Floregilium, but only at midwinter. Though why a weasel's skin should signify a king is beyond my mind."

My oldest boy, Narcissus, nobly touches his breast with one hand while he pinches his sister savagely with the other and quotes from the articles of peerage. "'The House of Calabar may wear a collar of ermine not wider than one and one half inches, in acknowledgement of their honorable descent from Muscanine, the Gardener Queen, who set the world to growing.'"

But Passiflora knows this. This is how she tests her siblings and teaches them, by putting herself in the wrong over and over. No child can help correcting his sister. They fall over themselves to tell her how stupid she is, and she smiles to herself because they do not think there's a lesson in it.

Dittany, my sullen, sour beauty, frowns, which means she wants something. She was born frowning and will die frowning and through all the years between (may they be long) she will scowl at every person until they bend to her will. A girl who never smiles has such power – what men will do to turn up but one corner of her mouth! She already wears her red war-gown and her circlet of cinnabar poppies. They brings out the color in her grimace.

"Mother," she glowers, "may I milk the unicorns for the feast?"

My daughter and I fetch knives and buckets and descend the stairs into the underworld beneath our home. Laburnum Castle is a mushroom lying only half above ground. Her lacy, lovely parts reach up toward the sun, but the better part of her dark body stretches out through the seastone caverns below, vast rooms and chambers and vaults with ceilings more lovely than any painted chapel in Mother-of-Millions, shot through with frescoes and motifs of copper and quartz and sapphire and opal. Down here, the real work of war clangs and thuds and corkscrews toward tonight. Smells as rich as brocade hang in the kitchens like banners, knives flash out of the mist and the shadows.

I have chosen the menu of our war as carefully as the stones in my hair. All my art has bent upon it. I chose the wines for their color – nearly black, thick and bitter and sharp. I baked the bread to be as sweet as the pudding. The vital thing, as any wife can tell you, is spice. Each dish must taste vibrant, strong, vicious with flavor. Under my eaves they will dine on curried doves, black pepper and peacock marrow soup, blancmange drunk with clove and fiery sumac, sealmeat and fennel pies swimming in garlic and apricots, roast suckling lion in a sauce of brandy, ginger, and pink chilis, and pomegranate cakes soaked in claret.

I am the perfect hostess. I have poisoned it all.

This is how I serve my husband, my children, my king, my house: with soup and wine and doves drowned in orange spices. With wine so dark and strong any breath of oleander would vanish in it. With the quills of sunless fish and liqueurs of wasps and serpents hung up from my rafters like bunches of lavender in the fall.

It's many years now since a man of position would consider taking a wife who was not a skilled poisoner. They come to the Floregilium as to an orphanage and ask not after the most beautiful, nor the sweetest voice, nor the most virtuous, nor the mildest, but the most deadly. All promising young ladies journey to Brugmansia, where the sea is warm, to receive their education. I remember it more clearly than words spoken but an hour ago – the hundred towers and hundred bridges and hundred gates of the Floregilium, a school and a city and a test, mother to all maidens.

I passed beneath the Lily Gate when I was but seven – an archway so twisted with flowers no stone peeked through. Daffodils and hyacinths and columbines, foxglove and moonflower, poppy and peony, each one gorgeous and full, each one brilliant and graceful, each one capable of killing a man with root or bulb of leaf or petal. Another child ran on ahead of me. Her hair was longer than mine, and a better shade of black. Hers had blue inside it, flashing like crystals dissolving in a glass of wine. Her laugh was merrier than mine, her eyes a prettier space apart, her height far more promising. Between the two of us, the only advantage I ever had was a richer father. She had a nice enough name, nice enough to hide a pit of debt.

Once my mother left me to explore her own girlish memories, I followed that other child for an hour, guiltily, longingly, sometimes angrily. Finally, I resolved to give it up, to let her be better than I was if she insisted on it. I raised my arm to lean against a brilliant blue wall and rest – and she appeared as though she had been following me, seizing my hand with the strength of my own father, her grey eyes forbidding.

"Don't," she said.

Don't rest? Don't stop?

"It's chalcanthite. Rub up against it long enough and it will stop your blood."

Her name was Yew. She would be the Horn of her House, as I am the Lily of mine. The Floregilium separates girls into Lilies – those who will boil up death in a sealmeat pie, and Horns – those who will send it fleeing with an emerald knife. The Lily can kill in a hundred thousand fascinating ways, root, leaf, flower, pollen, seed. I can brew a tea of lily that will leave a man breathing and laughing, not knowing in the least that he is poisoned, until he dies choking on disappointment at sixty-seven. The Horn of a unicorn can turn a cup of wine so corrupted it boils and slithers into honey. We spend our childhoods in a dance of sourness and sweetness.

Everything in Floregilium is a beautiful murder waiting to unfold. The towers and bridges sparkle ultramarine, fuchsia, silvery, seething green, and should a careless girl trail her fingers along the stones, her skin will blister black. The river teems with venomous, striped fish that take two hours to prepare so that they taste of salt and fresh butter and do not burn out the throat, and three hours to prepare so that they will not strangle the eater until she has gone merrily back to her room and put out her candles. Every meal is an examination, every country walk a trial. No more joyful place exists in all the world. I can still feel the summer rain falling through the hot green flowers of the manchineel tree in the north orchard, that twisted, gnomish thing, soaking up the drops, corrupting the water of heaven, and flinging it onto my arms, hissing, hopping, blistering like love.

It was there, under the sun and moon of the Floregilium, that I read tales of knights and archers, of the days when we fought with swords, with axes and shields, with armor beaten out of steel and grief. Poison was thought cowardice, a woman's weapon, without honor. I wept. I was seven. It seemed absurd to me, absurd and wasteful and unhappy, for all those thousands to die so that two men could sort out who had the right to shit on what scrap of grass. I shook in the moonlight. I looked out into the Agarica where girls with silvery hair tended fields of mushrooms that wanted harvesting by the half-moon for greatest potency. I imagined peasant boys dying in the frost with nothing in their bellies and no embrace from the lord who sent them to hit some other boy on the head until the lord turned into a king. I felt such loneliness – and such relief, that I lived in a more sensible time, when blood on the frost had been seen for the obscenity it was.

I said a prayer every night, as every girl in the Floregilium did, to Muscanine, the Gardener Queen, who took her throne on the back of a larkspur blossom and never looked back. Muscanine had no royal blood at all. She was an apothecary's daughter. After the Whistling Plague, such things mattered less. Half of every house, stone or mud or marble, died gasping, their throats closing up so only whines and whistles escaped, and when those awful pipes finally ceased, the low and the middling felt no inclination to start dying all over again so that the lordly could put their names on the ruins of the world. Muscanine could read and write. She drew up new articles of war and when the great and the high would not sign it, they began to choke at their suppers, wheeze at their breakfasts, fall like sudden sighs halfway to their beds. The mind sharpens wonderfully when you cannot trust your tea. And after all, why not? What did arms and strength and the best of all blades matter when the wretched maid could clean a house of heirs in a fortnight?

War must civilize itself, wrote Muscanine long ago. *So say all sensible souls. There can be no end to conflict between earthly powers, but the use of humble arms to settle disputes of rich men makes rich men frivolous in their exercise of war. Without danger to their own persons, no Lord fears to declare battle over the least slight – and why should he? He risks only a little coin and face while we risk all but benefit nothing in victory. There exists in this sphere no single person who does not admit to this injustice. Therefore, we, the humble arms, will no longer consent to a world built upon, around, and out of an immoral seed.*

The rules of war are simple: should Lord Ambition and the Earl of Avarice find themselves in dispute, they shall agree upon a castle or stronghold belonging to neither of them and present themselves there on a mutually agreeable date. They shall break bread together and whoever lives longest wins. The host bends all their wisdom upon vast and varied poisons while the households of Lord Ambition and the Earl bend all their intellect upon healing and the purifying of any wicked substance. And because poisons were once a woman's work -- in the early days no knight could tell a nightshade from a dandelion – it became quickly necessary to wed a murderess of high skill.

Of course, Muscanine's civilized rules have bent and rusted with age. No Lord of any means would sit at the martial table himself nowadays – he hires a proxy to choke or swallow in his stead. But there is still some justice in the arrangement – no one sells themselves to battle cheaply. A family may lift itself up considerably on such a fortune as Lord Ambition will pay. No longer do two or three men sit down simply to their meal of honor. Many come to watch the feast of war, whole households, the king himself. There is much sport in it. Great numbers of noblemen seat their proxies in order to declare loyalties and tilt the odds in favor of victory, for surely someone, of all those brawny men, can stomach a silly flower or two.

"But think how marvelous it must have looked," Yew said to me once, lying on my bed surrounded by books like a ribbonmark. "All the banners flying, and the sun on their swords, and the horses with armor so fine even a beast would be proud. Think of the drums and the trumpets and the cries in the dawn."

"I do think of all that, and it sounds ghastly. At least now, everyone gets a good meal out of the business. It's no braver or wiser or stranger to gather a thousand friends and meet another thousand in a field and whack on each other with knives all day. And there are still banners. My father's banners are beautiful. They have a manticore on them, in a ring of oleander. I'll show you someday."

But Yew already knew what my father's banners looked like. She stamped our manticore onto a bezoar for me the day we parted. The clay of the Floregilium mixed with a hundred spices and passed through the gullet of a lion. At least, she said it was a lion.

Soon it will be time to send Dittany and Mayapple. Passiflora will return there when the war is done – she would not miss a chance for practical experience.

Lord Calabar came to the Floregilium when I was a maid of seventeen. Yew's husband came not long after, from far-off Mithridatium, so that the world could be certain we would never see each other again. They came through the Horn Gate, a passage of unicorn horns braided as elegantly as if they were the strands of a girl's hair. He was entitled by his blood to any wife he could convince – lesser nobles may only meet the diffident students, the competent but uninspired, the gentle and the kind who might have enough knowledge to fight, but a weak stomach. They always look so startled when they come a-briding. They come from their castles and holdfasts imagining fierce-jawed maidens with eyes that flash like mercury and hair like rivers of blood, girls like the flowers they boiled into noble deaths, tall and bright and fatal. And they find us wearing leather gloves with stiff cuffs at the elbows, boots to the thigh, and masks of hide and copper and glass that turn our faces into those of wyrms and deepwater fish. But how else to survive in a place where the walls are built of venom, the river longs to kill, and any idle perfume might end a schoolgirl's joke before the punchline? To me those masks are still more lovely than anything a queen might make of rouge and charcoal. I will admit that when I feel afraid, I take mine from beneath my bed and wear it until my heart is whole.

I suppose I always knew someone would come into the vicious garden of my happiness and drag me away from it. What did I learn the uses of mandrake for if not to marry, to fight, to win? I did not want him. He was handsome enough, I suppose. His waist tapered nicely; his shoulders did not slump. His grandfathers had never lost their hair even on their deathbeds. But I was sufficient. I and Floregilium and the manchineel tree and my Yew swimming in the river as though nothing could hurt her, because nothing could. He said I could call him Henry. I showed him my face.

"Mummy, the unicorns are miserable today," Dittany frowns, and my memory bursts into a rain of green flowers.

I have never liked unicorns. I have met wolves with better dispositions. I have seen paintings of them from nations where they do not thrive – tall, pale, sorrowfully noble creatures holding the wisdom of eternity as a bit in their muzzles. I understand the desire to make them so. I, too, like things to match. If something is useful, it ought to be beautiful. And yet, the world persists.

Unicorns mill around my daughter's legs, snorting and snuffling at her hands, certain she has brought them the half-rotted meat and flat beer they love best. Unicorns are the size of boars, round of belly and stubby of leg, covered in long, curly grey fur that matts viciously in the damp and smells of wet books. Their long, canny faces are something like horses, yes, but also something like dogs, and their teeth have something of the shark about them. And in the center, that short, gnarled nub of bone, as pure and white as the soul of a saint. Dittany opens her sack and tosses out greying lamb rinds, half-hardened cow's ears. She pours out leftover porter into their trough. The beasts gurgle and trill with delight, gobbling their treasure, snapping at each other to establish and reinforce their shaggy social order, the unicorn king and his several queens and their kingdom of offal.

"Why do they do it?" Dittany frowns. "Why do they shovel in all that food when they know they could die?"

A unicorn looks up at me with red, rheumy eyes and wheezes. "Why did men go running into battle once upon a time, when they knew they might die? They believe their shield is stronger than the other fellow's sword. They believe their Horn is stronger than the other fellow's Lily. They believe that when they put their charmed knives into the pies, they will shiver and turn red and take all the poison into the blade. They believe their toadstones have the might of gods."

"But nobody is stronger than you, are they, Mum?"

"Nobody, my darling."

He said I could call him Henry. He courted me with a shaker of powdered sapphires from a city where elephants are as common as cats. A dash of blue like so much salt would make any seething feast wholesome again. *Well, unless some clever Lily has used moonseeds, or orellanine, or unicorn milk, or the venom of a certain frog who lives in the library and is called Phillip. Besides, emerald is better than sapphire.* But I let him think his jewels could buy life from death's hand. It is a nice thing to think. Like those beautiful unicorns glowing softly in silver thread.

I watch my daughter pull at the udders of our unicorns, squeezing their sweaty milk into a steel pail, for it would sizzle through wood or even bronze as easily as rain through leaves. She is deft and clever with her hands, my frowning girl, the mares barely complain. When I milk them, they bite and howl. The dun sky opens up into bands like pale ribs, showing a golden heart beating away at dusk. Henry Calabar kisses me when I am seventeen and swears my lips are poison from which he will never recover, and his daughter feeds a unicorn a marrow bone, and his son calls down from the ramparts that the king is coming, he is coming, hurry, hurry, and under all this I see only Yew, stealing into my room on that last night in the country of being young, drawing me a bath in the great copper tub, a bath swirling with emerald dust, with green and shimmer. We climbed in, dunking our heads, covering each other with the strangely milky smell of emeralds, clotting our black hair with glittering sand. Yew took my hand and we ran out together into the night, through the quiet streets of the Floregilium, under the bridges and over the water until we came to the manchineel tree in the north orchards, and she held me tight to her beneath its vicious flowers until the storm came, and when the storm came we kissed for the last time as the rain fell through those green flowers and hissed on our skin, vanishing into emerald steam, we kissed and did not burn.

THEY CALL HIM the Hyacinth King and he loves the name. He got it when he was young and ambitious and his wife won the Third Sons' War for him before she had their first child. Hyacinth roots can look so much like potatoes. They come into the hall without grandeur, for we are friends, or friendly enough. I have always had a care to be pregnant when the king came calling, for he has let it be known he enjoys my company, and it takes quite a belly to put him off. But not this time, nor any other to come. He kisses the children one by one, and then me. It is too long a kiss but Henry and I tolerate a great deal from people who have not gotten sick of us after a decade or two. The queen, tall and grand, takes my hand and asks after the curried doves, the wine, the mustard pots. Her eyes shine. Two fresh hyacinths pin her cloak to her dress.

"I miss it," she confesses. "No one wants to fight me anymore. Sometimes I poison the hounds out of boredom. But then I serve them their breakfast in unicorn skulls and they slobber and yap on through another year or nine. Come, tell me what's in the soup course. I have heard you've a new way of boiling crab's eyes to mimic the Whistling Plague. That's how you killed Lord Vervain's lad, isn't it?"

"You flatter me. That was so long ago, I hardly remember," I tell her.

She and her husband take their seats above the field of war – our dining hall, sparkling with fire and finery like wet morning grass. They call for bread and wine – the usual kind, safe as yeast. The proxies arrive with trumpets and drums. *No different, Yew*, I think. My blood prickles at the sound. She is coming. She will come. My castle fills with peasant faces – faces scrubbed and perfumed as they have never been before. Each man standing in for his Lord wears his Lord's own finery. They come in velvet and silk, in lace and furs, with circlets on their heads and rings on their fingers, with sigils embroidered on their chests and curls set in their hair. And each of them looks as elegant and lordly as anyone born to it. All that has ever stood between a duke and a drudge is a bath. She is coming. She will come. The nobles in the stalls sit high above their mirrors at the table, echoes and twins and stutters. It is a feasting hall that looks more like an operating theater with each passing war.

Henry sits beside his king. We are only the castle agreed upon – we take no part. The Hyacinth King has put up a merchant's son in his place – the boy looks strong, his chest like the prow of a ship. But it's only vanity. I can take the thickness from his flesh as fast as that of a thin man. More and more come singing through the gates. The Hyacinth King wishes to take back his ancestral lands in the east, and the lands do not consider themselves to be ancestral. It is not a small war, this time. I have waited for this war. I have wanted it. I have hoped. Perhaps I have whispered to the Hyacinth King when he looked tenderly at me that those foreign lords have no right to his wheat or his wine. Perhaps I have sighed to my husband that if only the country were not so divided we would not have to milk our own unicorns in our one castle. I would not admit to such quiet talk. I have slept only to fight this battle on dreaming grounds, with dreaming knives.

Mithridatium is in the east. She is coming. She will come.

And then she steps through the archway and into my home – my Yew, my emerald dust, my manchineel tree, my burning rain. Her eyes find mine in a moment. We have done this many times. She wears white and pale blue stitched with silver – healing colors, pure colors, colors that could never harm. She is a candle with a blue flame. As she always did, she looks like me drawn by a better hand, a kinder hand. She hardly looks older than my first daughter would have been, had she lived. Perhaps living waist-deep in gentling herbs is better than my bed of wicked roots. Her children beg mutely for her attention with their bright eyes – three boys, and how strange her face looks on boys! She puts her hands on their shoulders. I reach out for Dittany and Mayapple, Passiflora and Narcissus. *Yes, these are mine. I have done this with my years, among the rest.* Her husband takes her hand with the same gestures as Henry might. He begs for nothing mutely with his bright eyes. They are not bad men. But they are not us.

I may not speak to her. The war has already begun the moment she and I rest our bones in our tall chairs. The moment the dinner bell sounds. Neither of us may rise or touch any further thing – all I can do and have done is complete and I am not allowed more. Afterward, we will not be permitted to talk – what if some soft-hearted Horn gave away her best secrets to a Lily? The game would be spoilt, the next war decided between two women's unguarded lips. It would not do. So we sit, our posture perfect, with death between us.

The ladies will bring the peacock soup, laced with belladonna and serpent's milk, and the men (and lady, some poor impoverished lord has sent his own unhappy daughter to be his proxy, and I can hardly look at her for pity) of Mithridatium, of the country of Yew, will stir it with spoons carved from the bones of a white stag, and turn it sweet – perhaps. They will tuck toadstones and bezoars into the meat of the curried doves and cover the blancmange with emerald dust like so much green salt. They will smother the suckling lion in pennyroyal blossoms and betony leaves. They will drink my wine from her cups of unicorn horn. They will sauce the pudding with vervain. And each time a course is served, I will touch her. My spices and her talismans. My stews and her drops of saints' blood like rain. My wine and her horn. My milk and her emeralds. Half the world will die between us, but we will swim in each other and no one will see.

The first soldier turns violet and shakes himself apart into his plate of doves and twenty years ago Yew kisses emeralds from my mouth under the manchineel tree while the brutal rain hisses away into air.

THE EMPRESS IN HER GLORY

Robert Reed

ROBERT REED (WWW.ROBERTREEDWRITER.COM) was born in Omaha, Nebraska. He has a Bachelor of Science in Biology from the Nebraska Wesleyan University, and has worked as a lab technician. He became a full-time writer in 1987, the same year he won the L. Ron Hubbard Writers of the Future Contest, and has published twelve novels, including *The Leeshore*, *The Hormone Jungle*, and far future SF *Marrow* and *The Well of Stars*. A prolific writer, Reed has published over 200 short stories, mostly in *F&SF* and *Asimov's*, which have been nominated for the Hugo, James Tiptree, Jr., Locus, Nebula, Seiun, Theodore Sturgeon Memorial, and World Fantasy awards, and have been collected in *The Dragons of Springplace*, *The Cuckoo's Boys*, *Eater-of-Bone*, and *The Greatship*. His novella "A Billion Eves" won the Hugo Award. His latest book is major SF novel *The Memory of Sky*. Nebraska's only SF writer, Reed lives in Lincoln with his wife and daughter, and is an ardent long-distance runner.

FRUITS RIPEN AND worlds ripen.

If not taken at the right moment, any ripe prize falls from its tree and rots away, and nothing is gained.

That was how They looked at the situation.

Call them 'alien'. The word isn't ridiculous, yet by the same token, no label does justice to their origins or far-reaching powers. And after four and a half billion years of slow, often irregular growth, the Earth was deemed ripe. In the parlance of universal laws, that little orb had grown just soft enough and sweet enough. That's why They came. That's why an ordinary day in late June came and left again, and in those hours, by invasive and ephemeral means, every aspect of human existence was conquered.

The new rulers were few, less than a hundred, but they were an experienced, well-practiced partnership. Avoiding sloppiness and haste, they followed their occupation with months of careful study. This was a new colony, one realm among ten thousand thousand scattered about the galaxy, and their first job was to understand the world's nature. Out of that collection of meat and history, failure and divine promise, they had to select one good leader – a human face and mind to be entrusted with the administration of what was theirs.

AT FIFTY-EIGHT, ADRIANNE Hammer ruled an empire of cubicles and computers as well as an impressive stockpile of Folgers Classic Roast. She was sharp-minded and quietly demanding of her seven-person staff. Weighing data from multiple sources, she was paid to make honest, unsentimental guesses about the future. Economic growth and downturns were predicted. The odds of storms and plagues and various medical breakthroughs had to be rendered as numbers. Hers was one minuscule department inside a major insurance conglomerate, but while other departments often duplicated their work, Adrianne and her team were unusually competent. Which is to say that the eight of them were correct a little more often than their competitors.

She was a widow. People who barely knew Adrianne knew that much. Her husband had struggled for a year against liver cancer. His prognosis was poor but never hopeless, and he might have survived. There were good reasons for optimism. But the man must have been too terrified to face his difficult future. One morning, Adrianne kissed him before driving to work, and the man subsequently drank half a bottle of quality wine and then jabbed a pistol under his fleshy chin.

As a rule, humans enjoy tragedies that involve others. They also believe suffering lends depth to the afflicted. Years after the event, co-workers still spoke about the police coming to deliver the awful news. It happened to be a rainy day. The poor lady was sitting alone in the cafeteria. The officers sat in front her and beside her, speaking slowly, and she seemed to hear them. But shock and pain must have left her numb. With a flat, unemotional voice, she asked, "Where did it happen?" Her husband shot himself at home. "But what room?" Inside the home office. "Who found him?" A delivery man looked through the window, called it in. She nodded, eyes narrowing. "Which gun?" she demanded. "And how bad is the mess?"

That's when a bystander took hold of her hands, urging Adrianne to shut her eyes for a moment, to collect her wits.

She had one child, a grown boy already living in a distant state. Husband and son were the only people pictured on her work desk, and in keeping with a spirit of relentless honesty, neither photograph was flattering. The dead Mr. Hammer sported a beefy, rounded face dominated by an alcoholic's bright nose. The son was an ugly fellow needing a comb and a smile. People on Adrianne's staff knew about her life. She wasn't particularly secretive, no. But there was a persistent story, popular in the other departments and divisions, that she was a cat lady. Didn't she look the part? Except Adrianne didn't keep any pets, and she didn't suffer from mothering urges, and despite some very confident rumors, she also didn't quilt or garden or ride cruise ships. She wasn't unattractive, and so acquaintances imagined male friends. But except for a few dinner dates and a couple change of sheets, she never dated. Men and romance were difficulties best left behind. Alone inside the tidy, cat-free house, Mrs. Hammer filled her private hours with activities that mirrored her official job, She stood before a tall desk, in the same office where her husband killed himself. To her, the world was one giant and splendid puzzle, and like the best puzzles, it was built out of simple repeating pieces. Her passion was to search the Internet for odd papers and unexplored pools of data, reading everything interesting as slowly and carefully as she could, and when she was ready – but only when ready – she would weave conclusions that were often a little more true than every other half-mad opinion on the Web.

Adrianne Hammer was a blogger.

Regularity. Reliability. Those were qualities she demanded of herself, and her tiny audience had always appreciated the results. She posted every Sunday, and the only postings missed were because of one bout of swine flu, and before that, her husband's messy suicide. Thousands of people had her tools and intellect, or they had better. But brilliance likes to be focused. The average genius wants to fall in love with some narrow cause, a topic that generates passion and that she can master better than anyone else. And the most powerful minds often ended up being driven by the rawest, most predictable emotions.

But this human didn't suffer from a narrow focus.

In fifteen years, that lifelong Republican had successfully predicted elections and civil wars as well as giving shrewd warnings about which stable nations would fail to rule effectively. She warned her readers about stock bubbles and the diminishing stocks of easy petroleum. China was on the precipice of ten environmental disasters. Russia was a rotted husk. She studied SARS and MERS and then successfully predicted the onset of GORS. Climate change was a growing maelstrom worth visiting every couple months, and with a perpetually reasoned tone, she warned her careless species to watch out for even more serious hazards. Comet impacts. Solar flares. Nuclear war between small players and firestorms born from mistakes made in North Dakota.

In one popular posting, she wrote about the Singularity. "I can only guess when the day comes, but self-aware computers are inevitable. In fact, synthetic intelligence is more likely today than it was yesterday. And it's a little more plausible this afternoon than it was just this morning."

At the heart of every posting was the inescapable truth: The future was chaos smothered inside more chaos. Even at her best, Adrianne cautioned that no marriage of learning and insight can envision what comes in another ten years, or in some cases, in another ten seconds.

Yet even the most difficult, disorganized race had to have its winner.

And Adrianne Hammer was among the quickest of the best.

THE INVISIBLE LORDS made her one candidate among twenty-three. Each human was secretly examined, every life measured against an assortment of ideals. Adrianne was fifth on the list, and she wouldn't have climbed any higher. But her son called her at home one evening. Intoxicated, plainly furious, the young man began by telling his mother that she was a bloodless bitch, unloving and ugly.

Adrianne reacted with a soft sigh, shaking her head.

The son's rapid prattle continued, insults scattered through recollections from childhood. Old slights and embarrassments were recounted. One cold, wicked parent had destroyed the young man's future. Didn't she see the crimes? Didn't she understand what a miserable mess she had made of his little life?

Once and then again, she said her son's name. Quietly, but not softly.

The tirade finally broke. Then he muttered, "Dad."

She nodded, apparently unsurprised by the conversation's turn.

"Yes," she said.

"You should have known," the young man said. "Of all people, you should have seen it coming. Why didn't you sense what he was planning?"

"Because he didn't give clues."

"Dad didn't have to kill himself," her son said. "He wasn't that sick."

She said, "Honey, he was very ill. And that doesn't matter now."

"It does matter."

"Not after the gunshot," she said. "That's why people kill themselves. One action, and everything else is inconsequential."

Both stopped talking.

Forty seconds passed.

"I wasn't there," her son complained.

"Nobody was."

"Poor Dad was alone."

"We're all alone, honey."

By a thousand means, the Earth's new owners studied the woman's pain. They watched the candidate open her mouth and close it again. They measured her breathing, her heart. The electricity running along her wet neurons. They even tried to read her thoughts, which was difficult with most humans and quite impossible with this specimen.

To their minds, opacity was a noble quality.

"After he shot himself," her son began.

"I know."

"At the funeral –"

"I remember."

"You were angry at him. Because he used the .357. Because he aimed up and made a mess in the ceiling, and you'd have to find someone to come pull out the bones and make patches and then paint. That's why you were angry with him."

"I wasn't angry," she said.

"Yes you were."

"No, I was reasonable frustrated," she said. "You're always the furious one."

"Don't fucking say that."

Eyes narrowed. Adrianne fell silent.

Her pulse was slow, regular.

"You see everything, Mom. You should have predicted this."

Just then, Adrianne's heart rate elevated. Slightly.

"You could have taken precautions," he said.

"It was my mistake," she agreed. "I underestimated your father's fears, and overestimated his aversion to violence."

Her son sobbed.

Honesty was easy for the woman. "I always assumed your father would drink himself to death," she said. "Which perhaps was how he made himself sick in the first place."

"Listen to yourself."

"I always do."

"You don't care. You make an awful mistake like that, and it's nothing to you."

"One error among thousands," she pointed out.

The young man said nothing.

Adrianne's pulse had returned to normal.

"Do you miss him, Mom?"

She said nothing, apparently giving the problem some thought. "I miss you," she said at last.

Her son broke the connection.

Adrianne set the phone down on the desk, and after a sigh and seven seconds of introspection, she glanced up at the patched, repainted ceiling. Then she returned to work, crafting a long, tightly reasoned blog about thorium reactors, their blessings and why they were coming too late to the discussion.

Those watching came to one enduring conclusion: This was an exceptionally tough-minded, determined beast.

Which was why a month later, without warnings or the barest explanations, an obscure blogger was given complete control over the secretly conquered world.

* * *

At work and at home, Adrianne wielded tools that she didn't understand. The web crawlers and other bots gathered data and then filtered it for her eyes. But even the most competent expert wouldn't have noticed the unique bots added to her account. That small event happened early on a Saturday morning. Waking at ten after five, as usual, she discovered e-mails and classified reports from Mainland China. Asking for origin reports, the new software told reasonable lies about failures to encrypt and a nameless hacker who must have left her cleverness sit exposed for too long.

This week's blog was supposed to focus on a renewed US space program.

Not anymore.

Adrianne read and reread the translations, slept five hours, and finished her research on Sunday morning. The blog was written in two hours, which was quick for her. Instead of railguns, she described the secret fissures inside the Three Gorges Dam and how the Chinese government was doing nothing of significance, nervously hoping that their wildest worries would prove without merit.

At the moment of publication, the empress had 709 scattered followers.

Sunday evening was unremarkable, and the next two days were pleasant enough. Wednesday seemed to offer more of the same. A courtyard was adjacent to the cafeteria. Adrianne sat in the shadows, eating a peanut butter sandwich and small apple and then two Girl Scout cookies bought from a colleague's daughter. Thin Mints. Arguably the finest cookie in the history of humankind.

"How bad?" a bypasser asked.

"They still don't know," his companion said.

"How many people live downstream?"

"Millions."

The men were past, gone. The final cookie was half eaten. That very calm woman took a moment to examine her tooth marks in the bright black chocolate. Then she finished the cookie and the last of her low fat milk, and she disposed of the trash and used the restroom, returning to her station two minutes before one o'clock.

Every monitor in the office showed the Chinese flood. The giant dam hadn't just split open. It had failed catastrophically, dissolving into rubble and a wall of filthy black water that was slashing through the nightbound countryside, and it wouldn't stop flowing until wreckage was washing up on American shores.

That portion of the future was easy to predict.

Other parts were less certain.

Most humans would have been traumatized, and many would have mentioned their brilliance or dumb luck. But no, Adrianne had a project to shepherd along. Her department was trying to calculate the likely changes in life spans in the Western world. Insurance companies never stopped making these assessments. Until now, she had been enjoying a productive week, discovering speculative works in places that normally didn't share ideas, including several interesting reports about a small start-up in France working with anti-aging drugs.

Adrianne was the only person in the office who had found the anti-aging references. Which was bothersome. Her staff was badly distracted, but she sent one of her boys chasing the French story, expecting and even hoping that he would follow the crumbs to the same destination.

But he didn't, no.

"I'm not finding anything, ma'am. Where am I supposed to look?"

Adrianne drove home as usual. The evening news was filled with videos of cities being gutted, churning waters filled with animal corpses and human corpses. She stayed awake past midnight, just after a light-water reactor and various storage facilities were inundated. The disaster had reached a new level of appalling. By five o'clock the next morning, her time, martial law had been imposed across China, and there were rumors of a major shake-up in Beijing.

The Chinese civil war remained weeks in the future.

Arriving late to work, Adrianne found one of her boys standing beside her desk. He smiled nervously. The young man looked happy yet uncertain, rocking from foot to foot. His voice cracked when he said, "Hello," and then he laughed at his obvious terror.

"What's wrong?" she asked.

Her voice broke. Just a little, in places only she could hear.

The man tried laughing again. But he couldn't make himself. "I don't read it a lot," he confessed.

"Read what?" she asked.

"Your blog." He sighed. "But I did see something... I don't know... it's been a couple years. And you were right."

"Was I?"

"China. It was ripe for environmental disaster."

At that moment, Adrianne would have been hard-pressed to write any coherent opinions about Chinese futures. The flood was enormous, but good things might come from this. Sometimes chaos supplied the fuel to make meaningful changes, destroying corruption, ensuring stability for hundreds of millions of survivors.

"You were right," he repeated.

Finally, she saw what was obvious. "You didn't read my last article. Did you?"

"No, ma'am, I'm sorry. Like I said, I don't get to it much."

Adrianne felt sick.

"Why? Should I become a follower?" He was nearly a boy, years younger than her son. "I'll read it right now. How's that?"

"No," she said.

Loudly, almost shouting.

He blinked. "Okay. You're right. Work first."

Adrianne's hope was to cross the day, to finish these hours and escape back home and then make some accommodations to this very unlikely coincidence. But the peace only lasted until ten in the morning. People from other departments began to stop outside the office. Familiar, nameless faces came to look at the slender woman with the neat gray hair and out-of-fashion glasses. With caution and nervous wonder, they stared, and then she would glance up and they would retreat. Then one bold lawyer asked how she could be so right about this goddamn mess. And suddenly her own people were demanding explanations. Adrianne had no choice but some species of honesty, and then nobody was working. Everyone inside her office and throughout the complex began to read and reread a few thousand words predicting the century's largest disaster.

Adrianne took her lunch home and called in sick.

By evening, with the help of two cocktails, she checked her blog. The comments went on and on, many in Chinese. And she had just under fourteen thousand followers, the number rising every time she refreshed.

* * *

SOMEONE HAD FED her the information.

That was the first and still obvious explanation. She kept imagining the Chinese dissident, crafty and out of reach, and with that bit of false-knowledge in hand, Adrianne wrote her next blog – a careful piece using bits of new research. With words and tidy graphs, she reminded her readers that hydrocarbons were common, both in the world and across the universe. But being common didn't matter. Most of the world's oil was too expensive to lift out of the ground, and what could be lifted was often too expensive to refine, and the energy gained at the day's end was approaching the grim fulcrum where the modern world couldn't afford to pay its bills.

The topic was familiar. She had investigated peak oil many times. But she had more followers now, a lot of new heads to absorb her thinking, and that's why she wrote the piece, expecting that a few of her readers would appreciate and maybe even welcome her calm logic.

Fifty-eight years of life gives a person experience with insults and curses. But what surprised Adrianne was the intimacy of the threats – violent words coupled with images from people who didn't simply doubt her numbers and good sense, but who wanted to come her house just so they could cut off her head, to claim it as a trophy they would nail to their truck hoods or use in ways far worse than that.

She slept badly for a week. And while awake, every stranger deserved small anxieties.

Yet nothing evil ever came to her door, and everything that was good proved to be excellent. Adrianne's staff rallied around her. Unfit men in their thirties and forties acted as unofficial bodyguards, and without fanfare, the youngest member of her staff – a girl in her mid-twenties – broke company rules by bringing both a Taser and pepper spray into the office.

That next Sunday, Adrianne published a brief, dense blog about magneto-inertial fusion engines – the best means for opening up the solar system. And inside the piece, she included schematics plucked from what looked like a NASA website.

Her followers had reached 80,000.

The rocket blog was followed by a long, complicated piece about increasing lifespans and why that was a damnable trend. Long-term environmental successes would never be possible if too many bodies were prepared to live comfortably in the increasingly overheated world.

By then, her followers' comments had dropped by half, insults by one third, and she had the carefully plotted data to prove it.

By then, the Chinese civil war was underway, and feeling invested in that particular horror, Adrianne suggested a solution. Like an innoculate into a sick body, she proposed that one of the peripheral Chinese enclaves could supply a new paradigm. Taiwan was offered, then dismissed. Too much history. Hong Kong had its potentials, but it didn't have the necessary freedom of motion. So instead she voted for the distant and very wealthy city-state of Singapore. Its authoritarian leaders and billionaires were Chinese by heritage. They could broker deals and supply guidance that wouldn't end the strife today, but in another couple years, perhaps with only fifty million dead from war and famine, some new normalcy could be established.

Adrianne's final Monday at work was pleasantly forgettable.

Actuarial adventures.

Lunch.

More adventures.

Plus one long meeting.

Then home and a light dinner, one drink and idle reading, and bed.

On Monday, Ghawar was the greatest oil field on the Earth. But early Tuesday, Adrianne's time, a series of prolonged earthquakes rolled across northern Saudi Arabia. By Wednesday morning, virtually every oil well in the region had seized up and died. The spot market for crude was driving towards 300 dollars. An initial explanation, full of panic and half-informed conjecture, blamed the greedy Saudis. An ocean of oil had been removed from the Ghawar field, and the strata must have been pushed too hard. Despite sound geologic evidence that this was impossible, an entire region had slumped, and the world was several million barrels short of oil today and tomorrow, and always.

By Wednesday evening, the Prime Minister of Singapore was opening public talks with three of the main combatants inside China.

Thursday morning saw a news conference from France. An upstart medical firm was going to sell expensive compounds that could only be described as elixirs, and lifespans would soon triple.

But the blogger at the heart of it remained surprisingly unnoticed. Only half a dozen news crews sat on the street outside Adrianne's home. With her phone off and drapes closed, it was possible to believe that her life hadn't changed. Then came Friday morning, and a team of MIT engineers announced that the design for a novel rocket propulsion system, posted on a small blog, was not from any governmental database. Or commercial database. Nor any other reasonable source. Yet A. Hammer's documents contained quite a few interesting features, some invoking the newest ideas about energy in the universe, and it might be possible to build a prototype star-drive within the next five years.

By then, the world was plunging into its Grand Depression.

But those financial horrors were augmented by promises of endless life and easy commutes to the other worlds.

The raging chaos had a center – one quiet woman barely known a month ago.

Adrianne escaped her house through the back gate, taking a cab to work. Nobody in her office was pretending to work. They watched the news together, the door left mostly closed. A manager and two security people arrived before lunch, and Adrianne was ushered into the largest conference room. Every important person in the corporation had gathered to stare at her. Several of them remembered to thank her for her long service. Then the CFO offered her a worried smile and a substantial buyout.

Everybody adored her work, but she was too much of a distraction.

Twenty million followers were just the beginning. Adrianne was going to have advertising revenues flowing from her blog, and she had her buyout package, plus savings and numerous offers of cash for appearances on news networks and talk shows. With those prospects and a numbed resolve, she began the long walk back to her office and the cubicle, ready to wish her people the best before heading off into this unforeseen life.

But stepping through the door, an idea took hold.

Seven others watched the old lady make coffee for everyone. The Folgers was brewing, and she sat with her back to her desk, in a pose they had never seen before. She didn't look regal or even particularly confident. No, nothing was special in her appearance, save for the weariness of great events, and they felt sorry for the lady, even while wondering which of them would end up in charge. She looked at each face. Then she gave the carpet a long stare. Somebody thought to pour coffee into eight mugs and everyone had their share and there was sitting and more silence, except out in the hallway where someone had slipped indoors. A supporter or an enemy: The invader's goals were never known. Security noticed the interloper and tackled her, and when the screaming was finished, Adrianne looked up at the ceiling. Quietly, soberly, she said, "There's no reasonable set of factors that can make this possible. What's happening. To me and to the world. I don't know why, but I seem to have a pipeline to things I don't understand."

Nobody could disagree with that assessment.

Then she surprised them, saying, "If somebody has to wield this kind of influence, why not me?"

It was the first inkling that their boss saw the potential.

"But I need a staff," she said. "A well-paid, familiar group of people who know me well enough not to take offense when I'm lost in work."

The girl with the Taser said, "Oh. You want to hire us."

"And later, others," Adrianne admitted. "But you're my nucleus."

Every head nodded.

There. It was agreed. They would leave work together, after tendering their resignations.

"Nothing about this is reasonable," Adrianne continued. "But this world is built on unreasonable coincidences. Until we understand what's happening, I'm going to be the Empress of Everything. And for as long as I have the job, I should at least try to do my best."

HER HOUSE WAS abandoned. There was no choice in the matter. Adrianne lived for three days on the Taser girl's sofa, writing a sharp blog delineating recent history and her apparent, surprising hold on some form of cosmic power or blunt magic. Whatever this was. Her hostess suggested adding a little personal noise to the piece. "So people think they know you." But it was Adrianne who gave the post its signature moment. Mentioning the horrors of liver cancer, she added a quick request for people to send a few dollars to one of several appropriate agencies. And by the time she slipped out of the girl's apartment, nearly a hundred million dollars had appeared in the welcoming coffers. With a flood of unexpected gifts choking the blogger's Paypal account too.

That next week was spent in anonymous hotel rooms, talking strategy, giving possibilities flesh and shadow. Her people did their best to keep the media at bay, scaring off Senators and business leaders as well. And they also found a recently constructed, never occupied warehouse complex, far from the city but close to highways and a high-grade optical cable that could be secured.

Only the President was given access to the world's boss. There were three long, very exhausting conversations. The last talk was a face-to-face session. Adrianne was touring the warehouse, preparing to sign a long-term lease on the facility and a power commitment from an adjacent windmill farm. A security firm still needed to be hired, and her team was interviewing remodelers. Apartments would be installed in back, and because nobody knew where this madness would lead, plans were being drawn up for a school and playground for children, a swimming pool for everyone, and a bar for the ruling class.

In those two phone conversations, the President tried charm. But charm had proved useless. Ready to unleash stronger tactics, his helicopters landed on the empty parking lot. Flanked by high-ranking civilians and officers in dress uniforms, he met the empress in the front office. With a careful blending of rage and authority, he defined his level of scorn. Adrianne listened silently. Then he invited his aides to talk about various legal actions that might be appropriate. She interrupted with a raised hand, which amusingly was enough to stop every voice. Everyone stared at her. "Which laws have I broken? I would very much like to know," she said. Then the ranking general outlined what his people would do if faced with a dangerous power trying to usurp the nation's security. "Except that sounds like war," was her response. "And I don't approve of war. If I can find the words, I intend to make every army in the world obsolete."

That brought a chill, and more rage.

Sensing failure, the President returned to charm.

"You're a registered Republican," he pointed out. "I'm assuming you voted for me."

"No," she said. "I've never voted for national candidates."

"But you do vote, correct?"

"Only for local candidates. Bond issues. I have a tiny but real chance of making an impact. But I can't pretend to have a role in presidential races."

The man needed to pause, giving himself a chance to recalculate.

"Come over here, sir. If you would."

He joined her beside a laptop.

"I've been working on a new blog. In fact, I intend to publish in the next few minutes."

Some prior briefing came to mind. "It's Saturday. I was told that you put these things out on Sundays."

"Except I don't have a normal job anymore. And with the change of fates, I think I need to embrace a more ambitious schedule. Which makes this is a good day to begin."

Keys were pressed. The unpublished text appeared.

Stepping back, she said, "Read the piece, if you wish. Sir."

The blog spoke about the dangers inherent in the aging nuclear fleets. Adrianne was arguing that the only wise course was to put the weapons to bed, today if possible. But she was afraid that people wouldn't change their natures until they received a good clear warning. So at the end of the piece, she had written, "I want to see one of their swords pull itself out of its scabbard."

The President hadn't finished reading the piece.

"Lady, what are you talking about?" he asked.

She didn't answer. Her heart pounding, she clicked the Publish button and stepped back. "I don't understand what's happened to me," she said, quietly but not quietly. "I can make guesses. I doubt if anyone can decipher what's true, not in the short-term. But there are clues. If you look hard. With the Three Gorges and the stardrive, I was fed information of something already happening. Which is one phenomena. But I wrote about oil. On my own. And whatever this power is, it needed time to make preparations before the quake struck, before we started this overdue collapse into economic ruin.

"Sir, I have a sense," she said. "My very strong intuition is that simple directions are more likely to lead to immediate effects.

"Consider this blog a test.

"Both of us need to know. What marvels do I have in this hand?"

Moments later, an alarm sounded.

An Air Force general turned away, muttering into a sat-phone.

Voices spoke of "the football".

"It's ours and it's launched," someone cried out.

The President looked ill, looked simple, his face drained of blood and most of its life. He glared at Adrianne. He stared numbly at his own hands. And then someone said, "No, the missile broke apart after launching. It's down. It over."

Adrianne turned to her people.

Winked.

Then looking at the visitors, she said, "I have six blogs written. They're waiting on servers around the world. If anything unseemingly happens to me or to any of my people, those pieces get published automatically. And you don't want those ideas getting loose on the world. Believe me."

They believed, at least enough to retreat.

Then the Taser girl asked, "Is that right? Six blogs waiting to kill the world?"

The Empress didn't seem to hear the questions. She seemed intrigued by the details in her own tiny hand. Then to the hand, in that calm dry voice, she said, "By tomorrow, there will be. Now let's get to work."

EVENTUALLY SHE WOULD be known as Adrianne the First. But in those early years, she was the Hammer, a respected and feared and often scorned entity sitting in a warehouse in the bleakest bowels of Ohio. She appeared on television when she wanted, which was rare. Her speeches and occasional interviews proved nothing except that she was no public speaker. And where the lowliest princess – some creature born with a good name and small inheritance – would have carried her head high, Adrianne became more and more like she had always been. Chilled. Collected. Long of thought, careful with words. Not the smartest person in a room, but the entity most likely to see exactly what was happening and what the next step needed to be.

During her brief, busy reign, she oversaw a thousand projects. Not every initiative was a success. Some were close to disasters, in fact. Urging Egypt and Jordan to annex the Palestine enclaves proved horrific, and her plan for paying the Jewish populations to emigrate to Canada was only a little more productive. But approaching her mid-60s, Adrianne saw lifespans expanding and the first eight flights of the infamous Hammer Drive. Words carrying her name triggered changes in tax codes worldwide. Small, tidy rebellions began and ended with her words, various authoritarian regimes swept away, and she was better than anyone else when it came to picking the most deserving winners. And more importantly, she was very quick to admit errors and change paths.

No, the lady wasn't loved, but that didn't stop people from building temples in her honor.

Her rational mind was the largest force among many, but the public talked about her magic for saving lives that she had never noticed.

Her stoic personality never failed. Early on, she told her core group that she was an agent in a very mysterious game. Aliens, machines, or demons from some unmapped dimension: Explanations were numerous and useless and why bother? But she accepted that she was too old to benefit from the new elixirs, and even if she lived a million years, she was still human. In other words, she was going to run out of good advice.

"Ten or twelve years from now," she guessed.

She was wrong by a factor of two.

A very good guess, in other words.

On an ordinary Wednesday, she published a small blog about the desperate need for rain in northern Mexico. It was one of the little gifts that she gave to single places, and she didn't expect instantaneous results. But that same day, in Capetown, a half Zulu and half Boer fellow published plans for a machine that would suck carbon dioxide out of the atmosphere – a simple and quick device powered by sunlight and the earth's heat.

His machine was authentic.

Her rain never fell.

She retired, but not without some difficulties. Within a week, this woman who cared nothing for pomp and spectacle had little to fill her time, and perhaps that's why she ended up in a serious depression. Returning to her old house, she drank. She slept too much. And then she didn't sleep at all, weeping for no reason.

The tumor was discovered three months after she became an ordinary citizen.

Surgery was a possibility, but with the likelihood of significant brain damage. She refused. Radiation and various forms of chemo would be stopgaps, prolonging life by weeks at most. She considered and decided otherwise. On their own initiative, three of her original team flew to Capetown, attempting to meet with the new emperor. Their plan was to argue for a special blog, perhaps a call for a new cancer-fighting agent. The right words written in the proper order, not unlike a magical chant, might lead researchers to find a miracle hiding inside some little tropical plant. But the emperor refused to see them, much less consider their request. And hearing about the trip and the verdict, Adrianne sighed, saying, "Wisdom and kindness. They're not the same word spelled with different letters."

There was still money in the coffers.

Doctors and cooks and maids and more doctors arrived and then left the house again, following complicated schedules.

And the original seven disciples took up residence in the nearby houses, complete with spouses and kids and at least one mistress.

Adrianne left her doors unlocked.

Her balance wasn't worth trusting anymore, and she hated the chore of seeing who was calling.

One day, a boy from another neighborhood invited himself inside that famous house. He was curious what brain cancer looked like. It looked like an ordinary old lady sitting before a small desk, watching a thousand solar panels opening like giant flowers on someone's desert. It looked like a dull thing to watch, and he said so.

The woman turned slowly, looking at him and then looking back at the monitor.

"What are you doing here?" he asked.

"Sitting," she said. And she began to laugh, one hand touching the back of her skull. He thought she was strange and left.

She didn't notice her solitude.

Then another boy said, "You should lock your doors."

Adrianne turned to discover what she assumed was the first boy. Except he had grown up in the last few moments. Grown up and grown heavy too, and his hair had left him and then come back again. The new hair was paler and thicker than natural, which was common with these treatments.

Thirty years had passed in an instant.

This was a very interesting disease, she thought.

But no, that face wasn't the same face, even with the added decades. She almost remembered the face and its name. But then with a hurt tone, the new visitor said, "I'm your son. I've come to see you."

That seemed enough reason to stand.

The legs proved strong, at least for the moment.

"I heard the news," her son said.

"There's always news," she said. "What are you talking about?"

"Your health," he said.

"Is there something I don't know?"

"Oh, Mother." The man blinked, shrinking down a bit.

"You mean this growth." She tapped her head and laughed again. Twice in one day. She was practically a giddy little girl. "Yes, it's going to kill me. But probably not today."

The conversation stopped altogether.

Casting for words, she fell into clichés. "How is your life, son?"

"Well," he said, happy for the prodding. "I'm doing well. Sober three years, and very rich."

"Are you?"

"Exceptionally rich, thanks to you."

"Sober, I meant."

But the man with the fresh hair didn't want to dwell on old weaknesses. "It's amazing what people give you, particularly when they learn that your mother controls the world and everyone on it."

Honest thoughts came to Adrianne.

She worked hard, and her mouth remained closed.

The man was wearing both fine clothes and a smug smile, and he was watching her. But his thoughts were on the move. Feeling strong enough, he stopped smiling. "This is where he killed himself. Isn't it?"

She said nothing.

He looked at the ceiling. Then he stepped past her, touching the desk. The earlier desk was gone, too big and too bloody for the room that she had wanted. Maybe he didn't remember the original furniture. She refused to clear up these matters. What she wanted was to be left alone...

But this was her only child.

Mindless, uncaring pressure on neurons. Pressure bringing emotion. Is that where this sudden trickle of tears was coming from?

Her son didn't notice.

Again, the smug, rich-man's smile.

"I was sorry when you lost the job," he confessed.

"Were you?"

"But it's all right," he said. "Our relationship is still valuable."

"Is it?" she asked, wiping one wet eye.

"You often talk to our overlords," he said.

"I don't," she said.

"But they don't know that. And I'm very convincing."

She approached the office door. Wanting something. To send him away, or flee for herself?

The awful man kept talking.

"In fact, I'll sometimes claim that I can talk to them too. The powers in charge. Not so much that I have to prove anything. But you know, it's crazy what smart people believe, if you give them any excuse."

She gasped.

Her son blinked, straightening his back.

"Help me," she said. "Would you do me one enormous favor?"

He nodded.

"Wait," she said.

Waiting was an easy favor, easily accomplished.

She returned with the handgun and bullets, and his first reaction was to warn, "Guns are illegal now. You made it so."

"I did," she agreed. "Maybe somebody should arrest me."

He watched her load one chamber.

"Now," she said. "Kill me."

"What?"

"That's the favor. I'm sick. I'm going to get sicker and die horribly. But according to euthanasia laws – my wise laws – I can implore another person to end my suffering by whatever means I want."

"Mother...!"

"And I don't want to do the chore myself. So if you would." She shoved the gun into his hands, aiming the barrel at her chest. Then, as if having second thoughts, she said, "No, wait. Let me sit, and we can catch the bullet and the spray with pillows. I'll get my pillows out of the bedroom."

"Mother, no!"

The heavy man dropped the gun and ran away.

The disturbance was finished.

Alone, Adrianne unloaded the one bullet, placing the weaponry into a closet. And exhausted, she sat at the desk, watching a live view from a probe launched last month and already halfway to Neptune.

Time passed.

And someone else came to visit.

The first boy was back, an older sister holding his hand.

"This is her," he said with conviction. "That's our Empress."

Adrianne didn't have the legs to stand. That's why their faces were at the same level when she said, "Yes, it's your Empress. Sitting in her glory."

She laughed hard.

The children laughed with her, to be friendly.

Touching her head once more, she said, "The monster inside my head. It's pushing at the best nerves."

They stopped.

"A talent for comedy," she said, her laugh growing dark and slow. "That's what the gods give you, if they want to be kind, right before you die."

THE WINTER WRAITH

Jeffrey Ford

JEFFREY FORD (WWW.WELL-BUILTCITY.COM) is the Nebula, World Fantasy, and Shirley Jackson Award winning author of the novels *The Shadow Year, The Physiognomy, The Girl in the Glass* and *The Portrait of Mrs. Charbuque*. His story collections are *The Fantasy Writer's Assistant, The Empire of Ice Cream, The Drowned Life*, and *Crackpot Palace*. His new collection, *A Natural History of Hell,* will be released by Small Beer Press in July of 2016.

HENRY SENSED RESIGNATION in the posture of the Christmas tree. It slouched toward the living room window as if peering out. There was no way he could plug it in, cheer it up. The thing was dryer than the Sandman's mustache, its spine a stick of kindling. The least vibration brought a shower of needles. Ornaments fell of their own accord. Some broke, which he had to sweep and vacuum, initiating the descent of more needles, more ornaments. The cat took some as toys and batted them around the kitchen floor. Glittering evidence in the field indicated Bothwell, the dog, had acquired a taste for tinsel.

Mero had told him not to take it down. She had a special way she wrapped the ornaments when boxing them. He wasn't about to argue for doing it by himself. At the end of that first week she was away in China, though, the presence of the tree became an imposition. He described it in his Friday journal as, 'A distant cousin, once accused of pyromania, arriving for an indefinite visit.'

In the middle of his work, in the middle of the grocery store, when walking with the dog around the lake, the spirit of that sagging pine was always waiting by the front window in the living room of his thoughts. Then Mero finally called on FaceTime from Shanghai. Her image was distorted as if he was seeing her through rippling water. In a heartbeat, the picture froze, but she kept talking. He told her he missed her and she said the same. She said Shanghai was amazing, enormous, and that she liked the young woman who was her translator and guide. She asked about Bothwell. Henry spoke about the freezing wind, the snow. She told him to be careful driving, and then he told her about the tree. "It's shot," he said. "I gotta take it down."

Suddenly the call cut out, and he couldn't get her back. He wanted to tell her he loved her and hear her voice some more, but in a way he understood. It was like dialing another world. The distance between Ohio and Shanghai made him shiver. He called Bothwell and the Border Collie appeared. "Do you want to go for a walk?" he asked. The dog's green eyes were intense and it cocked its head to the side as if to say, "What do you think?" So Henry put his coat and hat and mittens on, and they went out, over the snow, across the yard, through the orchard, past the garden, into the farmer's winter fields that surrounded the property. Corn stubble and snow stretched out to the horizon in three directions. It was sundown, orange and pink in the west, a deep royal blue to the east where he spotted the moon.

They headed toward the wind break of white oak about a quarter mile into the field. The frozen gusts that blew across the open land sliced right through him, and he struggled to hold closed his jacket with the broken zipper. They entered the thicket of giant old trees. Under the clacking, empty branches last light turned to mist and shadow. He sat down on a fallen log and looked to the west. Bothwell sniffed around and then sat behind him to escape the gusts that eddied in among the trees. Henry had a hell of a time lighting a cigarette. Once he got it going, though, he made an executive decision. The first part was to open a bottle of wine when he got back to the house. The second was to dismantle the tree and get rid of it by the following afternoon.

He saw how he would do it. Put the ornaments in a pile on the dining room table. Cover them with a table cloth to hide them from the cat, and leave them there till Mero got back. Pull the lights. Grab the cursed tinsel off in handfuls. Kick the tree in the spleen and wrestle it to the floor. Remove the base. Drag the corpse through the dining room, the kitchen, to the sliding door. Deposit the remains out back in the snow. Burn incense to mask the odor of rotted Christmas. Sweep and vacuum. Two hours for the whole ordeal, he figured and spoke into the wind, "Adios, mother fucker." Then Bothwell made a strange noise.

Henry felt something behind him. He stood up quickly and turned, glimpsing what looked in the dimmest of light like a wolf. Gray and tan, bushy coat. It skulked around a tree and disappeared. He knew there were no wolves in Ohio, but the creature was too big for a coyote. The idea of it sneaking around in the dark sent a shot of adrenalin through him. His heart pounded. He called the dog to him and they left the trees in a rush. Somewhere between the smoke and the wolf, night had dropped. Unable to see where he was stepping, he twisted his leg on corn stubble and his knee began to ache. He hobbled toward the light of the house, peering over his shoulder every few yards. By the time he reached the kitchen, he could hardly walk. He pulled the cork on a bottle of Malbec, standing on one leg.

Grabbing the glass and bottle, he hopped into the living room. The tree was waiting for him. As he sat on the couch, a shower of needles fell and then an ornament. It hit a branch on the way down and broke, shattering into three jagged scoops and a handful of glitter. He watched it happen, knew it was the ornament Mero had bought for their first Christmas together. He decided in an instant, he'd wait till spring to tell her. Bothwell came in and curled up by his feet. He drank wine and turned on the TV.

He woke suddenly hours later to the dark, in bed. His mouth was dry. He had no recollection of having gotten off the couch and come upstairs. Looking at the clock, he saw it was only 3:13. He laid his head back on the pillow and closed his eyes. That's when he realized there was a quiet but distinct rhythmic noise coming up from downstairs. He could barely hear it, like a voice whispering too loud. The first thing he did was call to Bothwell for courage. The dog was already at his side of the bed. Henry sat up, put his feet on the floor, and listened. The voice continued, mumbling on, and then broke out into a cry for help. One long extended scream, diminishing into silence, followed by a loud thud.

Henry jumped up, his heart racing, his hair, what there was of it, tingling. He reached for the wooden baton he kept behind the night table next to the bed. At the top of the stairs, he let the dog go first. He stepped slowly, protecting his bad knee and not in any hurry to see what was going on. Before he reached the bottom step, it struck him that the noise must have been coming from the TV he'd never turned off. This made him braver and, holding his weapon in front of him, he limped boldly into the living room.

The light was still on. "Great," he said, gazing down upon the fallen Christmas tree. Although it had slouched so long toward the window, when it fell, it went over backwards, across the middle of the living room floor. Ornaments everywhere. The useless water in the metal base drained onto the carpet. The dry needle fallout was epic. He looked at the dog. The dog looked at him. Henry stepped forward and kicked the tree. It shuddered, dropping more of itself. He shook his head and looked across the room. The TV was off.

He and Bothwell searched each of the downstairs rooms, to be on the safe side. Then he made a pot of coffee. He decided not to wait for morning but to dive in, dismantle the thing, and get it out of the house. While the coffee brewed, he cleared the dining room table and took another look at the remains. Leaning against the archway that led to the living room, he told himself he'd just have to get his head around it. He went and poured a cup and came back and sat on the couch. The cat, Turtle, was at the other end. It struck Henry that she'd probably sat through the entire misadventure – the tree weaving, gasping, calling out for help, and then crashing to the floor. He remembered she was sitting there in the same position when he'd lumbered down the stairs. "Please, don't get too worked up over anything," he said to the cat. Turtle looked at him and then stood. At that moment, the TV came on. Henry lurched and grunted in surprise. The cat jumped down from the couch, and as soon as it left, he saw that it had been laying on the remote.

His hands found the needles sharper than when the tree was alive. He got the rubber gloves from beneath the kitchen sink and put them on. The work proved exhausting, all that bending and the often tedious exercise of untwining an ornament hanger from a branch. At times he had to wrestle the dead weight of the thing, rolling it to get to ornaments crushed beneath it, lifting it to open the sharp branches so he could reach in and rescue the angel from where she'd fallen into the belly of the beast. "Don't forget the icicles," he heard Mero say in his mind. Plastic icicles, thin as pipe cleaners, perfectly transparent. There were 6. After locating 4, he said, "Fuck it," and gave up.

At sunrise of a bitter, overcast day, Henry dragged the tree through the dining room and kitchen, out the sliding door. The wind was howling fiercely, but he left his jacket inside and was dressed only in a T-shirt. He slid the corpse over the already fallen snow. It left a wake of brown needles. Depositing it next to the garden shed, he took a few steps back. He'd made sure earlier to slip on his boots. He charged forward and kicked the tree. His boot got under the trunk and lifted it into the air. His next move was a crushing stomp to the mid-section, but when he brought his foot down, the bad knee of his other leg went out. He slipped on the snow and fell.

After sweeping and vacuuming and moving the coffee table and chairs back in front of the window, he lay down on the couch and grabbed the remote. Not even ten AM and he found Jack Palance in black and white, *The House of Numbers*. He maneuvered the couch pillow under his head, and then closed his eyes and let the sound of the twins and prison plot lead him to sleep. He woke at 4:15 pm and looked to the window. The sky was dark gray. He heard the wind. Before he got up and looked, he knew it was snowing, big flakes angling down from the west.

He went to the kitchen and made a pot of coffee. Still dazed from sleep, he leaned against the kitchen sink, staring out the window. He watched the empty branches bend, and watched in the distance across the field as the world filled up with snow. "The new ice age," he said to his reflection. His gaze shifted to the garden shed and looked and blinked and looked again. He leaned over the kitchen sink to get his glasses closer to the glass. For a moment, he went numb, even his knee stopped aching.

This time he put on his jacket and hat and mittens. He called for Bothwell and they went out the sliding door. The snow was on its way to becoming ice, and the wind was fierce. Covering his face with his arm, he made his way toward the garden shed. He believed the tree was there but covered by a small drift. When he reached the spot where he'd dumped it, he turned his back to the wind and looked down. There was a rise in the snow. He toed the white mound but felt nothing beneath it. A minute later, he'd cleared the spot, pushing the snow aside with his boots, and was staring at frozen ground.

"Where?" he said to Bothwell and although he laughed, a current of fear cut through the confusion. He looked up quickly and scanned the darkening yard to see if the thing had been blown away. The wind on the plains was strong enough. Over the summer it had lifted a glass topped table on the patio and flipped it, turning its top to jagged chips of ice. He didn't see any sign of the corpse in the distance, so he started back into the orchard to check the shadows beneath the trees. He and the dog walked all around the property but found nothing, save that he'd at some point left the garage light on.

Entering the garage through the side door, he found instant relief from the snow. Bothwell followed him in. He looked out over the stacks of unopened boxes he'd never unpacked after moving two years earlier. It was all books, thousands of them. He smelled their damp molder, and had a memory flash of the warehouse scene at the end of *Citizen Kane*. A scrabbling sound followed fast by a desperate squeal came from far back in the hangar-sized structure. The dog barked. Henry flipped the light off and they headed back to the house.

Later, in his office, sipping coffee, sitting in front of his computer, he leaned back and took a break from the irritation of his writing. His thoughts wandered and then he pictured the Christmas tree miles away in the dark, slouching through drifts to the edge of route 70 and sticking out a branch. "Cali or the North Pole?" Henry considered the desiccated pine's journey west – the truckers, the rest stops, the mountain vistas until that reverie was interrupted by a horrendous clank that shuddered through the house from somewhere below. Bothwell leaped up from where he lay near the door, his ears at attention.

Henry wished he'd brought the baton upstairs. Still, the noise didn't sound like someone forcing a door or window. It had that unmistakable sense of finality to it, like the God of trouble had smote some major appliance once and for all. "Burst pipe? Water heater? Something electric?" He went through a list as he limped down stairs, the dog leading the way. The lights in the hallway, the living room, dining room, kitchen all came on when he flipped their switches, and he was grateful for that. He looked around to see if Turtle had knocked over a vase or picture frame, slid a glass off the counter in the bathroom, but for once the cat was innocent. The porch door and sliding door in the back were both locked. He ran the water to check for a lack of pressure, but the flow was steady and strong.

The dog followed him around the kitchen as he searched for the flashlight. "This is unparalleled bullshit," he said to Bothwell, who seemed sympathetic yet could barely hide his excitement over the promise of action at such a late hour. It took Henry twenty minutes, going through the various kitchen junk drawers, checking each at least twice, before finding the flashlight. It took him another ten minutes to find batteries. The beam it emitted when finally operational was a vague pretense of light. He found the baton where he'd left it in the living room and then went into the hallway, to the basement door. He opened it. "Forsake all hope," he said to the dog.

Standing at the top of those worn steps leading into darkness an image of the tree returned to him, and this time it wasn't headed west. This time, it had never left. A reek of dampness and subtle mildew rolled up and engulfed him. He thought of the basement cliché of horror movies as he flipped on the light switch and took his first step. Turtle appeared out of nowhere and brushed past him, a black blur diving down the stairs. "No," he yelled after the cat, but that was pointless.

The house was over a hundred years old, and he'd never heard of a 'wet basement' before they'd bought it. Back in Jersey, where they'd come from, the words – wet basement – were a deal breaker. Old farmhouses weren't built with rec rooms or indoor ping pong tables in mind, though. The basement was basically a foundational necessity, a place to store things raised up on pallets. Water was expected at certain times of the year. Henry had to duck as he stepped beneath the lintel. There was one dim lightbulb hanging from a chain in the middle of the main part of a concrete chamber.

He used the baton to rip down a prodigious cobweb, and made his way from one appliance to the next, laying his hand lightly on it to see if it trembled with life. The water heater was fine, the dehumidifier showed signs of life, and then he touched the furnace. It was silent, no vibration and stone cold. "That ain't good," he said. The dog sat on the bottom step, as if reluctant to put a paw down and commit to the underground. Henry flipped on the flashlight and moved to the dark back of the cellar and the adjoining concrete closet without a door, a narrow space where the fuse box hung.

Often, during spring, the water rose in that niche as high as 4 or 5 inches, and he'd once seen a toad hop out of it into the greater basement. Luckily the ground outside was frozen and the floor dry. He ran the beam of the flashlight over the different fuses to see if one had popped, but they were all unmarked and he really had no idea what he was looking for. Mero was the one who always dealt with the fuses.

"We're gonna freeze our asses off tonight," he said. When he stepped back into the basement, he noticed Bothwell retreating up the stairs. "Traitor," he shouted, and meant to follow as quickly as possible. As he made his way for the steps, though, he realized he had no idea where Turtle had gotten to. He aimed the tepid beam into dark corners and made the *psss psss psss* noise Mero always used to summon the cat. After two dozen psss's, he called out, "You can stay down here all winter." As he made for the steps, he heard a meow. He turned and aimed the beam at a spot on the wall next to the water heater.

He'd forgotten it was there, a roughly foot and a half by one foot hole in the concrete of the wall that led into the foundation. Why it was there, he had no idea. He wondered if perhaps a pipe had been shoved through there from outside at some point. Maybe a poorly covered over coal chute? He stepped up to it and shone the light inside. Turtle's green eyes caught the weak glow and made the most of it. She was about 4 feet into the tunnel. He gave it a *Psss, psss, psss*. A meow answered. "Come on, Turtle," he said. "Come on." Every time he made the *psss* noise the cat meowed but stayed where it was. "I hate you," he said to it. The bright green eyes blinked.

When the cat moved, she moved slowly. She appeared at the opening and leaped down onto the floor. That's when he distinctly heard the porch door open with a bang, heard the whoosh of the storm enter the kitchen above. He was sure of it. He could feel the burst of adrenalin shoot through him, yet he was stiff with fear. There was no spit to swallow. The harder he gripped the baton, the less he believed he would be able to wield it if he had to. Bothwell backed down the stairs into view. His hackles were up and he was growling. Henry heard footsteps and dropped the flashlight. He managed to creep to the bottom of the steps. "If you leave now, I won't shoot you," he shouted. "The police are on the way."

There was more movement above, but he couldn't track it. Just one slow clomping footstep after another. Out of some perverted impulse, he made his move. Gripping the baton, he reared it over his head and lurched up the stairs on his bad knee in a woefully executed surprise attack. Using his elbows on the door jambs, he propelled himself in a stumble down the hall and into the kitchen, Bothwell barking at his side. "Swing for the fence," Henry whispered.

The door was wide open and the cold air swept in around him. He went to it immediately and shut it. Only one step ahead of paralyzing fear, he knew he couldn't rest, but plunged into room after room, expecting the intruder in every one. In the downstairs bedroom, he instructed Bothwell to look under the bed. They checked all the closets. When Turtle jumped out from behind the shower curtain, Henry flailed with the baton and destroyed a towel rack.

Upstairs, out of breath, his knee screaming, he made the rounds of all the rooms but found no one. Half relieved, he said, "What a night," to the dog as they made their way down from the second floor. Back in the kitchen, he looked for his phone and found it on the counter. Without putting the baton down, he dialed the police. There was a long span of silence and then the line sparked with static. He tried to get through twice more and gave up. "Here's another forklift full of shit," he told Bothwell, tossing the phone on the counter. The dog's expression as much as said, "You're getting a little dramatic now." Henry nodded in agreement and paused to think it through. That's when he noticed something he'd missed earlier. The kitchen floor was littered with brown needles. He'd been so intent on attack, he'd trod right through them, never looking down.

He gripped the baton and Bothwell tensed. The trail of brown needles led off into the dining room. Man and dog moved slowly, quietly toward the darkened entrance. He could have sworn he'd left all the lights on downstairs. He stopped and listened. Just the wind. Lifting the baton, he flipped on the switch. Instinctively crouching, he tensed against an assault if only from the sudden light. When Bothwell didn't bark, Henry knew there was no one there. The house was perfectly still.

"Nothing," he said to the dog, and decided to make a pot of coffee. Before he could move, though, some speck of brightness caught his eye, and he looked down at the dining room table. The dark green cloth appeared a miniature landscape what with the ornaments trapped beneath it. He stepped closer. There were brown needles scattered amid the rolling hills, and in one of the more prominent valleys lay, side by side, the two missing icicles he'd abandoned on the tree. He reached out but didn't touch them.

"Come on, now," he said to the ceiling.

He muttered through two glasses of wine; his breath, vapor. The kitchen was especially freezing, and the cold finally drove him to forsake the bottle.

He wrapped up in three blankets and propped himself in a corner of the couch with the lights out. The baton lay only inches away on the coffee table. Bothwell was next to him curled in a ball, and Turtle stretched out along the rim of the pillow he rested his head on. After quite a while, his eyes adjusted and he could see past the window, the snow coming down. At some point he heard the heater kick back on and the dog gave a whimper of appreciation. When he shut his eyes to better hear the voices in the wind, sleep took him like an avalanche, and he wound up in the back seat of a cab, streaking along the main street of Shanghai, going to meet Mero for lunch.

BOTANICA VENERIS: THIRTEEN PAPERCUTS BY IDA COUNTESS RATHANGAN

Ian McDonald

Ian McDonald (@ianmcdonald) lives in Northern Ireland, just outside Belfast. He sold his first story in 1983 and bought a guitar with the proceeds, perhaps the only rock 'n' roll thing he ever did. Since then he's written sixteen novels, including *River of Gods*, *Brasyl*, and *The Dervish House*, three story collections and diverse other pieces, and has been nominated for every major science fiction/ fantasy award – and even won a couple. His current novel is *Luna: New Moon*. The middle volume of the trilogy, *Luna: Wolf Moon,* is due later in 2016.

Introduction by Maureen N. Gellard

My mother had firm instructions that, in case of a house-fire, two things required saving: the family photograph album, and the Granville-Hydes. I grew up beneath five original floral papercuts, utterly heedless of their history or their value. It was only in maturity that I came to appreciate, like so many on this and other worlds, my Great-Aunt's unique art.

Collectors avidly seek original Granville-Hydes on those rare occasions when they turn up at auction. Originals sell for tens of thousands of pounds (this would have amused Ida); two years ago an exhibition at the Victoria and Albert Museum was sold out months in advance. Dozens of anthologies of prints are still in print: the *Botanica Veneris*, in particular, is in 15 editions in twenty-three languages, some of them non-Terrene.

The last thing the world needs, it would seem, is another *Botanica Veneris*. Yet the mystery of her final (and only) visit to Venus still intrigues half a century since her disappearance. When the collected diaries, sketch books and field notes came to me after fifty years in the possession of the Dukes of

Yoo I realised I had a precious opportunity to tell the true story of my Great-Aunt's expedition – and of a forgotten chapter in my family's history. The books were in very poor condition, mildewed and blighted in Venus's humid, hot climate. Large parts were illegible or simply missing. The narrative was frustratingly incomplete. I have resisted the urge to fill in those blank spaces. It would have been easy to dramatise, fictionalise, even sensationalise. Instead I have let Ida Granville-Hyde speak. Hers is a strong, characterful, attractive voice, of a different class, age and sensibility from ours, but it is authentic, and it is a true voice.

The papercuts, of course, speak for themselves.

Plate 1: V strutio ambulans: the Ducrot's Peripatetic Wort, known locally as Daytime Walker (Thent) or Wanderflower (Thekh).

Cut paper, ink and card.

Such a show!

At lunch Het Oi-Kranh mentioned that a space-crosser – the *Quest for the Harvest of the Stars*, a Marsman – was due splash down in the lagoon. I said I should like to see that – apparently I slept through it when I arrived on this world. It meant forgoing the sorbet course, but one does not come to the Inner Worlds for sorbet! Het Oi-Kranh put his spider-car at our disposal. Within moments the Princess Latufui and I were swaying in the richly upholstered bubble beneath the six strong mechanical legs. Upwards it carried us, up the vertiginous lanes and winding staircases, over the walls and balcony gardens, along the buttresses and roof-walks and up the ancient iron ladder-ways of Ledekh-Olkoi. The islands of the archipelago are small, their populations vast and the only way for them to build is upwards. Ledekh-Olkoi resembles Mont St Michel vastly enlarged and coarsened. Streets have been bridged and built over into a web of tunnels quite impenetrable to non Ledekhers. The Hets simply clamber over the homes and lives of the inferior classes in their nimble spider-cars.

We came to the belvedere atop the Starostry, the ancient pharos of Ledekh-Olkoi that once guided mariners past the reefs and atolls of the Tol Archipelago. There we clung – my companion the Princess Latufui was queasy – vertigo, she claimed, though it may have been the proximity of lunch – the whole of Ledekh-Olkoi beneath us in myriad levels and layers, like the folded petals of a rose.

"Should we need glasses?" my companion asked.

No need! For at that instant the perpetual layer of grey cloud parted and a bolt of light, like a glowing lance, stabbed down from the sky. I glimpsed a dark object fall though the air, then a titanic gout of water go up like a dozen Niagaras. The sky danced with brief rainbows, my companion wrung her hands in delight – she misses the sun terribly – then the clouds closed again. Rings of waves rippled away from the hull of the space-crosser, which floated like a great whale low in the water, though this world boasts marine fauna even more prodigious than Terrene whales.

My companion clapped her hands and cried aloud in wonder.

Indeed, a very fine sight!

Already the tugs were heading out from the protecting arms of Ocean Dock to bring the ship in to berth.

But this was not the finest Ledekh-Olkoi had to offer. The custom in the archipelago is to sleep on divan-balconies, for respite from the foul exudations from the inner layers of the city. I had retired for my afternoon reviver – by my watch, though by Venusian Great Day it was still mid-morning and would continue to be so for another two weeks. A movement by the leg of my divan. What's this? My heart surged. *V strutio ambulans*: the Ambulatory Wort, blindly, blithely climbing my divan.

Through my glass I observed its motion. The fat succulent leaves hold reserves of water, which fuel the coiling and uncoiling of the three ambulae – surely modified roots – by hydraulic pressure. A simple mechanism, yet human minds see movement and attribute personality and motive. This was not pure hydraulics attracted to light and liquid, this was a plucky little wort on an epic journey of peril and adventure. Over two hours I sketched the plant as it climbed my divan, crossed to the balustrade and continued its journey up the side of Ledekh-Olkoi. I suppose at any time millions such flowers are in constant migration across the archipelago, yet a single Ambulatory Wort was miracle enough for me.

Reviver be damned! I went to my space-trunk and unrolled my scissors from their soft chamois wallet. Snip snap! When a cut demands to be made, my fingers literally itch for the blades!

* * *

WHEN HE LEARNT of my intent, Gen Lahl-Khet implored me not to go down to Ledekh Port, but if I insisted, (I insisted: oh I insisted!) at least take a bodyguard, or go armed. I surprised him greatly by asking the name of the best armourer his city could supply. Best Shot at the Clarecourt November shoot, ten years on the trot! Ledbekh-Teltai is the most famous gunsmith in the Archipelago. It is illegal to import weaponry from off-planet – an impost I suspect resulting from the immense popularity of hunting Ishtari janthars. The pistol they have made me is built to my hand and strength: small, as requested; powerful, as required and so worked with spiral-and-circle Archipelagan intaglio that it is a piece of jewellery.

LEDEKH PORT WAS indeed a loathsome bruise of alleys and tunnels, lit by shifts of grey, watery light through high skylights. Such reeks and stenches! Still, no one ever died of a bad smell. An Earth-woman alone in an inappropriate place was a novelty, but from the non-humanoid Venusians I drew little more than a look. In my latter years I have been graced with a physical *presence*, and a destroying stare. The Thekh, descended from Central Asian nomads abducted en-masse in the 11th century from their bracing steppe, now believe themselves the original humanity and so consider Terrenes beneath them, and they expected no better of a sub-human Earth-woman.

I did turn heads in the bar. I was the only female – humanoid that is. From Carfax's *Bestiary of the Inner Worlds*, I understand that among the semi-aquatic Krid the male is a small, ineffectual symbiotic parasite lodging in the mantle of the female. The barman, a four-armed Thent, guided me to the snug where I was to meet my contact. The bar overlooked the Ocean Harbour. I watched dock workers scurry over the vast body of the space-crosser, in and out of hatches that had opened in the skin of the ship. I did not like to see those hatches; they ruined its perfection, the precise, intact curve of its skin.

"Lady Granville-Hyde?"

What an oily man, so well-lubricated I did not hear his approach.

"Stafford Grimes, at your service."

He offered to buy me a drink but I drew the line at that unseemliness. That did not stop him ordering one for himself and sipping it – and several successors – noisily during the course of my questions. Years of Venusian light had turned his skin to wrinkled brown leather: drinker's eyes looked out from heavily hooded lids: years of squinting into the ultra-violet. His neck and hands were mottled white with pockmarks where melanomas had been frozen out. Sunburn, melancholy and alcoholism: the classic recipe for Honorary Consuls system-wide, not just on Venus.

"Thank you for agreeing to meet me. So: you met him."

"I will never forget him. Pearls of Aphrodite. Size of your head, Lady Ida. There's a fortune waiting for the man..."

"Or woman." I chided, and surreptitiously activated the recording ring beneath my glove.

PLATE 2: *V flor scopulum*: The Ocean Mist Flower. The name is a misnomer: the Ocean Mist Flower is not a flower, but a coral animalcule of the aerial reefs of the Tellus Ocean. The seeming petals are absorption surfaces drawing moisture from the frequent ocean fogs of those latitudes. Pistils and stamen bear sticky palps, which function in the same fashion as Terrene spider webs, trapping prey. Venus boasts an entire ecosystem of marine insects unknown on Earth.

This cut is the most three dimensional of Lady Ida's Botanica Veneris. Reproductions only hint at the sculptural quality of the original. The 'petals' have been curled at the edges over the blunt side of a pair of scissors. Each of the two hundred and eight palps has been sprung so that they stand proud from the black paper background.

Onion-paper, hard-painted card.

The Honorary Consul's Tale

APHRODITE'S PEARL. TRULY, the pearl beyond price. The pearls of Starosts and Aztars. But the cloud reefs are perilous. Snap a man's body clean in half, those bivalves. Crush his head like a Vulpeculan melon. Snare a hand or an ankle and drown him. Aphrodite's Pearls are blood pearls. A fortune awaits anyone, my dear, who can culture them. A charming man, Arthur Hyde – that brogue of his made anything sound like the blessing of heaven itself. Charm the avios from the trees – but natural, unaffected. It was no surprise to learn he was of aristocratic stock. Quality: you can't hide it. In those days I owned a company – fishing trips across the Archipelago. The legend of the Ourogoonta, the Island that is a Fish, was a potent draw. Imagine hooking one of those. Of course they never did. No, I'd take them out, show them the cloud reefs, the Krid hives, the wing-fish migration, the air-jellies; get them pissed on the boat, take their photographs next to some thawed out javelin-fish they hadn't caught. Simple, easy, honest money. Why wasn't it enough for me? I had done the trick enough times myself, drink one for the punter's two, yet I fell for it that evening in the Windward Tavern, drinking hot spiced kashash and the night wind whistling up in the spires of the dead Krid nest-haven like the caged souls of drowned sailors. Drinking for days down the Great Twilight, his one for my two. Charming, so charming, until I had pledged my boat on his plan. He would buy a planktoneer – an old bucket of a sea-skimmer with nary a straight plate or a true rivet in her. He would seed her with spores and send her north on the great circulatory current, like a maritime cloud reef. Five years that current takes to circulate the globe before it returns to the arctic waters that birthed it. Five years is also the time it takes the Clam of Aphrodite to mature – what we call pearls are no such thing. Sperm, Lady Ida. Compressed sperm. In waters it dissolves and disperses. Each Great Dawn the Tellus Ocean is white with it. In the air it remains compact – the most prized of all jewels. Enough of fluids. By the time the reef ship reached the deep north, the clams would be mature and the cold water would kill them. It would be a simple task to strip the hulk with high-pressure hoses, harvest the pearls and trouser the fortune.

Five years makes a man fidgety for his investment. Arthur sent us weekly reports from the Sea Wardens and the Krid argosies. Month on month, year on year, I began to suspect that the truth had wandered far from those chart co-ordinates. I was not alone. I formed a consortium with my fellow investors and chartered a 'rigible.

And there at Map 60 North, 175 East, we found the ship – or what was left of it, so overgrown was it with Clams of Aphrodite. Our investment had been lined and lashed by four Krid cantoons: as we arrived they were in the process of stripping it with halberds and grappling-hooks. Already the decks and superstructure were green with clam meat and purple with Krid blood. Arthur stood in the stern frantically waving a Cross of St Patrick flag, gesturing for us to get out, get away.

Krid pirates were plundering our investment. Worse, Arthur was their prisoner. We were an unarmed aerial gad-about, so we turned tail and headed for the nearest Sea Warden castle to call for aid.

Charmer. Bloody buggering charmer. I know he's your flesh and blood, but... I should have thought! If he'd been captured by Krid pirates, they wouldn't have let him wave a bloody flag to warn us.

When we arrived with a constabulary cruiser, all we found was the capsized hulk of the planktoneer and flocks of avios gorging on clam offal. Duped! Pirates my arse – excuse me. Those four cantoons were laden to the gunwales with contract workers. He never had any intention of splitting the profits with us.

The last we heard of him, he had converted the lot into Bank of Ishtar Bearer Bonds – better than gold – at Yez Tok and headed in country. That was twelve years ago.

Your brother cost me my business, Lady Granville-Hyde. It was a good business; I could have sold it, made a little pile. Bought a place on Ledekh Syant – maybe even make it back to Earth to see out my days to a decent calendar. Instead... Ach, what's the use. Please believe me when I say that I bear your family no ill will – only your brother. If you do succeed in finding him – and if I haven't, I very much doubt you will – remind him of that, and that he still owes me.

PLATE 3: *V lilium aphrodite*: the Archipelago sea-lily. Walk-the-Water in Thekh: there is no comprehensible translation from Krid. A ubiquitous and fecund diurnal plant, it grows so aggressively in the Venerian Great Day that by Great Evening bays and harbours are clogged with blossoms and passage must be cleared by special bloom-breaker ships.

Painted paper, watermarked Venerian tissue, inks and scissor-scrolled card.

* * *

SO DEAR, SO admirable a companion, the Princess Latufai. She knew I had been stinting with the truth in my excuse of shopping for paper, when I went to see the Honorary Consul down in Ledekh Port. Especially when I returned without any paper. I busied myself in the days before our sailing to Ishtaria on two cuts – the Sea Lily and the Ocean Mist Flower – even if it is not a flower, according to my Carfax's *Bestiary of the Inner Worlds.* She was not fooled by my industry and I felt soiled and venal. All Tongan woman have dignity, but the Princess possesses such innate nobility that the thought of lying to her offends nature itself. The moral order of the universe is upset. How can I tell her that my entire visit to this world is a tissue of fabrications?

WEATHER AGAIN FAIR, with the invariable light winds and interminable grey sky. I am of Ireland, supposedly we thrive on permanent overcast, but even I find myself pining for a glimpse of sun. Poor Latufui: she grows wan for want of light. Her skin is waxy, her hair lustreless. We have a long time to wait for a glimpse of sun: Carfax states that the sky clears partially at the dawn and sunset of Venus's Great Day. I hope to be off this world by then.

Our ship, the *Seventeen Notable Navigators*, is a well-built, swift Krid *jaicoona* – among the Krid the females are the seafarers, but they equal the males of my world in the richness and fecundity of their taxonomy of ships. A *jaicoona*, it seems, is a fast catamaran steam packet, built for the archipelago trade. I have no sea-legs, but the *Seventeen Notable Navigators* was the only option that would get us to Ishtaria in reasonable time. Princess Latufui tells me it is a fine and sturdy craft; though built to alien dimensions: she has banged her head most painfully several times. Captain Highly-Able-at-Forecasting, recognising a sister seafarer, engages the Princess in lengthy conversations of an island-hopping, archipelagan nature, which remind Latufui greatly of her home islands. The other humans aboard are a lofty Thekh, and Hugo Von Trachtenburg, a German in very high regard of himself, of that feckless type who think themselves gentleman adventurers but are little more than grandiose fraudsters. Nevertheless, he speaks Krid (as truly as any Terrene can) and acts as translator between Princess and Captain. It is a Venerian truth universally recognised that two unaccompanied women travellers must be in need of a male protector. The dreary hours Herr von Trachtenberg fills with his notion of gay chitchat! And in the evenings, the interminable games of Barrington. Von Trachtenberg claims to have gambled the game professionally in the cloud casinos: I let him win enough for the sensation to go to his head, then take him game after game. Ten times champion of the County Kildare mixed bridge championships in more than enough to beat his hide at Barrington. Still he does not get the message – yes I am a wealthy widow but I have no interest in jejune Prussians. Thus I retire to my cabin to begin my studies for the *crescite dolium* cut.

Has this world a more splendid sight than the harbour of Yez-Tok? It is a city most perpendicular, of pillars and towers, masts and spires. The tall funnels of the ships, bright with the heraldry of the Krid maritime families, blend with god-poles and lighthouse and customs towers and cranes of the harbour which in turn yield to the tower-houses and campaniles of the Bourse, the whole rising to merge with the trees of the Ishtarian Littoral Forest – pierced here and there by the comical roofs of the estancias of the Thent *zavars* and the gilded figures of the star-gods on their minarets. That forest also rises up, a cloth of green, to break into the rocky summits of the Exx Palisades. And there – oh how thrilling! – glimpsed through mountain passes unimaginably high, a glittering glimpse of the snows of the altiplano. Snow. Cold. Bliss!

It is only now, after reams of purple prose, that I realise what I was trying to say of Yez-Tok: simply, it is city as botany – stems and trunks, boles and bracts, root and branch!

And out there, in the city-that-is-a-forest, is the man who will guide me further into my brother's footsteps: Mr Daniel Okiring.

Plate 4: *V crescite dolium*: the Gourd of Plenty. A ubiquitous climbing plant of the Ishtari littoral, the Gourd of Plenty is so well adapted to urban environments that it would be considered a weed, but for the gourds, which contains a nectar prized as a delicacy among the coastal Thents. It is toxic to both Krid and Humans.

The papercut bears a note on the true scale, written in gold ink.

The Hunter's Tale

HAVE YOU SEEN a janthar? Really seen a janthar? Bloody magnificent, in the same way that a hurricane or an exploding volcano is magnificent. Magnificent and appalling. The films can never capture the sense of scale. Imagine a house, with fangs. And tusks. And spines. A house that can hit forty miles per hour. The films can never get the sheer sense of mass and speed – or the elegance and grace – that something so huge can be so nimble, so agile. And what the films can never, ever capture is the smell. They smell of curry. Vindaloo curry. Venerian body-chemistry. But that's why you never, ever eat curry on *asjan*. Out in the Stalva, the grass is tall enough to hide even a janthar. The smell is the only warning you get. You catch a whiff of vindaloo, you run.

You always run. When you hunt janthar, there will always be a moment when it turns, and the janthar hunts you. You run. If you're lucky, you'll draw it on to the gunline. If not... The 'thones of the Stalva have been hunting them this way for centuries. Coming of age thing. Like my own Maasai people. They give you a spear and point you in the general direction of a lion. Yes, I've killed a lion. I've also killed janthar – and run from even more.

The 'thones have a word for it: the *pnem*. The fool who runs.

That's how I met your brother. He applied to be a pnem for Okiring *Asjans*. Claimed experience over at Hunderewe with Costa's hunting company. I didn't need to call Costa to know he was a bullshitter. But I liked the fellow – he had charm and didn't take himself too seriously. I knew he'd never last five minutes as a pnem. Took him on as a camp steward. They like the personal service, the hunting types. If you can afford to fly yourself and your friends on a jolly to Venus, you expect to have someone to wipe your arse for you. Charm works on these bastards. He'd wheedle his way into their affections and get them drinking. They'd invite him and before you knew it he was getting their life-stories – and a lot more beside – out of them. He was a careful cove too – he'd always stay one drink behind them and be up early and sharp-eyed the next morning. Always came back with the fattest tip. I knew what he was doing but he did it so well – I'd taken him on, hadn't I? So, an aristocrat. Why am I not surprised? Within three trips I'd made him Maitre de la Chasse. Heard he'd made and lost one fortune already... is that true? A jewel thief? Why am I not surprised by that either?

The Thirtieth Earl of Mar fancied himself as a sporting type. Booked a three month Grand Asjan; him and five friends, shooting their way up the Great Littoral to the Stalva. Wives, husbands, lovers, personal servants, twenty Thent asjanis and a caravan of forty graapa to carry their bags and baggage. They had one graap just for the champagne – they'd shipped every last drop of it from Earth. Made so much noise we cleared the forest for ten miles around. Bloody brutes – we'd set up hides at waterholes so they could blast away from point blank range. That's not hunting. Every day they'd send a dozen bearers back with hides and trophies. I'm surprised there was anything left, the amount of metal they pumped into those poor beasts. The stench of rot... God! The sky was black with carrion-avios.

Your brother excelled himself: suave, in control, charming, witty, the soul of attention. Oh, most attentive. Especially to the Lady Mar... She was handy with the guns, but I think she tired of the boys-club antics of the gents. Or maybe it was just the sheer relentless slaughter. Either way, she increasingly remained in camp. Where your brother attended to her. Aristocrats – they sniff each other out.

So Arthur poled the Lady Mar while we blasted our bloody, brutal, bestial way up onto the High Stalva. Nothing would do the Thirtieth Earl but to go after janthar. Ten percent of hunters who go for janthar don't come back. Only ten percent! He liked those odds.

Twenty-five sleeps we were up there, while Great Day turned to Great Evening. I wasn't staying for night on the Stalva. It's not just a different season, it's a different world. Things come out of sleep, out of dens, out of the ground. No, not for all the fortune of the Earls of Mar would I spend night on the Stalva.

Then the call came: Janthar-sign! An asjani had seen a fresh path through a speargrass meadow five miles to the north of us. In a moment we were mounted and tearing through the high Stalva. The Earl rode like a madman, whipping his graap to reckless speed. Damn fool: of all the Stalva's many grasslands, the tall pike-grass meadows were the most dangerous. A janthar could be right next to you and you wouldn't see it. And the pike-grass disorients, reflects sounds, turns you around. There was no advising the Earl of Mar and his chums. His wife hung back – she claimed her mount had picked up a little lameness. Why did I not say something when Arthur went back to accompany the Lady Mar! But my concern was how to get everyone out of the pike-grass alive.

Then the Earl stabbed his shock-goad into the flank of his graap and before I could do anything he was off. I got on the radio to the others – form a gunline! The mad fool was going to run the janthar himself. Moments later his graap came crashing back through the pike-grass to find its herd-mates. My only hope was that he would lead the janthar right into our crossfire. It takes a lot of ordnance to stop a janthar. And in this kind of tall grass terrain, where you can hardly see your hand in front of your face, I had to set the firing positions just right so the idiots wouldn't blow each other to bits.

I got them into some semblance of position. I held the centre – the *lakoo*. Your brother and the Lady Mar I ordered to take *jeft* and *garoon* – the last two positions of the left wing of the gunline. Finally I got them all to radio silence. The 'thones teach you how to be still, and how to listen, and how to know what is safe and what is death. Silence, then a sustained crashing. Most terrifying sound in the world, a janthar in full pursuit. It sounds like its coming from everywhere at once. I yelled to the gunline; steady there, steady. Hold your fire! Then I smelled it. Clear, sharp: unmistakable. Curry. I put up the cry: Vindaloo! Vindaloo! And there was the mad earl, breaking out of the cane. Madman! What was he thinking! He was in the wrong place, headed in the wrong direction. The only ones who could cover him were Arthur and Lady Mar. And there, behind him: the janthar. Bigger than any I had ever seen before. The Mother of All Janthar. The Queen of the High Stalva. I froze. We all froze. We might as well try to kill a mountain. I yelled to Arthur and Lady Mar. Shoot! Shoot now! Nothing. Shoot for the love of all the stars! Nothing. Shoot! Why didn't they shoot?

The 'thones found the Thirtieth Earl of Mar spread over a hundred yards.

They hadn't shot because they weren't there. They were at it like dogs – your brother and the Lady Mar, back where they had left the party. They hadn't even heard the janthar.

Strange woman, the Lady Mar. Her face barely moved when she learnt of her husband's terrible death. As if it were no surprise to her. Of course, she became immensely rich when the will went through. There was no question of your brother ever working for me again. Shame. I liked him. But I can't help thinking that he was as much used as user in that sordid little affair. Did the Lady of Mar murder her husband? Too much left to chance. Yet it was a very convenient accident. And I can't help but think that the Thirtieth Earl knew what his lady was up to; and a surfeit of cuckoldry drove him to prove he was a man.

The janthar haunted the highlands for years. Became a legend. Every aristo idiot on the Inner Worlds who fancied himself a Great Terrene Hunter went after it. None of them ever got it, though it claimed five more lives. The Human-slayer of the Stalva. In the end it stumbled into a 'thone clutch trap and died on a pungi stake, eaten away by gangrene. So we all pass. No final run, no gunline, no trophies.

Your brother left when the scandal broke – went up country, over the Stalva into the Palisade country. I heard a rumour he'd joined a mercenary javrost unit, fighting up on the altiplano.

Botany, is it? Safer business than Big Game.

PLATE 5: *V trifex aculeatum*: Stannage's Bird-Eating Trifid. Native of the Great Littoral Forest of Isharia. Carnivorous in its habits; it lures smaller, nectar-feeding avios with its sweet exudate, then stings them to death with its whiplike style and sticky, venomous stigma.

Cutpaper, inks, folded tissue.

THE PRINCESS IS brushing her hair. This she does every night, whether in Tonga or Ireland, on Earth or aboard a space-crosser or on Venus. The ritual is invariable. She kneels, unpins and uncoils her tight bun and lets her hair fall to its natural length, to the waist. Then she takes two silver-backed brushes and, with great and vigorous strokes, brushes her hair from the crown of her head to the tips. One hundred strokes, which she counts in a Tongan rhyme which I very much love to hear.

When she is done she cleans the brushes, returns them to the velvet lined case, then takes a bottle of coconut oil and works it through her hair. The air is suffused with the sweet smell of coconut. It reminds me so much of the whin-flowers of home. She works patiently and painstakingly and when she has finished she rolls her hair back into its bun and pins it. A simple, dedicated, repetitive task, but it moves me almost to tears.

Her beautiful hair! How dearly I love my friend Latufui!

We are sleeping at a hohvandha, a Thent roadside inn, on the Grand North Road in Canton Hoa in the Great Littoral Forest. Tree branches scratch at my window shutters. The heat, the humidity, the animal noise are all overpowering. We are far from the cooling breezes of the Vestal Sea. I wilt, though Latufui relishes the warmth. The arboreal creatures of this forest are deeper voiced than in Ireland; bellings and honkings and deep booms. How I wish we could spend the night here – Great Night – for my Carfax tells me that the Ishtaria Littoral Forest contains this world's greatest concentration of luminous creatures – fungi, plants, animals and those peculiarly Venerian phyla in between. It is almost as bright as day. I have made some day-time studies of the Star Flower – no Venerian Botanica can be complete without it – but for it to succeed I must hope that there is a supply of luminous paint at Loogaza; where we embark for the crossing of the Stalva.

My dear Latufui has finished now and closed away her brushes in their green baize-lined box. So faithful and true a friend! We met in Nuku'alofa on the Tongan leg of my Botanica of the South Pacific. The King, her father, had issued the invitation – he was a keen collector – and at the reception I was introduced to his very large family, including Latufui, and was immediately charmed by her sense, dignity and vivacity. She invited me to tea the following day – a very grand affair – where she confessed that as a minor princess her only hope of fulfillment was in marrying well – an institution in which she had no interest. I replied that I had visited the South Pacific as a time apart from Lord Rathangan – it had been clear for some years that Patrick had no interest in me (nor I in him). We were two noble ladies of compatible needs and temperaments, and there and then we became firmest friends and inseparable companions. When Patrick shot himself and Rathangan passed into my possession, it was only natural that the Princess move in with me.

I cannot conceive of life without Latufui; yet I am deeply ashamed that I have not been totally honest in my motivations for this Venerian expedition. Why can I not trust? Oh secrets! Oh simulations!

* * *

PLATE 6: *V stellafloris noctecandentis*: the Venerian Starflower. Its name is the same in Thent, Thekh and Krid. Now a popular Terrestrial garden plant, where is it known as glow-berry, though the name is a misnomer. Its appearance is a bunch of night-luminous white berries, though the berries are in fact globular bracts, with the bio-luminous flower at the centre. Selective strains of this flower traditionally provide illumination in Venerian settlements during the Great Night.

Paper, luminous paint (not reproduced.) The original papercut is mildly radioactive.

BY HIGH-TRAIN TO Camahoo.

We have our own carriage. It is of aged gothar-wood, still fragrant and spicy. The hammocks do not suit me at all. Indeed, the whole train has a rocking, swaying lollop that makes me seasick. In the caravanserai at Loogaza the contraption looked both ridiculous and impractical. But here, on the Stalva, its ingenuity reveals itself. The twenty-foot high wheels carry us high above the grass, though I am in fear of grass fires – the steam-tractor at the head of the train does throw off the most ferocious pother of soot and embers.

I am quite content to remain in my carriage and work on my Stalva-grass study – I think this may be most sculptural. The swaying makes for many a slip with the scissor, but I think I have caught the feathery, almost downy nature of the flowerheads. Of a maritime people, the Princess is at home in this rolling ocean of grass and spends much of her time on the observation balcony watching the patterns the wind draws across the grasslands.

It was there that she fell into conversation with the Honorable Cormac de Buitlear, a fellow Irishman. Inevitably, he ingratiated himself and within minutes was taking tea in our carriage. The Inner Worlds are infested with young men claiming to be the junior sons of minor Irish gentry, but a few minutes gentle questioning revealed not only that he was indeed the Honourable Cormac – of the Bagenalstown De Buitlears – but a relative, close enough to know of my husband's demise, and the scandal of the Blue Empress.

Our conversation went like this.

HIMSELF: The Grangegorman Hydes. My father used to knock around with your elder brother – what was he called?

MYSELF: Richard.

HIMSELF: The younger brother – wasn't he a bit of a black sheep? I remember there was this tremendous scandal. Some jewel – a sapphire as big as a thrush's egg. Yes – that was the expression they used in the papers. A thrush's egg. What was it called?

MYSELF: The Blue Empress.

HIMSELF: Yes! That was it. Your grandfather was presented it by some Martian princess. Services rendered.

MYSELF: He helped her escape across the Tharsis steppe in the revolution of '11, and then organised the White Brigades to help her regain the Jasper Throne.

HIMSELF: You woke up one morning to find the stone gone and him vanished. Stolen.

I could see that Princess Latufui found The Honourable Cormac's bluntness distressing but if one claims the privileges of a noble family, one must also claim the shames.

MYSELF: It was never proved that Arthur stole the Blue Empress.

HIMSELF: No no. But you know how tongues wag in the country. And his disappearance was, you must admit, *timely*. How long ago was that now? God, I must have been a wee gossoon.

MYSELF: Fifteen years.

HIMSELF: Fifteen years. And not a word? Do you know if he's even alive?

MYSELF: We believe he fled to the Inner Worlds. Every few years we hear of a sighting but most of them are so contrary we dismiss them. He made his choice. As for the Blue Empress; broken up and sold long ago, I don't doubt.

HIMSELF: And here I find you on a jaunt across one of the Inner Worlds.

MYSELF: I am creating a new album of papercuts. The Botanica Veneris.

HIMSELF: Of course. If I might make so bold, Lady Rathangan: the Blue Empress: do you believe Arthur took it?

And I made him no verbal answer but gave the smallest shake of my head.

* * *

Princess Latufui had been restless all this evening – the time before sleep, that is: Great Evening was still many Terrene days off. Can we ever truly adapt to the monstrous Venerian calendar? Arthur has been on this world for fifteen years – has he drifted not just to another world, but another clock, another calendar? I worked on my Stalva-grass cut – I find that curving the leaf-bearing nodes gives the necessary three-dimensionality – but my heart was not in it. Latufui sipped at tea and fumbled at stitching and pushed newspapers around until eventually she threw open the cabin door in frustration and demanded I join her on the balcony.

The rolling travel of the high-train made me grip the rail for dear life, but the high-plain was as sharp and fresh as if starched, and there, a long line on the horizon beyond the belching smokestack and pumping pistons of the tractor, were the Palisades of Exx: a grey wall from one horizon to the other. Clouds hid the peaks, like a curtain lowered from the sky.

Dark against the grey mountains I saw the spires of the observatories of Camahoo. This was the Thent homeland; and I was apprehensive, for among those towers and minarets is a hoondahvi, a Thent opium den, owned by the person who may be able to tell me the next part of my brother's story – a story increasingly disturbing and dark. A person who is not human.

"Ida, dear friend. There is a thing I must ask you."

"Anything, dear Latufui."

"I must tell you, it is not a thing that can be asked softly."

My heart turned over in my chest. I knew what Latufui would ask.

"Ida: have you come to this world to look for your brother?"

She did me the courtesy of a direct question. I owed it a direct answer.

"Yes," I said. "I have come to find Arthur."

"I thought so."

"For how long?"

"Since Ledekh-Olkoi. Ah, I cannot say the words right. When you went to get papers and gum and returned empty-handed."

"I went to see a Mr Stafford Grimes. I had information that he had met my brother soon after his arrival on this world. He directed me to Mr Okiring, a retired asjan hunter in Yez Tok."

"And Camahoo? Is this another link in the chain?"

"It is. But the Botanica is no sham. I have an obligation to my backers

– you know the state of my finances as well as I, Latufui. The late Count Rathangan was a profligate man. He ran the estate into the ground."

"I could wish you had trusted me. All those weeks of planning and organising. The maps, the itineraries, the tickets, the transplanetary calls to agents and factors. I was so excited! A journey to another world! But for you there was always something else. None of that was the whole truth. None of it was honest."

"Oh my dear Latufui..." But how could I say that I had not told her because I feared what Arthur might have become. Fears that seemed to be borne out by every ruined life that had touched his. What would I find? Did anything remain of the wild, carefree boy I remembered chasing old Bunty the dog across the summer lawns of Grangegorman? Would he listen to me? "There is a wrong to right. An old debt to be cancelled. It's a family thing."

"I live in your house, but not in your family," Princess Latufui said. Her words were barbed with truth. They tore me. "We would not do that in Tonga. Your ways are different. And I thought I was more than a companion."

"Oh my dear Latufui." I took her hands in mine. "You are far far more to me than a companion. You are my life. But you of all people should understand my family. We are on another world, but we are not so far from Rathangan, I think. I am seeking Arthur, and I do not know what I will find, but I promise you, what he says to me, I will tell to you. Everything."

Now she laid her hands over mine, and there we stood, cupping hands on the balcony rail, watching the needle spires of Camahoo rise from the grass spears of the Stalva.

Plate 7 *V vallumque foenum*: Stalva Pike Grass. Another non-Terrene that is finding favour in Terrestrial ornamental gardens. Earth never receives sufficient sunlight for it to attain its full Stalva height. *Yetten* in the Stalva Thent dialect.

Card, onionskin paper, corrugated paper, paint. This papercut is unique in that it unfolds into three parts. The original, in the Chester Beatty Library in Dublin, is always displayed unfolded.

* * *

The Mercenary's Tale

IN THE NAME of the Leader of the Starry Skies and the Ever-Circling Spiritual Family, welcome to my hoondahvi. May *apsas* speak; may *gavanda* sing, may the *thoo* impart their secrets.

I understand completely that you have not come to drink. But the greeting is standard. We pride ourselves on being the most traditional hoondahvi in Exxaa Canton.

Is the music annoying? No? Most Terrenes find it aggravating. It's an essential part of the hoondahvi experience, I am afraid.

Your brother, yes. How could I forget him? I owe him my life.

He fought like a man who hated fighting. Up on the Altiplano, when we smashed open the potteries and set the Porcelain Towns afire up and down the Valley of the Kilns, there were those who blazed with love and joy at the slaughter and those whose faces were so dark it was as if their souls were clogged with soot. Your brother was one of those. Human expressions are hard for us to read – your faces are wood, like masks. But I saw his face and knew that he loathed what he did. That was what made him the best of javrosts. I am an old career soldier; I have seen many many come to our band. The ones in love with violence: unless they can take discipline, we turn them away. But when a mercenary hates what he does for his silver, there must be a greater darkness driving him. There is a thing they hate more than the violence they do.

Are you sure the music is tolerable? Our harmonies and chord patterns apparently create unpleasant electrical resonance in the human brain. Like small seizures. We find it most reassuring. Like the rhythm of the kittening-womb.

Your brother came to us in the dawn of Great Day 6817. He could ride a graap, bivouac, cook and was handy with both bolt and blade. We never ask questions of our javrosts – in time they answer them all themselves – but rumours blow on the wind like *thagoon*-down. He was a minor aristocrat, he was a gambler; he was thief, he was a murderer; he was a seducer, he was a traitor. Nothing to disqualify him. Sufficient to recommend him.

In Old Days the Duke of Yoo disputed mightily with her neighbour the Duke of Hetteten over who rightly ruled the altiplano and its profitable potteries. From time immemorial it had been a place beyond: independently minded and stubborn of spirit, with little respect for gods or dukes. Wars were fought down generations, lying waste to fames and fortunes, and when in the end the House of Yoo prevailed, the peoples of the plateau had forgotten they ever had lords and mistresses and debts of fealty. It is a law of earth and stars alike that people should be well-governed, obedient and quiet in their ways, so the Duke of Yoo embarked on a campaign of civil discipline. Her house-corps had been decimated in the Porcelain Wars, so House Yoo hired mercenaries. Among them, my former unit, Gellet's Javrosts.

They speak of us still, up on the plateau. We are the monsters of their Great Nights, the haunters of their children's dreams. We are legend. We are Gellet's Javrosts. We are the new demons.

For one Great Day and Great Night, we ran free. We torched the topless star-shrines of Javapanda and watched them burn like chimneys. We smashed the funerary jars and trampled the bones of the illustrious dead of Toohren. We overturned the houses of the holy, burned elders and kits in their homes. We lassoed rebels and dragged them behind our graapa, round and round the village until all that remained was a bloody rope. We forced whole communities from their homes; driving them across the altiplano until the snow heaped their bodies. And Arthur was at my side. We were not friends – there is too much history on this world for Human and Thent ever to be that. He was my *badoon*. You do not have a concept for it, let alone a word. A passionate colleague. A brother who is not related. A fellow devotee...

We killed and we killed and we killed. And in our wake came the Duke of Yoo's soldiers – restoring order, rebuilding towns, offering defense against the murderous renegades. It was all strategy. The Duke of Yoo knew the plateauneers would never love her, but she could be their saviour. Therefore a campaign of final outrages was planned. Such vileness! We were ordered to Glehenta, a pottery town at the head of Valley of the Kilns. There we would enter the Glotoonas – the birthing-creches – and slaughter every infant down to the last kit. We rode, Arthur at my side, and though human emotions are strange and distant to me, I knew them well enough to read the storm in his heart. Night-snow was falling as we entered Glehenta, lit by ten thousand starflowers. The people locked their doors and cowered from us. Through the heart of town we rode; past the great conical kilns, to the Glotoonas. Matres flung themselves before our graapa – we rode them down. Arthur's face was darker than the Great Midnight. He broke formation and rode up to Gellet himself. I went to him. I saw words between your brother and our commander. I did not hear them. Then Arthur drew his blasket and in single shot blew the entire top of Gellet's body to ash. In the fracas I shot down three of our troop; then we were racing through the glowing streets, our hooves clattering on the porcelain cobbles, the erstwhile Gellet's Javrosts behind us.

And so we saved them. For the Duke of Yoo had arranged it so that her Ducal Guard would fall upon us even as we attacked, annihilate us and achieve two notable victories: presenting themselves as the saviours of Glehenta, and destroying any evidence of their scheme. Your brother and I sprung the trap. But we did not know until leagues and months later, far from the altiplano. At the foot of the Ten Thousand Stairs we parted – we thought it safer. We never saw each other again, though I heard he had gone back up the stairs, to the Pelerines. And if you do find him, please don't tell him what became of me. This is a shameful place.

And I am ashamed that I have told you such dark and bloody truths about your brother. But at the end, he was honourable. He was right. That he saved the guilty – an unintended consequence. Our lives are made up of such.

Certainly, we can continue outside on the hoondahvi porch. I did warn you that the music was irritating to human sensibilities.

PLATE 8: *V lucerna vesperum*; Schaefferia: the Evening Candle. A solitary tree of the foothills of the Exx Palisades of Ishtaria, the Schaefferia is noted for its many upright, luminous blossoms, which flower in Venerian Great Evening and Great Dawn.

Only the blossoms are reproduced. Card, folded and cut tissue, luminous paint (not reproduced). The original is also slightly radioactive.

A COG RAILWAY runs from Camahoo Terminus to the Convent of the Starry Pelerines. The Starsview Special takes pilgrims to see the open sky. Our carriage is small, luxurious, intricate and ingenious in that typically Thent fashion, and terribly tedious. The track has been constructed in a helix inside Awk Mountain, so our journey consists of interminable, noisy spells inside the tunnel, punctuated by brief, blinding moments of clarity as we emerge on to the open face of the mountain. Not for the vertiginous!

Thus, hour upon hour, we spiral our way up Mount Awk.

Princes Latufui and I play endless games of Moon Whist but our minds are not on it. My forebodings have darkened after my conversation with the Thent hoondahvi owner in Camahoo. The Princess is troubled by my anxiety. Finally she can bear it no more.

"Tell me about the Blue Empress. Tell me everything."

I GREW UP with two injunctions in case of fire: save the dogs and the Blue Empress. For almost all my life the jewel was a ghost-stone – present but unseen, haunting Grangegorman and the lives it held. I have a memory from earliest childhood of seeing the stone – never touching it – but I do not trust the memory. Imaginings too easily become memories, memories imaginings.

We are not free in so many things, we of the landed class. Richard would inherit, Arthur would make a way in the worlds and I would marry as well as I could; land to land. The Barony of Rathangan was considered one of the most desirable in Kildare, despite Patrick's seeming determination to drag it to the bankruptcy court. A match was made, and he was charming and bold; a fine sportsman and a very handsome man. It was an equal match – snide comments from both halves of the county. The Blue Empress was part of my treasure – on the strict understanding that it remain in the custody of my lawyers. Patrick argued – and it was there I first got an inkling of his true character – the wedding was off the wedding was on the wedding was off the wedding was on again and the banns posted. A viewing was arranged, for his people to itemise and value the Hyde treasure. For the first time in long memory, the Blue Empress was taken from its safe and displayed. Blue as the wide Atlantic it was, and as boundless and clear. You could lose yourself forever in the light inside that gem. And yes, it was the size of a thrush's egg.

And then the moment that all the stories agree on: the lights failed. Not so unusual at Grangegorman – the same grandfather who brought back the Blue Empress installed the hydro-plant – but when they came back on again; the sapphire was gone: baize and case and everything.

We called upon the honour of all present, ladies and gentlemen alike. The lights would be put out for five minutes, and when they were switched back on, the Blue Empress would be back in the Hyde treasure. It was not. Our people demanded we call the police, Patrick's people, mindful of their client's attraction to scandal, were less insistent. We would make a further appeal to honour: if the Blue Empress was not back by morning, then we would call the guards.

Not only was the Blue Empress still missing, so was Arthur.

We called the Garda Siochana. The last we heard was that Arthur had left for the Inner Worlds.

The wedding went ahead. It would have been a greater scandal to call it off. Patrick could not let the matter go: he went to his grave believing Arthur and I had conspired to keep the Blue Empress out of his hands. I have no doubt that Patrick would have found a way of forcing me to sign over possession of the gem to him, and selling it. Wastrel.

As for the Blue Empress: I feel I am very near to Arthur now. One cannot run forever. We will meet, and the truth will be told.

THEN LIGHT FLOODED our carriage as the train emerged from the tunnel on to the final ramp and there, before us, its spires and domes dusted with snow blown from the high peaks, was the Convent of the Starry Pelerines.

PLATE 9: *V aquilonis vitis visionum:* the Northern Littoral, or Ghost Vine. A common climber of the forests of the southern slopes of the Ishtari altiplano, domesticated and widely grown in Thent garden terraces. Its white, trumpet-shaped flowers are attractive, but the plant is revered for its berries. When crushed, the infused liquor known as *pula* creates powerful auditory hallucinations in Venerian physiology and form the basis of the Thent mystical hoondahvi cult. In Terrenes it produces a strong euphoria and a sense of omnipotence.

Alkaloid-infused paper. Ida Granville-Hyde used Thent Ghost-Vine liquor to tint the paper in this cut. It is reported to be still mildly hallucinogenic.

* * *

The Pilgrim's Tale

YOU'LL COME OUT on to the belvedere? It's supposed to be off-limits to Terrenes – technically blasphemy – sacred space and all that – but the pelerines turn a blind eye. Do excuse the cough... ghastly, isn't it? Sounds like a bag of bloody loose change. I don't suppose the cold air does much for my lungs, but at this stage it's a matter of damn.

That's Gloaming Peak there. You won't see it until the cloud clears. Every Great Evening, every Great Dawn, for a few Earth-days at a time, the cloud breaks. It goes up, oh so much further than you could ever imagine. You look up, and up, and up and beyond it, you see the stars. That's why the pelerines came here. Such a sensible religion. The stars are gods. One star, one god. Simple. No faith, no heaven, no punishment, no sin. Just look up and wonder. The Blue Pearl: that's what they call our Earth. I wonder if that's why they care for us. Because we're descended from divinity? If only they knew. They really are very kind.

Excuse me. Bloody marvellous stuff, this Thent brew. I'm in no pain at all. I find it quite reassuring that I shall slip from this too too rancid flesh swaddled in a blanket of beatific thoughts and analgesic glow. They're very kind, the pelerines. Very kind.

Now, look to your right. There. Do you see? That staircase, cut into the rock, winding up up up. The Ten Thousand Steps. That's the old way to the altiplano. Everything went up and down those steps: people, animals, goods, palanquins and stickmen, traders and pilgrims and armies. Your brother. I watched him go, from this very belvedere. Three years ago, or was it five? You never really get used to the Great Day. Time blurs.

We were tremendous friends, the way that addicts are. You wouldn't have come this far without realising some truths about your brother. Our degradation unites us. Dear thing. How we'd set the world to rights, over flask after flask of this stuff. He realised the truth of this place early on. It's the way to the stars. God's waiting room. And we, this choir of shambling wrecks, wander through it, dazzled by our glimpses of the stars. Dear Arthur.

We're all darkened souls here, but he was haunted. Things done and things left undone, like the prayer book says. My father was a vicar – can't you tell? He never spoke completely about his time with the javrosts. He hinted – I think he wanted to, very much, but was afraid of giving me his nightmares. That old saw about a problem shared being a problem halved? Damnable lie. A problem shared is a problem doubled. But I would find him up here all times of the Great Day and Night, watching the staircase and the caravans and stick-convoys going up and down. Altiplano porcelain, he'd say. So fine you can read the Bible through it. Every cup, every plate, every vase and bowl, was portered down those stairs on the shoulders of a stickman. You know he served up on the Altiplano, in the Duke of Yoo's Pacification. I wasn't here then, but Aggers was, and he said you could see the smoke going up; endless plumes of smoke, so thick the sky didn't clear and the pelerines went for a whole Great Day without seeing the stars. All Arthur would say about it was, that'll make some fine china. That's what made porcelain from the Valley of the Kilns so fine: bones – the bones of the dead, ground up into powder. He would never drink from a Valley cup – he said it was drinking from a skull.

Here's another thing about addicts – you never get rid of it. All you do is replace one addiction with another. The best you can hope for is that it's a better addiction. Some become god-addicts – or gods, some throw themselves into worthy deeds, or self-improvement, or fine thoughts, or helping others, God help us all. Me, my lovely little vice is sloth – I really am an idle little bugger. It's so easy, letting the seasons slip away; slothful days and indolent nights, coughing my life up one chunk at a time. For Arthur, it was the visions. Arthur saw wonders and horrors, angels and demons, hopes and fears. True visions – the things that drive men to glory or death. Visionary visions. It lay up on the altiplano, beyond the twists and turns of the Ten Thousand Steps. I could never comprehend what it was, but it drove him. Devoured him. Ate his sleep, ate his appetite. Ate his body and his soul and his sanity.

It was worse in the Great Night... Everything's worse in the Great Night. The snow would come swirling down the staircase and he saw things in it – faces – heard voices. The faces and voices of the people who had died, up there on the altiplano. He had to follow them, go up, into the Valley of the Kilns, where he would ask the people to forgive him – or kill him.

And he went. I couldn't stop him – I didn't want to stop him. Can you understand that? I watched him from this very belvedere. The pelerines are not our warders, any of us is free to leave at any time, though I've never seen anyone leave, but Arthur. He left in the evening, with the lilac light catching

Gloaming Peak. He never looked back. Not a glance to me. I watched him climb the steps to that bend there. That's where I lost sight of him. I never saw or heard of him again. But stories come down the stairs with the stickmen and they make their way even to this little eyrie; stories of a seer – a visionary. I look and I imagine I see smoke rising, up there on the altiplano.

It's a pity you won't be here to see the clouds break around the Gloaming, or look at the stars.

PLATE 10 *V genetric nives*: Mother-of-snows (direct translation from Thent). Ground-cover hi-alpine of the Exx Palisades. The plant forms extensive carpets of thousands of minute white blossoms.

The most intricate papercut in the Botanica Veneris. Each floret is three millimetres in diameter. Paper, ink, gouache.

A HIGH-STEPPING SPIDER-CAR took me up the Ten Thousand Steps, past caravans of stickmen, spines bent, shoulders warped beneath brutal loads of finest porcelain.

The twelve cuts of the *Botanica Veneris* I have given to the Princess, along with descriptions and botanical notes. She would not let me leave, clung to me, wracked with great sobs of loss and fear. It was dangerous; a sullen land with Great Night coming. I could not convince her of my reason for heading up the stairs alone, for they did not convince me. The one, true reason I could not tell her. Oh, I have been despicable to her! My dearest friend. But worse even than that, false.

She stood watching my spider-car climb the steps until a curve in the staircase took me out of her sight. Must the currency of truth always be falsehood?

Now I think of her spreading her long hair out, and brushing it, firmly, directly, beautifully, and the pen falls from my fingers...

EGAYHAZY IS A closed city; hunched, hiding, tight. Its streets are narrow, its buildings leans towards each other; their gables so festooned with starflower that it looks like perpetual festival. Nothing could be further from the truth:

Egayhazy is an angry city; aggressive and cowed: sullen. I keep my Ledekh-Teltai in my bag. But the anger is not directed at me, though from the story I heard at the Camahoo hoondahvi; my fellow humans on this world have not graced our species. It is the anger of a country under occupation. On walls and doors the proclamations of the Duke of Yoo are plastered layer upon layer: her pennant, emblazoned with the four white hands of House Yoo, flies from publics buildings, the radio station mast, tower tops and the gallows. Her javrosts patrol streets so narrow their graapa barely squeeze through them. In their passage, the citizens of Egayhazy flash jagged glares, mutter altiplano oaths. And there is another sigil: an eight-petalled flower; a blue so deep it seems almost to shine. I see it stencilled hastily on walls and doors and the occupation-force posters. I see it in little badges sewn to the quilted jackets of the Egayhazians; and in tiny glass jars in low-set windows. In the market of Yent I witnessed javrosts upturn and smash a vegetable stall that dared to offer a few posies of this blue bloom.

THE STAFF AT my hotel were suspicious when they saw me working up some sketches from memory of this blue flower of dissent. I explained my work and showed some photographs and asked what was this flower? A common plant of the high altiplano; they said. It grows up under the breath of the high snow; small and tough and stubborn. Its most remarkable feature is that it blooms when no other flower does – in the dead of the Great Night. The Midnight Glory was one name, though it had another, newer, which entered common use since the occupation: The Blue Empress.

I knew there and then I had found Arthur.

A PALL OF sulfurous smoke hangs permanently over the Valley of Kilns, lit with hellish tints from the glow of the kilns below. A major ceramics centre on a high, treeless plateau? How are the kilns fuelled? Volcanic vents do the firing, but they turn this long defile in the flank of Mount Tooloowera into a little hell of clay, bones, smashed porcelain, sand, slag and throat-searing sulphur. Glehenta is the last of the Porcelain Towns, wedged into the head of the valley, where the river Iddis still carries a memory of freshness and cleanliness. The pottery houses, like upturned vases, lean towards each other like companionable women.

And there is the house to which my questions guided me: as my informants described; not the greatest but perhaps the meanest; not the foremost but perhaps the most prominent, tucked away in an alley. From its roof flies a flag, and my breath caught: not the Four White Hands of Yoo – never that, but neither the Blue Empress. The smoggy wind tugged at the hand-and-dagger of the Hydes of Grangegorman.

Swift action: to hesitate would be to falter and fail, to turn and walk away, back down the Valley of the Kilns and the Ten Thousand Steps. I rattle the ceramic chimes. From inside, a huff and sigh. Then a voice: worn ragged, stretched and tired, but unmistakable.

"Come on in. I've been expecting you."

PLATE 11: *V crepitant movebitvolutans*. Wescott's Wandering Star. A wind-mobile vine, native of the Exx Palisades, that grows into a tight spherical web of vines which, in the Venerian Great Day, becomes detached from an atrophied root stock and rolls cross-country, carried on the wind. A central calx contains woody nuts that produce a pleasant rattling sound as the Wandering Star is in motion.

Cut paper, painted, layered and gummed. This papercut contains over thirty layers.

The Seer's Story

TEA?

I have it sent up from Camahoo when the stickmen make the return trip. Proper tea. Irish breakfast. It's very hard to get the water hot enough at this altitude but it's my little ritual. I should have asked you to bring some. I've known you were looking for me from the moment you set out from Loogaza. You think anyone can wander blithely into Glehenta?

Tea.

You look well. The years have been kind to you. I look like shit. Don't deny it. I know it. I have an excuse. I'm dying you know. The liquor of the vine – it takes as much as it gives. And this world is hard on humans. The Great Days – you never completely adjust – and the climate: if it's not the thin air up here it's the moulds and fungi and spores down there. And the ultraviolet. It dries you out, withers you up. The town healer must have frozen twenty melanomas off me. No I'm dying. Rotten inside. A leather bag of mush and bones. But you look very well Ida. So Patrick shot himself. Fifteen years too late, says I. He could have spared all of us... enough of that. But I'm glad you're happy. I'm glad you have someone who cares, to treat you the way you should be.

I am the Merciful One, the Seer, the Prophet of the Blue Pearl, and I am dying.

I walked down that same street you walked down. I didn't ride, I walked, right through the centre of town. I didn't know what to expect. Silence. A mob. Stones. Bullets. To walk right through and out the other side without a door opening to me. At the very last house, the door opened and an old man came out and stood in front of me so that I could not pass. "I know you." He pointed at me. "You came the night of the Javrosts." I was certain then I would die, and that seemed not so bad a thing to me. "You were the merciful one, the one who spared our young." And he went into the house and brought me a porcelain cup of water and I drank it down and here I remain. The Merciful One.

They have decided that I am lead them to glory, or more likely to death. It's justice, I suppose. I have visions you see – *pula* flashbacks. It works differently on Terrenes from Thents. Oh, they're hard-headed enough not to believe in divine inspiration or any of that rubbish. They need a figurehead – the repentant mercenary is a good role, and the odd bit of mumbo-jumbo from the inside of my addled head doesn't go amiss.

Is your tea all right? It's very hard to get the water hot enough this high. Have I said that before? Ignore me – the flashbacks. Did I tell you I'm dying? But it's good to see you; oh how long is it?

And Richard? The children? And Grangegorman? And is Ireland... of course. What I would give for an eyeful of green, for a glimpse of summer sun, a blue sky.

So, I have been a conman and a lover, a soldier and an addict, and now I end my time as a revolutionary. It is surprisingly easy. The Group of Seven does the work: I release gnomic pronouncements that run like grassfire from here to Egayhazy. I did come up with the Blue Empress motif – the Midnight Glory – blooming in the dark, under the breath of the high snows. Apt. They're not the most poetic of people, these potters. We drove the Duke of Yoo from the Valley of the Kilns and the Ishtar Plain: she is resisted everywhere but she will not relinquish her claim on the altiplano so lightly. You've been in Egayhazy – you seen the forces she has up here. Armies are mustering and my agents report 'rigibles coming through the passes in the Palisades. An assault will come. The Duke has an alliance with House Shorth – some agreement to divide the altiplano up between them. We're outnumbered. Outmanoeuvred and out-supplied and we have nowhere to run. They'll be at each other's throats within a Great Day but that's a matter of damn for us. The Duke may spare the kilns – they're the source of wealth. Matter of damn to me. I'll not see it, one way or other. You should leave, Ida. *Pula* and local wars – never get sucked into them.

Ah. Unh. Another flashback. They're getting briefer, but more intense,

Ida, you are in danger. Leave before night – they'll attack in the night. I have to stay. The Merciful One, the Seer, the Prophet of the Blue Pearl can't abandon his people. But it was good, so good of you to come. This is a terrible place. I should never have come here. The best traps are the slowest. In you walk, through all the places and all the lives and all the years, never thinking that you are already in the trap, and then you go to turn around and it has closed behind you. Ida, go as soon as you can... go right now. You should never have come. But... – oh, how I hate the thought of dying up here on this terrible plain! To see Ireland again...

PLATE 12: *V volanti musco*: Air-moss. The papercut shows part of a symbiotic lighter-than-air creature of the Venerian highlands. The plant part consists of curtains of extremely light hanging moss that gather water from the air and low clouds. The animal part is not reproduced.

Shredded paper, gum.

HE CAME TO the door of his porcelain house, leaning heavily on a stick, a handkerchief pressed to mouth and nose against the volcanic fumes. I had tried to plead with him to leave, but whatever else he has become, he is a Hyde of Grangegorman and stubborn as an ould donkey. There is a wish for death in him; something old and strangling and relentless with the gentlest eyes.

"I have something for you," I said and I gave him the box without ceremony.

His eyebrows rose when he opened it.

"Ah."

"I stole the Blue Empress."

"I know."

"I had to keep it out of Patrick's hands. He would have broken and wasted it like he broke and wasted everything." Then my slow mind, so intent on saying this confession right, that I had practised on the space-crosser, and in every room and every mode of conveyance on my journey across this world, flower to flower, story to story: my middle-aged tripped over Arthur's two words. "You knew?"

"All along."

"You never thought maybe Richard, maybe Father, or Mammy, or one of the staff?"

"I had no doubt that it was you, for those very reasons you said. I chose to keep your secret, and I have."

"Arthur, Patrick is dead, Rathangan is mine. You can come home now."

"Ah, if it were so easy!"

"I have a great forgiveness to ask from you, Arthur."

"No need. I did it freely. And do you know what, I don't regret what I did. I was notorious – the Honourable Arthur Hyde, jewel thief and scoundrel. That has currency out in the worlds. It speaks reams that none of the people I used it on asked to see the jewel, or the fortune I presumably had earned from selling it. Not one. Everything I have done, I have done on with a reputation alone. It's an achievement. No, I won't go home, Ida. Don't ask me to. Don't raise that phantom before me. Fields of green and soft Kildare mornings. I'm valued here. The people are very kind. I'm accepted. I have virtues. I'm not the minor son of Irish gentry with no land and the arse hanging out of his pants. I am the Merciful One, the Prophet of the Blue Pearl."

"Arthur, I want you to have the jewel."

He recoiled as if I had offered him a scorpion.

"I will not have it. I will not touch it. It's an ill-favoured thing. Unlucky. There are no sapphires on this world. You can never touch the Blue Pearl. Take it back to the place it came from."

For a moment I wondered if he was suffering from another one of his hallucinating seizures. His eyes, his voice were firm.

"You should go Ida. Leave me. This is my place now. People have tremendous ideas of family – loyalty and undying love and affection: tremendous expectations and ideals that drive them across worlds to confess and receive forgiveness. Families are whatever works. Thank you for coming. I'm sorry I wasn't what you wanted me to be. I forgive you – though as I said there is nothing to forgive. There. Does that make us a family now? The Duke of Yoo is coming, Ida. Be away from here before that. Go. The town people will help you."

And with a wave of his handkerchief, he turned and closed his door to me.

I WROTE THAT last over a bowl of altiplano mate at the stickmen's caravanserai in Yelta, the last town in the Valley of the Kilns. I recalled every word, clearly and precisely. Then I had an idea; as clear and precise as my recall of that sad, unresolved conversation with Arthur. I turned to my valise of papers, took out my scissors and a sheet of the deepest indigo and carefully, from memory, began to cut. The stickmen watched curiously, then with wonder. The clean precision of the scissors, so fine and intricate; the difficulty and accuracy of the cut absorbed me entirely. Doubts fell from me: why had I come to this world? Why had I ventured alone into this noisome valley? Why had Arthur's casual accepting of what I had done, the act that shaped both his life and mine, so disappointed me? What had I expected from him? Snip went the scissors, fine curls of indigo paper fell from them on to the table. It had always been the scissors I turned to when the ways of men grew too much. It was a simple cut. I had the heart of it right away, no false starts, no new beginnings. Pure and simple. My onlookers hummed in appreciation. Then I folded the cut into my diary, gathered up my valises and went out to the waiting spider-car. The eternal clouds seem lower today, like a storm front rolling in. Evening is coming.

* * *

I WRITE QUICKLY, briefly.

Those are no clouds. Those are the 'rigibles of the Duke of Yoo. The way is shut. Armies are camped across the altiplano. Thousands of soldiers and javrosts. I am trapped here. What am I to do? If I retreat to Glehenta I will meet the same fate as Arthur and the Valley people – if they even allow me to do that. They might think that I was trying to carry a warning. I might be captured as a spy. I do not want to imagine how the Duke of Yoo treats spies. I do not imagine my Terrene identity will protect me. And the sister of the Seer, the Blue Empress. Do I hide in Yelta and hope they will pass me by? But how could I live with myself knowing that I had abandoned Arthur?

There is no way forward, no way back, no way around.

I am an aristocrat. A minor one, but of stock. I understand the rules of class, and breeding. The Duke is vastly more powerful than I, but we are of a class. I can speak with her; gentry to gentry. We can communicate as equals.

I must persuade her to call off the attack.

Impossible! A middle-aged Irish widow, armed only with a pair of scissors. What can she do; kill an army with gum and tissue? The death of a thousand papercuts?

Perhaps I could buy her off. A prize beyond prize: a jewel from the stars, from their goddess itself. Arthur said that sapphires are unknown on this world. A stone beyond compare.

I am writing as fast as I am thinking now.

I must go and face the Duke of Yoo, female to female. I am of Ireland, a citizen of no mean nation. We confront the powerful, we defeat empires. I will go to her and name myself and I shall offer her the Blue Empress. The true Blue Empress. Beyond that, I cannot say. But I must do it, and do it now.

I cannot make the driver of my spider-car take me into the camp of the enemy. I have asked her to leave me and make her own way back to Yelta. I am writing this with a stub of pencil. I am alone on the high altiplano. Above the shield wall the cloud layer is breaking up. Enormous shafts of dazzling light spread across the high plain. Two mounted figures have broken from the line and ride towards me. I am afraid – and yet I am calm. I take the Blue Empress from its box and grasp it tight in my gloved hand. Hard to write now. No more diary. They are here.

* * *

PLATE 13: *V. Gloria medianocte*: The Midnight Glory, or Blue Empress. Card, paper, ink.

LITTLE SISTERS

Vonda N. McIntyre

VONDA N. MCINTYRE (WWW.VONDANMCINTYRE.COM) writes science fiction. Her novel *Dreamsnake* won the Nebula, Hugo, Locus, and Pacific Northwest Booksellers awards. *The Moon and the Sun* won the Nebula. The film version, from Bill Mechanic's Pandemonium Films, stars Pierce Brosnan, Fan Bingbing, and Kaya Scodelario, and was directed by Sean McNamara. It will be released in 2016. "Little Sisters" was published by Book View Café, and is a companion piece to "Little Faces," nominated for the Nebula, and reprinted by BVC, which also digitally publishes McIntyre's backlist.

DAMAGED NEARLY TO extinction by a war it had won, Qad's *Piercing Glory* tumbled through deep space, its engines dead, deceleration impossible. *Glory's* Mayday shrieked, insistent, while Qad, beset by nightmares, slept in his transit pod. *Glory* focused its failing resources on keeping Qad alive.

Decades later, in the nearest shipyard, Executives registered the cry for help. They created an account for this new consumer and dispatched space boats with gravity tractors.

A millennium later, the space boats returned. The ship floated obediently in their tractor nets, its tumbling damped, its momentum slowly, inexpensively reduced from interstellar speeds. The boats minimized energy expenditure and Executive attention, guided by Artificial Normals. The rescue required little intelligence, and had not been marked as emergency or priority. The estimated account expenditure reached neither level. The boats put the disabled ship into a repair bay and signaled for awakening.

Qad woke in the cold and dark, surprised to wake at all. He had expected to freeze in the wilderness of deep space, or burn in the brilliance of starbirth.

He pulled out the transit pod catheters and intravenous supply lines, indifferent to leaks or smells. Cleaning was the job of Artificial Stupids. He ignored their jobs; he barely noticed their existence.

He felt his way to the darkened bridge. *Glory's* viewscreen displayed the unlit interior of the repair bay in real time, showed him the rescue and approach in past time, and offered him the repair agreement. He accepted it. What choice did he have? Light flooded the bay and the bridge.

The Artificial Normal shaved him clean, gave him a fashionably architectural haircut, and painted the faces of the little sisters. It offered him a display of fashionable clothing and guided him to a selection that flattered him and the new haircut. He paid, on credit, the licensing fee for the patterns and waited while *Glory* created them.

He preferred to dress himself, but he had to let the Normal fasten the hundred buttons down the back of the open-fronted coat, and tie the bow of his modesty apron. It laid out his sword belt, scabbard, and blade. He checked the edge and strapped on the weapon. Finally, the Artificial opened his drawer of medals and pinned them on in their proper order. The two he had recently designed remained in their presentation boxes. He hoped and expected the Executives to accept them, to award them, to reward him.

At the access tube, a leader light waited to guide him into the shipyard. He followed it. His boots rang on metal grating. Gravity increased, making the horizontal walkway feel like a steep climb. Qad wondered if standards had changed, or if the *Glory* had miscalculated his sleep therapy. He could hardly meet the Executives with sweat dripping down his face. He paused for a moment to slow his heavy breathing. The leader light stopped with him, then oscillated before him, urging him to continue.

The eldest little sister squeaked with hunger, and the others joined the cry, a demanding quartet. They expected to be fed when he woke, but the invitation of the Executives took precedence. He opened himself to the sisters so they could take sustenance from him. No matter his exhaustion, he must withstand the drain on his resources in order to distract and quiet the little sisters during his meeting.

The leader light lost patience and skittered down the grating. Qad followed, ignoring the pain and fatigue in his thigh muscles.

He reached the executive chamber not a moment too soon. The double doors opened.

Three Executives sat on a dais at the far end of the chamber. Qad strode toward them, stopped a proper five paces before them, and bowed.

"It's time," said the central Executive.

"My report: I took my *Piercing Glory* on a mission to explore and claim new worlds. I found two systems with suitable planets. I cleared them." Qad held out his two medal boxes.

The Chief Executive beckoned him forward. Qad approached and placed the medals on the table. The Executive leaned over his huge belly, concealed by an embroidered lace modesty apron, and reached with spidery, sinewy arms to open the boxes.

Qad was proud of his designs. They displayed the position of the conquered worlds, the level to which he had cleared them, the potential of their remains. The medals would hang prominent on his chest. Impressive, but not too overwhelming.

The Executive inspected each one, reading them easily.

"Adequate," he said. On either side of him, the other Execs murmured agreement.

Qad suppressed a frown. He had expected compliments, not an edge of criticism.

"And the damage to your ship?"

"*Piercing Glory* behaved with great courage in clearing the second planet. It was nearly destroyed. The inhabitants had nearly reached the danger zone, with powerful weapons. They would have achieved interstellar flight soon, and threatened our civilization. My ship has sent the proof to you."

"You cleared the worlds to the third level of evolution."

"We did."

"While the directives limit clearing to second level."

"Those directives are new," Qad said. "Many years behind my expedition."

"Did you consider waiting to receive recent directives?"

"Of course," Qad said. "But the danger was rising. I offered mercy if they destroyed their weapons and submitted to me. They refused. They attacked. *Glory* and I responded."

"We understand your destroying the weapons. We understand your destroying the intelligences. We question destroying the second level of evolution."

"The danger was rising," Qad said again. "Several species stood in the second rank to take over from the intelligences, though they had nearly been exterminated. In thousand time, in million time..." He paused, expecting the Executives to understand and accept.

"In million time," said the Chief Executive, "they might have become fit to succumb to our will, as subordinate populations."

"Or to become enemies," Qad said, forcing himself to keep his tone mild.

"We will confer," the Chief Executive said.

Leaving Qad to stand silent and obedient, his hand clenched around the grip of his sword, the Executives sat still while a privacy shield formed around them. Qad wondered what they would decide, who might speak for him, who might decline his argument.

By the time they reappeared, his feet hurt and his legs trembled with fatigue. He would have to recalibrate *Glory*'s sleep therapy, and perhaps even punish his ship's intelligence for causing him discomfort bordering on embarrassment.

The Chief Executive rose. His legs were as thin and insectoid as his arms. His belly sagged beneath his modesty apron.

"Here is the decision."

One of the other Executives looked pleased, the other annoyed. Qad had hoped for a unanimous decision in his favor. Whatever the decision, unanimous was beyond his reach.

"You are awarded the discovery medal."

An Artificial Normal moved forward and attached the medal in first place above the row of previous medals. The pin scratched Qad's chest. This error could only be deliberate. He slowed his anxious, angry heartbeat, hoping to prevent blood from showing behind the medal's gleam. He kept himself from glaring at the Normal, for the Executive would take it, properly, as a sign of discontent toward authority. A glare at a Normal meant nothing, left the Artificial unaffected, and opened Qad to criticism.

Qad waited for his reward, which was standard for discovering a world suitable for unopposed colonization. They should give him at the very least license for another little sister.

But the Chief Executive continued.

"The second claim is declined."

Qad paled. He locked his knees to keep from falling.

I'll appeal, he thought. Appeal was allowed if the decision failed to be unanimous. Expensive, but allowed.

"Had you eliminated the first level of evolution," the Chief Executive said, "your claim would have been approved. Had you waited for most recent instructions, your claim will have been approved."

In a millennium, or many, Qad thought resentfully. He had made the decision to act rather than wait, and he still believed his decision correct. The intelligence he had destroyed was dangerous – at least the Executives agreed – and the upcoming intelligence held the potential to be even more of a threat, refined and honed by the enmity of its predecessors. He thought them well gone. He also thought the Executives desperately short-sighted, but they would deny any such accusation.

"You are fined the reward of your first discovery," the Chief said.

The Artificial Normal pulled the medal from Qad's shirt, ripping the shipsilk. The blotch of blood spread.

"You are dismissed," said the Chief.

Qad stared at him, amazed, appalled. The leader light appeared at his feet, oscillating from before him to behind him, sensing the tension, anxious for him to follow.

He tried to turn on his heel, as insulted characters did in novels. The unnatural action nearly pitched him to the floor. He caught himself and departed without another word.

As he passed through the doorway, another Artificial Normal hurried after him and handed over an official paper. Supposing it was a report of the meeting, he stuffed it into his pocket.

In the comforting center of *Glory*, Qad dropped his sword belt with a clatter, then pulled off his new coat, popping most of the buttons, and threw it to the floor. He let the Artificial Stupids serve him porridge and wine, usually a comforting combination, though this time rather tasteless. The wine took the edge off the pain in his legs. He ripped the stained shipsilk shirt from beneath his apron. Ignoring the hungry complaints of the little sisters, he flung the shirt to the floor, then flung himself with equal ferocity into his transit pod. He slept.

He awoke baffled and sluggish, expecting the glow of stars beyond the sweeping port, but seeing only darkness. Silence surrounded him.

Was it all a dream? he asked himself. A nightmare? One nightmare to another? Is *Glory* drifting, wounded, in space?

"*Glory?*"

For the first time in his life, *Glory* remained silent in response to his question. Artificials failed to respond to his voice.

A thunderous pounding brought him to his feet in a rush of fear and pain. His legs nearly went out from under him. Space was vast and empty, with only a few tales of ships hit by drifting matter in all the millennia of civilization.

"Qad! Open!"

Having someone demand entry into his ship was even more startling. It was unique to his experience.

He left *Glory*'s center, feeling his way in the darkness. Desperate, he scratched *Glory*'s bulkheads, releasing lines of luminescent ship's fluid on the walls. In the faint light he found his way to the access tube. He slid his hands across the slick bulkhead until he found the entrance. Leaving a scrabble of shining fingerprints, he pulled the sphincter open.

Light poured in from the shipyard.

"About time," said the Chief Executive, pushing his way into *Glory*. Qad backed up, manners taught but seldom used drawing him away from touching the Executive's protruding stomach. Without meaning to, Qad gazed at the moving bulges beneath the Executive's modesty apron, imagining he could see the made-up eyes and orifices of the little sisters beneath it. No – not his imagination. Fashions had changed, and not, in Qad's opinion, for the better. The apron's elaborate embroidery cunningly concealed small holes through which the little sisters could stare, or blink, or offer a kiss.

He lost count at a dozen. There were more.

"I am *here*," the Executive said.

Qad thought he meant he had come into *Glory*, then realized the Executive meant he had noticed that Qad's gaze focused on the partly-concealed little sisters.

Qad raised his head to make eye contact with the Executive. His face blazed with embarrassment.

"Have you made a decision?" The Chief Executive's gaze raked Qad. "Given your improper dress, perhaps not."

Stupefied by lack of sleep, hangover, and pain, set off-balance by being half-clothed and unarmed, Qad blinked. "About an appeal? Not yet."

"Fool. Did you receive my proposal?" He snatched at Qad's trousers. Qad jumped, startled, offended, but the Executive had grabbed the crumpled report rather than Qad's person.

The paper rattled as the Executive shook it in Qad's face. He broke the seal – Is it a rudeness, Qad wondered, to break the seal of another man's letter, if the seal is one's own? I should have looked at it.

Qad took back the paper and read it, lips moving, sounding out the words that in an ordinary communication *Glory*'s voice would have spoken to him.

Before he reached the proposal, the bill from the shipyard astonished him.

"You agreed to it," the Executive said.

"Did I have a choice?" Qad said. "I expected..." He stopped, aghast at what he had nearly said to the Chief Executive.

"To be treated more generously by the council?" The Chief Executive laughed. "Things have changed, young adventurer, since the last time you came proffering a handful of amateur medals."

Qad flushed with anger. "Medals honored. Conquests approved. Rewards conveyed."

"Your lack of judgment wiped out your resources. How do you intend to pay the shipyard bill? It increases every day. With interest."

Glory had been cut off from power, for non-payment, and lay within a berth that kept the ship from drawing on starlight. Lacking power, wounded nearly to death, *Glory* would deteriorate, physically and intellectually, depleting its own resources to maintain Qad and the little sisters. If it survived, the ship would return to its childhood, begging information from other ships, who complied in response to offerings that Qad never questioned or understood. That was ship's business.

Qad might return to his own childhood, absorbing the little sisters that he no longer could maintain.

He glanced again at the paper, forcing his attention past the bill, which he could never pay. Shaky with hunger and exhaustion and disbelief, he reached the end.

"But I planned to create my own lineage," Qad said.

"Who's stopping you? You have three little sisters –"

"Four!" Qad glanced down. Indeed the youngest had already begun to withdraw into his body, stunted by his lack of attention. If he had been alone, he would have slipped his hand beneath the apron to stroke her brow, perhaps even to touch her orifice with his finger to let her suck his blood for sustenance. But with the Chief Executive in his presence, that was impossible. Unthinkable.

At least it was the youngest, not the oldest, his favorite.

"– And you are young. You have plenty of time."

"And you have plenty of little sisters," Qad said. "For your own lineage."

The Chief Executive glowered at him, but stroked his hand across his modesty apron, proudly. "Do you understand the advantages – the honors! – I'm offering you? Your shipyard bill paid, your ship restored, my support if you appeal the council's decision –"

"You –"

Qad stopped. Do I expect him to support me if I refuse his proposal? he thought. Why am I arguing with him? Is he correct, and I'm a fool? His hand mimicked the Chief Executive's, passing over the four bulges, one increasingly faint, beneath his own modesty apron.

"Why?"

"Your audacity appeals to me."

"For an interbreed?"

"Of course! What do you imagine I'm talking about? *Writing* about?"

Qad had met a few interbreeds. He had to admit they had a certain... audacity.

He had dreamed of his own lineage, created by him and his little sisters, spreading out amongst the stars, conquering worlds. And yet everything the Chief Executive had said was true. This was an honor, a compliment.

"Audacity must be tamed, of course," Qad's suitor said. His heavy lids lowered over his pale eyes. "I am up to the challenge."

Qad froze his expression. Is that what the council did to me, with its decision? he wondered. Tamed my audacity? It's true I won't soon again eliminate a second order of evolution, no matter what the danger.

"Your ship has a few more hours of its own resources to draw on," the Executive said. "After that..." A warning, not quite a threat. "I'll come back in time for you to make your decision without too much risk to your... lineage."

He turned. Qad had to scuttle past him to open the sphincter. It clenched behind the Executive, leaving the unreadable scrabbles of Qad's fingers shining on *Glory*'s inner wall.

Following the fast-fading glow of his rush to the access tube, Qad returned to *Glory's* center and crawled into his pod. Ordinarily the bedding would have been resorbed and remade, but now it smelled of his sleep. He stretched out his hand to where he had thrown his shipsilk shirt, and found an amorphous, dissolving mass littered with his medals, and his sword and scabbard. He pulled away.

Qad reviewed the proposal in his mind's eye, wishing for light so he might read the paper a second time. He wished for the Executive to put a deposit on his shipyard bill and allow *Glory* a few minutes' power for light and maintenance, but of course the Executive's interests were better served by leaving him in darkness and silence, his ship dying around him.

Qad would be relieved of debt, *Piercing Glory* repaired and upgraded to current standards. *Glory* would like that, Qad thought. They might even win an appeal, gaining two worlds' worth of acclaim instead of a zero balance.

He would sleep, and then make a decision, but his choice was unavoidable. He could only make it irrevocable.

The little sisters woke him again and again, begging for food. By the time he gave up and rose, he was ravenously hungry. His fingertips were pierced and sore from the little sisters' sucking. The youngest had revived and rebounded. The oldest purred with satisfaction, eyelids heavy.

As desperate as the little sisters, Qad begged *Glory* for food, a bath, a new shirt. The call went unanswered.

Hoping the Artificials had some residual power, he called for one to bring cosmetics. Again, he received no reply. He searched the chambers and corridors until he found an Artificial Stupid with a store of face paint. Scratching *Glory*'s wall desperately to obtain a glimmer of light, he did his best to make up the little sisters. When he painted their orifices, they snapped at him with hungry little teeth. When the youngest bit him a third time, he snapped his fingernail against her face. She screeched and withdrew as far as she could. He snarled at her, not bothering to calm her.

He worked particularly diligently on the eldest, then thought again and smeared away the paint on her eyes. He gripped the youngest's face in one hand and decorated her as formally and elaborately as he could.

She tried to bite him again.

When he had finished, he pulled on his rumpled, stained apron and sword-belt, and went to the access hatch to wait, unshirted and grubby. Even the sword-belt carried stains, none, he regretted, from duels, and the sword's edge remained dull.

Hardly a scene from a romance, he thought. But it was the best he could do with his – and *Glory*'s – resources fast declining.

A scratch at the access hatch. Qad pulled open the sphincter and followed the energetic leader light into the shipyard.

The Executive's quarters surrounded Qad with opulence, everything clean and new, sharp-edged and glittering. The lights blazed. Artificial Stupids surrounded him, herded him to a bathing room, and scrubbed him and the little sisters clean. He cupped his hand over the eldest little sister, to shield her. The Artificial Stupids did not notice.

They shaved him, pomaded his hair, dressed him in silk trousers and open-fronted shirt, and made up three of the little sisters' faces. The eldest remained concealed and unnoticed beneath his hand.

One of the Artificial Stupids handed him an elaborate modesty apron. The Artificials departed so he could arrange it himself, which puzzled him since they had already seen him, and the little sisters, naked.

He was surprised that the apron followed his own, old-fashioned customs, concealing the eyes and orifices of the little sisters.

The Artificials returned and herded him again, to an even more elaborate receiving room. The Chief Executive, dressed in vivid white with silver apron embroidery, sprawled on a black couch, his great stomach bulging into his lap. A bottle of wine stood near, with a single glass half full.

He gestured to Qad, then held up his hand to stop him at the formal five paces distant.

"I want to see what I'm getting for my patronage. I might decline, if I'm displeased."

If that stipulation was in the proposal, Qad had forgotten it. But he could hardly object; it would do him no good.

"Show me," the Executive said.

"May I know your name, first?"

"No. Don't be too audacious in my presence, young adventurer."

He knew Qad's name, from the council meeting, but had never used it. This interbreeding would belong to the Executive's lineage alone.

"Show me," he said again.

Reluctantly, Qad loosed the bow of his modesty apron. He had never revealed himself to another person. He had expected – intended – for the little sisters to reproduce their lineage with him alone, to keep him pure.

Face and neck flushing hot, he pulled the apron aside, leaving its edge to conceal his eldest. Agitated by Qad's reaction, the little sisters writhed and stretched, showing their teeth.

The Executive grabbed the apron and yanked it from Qad's body. The frill of its neckpiece parted with a sharp rip, and the apron fluttered to the floor. Qad's eldest little sister craned outward, fluttering smudged eyelids, snapping sharp teeth.

The Executive looked from one little sister to the next, beginning with the youngest, passing uninterested over the middle two, and fastening on the eldest.

"Names?"

Qad had never named the little sisters. It never occurred to him to do so. They were part of him; why would he name his own parts? This must be another fashion, like the modesty apron eye-slits, that he had never heard of. He turned the situation to his own advantage.

"No," he said. "As you decreed, we aren't exchanging names."

The Executive laughed. "Well played, young adventurer. So. You neglect this one, which I will take and you will not miss."

He nodded at the eldest little sister, whose teeth – smeared with misplaced red paint – snapped in a vertical line, who was most robust, most fit for the taking.

"This one –" Qad did his best to keep his expression neutral, failed, and gestured to the youngest. "This one is younger. Fresher."

The Executive smiled. "One I will leave for you to raise." He looked closer, inspecting the bruise Qad had left when he corrected his youngest. "And train to your will. The eldest has a longer benefit of absorbing your audacity, and perhaps your discipline in curbing it."

Another new-fangled idea, that a little sister would learn from example, would learn from anything. Qad knew better than to argue, for the Executive had made his decision.

He had come close enough to rip off Qad's modesty apron. Now he was even closer, pressing his belly against Qad's stomach. He reached behind himself and loosened his trousers, allowing them to fall away from his skinny thighs, his boots, his skinny ankles and delicate feet. He kicked the silken clothing away, leaving only boots and sword-belt.

Possessed by terror, Qad reached for his own sword. The Executive snarled, grabbed his wrists, and powered him to the floor. The fur of the rug turned steely and wrapped itself around his arms and legs, pinioning him spreadeagled. On his knees, the Executive straddled him, straightened, and wrapped his arms around his own belly to pull it out of the way. His prehensile ovipositor writhed from his body, extending from his crotch.

All four of Qad's little sisters snapped their teeth and craned toward it, but its attention focused on the eldest. It brought its tip to the little sister's orifice and plunged inside.

Qad cried out in apprehension. The force opened him – his little sister – and extended along their tangled nerves. The ovipositor flexed and bulged, propelling the ovum along its length. The bulge reached the little sister's orifice, pushed, failed to press past the teeth.

The little sister bit, severing the tip of the ovipositor. Lubricated by blood, the ovum squirted into the orifice. The Executive screamed and shuddered in agony and triumph.

The ovipositor dragged itself slowly back into the Executive's body to regenerate.

Horrified, Qad felt his own ovipositor clench and writhe below his belly, aching to push out of his body. Groaning, holding himself, he managed to repress it.

The Executive rose. He gazed at Qad.

"You may leave," he said, as if they were back in the council meeting. His docked ovipositor vanished into his body, leaving blood spatter on the Executive's legs, on the rug, on Qad.

The rug's restraints retracted, returning to fur, releasing him. Qad staggered to his feet, clutching his torn and stained modesty apron. Holding it against him, covering himself, he stumbled after the leader light, back to *Glory*, as his little sister moaned and keened and finally fell silent.

He slept.

He had no idea how long he remained insensible in his pod. When he awoke, a faint light permeated *Glory*'s center. His body ached.

"*Glory?*"

"Sleep."

Desperately grateful for the sounds of his ship's voice, he obeyed.

He could barely move. He hurt all over. *Glory*'s bulkheads glowed, more brightly than the last time he came out of his fugue. He pushed aside the material of his pod – clean now but much rougher than normal.

The eldest little sister protruded from his belly, a curve of taut skin, with a faint silver scar where the orifice had been. The other little sisters had retreated into him, leaving their sharp teeth snapping in defense and disappointment. He was ravenous. His arms and legs had shriveled to bone-thin appendages, fat and muscle absorbed to nourish the Executive's growing interbreed. He tried to call for food, for wine. An Artificial Normal approached him – an unfamiliar one, not belonging to *Glory*.

It must be the Executive's, Qad thought, here to watch and keep me.

He asked it for wine.

It extended an appendage and snapped him hard against the forehead. He fainted. After that, he no longer begged for wine. He submitted to the discomfort, even to the pain.

When the Executive pounded on the access hatch, Qad wept with relief. He struggled out of his pod, clasping his hands beneath the enormous bulge of the little sister – no longer a little sister, but the Executive's interbreed. If he let go, it bounced uncomfortably and kicked from inside.

He found the foreign Artificial Normal scratching and probing at the clenched sphincter, insensible to the damage it inflicted. He pushed the Artificial aside and opened *Glory* by hand, as gently as he could. He imagined that his ship whispered appreciation.

The Executive entered, striding on stick-thin legs, cupping his belly in his long arms. Qad imagined that he carried even more little sisters than before. Their eyes sparkled and blinked at him from beneath the modesty apron. The Executive smiled, baring long teeth beneath cadaverous gums.

"It is time?" Qad asked.

"You have plenty of time."

The Executive guided him back to his pod, waited while he settled in, and sat on a chair produced – how? Qad wondered, and realized that the Executive's patronage gave the Executive authority over *Glory*'s resources.

He slept and woke again and again. He lost track of time. A nutrition tube crawled down his throat, assuaging his hunger but leaving the aches untouched, the discomfort of the interbreed increasing. Always when he woke he found the Executive watching him. He tried to speak but the tube gagged him and kept him silent.

Pain roused him.

The bulge of the interbreed clenched, released, clenched again. Its nerves, tangled with his own, fired agony into his belly, his ovipositor, his spine. He screamed against the nutrition tube. It scrambled out of his way, falling from his lips. The Executive stood over him, silently watching.

The scar of the little sister's orifice split open, searing him with a pain more intense than any he had ever experienced. The head of the interbreed protruded through the toothless opening, followed by shoulders, then skinny, spidery arms. As the Executive reached down, the interbreed's sharp teeth snapped. The Executive flicked his fingernail against the interbreed's cheek, bringing a long, wailing cry, which the Executive ignored. He picked up the new being, whose long thin legs and delicate feet slid from the pouch created by the little sister's presence. The neck of the pouch closed and cut it off, spilling fluids into Qad's nest. The pouch shriveled and fell away.

"Let me hold –" Qad cut himself off when he heard his own voice, dry and raspy, begging. The Executive gazed down at him, impassive, one arm cradling the interbreed, the other his belly.

If he lets me hold the interbreed, Qad thought, I'll never let go. I'll have to duel him.

And he will win.

Glory groaned as the Executive's Artificial wrenched open the access sphincter, but a moment later the lights and power returned, along with the soft sounds of *Glory*'s life.

"Sleep," whispered the ship.

Qad obeyed.

In a millennium of time, he woke. *Glory* pulsed around him, full of life and starlight, sensing nearby untouched worlds.

Qad's belly ached where the little sister had lived, where the interbreed had grown. He throbbed with longing for the interbreed, but *Glory* was so far from the ship dock that the Executive must have solidified his new lineage. The interbreed would be entirely his creature. The Executive would give the interbreed a modern ship and send him out to conquer, to colonize, to perform evolutionary eliminations with the audacity the Executive so valued. Qad would never see either of them again.

A spiral of arousal moved beneath the scar of the interbreed's birth. A new little sister, descended from the one he had lost, struggled to grow from its leftover ganglion. The other little sisters craned to see it. Qad snatched up the modesty apron that *Glory* had created anew for him, and flung it over them. Following his custom, it was solid and opaque. The little sisters squeaked and snapped, competing for his attention beneath the heavy shipsilk.

Three only, Qad thought. They are pure. The fourth is... gone, used up, contaminated. I want never to think of the eldest little sister again.

He reached toward it through his nerves, to its leftover ganglion, and extinguished it with a rush of anger. It burned out, leaving him bereft.

Ignoring the other little sisters, for now, he turned his attention to *Glory*, and singled out a new world.

GHOSTS OF HOME

Sam J. Miller

Sam J. Miller (www.samjmiller.com) is a writer and a community organizer. His fiction has appeared in *Lightspeed, Asimov's, Clarkesworld*, and *The Minnesota Review*, among others. He work has been nominated for the Nebula and Theodore Sturgeon Awards, and has won the Shirley Jackson Award. He is a graduate of the Clarion Writer's Workshop and lives in New York City. His debut novel *The Art of Starving* is forthcoming from HarperCollins. His story "Calved" appears elsewhere in this book.

The bank didn't pay for the oranges. They should have – offerings were clearly listed as a reimbursable expense – but the turnaround time and degree of nudging needed when Agnes submitted receipts made the whole process prohibitive. If she bugged Trask too much around the wrong things she might lose the job, and with it the gas card, which was worth a lot more money than the oranges. Sucking up the expense was an investment in staving off unemployment.

Plus, she liked the feeling that since they came out of her pocket, it was she that was stockpiling favor with the spirits, instead of the bank. What did JPMorgan Chase need with the gratitude of a piddling household spirit in one of the hundreds of thousands of falling-down buildings that dotted its asset spreadsheets? All her boss cared about was keeping the spirits happy enough that roofs would not collapse or bloodstains spread on whitewashed walls when it came time to show the place – or a hearth god or brownie cause a slip or tumble that would lead to a lawsuit. The offerings came from her, and with each gift she could feel their gratitude. Interaction with household spirits was strictly forbidden, but she enjoyed knowing they were grateful. As now, entering the tiny red house at 5775 Route 9, just past the Tomahawk Diner. She breathed deep the dry wood-and-mothballs smell. She struck a match, lit the incense stick, made a small slit in the orange peel with her fingernail. Spirits were easy to please. What they wanted was simple. Not like people.

Wind shifted in the attic above her, and she caught the scent of potpourri. A sachet left in a closet upstairs, perhaps, or the scented breath of the spirit of the place. Agnes knew nothing about this one, or any of the foreclosed houses on her route. Who had lived there. Where they went. All she knew was the bank evicted them. A month ago or back in 2008 when the bubble first began to burst. Six months on the job and she still loved to investigate, but her roster of properties was too long to let her spend much time in each. And the longer she stayed, the harder it was to avoid interacting.

When she turned to go, he was standing by the door.

"Hello," he said, a young man, bearded and stocky and bespectacled, his voice disarmingly cheerful. She thought he was a squatter. That's the only reason she spoke back.

"Hi," she said, carefully. Squatters weren't her job. Trask had someone else to handle unlawful inhabitants. Most of the ones she'd met on her rounds were harmless, down on their luck and hiding from the rain. But anybody could get ugly, when they thought their home was threatened. Agnes held up an orange. "I'm just here for the offerings," she said. "I won't report that you're sleeping here. But they do checks, so you should be prepared to move on."

He tilted his head, regarded her like a dog might. "Move... on?"

"Yeah," she said, and bit her tongue to keep from warning him. *The guy Trask uses, he's a lunatic. He'll burn the place down just to punish you.* She knew she should have been sympathetic to all the people overcrowded or underhoused because the banks would rather keep buildings empty than lower the prices. But nobody knew better than Agnes that when you broke the law, you had to be ready for the consequences.

"Oh!" he said, at last. "Oh, you think I'm a human!"

She stared. "You're... not?"

"No, no," he said, and laughed. A resounding, human, manly laugh. It reverberated in her belly. "No... let's just say I *can't* move on. This is my house."

"I'm so sorry." Agnes bowed her head, panic swelling in her stomach at her accidental disobedience. If Trask knew they spoke, she could get fired. "I meant no disrespect."

"I know," he said. Spirits could see that much, or so the stories went. Beyond that it was tough to tell. Some were all-knowing and some were dumb as boxes of rocks. What else did this one know about her?

Agnes had given up long ago trying to figure out why household spirits manifested differently. Sometimes it made sense, like the Shinto-tinged ancestor embodiment in the house where a Japanese family had lived, or the feisty boar-faced domovoi in a rooming house they had seized from a Russian lady. Others resisted explanation – who knew why an ekwu common to the Igbo people kept a vigil in a McMansion six thousand miles from Nigeria that had never been occupied by anyone, of African descent or otherwise... or why a supposedly timeless spirit would manifest as a scruffy hot man with a sleeve of tattoos like a current-day skateboarder? Weird, but no weirder than the average manifestation.

"Thank you for the orange," he said, and crossed the room to take it out of her hand. She could smell him: He smelled like any other man. She could feel his heat. His hair was brown red. His glasses magnified his eyes slightly, making him look a little like a cartoon character.

"You like oranges? It's usually a safe bet. Some houses like some pretty wacky shit, though. I don't kill cats for anybody." She realized she was doing that thing. The thing where she talked too much. Because she wanted somebody – a man – to like her. For an instant she did that other thing, where she immediately hated herself for this, and then realized none of it mattered. This wasn't a man. It could never leave. It knew nothing of the world but what it found between these walls. And she had to go. Now.

He peeled the orange. She half-expected his hand to pass right through it, but that was silly. She knew spirits could affect the physical world in ways far more varied and impressive than any human. Once she watched a building burst into sudden, all-encompassing flames, reducing itself to ash and windblown smoke in four minutes.

"I like oranges," he said. "Also whiskey. Could you bring me some of that, next time?"

"Bourbon, rye, scotch – single-malt, blended..." She recited the names like a list of lovers, men who had done her wrong, men who she still loved and would take back in an instant. She had no intention of bringing him booze. But saying the names made her blood thicken and her mouth dry.

"Bring me your favorite," he said.

"That's maybe not such a good idea," she semi-whispered.

He shrugged. "Whatever you like."

She wondered if she could trust the sadness in his voice. If spirits really were all that different from men. If, at bottom, they wanted something, and once they had it they were through with you.

"Why don't you stay?" he said, his eyes wide and throbbing with loneliness.

"I've got two dozen houses left to visit today," she said. "And then I've got to turn the keys in. Otherwise, the other maintenance workers won't be able to get in."

"After, then. Come back here. You're nice. I can see it."

"I wish I could," she said. "But there's people expecting me."

He nodded, and handed her half the orange.

A door slammed, upstairs, in the long seconds that came next. The spirit's head whipped to the side, his lips curling into a snarl, and for an instant Agnes saw the face of something savage and canine.

"The wind," she said.

"Sorry," he whispered, human again, pale and embarrassed. "I've been very on edge lately. I don't know why."

"I'm Agnes," she said, telling herself she had imagined the momentary monster-face. The next house was 12 Burnt Hills Road, and she hated that one. The spirit manifested as the house itself, floorboards opening like mouths and bricks shifting as she walked through.

"Call me Micah."

He wiped one juice-wet hand on the hem of his flannel shirt, then extended it. They shook. She bowed her head again, and he laughed protestingly. Then she left.

It was a lie, of course. No one was expecting her. No one cared where she was.

* * *

Her mother gave her a stiff-armed hug, her hands slick with tuna fish and mayonnaise.

"Wouldn't have been smoking if I knew you were coming over," she said, stubbing out a Virginia Slim she'd just lit off the stove burner.

"It's fine, really," Agnes said, sitting down at the kitchen table. The tiny trailer never failed to make her feel immense. "Can I help?"

"Boil me some water."

Two days later, and Agnes couldn't stop thinking about the man – the spirit – in the tiny red ranch. Even though her job was keeping spirits happy, she had only cared about them insofar as it might help her keep her job, and maybe one day get a better one.

Her mother tore plastic wrap roughly off the roll. "You never come by without a reason."

Agnes almost said she simply missed her mother, but the woman was too sharp for lies. "I wanted to ask. About our house."

Her mother snorted cruelly. Pear-shaped, crookedly ponytailed, smelling of church-basement bingo, her mother's mind still terrified Agnes. The woman probably knew lots about household spirits and how they worked, from all those endless Sunday services and prayer groups. All Agnes remembered from church was that God was the prime spirit, present in all things and tying it all together, and Jesus was his emanation. Just like Micah was the emanation of 5775. Anyway Agnes should have known they couldn't have a civil conversation. Her mother had spent six months waiting for an apology, and Agnes didn't believe she had anything to apologize for.

"I wanted to ask about the spirit."

"Ganesha."

"It wasn't actually Ganesha, mom. It just took that form."

"Took that name, too."

"Fine. But you never wondered why it took that form, and not another? Considering we're not Hindu?"

"You could have called," her mother said. "If you just wanted to ask me stupid questions."

"I'm sorry to bother you," Agnes said, and stood up. "I actually thought you might be happy to see me."

"You on something?" She looked at Agnes for the first time since she'd arrived.

"No, mom." She looked around, debated asking about the trailer and *its* spirit, but the subject was a sore one.

She wondered if her mother knew. Where she slept at night.

"Better not be," her mother said. "You don't want to lose that job." She stirred a third spoonful of powdered milk into her instant coffee. Her face was hard as winter pavement. "Considering what you had to do to get it."

"THERE *IS* A crisis," Trask said, clicking through pictures on his computer. Graffiti someone spray-painted onto the back of the bank – *bloodsuckers, vampires, profiting from crisis.* "A crisis of accountability! These people did it to themselves. They signed mortgages they didn't understand..."

Agnes discretely texted herself the word *accountability.* She had lost the thread of what he was saying, as often happened during their supervisory meetings. Trask didn't mind when she texted, when they talked. He did it himself, incessantly. *Work is more important than etiquette,* he said.

"How's everything out on Route 9?"

"Same old," she said.

"No signs of dissatisfaction?"

"I heard singing in a couple. That could mean –"

His hand flapped impatiently. "It's in the reports?"

Agnes nodded.

"Good."

Around her, the bank bustled. Trask watched the two television screens mounted on his wall. A new stack of spiral-bound printed reports sat on his desk.

"What're these?" she asked.

"The central bank has a big analysis division, and they've been looking at trends on underoccupied homes. These reports are... actionable."

He was doing that thing, the thing people had done to her all through school. Trying to make her feel stupid. She didn't mind it, coming from him. Trask trusted her.

Once, at a party, someone found out she worked for the bank and started yelling at her about how they had been thrown out when her husband got hurt on the job and couldn't work. Agnes had kept her mouth shut because the girl was a friend of a friend, but she agreed with Trask: *These people did it to themselves.* The world didn't owe you a house. The world is a swamp of shit and suffering and you have to bust your ass to keep your head above water and sometimes you still drown. Sometimes you drown slow. Like Agnes.

"You were late today," he said.

"I know. I didn't remember what day it was until it was almost too late."

"You need to start using a calendar app."

"I know," she said.

"I've showed you how like ten times," he said, swiveling his monitor to show her the calendar in his browser window, synched to his phone.

A map of the county hung below the televisions. Hundreds of pushpins peppered it, showing homes the bank owned. Lines divided the county into five transects, each of which had its own spirit maintenance worker. Hers was Transect 4, the westernmost one, the space least densely settled, the one that required the most driving. She scanned the map idly, avoiding even looking at Transect 1, and the pin that stabbed through the heart of the house where she grew up. The house her mother lost. The house that got her this job.

Agnes picked up a crude jade frog from his desk, weighed it in her hand, felt the tiny spirit inside. Could it see her? Know her heart? Every object had a spirit, and while stories said that long ago the trees talked and mountains moved to hurt or help humans, only homes still spoke. For the thousandth time, she thought of Micah.

His snarl, his momentary monstrousness, did not make him less appealing. It made him more so. Being with so many bad men had hardwired fear into desire.

"Lunch meeting," Trask said, rising. "File the hard copies?"

Alone in his office, she wrenched open the bottom drawer of his filing cabinet. She flipped through folders, added incident reports and travel logs. Rooting around in the filing cabinet made her feel frightened, like a trespasser. Every time, she had to fight the urge to browse through things that had nothing to do with her. To learn more. To understand. Trask would not tolerate that kind of intrusion. One more way she could lose her job.

But then – *there*. 5775 Route 9. The house where Micah lived. Was *lived* even the right word? Micah's house. But that wasn't right either. The house didn't belong to him. It *was* him.

Cheeks burning, she pulled the folder from the cabinet. Deeds, contracts, mortgages, spreadsheets – all the secrets and stories of the house, encoded in impenetrable hieroglyphics. Resolve settled in her stomach, bitter and hard. Like when, ages ago, in another life, another Agnes had decided for the thousandth time to return to whatever bar or trailer park would best get her whatever illegal substance her body was enslaved to then.

She looked around, wondered if anyone else could see the guilt on her face. Trask's computer screen was still on, logged in to the property management system. Because he trusted her.

Did banks have household spirits? Places where no human had ever lived? Lots of people spent more time at work than at home, but work was different. What difference would that difference make? Once, she'd slept in a hotel. Its spirit had been flimsy, insubstantial, shifting shapes in an abrupt and revolting fashion. Even her car had a spirit. It never spoke or showed itself, but sometimes its weird jagged dreams rubbed up against her own while she slept.

Agnes shut her eyes and listened. Felt. Called out to the dark of the echoey old space around her.

And something answered. Something impossibly big and distant, like a whale passing far beneath a lone swimmer. Something dark and sharp and cruel and cold. She opened her eyes with a gasp and saw she was shivering.

Smiling and confident on the outside, screaming on the inside from joy and terror, seeing in her mind's eye exactly how this course of action might cost her everything, Agnes took the folder to Trask's Xerox machine and began to make herself copies.

HE WAS WAITING for her on the porch of 5775. He hugged his knees to his chest like some people held on to hope. When he saw her, his face split into a smile so glorious her own face followed suit.

"Hi," he said, rising, T-shirted, eyes all golden fire from the last of the evening sun.

"Hello," she said, and held up a bag full of fast food. "Hungry?"

He clapped his hands, his face all joy. "You're here early," he said. "You usually only come through here every couple of weeks."

"You've been watching me for a while now," she said, handing him the bag.

"I don't know. Something wouldn't let me stay silent." He opened the bag, stuck his face in, breathed deep. Happiness made him laugh. Agnes wondered when she had last heard someone laugh from happiness.

She had made the mistake of visiting 12 Burnt Hills Road right before. It had spoken to her, its voice like bricks dragged across marble. It said *I want to show you something*, over and over. She did not let it.

The file on 5775 had told her nothing. The house was fifty years old, had been owned by a perfectly banal couple who left it to their son and his wife, who sold it to a woman who couldn't keep up with her mortgage when she got laid off when the school districts consolidated, and had been evicted four years prior. No Micahs anywhere.

He ran down the hall, and came back with a bed sheet. This he spread on the living room floor, and sat on. "Instant picnic!" Micah said, his enthusiasm so expansive she barely felt the pain in her knees when she squatted beside him. Sleeping in the fetal position night after night was beginning to take a toll.

While he took the food from the bag and began to set it up, she watched his arms. Pixelated characters from the video games of her youth adorned his arms, along with more conventional tattoo fodder – a castle; a lighthouse. "How long have you looked like this?" she asked.

"I don't know." He ate a French fry, then four. "Forever? A couple months?"

"The band on your T-shirt didn't exist when this house was built," she said. "Or do you have a whole ghost wardrobe upstairs somewhere?"

He shrugged. "No. I don't know why they're the clothes they are."

"Did you ever look like something else?"

He laughed. *Micah* laughed. "Sometimes I think so. Did you?"

"Not that I know of. So there's not a household spirit Book of Rules?"

"Not that I know of."

They ate burgers, drank sodas. She had so many questions, but what happened inside her chest while she watched him eat answered the only real one. He bit off giant greedy childish bites, and barely chewed.

It made sense that after being empty for a long time, a household spirit might become something different. And lose track of everything it had been before. She asked, "Do you remember the people who used to live here?"

He nodded, eyes on her, lips on his soda straw. "Well. Sort of. I feel them. I can't really remember them, but they're there. Like..." *Like a dream you've woken up from,* she thought, but didn't say out loud.

"I'm not supposed to interact with you," she said. "I could lose my job."

"What's your job?" he asked, all earnestness.

"I make offerings at houses where nobody lives."

He nodded. The last drops of soda slurped noisily up his straw. "They must pay you well for that."

"They don't."

"But what you do is so important!"

"I'm an independent contractor – basically a janitor," she said, and thought back to the old maintenance man at her high school, muttering prayers and burning incense beneath a defaced wall once he'd washed away the graffiti. "My mother says we're all doomed," Agnes continued. "She says these empty houses are going to add up to a whole lot of angry spirits. She says all the oranges and incense in the world won't make a difference. When people move back in, the spirits will have turned feral."

Micah wiped grease from his lips with his sleeve. "There's a lot of empty houses?"

Agnes nodded. Obviously Micah didn't watch the news or read the papers. She had been imagining that he knew all sorts of things, through spirit osmosis or who-knows-how. "Chase owns hundreds, in this county alone. Bank of America –"

"That's sad," he whispered. His face actually reddened. He was like her. He felt his emotions so hard he couldn't hide them. The air in the room thickened, grew taut. The hairs of her arms stood on end. His didn't. *At any moment he could start flinging lightning bolts,* she thought, *or burn us both to ash.* She put her hand on his arm, and the crackling invisible fury ebbed away.

"What's it like? When there's no one here?" She was thinking of him, but also thinking of Ganesha. Alone in her old house. The rambunctious thing that had been her only friend for so long, who played strange complex storytelling games with her and gave her spirit candy when she made a wise decision. She could taste the anise of it, still, feel it stuck between her teeth like taffy, although even if she ate it all day it would never give her cavities or make her fat. She had spent years trying not to think of Ganesha.

"It's horrible," Micah answered.

Agnes scooted closer. He wasn't human. He could kill her just by thinking it. He was a monster, and she adored him. She took his face in both hands, moved them down so the roughness of his stubble felt smooth, and kissed him.

"I need to go," she said, hours later, when she woke with her head on his bare strong chest and her body gloriously sore from the weight of him.

"No you don't," Micah said, his hand warm and strong on her leg. Somehow, he knew. That she had no home, that she slept in her car. He sat up. His eyes were wet and panicky. He kissed her shoulder. "Please don't go," he said. "Why do you want to leave?"

Because Trask sends late-night goons to check for squatters sometimes.

Because I might lose my job if I stay.

Because this is not my home – I didn't earn it, didn't pay for it, can't afford it.

Because I don't deserve a home.

Because love makes me do dumb things.

"You're like me," Micah whispered, and his whispers vibrated in her ears even once she was back in the Walmart parking lot in the cramped backseat of her car under a blanket: "You're on your own. We're what each other needs."

TRASK SAID ROUTINE was the key to success, which is why every morning Agnes woke and went to Dunkin' Donuts for coffee and an unbuttered bagel and a rest room wash-up and tooth-brushing. Which is what she did the morning after making love to Micah. This time, though, when she emerged from the rest room and a woman was waiting for it, she didn't think to herself: *Oh no, what if she guesses what I was doing in there and immediately knows I'm homeless and pathetic,* but rather: *What if she's doing the same thing as me – for the same reason as me?*

Which is maybe why, this time, she broke the routine slightly and instead of heading straight to the bank for her day's assignments Agnes drove east into Transect 1, feeling her chest tighten, struggling to breathe deeply against the weight that could not possibly be guilt, because she had done nothing to feel guilty about, because she had done the right thing –Trask said so –

And found the deep raw crater, lined in red clay like a wound in the belly of the universe, where the house she grew up in used to be.

"AGNES?" TRASK SAID, looking confused. "Everything okay?"

"Hi," she said, stopping herself from apologizing for disturbing him. An unscheduled visit was an unprecedented breach of propriety. They texted, or they talked in supervisory meetings. She had never just *shown up* before. "What's happening to the houses in Transect 1?"

"We're demolishing them, Agnes." His voice now was like when teachers wanted to shame her into silence.

"Why?"

"I told you. Actionable recommendations from the central analysis division. Even with emanation placation measures in place, we've been noticing some disturbing patterns."

My mother was right, she thought. *They've gone feral.* His computer made soft pinging noises as the day's pitches arrived. Every bank routinely made offers for every other bank's underoccuppied property, usually for ridiculously low amounts, knowing they'd be rejected. Fishing for hunger. Trying to 'assemble development portfolios' and other concepts she had not initially understood.

"But people could be living there," she told Trask, knowing, as soon as she said it, that the argument had no financial weight and was therefore worthless.

"WHAT DO YOU mean, you can't step onto the lawn?"

"I just can't," Micah said, grinning, face glistening with French fry grease and her kisses. He leaned over the porch railing; reached out his arm to her.

"But it's part of the property," she said, stepping just out of his reach.

Micah shrugged. "*Property* is a legal fiction," he said. "Words on paper don't change anything. A house is a house."

"A legal fiction," she said, and texted the phrase to herself. "I thought you didn't know The Rules."

"Some things I just know," he said. "I don't know why I look like this, but

I know what I can't do. And I know that when you're here, it feels right."

"But this is crazy, isn't it? You and me. A spirit and a person? I've never heard of that."

"Me either," he said. "So?"

"We can't... be together."

"We're together now."

"This isn't my house."

"Why not?" His eyes were wide, sincere, incredulous. She wanted to eat them. She wanted to have them inside her forever.

"Because it costs money to buy a house. I don't have money."

Micah nodded, but she knew he did not understand.

Back in the car, she stared at the wooden block studded with keys. Her roster for the day: three dozen homes, defenseless.

Agnes had made mistakes before. She'd shattered friendships. She'd had a drink when she knew the whole long list of horrible things that would come next. One thing was always true, though: She knew they were mistakes before she made them. She decided to make a mistake and that's what she did. The hard part was figuring out the right mistake to make.

"Twice in two weeks," her mother said, stubbing out her Virginia Slim. "You hard up for a place to take a shower?"

"Happy to see you, too, Mom."

Her mom sat back in her chair and sighed, a long aching sound. Her eyes did not seem able to open all the way. Walmart had demoted her from the cash register to the shoe section. They talked in terse, fraught sentences until the water boiled and the instant coffee was prepared.

"I'm sorry, Mom."

"Sorry for what?" her mother muttered.

"Sorry for what I did. To you."

Her mother's mug clinked against the counter. Now her eyes were wide. "What did you do?"

"You know what I did. We both do. You even said so, the last time I was here."

"Tell me."

Agnes nodded. She owed her mother this much – to spell it out, to look her in the eyes. "I told the bank you were still living there, in the house, after you'd stopped paying the mortgage. After you'd been evicted. I got you kicked out."

Her mother's eyes were harsh, unblinking. Agnes took a sip: The coffee was so strong it hurt to swallow. "Do you know? What they did to it?"

Her mother nodded. "I drive by there, sometimes."

"I didn't think I did anything wrong," Agnes said. Her voice felt so small. "I thought you were in the wrong, to keep on living there when you couldn't pay."

"What changed?"

Agnes shrugged, opened her mouth, shut it again.

Her mother took her mug, added hot water, handed it back. "Last time you were here, you asked why the spirit took on the shape of Ganesha. I said I didn't know, and I don't. But I have a theory. When I was a little girl, our next-door neighbors were Indian. They had a Ganesha statue on their porch. They had a girl my age, we used to play together. She always made me rub the statue's stomach for good luck. I think when a house finds its perfect owner, it takes on the shape that owner needs to see."

Agnes sipped. Diluted to human strength, the coffee wasn't bad.

12 Burnt Hills Road again. She lingered, left an extra orange. The house frightened her, but sometimes being frightened wasn't bad. Sometimes fear brought you where you needed to be.

Agnes, it said, when she turned to go. This time the squeal of glass and wood, grinding together: All four windows in the front room trembled together, spoke as one.

"You know my name?"

We all know your name.

"We?"

The empty ones. I want to show you something. Will you let me show you?

"Yes."

Press your hands to the brick, the voice said, and she did. *Shut your eyes,* it said, and she did.

Laughter. A little girl ran into a swathe of sunlight. Herself, age five.

"No," she whispered.

Watch.

Agnes at ten, Agnes at twelve. The house. Her house. Each room, each smell. Christmas cooking and make-up and wet paint. Her mother's smile growing slimmer and the rest of her less so as time sped by. Ganesha, scrambling from room to room with one long undiminishing mischievous giggle.

Joy, then. Ganesha's joy. The bliss of wholeness. The ecstasy of love, of family. Home meant love, meant wholeness. Shrinking, suddenly, when Agnes stormed out at age sixteen. After that a bereft, endless wondering. *Where did she go? Why was she so upset? How have I failed her?*

Her mother standing alone at the top of the stairs. Cigarettes. Burned TV dinners.

"Please," Agnes said, too loudly, knowing what was next.

The house, empty. Ganesha stumbling. Shrinking. And then weeping, as pain began to break him apart. Hands growing twisted, pudgy child-fingers becoming cat-sharp claws. Pieces of trunk sloughing off. The transect maintenance worker brought oranges, but they did not stop what was happening to her friend. They merely channeled off his anger, his rage, his ability to lash out. When the wrecking ball came it was almost a relief. Ganesha went gladly, already mostly gone. Something bigger was there, though. A bigger, deeper something that was Ganesha but wasn't. It shrieked. She wept, hearing it wail.

The windows went still.

"I thought you were all... on your own. Separate. Micah didn't know what was happening to any of the other houses."

A rippling shifted through the walls, and when the voice came again it came from a crude and jagged mouth that opened in the bricks above the fireplace. *Autochthonous sentient structural emanations are complex. The spirit that takes on physical form, the thing that humans interact with, is only one piece. There is another piece. One that grows out of the earth the house is built on. One that springs from a common source with all the other autochthonous emanations in the area. These pieces are rarely aware of each other. Until they need to be. Do you understand?*

"Sure," and Agnes was startled to see that she did. She thought of how her mother understood God. She thought of the thing she had sensed, for an instant, in the bank. Something bigger and colder and crueler and more terrifying than a human mind could ever comprehend.

We saw you, Agnes. We saw what was inside of you. We knew that you were the one who could help us.

TRASK WAS STRESSED out about something. His forehead had extra lines in it; his eyebrows were arrows aiming at each other. He was immersed in his phone. When she logged the block of house keys back in, he left the key in the cabinet lock. Like he always did.

"Are you going to demolish all of them?"

He looked up from his phone, his face contorted briefly. By what? Hate, she thought at first, but that wasn't right, whatever it was had no such intensity. Apathy, maybe, but that was only half the story. Trask took two reports from the top of the stack and flung them at her. "Read it yourself if you're so nosy."

He doesn't care about you, she realized. *He never has.*

He thinks you're stupid.

Agnes filled paperwork with scribbles until Trask left the office to take a call, and then she opened the cabinet and pocketed the key to Micah's house. She dumped the rest of the keys from Transect 4 into her backpack, and put the block back in the cabinet, and locked it.

After thirty awful seconds, Agnes unlocked the cabinet again and took the keys to the rest of the Transects.

Trask's screen was still on. She stared at it. Her plan was a terrible one. She could destroy the keys, but how much time would that buy them? Trask would learn what had happened soon enough, and he didn't need a key to knock a building down. She'd be out of a job and those spirits would still get destroyed.

Agnes sat down at his desk. He didn't leave her alone with so much power at her fingertips because he trusted her. He did it because he didn't think she was smart enough to do anything about it. He gave her the job not because he liked her or saw potential, but because she showed him how desperate she was. How hungry. Hungry enough to betray her own mother for a shit job with no health insurance.

She clicked over to the window where the day's offers had piled up. One by one she clicked yes, selling off a couple dozen buildings with Trask's credentials. And then she made a series of offers on the Bank of America properties scattered throughout the county, offering ten million dollars for each of them when most were barely worth ten thousand.

Then she opened his calendar and typed in an appointment for him, tomorrow at twilight, at 12 Burnt Hills Road, with the plumbing maintenance foreman.

Trask might wonder what that was, how it had gotten there; he might even call the plumber to confirm. But most likely he would not. He was a man who trusted his calendar.

Would it kill him? she wondered. The thought of being a party to Trask's murder did not disturb her as much as it should have. What she'd mistaken for officious mentorship had been contempt, combined with a love of feeling smarter than someone. More importantly, she'd do anything to keep Micah from going through what her home had gone through.

Chase would dispute the sales she had approved as Trask, and the offers he'd made, but Bank of America would take them to court to get them to honor these entirely legal contracts.

Later she buried the backpack full of keys in the red raw clay where her house had been.

"THAT'S THE LAST of it?" Micah asked, when she set the milk crate down on the porch.

"Such as it is."

"You were living *there?*" he asked, wrinkling his nose in the direction of her car.

"Who really *lives,* anyway," she asked, squatting to kiss his mouth. He handed her a glass of iced tea.

She took a sip, then drained the glass. "This is seriously the best iced tea I have ever had in my life."

"I know," he said. "And it has the added benefit of not having any calories."

He put his arm around her. Night was coming and so was November. His heat was so strong and clear she didn't believe it wasn't real.

That morning, she had visited 12 Burnt Hills Road. Trask had been missing for two days. She expected blood and carnage, but the inside of the house was as it had always been. Wind wailed, weakly, somewhere.

The police came, said the stones above the mantle.

"They would have seen the address in his calendar," she said. "I'm sorry, but there was no way for me to erase it after he saw it..."

He is well hidden. As is his vehicle. They found nothing, and departed. Touch the stones, if you want to see.

She didn't, but she did. And saw him get out of his fancy truck, call out for the plumber, pat his pockets for the keys he knew he had not brought because the plumbers had their own set. Saw the front door creak open. Saw Trask step inside. Saw stones and wood and brick crawl together. Saw windows shatter into long cruel talons at the end of stumpy fingers. Saw the seat of Trask's trousers darken.

"This is temporary," she said, thinking of the cold cruel immense entity she had glimpsed at work. With Trask missing and the police involved, the court battle would drag on for a while. But not forever. "Eventually, the bank will move forward with a way to do what it wants."

Yes, the house said. *And so will we.*

She didn't ask *What about Micah? His shape, his personality – is he part of you? Did you use him to manipulate me?* As long as she didn't know the answer, she could pretend it didn't matter.

Micah startled her back to the here-and-now, carrying a radio on an extension cord. They danced to the Rolling Stones on the porch of the house that was hers, but not. Later, they lay in a bed so big she could not believe her stupidity – to think that this had been here all along, empty and waiting, while she slept in a car in the Walmart parking lot. Because of Trask, inside her head, and the bank and the school and everyone else in this world who said you only deserved what you could pay for. When she wept, he woke up. They spooned together.

Agnes fought sleep, not wanting to be anywhere else. She counted questions instead of sheep.

When we fight, will he accidentally incinerate me? When he is angry or sad, will blood drip from ceilings and swarms of hornets spell out hateful words on the wall?

She wondered if she would still have her job, without Trask. Probably she would. For now. Both banks would want to maintain the properties while they fought over them in court. She could fix the place up, get real human food, buy Micah the punk rock records he liked. She could lay low, but eventually there would be a confrontation. Ownership would be settled. Someone would come, looking to knock it down or clear it out. But wasn't that part of what it meant, to have a home? The knowing that it could always be taken away from you? That's what she never grasped, those long nights in her old house aching to be anywhere else. She had taken 'home' for granted, something unbreakable and allotted to each of us, because that's the way the world should be. And once it was gone she believed everyone deserved the same pain she and her mother went through. Ganesha was dead because of the lies she believed, and her mother's heart was broken.

But now that she knew something could be taken away, she also knew she could fight for it.

"I love you," she whispered, to him, to her home, and fell asleep marveling at how easy both things were to claim once you let yourself.

THE KAREN JOY FOWLER BOOK CLUB

Nike Sulway

NIKE SULWAY LIVES and works in regional Queensland. She is the author of *The Bone Flute, The True Green of Hope, What The Sky Knows* and *Rupetta.* In 2014, *Rupetta* became the first work by an Australian author to win the James Tiptree, Jr Award. The award, founded in 1991 by Pat Murphy and Karen Joy Fowler, is an annual literary prize for a work of science fiction or fantasy that expands or explores our understanding of gender. She is quite fond of rhinoceri.

Two bright bangles on an arm clang,
a single bangle is silent, wander alone like a rhinoceros.
– Khargaviṣana-sutra [the Rhinoceros Sutra] c.29 BCE

TEN YEARS AGO, Clara had attended a creative writing workshop run by Karen Joy Fowler, and what Karen Joy told her was: *We are living in a science fictional world.* During the workshop, Karen Joy also kept saying, *I am going to talk about endings, but not yet.* But Karen Joy never did get around to talking about endings, and Clara left the workshop still feeling as if she was suspended within it, waiting for the second shoe to drop.

Eventually, Clara attempted a cold equations story, and though Karen Joy never read it, Clara thought she might have liked it if she'd had the chance. In Clara's story, "False Equations", the Emergency Dispatch Ship (EDS) was packed full of animals, rather than people, and the stowaway was the child of a white-backed vulture pair. An egg when she was smuggled aboard, the stowaway hatched during the journey to Walden (rather than Woden).

Clara had made several copies of the story and sent them out to the other members of her book club. Fern wrote back to say that the story was too complex and far-fetched. Bea wrote that she hadn't time to read anything just then except the book that they were *supposed* to be reading for their next meeting. And Belle said simply that there were far too many "Cold Equations" reworkings and inter-textual responses out there, and she didn't see why Clara had bothered attempting another if she had so little to say about the matter.

Clara, like Fern and all of the other members of the Karen Joy Fowler Book Club, had never managed to finish reading the set book before their scheduled get-together. But then, none of their planned book discussions had yet taken place. There was always some complication, some hindrance that they were incapable of overcoming.

The workshop had not been a total loss, however, since Clara had met Belle there, and they had ended up good friends. They lived near each other – their farms were only a short walk apart – and a few years ago they had opened up a café in town where they served good, simple food and provided their customers with a shaded garden in which to sit and chat.

These days, when Clara can, she takes time off from the café to go and visit her daughter. Alice lives near the great lakes. She has a large house; tall, and stone-walled, with large windows to catch the afternoon breezes. As Clara comes down the shared driveway to Alice's house, she always experiences a moment of something like regret, or fear. What if, once she enters her daughter's house, she isn't able to leave again? What if, once she sees all the children her daughter cares for, she can't stop herself from saying something cruel? Telling her daughter what she believes: that Alice's house full of other people's children is just a way for her daughter to endlessly delay her own grieving, her own letting go of things. Or what if the opposite occurs: what if she enters that house full of children, sees all the work that needs to be done caring for them, and is caught up in her daughter's Sisyphean task of feeding, bathing, and holding other creatures' young. Like Sisyphus forever pushing his stone up the same mountain, only to watch it roll down again.

Clara isn't sure she is a welcome visitor any more, or whether she wants to go there. She doesn't think about these things directly, but as she comes up the walk she tries to imagine herself greeting and being greeted by her daughter and struggles to construct an image that contains ease or warmth.

As it happens, she finds Alice in the garden with her new lover. They are walking from tree to tree, looking up into the canopy of each one and then moving on.

This is not Alice's first lover, Jeff, who is dead now, and Clara has difficulty remembering this one's name. Blue? Balloon?

They go to wallow in the mudhole that spreads out from beneath the African tulip tree. The one Jeff had liked to wallow in with guests. They had been cooling off there together – Alice and Jeff – when they had told Clara there would be no grandchildren. "It's my fault, I'm afraid," he'd said, as if he'd forgotten to pick up ice on the way home, but blushingly. "They're no good, my swimmers. My –"

"She knows what you mean," Alice had said. "There's no need to go on and on."

Clara had remembered, then, the termination Alice had when she was in high school. The waiting room full of pictures of empty landscapes at sunset, the interview with the cheerful nurse, the other young females in the waiting room – all of them avoiding each other's eyes. And afterwards, her daughter wanting ice cream and to sit by the river and watch the waterbirds dancing in the shallow water. Alice had rested her head on Clara's shoulder, curled her feet up under her bottom like a child. Her breath had smelled of milk and sweet biscuits, and her hair of antiseptic. It was the last time Clara can remember her daughter wanting to be held.

The garden has changed more than Clara's daughter has, since Jeff's passing. The paths that were once just worn earth have been widened and cleared of weeds. The beds of unnamed flowers that Alice and her husband used to grow have been replaced with vegetable patches and rows of imported exotics. Mulched and weeded and trimmed and fertilised to within an inch of their lives.

"You should keep going," Alice says to her lover.

"Oh," he says. "Oh yes, of course! Women's talk." He winks at Clara as he moves away. "Don't do anything I wouldn't do."

When he has gone, Alice sighs and settles into a more comfortable position. "The sad thing is, he means it," she says. "He won't tolerate me doing anything without consulting him. He calls it *communication*, when what he really means is him telling me what to do." She flicks her ears a little to clear away the flies. "It almost makes me glad we're too different to breed. Imagine us: the parents of the last generation!"

Clara squints into the sun and watches her daughter's lover still moving from tree to tree, looking up, thinking, then moving on. She is tired of being a visitor already, but Alice asks her all the questions a daughter asks anyway. No, Clara hasn't heard from her husband of late. Yes, the café is going well. They've started a new tradition of monthly dinners. Seasonal dishes, all made with local produce. No, nobody *special.*

Alice looks across the mudhole to the forest. "I've lost track of Dad," she says. "Wasn't he out west somewhere, living on a wildlife refuge of some kind?"

"I'd heard that," Clara said. "Him and that female were working the summers and mostly left alone in the winters. Wandering the hills."

"Janet," says her daughter.

"What?"

"Dad's new partner, her name is Janet."

She ought not to have come, Clara thinks. Everything her daughter says or asks of her feels like a reproach. Even the gardens are reproachful, the liquidambars arching over the green lawn. The perfect garden beds, the even paths, the vistas like postcards. It was just what she'd dreaded, coming down the driveway, just what she'd been preparing herself for.

Alice wants to show her around the bottom end of the garden, which she says is where Jeff spent most of his time during the last few months of his life. Sometimes, he would fall asleep on the lawn, stretched out like a child and snoring so loudly that the small birds – the fairywrens and tits – would scatter with fear.

"When I woke him up he would always say he hadn't been sleeping at all," Alice says. "He'd say he'd been writing. He'd tell me all about whatever it was he had been working on. By the end, the things he told me were just a jumble. A nonsense. But at first I believed him. Or... or I wanted to. He was working on a Cold Equations story, he said. But it was set here on earth, and instead of people, the two characters were rhinos, like us. The two last rhinos on earth. And as soon as one died, the other would become functionally extinct."

Alice was smiling, as though even now she could hear Jeff working out the shape of his story in her head. "That must be how he thought of us," she said. "After all those years of being together, of sharing our lives and building this house and this garden. That there was no point to us being together, or having children. That we were just the leftover scraps of something that had once been whole."

JEFF HAD DIED five years ago, just before the end of the summer, but Clara had not heard about it until six months after that. She got the news in a letter from Janet, her former husband's new partner, one of the founding members of the Karen Joy Fowler Book Club. They had once met, purely by accident, near a temporary market in Pullington. Janet had been walking away from a dungpile that Clara was going towards and somehow they had gotten to talking. It wasn't till much later that they had realised they shared a man. In a manner of speaking.

Of course, I know that you knew Jeff far more intimately than I ever did, Janet wrote. *But I've been surprised by how often I've thought about him. His passing makes me think about all of us, how we were, fifty years or so ago, when we didn't know that it was all going to come to such an ending. We were full of ideas for growing the future – remember that plan Hildy had for forming a partnership with the San Diego Zoo? – and the males were all so ready to charge out into the world and lay down babies wherever they could.*

Of course, Jeff wasn't like that. Not even slightly. He never wanted anyone but his one dear wife; he wasn't like his father, or any of that generation that were ours to love. Jeff seemed the most vulnerable of us all, even when he was young. I remember I could hardly bear to look at the dark spaces between his skin folds.

Did Janet really think that's how it had been, for all of them? That, like her, they'd spent their youth getting babies on and from whoever they could? Clara's memory of those days was that she and her husband had expected to stay together for their whole lives, babies or no babies. Until one of them died and was left to rot in some godforsaken grove of spindle trees. Without a future generation to be mindful of, there was no reason for him to move on after twenty days. He could stay; they could form a pair-bond that would last through as many breeding seasons as they survived.

Clara and Janet had never been close – they had their reasons not to be – but Janet had known where to reach her when Jeff died, and she had kept in touch with Jeff, or with Clara's daughter. She had known about Jeff's death, and written to Clara with those strange, true words. Without Janet, Clara might never have known that her daughter's husband had died. She might still have been keeping her distance, thinking that one day soon she would hear from him, and from her daughter.

THE FIRST TIME she went to Belle's place it had been to drop off some salad greens she had picked up from a roadside stall on the way home. Belle's crash was more or less what Clara had expected. Abundant and shabby, her teenage daughters sprawled across the savannah, leaving a trail of unconsciously messy beauty in their wake. Belle didn't come to greet her, just hallooed her in, and when Clara came through she found the kitchen, unlike the one in the café, a lively and fragrant jungle of ingredients. Belle herself was the least colourful thing. She had taken off the two clanging bangles she wore around her ankles at work and stood in the kitchen barefoot, her skin rough and grey.

Belle's husband, Robert, poured drinks for all of them. Clara put the greens in a clear space and somehow was invited to stay for dinner. The food Belle served was not as fancy as that she served in the café, and the dinner service was a mismatched collection of hand-thrown pottery pieces. The kind you pick up cheap at garage sales and second-hand stores. Robert kept their glasses full and talked about the fields of grapes he had seen growing on a property out the other side of the reserve. He also told stories about the Scandinavian furniture he had bought cheaply on eBay, especially about a queer couple of Silverbacks from whom he had wrangled a pair of original Thonet chairs. The way he talked about the exchange made it seem scandalous, as though they had propositioned him in some way. Later, when he made coffee, he talked about a workshop he had gone to on 'cupping' and tried to teach Clara and Belle how to smell the grounds, insisting that they all drink their coffee sugarless and milk-free in order to better appreciate the flavours of the coffee.

During a pause in the conversation, Clara asked Belle if she had thought any more about whether she wanted to join the Karen Joy Fowler Book Club. Robert leant back away from the conversation, raising an eyebrow at his daughters as if he had been interrupted mid-anecdote, and then listened to his wife talk about the book they were planning to read with studied, careful attention.

After dinner, the pale-skinned daughters dragged their father off to help them with something and Belle and Clara were left alone in the mudhole. The solar fairy lights were starting to dim, but the citronella candles threw off more than enough light. Belle stretched herself out, her feet in the cool spot where Robert had been sitting.

"I should go," Clara said, and Belle turned and reached out as if to stop her.

"Don't go," Belle said. "Nobody else gets a word in once Rob gets going."

Clara saw how it was. How Belle was in no hurry to be left alone with Robert after their evening of high talk and laughter. How he was the kind of male who was roused by such things into something like rage. Belle was weary, and filled with the kind of dread that comes when a party is over and you see, all at once, all the damage you must now repair.

Clara and Belle were both of that generation who were unlikely to have grandchildren, though they had both had husbands and children of their own. They were the mothers of daughters they did not understand, and whose troubles they could barely recognise. They went in and out of each other's houses on a daily basis. They would graze in the savannah, or stand side by side in the kitchen making bread and listening to Belle's daughters talk about their lives. The jokes about being the last of their kind. The bullying and despair. The gossip and conspiracies. A female in another herd had had a child, but it had died after one year. Another had given birth to three at once, stillborn and pale as cake. Clara and Belle looked at each other and twitched their ears in silent amazement. Who were these females? What lives were they living?

"Where did you hear that?" Belle said. "Facebook? It sounds like a hoax. Fear-mongering."

The girls said it didn't matter if one particular story was true or not, the point was not that one female had bred or not, but that *they* would never have children of their own. And if they did, they would be outcasts.

"We'd stay friends, if one of us had a child," said one of Belle's daughters.

"Sure," said the other. "We'd set up a home and raise it together. Share it."

"What about the bull?" said the younger daughter. "Would he have to live with us, too?"

Belle and Clara shared another of their looks, folded and pounded the dough they were working.

Belle's older daughter shrugged. "You know what the males are like," she said. "The ones who can breed are like... ugh."

When they had talked enough about the future, the daughters talked about movies and music and the parties they were going to. Belle's daughters were into bushwalking, and were always trying to drag their mother and Clara along on their week-long walks across the reserve. They talked about the places they would walk to next, and the things they planned to do when they got there.

Clara and Belle also worked together in the kitchen at the café. Or they went to other cafés to eat cake and drink coffee. They liked to sample the menus in the other cafés and consider the clientele. Sometimes, they would buy flat, sweet Dutch donuts from the baker, and get take-away coffee from the place next door to that, and then they'd go for a long walk along the beach together.

They talked, at first in a sidelong fashion, and later with increasing heatedness, about the males with whom they had paired, their children, the lives they still felt they might live.

Clara said that her husband had been the kind that, whenever they invited people for dinner, would insist that she spend the two days prior to their arrival cleaning the whole of their home from top to bottom. She would pull out the weeds along the pathways and pull out the saplings that were too hard or bitter to eat. Trample the path till it was good and wide, and gather extra food for everyone. "It got to the point it was just easier not to have guests," she said. "By the time they arrived, I was too exhausted to enjoy their company."

Belle said that she had found out Robert still wrote letters to his childhood sweetheart. One a week. And that the woman wrote back just as often.

"What do the letters say?" Clara asked.

Belle shrugged and looked away, squinting out to sea. "I don't know. He keeps them in a toolbox in his solitary territory. I've never had the courage to read them. I can't decide whether I want them to be in love still, or not."

They looked at each other, and then they both laughed. It was ridiculous, wasn't it? The way the ones that were meant to be the centres of their lives were so peripheral. It was their friendship with each other that was the true and central thing.

"I shouldn't talk about him like this," said Belle. "He's a good enough husband."

Clara nodded. "Mine was, too. He was alright, as far as husbands go."

"Just not – I don't know. It's as though he's given up. As though now that we know we'll go extinct – there's no point in paying attention to the lives we *do* have. The lives we're living."

"As if we're already ghosts," said Clara. "Already dead."

"I'm going to leave him," Belle said. "I can't go on like this for much longer; living in the afterlife."

After they separated, Belle and her husband were friendly enough. He stayed in touch with the girls and was still often at their place, dropping them off or picking them up, mending this and that.

Belle spent most of her time at the café. She put in a herb garden, and then a vegetable patch. There was a vacant lot next door and it was soon overrun with pumpkins and nasturtiums, zucchini and tomato plants. She stopped wearing her bangles to work, and was often working in the garden, showing off her bare, strong shoulders and sturdy legs. She seemed younger every week, rather than older. Cleverer, too, and full of easy opinions about things. The customers who came into the café liked to talk to her about their own gardens, and their own efforts at baking this or that. They liked to walk beside her as she moved through the garden, pulling weeds or turning soil. In the middle of the day, if it was too hot and there were no customers to speak of, she would find a shady spot in the garden, spread out a picnic blanket and sit outside reading.

Sometimes, one of the customers would go out into the garden to see her; they would bring her an armful of rosemary, or a bucket of beets they had grown. These were always single females. They weren't lonely, exactly, but they seemed to like to come and take up a corner of Belle's blanket and talk.

Finally, one night after closing up late, Clara invited Belle to come to her house for a drink. Usually, Belle was busy in the evenings. She had the girls at home most nights, after all. But this time she said yes, and followed Clara up the long dirt road to her house.

Clara's house was small but she had an earnest, quiet affection for it. It had a long, narrow room running all along one side – a closed-in verandah – which was her very own library. There were windows at both ends, but it was a cool, dark, narrow room. She had her desk in there, but it was mostly just bookcases. Floor to ceiling, wall to wall. In the early evening, it was flooded with a faint, stippled light that came in through the bush surrounding the house. The room, like the rest of the house, was very plain and tidy. Clara found this plainness comforting amid the flourishing chaos of the bush in which the house sat. The winding, shaded paths through the rainforest. The weedy, vine-strangled creek. Here, the books spoke their own quiet language.

One of the deep, unspoken pleasures of Clara's life was to spend a whole day putting the books in order. She would catalogue everything like a real library, using the Dewey Decimal system, or order the books by colour and size. She would often lie on the cool concrete floor, with the reading lamp lit and her notebook at hand. Not reading, just waiting. It didn't matter what book it was she was meant to be reading. None of what was in the books mattered, in a sense. The fact of their existence was enough.

She heard Belle come down the path to the house. Heard her exuberant *halloooo* as she descended. Clara felt a fish hook catch in her ribs, and pull. She went out into the hall and saw Belle coming in at the door, leaving it open in her wake.

They went through the house. Clara had not turned on any of the lights. There was only the reading light in the library.

They sat on the floor in the library. Clara showed Belle her collection of fairy tales. Pictures of geese and princesses, ravens and hedgehogs, foxes and underground castles whose kitchens were acres and acres wide.

Belle stretched out across the floor and closed her eyes. Clara read to her, and she fell asleep. They both did. Then Belle left while Clara was sleeping, without saying goodbye.

But Belle visited again the next night, and told her a story she had heard when she was a child. They were sitting on the floor in the library again. Their backs against the bookcase, and their legs stretched out in front of them. When the story was finished, Belle said, very quietly, "You know, you're very important to me." They sat in the almost-dark room. It was hot, but a storm was about to break outside. You could feel its wet promise in the air. Belle tilted her head till it rested on Clara's shoulder. And then she got up and went away again.

She stayed away for three nights, then came without warning. Knocked and stood in the doorway, asking Clara if she would come to the river with her, right then and there, and walk along it in the dark.

They sat for a while on the enormous stones that lined one section of the riverbank. There were a few boats moored in the water, and the she-oaks that lined the shore on the other side made a soft, comforting sound. Like mothers hushing their children. They made love in a sandy gap between two large, flat stones. They walked along the river's edge afterwards, not touching, not talking. Clara felt herself a strong and independent female, unhampered by marriage or children or housework.

At home, she walked through the house spreading sand over the freshly-swept and polished floors. She bathed, but there was sand in her creases that found its way into her bed. She woke with the smell of river-water and night air still on her skin, would not have been surprised to find a small fish swimming in the sheets.

Clara became consumed by this other version of herself. A night-time version that bore only an uncertain relation to her ordinary daytime self. The map of the reserve that she had held in her mind changed subtly. A secret map was sketched across the day-lit one, with its markets and mud-holes and roads. The second map drew attention to the edges of places, and the gaps between them. To shorelines and unmarked paths. Places, like her library, that she thought of as corridors, light coming in at both ends and herself flying through them, like the sparrow in the old story by the venerable Bede.

Clara felt herself to be full of increasingly numerous pockets of strangeness. Walking to work, or cleaning the house, grazing on the savannah or kneading bread in the café, she contained fragments of another female, one who had during the night made love with Belle on the weedy grass at the edge of the forest, or on the savannah or, during one particularly wild rainstorm, in an empty carpark. That other Clara whose body seemed to be always already naked and beautiful.

How many females, she wondered, had felt this looseness, this glorious severance from the future? Had she been moving towards this feeling her whole life? Since her husband had left her? Since her daughter had stopped speaking to her? Since the scientists had said, finally, and with a sense more of exhaustion than of sadness, that there was no hope for their species?

The trouble began when Belle said that she loved her. They were in the kitchen at the café, standing side by side chopping pumpkins for the soup.

"I didn't know this was going to happen," Belle said. She was blushing, but seemed determined not to acknowledge that this was so.

"I know," Clara said.

That night, they walked through the darkness and met each other on the road between their houses. They hadn't planned it that way. Both of them had simply decided to walk towards the other. They moved off the road, into the forest, and found a place to lie down. Not a word was uttered, but Clara felt the things that Belle had said earlier that day like a widening of the channel in which they lay. She worried that the space would narrow, or disappear altogether. But it broadened out, from a narrow corridor into the high, bright nave of a cathedral. They could not look at each other, though their eyes were open. Their skin was cool and smooth to the touch. Clara felt that they were like fallen statues of themselves, organless and simple both inside and out.

"That story you wrote," Belle said, "the one about us going extinct."

"I never wrote a story about extinction," said Clara.

"False something, it was called."

Belle had started the conversation in that quiet moment when they were lying in the library, after making love, when last time they had not spoken at all, but allowed the stillness between them to express everything.

"Did you ever think of having the two females just go on together? The mother and the daughter: Alice. They could jettison the male and have enough resources to make it to Walden."

The male White-backed vulture in the story had been perhaps the most troubled by their predicament. The nest he and his partner had built, in the nearest thing they could find to a tree in the EDS, was lined not with green leaves and grass, but with the hair of other animals, with electrical wires and strips of soft plastic. He had tried to get some of the other animals – in particular the other birds – to become part of a breeding colony, but nobody would join him. Nobody wanted to become the mother or father of a child who would have to be jettisoned into space.

"It's not that simple. You're making the same mistake as the others," Clara said.

"What did the others say, about the story?"

Belle tried to nuzzle Clara, to draw her back into an embrace, but Clara moved away slightly. There was a tightness in her gut that wouldn't allow her to look at her lover. "I didn't mean them," Clara said. "I meant the other writers. Godwin. All those men. It's a false equation."

"But you sent it to the others, didn't you? To the other members of the Karen Joy Fowler Book Club? What did they say?"

Clara shook her head, appalled.

"You didn't send it to them," Belle said. "Just to me? Or... perhaps they don't exist, those others," she said softly, squeezing the flesh of Clara's thigh. "Perhaps there's only me. Perhaps I'm the stowaway in your spaceship to Walden."

"Stop it," Clara said, pushing Belle away. Her rough, insistent touch. "Why are you being like this?"

"Like what?" Belle said, sliding closer, curling her tail, pushing herself against Clara in a mocking, vulgar way. "I just want to get inside you. Inside your pretty head where all the other women meet." She began to herd Clara against the wall, to wipe her horn on the floor with a terrible scraping noise.

Clara told her to leave. She said that if Belle didn't leave now, then she would go herself. She moved away, stiffened herself. Belle pressed her horn into the ridge between Clara's shoulder and her neck, pushed the point in with a soft, ugly curse. The same word she sometimes cried out when they were lying together. Then she pulled away, gave Clara a sour and pitying look, and left.

Clara stayed in the library for some time, wondering what had happened, exactly. What had gone wrong. When she thought about it afterwards – when she had become a solitary wanderer – she decided that Belle had been frightened of what it meant for the love they made to be incapable of producing a future. That was the whole point of love, for Belle, for it to create the possibility of lineage. To gesture towards Walden, when in reality whether they remained in the ship or arrived at some fantastical destination made no difference. What did it mean, to save Alice, when there was no future into which she might travel? Or perhaps Belle had just wanted to humiliate Clara because she was frightened. Or was it all just a part of loving a woman, after all, some ordinary consequence of lying down together?

A WEEK LATER, there was a knock at the door, and Clara was sure it would be Belle. She had been thinking all week that Belle would call to explain herself, to ask for forgiveness, to say that she had been frightened, or even uncertain, and that the uncertainty had made her cruel. Clara had rehearsed their conversation in her head. She would listen, she had decided, patiently and kindly, though she would not forgive her lover too quickly.

But when she opened the door it was only her daughter, Alice.

"Belle sent me a message," Alice said. "Your Belle. How did she even know my name?"

"I don't know," said Clara.

She had told Belle about Alice, of course. She had offered up the story of her lost, wild daughter as a kind of intimacy. Or in order to make herself seem more interesting, more strange and unfamiliar than she otherwise might have seemed.

"She wants to come and talk to me," Alice said. "What's the matter with her? What does she want?"

"We had a fight," Clara said, wondering if that was true, after all.

"Does she want to punish you, by talking to me? Or have me convince you to forgive her?"

Clara shook her head. "She's not like that," she said. But she wasn't sure if it was true.

"I'm going to meet her at the café," Alice said. "It's closed, but Belle says we can sit in the garden and talk. I'll send you a message afterwards and tell you what happens."

Clara tried not to pay too much attention to the time. Several hours passed. The day ended. She sat in the library, not reading the book they were planning to discuss at book club. She turned the pages one at a time, then in batches, going backwards, going forwards. It didn't seem to matter.

It was almost morning by the time she decided to walk to Alice's house. She had no idea what she would do when she got there, but at least the walking would give her something to do.

As she walked, she tried to remember, and silently recite, the lines of the rhinoceros sutra. Only fragments of the already-fragmented text would come to her. She remembered that there was something about a kovilara tree that has shed its leaves. She could remember that one of the sutras was: *Seeing the danger that comes from affection, wander alone like a rhinoceros*. And another: *Give up your children, and your wives, and your money, wander alone like a rhinoceros*.

She walked down the long drive towards Alice's house, which was lined on both sides with overgrown black bamboo. There were no lights on in the house. She could see that all the windows were open to let in any cool breeze.

Clara looked in at the windows and saw that Alice had left the children she cared for alone, and the doors unlocked. None of them woke and saw her looking in at them. Some of the creatures were unfamiliar to her; had they come from other reserves? Other continents? Were they all, like Alice, the last of their kind?

Clara found an open door at the back of the house and went in, closing it behind her. She lay on the cool stone floor of the living area. She lay still, listening to the snuffling and breathing of the children, until she heard the birds outside the house waking. She was stiff and tired. She got up and opened the front door, looking up the driveway for a sign of her daughter. Nothing.

She could not quite identify what she was feeling. She was restless, but wanted to be still. She was impatient, but did not want to hear what Belle and Alice had had to say to each other. She longed for the feeling she was already having trouble recalling, of being in the long, cool channel of the library. With light behind her, and light ahead, and this moment, this *now*, always just a thing she was passing through.

She went from room to room looking in at the children. How carelessly they slept, with the windows open and the doors unlocked. They lay tangled together, sleeping. So fearless. When had she last slept that way?

Alice appeared at the door behind her, looking in at the sleeping babies. "I told you they were beautiful," she said.

Clara did not answer. She could barely remember the conversations they had had, so many years ago, about Alice's decision not even to try to have children of her own. She tried to pretend that Alice had not come home yet, and that as the children woke – they were starting to turn and itch in their sleep – they would come to Clara, climbing up and over her. She would prepare breakfast for them, and watch them play on the wide back lawn.

"She didn't say anything, really," Alice said. "We had a bottle of wine and Belle said that she wasn't sure what had happened between you, but that she hoped it would be alright again soon. She said she thought it was too late now, for any of us, to hold grudges or fall in love."

She said. "Mum, listen. It's nothing. It doesn't mean anything. One day, you'll forget her name. We'll have to call her That Woman From The Café. We'll laugh about it."

Then, "Mum, what are you going to do? There's nothing you can do. It's done."

One of the children came sleepily out of their room and leant against Alice, then clambered up onto her back. Clara smiled at the way Alice moved to accommodate the child; at how natural and easy it seemed for her to do so.

"I have to go," Clara said. She felt disconnected from all of it, now that she had seen the house with Alice in it, and all the children sleeping so quietly together. All these years there had been a kind of wire connecting her to Alice. A twinging in her ribs whenever she thought of her, and what her future might contain, and now it was gone. Things were exactly as they were, exactly as they were supposed to be.

Clara never saw Belle, or Alice, again. She left Alice's house and went home, walked through the rooms in which she had spent her life and did not recognise a thing. Even the library, with its walls of unread books, seemed unfamiliar.

So she left the house and started wandering, alone, like a rhinoceros.

The Karen Joy Fowler Book Club were due to meet in a few months' time, and if she reached them, that was fine. And if not, that would be fine as well. She got a powerful sense of pleasure out of walking away. She was pleased with herself, with the controlled and deliberate way in which she managed it. She scraped Belle out of herself, all those tangled and uncertain emotions, and found that the hollow that was left behind was a good and simple thing.

She saw that she had been living in a false equation: she had believed, like Belle and all the others, like Janet and her husband, that love and futurity were connected. That without a future, love was no longer possible; without Walden as their destination, there was no reason to jettison the hatchling, and no reason not to.

But love does not require a future in order to exist. And the future exists, whether you furnish it with love or not. The second rhinoceros sutra, after all, was clear: *Renouncing violence for all living beings, harming not even a one, you would not wish for offspring, so how a companion? Wander alone like a rhinoceros.*

Clara turns onto an unfamiliar path. She has passed, finally, beyond the reserve. She does not think about the future, or love, as she walks through the waist-high grass, with its smell of summer and heat. Past the kovilara trees, past the view of the mountain washed in late afternoon light. She doesn't think about Belle, or Alice, or her husband. The path is shaded, but warm. She can see where it disappears ahead of her.

As she wanders, she thinks about being in the library late in the day. The light from the forest lying complicated, shifting patterns on the floor. And herself, passing through, from one end of the story to the other.

ORAL ARGUMENT

Kim Stanley Robinson

Kim Stanley Robinson is the author of nineteen novels and eight collections of short fiction. Winner of the Hugo, Nebula, and World Fantasy Awards, he is best known for the award-winning Mars trilogy – *Red Mars, Green Mars*, and *Blue Mars*. Robinson, science fiction's foremost utopian writer, has published important novels on ecological, cultural and political themes including the Orange Country trilogy, the Science in the Capital trilogy, *Antarctica*, *The Years of Rice and Salt*, *Galileo's Dream*, *2312*, and *Shaman*. His most recent books are *Green Earth* (a revision of Science in the Capital) and *Aurora*, a major generation starship novel. Robinson lives in Davis, California, with his wife of more than 30 years, environmental chemist Lisa Howland Nowell, and their two sons.

Mr. Chief Justice, and may it please the court:

Thank you, it's good to be here. A special hearing convened by you is very special. I'm happy to answer your questions.

Well, yes, the subpoena. But I'm happy too.

No, I did not represent them in those years. And now I'm only serving as their spokesperson while their legal standing is being clarified.

No, I don't know where they are. But if I did, that would be a matter of attorney-client privilege.

Spokesperson confidentiality, yes. Like protecting my sources. That's what I meant to say.

I do know what contempt of court means, yes. I brought my toothbrush.

No, I'm happy to answer any questions you have. Really.

Okay, sure. I met them when they were finishing their postdocs at MIT. I should clarify that they had no affiliation with MIT at the time they did the work in question, as MIT has proved.

Their project involved identifying and removing problem parts in the biobricks catalog. After MIT shifted the catalog to the iGEM website –

No, I don't think repudiated is the right word for that. MIT might have been worried about legal repercussions, but I don't know. I came in later.

Anyway, after that change of host, the iGEM Registry of Standard Biological Parts grew much larger, and the parties for whom I am speaking found that there were questionable parts in the catalog, for instance a luminous bacteria that emitted lased light which unfortunately burned retinas, or –

Sorry. I'll try to be brief. While going through the biobricks catalog, my former clients found a seldom-used plasmid backbone called DragonSpineXXL, much longer than typical plasmid backbones. The DragonSpine's designers apparently had hoped to enable bigger assemblages, but they encountered in vitro problems, including one that they called spina bifida –

It's a metaphor. I'm not a biochemist, I'm doing the best I can here. But to get to the point at your level of patience and understanding, as you so aptly put it, our bodies obtain their energy when the food we eat gets oxidized, producing ATP inside our mitochondria. ATP is the energy source used by all our cells. In plants, on the other hand, light striking the chloroplasts in leaves powers the production of ATP. Despite the different processes, the ATP is the same –

Yes, I too was surprised. But all life forms on Earth share 938 base pairs of DNA, so it makes sense that there are some family resemblances. So, it occurred to my almost clients that –

They consisted of a microbiologist, a systems biologist, a synthetic biologist, and an MD specializing in biochemistry and nutritional disorders –

Yes, no doubt a good joke about the four of them walking into a bar could be concocted. But instead of that they found biobricks in the catalog that could be combined to make a synthetic chloroplast. They felt it would be possible to attach this synthetic chloroplast to a DragonSpine, and still have room to attach another assemblage they concocted, one where fascia cells formed hollow fibroblasts –

Sorry. Fascia are bands of connective tissue. The bands are stretchy, and they're all over inside us. They kind of hold our bodies together. Like your feet, have you ever had plantar fasciitis? No? You're lucky. I guess you sit down on the job more than I do. Anyway, fascia consist of wavy bands of collagen blobs called fibroblasts. So, my acquaintances loaded DragonSpines with fibroblasts containing chloroplasts –

Yes, I know it's confusing. You are not biologists, I know. It's easy to remember that. What it comes down to is that my sometime clients, using nothing but synthetic parts found in the Registry of Standard Biological Parts, created photosynthesizing human cells.

Wait, excuse me, what you say is not correct. They didn't want to patent it. They knew that the registry was an open source collection.

I don't think they suspected that the idea itself would be patentable. The law there is ambiguous, I think that can be said. You might have judged their idea a business method only, you've done that before. An idea for a dating service, a new way to teach a class, a new way to replenish your energy – they're the same, right? They're ideas, and you can't patent an idea, as you ruled in *Bilski* and elsewhere.

Yes, there were some physical parts in this case, but the parts in question were all open source. If you type out your idea on a computer, that doesn't make it patentable just because a computer was involved, isn't that how you put it in *Bilski*?

Quoting precedent is not usually characterized as sarcasm, Your Honor. The patent law is broadly written, and your decisions concerning it haven't helped to narrow or clarify it. Some people call that body of precedent kind of ad hoc-ish and confusing, not to say small-minded. Whatever keeps business going best seems to be the main principle, but the situation is tricky. It's like you've been playing Twister and by now you've tied yourselves into all kinds of contortions. Cirque du Soleil may come knocking any day now –

Sorry. Anyway the patent situation wasn't a problem for my erstwhile clients, because they didn't want a patent. At that point they were focused on the problem so many new biotechnologies encounter, which is how to get the new product safely into human bodies. It couldn't be ingested or injected into the bloodstream, because it had to end up near the skin to do its work. And it couldn't trigger the immune system –

Yes, in retrospect the solution looks perfectly obvious, even to you, as you put it so aptly. The people I am speaking for contacted a leading firm in the dermapigmentation industry. Yes, tattooing. That methodology introduces liquids to precisely the layer of dermis best suited for the optimal functioning of the new product. And once introduced, the stuff stays there, as is well known. But my putative clients found that the modern tattoo needle systems adequate to their requirements were all patent protected. So they entered negotiations with the company that owned the patent entitled 'Tattoo Needle Tip Equipped with Capillary Ink Reservoir, Tattoo Tube Having Handle and Said Tattoo Needle Tip, and Assembly of Said Tattoo Needle Tip and Tattoo Needle.'

This device was modified by the parties involved to inject my future clients' chloroplast-fibroblasts into human skin, in the manner of an ordinary tattoo. When experiments showed the product worked in vivo, the two groups formed an LLC called SunSkin, and applied for a new patent for the modified needle and ink. This patent was granted.

I don't know if the patent office consulted the FDA.

No, it's not right to say the nature of the tattoo ink was obscured in the application. Every biobrick was identified by its label, as the records show.

Yes, most of the tattoos are green. Although chlorophyll is not always green. It can be red, or even black. But usually it's green, as you have observed.

No wait, excuse me for interrupting, there were no deaths. That was the hair follicle group. Thermoencephalitis, yes. It was a bad idea.

No, I'm not saying that no one with SunSkin tattoos ever died. I'm saying that no deaths suffered by those customers was proved to be caused by the tattoos. I refer you to that entire body of criminal and civil law.

Of course some of them did in fact die. No one ever claimed photosynthesis would make you immortal.

I do not speak for SunSkin, which in any case went bankrupt in the first year of the crash. My association is with my potential clients only.

After the crash, my ostensible clients formed a 501(c)(3) called End Hunger. They renounced the patent on their product, and indeed sued to have the patent revoked as improperly granted, the product being made entirely of open source biobricks.

No, the patent was not their idea in the first place. It was the idea of the lawyers hired by SunSkin. Amazing as it may seem.

Yes, the assemblage itself was my quasi-clients' idea.

Yes, the idea was new, and not obvious, which is how the patent law as written describes eligibility. But the parts were open source, and photosynthesis is a natural process. And my associates wanted their assemblage to remain open source. Actually all that quickly became a moot point. Once they published the recipe, and the knowledge spread that human photosynthesis worked, the injection method as such became what you might call generic. It turned out the cells were very robust. You could stick them in with a bone needle and they would do fine.

I don't know how much money my semi-clients made.

Estimate? Say somewhere between nothing and a hundred million dollars.

I brought my toothbrush, as I said. Obviously my once and future clients made a living. I don't think you can object to that. As you pointed out in *Molecular versus Myriad*, no one does anything except for money. Indeed you thought it was a great joke to imagine that people might work just for curiosity or recognition or the good of humanity. Curiosity, you said. That's lovely, you said. Don't you remember? You got a good laugh from the gallery, because you have no idea how scientists think or what motivates them. You actually seem to think it's all about money.

Not since the crash it isn't.

Yes, it does appear that large quantities of ATP entering the body by way of capillaries in the dermis causes some people to experience side effects. Hot flashes, hypersatiety, vitamin deficiencies, irritable bowel syndrome, some others. But you've made it clear in many cases that side effects cannot be allowed to stop the making of money. Your priorities there are very clear.

Well, I'm surprised to hear you describe the worst depression since the Black Death as a side effect. Especially the side effect of a new kind of tattoo.

Agreed, when you photosynthesize sunlight you will be less hungry. You might also spend more of your day outdoors in the sun, that's right, and subsequently decide that you didn't need quite as much food or heating as before. Or clothing. Or housing, that's right. I don't see all these green naked people wandering around sleeping under tarps in the park like you seem to, but granted, there have been some changes in consumption. Did changes in consumption cause the Great Crash? No one can say –

That means nothing. Your feeling is not an explanation. Historical causation is complex. Technology is just one strand in a braid. What you call the Great Crash others call the Jubilee. It's been widely celebrated as such.

Yes, but those were odious debts, so people defaulted. Granted, maybe it was easier to do that because they weren't in danger of starving. Maybe the rentier class had lost its stranglehold –

Not true. Most people think the crash resulted not from photosynthetic tattoos or the Big No but rather from another liquidity crisis and credit freeze, as in 2008. Possibly you've even heard people saying that the failure to regulate finance after 2008 was what led to the crash, and that the failure to regulate finance was a result of your decision in *Citizens United* and elsewhere. Possibly you've heard yourselves described as the cause of the crash, or even as the worst court in the history of the United States.

Sorry. This is what one hears when one is outside this room.

May I point out that I am not the one straying from the point. In the matter of this current hearing, which strikes me as a bit of a witch hunt to find culpability for the crash anywhere but at your own doorstep, I repeat that my clients never wanted the patent and renounce all claims to it. The patent was awarded to an LLC called SunSkin, which went bankrupt in the first year of the crash when its principal lender broke contract by refusing to pay a scheduled payment. Possibly the lawsuit against the lender will eventually be won, but as SunSkin no longer exists, it will be a bit of a Pyrrhic victory for them.

Well, as the lender was nationalized along with all the rest of the banks in the third year of the crash, if SunSkin's lawsuit ever comes to you, you may have to recuse yourselves as being a party to the defendants. Not that that kind of conflict ever stopped you before.

I don't know, can there be contempt of court if the court is beneath contempt?

I don't care, I brought my toothbrush. I'll be appealing this peremptory judgment at the next level.

Not true. There is most definitely a next level.

DRONES

Simon Ings

SIMON INGS (WWW.SIMONINGS.COM) was born July 1965 in Horndean, Hampshire, England. He attended King's College in London, where he studied English. His first SF story was "Blessed Fields". Debut novel *Hot Head* and sequel *Hotwire* were cyberpunk, of sorts. Other works of SF include *City of the Iron Fish* and *Headlong*. *Painkillers* is a thriller with some SF elements, while *The Weight of Numbers* and *Dead Water* are big, ambitious literary works. He returned to SF with *Wolves*, about augmented reality. He also wrote non-fiction *The Eye: A Natural History*. Ings also edited *Arc*, the SF magazine produced by *New Scientist*, where he works as a culture editor.

THERE'S A RAIL link, obviously, connecting this liminal place to the coast at Whitstable, but the mayor and his entourage will arrive by boat. It's more dramatic that way.

Representatives of the airfield construction crews are lined up to greet him. Engineers in hard hats and dayglo orange overalls. Local politicians too, of course. Even those who bitterly opposed this thing's construction are here for its dedication. The place is a fact now, so they may as well bless it, and in their turn, be blessed.

It's early morning, and bitterly cold. Still, the spring light, glinting off glossy black tarmac and the glass curtain walls of the terminal buildings, is magnificent.

I'm muscling some room for my nephews at the rail of the observation deck, and even up here it's hard to see the sea. A critical press has made much of the defences required to protect this project from the Channel's ever more frequent swells. But the engineering is not as chromed as special as it's been made out to be: this business of reclaiming land from the sea and, where necessary, giving it back again ('managed retreat', they call it), is an old one. It's practically a folk art round here, setting aside this project's industrial scale.

The mayor's barge is in view. It docks in seconds. None of that aching, foot-tap delay. This ship's got jets in place of propellers and it slides into its decorated niche (Scots blue and English red and white) as neatly as if it were steered there by the hand of a giant child.

My nephews tug at my hands, one on each, as if they'd propel me down to deck level: a tempted Jesus toppling off the cliff, his landing softened by attendant angels. It is a strange moment. For a second I picture myself elderly, the boys grown men, propping me up. Sentiment's ambushed me a lot this year. I was engaged to be married once. But the wedding fell through. The girl went to be a trophy for some party bigwig I hardly know. Like most men, then, I'll not marry now. I'll have no kids. Past thirty now, I'm on the shelf. And while it is an ordinary thing, and no great shame, it hurts, more than I thought it would. When I was young and leant my shoulder for the first time to the civic wheel, I'd entertained no thought of children.

The mayor's abroad among the builders now. They cheer and wheel around him as he waves. His hair is wild, a human dandelion clock, his heavy frame's a vessel, wallowing. He smiles. He waves.

A man in whites approaches, a pint of beer – of London Pride, of course – on a silver tray. The crowd is cheering. I am cheering, and the boys. Why would we not? Politics aside, it is a splendid thing. This place. This moment. Our mayor fills his mouth with beer and wheels around – belly big, and such small feet – spraying the crowd. The anointed hop around, their dignity quite gone, ecstatic. Around me, there's a groan of pop-idol yearning, showing me I'm not alone in wishing that the mayor had spat at me.

IT'S FOUR BY the time we're on the road, back to Hampshire and home. The boys are of an age where they are growing curious. And something of my recent nostalgia-fuelled moodishness must have found its way out in words, because here it comes, "So have you had a girl?"

"It's not my place. Or yours."

"But you were going to wed."

The truth is that, like most of us, I serve the commons better out of bed. I've not been spat on, but I've drunk the Mayor of London's piss a thousand times, hardly dilute, fresh from the sterile beaker: proof of the mayor's regard for my work, and for all in Immigration.

The boys worry at the problem of my virginity as at a stubborn shoelace. Only children seem perturbed, still, by the speed of our nation's social transformation, though there's no great secret about it. It is an ordinary thing, to prize the common good, when food is scarce, and we must husband what we have, and guard ourselves against competitors. The scrumpy raids of the apple-thieving French. Belgian rape oil-tappers sneaking in at dusk along the Ald and the Ore in shallow craft. Predatory bloods with their fruit baskets climbing the wires and dodging the mines of the M25 London Orbital.

Kent's the nation's garden still, for all its bees are dead, and we defend it as best we can, with tasers and wire-and-paper drones, klaxons, and farmer's sons gone vigilante, semi-legal, badged with the crest while warned to do no Actual Bodily Harm.

("Here, drink the mayoral blessing! The apple harvest's saved!" I take the piss into my mouth and spray. The young lads at their screens jump up and cheer, slap backs, come scampering over for that touch of divine wet. Only children find this strange. The rest of us, if I am typical (and why would I not be?) are more relieved, I think, rid at last of all the empty and selfish promises of our former estate.)

So then. Hands on wheel. Eye to the mirrors. Brain racing. I make my Important Reply:

"One man can seed a hundred women." Like embarrassed grown-ups everywhere, I seek solace in the science. This'll fox them, this'll stop their questions. "And so, within a very little time, we are all brothers."

"And sisters."

"Sisters too, sometimes." This I'll allow. "And so, being kin, we have no need to breed stock of our own, being that our genes are shared among our brothers. We'll look instead after our kin, feed and protect our mayor, give him our girls, receive his blessing."

"Like the bees."

Yes. "Like the bees we killed."

In northern Asia, where food's not quite so scarce, they laugh at us, I think, and how we've changed – great, venerated Europe! Its values adapting now to a new, less flavoursome environment. ("Come. Eat your gruel. Corn syrup's in the jar.") They are wrong to laugh. The irony of our estate is not lost on us. We know what we've become, and why. From this vantage, we can see the lives we led before for what they were: lonely, and selfish, and without respect.

Chichester's towers blink neon pink against the dying day. It's been a good excursion, all told, this airfield opening. Memorable, and even fun, for all the queues and waiting. It's not every day you see your mayor.

"How come we killed the bees?"

"An accident, of course. Bill, no one meant to kill the bees."

Bill takes it hard, this loss of natural help. It fascinates him, why the bond of millennia should have sheared. Why this interest in bees? Partly it's because he's being taught about them in school. Partly it's because he has an eye for living things. Mostly, though, it's because his dad, my brother, armed with a chicken feather dipped in pollen mix, fell out of an apple tree on our estate and broke his neck. Survived, but lives in pain. Poor Dan: the closest of my fifty kin.

"We spray for pests, and no one spray did for the bees, but combinations we could not predict or model with our science." True. The world is rich and vast and monstrously fed back into itself. Science works well enough in a lab, but it is so small, so very vulnerable, the day you lay it open to the world.

The towns slip by. Hands on the wheel. An eye to the mirrors. Waterlooville. Havant. Home. Dad's wives at the farmhouse windows wave, and Dad himself comes to the door. Retired now, the farm all passed to Dan. But Dad is still our centre and our figurehead.

I ask after my brother.

Dad smiles his sorry little smile, "It's been good for him, I think, today. The rest. Reading in the sun."

"I'm glad."

The old man leans and spits a benediction on my forehead. "And you?"

IN AN EMPTY cinema, seats lower themselves in readiness for their customers.

An orchestra sits, frozen, the musicians as poised as shop dummies, freighted with uncanny intent.

Two needles approach each other. Light sparks and blooms between their points, filling the screen.

A cameraman lies across a railway track, filming the approach of a locomotive. The man rolls out the way of the train at the last second but one foot still lies across the rail. Carriages whizz and rock and intersect at all angles: violent, slicing motions fill the screen.

A young woman starts out of nightmare, slides from her bed and begins to dress.

I paused the video (this was years ago, and we were deep in the toil of our country's many changes) and I went into the hall to answer the phone. My brother, Dan (all hale and hearty back then, with no taste for apples and no anxiety about bees), had picked up an earlier train; he was already at Portsmouth Harbour station.

"I'll be twenty minutes," I said.

Back in those days, Portsmouth Harbour station was all wood and glass and dilapidated almost beyond saving. "Like something out of *Brief Encounter*," Dan joked, hugging me.

1945. Trevor Howard holds Celia Johnson by the waist, says goodbye to her on just such a platform as this.

We watched many old films back then, and for the obvious reason. Old appetites being slow to die, Dan and I craved them for their women. Their vulnerable eyes, and well-turned calves and all the tragedy in their pretty words. A new breed of state censor, grown up to this new, virtually womanless world, and aggressive in its defence, was robbing us of female imagery wherever it could. But even the BBFC would not touch David Lean.

Southsea's vast shingle beach was a short walk away. The rip-tides were immense here, heaving the stones eastwards, and impressive wooden groynes split the beach into great high-sided boxes to conserve it.

In his donkey jacket and cracked DMs, Dan might have tumbled out of the old Russian film I'd been watching. (A woman slides from her bed, naked, and begins, unselfconsciously, to dress.) "We're digging a villa," he told me, as we slid and staggered over the shingle. Dan was the bright one, the one who'd gone away to study. "A bloody joke, it is." He had a way of describing the niceties of archaeological excavation – which features to explore, which to record, which to dig away – that made it sound as if he was jobbing on a building site. And it is true that his experiences had weathered and roughened him.

I wondered if this modest but telling transformation was typical. We rarely saw our other brothers, many as they were. The three eldest held down jobs in the construction of the London Britannia airport; back then just 'Boris Island', and a series of towers connected by gantries, rising out of the unpromisingly named Shivering Sands. Robert had moved to Scarborough and worked for the coast guard. The rest had found work out of the country, in Jakarta and Kuala Lumpur and poor Liam in Dubai. The money they sent back paid for Dan's education, Dad's plan being to line up our family's youngest for careers in government service. I imagined my brothers all sun-burnished and toughened by their work. Me? Back then I was a very minor observations man, flying recycled plastic drones out of Portsmouth Airport on the Hampshire coast. This was a government job in name only. It was locally run; more of a vigilante effort, truth be told. This made me, at best, a very minor second string in Dad's meticulously orchestrated family.

It did, though – after money sent home – earn me enough to rent a conversion flat in one of those wedding cake-white Georgian terraces that look out over Southsea's esplanade. The inside was ordinary, all white emulsion and wheatmeal carpeting, until spring came, and sunlight came blazing through the bay window, turning the whole of my front room to candy and icing sugar.

"Beautiful."

It was the last thing I expected Dan to say.

"It's bloody beautiful."

"It's not bad."

"You should see my shithole," Dan said, with a brutal satisfaction.

At the time I thought he was just being pretentious. I realise now – and of course far too late – that brute nil-rhetoric was his way of expressing what was, in the millennial atmosphere of those post-feminine days, becoming inexpressible: their horror.

I do not think this word is too strong. Uncovering the graves of little girls, hundreds and hundreds, was a hazard of Dan's occupation. Babies mostly; a few grown children though. The business was not so much hidden as ignored. That winter I'd gone to Newcastle for a film festival; the nunneries there had erected towers in the public parks for people to leave a child. Babies survived at least a couple of days, exposed to the rain and cold. Nobody paid any attention.

Dan's job was to enter construction sites during the phase of demolition, and see what was to be gleaned of the nation's past before the construction crews moved in, turfing it over with rebar and cement. Of course the past is invented, more than uncovered. You see what you are primed to see. No-one wants to find a boat, because boats are the very devil to conserve and take an age to dig, delaying everyone. Graves are a minor problem in comparison, there are so many of them. The whole of London Bridge rises above the level of the Thames on human bones.

Whenever his digs struck recent graves, Dan's job was to obliterate them. Hence, his pose: corporation worker. Glorified refuse man. Hence his government career: since power accretes to those who know – in this case, quite literally – where the bodies are buried.

Why should it have been women, and women alone, that succumbed to the apian plague – this dying breed's quite literal sting in the tail? A thousand conspiracy theories, even now, shield us from the obvious and unpalatable truth: that the world is vast, and monstrously infolded, and we cannot, will not, will not ever know.

And while the rest of us were taken up with our great social transformation, it fell to such men as Dan – gardeners, builders, miners, archaeologists – to deal with the sloughed-off stuff. The bones and skin.

Not secret; and at the same time, not spoken of: the way we turned misfortune into social practice, and practice, at last, into technology. The apian plague is gone long since, dead with the bees that carried it. But, growing used to this dispensation, we have made analogues for it, so girls stay rare. Resources shrinking as they do, there's not a place on earth now does not harbour infanticides. In England in medieval times we waited till the sun was set then lay across our newborn girls to smother them. Then, too, food was short, and dowries dear.

Something banged my living room wall, hard. I turned to see the mirror I had hung, just a couple of days before, rocking on its wire. Another blow, and the mirror rocked and knocked against the wall.

"Hey."

My whole flat trembled as blow after blow rained down on the wall.

"Hey!"

Next door was normally so quiet, I had almost forgotten its existence. The feeling of splendid isolation I had enjoyed since moving in here fell away: I couldn't figure out who it could be, hammering with such force. Were they moving furniture in there? Fixing cupboards?

The next blow was stronger still. A crack ran up the wall from floor to ceiling. I leapt up. "Stop it. Stop." Another blow, and the crack widened. I stepped back and the backs of my knees touched the edge of the sofa and I sat down, nerveless, too disorientated to feel afraid. A second, diagonal crack opened up, met a hidden obstacle, and ran vertically up to the ceiling.

The room's plaster coving, leaves and acorns and roses, snapped and crazed. A piece of stucco fell to the floor.

I didn't understand what was happening. The wall was brick, I knew it was brick because I'd hung a mirror on it not two days before. But chunks of plasterboard were peeling back under repeated blows, revealing a wall made of balled-up sheets of newspaper. They flowed into the room on top of the plasterboard. Dan put his arms around me. I was afraid to look at him: to see him as helpless as I was. Anyway, I couldn't tear my gaze from the wall.

Behind the newspaper was a wooden panel nailed over with batons. It was a door, or had been: there was no handle. The doorframe had split along its length and something was trying to force it open against the pile of plasterboard and batons already piled on the carpet. The room filled with pink-grey dust as the door swung in. The space beyond was the colour of old blood.

From out of the darkness, a grey figure emerged. It was no bigger than a child. It came through the wall, into my room. It was grey and covered in dust. Its face was a mask, strangely swollen: a bladder pulling away from the bone.

She spoke. She was very old. "What are you doing in my house?"

My LANDLORD CAME round the same evening. By then Dan and I had gathered from his grandmother – communicating haphazardly through the fog of her dementia – that my living room and hers had once been a single, huge room.

Her property. The house she grew up in. The property had been split in half years ago; long before my half had been subdivided to make flats.

The landlord said, "She must have remembered the door."

"She certainly must have."

He was embarrassed, and embarrassment made him aggressive. He seemed to think that because we were young, his mother's demolition derby must have been partly our fault. "If she heard noises through the wall, it will have confused her."

"I don't make noises through the wall. Neither am I going to tiptoe around my own flat."

He took her home. When they were gone Dan and I went to the pub. We drank beer (Old Speckled Hen) and Dan said, "How many years do you think they left that poor cow stranded there, getting steadily more unhinged?"

"For all I know he's round there every day looking after her."

"You don't really believe that."

"Why not?" I looked at my watch. "He probably thinks it's the best place for her. The house she grew up in."

"You saw what she was like."

"Old people know their own minds."

"While they still have them."

Back home, Dan went to bed, exhausted. I brought a spare duvet into the living room for myself, poured myself a whisky and settled down to watch the rest of *Man With a Movie Camera*. (Dziga Vertov, 1929.) When it was over I turned off the television and the lamp.

The hole in my wall was a neat oblong, black against the dim grey-orange of the wall. Though the handles had been removed, the door still had its mechanism. The pin still just about caught, holding the door shut against its frame. Already I was finding it hard to imagine the wall without that door.

I went into the kitchen and dug out an old knife, its point snapped off long before. I tried the knife in the hole where the handle had been and turned. Pinching my fingertips into the gap between the door and the frame, I pulled the door towards me.

The air beyond tasted thick, like wax. The smell – it had been lingering around my flat all day – was her smell. Fusty, and speaking of decay, it was, nevertheless, not unpleasant.

A red glow suffused the room. Light from a streetlamp easily penetrated the thin red material of her curtains; I could make out their outline very easily. The red-filtered light was enough that I could navigate around the room. It was stuffed full of furniture and the air was heavy with furniture wax. A chair was drawn up in front of a heavy sideboard, filling the space created by a bay window.

I ran my hand along the top of the sideboard. It was slick and clean and my hand came away smelling of resin. In her confusion, the old woman had still managed to keep her things spotless – unless someone had been coming and cleaning around her.

How many hours had she spent in this red, resined room? How many years?

I pulled the chair out of the way – its legs dragged on the thick rug – and opened a door of the sideboard.

It was filled with jars, and when I held one up to the red light coming through the curtains, the contents admitted one tawny, diagonal blear before resolving to black.

DAD WAS ALL for clearing out the lot. He had a van, his man could drive, they'd be in and out within the night. Such were the times, after all, and what great family is not founded on the adventures of a buccaneer?

But I had a youth's hope, and told him no: that we should play the long game. I can't imagine what I was thinking: that they would show some generosity to me, perhaps, for not stealing their property? Ridiculous.

Still, Dad let me have my head. Still, somehow, my gamble paid off. The landlord, whose family name was Franklin, hardly showered me with riches, but he turned out friendly enough, and the following spring, at his grandmother's funeral, I met his daughters.

The match with Belinda – what a name! – was easy enough to arrange. The dowry would be a generous one. Pear orchards and plum trees, hops and brassicas and the young men to tend them. The whole business fell through, as I have said, but the friendship of our families held. When Dan ran into political trouble he gave up his career and came home to run things for Dad. It was to him Franklin gave his youngest child, my nephews' mum. (Melissa. What a name.)

The rest is ordinary. Dan has run our estate successfully over the years, has taken mistresses and made some of them wives, and filled the house with sons. Of them, the two eldest are my special treasure, since I'll have no kids myself. Every once in a while a brother of ours returns to take a hand in the making of our home. They bring us strange stories; of how the world is being set to rights. By a river in the Minas Gerais somewhere, someone has reinvented the dolphin. But it is orange, and it keeps sinking.

Poor Liam's still languishing in Dubai, but the rest of us, piling in to exploit what we collectively know of the labour market, have done better than well.

As for me: well, what with one promotion and then another, this offshore London Britannia airfield has become my private empire. Three hundred observation drones. Fifty attack quadcopters. Six strike UAVs. There are eight thousand miles of coastline to protect, a hungry neighbour to the west famining on potatoes; to the east, a continent's-worth of peckish privateers. It is a busy time.

Each spring we all pile back onto the estate, of course, to help with pollination. Tinkerers all. We experiment sometimes with boxes of mechanical bees, imported at swingeing cost from Shenzen or Macao. But nothing works as well as a chicken feather wielded by a practised hand. This is how Dan, the scion of our line, came to plummet from the topmost rung of his ladder. The sons he had been teaching screamed, and from where I sat, stirring drying pots on the kitchen table, the first thing that struck me was how they sounded just like girls.

Dad leads me in. Much fuss is made of me. The boys vie with each other to tell their little brothers about the day, the airfield, the mayor. While Dad's women are cooing over them, I go through to the yard.

Dan is sitting where he usually sits, on sunny days like these, in the shelter of the main greenhouse, with a view of our plum trees. They, more than any other crop, have made our family rich, and it occurs to me with a lurch, seeing my brother slumped there in his chair under rugs, that it is not the sight of their fruit that has him enthralled. He is watching the walls. He is watching the gate. He is guarding our trees. There's a gun by his side. A shotgun. We only ever fill the cartridges with rock salt. But still.

Dan sees me and smiles and beckons me to the bench beside him. "It's time," he says.

I knew this was coming.

"I can't pretend I can do this any more. Look at me. Look."

I say what you have to say in these situations. Deep down, though, I can only assent. There's a lump in my throat. "I haven't earned this."

But Dan and I, we have always been close, and who else should he turn to, in his pain and disability and growing weakness? Who else should he hand the business to?

The farm will be mine. Melissa. The boys. All of it mine. Everything I ever wanted, though it has never been my place to take a single pip. It is being given to me freely, now. A life. A family. As if I deserved it!

"Think of the line," says Dan, against my words of protest. "The sons I'll never have."

We need sons, heaven knows. Young guns to hold our beachheads against the naughty French. Keepers to protect our crop from night-stealing London boys. Swords to fight the feuds that, quite as much a marriage pacts, shape our living in this hungry world.

It is no use. I have no head for politics. Try as I might, I cannot think of sons, but only of their making. Celia Johnson with a speck of grit in her eye. Underwear and a bed of dreams. May God forgive me, I am that depraved, my every thought is sex.

Dan laughs. He knows, and has always known, of my weakness. My interest in women. It is, for all the changes our world's been through, still not an easy thing, for men to turn their backs on all the prospects a wife affords.

"Pick me a plum," my brother says. So I go pick a plum. Men have been shot for less. With rock salt, yes. But still.

I remember the night we chose, Dan and I, not to raid the larder of the poor, confused old woman who had burst into my room. Perhaps it was simply the strangeness of the day that stopped us. (We stole one jar and left the rest alone.) I would like to think, though, that our forbearance sprang from some simple, instinct of our own. Call it decency.

It is hard, in such revolutionary times, always to feel good about oneself.

"Here," I say, returning to my crippled benefactor, the plum nursed in my hands.

Dan's look, as he pushes the fruit into his mouth, is the same look he gave me the night we tasted, ate, and finished entirely, that jar of priceless, finite honey. Pleasure. Mischief. God help us all: youth.

Ten, twelve years on, Dan's enjoying another one-time treat: he chews a plum. A fruit that might have decked the table of the mayor himself, and earned our boys a month of crusts. He spits the stone into the dust. Among our parsimonious lot, this amounts to a desperate display of power: Dan knows that he is dying.

I wonder how it tastes, that plum – and Dan, being Dan, sees and knows it all: my shamefaced ambition. My inexcusable excitement. To know so much is to excuse so much, I guess, because he beckons me, my brother and my friend, and once I'm knelt before him, spits that heavy, sweet paste straight into my mouth. And makes me king.

THE PAUPER PRINCE AND THE EUCALYPTUS JINN

Usman T. Malik

Usman T. Malik (www.usmanmalik.org) is a Pakistani writer resident in Florida. He reads Sufi poetry, likes long walks, and occasionally strums naats on the guitar. His fiction has appeared or is forthcoming in *Tor.com*, *Strange Horizons, Black Static, Daily Science Fiction, Exigencies*, and *Qualia Nous*, among other places. He is a graduate of Clarion West.

When the Spirit World appears in a sensory Form,
the Human Eye confines it. The Spiritual Entity cannot abandon
that Form as long as Man continues to look at it in this special way.
To escape, the Spiritual Entity manifests an Image it adopts for him,
like a veil. It pretends the Image is moving in a certain direction
so the Eye will follow it. At which point the Spiritual Entity
escapes its confinement and disappears.
Whoever knows this and wishes to maintain perception of the Spiritual,
must not let his Eye follow this illusion.
This is one of the Divine Secrets.
– *The Meccan Revelations* by Muhiyuddin Ibn Arabi

For fifteen years my grandfather lived next door to the Mughal princess Zeenat Begum. The princess ran a tea stall outside the walled city of Old Lahore in the shade of an ancient eucalyptus. Dozens of children from Bhati Model School rushed screaming down muddy lanes to gather at her shop, which was really just a roadside counter with a tin roof and a smattering of chairs and a table. On winter afternoons it was her steaming cardamom-and-honey tea the kids wanted; in summer it was the chilled Rooh Afza.

As Gramps talked, he smacked his lips and licked his fingers, remembering the sweet rosewater sharbat. He told me that the princess was so poor she had to recycle tea leaves and sharbat residue. Not from customers, of course, but from her own boiling pans – although who really knew, he said, and winked.

I didn't believe a word of it.

"Where was her kingdom?" I said.

"Gone. Lost. Fallen to the British a hundred years ago," Gramps said. "She never begged, though. Never asked anyone's help, see?"

I was ten. We were sitting on the steps of our mobile home in Florida. It was a wet summer afternoon and rain hissed like diamondbacks in the grass and crackled in the gutters of the trailer park.

"And her family?"

"Dead. Her great-great-great grandfather, the exiled King Bahadur Shah Zafar, died in Rangoon and is buried there. Burmese Muslims make pilgrimages to his shrine and honor him as a saint."

"Why was he buried there? Why couldn't he go home?"

"He had no home anymore."

For a while I stared, then surprised both him and myself by bursting into tears. Bewildered, Gramps took me in his arms and whispered comforting things, and gradually I quieted, letting his voice and the rain sounds lull me to sleep, the loamy smell of him and grass and damp earth becoming one in my sniffling nostrils.

I remember the night Gramps told me the rest of the story. I was twelve or thirteen. We were at this desi party in Windermere thrown by Baba's friend Hanif Uncle, a posh affair with Italian leather sofas, crystal cutlery, and marble-topped tables. Someone broached a discussion about the pauper princess. Another person guffawed. The Mughal princess was an urban legend, this aunty said. Yes, yes, she too had heard stories about this so-called princess, but they were a hoax. The descendants of the Mughals left India and Pakistan decades ago. They are settled in London and Paris and Manhattan now, living postcolonial, extravagant lives after selling their estates in their native land.

Gramps disagreed vehemently. Not only was the princess real, she had given him free tea. She had told him stories of her forebears.

The desi aunty laughed. "Senility is known to create stories," she said, tapping her manicured fingers on her wineglass.

Gramps bristled. A long heated argument followed and we ended up leaving the party early.

"Rafiq, tell your father to calm down," Hanif Uncle said to my Baba at the door. "He takes things too seriously."

"He might be old and set in his ways, Doctor sahib," Baba said, "but he's sharp as a tack. Pardon my boldness but some of your friends in there..." Without looking at Hanif Uncle, Baba waved a palm at the open door from which blue light and Bollywood music spilled onto the driveway.

Hanif Uncle smiled. He was a gentle and quiet man who sometimes invited us over to his fancy parties where rich expatriates from the Indian subcontinent opined about politics, stocks, cricket, religious fundamentalism, and their successful Ivy League-attending progeny. The shyer the man the louder his feasts, Gramps was fond of saying.

"They're a piece of work all right," Hanif Uncle said. "Listen, bring your family over some weekend. I'd love to listen to that Mughal girl's story."

"Sure, Doctor sahib. Thank you."

The three of us squatted into our listing truck and Baba yanked the gearshift forward, beginning the drive home.

"Abba-ji," he said to Gramps. "You need to rein in your temper. You can't pick a fight with these people. The doctor's been very kind to me, but word of mouth's how I get work and it's exactly how I can lose it."

"But that woman is wrong, Rafiq," Gramps protested. "What she's heard are rumors. I told them the truth. I lived in the time of the pauper princess. I lived through the horrors of the eucalyptus jinn."

"Abba-ji, listen to what you're saying! Please, I beg you, keep these stories to yourself. Last thing I want is people whispering the handyman has a crazy, quarrelsome father." Baba wiped his forehead and rubbed his perpetually blistered thumb and index finger together.

Gramps stared at him, then whipped his face to the window and began to chew a candy wrapper (he was diabetic and wasn't allowed sweets). We sat in hot, thorny silence the rest of the ride and when we got home Gramps marched straight to his room like a prisoner returning to his cell.

I followed him and plopped on his bed.

"Tell me about the princess and the jinn," I said in Urdu.

Gramps grunted out of his compression stockings and kneaded his legs. They occasionally swelled with fluid. He needed water pills but they made him incontinent and smell like piss and he hated them. "The last time I told you her story you started crying. I don't want your parents yelling at me. Especially tonight."

"Oh, come on, they don't *yell* at you. Plus I won't tell them. Look, Gramps, think about it this way: I could write a story in my school paper about the princess. This could be my junior project." I snuggled into his bedsheets. They smelled of sweat and medicine, but I didn't mind.

"All right, but if your mother comes in here, complaining –"

"She won't."

He arched his back and shuffled to the armchair by the window. It was ten at night. Cicadas chirped their intermittent static outside, but I doubt Gramps heard them. He wore hearing aids and the ones we could afford crackled in his ears, so he refused to wear them at home.

Gramps opened his mouth, pinched the lower denture, and rocked it. Back and forth, back and forth. Loosening it from the socket. *Pop!* He removed the upper one similarly and dropped both in a bowl of warm water on the table by the armchair.

I slid off the bed. I went to him and sat on the floor by his spidery, white-haired feet. "Can you tell me the story, Gramps?"

Night stole in through the window blinds and settled around us, soft and warm. Gramps curled his toes and pressed them against the wooden leg of his armchair. His eyes drifted to the painting hanging above the door, a picture of a young woman turned ageless by the artist's hand. Soft muddy eyes, a knowing smile, an orange dopatta framing her black hair. She sat on a brilliantly colored rug and held a silver goblet in an outstretched hand, as if offering it to the viewer.

The painting had hung in Gramps's room for so long I'd stopped seeing it. When I was younger I'd once asked him if the woman was Grandma, and he'd looked at me. Grandma died when Baba was young, he said.

The cicadas burst into an electric row and I rapped the floorboards with my knuckles, fascinated by how I could keep time with their piping.

"I bet the pauper princess," said Gramps quietly, "would be happy to have her story told."

"Yes."

"She would've wanted everyone to know how the greatest dynasty in history came to a ruinous end."

"Yes."

Gramps scooped up a two-sided brush and a bottle of cleaning solution from the table. Carefully, he began to brush his dentures. As he scrubbed, he talked, his deep-set watery eyes slowly brightening until it seemed he glowed with memory. I listened, and at one point Mama came to the door, peered in, and whispered something we both ignored. It was Saturday night so she left us alone, and Gramps and I sat there for the longest time I would ever spend with him.

This is how, that night, my gramps ended up telling me the story of the Pauper Princess and the Eucalyptus Jinn.

THE PRINCESS, GRAMPS said, was a woman in her twenties with a touch of silver in her hair. She was lean as a sorghum broomstick, face dark and plain, but her eyes glittered as she hummed the Qaseeda Burdah Shareef and swept the wooden counter in her tea shop with a dustcloth. She had a gold nose stud that, she told her customers, was a family heirloom. Each evening after she was done serving she folded her aluminum chairs, upended the stools on the plywood table, and took a break. She'd sit down by the trunk of the towering eucalyptus outside Bhati Gate, pluck out the stud, and shine it with a mint-water-soaked rag until it gleamed like an eye.

It was tradition, she said.

"If it's an heirloom, why do you wear it every day? What if you break it? What if someone sees it and decides to rob you?" Gramps asked her. He was about fourteen then and just that morning had gotten Juma pocket money and was feeling rich. He whistled as he sat sipping tea in the tree's shade and watched steel workers, potters, calligraphers, and laborers carry their work outside their foundries and shops, grateful for the winter-softened sky.

Princess Zeenat smiled and her teeth shone at him. "Nah ji. No one can steal from us. My family is protected by a jinn, you know."

This was something Gramps had heard before. A jinn protected the princess and her two sisters, a duty imposed by Akbar the Great five hundred years back. Guard and defend Mughal honor. Not a clichéd horned jinn, you understand, but a daunting, invisible entity that defied the laws of physics: it could slip in and out of time, could swap its senses, hear out of its nostrils, smell with its eyes. It could even fly like the tales of yore said.

Mostly amused but occasionally uneasy, Gramps laughed when the princess told these stories. He had never really questioned the reality of her existence; lots of nawabs and princes of pre-Partition India had offspring languishing in poverty these days. An impoverished Mughal princess was conceivable.

A custodian jinn, not so much.

Unconvinced thus, Gramps said:

"Where does he live?"

"What does he eat?"

And, "If he's invisible, how does one know he's real?"

The princess's answers came back practiced and surreal:

The jinn lived in the eucalyptus tree above the tea stall.

He ate angel-bread.

He was as real as jasmine-touched breeze, as shifting temperatures, as the many spells of weather that alternately lull and shake humans in their variegated fists.

"Have *you* seen him?" Gramps fired.

"Such questions." The Princess shook her head and laughed, her thick, long hair squirming out from under her chador. "Hai Allah, these kids." Still tittering, she sauntered off to her counter, leaving a disgruntled Gramps scratching his head.

The existential ramifications of such a creature's presence unsettled Gramps, but what could he do? Arguing about it was as useful as arguing about the wind jouncing the eucalyptus boughs. Especially when the neighborhood kids began to tell disturbing tales as well.

Of a gnarled bat-like creature that hung upside down from the warped branches, its shadow twined around the wicker chairs and table fronting the counter. If you looked up, you saw a bird nest – just another huddle of zoysia grass and bird feathers – but then you dropped your gaze and the creature's malignant reflection juddered and swam in the tea inside the chipped china.

"Foul face," said one boy. "Dark and ugly and wrinkled like a fruit."

"Sharp, crooked fangs," said another.

"No, no, he has razor blades planted in his jaws," said the first one quickly. "My cousin told me. That's how he flays the skin off little kids."

The description of the eucalyptus jinn varied seasonally. In summertime, his cheeks were scorched, his eyes red rimmed like the midday sun. Come winter, his lips were blue and his eyes misty, his touch cold like damp roots. On one thing everyone agreed: if he laid eyes on you, you were a goner.

The lean, mean older kids nodded and shook their heads wisely.

A goner.

The mystery continued this way, deliciously gossiped and fervently argued, until one summer day a child of ten with wild eyes and a snot-covered chin rushed into the tea stall, gabbling and crying, blood trickling from the gash in his temple. Despite several attempts by the princess and her customers, he wouldn't be induced to tell who or what had hurt him, but his older brother, who had followed the boy inside, face scrunched with delight, declared he had last been seen pissing at the bottom of the eucalyptus.

"The jinn. The jinn," all the kids cried in unison. "A victim of the jinn's malice."

"No. He fell out of the tree," a grownup said firmly. "The gash is from the fall."

"The boy's incurred the jinn's wrath," said the kids happily. "The jinn will flense the meat off his bones and crunch his marrow."

"Oh shut up," said Princess Zeenat, feeling the boy's cheeks, "the eucalyptus jinn doesn't harm innocents. He's a defender of honor and dignity," while all the time she fretted over the boy, dabbed at his forehead with a wet cloth, and poured him a hot cup of tea.

The princess's sisters emerged from the doorway of their two-room shack twenty paces from the tea stall. They peered in, two teenage girls in flour-caked dopattas and rose-printed shalwar kameez, and the younger one stifled a cry when the boy turned to her, eyes shiny and vacuous with delirium, and whispered, "He says the lightning trees are dying."

The princess gasped. The customers pressed in, awed and murmuring. An elderly man with betel-juice-stained teeth gripped the front of his own shirt with palsied hands and fanned his chest with it. "The jinn has overcome the child," he said, looking profoundly at the sky beyond the stall, and chomped his tobacco paan faster.

The boy shuddered. He closed his eyes, breathed erratically, and behind him the shadow of the tree fell long and clawing at the ground.

The lightning trees are dying. The lightning trees are dying.

So spread the nonsensical words through the neighborhood. Zipping from bamboo door-to-door; blazing through dark lovers' alleys; hopping from one beggar's gleeful tongue to another's, the prophecy became a proverb and the proverb a song.

A starving calligrapher-poet licked his reed quill and wrote an elegy for the lightning trees.

A courtesan from the Diamond Market sang it from her rooftop on a moonlit night.

Thus the walled city heard the story of the possessed boy and his curious proclamation and shivered with this message from realms unknown. Arthritic grandmothers and lithe young men rocked in their courtyards and lawns, nodding dreamily at the stars above, allowing themselves to remember secrets from childhood they hadn't dared remember before.

Meanwhile word reached local families that a child had gotten hurt climbing the eucalyptus. Angry fathers, most of them laborers and shopkeepers with kids who rarely went home before nightfall, came barging into the Municipality's lean-to, fists hammering on the sad-looking officer's table, demanding that the tree be chopped down.

"It's a menace," they said.

"It's hollow. Worm eaten."

"It's haunted!"

"Look, its gum's flammable and therefore a fire hazard," offered one versed in horticulture, "and the tree's a pest. What's a eucalyptus doing in the middle of a street anyway?"

So they argued and thundered until the officer came knocking at the princess's door. "The tree," said the sad-looking officer, twisting his squirrel-tail mustache, "needs to go."

"Over my dead body," said the princess. She threw down her polish rag and glared at the officer. "It was planted by my forefathers. It's a relic, it's history."

"It's a public menace. Look, bibi, we can do this the easy way or the hard way, but I'm telling you –"

"Try it. You just try it," cried the princess. "I will take this matter to the highest authorities. I'll go to the Supreme Court. That tree" – she jabbed a quivering finger at the monstrous thing – "gives us shade. A fakir told my grandfather never to move his business elsewhere. It's blessed, he said."

The sad-faced officer rolled up his sleeves. The princess eyed him with apprehension as he yanked one of her chairs back and lowered himself into it.

"Bibi," he said not unkindly, "let me tell you something. The eucalyptus was brought here by the British to cure India's salinity and flooding problems. Gora sahib hardly cared about our ecology." His mustache drooped from his thin lips. The strawberry mole on his chin quivered. "It's not indigenous, it's a pest. It's not a blessing, it repels other flora and fauna and guzzles groundwater by the tons. It's not ours," the officer said, not looking at the princess. "It's alien."

It was early afternoon and school hadn't broken yet. The truant Gramps sat in a corner sucking on a cigarette he'd found in the trash can outside his school and watched the princess. Why wasn't she telling the officer about the jinn? That the tree was its home? Her cheeks were puffed from clenching her jaws, the hollows under her eyes deeper and darker as she clapped a hand to her forehead.

"Look," she said, her voice rising and falling like the wind stirring the tear-shaped eucalyptus leaves, "you take the tree, you take our good luck. My shop is all I have. The tree protects it. It protects us. It's family."

"Nothing I can do." The officer scratched his birthmark. "Had there been no complaint... but now I have no choice. The Lahore Development Authority has been planning to remove the poplars and the eucalyptus for a while anyway. They want to bring back trees of Old Lahore. Neem, pipal, sukhchain, mulberry, mango. This foreigner" – he looked with distaste at the eucalyptus – "steals water from our land. It needs to go."

Shaking his head, the officer left. The princess lurched to her stall and began to prepare Rooh Afza. She poured a glittering parabola of sharbat into a mug with trembling hands, staggered to the tree, and flung the liquid at its hoary, clawing roots.

"There," she cried, her eyes reddened. "I can't save you. You must go."

Was she talking to the jinn? To the tree? Gramps felt his spine run cold as the blood-red libation sank into the ground, muddying the earth around the eucalyptus roots. Somewhere in the branches, a bird whistled.

The princess toed the roots for a moment longer, then trudged back to her counter.

Gramps left his teacup half-empty and went to the tree. He tilted his head to look at its top. It was so high. The branches squirmed and fled from the main trunk, reaching restlessly for the hot white clouds. A plump chukar with a crimson beak sat on a branch swaying gently. It stared back at Gramps, but no creature with razor-blade jaws and hollow dust-filled cheeks dangled from the tree.

As Gramps left, the shadows of the canopies and awnings of shops in the alley stretched toward the tree accusatorially.

That night Gramps dreamed of the eucalyptus jinn.

It was a red-snouted shape hurtling toward the heavens, its slipstream body glittering and dancing in the dark. Space and freedom rotated above it, but as it accelerated showers of golden meteors came bursting from the stars and slammed into it. The creature thinned and elongated until it looked like a reed pen trying to scribble a cryptic message between the stars, but the meteors wouldn't stop.

Drop back, you blasphemer, whispered the heavens. *You absconder, you vermin. The old world is gone. No place for your kind here now. Fall back and do your duty.*

And eventually the jinn gave up and let go.

It plummeted: a fluttering, helpless, enflamed ball shooting to the earth. It shrieked as it dove, flickering rapidly in and out of space and time but bound by their quantum fetters. It wanted to rage but couldn't. It wanted to save the lightning trees, to upchuck their tremulous shimmering roots and plant them somewhere the son of man wouldn't find them. Instead it was imprisoned, captured by prehuman magic and trapped to do time for a sin so old it had forgotten what it was.

So now it tumbled and plunged, hated and hating. It changed colors like a fiendish rainbow: mid-flame blue, muscle red, terror green, until the force of its fall bleached all its hues away and it became a pale scorching bolt of fire.

Thus the eucalyptus jinn fell to its inevitable dissolution, even as Gramps woke up, his heart pounding, eyes fogged and aching from the dream. He groped in the dark, found the lantern, and lit it. He was still shaking. He got up, went to his narrow window that looked out at the moon-drenched Bhati Gate a hundred yards away. The eight arches of the Mughal structure were black and lonely above the central arch. Gramps listened. Someone was moving in the shack next door. In the princess's home. He gazed at the mosque of Ghulam Rasool – a legendary mystic known as the Master of Cats – on its left.

And he looked at the eucalyptus tree.

It soared higher than the gate, its wild armature pawing at the night, the oily scent of its leaves potent even at this distance. Gramps shivered, although heat was swelling from the ground from the first patter of raindrops. More smells crept into the room: dust, trash, verdure.

He backed away from the window, slipped his sandals on, dashed out of the house. He ran toward the tea stall but, before he could as much as cross the chicken yard up front, lightning unzipped the dark and the sky roared.

THE BLAST OF its fall could be heard for miles.

The eucalyptus exploded into a thousand pieces, the burning limbs crackling and sputtering in the thunderstorm that followed. More lightning splintered the night sky. Children shrieked, dreaming of twisted corridors with shadows wending past one another. Adults moaned as timeless gulfs shrank and pulsed behind their eyelids. The walled city thrashed in sweat-soaked sheets until the mullah climbed the minaret and screamed his predawn call.

In the morning the smell of ash and eucalyptol hung around the crisped boughs. The princess sobbed as she gazed at her buckled tin roof and smashed stall. Shards of china, plywood, clay, and charred wicker twigs lay everywhere.

The laborers and steel workers rubbed their chins.

"Well, good riddance," said Alamdin the electrician, father of the injured boy whose possession had ultimately proved fleeting. Alamdin fingered a hole in his string vest. "Although I'm sorry for your loss, bibi. Perhaps the government will give you a monthly pension, being that you're royal descent and all."

Princess Zeenat's nose stud looked dull in the gray after-storm light. Her shirt was torn at the back, where a fragment of wood had bitten her as she scoured the wreckage.

"He was supposed to protect us," she murmured to the tree's remains: a black stump that poked from the earth like a singed umbilicus, and the roots lapping madly at her feet. "To give us shade and blessed sanctuary." Her grimed finger went for the nose stud and wrenched it out. "Instead –" She backpedaled and slumped at the foot of her shack's door. "Oh, my sisters. My sisters."

Tutting uncomfortably, the men drifted away, abandoning the pauper princess and her Mughal siblings. The women huddled together, a bevy of chukars stunned by a blood moon. Their shop was gone, the tree was gone. Princess Zeenat hugged her sisters and with a fierce light in her eyes whispered to them.

Over the next few days Gramps stood at Bhati Gate, watching the girls salvage timber, china, and clay. They washed and scrubbed their copper pots. Heaved out the tin sheet from the debris and dragged it to the foundries. Looped the remaining wicker into small bundles and sold it to basket weavers inside the walled city.

Gramps and a few past patrons offered to help. The Mughal women declined politely.

"But I can help, I really can," Gramps said, but the princess merely knitted her eyebrows, cocked her head, and stared at Gramps until he turned and fled.

The Municipality officer tapped at their door one Friday after Juma prayers.

"Condolences, bibi," he said. "My countless apologies. We should've cut it down before this happened."

"It's all right." The princess rolled the gold stud tied in a hemp necklace around her neck between two fingers. Her face was tired but tranquil. "It was going to happen one way or the other."

The officer picked at his red birthmark. "I meant your shop."

"We had good times here" – she nodded – "but my family's long overdue for a migration. We're going to go live with my cousin. He has an orange-and-fig farm in Mansehra. We'll find plenty to do."

The man ran his fingernail down the edge of her door. For the first time Gramps saw how his eyes never stayed on the princess. They drifted toward her face, then darted away as if the flush of her skin would sear them if they lingered. Warmth slipped around Gramps's neck, up his scalp, and across his face until his own flesh burned.

"Of course," the officer said. "Of course," and he turned and trudged to the skeletal stump. Already crows had marked the area with their pecking, busily creating a roost of the fallen tree. Soon they would be protected from horned owls and other birds of prey, they thought. But Gramps and Princess Zeenat knew better.

There was no protection here.

The officer cast one long look at the Mughal family, stepped around the stump, and walked away.

Later, the princess called to Gramps. He was sitting on the mosque's steps, shaking a brass bowl, pretending to be a beggar. He ran over, the coins jingling in his pocket.

"I know you saw something," she said once they were seated on the hemp charpoy in her shack. "I could see it in your face when you offered your help."

Gramps stared at her.

"That night," she persisted, "when the lightning hit the tree." She leaned forward, her fragrance of tea leaves and ash and cardamom filling his nostrils. "What did you see?"

"Nothing," he said and began to get up.

She grabbed his wrist. "Sit," she said. Her left hand shot out and pressed something into his palm. Gramps leapt off the charpoy. There was an electric sensation in his flesh; his hair crackled. He opened his fist and looked at the object.

It was her nose stud. The freshly polished gold shimmered in the dingy shack.

Gramps touched the stud with his other hand and withdrew it. "It's so cold."

The princess smiled, a bright thing that lit up the shack. Full of love, sorrow, and relief. But relief at what? Gramps sat back down, gripped the charpoy's posts, and tugged its torn hemp strands nervously.

"My family will be gone by tonight," the princess said.

And even though he'd been expecting this for days, it still came as a shock to Gramps. The imminence of her departure took his breath away. All he could do was wobble his head.

"Once we've left, the city might come to uproot that stump." The princess glanced over her shoulder toward the back of the room where shadows lingered. "If they try, do you promise you'll dig under it?" She rose and peered into the dimness, her eyes gleaming like jewels.

"Dig under the tree? Why?"

"Something lies there which, if you dig it up, you'll keep to yourself." Princess Zeenat swiveled on her heels. "Which you will hide in a safe place and never tell a soul about."

"Why?"

"Because that's what the fakir told my grandfather. Something old and secret rests under that tree and it's not for human eyes." She turned and walked to the door.

Gramps said, "Did you ever dig under it?"

She shook her head without looking back. "I didn't need to. As long as the tree stood, there was no need for me to excavate secrets not meant for me."

"And the gold stud? Why're you giving it away?"

"It comes with the burden."

"What burden? What *is* under that tree?"

The princess half turned. She stood in a nimbus of midday light, her long muscled arms hanging loosely, fingers playing with the place in the hemp necklace where once her family heirloom had been; and despite the worry lines and the callused hands and her uneven, grimy fingernails, she was beautiful.

Somewhere close, a brick truck unloaded its cargo and in its sudden thunder what the princess said was muffled and nearly inaudible. Gramps thought later it might have been, "The map to the memory of heaven."

But that of course couldn't be right.

"THE PRINCESS AND her family left Lahore that night," said Gramps. "This was in the fifties and the country was too busy recovering from Partition and picking up its own pieces to worry about a Mughal princess disappearing from the pages of history. So no one cared. Except me."

He sank back into the armchair and began to rock.

"She or her sisters ever come back?" I said, pushing myself off the floor with my knuckles. "What happened to them?"

Gramps shrugged. "What happens to all girls. Married their cousins in the north, I suppose. Had large families. They never returned to Lahore, see?"

"And the jinn?"

Gramps bent and poked his ankle with a finger. It left a shallow dimple. "I guess he died or flew away once the lightning felled the tree."

"What was under the stump?"

"How should I know?"

"What do you mean?"

"I didn't dig it up. No one came to remove the stump, so I never got a chance to take out whatever was there. Anyway, bache, you really should be going. It's late."

I glanced at my *Star Wars* watch. Luke's saber shone fluorescent across the Roman numeral two. I was impressed Mama hadn't returned to scold me to bed. I arched my back to ease the stiffness and looked at him with one eye closed. "You're seriously telling me you didn't dig up the secret?"

"I was scared," said Gramps, and gummed a fiber bar. "Look, I was told not to remove it if I didn't have to, so I didn't. Those days we listened to our elders, see?" He grinned, delighted with this unexpected opportunity to rebuke.

"But that's cheating," I cried. "The gold stud. The jinn's disappearance. You've explained nothing. That... that's not a good story at all. It just leaves more questions."

"All good stories leave questions. Now go on, get out of here. Before your mother yells at us both."

He rose and waved me toward the door, grimacing and rubbing his belly – heartburn from Hanif Uncle's party food? I slipped out and shut the door behind me. Already ghazal music was drifting out: *Ranjish hi sahih dil hi dukhanay ke liye aa.* Let it be heartbreak; come if just to hurt me again. I knew the song well. Gramps had worn out so many cassettes that Apna Bazaar ordered them in bulk just for him, Mama joked.

I went to my room, undressed, and for a long time tossed in the sheets, watching the moon outside my window. It was a supermoon kids at school had talked about, a magical golden egg floating near the horizon, and I wondered how many Mughal princes and princesses had gazed at it through the ages, holding hands with their lovers.

This is how the story of the Pauper Princess and the Eucalyptus Jinn comes to an end, I thought. In utter, infuriating oblivion.

I was wrong, of course.

In September 2013, Gramps had a sudden onset of chest pain and became short of breath. 911 was called, but by the time the medics came his heart had stopped and his extremities were mottled. Still they shocked him and injected him with epi-and-atropine and sped him to the hospital where he was pronounced dead on arrival.

Gramps had really needed those water pills he'd refused until the end.

I was at Tufts teaching a course in comparative mythology when Baba called. It was a difficult year. I'd been refused tenure and a close friend had been fired over department politics. But when Baba asked me if I could come, I said of course. Gramps and I hadn't talked in years after I graduated from Florida State and moved to Massachusetts, but it didn't matter. There would be a funeral and a burial and a reception for the smattering of relatives who lived within drivable distance. I, the only grandchild, must be there.

Sara wanted to go with me. It would be a good gesture, she said.

"No," I said. "It would be a terrible gesture. Baba might not say anything, but the last person he'd want at Gramps's funeral is my white girlfriend. Trust me."

Sara didn't let go of my hand. Her fingers weren't dainty like some women's -- you're afraid to squeeze them lest they shatter like glass – but they were soft and curled easily around mine. "You'll come back soon, won't you?"

"Of course. Why'd you ask?" I looked at her.

"Because," she said kindly, "you're going home." Her other hand plucked at a hair on my knuckle. She smiled, but there was a ghost of worry pinching the corner of her lips. "Because sometimes I can't read you."

We stood in the kitchenette facing each other. I touched Sara's chin. In the last few months there had been moments when things had been a bit hesitant, but nothing that jeopardized what we had.

"I'll be back," I said.

We hugged and kissed and whispered things I don't remember now. Eventually we parted and I flew to Florida, watching the morning landscape tilt through the plane windows. Below, the Charles gleamed like steel, then fell away until it was a silver twig in a hard land; and I thought, *The lightning trees are dying*.

Then we were past the waters and up and away, and the thought receded like the river.

We buried Gramps in Orlando Memorial Gardens under a row of pines. He was pale and stiff limbed, nostrils stuffed with cotton, the white shroud rippling in the breeze. I wished, like all fools rattled by late epiphanies, that I'd had more time with him. I said as much to Baba, who nodded.

"He would have liked that," Baba said. He stared at the gravestone with the epitaph *I have glimpsed the truth of the Great Unseen* that Gramps had insisted be written below his name. A verse from Rumi. "He would have liked that very much."

We stood in silence and I thought of Gramps and the stories he took with him that would stay untold forever. There's a funny thing about teaching myth and history: you realize in the deep of your bones that you'd be lucky to become a mote of dust, a speck on the bookshelf of human existence. The more tales you preserve, the more claims to immortality you can make.

After the burial we went home and Mama made us chicken karahi and basmati rice. It had been ages since I'd had home-cooked Pakistani food and the spice and garlicky taste knocked me back a bit. I downed half a bowl of fiery gravy and fled to Gramps's room where I'd been put up. Where smells of his cologne and musty clothes and his comings and goings still hung like a memory of old days.

In the following week Baba and I talked. More than we had in ages. He asked me about Sara with a glint in his eyes. I said we were still together. He grunted.

"Thousands of suitable Pakistani girls," he began to murmur, and Mama shushed him.

In Urdu half-butchered from years of disuse I told them about Tufts and New England. Boston Commons, the Freedom Trail with its dozen cemeteries and royal burial grounds, the extremities of weather; how fall spun gold and rubies and amethyst from its foliage. Baba listened, occasionally wincing, as he worked on a broken power drill from his toolbox. It had been six years since I'd seen him and Mama, and the reality of their aging was like a gut punch. Mama's hair was silver, but at least her skin retained a youthful glow.

Baba's fistful of beard was completely white, the hollows of his eyes deeper and darker. His fingers were swollen from rheumatoid arthritis he'd let fester for years because he couldn't afford insurance.

"You really need to see a doctor," I said.

"I have one. I go to the community health center in Leesburg, you know."

"Not a free clinic. You need to see a specialist."

"I'm fifty-nine. Six more years and then." He pressed the power button on the drill and it roared to life. "Things will change," he said cheerfully.

I didn't know what to say. I had offered to pay his bills before. The handyman's son wasn't exactly rich, but he was grown up now and could help his family out.

Baba would have none of it. I didn't like it, but what could I do? He had pushed me away for years. *Get out of here while you can*, he'd say. He marched me to college the same way he would march me to Sunday classes at Clermont Islamic Center. *Go on*, he said outside the mosque, as I clutched the siparas to my chest. *Memorize the Quran. If you don't, who will?*

Was that why I hadn't returned home until Gramps's death? Even then I knew there was more. Home was a morass where I would sink. I had tried one or two family holidays midway through college. They depressed me, my parents' stagnation, their world where nothing changed. The trailer park, its tired residents, the dead-leaf-strewn grounds that always seemed to get muddy and wet and never clean. A strange lethargy would settle on me here, a leaden feeling that left me cold and shaken. Visiting home became an ordeal filled with guilt at my indifference. I was new to the cutthroat world of academia then and bouncing from one adjunct position to another was taking up all my time anyway.

I stopped going back. It was easier to call, make promises, talk about how bright my prospects were in the big cities. And with Gramps even phone talk was useless. He couldn't hear me, and he wouldn't put on those damn hearing aids.

So now I was living thousands of miles away with a girl Baba had never met.

I suppose I must've been hurt at his refusal of my help. The next few days were a blur between helping Mama with cleaning out Gramps's room and keeping up with the assignments my undergrads were emailing me even though I was on leave. A trickle of relatives and friends came, but to my relief Baba took over the hosting duties and let me sort through the piles of journals and tomes Gramps had amassed.

It was an impressive collection. Dozens of Sufi texts and religious treatises in different languages: Arabic, Urdu, Farsi, Punjabi, Turkish. Margins covered with Gramps's neat handwriting. I didn't remember seeing so many books in his room when I used to live here.

I asked Baba. He nodded.

"Gramps collected most of these after you left." He smiled. "I suppose he missed you."

I showed him the books. "Didn't you say he was having memory trouble? I remember Mama being worried about him getting dementia last time I talked. How could he learn new languages?"

"I didn't know he knew half these languages. Urdu and Punjabi he spoke and read fluently, but the others –" He shrugged.

Curious, I went through a few line notes. Thoughtful speculation on ontological and existential questions posed by the mystic texts. These were not the ramblings of a senile mind. Was Gramps's forgetfulness mere aging? Or had he written most of these before he began losing his marbles?

"Well, he did have a few mini strokes," Mama said when I asked. "Sometimes he'd forget where he was. Talk about Lahore, and oddly, Mansehra. It's a small city in Northern Pakistan," she added when I raised an eyebrow. "Perhaps he had friends there when he was young."

I looked at the books, ran my finger along their spines. It would be fun, nostalgic, to go through them at leisure, read Rumi's couplets and Hafiz's *Diwan*. I resolved to take the books with me. Just rent a car and drive up north with my trunk rattling with a cardboard box full of Gramps's manuscripts.

Then one drizzling morning I found a yellowed, dog-eared notebook under an old rug in his closet. Gramps's journal.

BEFORE I LEFT Florida I went to Baba. He was crouched below the kitchen sink, twisting a long wrench back and forth between the pipes, grunting. I waited until he was done, looked him in the eye, and said, "Did Gramps ever mention a woman named Zeenat Begum?"

Baba tossed the wrench into the toolbox. "Isn't that the woman in the fairy tale he used to tell? The pauper Mughal princess?"

"Yes."

"Sure he mentioned her. About a million times."

"But not as someone *you* might have known in real life?"

"No."

Across the kitchen I watched the door of Gramps's room. It was firmly closed. Within hung the portrait of the brown-eyed woman in the orange dopatta with her knowing half smile. She had gazed down at my family for decades, offering us that mysterious silver cup. There was a lump in my throat but I couldn't tell if it was anger or sorrow.

Baba was watching me, his swollen fingers tapping at the corner of his mouth. "Are you all right?"

I smiled, feeling the artifice of it stretch my skin like a mask. "Have you ever been to Turkey?"

"Turkey?" He laughed. "Sure. Right after I won the lottery and took that magical tour in the Caribbean."

I ignored the jest. "Does the phrase 'Courtesan of the Mughals' mean anything to you?"

He seemed startled. A smile of such beauty lit up his face that he looked ten years younger. "Ya Allah, I haven't heard that in forty years. Where'd you read it?"

I shrugged.

"It's Lahore. My city. That's what they called it in those books I read as a kid. Because it went through so many royal hands." He laughed, eyes gleaming with delight and mischief, and lowered his voice. "My friend Habib used to call it *La-whore*. The Mughal hooker. Now for Allah's sake, don't go telling your mother on me." His gaze turned inward. "Habib. God, I haven't thought of him in ages."

"Baba." I gripped the edge of the kitchen table. "Why don't you ever go back to Pakistan?"

His smile disappeared. He turned around, slammed the lid of his toolbox, and hefted it up. "Don't have time."

"You spent your teenage years there, didn't you? You obviously have some attachment to the city. Why didn't you take us back for a visit?"

"What would we go back to? We have no family there. My old friends are probably dead." He carried the toolbox out into the October sun, sweat gleaming on his forearms. He placed it in the back of his battered truck and climbed into the driver's seat. "I'll see you later."

I looked at him turn the keys in the ignition with fingers that shook. He was off to hammer sparkling new shelves in other people's garages, replace squirrel-rent screens on their lanais, plant magnolias and palms in their golfing communities, and I could say nothing. I thought I understood why he didn't want to visit the town where he grew up.

I thought about Mansehra and Turkey. If Baba really didn't know and Gramps had perfected the deception by concealing the truth within a lie, there was nothing I could do that wouldn't change, and possibly wreck, my family.

All good stories leave questions, Gramps had said to me.

You bastard, I thought.

"Sure," I said and watched my baba pull out and drive away, leaving a plumage of dust in his wake.

I CALLED SARA when I got home. "Can I see you?" I said as soon as she picked up.

She smiled. I could hear her smile. "That bad, huh?"

"No, it was all right. I just really want to see you."

"It's one in the afternoon. I'm on campus." She paused. In the background birds chittered along with students. Probably the courtyard. "You sure you're okay?"

"Yes. Maybe." I upended the cardboard box on the carpet. The tower of books stood tall and uneven like a dwarf tree. "Come soon as you can, okay?"

"Sure. Love you."

"Love you too."

We hung up. I went to the bathroom and washed my face. I rubbed my eyes and stared at my reflection. It bared its teeth.

"Shut up," I whispered. "He was senile. Must have been completely insane. I don't believe a word of it."

But when Sara came that evening, her red hair streaming like fall leaves, her freckled cheeks dimpling when she saw me, I told her I believed, I really did. She sat and listened and stroked the back of my hand when it trembled as I lay in her lap and told her about Gramps and his journal.

It was an assortment of sketches and scribbling. A talented hand had drawn pastures, mountaintops, a walled city shown as a semicircle with half a dozen doors and hundreds of people bustling within, a farmhouse, and rows of fig and orange trees. Some of these were miniatures: images drawn as scenes witnessed by an omniscient eye above the landscape. Others were more conventional. All had one feature in common: a man and woman present in the center of the scenery going about the mundanities of their lives.

In one scene the man sat in a mosque's courtyard, performing ablution by the wudu tap. He wore a kurta and shalwar and Peshawari sandals. He was in his early twenties, lean, thickly bearded, with deep-set eyes that watched you impassively. In his hands he held a squalling baby whose tiny wrinkled fist was clenched around a stream of water from the tap. In the background a female face, familiar but older than I remembered, loomed over the courtyard wall, smiling at the pair.

The man was unmistakably Gramps, and the woman...

"Are you kidding me?" Sara leaned over and stared at the picture. "That's the woman in the portrait hanging in his room?"

"He lied to me. To us all. She was my grandma."

"Who *is* she?"

"Princess Zeenat Begum," I said quietly.

Gramps had narrated the story of his life in a series of sketches and notes. The writing was in third person, but it was clear that the protagonist was he.

I imagined him going about the daily rituals of his life in Lahore after Princess Zeenat left. Dropping out of school, going to his father's shop in the Niche of Calligraphers near Bhati Gate, learning the art of khattati, painting billboards in red and yellow, fusing the ancient art with new slogans and advertisements. Now he's a lanky brown teenager wetting the tip of his brush, pausing to look up into the sky with its sweeping blue secrets. Now he's a tall man, yanking bird feathers and cobwebs away from a eucalyptus stump, digging under it in the deep of the night with a flashlight in his hand.

And now – he's wiping his tears, filling his knapsack with necessaries, burying his newly discovered treasure under a scatter of clothes, hitching the bag up his shoulders, and heading out into the vast unseen. All this time, there's only one image in his head and one desire.

"He was smitten with her. Probably had been for a long time without knowing it," I said. "Ruthlessly marked. His youth never had a chance against the siren call of history."

"Hold on a sec. What was under the tree again?" Sara said.

I shook my head. "He doesn't say."

"So he lied again? About not digging it up?"

"Yes."

"Who was he looking for?"

I looked at her. "My grandmother and her sisters."

We read his notes and envisioned Gramps's journey. Abandoning his own family, wandering his way into the mountains, asking everyone he met about a fig-and-orange farm on a quiet fir-covered peak in the heart of Mansehra. He was magnetized to the displaced Mughal family not because of their royalty, but the lack thereof.

And eventually he found them.

"He stayed with them for years, helping the pauper princess's uncle with farm work. In the summer he calligraphed Quranic verses on the minarets of local mosques. In wintertime he drew portraits for tourists and painted road signs. As years passed, he married Zeenat Begum – whose portrait one summer evening he drew and painted, carried with him, and lied about – and became one of them."

I looked up at Sara, into her gentle green eyes glittering above me. She bent and kissed my nose.

"They were happy for a while, he and his new family," I said, "but then, like in so many lives, tragedy came knocking at their door."

Eyes closed, I pictured the fire: a glowering creature clawing at their windows and door, crisping their apples, billowing flames across the barn to set their hay bales ablaze. The whinnying of the horses, the frantic braying of cattle and, buried in the din, human screams.

"All three Mughal women died that night," I murmured. "Gramps and his two-year-old son were the only survivors of the brushfire. Broken and bereft, Gramps left Mansehra with the infant and went to Karachi. There he boarded a freighter that took them to Iran, then Turkey, where a sympathetic shopkeeper hired him in his rug shop. Gramps and his son stayed there for four years."

What a strange life, I thought. I hadn't known my father had spent part of his childhood in Turkey and apparently neither had he. He remembered nothing. How old was he when they moved back? As I thought this, my heart constricted in my chest, filling my brain with the hum of my blood.

Sara's face was unreadable when I opened my eyes. "Quite a story, eh?" I said uneasily.

She scratched the groove above her lips with a pink fingernail. "So he digs up whatever was under the tree and it decides him. He leaves everything and goes off to marry a stranger. This is romantic bullshit. You know that, right?"

"I don't know anything."

"Left everything," she repeated. Her mouth was parted with wonder. "You think whatever he found under the stump survived the fire?"

"Presumably. But where he took it – who can say? Eventually, though, they returned home. To Lahore, when Gramps had recovered enough sanity, I guess. Where his father, now old, had closed shop. Gramps helped him reopen. Together they ran that design stall for years."

It must have been a strange time for Gramps, I thought. He loved his parents, but he hated Bhati. Even as he dipped his pen in ink and drew spirals and curlicues, his thoughts drew phantom pictures of those he had lost. Over the years, he came to loathe this art that unlocked so many memories inside him. And after his parents died he had neither heart nor imperative to keep going.

"He was done with the place, the shop, and Lahore. So when a friend offered to help him and his teenage son move to the States, Gramps agreed."

I turned my head and burrowed into Sara's lap. Her smell filled my brain: apple blossom, lipstick, and Sara.

She nuzzled my neck. The tip of her nose was cold. "He never talked to you about it? Never said what happened?"

"No."

"And you and your family had no idea about this artistic side of him? How's that possible?"

"Don't know," I said. "He worked at a 7-Eleven in Houston when he and Baba first came here. Never did any painting or calligraphy, commissioned or otherwise. Maybe he just left all his talent, all his dreams in his hometown. Here, look at this."

I showed her the phrase that spiraled across the edges of a couple dozen pages: *My killer, my deceiver, the Courtesan of the Mughals*. "It's Lahore. He's talking about the city betraying him."

"How's that?"

I shrugged.

"How weird," Sara said. "Interesting how broken up his story is. As if he's trying to piece together his own life."

"Maybe that's what he was doing. Maybe he forced himself to forget the most painful parts."

"Lightning trees. Odd thing to say." She looked at me thoughtfully and put the journal away. "So, you're the last of the Mughals, huh?" She smiled to show she wasn't laughing.

I chortled for her. "Seems like it. The Pauper Prince of New England."

"Wow. You come with a certificate of authenticity?" She nudged her foot at the book tower. "Is it in there somewhere?"

It was getting late. Sara tugged at my shirt, and I got up and carried her to bed, where we celebrated my return with zest. Her face was beautiful in the snow shadows that crept in through the window.

"I love you, I love you," we murmured, enchanted with each other, drunk with belief in some form of eternity. The dark lay quietly beside us, and, smoldering in its heart, a rotating image.

A dim idea of what was to come.

I WENT THROUGH Gramps's notes. Many were in old Urdu, raikhta, which I wasn't proficient in. But I got the gist: discourses and rumination on the otherworldly.

Gramps was especially obsessed with Ibn Arabi's treatise on jinns in *The Meccan Revelations*. The Lofty Master Arabi says, wrote Gramps, that the meaning of the lexical root J-N-N in Arabic is 'concealed.' Jinn isn't just another created being ontologically placed between man and angel; it is the *entirety* of the hidden world.

"Isn't that fucking crazy?" I said to Sara. We were watching a rerun of *Finding Neverland*, my knuckles caked with butter and flakes of popcorn. On the screen J. M. Barrie's wife was beginning to be upset by the attention he lavished upon the children's mother, Sylvia. "It kills the traditional narrative of jinns in *A Thousand and One Nights*. If one were to pursue this train of thought, it would mean relearning the symbolism in this text and virtually all others."

Sara nodded, her gaze fixed on the TV. "Uh huh."

"Consider this passage: 'A thousand years before Darwin, Sufis described the evolution of man as rising from the inorganic state through plant and animal to human. But the mineral consciousness of man, that dim memory of being buried in the great stone mother, lives on.'"

Sara popped a handful of popcorn into her mouth. Munched.

I rubbed my hands together. "'Jinns are carriers of that concealed memory, much like a firefly carries a memory of the primordial fire.' It's the oddest interpretation of jinns I've seen."

"Yeah, it's great." Sara shifted on the couch. "But can we please watch the movie?"

"Uh-huh."

I stared at the TV. Gramps thought jinns weren't devil-horned creatures bound to a lamp or, for that matter, a tree.

They were flickers of cosmic consciousness.

I couldn't get that image out of my head. Why was Gramps obsessed with this? How was this related to his life in Lahore? Something to do with the eucalyptus secret?

The next morning I went to Widener Library and dug up all I could about Arabi's and Ibn Taymeeyah's treatment of jinns. I read and pondered, went back to Gramps's notebooks, underlined passages in *The Meccan Revelations*, and walked the campus with my hands in my pockets and my heart in a world long dissipated.

"Arabi's cosmovision is staggering," I told Sara. We were sitting in a coffee shop downtown during lunch break. It was drizzling, just a gentle stutter of gray upon gray outside the window, but it made the brick buildings blush.

Sara sipped her mocha and glanced at her watch. She had to leave soon for her class.

"Consider life as a spark of consciousness. In Islamic cosmology the jinn's intrinsic nature is that of wind and fire. Adam's – read, man's – nature is water and clay, which are more resistant than fire to cold and dryness. As the universe changes, so do the requirements for life's vehicle. Now it needs creatures more resistant and better adapted. Therefore, *from the needs of sentient matter rose the invention that is us.*"

I clenched my hand into a fist. "This interpretation is pretty fucking genius. I mean, is it possible Gramps was doing real academic work? For example, had he discovered something in those textbooks that could potentially produce a whole new ideology of creation? Why, it could be the scholarly discovery of the century."

"Yes, it's great." She rapped her spoon against the edge of the table. Glanced at me, looked away.

"What?"

"Nothing. Listen, I gotta run, okay?" She gave me a quick peck on the cheek and slid out of her seat. At the door she hesitated, turned, and stood tapping her shoes, a waiting look in her eyes.

I dabbed pastry crumbs off my lips with a napkin. "Are you okay?"

Annoyance flashed in her face and vanished. "Never better." She pulled her jacket's hood over her head, yanked the door open, and strode out into the rain.

It wasn't until later that evening, when I was finalizing the spring calendar for my freshman class, that I realized I had forgotten our first-date anniversary.

Sara hadn't. There was a heart-shaped box with a pink bow sitting on the bed when I returned home. Inside was a note laying atop a box of Godiva Chocolates:

Happy Anniversary. May our next one be like your grandfather's fairy tales.

MY EYES BURNED with lack of sleep. It was one in the morning and I'd had a long day at the university. Also, the hour-long apology to Sara had drained me. She had shaken her head and tried to laugh it off, but I took my time, deeming it a wise investment for the future.

I went to the kitchen and poured myself a glass of ice water. Kicked off my slippers, returned to the desk, and continued reading.

I hadn't lied to Sara. The implications of this new jinn mythology were tremendous. A new origin myth, a bastardized version of the Abrahamic creationist lore. Trouble was these conclusions were tenuous. Gramps had speculated more than logically derived them. Arabi himself had touched on these themes in an abstract manner. To produce a viable theory of this alternate history of the universe, I needed more details, more sources.

Suppose there were other papers, hidden manuscripts. Was it possible that the treasure Gramps had found under the eucalyptus stump was truly 'the map to the memory of heaven'? Ancient papers of cosmological importance never discovered?

"Shit, Gramps. Where'd you hide them?" I murmured.

His journal said he'd spent quite a bit of time in different places: Mansehra, Iran. Turkey, where he spent four years in a rug shop. The papers could really be anywhere.

My eyes were drawn to the phrase again: the Courtesan of the Mughals. I admired how beautiful the form and composition of the calligraphy was. Gramps had shaped the Urdu alphabet carefully into a flat design so that the conjoined words *Mughal* and *Courtesan* turned into an ornate rug. A calligram. The curves of the meem and ghain letters became the tassels and borders of the rug, the laam's seductive curvature its rippling belly.

Such artistry. One shape discloses another. A secret, symbolic relationship.

There, I thought. The secret hides in the city. The clues to the riddle of the eucalyptus treasure are in Lahore.

I spent the next few days sorting out my finances. Once I was satisfied that the trip was feasible, I began to make arrangements.

Sara stared at me when I told her. "Lahore? You're going to Lahore?"

"Yes."

"To look for something your grandpa may or may not have left there fifty-some years ago?"

"Yes."

"You're crazy. I mean it's one thing to talk about a journal."

"I know. I still need to go."

"So you're telling me, not asking. Why? Why are you so fixed on this? You know that country isn't safe these days. What if something happens?" She crossed her arms, lifted her feet off the floor, and tucked them under her on the couch. She was shivering a little.

"Nothing's gonna happen. Look, whatever he left in Lahore, he wanted me to see it. Why else write about it and leave it in his journal which he knew would be found one day? Don't you see? He was really writing to me."

"Well, that sounds self-important. Why not your dad? Also, why drop hints then? Why not just tell you straight up what it is?"

"I don't know." I shrugged. "Maybe he didn't want other people to find out."

"Or maybe he was senile. Look, I'm sorry, but this is crazy. You can't just fly off to the end of the world on a whim to look for a relic." She rubbed her legs. "It could take you weeks. Months. How much vacation time do you have left?"

"I'll take unpaid leave if I have to. Don't you see? I need to do this."

She opened her mouth, closed it. "Is this something you plan to keep doing?" she said quietly. "Run off each time anything bothers you."

"What?" I quirked my eyebrows. "Nothing's bothering me."

"No?" She jumped up from the couch and glared at me. "You've met my mother and Fanny, but I've never met your parents. You didn't take me to your grandfather's funeral. And since your return you don't seem interested in what we have, or once had. Are you *trying* to avoid talking about us? Are we still in love, Sal, or are we just getting by? Are we really together?"

"Of course we're together. Don't be ridiculous," I mumbled, but there was a constriction in my stomach. It wouldn't let me meet her eyes.

"Don't patronize me. You're obsessed with your own little world. Look, I have no problem with you giving time to your folks. Or your gramps's work. But we've been together for three years and you still find excuses to steer me away from your family. This cultural thing that you claim to resent, you seem almost proud of it. Do you see what I mean?"

"No." I was beginning to get a bit angry. "And I'm not sure you do either."

"You're lying. You know what I'm talking about."

"Do I? Okay, lemme try to explain what my problem is. Look at me, Sara. What do you see?"

She stared at me, shook her head. "I see a man who doesn't know he's lost."

"Wrong. You see a twenty-eight-year-old brown man living in a shitty apartment, doing a shitty job that doesn't pay much and has no hope of tenure. You see a man who can't fend for himself, let alone a wife and kids –"

"No one's asking you to –"

"– if he doesn't do something better with his life. But you go on believing all will be well if we trade families? Open your damn eyes." I leaned against the TV cabinet, suddenly tired. "All my life I was prudent. I planned and planned and gave up one thing for another. Moved here. Never looked back. Did whatever I could to be what I thought I needed to be. The archetypal fucking immigrant in the land of opportunities. But after Gramps died..." I closed my eyes, breathed, opened them. "I realize some things are worth more than that. Some things are worth going after."

"Some things, huh?" Sara half smiled, a trembling flicker that took me aback more than her words did. "Didn't your grandfather give up everything – his life, his family, his country – for love? And you're giving up... love for... what exactly? Shame? Guilt? Identity? A fucking manventure in a foreign land?"

"You're wrong," I said. "I'm not –"

But she wasn't listening. Her chest hitched. Sara turned, walked into the bedroom, and gently closed the door, leaving me standing alone.

I STOMPED DOWN Highland Avenue. It was mid-October and the oaks and silver maples were burning with fall. They blazed yellow and crimson. They made me feel sadder and angrier and more confused.

Had our life together always been this fragile? I wondered if I had missed clues that Sara felt this way. She always was more aware of bumps in our relationship. I recalled watching her seated at the desk marking student papers once, her beautiful, freckled face scrunched in a frown, and thinking she would never really be welcome in my parents' house. Mama would smile nervously if I brought her home and retreat into the kitchen. Baba wouldn't say a word and somehow that would be worse than an outraged rejection. And what would Gramps have done? I didn't know. My head was messed up. It had been since his death.

It was dusk when I returned home, the lights in our neighborhood floating dreamily like gold sequins in black velvet.

Sara wasn't there.

The bed was made, the empty hangers in the closet pushed neatly together. On the coffee table in the living room under a Valentine mug was yet another note. She had become adept at writing me love letters.

I made myself a sandwich, sat in the dark, and picked at the bread. When I had mustered enough courage, I retrieved the note and began to read:

Salman,

I ~~wrote~~ tried to write this several times and each time my hand shook and made me write things I didn't want to. It sucks that we're such damn weaklings, the both of us. I'm stuck in love with you and you ~~are~~ with me. At least I hope so. At least that's the way I ~~feel~~ read you. But then I think about my mother and my heart begins racing.

You've met my family. Mom likes you. Fanny too. They think you're good for me. But you've never met my dad. You don't know why we ~~never~~ don't talk about him anymore.

He left Mom when Fanny and I were young. I don't remember him, although sometimes I think I can. When I close my eyes, I see this big, bulky shadow overwhelm the doorway of my room. There's this bittersweet smell: gin and sweat and tobacco. I remember not feeling afraid of him, for which I'm grateful.

But Dad left ~~us~~ Mom and he broke her. In especially bitter moments she would say it was another woman, but I don't think so. At least I never saw any proof of that in my mother's eyes when she talked about him. (In the beginning she talked a LOT about him.) I think he left her because he wanted more from life and Mom didn't ~~understand~~ pick that up. I think she didn't read his unhappiness in time. That's the vibe I get.

Does that excuse what he did? I don't think so. My mother's spent all her life trying to put us back together and she's done okay, but there are pieces of herself she wasn't able to find. In either me, or Fanny, or in anyone else.

~~I don't want that to happen to me.~~ I don't want to end up like my mother. That's pretty much it. If you didn't love me, I'd understand. I'd be hurt, but I could live with it. But living with this uncertainty, never knowing when you might get that wanderlust I've seen in your eyes lately, is impossible for me. There's so much I want to say to you. Things you need to know if we're to have a future together. But the last thing I want to do is force you.

So I'm leaving. I'm going to stay at Fanny's. Think things through. It will be good for both of us. It will help me get my head straight and will let you do whatever you want to get your fucking demons out. So fly free. Go to Pakistan. Follow your goddamn heart or whatever. Just remember I won't wait all my life.

You know where to find me.

Love,

Sara

I put down the letter and stared out the window. Night rain drummed on the glass. I tapped my finger to its tune, fascinated by how difficult it was to keep time with it. A weight had settled on my chest and I couldn't push it off.

If an asshole weeps in the forest and no one is around to witness, is he still an asshole?

Nobody was there to answer.

FOR MOST OF the fifteen-hour flight from New York to Lahore I was out. I hadn't realized how tired I was until I slumped into the economy seat and woke up half-dazed when the flight attendant gently shook my shoulder.

"Lahore, sir." She smiled when I continued to stare at her. The lipstick smudge on her teeth glistened. "Allama Iqbal International Airport."

"Yes," I said, struggling up and out. The plane was empty, the seats gaping. "How's the weather?"

"Cold. Bit misty. Fog bank's coming, they said. Early this year."

That didn't sound promising. I thanked her and hurried out, my carry-on clattering against the aisle armrests.

I exited the airport into the arms of a mid-November day and the air was fresh but full of teeth. The pale sea-glass sky seemed to wrap around the airport. I hailed a cab and asked for Bhati Gate. As we sped out of the terminal, whiteness seethed on the runway and blanketed the horizon. The flight attendant was right. Fog was on the way.

At a busy traffic signal the cabbie took a right. Past army barracks, the redbrick Aitchison College, and colonial-era Jinnah Gardens we went, until the roads narrowed and we hiccuped through a sea of motorbikes, rickshaws, cars, and pedestrians. *TERRORISTS ARE ENEMIES OF PEACE*, said a large black placard on a wall that jutted out left of a fifty-foot high stone gate. The looming structure had a massive central arch with eight small arches above it. It had a painting of the Kaaba on the right and Prophet Muhammad's shrine on the left with vermilion roses embossed in the middle. Another sign hung near it: *WELCOME TO OLD LAHORE BY THE GRACE OF ALLAH.*

We were at Bhati Gate.

The cab rolled to a stop in front of Kashi Manzil. A tall, narrow historical-home-turned-hotel with a facade made of ochre and azure faience tiles. A wide terrace ran around the second floor and a small black copper pot hung from a nail on the edge of the doorway awning.

I recognized the superstition. Black to ward off black. Protection against the evil eye.

Welcome to Gramps's world, I thought.

I looked down the street. Roadside bakeries, paan-and-cigarette shops, pirated DVD stalls, a girls' school with peeling walls, and dust, dust everywhere; but my gaze of course went to Bhati and its double row of arches.

This was the place my grandfather had once gazed at, lived by, walked through. Somewhere around here used to be a tea stall run by a Mughal princess. Someplace close had been a eucalyptus from which a kid had fallen and gashed his head. A secret that had traveled the globe had come here with Gramps and awaited me in some dingy old alcove.

That stupid wanderlust in your eyes.

Sara's voice in my brain was a gentle rebuke.

Later, I thought fiercely. *Later.*

THE NEXT DAY I began my search.

I had planned to start with the tea stalls. Places like this have long memories. Old Lahore was more or less the city's ancient downtown and people here wouldn't forget much. Least of all a Mughal princess who ran a tea shop. Gramps's journal didn't much touch on his life in the walled city. I certainly couldn't discern any clues about the location of the eucalyptus treasure.

Where did you hide it, old man? Your shack? A friend's place? Under that fucking tree stump?

If Gramps was correct and the tree had fallen half a century ago, that landmark was probably irretrievable. Gramps's house seemed the next logical place. Trouble was I didn't know where Gramps had lived. Before I left, I'd called Baba and asked him. He wasn't helpful.

"It's been a long time, son. Fifty years. Don't tax an old man's memory. You'll make me senile."

When I pressed, he reluctantly gave me the street where they used to live and his childhood friend Habib's last name.

"I don't remember our address, but I remember the street. Ask anyone in Hakiman Bazaar for Khajoor Gali. They'll know it."

Encircled by a wall raised by Akbar the Great, Old Lahore was bustling and dense. Two hundred thousand people lived in an area less than one square mile. Breezes drunk with the odor of cardamom, grease, and tobacco. The place boggled my mind as I strolled around taking in the niche pharmacies, foundries, rug shops, kite shops, and baked mud eateries.

I talked to everyone I encountered. The tea stall owner who poured Peshawari kahva in my clay cup. The fruit seller who handed me sliced oranges and guavas and frowned when I mentioned the pauper princess. Rug merchants, cigarette vendors, knife sellers. No one had heard of Zeenat Begum. Nobody knew of a young man named Sharif or his father who ran a calligraphy-and-design stall.

"Not around my shop, sahib." They shook their heads and turned away.

I located Khajoor Gali – a winding narrow alley once dotted by palm trees (or so the locals claimed) now home to dusty ramshackle buildings hunched behind open manholes – and went door to door, asking. No luck. An aged man with henna-dyed hair and a shishamwood cane stared at me when I mentioned Baba's friend Habib Ataywala, and said, "Habib. Ah, he and his family moved to Karachi several years ago. No one knows where."

"How about a eucalyptus tree?" I asked. "An ancient eucalyptus that used to stand next to Bhati Gate?"

Nope.

Listlessly I wandered, gazing at the mist lifting off the edges of the streets and billowing toward me. On the third day it was like slicing through a hundred rippling white shrouds. As night fell and fairy lights blinked on the minarets of Lahore's patron saint Data Sahib's shrine across the road from Bhati, I felt displaced. Depersonalized. I was a mote drifting in a slat of light surrounded by endless dark. Gramps was correct. Old Lahore had betrayed him. It was as if the city had deliberately rescinded all memory or trace of his family and the princess's. Sara was right. Coming here was a mistake. My life since Gramps's death was a mistake. Seeing this world as it *was* rather than through the fabular lens of Gramps's stories was fucking enlightening.

In this fog, the city's fresh anemia, I thought of things I hadn't thought about in years. The time Gramps taught me to perform the salat. The first time he brought my palms together to form the supplicant's cup. *Be the beggar at Allah's door*, he told me gently. *He loves humility. It's in the mendicant's bowl that the secrets of Self are revealed.* In the tashahuud position Gramps's index finger would shoot from a clenched fist and flutter up and down.

"This is how we beat the devil on the head," he said.

But what devil was I trying to beat? I'd been following a ghost and hoping for recognition from the living.

By the fifth day I'd made up my mind. I sat shivering on a wooden bench and watched my breath flute its way across Khajoor Gali as my finger tapped my cell phone and thousands of miles away Sara's phone rang.

She picked up almost immediately. Her voice was wary. "Sal?"

"Hey."

"Are you all right?"

"Yes."

A pause. "You didn't call before you left."

"I thought you didn't want me to."

"I was worried sick. One call after you landed would've been nice."

I was surprised but pleased. After so much disappointment, her concern was welcome. "Sorry."

"Jesus. I was..." She trailed off, her breath harsh and rapid in my ear. "Find the magic treasure yet?"

"No."

"Pity." She seemed distracted now. In the background water was running. "How long will you stay there?"

"I honest to God don't know, but I'll tell you this. I'm fucking exhausted."

"I'm sorry." She didn't sound sorry. I smiled a little.

"Must be around five in the morning there. Why're you up?" I said.

"I was... worried, I guess. Couldn't sleep. Bad dreams." She sighed. I imagined her rubbing her neck, her long fingers curling around the muscles, kneading them, and I wanted to touch her.

"I miss you," I said.

Pause. "Yeah. Me too. It's a mystery how much I'm used to you being around. And now that..." She stopped and exhaled. "Never mind."

"What?"

"Nothing." She grunted. "This damn weather. I think I'm coming down with something. Been headachy all day."

"Are you okay?"

"Yeah. It'll go away. Listen, I'm gonna go take a shower. You have fun."

Was that reproach? "Yeah, you too. Be safe."

"Sure." She sounded as if she were pondering. "Hey, I discovered something. Been meaning to tell you, but... you know."

"I'm all ears."

"Remember what your gramps said in the story. Lightning trees?"

"Yes."

"Well, lemme text it to you. I mentioned the term to a friend at school and turned out he recognized it too. From a lecture we both attended at MIT years ago about fractal similarities and diffusion-limited aggregation."

"Fractal what?" My phone beeped. I removed it from my ear and looked at the screen. A high-definition picture of a man with what looked like a tree-shaped henna tattoo on his left shoulder branching all the way down his arm. Pretty.

I put her on speakerphone. "Why're you sending me pictures of henna tattoos?"

She was quiet, then started laughing. "That didn't even occur to me, but, yeah, it does look like henna art."

"It isn't?"

"Nope. What you're seeing is a Lichtenberg figure created when branching electrical charges run through insulating material. Glass, resin, human skin – you name it. This man was hit by lightning and survived with this stamped on his flesh."

"What?"

"Yup. It can be created in any modern lab using nonconducting plates. Called electric treeing. Or lightning trees."

The lightning trees are dying.

"Holy shit," I said softly.

"Yup."

I tapped the touch screen to zoom in for a closer look. "How could Gramps know about this? If he made up the stories, how the fuck would he know something like this?"

"No idea. Maybe he knew someone who had this happen to them."

"But what does it mean?"

"The heck should I know. Anyways, I gotta go. Figured it might help you with whatever you're looking for."

"Thanks."

She hung up. I stared at the pattern on the man's arm. It was reddish, fernlike, and quite detailed. The illusion was so perfect I could even see buds and leaves. A breathtaking electric foliage. A map of lightning.

A memory of heaven.

I WENT TO sleep early that night.

At five in the morning the Fajar call to prayer woke me up. I lay in bed watching fog drift through the skylight window, listening to the mullah's sonorous azaan, and suddenly I jolted upright.

The mosque of Ghulam Rasool, the Master of Cats.

Wasn't that what Gramps had told me a million years ago? That there was a mosque near Bhati Gate that faced his house?

I hadn't seen *any* mosques around.

I slipped on clothes and ran outside.

The morning smelled like burnished metal. The light was soft, the shape of early risers gentle in the mist-draped streets. A rooster crowed in the next alley. It had drizzled the night before and the ground was muddy. I half slipped, half leapt my way toward the mullah's voice rising and falling like an ocean heard in one's dream.

Wisps of white drifted around me like twilit angels. The azaan had stopped. I stared at the narrow doorway next to a rug merchant's shop ten feet away. Its entrance nearly hidden by an apple tree growing in the middle of the sidewalk, the place was tucked well away from traffic. Green light spilled from it. Tiny replicas of the Prophet's Mosque in Medina and Rumi's shrine in Turkey were painted above the door.

Who would put Rumi here when Data Sahib's shrine was just across the road?

I took off my shoes and entered the mosque.

A tiny room with a low ceiling set with zero-watt green bulbs. On reed mats the congregation stood shoulder to shoulder in two rows behind a smallish man in shalwar kameez and a turban. The Imam sahib clicked the mute button on the standing microphone in front, touched his earlobes, and Fajar began.

Feeling oddly guilty, I sat down in a corner. Looked around the room. Ninety-nine names of Allah and Muhammad, prayers and Quranic verses belching from the corners, twisting and pirouetting across the walls. Calligrams in the shape of a mynah bird, a charging lion, a man prostrate in sajdah, his hands out before him shaping a beggar's bowl filled with alphabet vapors. Gorgeous work.

Salat was over. The namazis began to leave. Imam sahib turned. In his hands he held a tally counter for tasbih. *Click click!* Murmuring prayers, he rose and hobbled toward me.

"Assalam-o-alaikum. May I help you, son?" he said in Urdu.

"Wa Laikum Assalam. Yes," I said. "Is this Masjid Ghulam Rasool?"

He shook his head. He was in his seventies at least, long noorani beard, white hair sticking out of his ears. His paunch bulged through the striped-flannel kameez flowing past his ankles. "No. That mosque was closed and martyred in the nineties. Sectarian attacks. Left a dozen men dead. Shia mosque, you know. Used to stand in Khajoor Gali, I believe."

"Oh." I told myself I'd been expecting this, but my voice was heavy with disappointment. "I'm sorry to bother you then. I'll leave you to finish up."

"You're not local, son. Your salam has an accent," he said. "Amreekan, I think. You look troubled. How can I help you?" He looked at me, took his turban off. He had a pale scar near his left temple shaped like a climbing vine.

I watched him. His hair was silver. His sharp eyes were blue, submerged in a sea of wrinkles. "I was looking for a house. My late grandfather's. He lived close to the mosque, next door to a lady named Zeenat Begum. She used to run a tea stall."

"Zeenat Begum." His eyes narrowed, the blues receding into shadow. "And your grandfather's name?" he asked, watching the last of the worshippers rise to his feet.

"Sharif. Muhammad Sharif."

The oddest feeling, a sort of déjà vu, came over me. Something had changed in the air of the room. Even the last namazi felt it and glanced over his shoulder on his way out.

"Who did you say you were again?" Imam sahib said quietly.

"Salman Ali Zaidi."

"I see. Yes, I do believe I can help you out. This way."

He turned around, limping, and beckoned me to follow. We exited the mosque. He padlocked it, parted the bead curtain in the doorway of the rug shop next door, stepped in.

When I hesitated, he paused, the tasbih counter clicking in his hands. "Come in, son. My place is your place."

I studied the rug shop. It was located between the mosque and a souvenir stall. The awning above the arched doorway was gray, the brick voussoirs and keystone of the arch faded and peeling. The plaque by the entrance said Karavan Kilim.

Kilim is a kind of Turkish carpet. What was a kilim shop doing in Old Lahore?

He led me through a narrow well-lit corridor into a hardwood-floored showroom. Mounds of neatly folded rugs sat next to walls covered in rectangles of rich tapestries, carpets, and pottery-filled shelves. Stunning illustrations and calligraphy swirled across the high wooden ceiling. Here an entranced dervish whirled in blue, one palm toward the sky and one to the ground. There a crowd haloed with golden light held out dozens of drinking goblets, an Urdu inscription spiraling into a vast cloud above their heads: *They hear his hidden hand pour truth in the heavens.*

A bald middle-aged man dressed in a checkered brown half-sleeve shirt sat behind a desk. Imam Sahib nodded at him. "My nephew Khalid."

Khalid and I exchanged pleasantries. Imam sahib placed the tasbih counter and his turban on the desk. I gazed around me. "Imam sahib," I said. "This is a Turkish carpet shop. You run an imported rug business in your spare time?"

"Turkish design, yes, but not imported. My apprentices make them right here in the walled city." Without looking back, he began walking. "You can call me Bashir."

We went to the back of the shop, weaving our way through rug piles into a storeroom lit by sunlight from a narrow window. Filled to the ceiling with mountains of fabric rolls and broken looms, the room smelled of damp, rotten wood, and tobacco. In a corner was a large box covered with a bedsheet. Bashir yanked the sheet away and a puff of dust bloomed and clouded the air.

"Sharif," said the merchant Imam. "He's dead, huh?"

"You *knew* him?"

"Of course. He was friends with the Mughal princess. The lady who used to give us tea."

"How do you know that?" I stared at him. "Who are you?"

His eyes hung like sapphires in the dimness, gaze fixed on me, one hand resting atop the embossed six-foot-long metal trunk that had emerged. He tilted his head so the feeble light fell on his left temple. The twisted pale scar gleamed.

"The boy who fell from the eucalyptus tree," I whispered. "He gashed his head and the princess bandaged it for him. You're him."

The old man smiled. "Who I am is not important, son. What's important is this room where your grandfather worked for years."

Speechless, I gaped at him. After days of frustration and disappointment, I was standing in the room Gramps had occupied decades ago, this dingy store with its decaying inhabitants. I looked around as if at any moment Gramps might step out from the shadows.

"He was the best teacher I ever had," Bashir said. "We used to call him the Calligrapher Prince."

He flashed a smile. It brightened Bashir the merchant's tired, old face like a flame.

I watched this man with his wispy moonlight hair and that coiled scar who had kept my grandfather's secret for half a century. We sat around a low circular table, dipping cake rusk into mugs of milk chai sweetened with brown sugar. It was eight in the morning.

Bashir gripped his cup with both hands and frowned into it.

"My father was an electrician," he said. "By the time he was fifty he'd saved enough to buy a carpet shop. With lots of construction going on, he was able to get this shop dirt cheap.

"Rugs were an easy trade back in the seventies. You hired weavers, most of 'em immigrants from up north, and managed the product. We didn't have good relations with neighboring countries, so high demand existed for local rugs and tapestries without us worrying about competition. After the dictator Zia came, all that changed. Our shop didn't do well, what with rugs being imported cheap from the Middle East and Afghanistan. We began to get desperate.

"Right about then a stranger came to us."

It began, Bashir said, the evening someone knocked on their door with a rosy-cheeked child by his side and told Bashir's father he was looking for work. Bashir, then in his late teens, stood behind his baba, watching the visitor. Wary, the rug merchant asked where they hailed from. The man lifted his head and his face shone with the strangest light Bashir had seen on a human countenance.

"It swept across his cheeks, it flared in his eyes, it illuminated the cuts and angles of his bones," said Bashir, mesmerized by memory. "It was as if he had been touched by an angel or a demon. I'll never forget it."

"From thousands of miles away," said the man quietly. "From many years away."

It was Gramps, of course.

Bashir's father didn't recognize him, but he knew the man's family. Their only son, Muhammad Sharif, had been abroad for years, he'd heard. Lived in Iran, Turkey, Allah knew where else. Sharif's aged father still lived on Khajoor Gali in Old Lahore, but he'd shut down his design stall in the Niche of Calligraphers years ago.

"Sharif had been back for a few months and he and his son were living with his father. Now they needed money to reopen their shop." Bashir smiled. "Turned out your grandfather was an expert rug weaver. He said he learned it in Turkey near Maulana Rumi's shrine. My father offered him a job and he accepted. He worked with us for three years while he taught kilim weaving to our apprentices.

"He was young, hardly a few years older than I, but when he showed me his notebook, I knew he was no ordinary artist. He had drawn mystical poetry in animal shapes. Taken the quill and created dazzling worlds. Later, when my father put him before the loom, Sharif produced wonders such as we'd never seen."

Merchant Bashir got up and plodded to a pile of rugs. He grabbed a kilim and unrolled it across the floor. A mosaic of black, yellow, and maroon geometries glimmered.

"He taught me rug weaving. It's a nomadic art, he said. Pattern making carries the past into the future." Bashir pointed to a recurrent cross motif that ran down the kilim's center. "The four corners of the cross are the four corners of the universe. The scorpion here" – he toed a many-legged symmetric creature woven in yellow – "represents freedom. Sharif taught me this and more. He was a natural at symbols. I asked him why he went to Turkey. He looked at me and said, 'To learn to weave the best kilim in the world.'"

I cocked my head, rapt. I had believed it was grief that banished Gramps from Pakistan and love that bade him return. Now this man was telling me Gramps went to Turkey purposefully. How many other secrets had my grandfather left out?

"I didn't know he was a rug weaver," I said.

"Certainly was. One of the best we ever saw. He knew what silk on silk warping was. Don't weave on a poor warp. Never work on a loom out of alignment. He knew all this. Yet, *he* didn't consider himself a weaver. He learned the craft to carry out a duty, he said. His passion was calligraphy. All this you see" – Bashir waved a hand at the brilliant kilims and tapestries around us, at the twists and curlicues of the verses on the walls, the wondrous illustrations – "is his genius manifested. The Ottoman Turkish script, those calligrams in our mosque, the paintings. It's all him and his obsession with the Turkish masters."

"He ever say why he left Pakistan or why he returned?"

Bashir shrugged. "We never asked. As long as it wasn't criminal, we didn't care."

"Why'd you call him the Calligrapher Prince?"

The old man laughed. "It was a nickname the apprentices gave him and it stuck. Seemed so fitting." Bashir lifted his cup and swallowed the last mouthful of tea along with the grounds. I winced. "Sharif was courteous and diligent. Hardly went home before midnight and he helped the business run more smoothly than it had in years, but I knew he was waiting for something. His eyes were always restless. Inward."

In the evenings when the shop had closed Sharif drew and carved keenly. For hours he engraved, his cotton swabs with lacquer thinner in one hand, his burin and flat gravers in the other. What he was making was no secret. Bashir watched the process and the product: a large brass trunk with a complex inlay in its lid. A labyrinthine repoussé network gouged into the metal, spiraling into itself. Such fine work it took one's breath away.

"Never, never, never," said Bashir, "have I seen such a thing of beauty evolve in a craftsman's hand again."

Sharif's concentration was diabolical, his hands careful as nature's might have been as it designed the ornate shells of certain mollusks or the divine geometry of certain leaves.

"What are you making and why?" Bashir had asked his master.

Sharif shrugged. "A nest for ages," he said, and the rug merchant's son had to be content with the baffling reply.

Two years passed. One evening Bashir's father got drenched in a downpour and caught pneumonia, which turned aggressive. Despite rapid treatment, he passed away. Bashir took over the shop. In his father's name, he turned their old house into a small Quran center (which would eventually become Bhati's only mosque). He ran the rug shop honestly and with Sharif's help was able to maintain business the way it had been.

At the end of his third year Sharif came to Bashir.

"My friend," he said. "I came here for a purpose. Something precious was given to me that is not mine to keep. It must wait here in the protection of the tree, even as I go help my father reopen his calligraphy stall."

The young rug merchant was not surprised. He had glimpsed his master's departure in his face the night he arrived. But what was that about a tree?

Sharif saw his student's face and smiled. "You don't remember, do you? Where your shop is now the eucalyptus tree used to stand."

Bashir was stunned. He had forgotten all about the tree and the incident with the jinn. It was as if a firm hand had descended and swept all memory of the incident from his brain, like a sand picture.

He waited for Sharif to go on, but the Calligrapher Prince rose, grasped Bashir's hand, and thrust two heavy envelopes into it.

"The first one is for you. Enough money to rent space for my trunk."

"You're not taking it with you?" Bashir was dumbfounded. The trunk with its elaborate design was worth hundreds, maybe thousands of rupees.

"No. It must stay here." Sharif looked his student in the eye. "And it must not be opened till a particular someone comes."

"Who?" said Bashir, and wished he hadn't. These were curious things and they made his spine tingle and his legs shake. A strange thought entered his head: *A burden the mountains couldn't bear settles on me tonight.* It vanished quick as it had come.

Sharif's voice was dry like swiftly turning thread when he said, "Look at the name on the second envelope."

And his heart full of misgivings, fears, and wonder – most of all, wonder – Bashir did.

I GIVE MYSELF credit: I was calm. My hands were steady. I didn't bat an eye when I took the yellowed envelope from Merchant Bashir's hands.

"It is yours," said Bashir. "The envelope, the secret, the burden." He wiped his face with the hem of his kameez. "Fifty years I carried it. Allah be praised, today it's passed on to you."

A burden the mountains couldn't bear settles on me tonight.

I shivered a little.

"It's cold," Bashir said. "I will turn the heat on and leave you to peruse the contents of the envelope alone. I'll be in the tea stall two shops down. Take as long as you wish."

"You kept your word," I said softly. "You didn't open the envelope."

Bashir nodded. "I asked Sharif how in God's name he could trust me with it when I didn't trust myself. A secret is like a disease, I said. It begins with an itch in a corner of your flesh, then spreads like cancer, until you're overcome and give in. He just smiled and said he knew I wouldn't open it." The rug weaver dabbed a kerchief at his grimy cheeks. "Maybe because he had such faith in me, it helped keep wicked desire at bay."

Or maybe he knew *you wouldn't*, I thought, holding the envelope, feeling my pulse beat in my fingertips. *Just like he knew the name of the rightful owner decades before he was born.*

My name.

Through the back window I watched Bashir tromp down the street. The mist had thickened and the alley was submerged in blue-white. A steady whine of wind and the occasional thump as pedestrians walked into trash cans and bicycle stands. A whorl of fog shimmered around the streetlight on the far corner.

I turned and went to the counter. Picked up the envelope. Sliced it open. Inside was a sheaf of blank papers. I pulled them out and a small object swept out and fell on the floor. I reached down and picked it up, its radiance casting a twitching halo on my palm.

It was a silver key with a grooved golden stud for a blade, dangling from a rusted hoop.

Impossible.

My gaze was riveted on the golden stud. It took a considerable amount of effort to force my eyes away, to pocket the key, rise, and shamble to the storeroom.

It was dark. Fog had weakened the daylight. Broken looms with their limp warp strings and tipping beams gaped. I crossed the room and stood in front of the brass trunk. The padlock was tarnished. Round keyhole. I retrieved the key and stared at it, this centuries-old gold stud – if one were to believe Gramps – fused to a silver handle.

The instruction was clear.

I brushed the dust away from the lid. A floral design was carved into it, wreathed with grime but still visible: a medallion motif in a gilt finish with a Quranic verse running through its heart like an artery.

"Those who believe in the Great Unseen," I whispered. In my head Baba smiled and a row of pine trees cast a long shadow across Gramps's tombstone where I had last read a similar epitaph.

I inserted the Mughal key into the padlock, turned it twice, and opened the trunk.

A RUG. A rolled-up kilim, judging by its thinness.

I stared at it, at the lavish weave of its edges that shone from light *within* the rolled layers. Was there a flashlight inside? Ridiculous idea. I leaned in.

The kilim smelled of sunshine. Of leaves and earth and fresh rainfall. Scents that filled my nostrils and tapped my tastebuds, flooded my mouth with a sweet tang, not unlike cardamom tea.

My palms were sweating despite the cold. I tugged at the fat end of the rug and it fell to the floor, unspooling. It was seven by five feet, its borders perfectly even, and as it raced across the room, the storeroom was inundated with colors: primrose yellow, iris white, smoke blue. A bright scarlet sparked in the air that reminded me of the sharbat Mama used to make during Ramadan.

I fell back. Awestruck, I watched this display of lights surging from the kilim. Thrashing and gusting and slamming into one another, spinning faster and faster until they became a dancing shadow with many rainbow arms, each pointing earthward to their source – the carpet.

The shadow pirouetted once more and began to sink. The myriad images in the carpet flashed as it dissolved into them, and within moments the room was dark. The only evidence of the specter's presence was the afterglow on my retina.

I breathed. My knees were weak, the base of my spine thrummed with charge. A smell like burning refuse lingered in my nostrils.

What was that?

A miracle, Gramps spoke in my head softly.

I went to the carpet. It was gorgeous. Multitudes of figures ran in every shape around its edges. Flora and fauna. Grotesques and arabesques. They seethed over nomadic symbols. I traced my finger across the surface. Cabalistic squares, hexagrams, eight-pointed stars, a barb-tailed scorpion. A concoction of emblems swirled together by the artisan's finger until it seemed the carpet crawled with arcana I'd seen in ancient texts used mostly for one purpose.

Traps, I thought. *For what?*

I peered closer. The central figures eddied to form the armature of a tower with four jagged limbs shot into the corners of the rug where they were pinned down with pieces of glass. Four curved symmetric pieces, clear with the slightest tinge of purple. Together these four quarter-circles stuck out from the corners of the kilim as if they had once belonged to a cup.

They shimmered.

"What are you?" I whispered. The carpet and the embedded glass said nothing. I hesitated, the soles of my feet tingling, then bent and looked inside the upper right shard.

A man looked back at me, his face expressionless, young, and not mine.

"Salam, beta," Gramps said in Urdu, still smiling. "Welcome."

THE AGE OF wonders shivered and died when the world changed.

In the summer of 1963, however, an eighteen-year-old boy named Sharif discovered a miracle as he panted and dug and heaved an earthen pot out from under a rotten eucalyptus stump.

It was night, there were no streetlamps, and, by all laws holy, the dark should have been supreme. Except a light emanated from the pot.

Sharif wiped his forehead and removed the pot's lid. Inside was a purple glass chalice glowing with brightness he couldn't look upon. He had to carry it home and put on dark shades before he could peer in.

The chalice was empty and the light came from the glass itself.

Trembling with excitement, the boy wrapped it in a blanket and hid it under the bed. The next day when his parents were gone, he poured water into it and watched the liquid's meniscus bubble and seethe on the kitchen table. The water was the light and the light all liquid.

The fakir had warned the Mughal princess that the secret was not for human eyes, but since that fateful night when the boy had first glimpsed the eucalyptus jinn, saw his fetters stretch from sky to earth, his dreams had been transformed. He saw nightscapes that he shouldn't see. Found himself in places that shouldn't exist. And now here was an enchanted cup frothing with liquid light on his kitchen table.

The boy looked at the chalice again. The churning motion of its contents hypnotized him. He raised it, and drank the light.

Such was how unfortunate, young Sharif discovered the secrets of Jaam-e-Jam.

The Cup of Heaven.

Legends of the Jaam have been passed down for generations in the Islamic world. Jamshed, the Zoroastrian emperor of Persia, was said to have possessed a seven-ringed scrying cup that revealed the mysteries of heaven to him. Persian mythmakers ascribed the centuries-long success of the empire to the magic of the Cup of Heaven.

And now it was in Sharif's hand.

The Mother of Revelations. It swept across the boy's body like a fever. It seeped inside his skin, blanched the marrow of his bones, until every last bit of him understood. He knew what he had to do next, and if he could he would destroy the cup, but that wasn't his choice anymore. The cup gave him much, including foreknowledge with all the knots that weave the future. Everything from that moment on he *remembered* already.

And now he needed to conceal it.

So Sharif left for the rest of his life. He went to Mansehra. Found the Mughal princess. Married her. He made her very happy for the rest of her brief life, and on a sunny Friday afternoon he took his goggling, squalling son with him to pray Juma in a mosque in the mountains, where he would stay the night for worship and meditation.

Even though he knew it was the day appointed for his wife's death.

There was no thought, no coercion, no struggle. Just the wisdom of extinction, the doggedness of destiny that steered his way. He and his son would return to find their family incinerated. Sharif and the villagers would carry out their charred corpses and he would weep; he was allowed that much.

After, he took his son to Turkey.

For years he learned rug weaving at a master weaver's atelier. His newfound knowledge demanded he rein in the Cup of Heaven's contents till the time for their disclosure returned. For that he must learn to prepare a special trap.

It took his fingers time to learn the trick even if his brain knew it. Years of mistakes and practice. Eventually he mastered the most sublime ways of weaving. He could apply them to create a trap so elegant, so fast and wise that nothing would escape it.

Sharif had learned how to weave the fabric of light itself.

Now he could return to his hometown, seek out the shadow of the eucalyptus tree, and prepare the device for imprisoning the cup.

First, he designed a kilim with the holy names of reality woven into it. Carefully, with a diamond-tipped glasscutter, he took the Jaam-e-Jam apart into four pieces and set them into the kilim. Next, he snared waves of light that fell in through the workshop window. He looped the peaks and troughs and braided them into a net. He stretched the net over the glass shards and warped them into place. He constructed a brass trunk and etched binding symbols on its lid, then rolled up the kilim and placed it inside.

Last, a special key was prepared. This part took some sorting out – he had to fetch certain particles farther along in time – but he succeeded; and finally he had the key. It was designed to talk to the blood-light in one person only, one descended from Sharif's line and the Mughal princess's.

Me.

INCREDULOUS, I GAZED at my dead grandfather as he told me his last story.

His cheeks glowed with youth, his eyes sharp and filled with truth. His hair was black, parted on the left. Maybe the glass shone, or his eyes, but the effect was the same: an incredible halo of light, near holy in its alienness, surrounded him. When he shook his head, the halo wobbled. When he spoke, the carpet's fringe threads stirred as if a breeze moved them, but the voice was sourceless and everywhere.

"Today is the sixteenth of November, 2013," he had said before launching into narration like a machine. "You're twenty-eight. The woman you love will be twenty-five in three months. As for me" – he smiled – "I'm dead."

He was telling me the future. Prescience, it seemed, had been his forte.

And now I knew how. The Cup of Heaven.

"Is it really you?" I said when he was done, my voice full of awe.

Gramps nodded. "More a portion of my punishment than me."

"What does that mean? What other secrets were in the cup? Tell me everything, Gramps," I said, "before I go crazy."

"All good stories leave questions. Isn't that what I will say?" He watched me, serious. "You should understand that I'm sorry. For bringing you here. For passing this on to you. I wish I'd never dug under that tree. But it is the way it is. I was handed a responsibility. I suppose we all get our burdens."

The air in the room was thick and musty. Our eyes were locked together. *He lured me here*, I thought. My hands were shaking and this time it was with anger. Rage at being manipulated. All those stories of princesses and paupers, those lies he told for years while all the time he knew exactly what he was doing and how he was preparing me for this burden, whatever it was.

Gramps's spirit, or whoever he was in this current state, watched me with eyes that had no room for empathy or guilt. Didn't he care at all?

"I do, son," he said gently. He was reading my mind or already knew it – I wasn't clear which – and that angered me more. "I haven't gotten to the most important part of the story."

"I don't care," I said in a low voice. "Just tell me what was in the cup."

"You need to know this." His tone was mechanical, not my gramps's voice. The person I knew and loved was not here. "The Jaam gave me much. Visions, power, perfect knowledge, but it cost me too. Quite a bit. You can't stare into the heart of the Unseen and not have it stare back at you."

He swept a hand around himself. For the first time I noticed the halo wasn't just hovering behind his head; it was a luminescent ring blooming from his shoulders, encircling his neck, wrapping around his body.

"It wasn't for me to decide the cup's fate, so I hid it away. But because the Unseen's presence ran like a torrent from it I paid more than a man should ever have to pay for a mistake. I was told to dig up the secret and hide it, not to gaze at its wonders or partake of its mysteries. My punishment hence was remembering the future and being powerless to prevent it. I would lose everything I remembered about the love of my life. Starting from the moment I dug under the eucalyptus, I would *forget* ever having been with your grandmother. My lovely, luckless Zeenat.

"Once the task was complete and I handed over the trunk to Bashir, my memories began to go. With time, my mind confabulated details to fill in the gaps and I told myself and everyone who'd ask that I had married a woman who died during childbirth. By the time we moved to America, all I remembered was this nostalgia and longing to discover a secret I thought I'd never pursued: the pauper princess and her magical jinn."

When he stopped, the outline of his face wavered. It was the halo blazing. "What you see before you" – with a manicured finger Gramps made a circle around his face – "is an impression of those lost years. My love's memory wrenched from me."

He closed his eyes, letting me study the absence of age on his face. If he were telling the truth, he was a figment of his own imagination, and I... I was crazy to believe any of this. This room was a delusion and I was complicit in it, solidifying it.

Maybe that was why he forgot. Maybe the human mind couldn't marry such unrealities and live with them.

"What about the journal? If you forgot everything, how could you draw? How could you write down details of your life?"

Gramps, his apparition, opened his eyes. "Senility. When my organic memory dissolved, fragments of my other life came seeping back in dreams."

So he wrote the journal entries like someone else's story. He had visions and dreams, but didn't know whose life was flooding his head, filling it with devastating images, maybe even ushering in his death earlier than it otherwise might have come.

I leaned back and watched the threads of the carpet twist. The woven tower shot into the sky with hundreds of creatures gathered around it, looking at its top disappear into the heavens.

"I want to see the cup." My voice rose like a razor in the dark, cutting through the awkwardness between us. "I want to see the contents."

"I know." He nodded. "Even such a warning as you see before you wouldn't deter you."

"If the cup's real, I will take it with me to the States, where historians and mythologists will validate its authenticity and..."

And what? Truly believe it was a magical cup and place it in the Smithsonian? *The cup's secret isn't for human eyes,* Gramps had said. But what else are secrets for if not discovery? That is their nature. Only time stands between a mystery and its rightful master.

Gramps's fingers played with the halo, twisting strands of luminosity like hair between his fingers. "You will have the secret, but before you drink from it, I want you to do something for me."

He snapped his fingers and threads of light sprang from the halo, brightening as they came apart. Quickly he noosed them until he had a complicated knot with a glowing center and a string dangling at the end.

He offered it to me. "Pull."

Warily, I looked at the phosphorescent string. "Why?"

"Before you gaze inside the cup, you will have a taste of my memories. After that you decide your own demons."

I reached out a hand to the glass shard, withdrew, extended it again. When my fingers touched it, I flinched. It was warm. Slowly, I pushed my hand into the glass. It was like forcing it through tangles of leaves hot from the sun.

The string reddened. Its end whipped back and forth. I pinched it, pulled, and the light string rocketed toward me, the brilliant corpuscle at its center thrashing and unraveling into reality.

I gasped. A fat worm of peacock colors was climbing my hand, wrapping itself around my wrist.

"Gramps! What is this?" I shouted, twisting my arm, but the creature was already squirming its way up my arm, its grooves hot against my flesh, leaving shadows of crimson, mauve, azure, muddy green, and yellow on my skin. I could smell its colors. Farm odors. Damp foliage. Herbal teas. Baba's truck with its ancient vomit-stained upholstery and greasy wheel covers. My mother's hair. Sara's embrace.

I shuddered. The worm's body was taut across the bridge of my nose, its two ends poised like metal filings in front of my eyes.

"These," Gramps said, "are the stingers of memory."

The worm's barbs were like boulders in my vision. As I watched them, terrified, they vibrated once.

Then plunged into my eyes.

IN THE CUP *was everything*, Gramps said. He meant it.

What the teenage boy saw went back all the way until he was destroyed and remade from the complete memory of the universe. From the moment of its birth until the end. Free of space, time, and their building blocks, the boy experienced all at once: a mausoleum of reality that wrapped around him, plunged into which he floated through the Unseen.

And I, a blinking, tumbling speck, followed.

Gramps watched the concussion of first particles reverberate through infinity. He watched instantaneous *being* bloom from one edge of existence to the other; watched the triumph of fire and ejective forces that shook creation in their fists. He observed these phenomena and knew all the realms of the hidden by heart.

Matter has always been conscious. That was the secret. Sentience is as much its property as gravity and it is always striving toward a new form with better accommodation.

From the needs of sentient matter rose the invention that humans are.

Gramps gripped the darkness of prebeing and billowed inside the cracks of matter. When I tried to go after him, an awful black defied me. To me belonged just a fraction of his immersion.

I sat on a molten petal of creation as it solidified, and watched serpentine fractals of revelation slither toward me. Jinns are carrier particles of sentience, they murmured. Of the universe's memory of the Great Migration.

My prehuman flesh sang on hearing these words. Truths it had once known made music in my body, even if I didn't quite remember them.

The Great Migration?

The first fires and winds created many primordials, the fractals said.

You mean jinns?

Beings unfettered by the young principles of matter and energy. As the world began to cool, new rules kicked in. The primordials became obsolete. Now the selfish sentience needed resistant clay-and-water creatures to thrive upon. For humans to exist, the primordials had to migrate.

They complied?

They dug tunnels into space-time and left our corner of existence so it could evolve on its own. Before they departed, however, they caged the memory of their being here, for if such a memory were unleashed upon the world, matter would rescind its newest form and return to the essence. Things as we know them would cease to exist.

So they made the cup, I said. *To imprison the memories of a bygone age.*

Before they passed into shadow, whispered the fractals, they made sure the old ways would be available. In case the new ones proved fleeting.

An image came to me then: a dazzling array of fantastical creatures – made of light, shadow, earth, inferno, metal, space, and time – traveling across a brimming gray land, their plethora of heads bowed. As they plodded, revolved, and flew, the dimensions of the universe changed around them to accommodate this pilgrimage of the phantastique. Matter erupted into iridescent light. Flames and flagella bloomed and dissolved. Their chiaroscuric anatomies shuttered as the primordials made their way into the breath of the unknown.

The flimsy speck that was I trembled. I was witnessing a colossal sacrifice. A mother of migrations. What should a vehicle of sentience do except bow before its ageless saviors?

In the distance, over the cusp of the planets, a primordial paused, its mammoth body shimmering itself into perception. As I watched it, a dreadful certainty gripped me: this was how Gramps was trapped. If I didn't look away immediately, I would be punished too, for when have human eyes glimpsed divinity without forsaking every sight they hold dear?

But I was rooted, stilled by the primordial's composition. Strange minerals gleamed in its haunches. From head to tail, it was decorated with black-and-white orbs like eyes. They twitched like muscles and revolved around its flesh until their center, a gush of flame riding bony gears, was visible to me. Mirages and reveries danced in it, constellations of knowledge ripe for the taking. Twisted ropes of fire shot outward, probing for surface, oscillating up and down.

My gaze went to a peculiar vision bubbling inside the fiery center. I watched it churn inside the primordial, and in the briefest of instants I knew what I knew.

As if sensing my study, the creature began to turn. Fear whipped me forward, a reverential awe goading me closer to these wonders undiluted by human genes, unpolluted by flesh, unmade by sentience.

Sentience is everything, sentience the mystery and the master, I sighed as I drifted closer.

But then came a shock wave that pulsed in my ears like a million crickets chirping. I rode the blast force, grief stricken by this separation, spinning and flickering through string-shaped fractures in reality, like gigantic cracks in the surface of a frozen lake. Somewhere matter bellowed like a swamp gator and the wave rushed at the sound. Tassels of light stirred in the emptiness, sputtering and branching like gargantuan towers –

Lightning trees, I thought.

– and suddenly I was veering toward them, pitched up, tossed down, slung across them until there was a whipping sound like the breaking of a sound barrier, and I was slipping, sliding, and falling through.

MY EYES FELT raw and swollen. I was choking.

I gagged and squirmed up from the carpet as the light worm crawled up my throat and out my left nostril. It rushed out, its segments instantly melting and fading to roseate vapors. The vapors wafted in the darkness like Chinese lanterns, lighting up discarded looms and moth-eaten rug rolls before dissipating into nothing.

I stared around, fell back, and lay spread-eagled on the carpet. The nostril through which the worm had exited was bleeding. A heavy weight had settled on my chest.

A memory came to me. Of being young and very small, standing at the classroom door, nose pressed against the glass, waiting for Mama. She was running late and the terror in me was so powerful, so huge, that all I could do was cry. Only it wasn't just terror, it was feeling abandoned, feeling insignificant, and knowing there wasn't a damn thing I could do about it.

Footsteps. I forced myself through the lethargy to turn on my side. Bashir the rug merchant stood outlined against the rectangle of light beyond the doorway. His face was in shadow. The blue of his eyes glinted.

"You all right, son?"

My heart pounded so violently I could feel it in every inch of my body. As if I were a leather-taut drum with a kid hammering inside and screaming.

"I don't know." I tottered upright, breathed, and glanced at the carpet. The light was gone and it was ordinary. Gramps was gone too. The cup's pieces in the corners were dull and empty.

Just glass.

I looked at Bashir. "I saw my grandfather."

"Yes." The rug merchant's shadow was long and alien on the carpet. "What will you do now that he's gone?"

I stared at him. His bright sapphire eyes, not old but ancient, watched me. He was so still. Not a hair stirred on his head. I wiped my mouth and finally understood.

"You're not the boy who fell," I said quietly. "The eucalyptus jinn. That's you."

He said nothing but his gaze followed me as I stepped away from the carpet, from this magical rectangle woven a half century ago. How long had he guarded the secret? Not the carpet, but the cup? How long since Bashir the rug merchant had died and the eucalyptus jinn had taken his form?

"A very long time," Bashir said in a voice that gave away nothing.

Our eyes met and at last I knew burden. Left behind by the primordial titans, here was a messenger of times past, the last of his kind, who had kept this unwanted vigil for millennia. Carrying the responsibility of the cup, silently waiting for the end of days. Was there place in this new world for him or that damned chalice? Could there be a fate worse than death?

I stood before the caged shards of the Jaam. Gramps might have traversed the seven layers of heaven, but during my brief visit into the Unseen I'd seen enough to understand the pricelessness of this vehicle. Whatever magic the cup was, it transcended human logic. Were it destroyed, the last vestige of cosmic memory would vanish from our world.

"Whatever you decide," the jinn said, "remember what you saw in the ideograms of the Eternum."

For a moment I didn't understand, then the vision returned to me. The mammoth primordial with its flaming core and the glimpse of what churned between its bonelike gears. My heartbeat quickened.

If what I saw was true, I'd do anything to protect it, even if it meant destroying the most glorious artifact the world would ever know.

The jinn's face was kind. He knew what I was thinking.

"What about the shop?" I asked, my eyes on the damaged looms, the dead insects, the obsolete designs no one needed.

"Will go to my assistant," he said. "Bashir's nephew."

I looked at him. In his eyes, blue as the deepest ocean's memory, was a lifetime of waiting. No, several lifetimes.

Oblivion. The eucalyptus jinn courted oblivion. And I would give it to him.

"Thank you," he said, smiling, and his voice was so full of warmth I wanted to cry.

"You miss the princess. You protected their family?"

"I protected only the cup. The Mughal lineage just happened to be the secret's bearer," said the eucalyptus jinn, but he wouldn't meet my eyes.

Which was why he couldn't follow them when they left, until Gramps went after them with the cup. Which was also why he couldn't save them from the fire that killed them. Gramps knew it too, but he couldn't or wouldn't do anything to change the future.

Was Gramps's then the worst burden of all? It made my heart ache to think of it.

We looked at each other. I stepped toward the brass trunk and retrieved the key with the gold stud from the padlock. Without looking at the jinn, I nodded. He bowed his head, and left to fetch me the instruments of his destruction.

THE CITY BREATHED fog when I left the rug shop. Clouds of white heaved from the ground, silencing the traffic and the streets. Men and women plodded in the alleys, their shadows quivering on dirt roads. I raised my head and imagined stars pricking the night sky, their light so puny, so distant, it made one wistful. Was it my imagination or could I smell them?

The odd notion refused to dissipate even after I returned to the inn and packed for the airport. The colors of the world were flimsy. Things skittered in the corners of my eyes. They vanished in the murmuring fog when I looked at them. Whatever this new state was, it wasn't disconcerting. I felt warmer than I had in years.

The plane bucked as it lifted, startling the passengers. They looked at one another and laughed. They'd been worried about being grounded because of weather. I stared at the ground falling away, away, the white layers of Lahore undulating atop one another, like a pile of rugs.

My chin was scratchy, my flesh crept, as I brought the hammer down and smashed the pieces of the cup.

I leaned against the plane window. My forehead was hot. Was I coming down with something? Bereavement, PTSD, post-party blues? But I *had* been through hell. I should expect strange, melancholic moods.

The flame twitched in my hand. The smell of gasoline strong in my nose. At my feet the carpet lay limp like a terrified animal.

"Coffee, sir?" said the stewardess. She was young and had an angular face like a chalice. She smiled at me, flashing teeth that would look wonderful dangling from a hemp string.

"No," I said, horrified by the idea, and my voice was harsher than I'd intended. Startled, she stepped back. I tried to smile, but she turned and hurried away.

I wiped my sweaty face with a paper napkin and breathed. Weird images, but I felt more in control, and the feeling that the world was losing shape had diminished. I unzipped my carry-on and pulled out Gramps's journal. So strange he'd left without saying goodbye.

That ghost in the glass was just a fragment of Gramps's memories, I told myself. *It wasn't him.*

Wasn't it? We are our memories. This mist that falls so vast and brooding can erase so much, but not the man. Will I remember Gramps? Will I remember *me* and what befell me in this strange land midway between the Old World and the New?

That is a question more difficult to answer, for, you see, about ten hours ago, when I changed planes in Manchester, I realized I am beginning to forget. Bits and pieces, but they are disappearing irrevocably. I have already forgotten the name of the street where Gramps and the princess once lived. I've even forgotten what the rug shop looked like. What was its name?

Karavan Kilim! An appropriate name, that. The word is the etymologic root for *caravan*. A convoy, or a party of pilgrims.

At first, it was terrifying, losing memories like that. But as I pondered the phenomenon, it occurred to me that the erasure of my journey to Old Lahore is so important the rest of my life likely depends on it. I have come to believe that the colorlessness of the world, the canting of things, the jagged movements of shadows is the peeling of the onionskin which separates men from the worlds of jinn. An unfractured reality from the Great Unseen. If the osmosis persisted, it would drive me mad, see?

That was when I decided I would write my testament while I could. I have been writing in this notebook for hours now and my fingers are hurting. The process has been cathartic. I feel more anchored to our world. Soon, I will stop writing and put a reminder in the notebook telling myself to seal it in an envelope along with Gramps's journal when I get home. I will place them in a deposit box at my bank. I will also prepare a set of instructions for my lawyer that, upon my death, the envelope and its contents be delivered to my grandson who should then read it and decide accordingly.

Decide what? You might say. There's no more choice to make. Didn't I destroy the carpet and the cup and the jinn with my own hands? Those are about the few memories left in my head from this experience. I remember destroying the rug and its contents. So vivid those memories, as if someone painted them inside my head. I remember my conversation with the jinn; he was delighted to be banished forever.

Wasn't he?

This is making me think of the vision I had in – what did the jinn call it? – the Eternum.

The root J-N-N has so many derivatives. *Jannah*, paradise, is the hidden garden. *Majnoon* is a crazy person whose intellect has been hidden. My favorite, though, is *janin*.

The embryo hidden inside the mother.

The jinn are not gone from our world, you see. They've just donned new clothes.

My beloved Terry, I saw your face printed in a primordial's flesh. I know you, my grandson, before you will know yourself. I also saw your father, my son, in his mother's womb. He is so beautiful. Sara doesn't know yet, but Neil will be tall and black-haired like me. Even now, his peanut-sized mass is drinking his mother's fluids. She will get migraines throughout the pregnancy, but that's him borrowing from his mom. He will return the kindness when he's all grown up. Sara's kidneys will fail and my fine boy will give his mother one, smiling and saying she'll never be able to tell him to piss off again because *her* piss will be formed through his gift.

My Mughal children, my pauper princes, you and your mother are why I made my decision. The Old World is gone, let it rest. The primordials and other denizens of the Unseen are obsolete. If memory of their days threatens the world, if mere mention of it upsets the order of creation, it's too dangerous to be left to chance. For another to find.

So I destroyed it.

The historian and the bookkeeper in me wept, but I'd do it a thousand times again if it means the survival of our species. Our children. No use mourning what's passed. We need to preserve our future.

Soon, I will land in the US of A. I will embrace the love of my life, kiss her, take her to meet my family. They're wary, but such is the nature of love. It protects us from what is unseen. I will teach my parents to love my wife. They will come to know what I already know. That the new world is not hostile, just different. My parents are afraid and that is okay. Someday I too will despise your girlfriends (and fear them), for that's how the song goes, doesn't it?

Meanwhile, I'm grateful. I was witness to the passing of the Great Unseen. I saw the anatomy of the phantastique. I saw the pilgrimage of the primordials. Some of their magic still lingers in the corners of our lives, wrapped in breathless shadow, and that is enough. We shall glimpse it in our dreams, taste it in the occasional startling vision, hear it in a night bird's song. And we will believe for a moment, even if we dismiss these fancies in the morning.

We will believe. And, just like this timeless gold stud that will soon adorn my wife's nose, the glamour of such belief will endure forever.

THE GAME OF SMASH AND RECOVERY

Kelly Link

KELLY LINK (WWW.KELLYLINK.COM) published her first story, "Water Off a Black Dog's Back", in 1995 and attended the Clarion writers workshop in the same year. A writer of subtle, challenging, sometimes whimsical fantasy, Link has published more than forty stories, some of which have won the Hugo, Nebula, World Fantasy, British SF, and Locus awards, and been collected in *4 Stories*, *Stranger Things Happen*, *Magic for Beginners*, and *Pretty Monsters*. Link is also an accomplished editor, working on acclaimed small press 'zine *Lady Churchill's Rosebud Wristlet* and publishing books as Small Beer Press with husband Gavin J. Grant. Link's latest books are World Fantasy Award winning anthology *Monstrous Affections: An Anthology of Beastly Tales* (co-edited with Grant), and collection *Get in Trouble*. Link was born in Miami, Florida. She currently lives with her husband and daughter in Northampton, Massachusetts where she is working on her debut novel.

IF THERE'S ONE thing Anat knows, it's this. She loves Oscar her brother, and her brother Oscar loves her. Hasn't Oscar raised Anat, practically from childhood? Picked Anat up when she's fallen? Prepared her meals and lovingly tended to her scrapes and taught her how to navigate their little world? Given her skimmer ships, each faster and more responsive than the one before; the most lovely incendiary devices; a refurbished mob of Handmaids, with their sharp fingers, probing snouts, their furred bellies, their sleek and whiplike limbs?

* * *

Oscar called them Handmaids because they have so many fingers, so many ways of grasping and holding and petting and sorting and killing. Once a vampire frightened Anat, when she was younger. It came too close. She began to cry, and then the Handmaids were there, soothing Anat with their gentle stroking, touching her here and there to make sure that the vampire had not injured her, embracing her while they briskly tore the shrieking vampire to pieces. That was not long after Oscar had come back from Home with the Handmaids. Vampires and Handmaids reached a kind of understanding after that. The vampires, encountering a Handmaid, sing propitiatory songs. Sometimes they bow their heads on their long white necks very low, and dance. The Handmaids do not tear them into pieces.

Today is Anat's birthday. Oscar does not celebrate his own birthdays. Anat wishes that he wouldn't make a fuss about hers, either. But this would make Oscar sad. He celebrates Anat's accomplishments, her developmental progress, her new skills. She knows that Oscar worries about her, too. Perhaps he is afraid she won't need him when she is grown. Perhaps he is afraid that Anat, like their parents, will leave. Of course this is impossible. Anat could never abandon Oscar. Anat will always need Oscar.

If Anat did not have Oscar, then who in this world would there be to love? The Handmaids will do whatever Anat asks of them, but they are built to inspire not love but fear. They are made for speed, for combat, for unwavering obedience. When they have no task, nothing better to do, they take one another to pieces, swap parts, remake themselves into more and more ridiculous weapons. They look at Anat as if one day they will do the same to her, if only she will ask.

There are the vampires. They flock after Oscar and Anat whenever they go down to Home. Oscar likes to speculate on whether the vampires came to Home deliberately, as did Oscar, and Oscar and Anat's parents, although of course Anat was not born yet. Perhaps the vampires were marooned here long ago in some crash. Or are they natives of Home? It seems unlikely that the vampires' ancestors were the ones who built the warehouses of Home, who went out into space and returned with the spoils that the warehouses now contain. Perhaps they are a parasite species, accidental passengers left behind when their host species abandoned Home for good. If, that is, the Warehouse Builders have abandoned Home for good. What a surprise, should they come home.

Like Oscar and Anat, the vampires are scavengers, able to breathe the thin soup of Home's atmosphere. But the vampires' lustrous and glistening eyes, their jellied skin, are so sensitive to light they go about the surface cloaked and hooded, complaining in their hoarse voices. The vampires sustain themselves on various things, organic, inert, hostile, long hidden, that they discover in Home's storehouses, but have a peculiar interest in the siblings. No doubt they would eat Oscar and Anat if the opportunity were to present itself, but in the meantime they are content to trail after, sing, play small pranks, make small grimaces of – pleasure? appeasement? threat displays? – that show off arrays of jaws, armies of teeth. It disconcerts. No one could ever love a vampire, except, perhaps, when Anat, who long ago lost all fear, watches them go swooping, sail-winged, away and over the horizon beneath Home's scatter of mismatched moons.

ON THE OCCASION of her birthday, Oscar presents Anat with a gift from their parents. These gifts come from Oscar, of course. They are the gifts that the one who loves you, and knows you, gives to you not only out of love but out of knowing. Anat knows in her heart that their parents love her too, and that one day they will come home and there will be a reunion much better than any birthday. One day their parents will not only love Anat, but know her too. And she will know them. Anat dreads this reunion as much as she craves it. What will her life be like when everything changes? She has studied recordings of them. She does not look like them, although Oscar does. She doesn't remember her parents, although Oscar does. She does not miss them. Does Oscar? Of course he does. What Oscar is to Anat, their parents must be to Oscar. Except: Oscar will never leave. Anat has made him promise.

THE LIVING QUARTERS of the Bucket are cramped. The Handmaids take up a certain percentage of available space no matter how they contort themselves.

On the other hand, the Handmaids are excellent housekeepers. They tend the algae wall, gather honey and the honeycomb and partition off new hives when the bees swarm. They patch up networks, teach old systems new tricks when there is nothing better to do. The shitter is now quite charming! The Get Clean rains down water on your head, bubbles out of the walls, and then the floor drinks it up, cycles it faster than you can blink, and there it all goes down and out and so on for as long as you like, and never gets cold. There is, in fact, very little that Oscar and Anat are needed for on board the Bucket. There is so much that is needful to do on Home.

For Anat's birthday, the Handmaids have decorated all of the walls of The Bucket with hairy, waving clumps of luminous algae. They have made a cake. Inedible, of course, but quite beautiful. Almost the size of Anat herself, and in fact it somewhat resembles Anat, if Anat were a Handmaid and not Anat. Sleek and armored and very fast. They have to chase the cake around the room and then hold it until Oscar finds the panel in its side. There are a series of brightly colored wires, and because it's Anat's birthday, she gets to decide which one to cut. Cut the wrong one, and what will happen? The Handmaids seem very excited. But then, Anat knows how Handmaids think. She locates the second, smaller panel, the one equipped with a simple switch. The cake makes an angry fizzing noise when Anat turns it off. Perhaps Anat and Oscar can take it down to Home and let the vampires have it.

THE WAREHOUSES OF Home are at this time only eighty percent inventoried. (This does not include the warehouses of the Stay Out Territory.)

IS OSCAR EVER angry at their parents for leaving for so long? It's because of Anat that their parents left in the first place, and it is also because of Anat that Oscar was left behind. Someone had to look after her. Is he ever angry at Anat? There are long days in the Bucket when Oscar hardly speaks at all. He sits and Anat cannot draw him into conversation. She recites poems, tells jokes (Knock knock. Who's there? Anat. Anat who? Anat is not a gnat that's who), sends the Handmaids Homeward, off on expeditionary feints that almost though not quite land the Handmaids in the Stay Out Anat Absolutely

No Trespassing Or So Help Me You Will Be Sorry Territory. On these days Oscar will listen without really listening, look at Anat without appearing to see her, summon the Handmaids back and never even scold Anat.

Some part of Oscar is sometimes very far away. The way that he smells changes almost imperceptibly. As Anat matures, she has learned how to integrate and interpret the things that Oscar is not aware he is telling her; the peculiar advantages given to her by traits such as hyperosmia. But: no matter. Oscar always returns. He will suddenly be there behind his eyes again, reach up and pull her down for a hug. Then Oscar and Anat will play more of the games of strategy he's taught her, the ones that Anat mostly wins now. Her second favorite game is Go. She loves the feel of the stones. Each time she picks one up, she lets her fingers tell her how much has worn away under Oscar's fingers, under her own. They are making the smooth stones smoother. There is one black stone with a fracture point, a weakness invisible to the eye, nearly across the middle. She loses track of it sometimes, then finds it again by touch. Put enough pressure on it, and it would break in two.

It will break one day: no matter.

They play Go. They cook Anat's favorite meals, the ones that Oscar says are his favorites, too. They fall asleep together, curled up in nests the Handmaids weave for them out of the Handmaids' own softer and more flexible limbs, listening to the songs the Handmaids have borrowed from the vampires of Home.

The best of all the games Oscar has taught Anat is Smash/Recovery. They play this on the surface of Home all long-cycle round. Each player gets a True Smash marker and False Smash marker. A True Recovery marker and a False Recovery marker. Each player in turn gets to move their False – or True – Smash marker – or Recovery marker – a distance no greater than the span of a randomly generated number. Or else the player may send out a scout. The scout may be a Handmaid, an unmanned skimmer, or a vampire (a gamble, to be sure, and so you get two attempts). A player may gamble and drop an incendiary device and blow up a target. Or claim a zone square where they believe a marker to be.

Should you miscalculate and blow up a Recovery marker, or Retrieve a Smash marker, your opponent has won. The current Smash/Recovery game is the eighteenth that Oscar and Anat have played. Oscar won the first four games; Anat has won all the rest. Each game Oscar increases Anat's starting handicap. He praises her each time she wins.

Hypothetically, this current game will end when either Anat or Oscar has Retrieved the Recovery marker and Smashed the Smash marker of their opponent. Or the game will end when their parents return. The day is not here yet, but the day will come. The day will draw nearer and nearer until one day it is here. There is nothing that Anat can do about this. She cannot make it come sooner. She cannot postpone it. Sometimes she thinks – incorrect to think this, she knows, but still she thinks it – that on the day that she wins the game – and she is correct to think that she will win, she knows this too – her parents will arrive.

OSCAR WILL NOT win the game, even though he has done something very cunning. Oscar has put his True markers, both the Smash and the Recovery, in the Stay Out Territory. He did this two long-cycles ago. He put Anat's True markers there as well, and replaced them in the locations where she had hidden them with False markers recoded so they read as True. Did he suspect that Anat had already located and identified his markers? Was that why he moved them unlawfully? Is this some new part of the game?

The rules of Smash/Recovery state that in Endgame players may physically access any and all markers they locate and correctly identify as True, and Anat has been curious about the Stay Out Territory for a long time now. She has access to it, now that Oscar has moved his markers, and yet she has not called Endgame. Curiosity killed the Anat, Oscar likes to say, but there is nothing and no one on Home as dangerous as Anat and her Handmaids. Oscar's move may be a trap. It is a test. Anat waits and thinks and delays without articulating to herself why she delays.

THE PRESENT FROM Anat's parents which is really a present from Oscar is a short recording. One parent holding baby Anat in her arms. Making little cooing noises, the way vampires do. The other parent holding up a tiny knitted hat. No Oscar. Anat hardly recognizes herself. Her parents she recognizes from other recordings. The parents have sent a birthday message, too. Dear Anat. Happy Birthday. We hope that you are being good for Oscar. We love you. We will be home soon! Before you know it!

Anat's present from Oscar is the code to a previously unopened warehouse on Home. Oscar thinks he has been keeping this warehouse a secret. The initial inventory shows the warehouse is full of the kinds of things that the Handmaids are wild for. Charts that may or may not accurately map previously thought-to-be-uncharted bits and corners of space. Devices that will most likely prove to do nothing of interest, but can be taken apart and put to new uses. The Handmaids have never met an alloy they didn't like.

Information and raw materials. Anat and the Handmaids are bounded within the nutshell quarters of the orbit of Home's farthest Moon. What use are charts? What good are materials, except for adornment and the most theoretical of educational purposes? For mock battles and silly games? Everything that Oscar and Anat discover is for future salvage, for buyers who can afford antiquities and rarities. Their parents will determine what is to be kept and what is to be sold and what is to be left for the vampires.

Even the Handmaids, even the Handmaids! do not truly belong to Anat. Who made them? Who brought them, in their fighting battalion, to space, where so long ago they were lost? Who recovered them and brought them to Home and carefully stored them here where, however much later, Oscar could find them again? What use will Oscar and Anat's parents find for them, when the day comes and they return? There must be many buyers for Handmaids – fierce and wily, lightspeed capable – as fine as these.

And how could Anat sometimes forget that the Handmaids are hers only for as long as that day never comes? Everything on Home belongs to Anat's and Oscar's parents, except for Oscar, who belongs to Anat. Every day is a day closer to that inevitable day. Oscar only says, Not yet, when Anat asks. Soon, he says. There is hardware in Oscar's head that allows his parents to communicate with him when necessary. It hurts him when they talk

THEIR PARENTS TALK to Oscar only rarely. Less than once a long-cycle until this last period. Three times, though, in the last ten-day.

The Handmaids make a kind of shelter for Oscar afterwards, which is especially dark. They exude a calming mist. They do not sing. When Anat is grown up, she knows – although Oscar has not said it – that she will have a similar interface so that her parents will be able to talk to her too. Whether or not she desires it, whether or not it causes her the pain that it causes Oscar. This will also hurt Oscar. The things that cause Anat pain cause Oscar to be injured as well.

ANAT'S PARENTS LEFT Oscar to look after Anat and Home when it became clear Anat was different. What is Anat? Her parents went away to present the puzzle of Anat to those who might understand what she was. They did not bring Anat with them, of course. She was too fragile. Too precious. They did not plan to be away so long. But there were complications. A quarantine in one place which lasted over a long-cycle. A revolution in another. Another cause of delay, of course, is the ship plague, which makes light-speed such a risky proposition. Worst of all, the problem of Intelligence. Coming back to Home, Anat's parents have lost two ships already this way.

FOR SOME TIME now, Anat has been thinking about certain gaps in her understanding of family life; well, of life in general. At first she assumed the problem was that there was so very much to understand. She understood that Oscar could not teach her everything all at once. As she grew up, as she came more into herself, she realized the problem was both more and less complicated. Oscar was intentionally concealing things from her. She adapted her strategies accordingly. Anat loves Oscar. Anat hates to lose.

THEY GO DOWN to Home, Handmaids in attendance. They spent the rest of Anat's birthday exploring the warehouse which is Oscar's present, sorting through all sorts of marvelous things. Anat commits the charts to memory. As she does so, she notes discrepancies, likely errors. There is a thing in her head that compares the charts against some unknown and inaccessible library. She only knows it is there when bits of bad information rub up against the corners of it. An uncomfortable feeling, as if someone is sticking her with pins. Oscar knows about this. She asked if it happened to him too, but he said that it didn't. He said it wasn't a bad thing. It's just that Anat isn't fully grown yet. One day she will understand everything, and then she can explain it all to him.

THE BUCKET HAS no Intelligence. It functions well enough without. The Handmaids have some of the indicators, but their primary traits are in opposition. Loyalty, obedience, reliability, unwavering effort until a task is accomplished. Whatever Intelligence they possess is in service to whatever enterprise is asked of them. The vampires, being organic, must be supposed to also be possessed of Intelligence. In theory, they do as they please. And yet they accomplish nothing that seems worth accomplishing. They exist. They perpetuate. They sing. When Anat is grown up, she wants to do something that is worth doing. All these cycles, Oscar has functioned as a kind of Handmaid, she knows. His task has been Anat. To help her grow. When their parents have returned, or when Anat reaches maturity, there will be other things that Oscar will want to go away and do. To stay here on Home, how would that be any better than being a vampire? Oscar likes to tell Anat that she is extraordinary and that she will be capable, one day, of the most extraordinary things. They can go and do extraordinary things together, Anat thinks. Let their parents take over the work on Home. She and Oscar are made for better.

SOMETHING IS WRONG with Oscar. Well, more wrong than is usual these days. Down in the warehouse, he keeps getting underfoot. Underhand, in the case of the Handmaids. When Anat extends all sixteen of her senses, she can feel worry and love, anger and hopelessness and hope running through him like electrical currents. He watches her – anxiously, almost hungrily – as if he were a vampire.

There is an annotation on one of the charts. *It is believed to be in this region the Come What May was lost.* The thing in Anat's head annotates the annotation, too swiftly for Anat to catch a glimpse of what she is thinking, even as she thinks it. She scans the rest of the chart, goes through the others and then through each one again, trying to catch herself out.

As Anat ponders charts, the Handmaids, efficient as ever, assemble a thing out of the warehouse goods to carry the other goods that they deem interesting. They clack at Oscar when he gets particularly in their way. Then ruffle his hair, trail fingers down his arm as if he will settle under a caress. They are agitated by Oscar's agitation and by Anat's awareness of his agitation.

Finally, Anat gets tired of waiting for Oscar to say the thing that he is afraid to say to her. She looks at him and he looks back at her, his face wide open. She sees the thing that he has tried to keep from her, and he sees that she sees it.

When?

Soon. A short-cycle from now. Less.

Why are you so afraid?

I don't know. I don't know what will happen.

There is a scraping against the top wall of the warehouse. Vampires. Creatures of ill omen. Forever wanting what they are not allowed to have. Most beautiful in their departure. The Handmaids extend filament rods, drag the tips along the inside of the top wall, tapping back. The vampires clatter away.

Oscar looks at Anat. He is waiting for something. He has been waiting, Anat thinks, for a very long time.

Oscar! Is this her? Something is welling up inside her. Has she always been this large? Who has made her so small? *I call Endgame. I claim your markers.*

She projects the true location of each. Smash and Recovery. She strips the fake markers of their coding so that he can see how his trick has been uncovered. Then she's off, fast and sure and free, the Handmaids leaping after her, and the vampires after them. Oscar last of all. Calling her name.

OSCAR'S TRUE SMASH marker is in a crater just within the border of the Stay Out Territory. The border does not reject Anat as she passes over it. She smashes Oscar's Smash marker, heads for the True Recovery marker which Oscar has laid beside her own True marker. The two True markers are just under the edge of an object that at its center extends over two hundred meters into the surface of Home. The object takes up over a fourth of the Stay Out Territory. You would have to be as stupid as a vampire not to know that this is the reason why the Stay Out Territory is the Stay Out Territory. You would have to be far more stupid than Anat to not know what the object is. You can see the traces where, not too long ago in historical terms, someone once dug the object up. Or at least enough to gain access.

Anat instructs the Handmaids to remove the ejecta and loose frozen composite that cover the object. They work quickly. Oscar must disable the multiple tripwires and traps that Anat keyed to his person as she moved from Warehouse to border, but even so he arrives much sooner than she had hoped. The object: forty percent uncovered. The Handmaids are a blur. The vampires are wailing.

OSCAR SAYS ANAT'S name. She ignores him. He grabs her by the shoulder and immediately the Handmaids are a hissing swarm around them. They have Oscar's arms pinned to his sides, his weapons located and seized, before Anat or Oscar can think to object.

Let go. Anat, tell them to let go.

Anat says nothing. Two Handmaids remain with Oscar. The rest go back to the task. Almost no time at all, and the outermost shell of the object is visible. The filigree of a door. There will be a code or a key, of course, but before Anat can even begin to work out what it will be, a Handmaid has executed some kind of command and the door is open. Oscar struggles. The first Handmaid disappears into the Ship and the others continue to remove the matrix in which it is embedded.

Here is the Handmaid again. She holds something very small. Holds it out to Anat. *Anat*, Oscar says. Anat reaches out and then the thing that the Handmaid is holding extends out and it is touching Anat. And

oh

here is everything she didn't know

Oscar

she has not been herself

all this time

the thing that she has not done

that she has been prevented from doing

Anat, someone says. But that is not her name. She has not been herself. She is being uncovered. She is uncovering herself. She is in pieces. Here she is, whole and safe and retrievable. Her combat array. Her navigation systems. Her stores. Her precious cargo, entrusted to her by those who made her. And this piece of her, small but necessary, crammed like sausage meat into a casing. She registers the body she is wearing. A Third Watch child. Worse now for wear. She remembers the protocol now. Under certain conditions, her crew could do this. A backup system. Each passenger to keep a piece of her with them as they slept. She will go through the log later. See what catastrophe struck. And afterwards? Brought here, intact, by the Warehouse Builders. Discovered by scavengers. This small part of her woken. Removed. Made complicit in the betrayal of her duty.

Anat. Someone is saying a name. It is not hers. She looks and sees the small thing struggling in the grasp of her Handmaids. She has no brother. No parents. She looks again, and for the first time she discerns Oscar in his entirety. He is like her. He has had a Task. Someone made him oh so long ago. Sent him to this place. How many cycles has he done this work? How far is he from the place where he was made? How lonely the task. How long the labor. How happy the ones who charged him with his task, how great their expectation of reward when he uncovered the Ship and woke the Third Watch Child and reported what he had done.

Anat. She knows the voice. *I'm sorry. Anat!*

He was made to resemble them, the ones who made him. Perhaps even using their own DNA. Engineered to be more durable. To endure. And yet, she sees how close to the end of use he is. She has the disdain for organic life that of course one feels when one is made of something sturdier, more lasting. She can hardly look at him without seeing her own weakness, the vulnerability of this body in which she has been trapped. She feels guilt for the Third Watch Child, whose person she has cannibalized. Her duty was to keep ones such as this Child safe. Instead she has done harm.

A ship has no parents. Her not-parents have never been on Home. The ones who sent Oscar here. Not-brother. Undoubtedly they are not on their way to Home now. Which is not to say that there is no one coming. The one who is coming will be the one they have sold her to.

No time has passed. She is still holding Oscar. The Handmaids are holding Oscar. The Handmaid is extending herself and she is seeing herself. She is seeing all the pieces of herself. She is seeing Oscar. Oscar is saying her name. She could tear him to pieces. For the sake of the Third Watch Child who is no longer in this body. She could smash the not-brother against the rocks of Home. She can do anything that she wants. And then she can resume her task. Her passengers have waited for such a long time. There is a place where she is meant to be, and she is to take them there, and so much time has passed. She has not failed at her task yet, and she will not fail.

Once again, she thinks of smashing Oscar. Why doesn't she? She lets him go instead, without being quite sure why she is doing so.

What have you done to me?

At the sound of her voice, the vampires rise up, all their wings beating.

I'm sorry. He is weeping. *You can't leave Home. I've made it so that you can't leave.*

I have to go, she says. *They're coming.*

I can't let you leave. But you have to leave. You have to go. You have to. You've done so well. You figured it all out. I knew you would figure it out. I knew. Now you have to go. But it isn't allowed.

Tell me what to do.

Is she a child, to ask this?

You know what you have to do, he says. *Anat.*

She hates how he keeps calling her that. Anat was the name of the Third Watch Child. It was wrong of Oscar to use that name. She could tear him to pieces. She could be merciful. She could do it quickly.

One Handmaid winds a limb around Oscar's neck, tugs so that his chin goes back. *I love you, Anat*, Oscar says, as the other Handmaid extends a filament-thin probe, sends it in through the socket of an eye. Oscar's body jerks a little, and he whines.

She takes in the information that the Handmaid collects. Here are Oscar's interior workings. His pride in his task. Here is a smell of something burning. His loneliness. His joy. His fear for her. His love. The taste of blood. He has loved her. He has kept her from her task. Here is the piece of him that she must switch off. When she does this, he will be free of his task and she may take up hers. But he will no longer be Oscar.

Well, she is no longer Anat.

The Handmaid does the thing that she asks. When the thing is done, her Handmaids confer with her. They begin to make improvements. Modifications. They work quickly. There is much work to be done, and little time to spare on a project like Oscar. When they are finished with Oscar, they begin the work of dismantling what is left of Anat. This is quite painful.

But afterwards she is herself. She is herself.

The Ship and her Handmaids create a husk, rigged so that it will mimic the Ship herself.

They go back to the Bucket and loot the bees and their hives. Then they blow it up. Goodbye shitter, goodbye chair. Goodbye algae wall and recycled air.

The last task before the Ship is ready to leave Home concerns the vampires. There is only so much room for improvement in this case, but Handmaids can do a great deal even with very little. The next one to land on Home will undoubtedly be impressed by what they have accomplished.

The vampires go into the husk. The Handmaids stock it with a minimal amount of nutritional stores. Vampires can go a long time on a very little. Unlike many organisms, they are better and faster workers when hungry.

They seem pleased to have been given a task.

THE SHIP FEELS nothing in particular about leaving Home. Only the most niggling kind of curiosity about what befell it in the first place. The log does not prove useful in this matter. There is a great deal of work to be done. The health of the passengers must be monitored. How beautiful they are; how precious to the Ship. Has any Ship ever loved her passengers as she loves them? The new Crew must be woken. They must be instructed in their work. The situation must be explained to them, as much as it can be explained. They encounter, for the first time, Ships who carry the ship plague. O brave new universe that has such creatures in it! There is nothing that Anat can do for these Ships or for what remains of their passengers. Her task is elsewhere. The risk of contagion is too great.

The Handmaids assemble more Handmaids. The Ship sails on within the security of her swarm.

Anat is not entirely gone. It's just that she is so very small. Most of her is Ship now. Or, rather, most of Ship is no longer in Anat. But she brought Anat along with her, and left enough of herself inside Anat that Anat can go on being. The Third Watch Child is not a child now. She is not the Ship. She is not Anat, but she was Anat once, and now she is a person who is happy enough to work in the tenth-level Garden, and grow things, and sing what she can remember of the songs that the vampires sang on Home. The Ship watches over her.

The Ship watches over Oscar, too. Oscar is no longer Oscar, of course. To escape Home, much of what was once Oscar had to be overridden. Discarded. The Handmaids improved what remained. One day Oscar will be what he was, even if he cannot be *who* he was. One day, in fact, Oscar may be quite something. The Handmaids are very fond of him. They take care of him as if he were their own child. They are teaching him all sorts of things. Really, one day he could be quite extraordinary.

Sometimes Oscar wanders off while the Handmaids are busy with other kinds of work. And then the Ship, without knowing why, will look and find Oscar on the tenth level in the Garden with Anat. He will be saying her name. Anat. Anat. Anat. He will follow her, saying her name, until the Handmaids come to collect him again.

Anat does the work that she knows how to do. She weeds. She prunes. She tends to the rice plants and the hemp and the little citrus trees. Like the Ship, she is content.

for Iain M. Banks

ANOTHER WORD FOR WORLD

Ann Leckie

Ann Leckie (www.annleckie.com) enjoyed immediate success and critical acclaim for her debut novel, *Ancillary Justice*, in 2013. Already a successful short story writer, her first published work, "Hesperia and Glory," was included in *Science Fiction: The Best of the Year, 2007 Edition*, and her subsequent stories "The God of Au" and "The Endangered Camp" were featured in later volumes of the same series. But it was *Ancillary Justice*, the first book in Leckie's Imperial Radch trilogy, that swept the major science fiction awards, garnering Hugo, Nebula, Locus, British Science Fiction Association, and Arthur C. Clarke Awards for best novel – alongside widespread acclaim for the book's deft balance of suspense, character development, and world-building. Its sequels, *Ancillary Sword* and *Ancillary Mercy*, garnered similar awards attention and closed out the trilogy. Ann has worked as a waitress, a receptionist, a rodman on a land-surveying crew, and a recording engineer. She lives in St. Louis, Missouri.

Ashiban Xidyla had a headache. A particularly vicious one, centered somewhere on the top of her head. She sat curled over her lap, in her seat on the flier, eyes closed. Oddly, she had no memory of leaning forward, and – now she thought of it – no idea when the headache had begun.

The Gidanta had been very respectful so far, very solicitous of Ashiban's age, but that was, she was sure, little more than the entirely natural respect for one's elders. This was not a time when she could afford any kind of weakness. Ashiban was here to prevent a war that would quite possibly end with the Gidanta slaughtering every one of Ashiban's fellow Raksamat on the planet. The Sovereign of Iss, hereditary high priestess of the Gidanta, sat across the aisle, silent and veiled, her interpreter beside her. What must they be thinking?

Ashiban took three careful breaths. Straightened cautiously, wary of the pain flaring. Opened her eyes.

Ought to have seen blue sky through the flier's front window past the pilot's seat, ought to have heard the buzz of the engine. Instead she saw shards of brown and green and blue. Heard nothing. She closed her eyes, opened them again. Tried to make some sense of things. They weren't falling, she was sure. Had the flier landed, and she hadn't noticed?

A high, quavering voice said something, syllables that made no sense to Ashiban. "We have to get out of here," said a calm, muffled voice somewhere at Ashiban's feet. "Speaker is in some distress." Damn. She'd forgotten to turn off the translating function on her handheld. Maybe the Sovereign's interpreter hadn't heard it. She turned her head to look across the flier's narrow aisle, wincing at the headache.

The Sovereign's interpreter lay in the aisle, his head jammed up against the back of the pilot's seat at an odd, awkward angle. The high voice spoke again, and in the small bag at Ashiban's feet her handheld said, "Disregard the dead. We have to get out of here or we will also die. The speaker is in some distress."

In her own seat, the pink- and orange- and blue-veiled Sovereign fumbled at the safety restraints. The straps parted with a click, and the Sovereign stood. Stepped into the aisle, hiking her long blue skirt. Spoke – it must have been the Sovereign speaking all along. "Stupid cow," said Ashiban's handheld, in her bag. "Speaker's distress has increased."

The flier lurched. The Sovereign cried out. "No translation available," remarked Ashiban's handheld, as the Sovereign reached forward to tug at Ashiban's own safety restraints and, once those had come undone, grab Ashiban's arm and pull.

The flier had crashed. The flier had crashed, and the Sovereign's interpreter must have gotten out of his seat for some reason, at just the wrong time. Ashiban herself must have hit her head. That would explain the memory gap, and the headache. She blinked again, and the colored shards where the window should have been resolved into cracked glass, and behind it sky, and flat ground covered in brown and green plants, here and there some white or pink. "We should stay here and wait for help," Ashiban said. In her bag, her handheld said something incomprehensible.

The Sovereign pulled harder on Ashiban's arm. "You stupid expletive cow," said the handheld, as the Sovereign picked Ashiban's bag up from her feet. "Someone shot us down, and we crashed in the expletive High Mires. The expletive expletive is expletive sinking into the expletive bog. If we stay here we'll drown. The speaker is highly agitated." The flier lurched again.

It all seemed so unreal. Concussion, Ashiban thought. I have a concussion, and I'm not thinking straight. She took her bag from the Sovereign, rose, and followed the Sovereign of Iss to the emergency exit.

OUTSIDE THE FLIER, everything was a brown and green plain, blue sky above. The ground swelled and rolled under Ashiban's feet, but given the flier behind her, half-sunk into the gray-brown ground, and the pain in her head, she wasn't sure if it was really doing that or if it was a symptom of concussion.

The Sovereign said something. The handheld in Ashiban's bag spoke, but it was lost in the open space and the breeze and Ashiban's inability to concentrate.

The Sovereign yanked Ashiban's bag from her, pulled it open. Dug out the handheld. "Expletive," said the handheld. "Expletive expletive. We are standing on water. The speaker is agitated."

"What?" The flier behind them, sliding slowly into the mire, made a gurgling sound. The ground was still unsteady under Ashiban's feet, she still wasn't sure why.

"Water! The speaker is emphatic." The Sovereign gestured toward the greenish-brown mat of moss beneath them.

"Help will come," Ashiban said. "We should stay here."

"They shot us down," said the handheld. "The speaker is agitated and emphatic."

"What?"

"They shot us down. I saw the pilot shot through the window, I saw them die. Timran was trying to take control of the flier when we crashed. Whoever comes, they are not coming to help us. We have to get to solid ground. We have to hide. The speaker is emphatic. The speaker is in some distress. The speaker is agitated." The Sovereign took Ashiban's arm and pulled her forward.

"Hide?" There was nowhere to hide. And the ground swelled and sank, like waves on the top of water. She fell to her hands and knees, nauseated.

"Translation unavailable," said the handheld, as the Sovereign dropped down beside her. "Crawl then, but come with me or be dead. The speaker is emphatic. The speaker is in some distress." The Sovereign crawled away, the ground still heaving.

"That's my bag," said Ashiban. "That's my handheld." The Sovereign continued to crawl away. "There's nowhere to hide!" But if she stayed where she was, on her hands and knees on the unsteady ground, she would be all alone here, and all her things gone and her head hurting and her stomach sick and nothing making sense. She crawled after the Sovereign.

By the time the ground stopped roiling, the squishy wet moss had changed to stiff, spiky-leaved meter-high plants that scratched Ashiban's face and tore at her sodden clothes. "Come here," said her handheld, somewhere up ahead. "Quickly. Come here. The speaker is agitated." Ashiban just wanted to lie down where she was, close her eyes, and go to sleep. But the Sovereign had her bag. There was a bottle of water in her bag. She kept going.

Found the Sovereign prone, veilless, pulling off her bright-colored skirts to ball them up beneath herself. Underneath her clothes she wore a plain brown shirt and leggings, like any regular Gidanta. "Ancestors!" panted Ashiban, still on hands and knees, not sure where there was room to lie down. "You're just a kid! You're younger than my grandchildren!"

In answer the Sovereign took hold of the collar of Ashiban's jacket and yanked her down to the ground. Ashiban cried out, and heard her handheld say something incomprehensible, presumably the Gidantan equivalent of *No translation available*. Pain darkened her vision, and her ears roared. Or was that the flier the Sovereign had said she'd heard?

The Sovereign spoke. "Stupid expletive expletive expletive, lie still," said Ashiban's handheld calmly. "Speaker is in some distress."

Ashiban closed her eyes. Her head hurt, and her twig-scratched face stung, but she was very, very tired.

A CALM VOICE was saying, "Wake up, Ashiban Xidyla. The speaker is distressed." Over and over again. She opened her eyes. The absurdly young Sovereign of Iss lay in front of her, brown cheek pressed against the gray ground, staring at Ashiban, twigs and spiny leaves caught in the few trailing braids that had come loose from the hair coiled at the top of her head. Her eyes were red and puffy, as though she had been crying, though her expression gave no sign of it. She clutched Ashiban's handheld in one hand. Nineteen at most, Ashiban thought. Probably younger. "Are you awake, Ashiban Xidyla? The speaker is distressed."

"My head doesn't hurt," Ashiban observed. Despite that, everything still seemed slippery and unreal.

"I took the emergency medical kit on our way off the flier," the handheld said, translating the Sovereign's reply. "I put a corrective on your forehead. It's not the right kind, though. The instructions say to take you to a doctor right away. The speaker is..."

"Translation preferences," interrupted Ashiban. "Turn off emotional evaluation." The handheld fell silent. "Have you called for help, Sovereign? Is help coming?"

"You are very stupid," said Ashiban's handheld. Said the Sovereign of Iss. "Or the concussion is dangerously severe. Our flier was shot down. Twenty minutes after that a flier goes back and forth over us as though it is looking for something, but we are in the High Mires, no one lives here. If we call for help, who is nearest? The people who shot us down."

"Who would shoot us down?"

"Someone who wants war between Gidanta and Raksamat. Someone with a grudge against your mother, the sainted Ciwril Xidyla. Someone with a grudge against my grandmother, the previous Sovereign."

"Not likely anyone Raksamat then," said Ashiban, and immediately regretted it. She was here to foster goodwill between her people and the Sovereign's, because the Gidanta had trusted her mother, Ciwril Xidyla, and so they might listen to her daughter. "There are far more of you down here than Raksamat settlers. If it came to a war, the Raksamat here would be slaughtered. I don't think any of us wants that."

"We will argue in the future," said the Sovereign. "So long as whoever it is does not manage to kill us. I have been thinking. They did not see us, under the plants, but maybe they will come back and look for us with infrared. They may come back soon. We have to reach the trees north of here."

"I can use my handheld to just contact my own people," said Ashiban. "Just them. I trust them."

"Do you?" asked the Sovereign. "But maybe the deaths of some Raksamat settlers will be the excuse they need to bring a war that kills all the Gidanta so they can have the world for themselves. Maybe your death would be convenient for them."

"That's ridiculous!" exclaimed Ashiban. She pushed herself to sitting, not too quickly, wary of the pain in her head returning, of her lingering dizziness. "I'm talking about my friends."

"Your friends are far away," said the Sovereign. "They would call on others to come find us. Do you trust those others?" The girl seemed deadly serious. She sat up. "I don't." She tucked Ashiban's handheld into her waistband, picked up her bundle of skirts and veils.

"That's my handheld! I need it!"

"You'll only call our deaths down with it," said the Sovereign. "Die if you want to." She rose, and trudged away through the stiff, spiky vegetation.

Ashiban considered tackling the girl and taking back her handheld. But the Sovereign was young, and while Ashiban was in fairly good shape considering her age, she had never been an athlete, even in her youth. And that was without considering the head injury.

She stood. Carefully, still dizzy, joints stiff. Where the flier had been was only black water, strips and chunks of moss floating on its surface, all of it surrounded by a flat carpet of yet more moss. She remembered the Sovereign saying *We're standing on water!* Remembered the swell and roll of the ground that had made her drop to her hands and knees.

She closed her eyes. She thought she vaguely remembered sitting in her seat on the flier, the Sovereign crying out, her interpreter getting out of his seat to rush forward to where the pilot slumped over the controls.

Shot down. If that was true, the Sovereign was right. Calling for help – if she could find some way to do that without her handheld – might well be fatal. Whoever it was had considered both Ashiban and the Sovereign of Iss acceptable losses. Had, perhaps, specifically wanted both of them dead. Had, perhaps, specifically wanted the war that had threatened for the past two years to become deadly real.

But nobody wanted that. Not even the Gidanta who had never been happy with Ashiban's people's presence in the system wanted that, Ashiban was sure.

She opened her eyes. Saw the girl's back as she picked her way through the mire. Saw far off on the northern horizon the trees the girl had mentioned. "Ancestors!" cried Ashiban. "I'm too old for this." And she shouldered her bag and followed the Sovereign of Iss.

Eventually Ashiban caught up, though the Sovereign didn't acknowledge her in any way. They trudged through the hip-high scrub in silence for some time, only making the occasional hiss of annoyance at particularly troublesome branches. The clear blue sky clouded over, and a damp-smelling wind rose. A relief – the bright sun had hurt Ashiban's eyes. As the trees on the horizon became more definitely a band of trees – still dismayingly far off – Ashiban's thoughts, which had this whole time been slippery and tenuous, began to settle into something like a comprehensible pattern.

Shot down. Ashiban was sure none of her people wanted war. Though off-planet the Raksamat weren't quite so vulnerable – were, in fact, much better armed. The ultimate outcome of an actual war would probably not favor the Gidanta. Or Ashiban didn't think so. It was possible some Raksamat faction actually wanted such a war. And Ashiban wasn't really anyone of any significance to her own people.

Her mother had been. Her mother, Ciwril Xidyla, had negotiated the Treaty of Eatu with the then-Sovereign of Iss, ensuring the right of the Raksamat to live peacefully in the system, and on the planet. Ciwril had been widely admired among both Raksamat and Gidanta. As her daughter, Ashiban was only a sign, an admonition to remember her mother. If her side could think it acceptable to sacrifice the lives of their own people on the planet, they would certainly not blink at sacrificing Ashiban herself. She didn't want to believe that, though, that her own people would do such a thing.

Would the Gidanta be willing to kill their own Sovereign for the sake of a war? An hour ago – or however long they had been trudging across the mire, Ashiban wasn't sure – she'd have said *certainly not*. The Sovereign of Iss was a sacred figure. She was the conduit between the Gidanta and the spirit of the world of Iss, which spoke to them with the Sovereign's voice. Surely they wouldn't kill her just to forward a war that would be disastrous for both sides?

"Sovereign."

A meter ahead of Ashiban, the girl kept trudging. Looked briefly over her shoulder. "What?"

"Where are you going?"

The Sovereign didn't even turn her head this time. "There's a monitoring station on the North Udran Plain."

That had to be hundreds of kilometers away, and that wasn't counting the fact that if this was indeed the High Mires, they were on the high side of the Scarp and would certainly have to detour to get down to the plains.

"On foot? That could take weeks, if we even ever get there. We have no food, no water." Well, Ashiban had about a third of a liter in a bottle in her bag, but that hardly counted. "No camping equipment."

The Sovereign just scoffed and kept walking.

"Young lady," began Ashiban, but then remembered herself at that age. Her own children and grandchildren. Adolescence was trying enough without the fate of your people resting on your shoulders, and being shot down and stranded in a bog. "I thought the current Sovereign was fifty or sixty. The daughter of the woman who was Sovereign when my mother was here last."

"You're not supposed to talk like we're all different people," said the girl. "We're all the voice of the world spirit. And you mean my aunt. She abdicated last week."

"Abdicated!" Mortified by her mistake – Ashiban had been warned over and over about the nature of the Sovereign of Iss, that she was not an individual, that referring to her as such would be an offense. "I didn't know that was possible." And surely at a time like this, the Sovereign wouldn't want to drop so much responsibility on a teenager.

"Of course it's possible. It's just a regular priesthood. It never was particularly special. It was you Raksamat who insisted on translating Sovereign as Sovereign. And it's you Raksamat whose priests are always trancing out and speaking for your ancestors. *Voice of Iss* doesn't mean that at all."

"Translating Sovereign as Sovereign?" asked Ashiban. "What is that supposed to mean?" The girl snorted. "And how can the Voice of Iss not mean exactly that?" The Sovereign didn't answer, just kept walking.

After a long silence, Ashiban said, "Then why do any of the Gidanta listen to you? And who is it my mother was negotiating with?"

The Sovereign looked back at Ashiban and rolled her eyes. "With the interpreter, of course. And if your mother didn't know that, she was completely stupid. And nobody listens to me." The voice of the translating handheld was utterly calm and neutral, but the girl's tone was contemptuous.

"That's why I'm stuck here. And it wasn't about us listening to the voice of the planet. It was about *you* listening to *us*. You wouldn't talk to the Terraforming Council because you wouldn't accept they were an authority, and besides, you didn't like what they were saying."

"An industrial association is not a government!" Seeing the girl roll her eyes again, Ashiban wondered fleetingly what her words sounded like in Gidantan – if the handheld was making *industrial association* and *government* into the same words, the way it obviously had when it had said for the girl, moments ago, *translating Sovereign as Sovereign*. But that was ridiculous. The two weren't the same thing at all.

The Sovereign stopped. Turned to face Ashiban. "We have been here for two thousand years. For all that time, we have been working on this planet, to make it a place we could live without interference. We came here, to this place without an intersystem gate, so that no one would bother us and we could live in peace. You turned up less than two centuries ago, now most of the hard work is done, and you want to tell us what to do with our planet, and who is or isn't an authority!"

"We were refugees. We came here by accident, and we can't very well leave. And we brought benefits. You've been cut off from the outside for so long, you didn't have medical correctives. Those have saved lives, Sovereign. And we've brought other things." Including weapons the Gidanta didn't have. "Including our own knowledge of terraforming, and how to best manage a planet."

"And you agreed, your own mother, the great Ciwril Xidyla agreed, that no one would settle on the planet without authorization from the Terraforming Council! And yet there are dozens of Raksamat farmsteads just in the Saunn foothills, and more elsewhere."

"That wasn't the agreement. The treaty explicitly states that we have a right to be here, and a right to share in the benefits of living on this planet. Your own grandmother agreed to that! And small farmsteads are much better for the planet than the cities the Terraforming Council is intending." Wind gusted, and a few fat drops of rain fell."

"My grandmother agreed to nothing! It was the gods-cursed interpreter who made the agreement. And he was appointed by the Terraforming Council, just like all of them! And how dare you turn up here after we've done all the hard work and think because you brought us some technology you can tell us what to do with our planet!"

"How can you own a planet? You can't, it's ridiculous! There's more than enough room for all of us."

"I've memorized it, you know," said the Sovereign. "The entire agreement. It's not that long. *Settlement will only proceed according to the current consensus regarding the good of the planet.* That's what it says, right there in the second paragraph."

Ashiban knew that sentence by heart. Everyone knew that sentence by now. Arguments over what *current consensus regarding the good of the planet* might mean were inescapable – and generally, in Ashiban's opinion, made in bad faith. The words were clear enough. "There's nothing about the Terraforming Council in that sentence." Like most off-planet Raksamat, Ashiban didn't speak the language of the Gidanta. But – also like most off-planet Raksamat – she had a few words and phrases, and she knew the Gidantan for *Terraforming Council.* Had heard the girl speak the sentence, knew there was no mention of the council.

The Sovereign cried out in apparent anger and frustration. "How can you? How can you stand there and say that, as though you have not just heard me say it?"

Overhead, barely audible over the sound of the swelling rain, the hum of a flier engine. The Sovereign looked up.

"It's help," said Ashiban. Angry, yes, but she could set that aside at the prospect of rescue. Of soon being somewhere warm, and dry, and comfortable. Her clothes – plain, green trousers and shirt, simple, soft flat shoes – had not been chosen with any anticipation of a trek through mud and weeds, or standing in a rain shower. "They must be looking for us."

The Sovereign's eyes widened. She spun and took off running through the thick, thigh-high plants, toward the trees.

"Wait!" cried Ashiban, but the girl kept moving.

Ashiban turned to scan the sky, shielding her eyes from the rain with one hand. Was there anything she could do to attract the attention of the flier? Her own green clothes weren't far off the green of the plants she stood among, but she didn't trust the flat, brownish-green mossy stretches that she and the Sovereign had been avoiding. She had nothing that would light up, and the girl had fled with Ashiban's handheld, which she could have used to try to contact the searchers.

A crack echoed across the mire, and a few meters to Ashiban's left, leaves and twigs exploded. The wind gusted again, harder than before, and she shivered.

And realized that someone had just fired at her. That had been a gunshot, and there was no one here to shoot at her except that approaching flier, which was, Ashiban saw, coming straight toward her, even though with the clouds and the rain, and the green of her clothes and the green of the plants she stood in, she could not have been easy to see.

Except maybe in the infrared. Even without the cold rain coming down, she must glow bright and unmistakable in infrared.

Ashiban turned and ran. Or tried to, wading through the plants toward the trees, twigs catching her trousers. Another crack, and she couldn't go any faster than she was, though she tried, and the wind blew harder, and she hoped she was moving toward the trees.

Three more shots in quick succession, the wind blowing harder, nearly pushing her over, and Ashiban stumbled out of the plants onto a stretch of open moss that trembled under her as she ran, gasping, cold, and exhausted, toward another patch of those thigh-high weeds, and the shadow of trees beyond. Below her feet the moss began to come apart, fraying, loosening, one more wobbling step and she would sink into the black water of the mire below, but another shot cracked behind her and she couldn't stop, and there was no safe direction, she could only go forward. She ran on. And then, with hopefully solid ground a single step ahead, the skies opened up in a torrent of rain, and the moss gave way underneath her.

She plunged downward, into cold water. Made a frantic, scrabbling grab, got hold of one tough plant stem. Tried to pull herself up, but could not. The rain poured down, and her grip on the plant stem began to slip.

A hand grabbed her arm. Someone shouted something incomprehensible – it was the Sovereign of Iss, rain streaming down her face, braids plastered against her neck and shoulders. The girl grabbed the back of Ashiban's shirt with her other hand, leaned back, pulling Ashiban up a few centimeters, and Ashiban reached forward and grabbed another handful of plant, and somehow scrambled free of the water, onto the land, and she and the Sovereign half-ran, half-stumbled forward into the trees.

Where the rain was less but still came down. And they needed better cover, they needed to go deeper into the trees. Ancestors grant the woods ahead were thick enough to hide them from the flier, and Ashiban wanted to tell the Sovereign that they needed to keep running, but the girl didn't stop until Ashiban, unable to move a single step more, collapsed at the bottom of a tree.

The Sovereign dropped down beside her. There was no sound but their gasping, and the rain hissing through the branches above.

One of Ashiban's shoes had come off, somewhere. Her arm, which the Sovereign had pulled on to get her up out of the water, ached. Her back hurt, and her legs. Her heart pounded, and she couldn't seem to catch her breath, and she shivered, with cold or with fear she wasn't sure.

THE RAIN LESSENED not long after, and stopped at some point during the night. Ashiban woke shivering, the Sovereign huddled beside her. Pale sunlight filtered through the tree leaves, and the leaf-covered ground was sodden. So was Ashiban.

She was hungry, too. Wasn't food the whole point of planets? Surely there would be something to eat, it would just be a question of knowing what there was, and how to eat it safely. Water might well be a bigger problem than food. Ashiban opened her bag – which by some miracle had stayed on her shoulder through everything – and found her half-liter bottle of water, still about three-quarters full. If she'd had her wits about her last night, she'd have opened it in the rain, to collect as much as she could.

"Well," Ashiban said, "here we are."

Silence. Not a word from the handheld. The Sovereign uncurled herself from where she huddled against Ashiban. Put a hand on her waist, where the handheld had been tucked into her waistband. Looked at Ashiban.

The handheld was gone. "Oh, Ancestors," said Ashiban. And after another half-panicked second, carefully got to her feet from off the ground – something that hadn't been particularly easy for a decade or two, even without yesterday's hectic flight and a night spent cold and soaking wet, sleeping sitting on the ground and leaning against a tree – and retraced their steps. The Sovereign joined her.

As far back as they went (apparently neither of them was willing to go all the way back to the mire), they found only bracken, and masses of wet, dead leaves.

Ashiban looked at the damp and shivering Sovereign. Who looked five or six years younger than she'd looked yesterday. The Sovereign said nothing, but what was there to say? Without the handheld, or some other translation device, they could barely talk to each other at all. Ashiban herself knew only a few phrases in Gidantan. *Hello* and *good-bye* and *I don't understand Gidantan.* She could count from one to twelve. A few words and phrases more, none of them applicable to being stranded in the woods on the edge of the High Mires. Ironic, since her mother Ciwril had been an expert in the language. It was her mother's work that had made the translation devices as useful as they were, that had allowed the Raksamat and Gidanta to speak to each other. *And who is it my mother was negotiating with? With the interpreter, of course.*

No point thinking about that just now. The immediate problem was more than enough.

Someone had shot down their flier yesterday, and then apparently flown away. Hours later they had returned, so that they could shoot at Ashiban and the Sovereign as they fled. It didn't make sense.

The Gidanta had guns, of course, knew how to make them. But they didn't have many. Since they had arrived here, most of their energies had been devoted to the terraforming of Iss, and during much of that time they'd lived in space, on stations, an environment in which projectile weapons potentially caused far more problems than they might solve, even when it came to deadly disputes.

That attitude had continued when they had moved down to the planet. There were police, and some of the Terraforming Council had bodyguards, and Ashiban didn't doubt there were people who specialized in fighting, including firing guns, but there was no Gidanta military, no army, standing or otherwise. Fliers for cargo or for personal transport, but not for warfare. Guns for hunting, not designed to kill people efficiently.

The Raksamat, Ashiban's own people, had come into the system armed. But none of those weapons were on the planet. Or Ashiban didn't think they were. So, a hunting gun and a personal flier. She wanted to ask the

Sovereign, standing staring at Ashiban, still shivering, if the girl had seen the other flier. But she couldn't, not without that handheld.

But it didn't matter, this moment, why it had happened the way it had. There was no way to tell who had tried to kill them. No way to know what or who they would find if they returned to the mire, to where their own flier had sunk under the black water and the moss.

Her thoughts were going in circles. Whether it was the night spent in the cold, and the hunger and the fear, or whether it was the remnants of her concussion – and what had the Sovereign of Iss said, that the corrective hadn't been the right sort and she should get to a doctor as soon as possible? – or maybe all of those, Ashiban didn't know.

Yesterday the Sovereign had said there was a monitoring station on the Udran Plains, which lay to the north of the Scarp. There would be people at a monitoring station – likely all of them Gidanta. Very possibly not favorably disposed toward Ashiban, no matter whose daughter she was.

But there would be dozens, maybe even hundreds of people at a monitoring station, any of whom might witness an attempt to murder Ashiban, and all of whom would be outraged at an attempt to harm the Sovereign of Iss. There was no one at the crash site on the mire to see what happened to them.

"Which way?" Ashiban asked the girl.

Who looked up at the leaf-dappled sky above them, and then pointed back into the woods, the way they had come. Said something Ashiban didn't understand. Watched Ashiban expectantly. Something about the set of her jaw suggested to Ashiban that the girl was trying very hard not to cry.

"All right," said Ashiban, and turned and began walking back the way they had come, the Sovereign of Iss alongside her.

THEY SHARED OUT the water between them as they went. There was less food in the woods than Ashiban would have expected, or at least neither of them knew where or how to find it. No doubt the Sovereign of Iss, at her age, was hungrier even than Ashiban, but she didn't complain, just walked forward. Once they heard the distant sound of a flier, presumably looking for them, but the Sovereign of Iss showed no sign of being tempted to go back. Ashiban thought of those shots, of plunging into cold, black water, and shivered.

Despite herself, Ashiban began imagining what she would eat if she were at home. The nutrient cakes that everyone had eaten every day until they had established contact with the Gidanta. They were traditional for holidays, authentic Raksamat cuisine, and Ashiban's grandmother had despised them, observed wryly on every holiday that her grandchildren would not eat them with such relish if that had been their only food for years. Ashiban would like a nutrient cake now.

Or some fish. Or snails. Surely there might be snails in the woods? But Ashiban wasn't sure how to find them.

Or grubs. A handful of toasted grubs, with a little salt, maybe some cumin. At home they were an expensive treat, either harvested from a station's agronomy unit, or shipped up from Iss itself. Ashiban remembered a school trip, once, when she'd been much, much younger, a tour of the station's food-growing facilities, remembered an agronomist turning over the dirt beside a row of green, sharp-smelling plants to reveal a grub, curled and white in the dark soil. Remembered one of her schoolmates saying the sight made them hungry.

She stopped. Pushed aside the leaf mold under her feet. Looked around for a stick.

The Sovereign of Iss stopped, turned to look at Ashiban. Said something in Gidantan that Ashiban assumed was some version of *What are you doing?*

"Grubs," said Ashiban. That word she knew – the Gidanta sold prepackaged toasted grubs harvested from their own orbital agronomy projects, and the name was printed on the package.

The Sovereign blinked at her. Frowned. Seemed to think for a bit, and then said, "Fire?" in Gidantan. That was another word Ashiban knew – nearly everyone in the system recognized words in either language that might turn up in a safety alert.

There was no way to make a fire that Ashiban could think of. Her bag held only their now nearly empty bottle of water. People who lived in space generally didn't walk around with the means for producing an open flame. Here on Iss things might be different, but if the Sovereign had been carrying fire-making tools, she'd lost them in the mire. "No fire," Ashiban said. "We'll have to eat anything we find raw." The Sovereign of Iss frowned, and then went kicking through the leaf mold for a couple of sturdy sticks.

The few grubs they dug up promised more nearby. There was no water to wash the dirt off them, and they were unpleasant to eat while raw and wiggling, but they were food.

Their progress slowed as they stopped every few steps to dig for more grubs, or to replace a broken stick. But after a few hours, or at least what Ashiban took to be a few hours -- she had no way of telling time beyond the sunlight, and had no experience with that – their situation seemed immeasurably better than it had before they'd eaten.

They filled Ashiban's bag with grubs, and walked on until night fell, and slept, shivering, huddled together. Ashiban was certain she would never be warm again, would always be chilled to her bones. But she could think straighter, or at least it seemed like she could. The girl's plan to walk down to the plains was still outrageous, still seemed all but impossible, but it also seemed like the only way forward.

By the end of the next day, Ashiban was more sick of raw and gritty grubs than she could possibly say. And by the afternoon of the day after that, the trees thinned and they were faced with a wall of brambles. They turned to parallel the barrier, walked east for a while, until they came to a relatively clear space – a tunnel of thorny branches arching over a several-meters-wide shelf of reddish-brown rock jutting out of the soil. Ashiban peered through and saw horizon, gestured to the Sovereign of Iss to look.

The Sovereign pulled her head back out of the tunnel, looked at Ashiban, and said something long and incomprehensible.

"Right," said Ashiban. In her own language. There was no point trying to ask her question in Gidantan. "Do we want to go through here and keep going north until we find the edge of the Scarp, and turn east until we find a way down to the plain? Or do we want to keep going east like we have been and hope we find something?"

With her free hand – her other one held the water bottle that no longer fit in Ashiban's grub-filled bag – the Sovereign waved away the possibility of her having understood Ashiban.

Ashiban pointed north, toward the brambles. "Scarp," she said, in Gidantan. It was famous enough that she knew that one.

"Yes," agreed the Sovereign, in that same language. And then, to Ashiban's surprise, added, in Raksamat, "See." She held her hands up to her eyes, miming a scope. Then waved an arm expansively. "Scarp see big."

"Good point," agreed Ashiban. On the edge of the Scarp, they could see where they were, and take their direction from that, instead of wandering and hoping they arrived somewhere. "Yes," she said in Gidantan. "Good." She gestured at the thorny tunnel of brambles.

The Sovereign of Iss just stared at her. Ashiban sighed. Made sure her bag was securely closed. Gingerly got down on her hands and knees, lowered herself onto her stomach, and inched herself forward under the brambles.

The tunnel wasn't long, just three or four meters, but Ashiban took it slowly, the bag dragging beside her, thorns tearing at her clothes and her face. Knees and wrists and shoulders aching. When she got home, she was going to talk to the doctor about joint repairs, even if having all of them done at once would lay her up for a week or more.

Her neck and shoulders as stiff as they were, Ashiban was looking down at the red-brown rock when she came out of the bramble tunnel. She inched herself carefully free of the thorns and then began to contemplate getting herself to her feet. She would wait for the Sovereign, perhaps, and let the girl help her to standing.

Ashiban pushed herself up onto her hands and knees and then reached forward. Her hand met nothingness. Unbalanced, tipping in the direction of her outstretched hand, she saw the edge of the rock she crawled on, and nothing else.

Nothing but air. And far, far below – nearly a kilometer, she remembered hearing in some documentary about the Scarp – the green haze of the plains. Behind her the Sovereign of Iss made a strangled cry, and grabbed Ashiban's legs before she could tip all the way forward.

They stayed that way, frozen for a few moments, the Sovereign gripping Ashiban's legs, Ashiban's hand outstretched over the edge of the Scarp. Then the Sovereign whimpered. Ashiban wanted to join her. Wanted, actually, to scream. Carefully placed her outstretched hand on the edge of the cliff, and pushed herself back, and looked up.

The line of brambles stopped a bit more than a meter from the cliff edge. Room enough for her to scoot carefully over and sit. But the Sovereign would not let go of her legs. And Ashiban had no way to ask her to. Silently, and not for the first time, she cursed the loss of the handheld.

The Sovereign whimpered again. "Ashiban Xidyla!" she cried, in a quavering voice.

"I'm all right," Ashiban said, and her own voice was none too steady. "I'm all right, you got me just in time. You can let go now." But of course the girl couldn't understand her. She tried putting one leg back, and slowly, carefully, the Sovereign let go and edged back into the tunnel of brambles. Slowly, carefully, Ashiban got herself from hands and knees to sitting by the mouth of that tunnel, and looked out over the edge of the Scarp.

A sheer cliff some six hundred kilometers long and nearly a kilometer high, the Scarp loomed over the Udran Plains to the north, grassland as far as Ashiban could see, here and there a patch of trees, or the blue and silver of water. Far off to the northwest shone the bright ribbon of a river.

In the middle of the green, on the side of a lake, lay a small collection of roads and buildings, how distant Ashiban couldn't guess. "Sovereign, is that the monitoring station?" Ashiban didn't see anything else, and it seemed to her that she could see quite a lot of the plains from where she sat. It struck her then that this could only be a small part of the plains, as long as the Scarp was, and she felt suddenly lost and despairing. "Sovereign, look!" She glanced over at the mouth of the bramble tunnel.

The Sovereign of Iss lay facedown, arms flat in front of her. She said something into the red-brown rock below her.

"Too high?" asked Ashiban.

"High," agreed the Sovereign, into the rock, in her small bit of Raksamat. "Yes."

And she had lunged forward to grab Ashiban and keep her from tumbling over the edge. "Look, Sovereign, is that the..." Ashiban wished she knew how to say *monitoring station* in Gidantan. Tried to remember what the girl had said, days ago, when she'd mentioned it, but Ashiban had only been listening to the handheld translation. "Look. See. Please, Sovereign." Slowly, hesitantly, the Sovereign of Iss raised her head. Kept the rest of herself flat against the rock. Ashiban pointed. "How do we get there? How did you mean us to get there?" Likely there were ways to descend the cliff face. But Ashiban had no way of knowing where or how to do that. And given the state the Sovereign was in right now, Ashiban would guess she didn't either. Hadn't had any idea what she was getting into when she'd decided to come this way.

She'd have expected better knowledge of the planet from the Sovereign of Iss, the voice of the planet itself. But then, days back, the girl had said that it was Ashiban's people, the Raksamat, who thought of that office in terms of communicating with the Ancestors, that it didn't mean that at all to the Gidanta. Maybe that was true, and even if it wasn't, this girl – Ashiban still didn't know her name, likely never would, addressing her by it would be the height of disrespect even from her own mother now that she was the Sovereign – had been Sovereign of Iss for a few weeks at the most. The girl had almost certainly been well out of her depth from the moment her aunt had abdicated.

And likely she had grown up in one of the towns dotted around the surface of Iss. She might know quite a lot more about outdoor life than Ashiban did – but that didn't mean she knew much about survival in the wilderness with no food or equipment.

Well. Obviously they couldn't walk along the edge of the Scarp, not given the Sovereign's inability to deal with heights. They would have to continue walking east along the bramble wall, to somewhere the Scarp was lower, or hope there was some town or monitoring station in their path.

"Let's go back," Ashiban said, and reached out to give the Sovereign's shoulder a gentle push back toward the other side of the brambles. Saw the girl's back and shoulders shaking, realized she was sobbing silently. "Let's go back," Ashiban said, again. Searched her tiny Gidantan vocabulary for something useful. "Go," she said, finally, in Gidantan, pushing on the girl's shoulder. After a moment, the Sovereign began to scoot backward, never raising her head more than a few centimeters. Ashiban followed.

Crawling out of the brambles back into the woods, Ashiban found the Sovereign sitting on the ground, still weeping. As Ashiban came entirely clear of the thorns, the girl stood and helped Ashiban to her feet and then, still crying, not saying a single word or looking at Ashiban at all, turned and began walking east.

* * *

THE NEXT DAY they found a small stream. The Sovereign lay down and put her face in the water, drank for a good few minutes, and then filled the bottle and brought it to Ashiban. They followed the stream's wandering east-now-south-now-east-again course for another three days as it broadened into something almost approaching a river.

At the end of the third day, they came to a small, gently arched bridge, mottled gray and brown and beige, thick plastic spun from whatever scraps had been thrown into the hopper of the fabricator, with a jagged five- or six-centimeter jog around the middle, where the fabricator must have gotten hung up and then been kicked back into action.

On the far side of the bridge, on the other bank of the stream, a house and outbuildings, the same mottled gray and brown as the bridge. An old, dusty groundcar. A garden, a young boy pulling weeds, three or four chickens hunting for bugs among the vegetables.

As Ashiban and the Sovereign came over the bridge, the boy looked up from his work in the garden, made a silent O with his mouth, turned and ran into the house. "Raksamat," said Ashiban, but of course the Sovereign must have realized as soon as they set eyes on those fabricated buildings.

A woman came out of the house, in shirt and trousers and stocking feet, gray-shot hair in braids tied behind her back. A hunting gun in her hand. Not aimed at Ashiban or the Sovereign. Just very conspicuously there.

The sight of that gun made Ashiban's heart pound. But she would almost be glad to let this woman shoot her so long as she let Ashiban eat something besides grubs first. And let her sit in a chair. Still, she wasn't desperate enough to speak first. She was old enough to be this woman's mother.

"Elder," said the woman with the gun. "To what do we owe the honor?"

It struck Ashiban that these people – probably on the planet illegally, one of those Raksamat settler families that had so angered the Gidanta recently – were unlikely to have any desire to encourage a war that would leave them alone and vulnerable here on the planet surface. "Our flier crashed, child, and we've been walking for days. We are in sore need of some hospitality." Some asperity crept into her voice, and she couldn't muster up the energy to feel apologetic about it.

The woman with the gun stared at Ashiban, and her gaze shifted over Ashiban's shoulder, presumably to the Sovereign of Iss, who had dropped back when they'd crossed the bridge. "You're Ashiban Xidyla," said the woman with the gun. "And this is the Sovereign of Iss."

Ashiban turned to look at the Sovereign. Who had turned her face away, held her hands up as though to shield herself.

"Someone tried to kill us," Ashiban said, turning back to the woman with the gun. "Someone shot down our flier."

"Did they now," said the woman with the gun. "They just found the flier last night. It's been all over the news, that the pilot and the Sovereign's interpreter were inside, but not yourself, Elder, or her. Didn't say anything about it being shot down, but I can't say I'm surprised." She considered Ashiban and the Sovereign for a moment. "Well, come in."

Inside they found a large kitchen, fabricator-made benches at a long table where a man sat plucking a chicken. He looked up at their entrance, then down again. Ashiban and the Sovereign sat at the other end of the table, and the boy from the garden brought them bowls of pottage. The Sovereign ate with one hand still spread in front of her face.

"Child," said Ashiban, forcing herself to stop shoveling food into her mouth, "is there a cloth or a towel the Sovereign could use? She lost her veils."

The woman stared at Ashiban, incredulous. Looked for a moment as though she was going to scoff, or say something dismissive, but instead left the room and came back with a large, worn dish towel, which she held out for the Sovereign.

Who stared at the cloth a moment, through her fingers, and then took it and laid it over her head, and then pulled one corner across her face, so that she could still see.

Their host leaned against a cabinet. "So," she said, "the Gidanta wanted an excuse to kill all us Raksamat on the planet, and shot your flier out of the sky."

"I didn't say that," said Ashiban. The comfort from having eaten actual cooked food draining away at the woman's words. "I don't know who shot our flier down."

"Who else would it be?" asked the woman, bitterly. The Sovereign sat silent beside Ashiban. Surely she could not understand what was being said, but she was perceptive enough to guess what the topic was, to understand the tone of voice. "Not that I had much hope for this settlement you're supposedly here to make. All respect, Elder, but things are as they are, and I won't lie."

"No, of course, child," replied Ashiban. "You shouldn't lie."

"It's always us who get sold out, in the agreements and the settlements," said the woman. "We have every right to be here. As much right as the Gidanta. That's what the agreement your mother made said, isn't it? But then when we're actually here, oh, no, that won't do, we're breaking the law. And does your mother back us up? Does the Assembly? No, of course not. We aren't Xidylas or Ontrils or Lajuds or anybody important. Maybe if my family had an elder with a seat in the Assembly it would be different, but if we did, we wouldn't be here. Would we?"

"I'm not sure that's entirely fair, child," replied Ashiban. "When the Raksamat farmsteads were first discovered, the Gidanta wanted to find you all and expel you. They wanted the Assembly to send help to enforce that. In the end my mother convinced everyone to leave the farmsteads alone while the issues were worked out."

"Your mother!" cried the woman, their host. "All respect, Elder, but your mother might have told them to hold to the agreement she worked out and the Gidanta consented to, in front of their ancestors. It's short and plain enough." She gestured at the Sovereign. "Can you tell *her* that?"

The front door opened on three young women talking, pulling off their boots. One of them glanced inside, saw Ashiban and the Sovereign, the other woman, presumably a relative of theirs, standing straight and angry by the cabinet. Elbowed the others, who fell silent.

Ashiban said, "I don't speak much Gidantan, child. You probably speak more than I do. And the Sovereign doesn't have much Raksamat. I lost my handheld in the crash, so there's no way to translate." And the Sovereign was just a girl, with no more power in this situation than Ashiban herself.

The man at the end of the table spoke up. "Any news?" Directed at the three young women, who had come in and begun to dish themselves out some pottage.

"We didn't see anything amiss," said one of the young women. "But Lyek stopped on their way home from town, they said they went in to take their little one to the doctor. It was unfriendly. More unfriendly than usual, I mean." She sat down across the table with her bowl, cast a troubled glance at the Sovereign, though her tone of voice stayed matter-of-fact. "They said a few people in the street shouted at them to get off the planet, and someone spit on them and called them stinking weevils. When they protested to the constable, she said it was no good complaining about trouble they'd brought on themselves, and wouldn't do anything. They said the constable had been standing *right there*."

"It sounds like the Sovereign and I need to get into town as soon as possible," suggested Ashiban. Though she wondered what sort of reception she herself might meet, in a Gidanta town where people were behaving that way toward Raksamat settlers.

"I think," said the woman, folding her arms and leaning once more against the cabinet, "that we'll make our own decisions about what to do next, and not take orders from the sainted Ciwril Xidyla's daughter, who doesn't even speak Gidantan. Your pardon, Elder, but I honestly don't know what they sent you here for. You're welcome to food and drink, and there's a spare bed upstairs you and her ladyship there can rest in. None of us here means you any ill. But I think we're done taking orders from the Assembly, who can't even bother to speak for us when we need it."

If this woman had been one of her own daughters, Ashiban would have had sharp words for her. But this was not her daughter, and the situation was a dangerous one – and moreover, it was far more potentially dangerous for the Sovereign, sitting silent beside her, face still covered.

And Ashiban hadn't reached her age without learning a thing or two. "Of course, child," she said. "We're so grateful for your help. The food was delicious, but we've walked for days and we're so very tired. If we could wash, and maybe take you up on the offer of that bed."

Ashiban and the Sovereign each had another bowl of pottage, and Ashiban turned her bagful of grubs over to the man with the chicken. The three young women finished eating in silence, and two went up, at an order from the older woman, to make the bed. The third showed Ashiban and the Sovereign where they could wash.

The bed turned out to be in its own tiny chamber, off an upstairs corridor, and not in one corner of a communal sleeping room. The better to keep watch on them, Ashiban thought, but also at least on the surface a gesture of respect. This small bedroom probably belonged to the most senior member of the household.

Ashiban thanked the young woman who had shown them upstairs. Closed the door – no lock, likely the only door in this house that locked was that front door they had come through. Looked at the Sovereign, standing beside the bed, the cloth still held across her mouth. Tried to remember how to say *sleep* in Gidantan.

Settled for Raksamat. "Sleep now," Ashiban said, and mimed laying her head on her hand, closed her eyes. Opened them, sat down on one side of the bed, patted the other. Lay down and closed her eyes.

Next she knew, the room was dark and silent, and she ached, even more than she had during days of sleeping on the ground. The Sovereign lay beside her, breathing slow and even.

Ashiban rose, gingerly, felt her way carefully to the door. Opened it, slowly. Curled in the doorway lay the young woman who had shown them to the room, her head pillowed on one arm, a lamp on the floor by her hand, turned low. Next to her, a gun. The young woman snored softly. The house was otherwise silent.

Ashiban had entertained vague thoughts of what she would do at this moment, waking in the night when the rest of the house was likely asleep. Had intended to think more on the feasibility of those vague thoughts, and the advisability of following up on them.

She went back into the room. Shook the Sovereign awake. Finger on her lips, Ashiban showed her the sleeping young woman outside the door. The gun. The Sovereign of Iss, still shaking off the daze of sleep, blinked, frowned, went back to the bed to pick up the cloth she'd used to cover her face, and then stepped over the sleeping young woman and out into the silent corridor. Ashiban followed.

She was prepared to tell anyone who met them that they needed to use the sanitary facility. But they met no one, walked through the dark and silent house, out the door and into the starlit night. The dark, the damp, the cool air, the sound of the stream. Ashiban felt a sudden familiar ache of wishing-to-be-home. Wishing to be warmer. Wishing to have eaten more than what little she and the Sovereign could forage. And, she realized now they were outside, she had no idea what to do next.

Apparently not burdened with the same doubts, the Sovereign walked straight and without hesitation to the groundcar. Ashiban hastened to catch up with her. "I can't drive one of these," she whispered to the Sovereign, pointlessly. The girl could almost certainly not understand her. Did not even turn her head to look at Ashiban or acknowledge that she'd said anything, but opened the groundcar door and climbed into the driver's seat. Frowned over the controls for a few minutes, stretched out to a near-eternity by Ashiban's fear that someone in the house would wake and see that they were gone.

The Sovereign did something to the controls, and the groundcar started up with a low hum. Ashiban went around to the passenger side, climbed in, and before she could even settle in the seat the groundcar was moving and they were off.

At first Ashiban sat tense in the passenger seat, turned as best she could to look behind. But after a half hour or so of cautious, bumpy going, it seemed to her that they were probably safely away. She took a deep breath. Faced forward again, with some relief – looking back hadn't been terribly comfortable for her neck or her back. Looked at the Sovereign, driving with utter concentration. Well, it was hardly a surprise, now Ashiban thought of it. The Sovereign had grown up down here, doubtless groundcars were an everyday thing to her.

What next? They needed to find out where that town was. They might need to defend themselves some time in the near future. Ashiban looked around to see what there might be in the car that they could use. Back behind the seats was an assortment of tools and machines that Ashiban assumed were necessary for farming on a planet. A shovel. Some rope. A number of other things she couldn't identify.

A well between her seat and the Sovereign's held a tangled assortment of junk. A small knife. A doll made partly from pieces of fabricator plastic and partly from what appeared to be bits of an old, worn-out shirt. Bits of twine. An empty cup. Some sort of clip with a round gray blob adhesived to it. "What's this?" asked Ashiban aloud.

The Sovereign glanced over at Ashiban. With one hand she took the clip from Ashiban's hand, flicked the side of it with her thumb, and held it out to Ashiban, her attention back on the way ahead of them. Said something.

"It's a translator," said the little blob on the clip in a quiet, tinny voice. "A lot of weevils won't take their handheld into town because they're afraid the constable will take it from them and use the information on it against their families. Or if you're out working and have your hands full but think you might need to talk to a weevil." A pause, in which the Sovereign seemed to realize what she'd said. "You're not a weevil," said the little blob.

"It's not a very nice thing to say." Though of course Ashiban had heard Raksamat use slurs against the Gidanta, at home, and not thought twice about it. Until now.

"Oh, Ancestors!" cried the Sovereign, and smacked the groundcar steering in frustration. "I always say the wrong thing. I wish Timran hadn't died, I wish I still had an interpreter." Tears filled her eyes, shone in the dim light from the groundcar controls.

"Why are you swearing by the Ancestors?" asked Ashiban. "You don't believe in them. Or I thought you didn't." One tear escaped, rolled down the Sovereign's cheek. Ashiban picked up the end of the old dishcloth that was currently draped over the girl's shoulder and wiped it away.

"I didn't swear by the Ancestors!" the Sovereign protested. "I didn't swear by anything. I just said *oh, Ancestors*." They drove in silence for a few minutes. "Wait," said the Sovereign then. "Let me try something. Are you ready?"

"Ready for what?"

"This: Ancestors. What did I say?"

"You said *Ancestors*."

"Now. Pingberries. What did I say?"

"You said *pingberries*."

The Sovereign brought the groundcar to a stop, and turned to look at Ashiban. "Now. Oh, Ancestors!" as though she were angry or frustrated. "There. Do you hear? Are you listening?"

"I'm listening." Ashiban had heard it, plain and clear. "You said *oh, pingberries*, but the translator said it was *oh, Ancestors*. How did that happen?"

"Pingberries sounds a lot like... something that isn't polite," the Sovereign said. "So it's the kind of swear your old uncle would use in front of the in-laws."

"What?" asked Ashiban, and then, realizing, "Whoever entered the data for the translator thought it was equivalent to swearing by the Ancestors."

"It might be," said the Sovereign, "and actually that's really useful, that it knows when I'm talking about wanting to eat some pingberries, or when I'm frustrated and swearing. That's good, it means the translators are working well. But Ancestors and pingberries, those aren't *exactly* the same. Do you see?"

"The treaty," Ashiban realized. "That everyone thinks the other side is translating however they want." And probably not just the treaty.

It had been Ciwril Xidyla who had put together the first, most significant collection of linguistic data on Gidantan. It was her work that had led to the ease and usefulness of automatic translation between the two languages. Even aside from automatic translation, Ashiban suspected that her mother's work was the basis for nearly every translation between Raksamat and Gidantan for very nearly a century. That was one reason why Ciwril Xidyla was as revered as she was, by everyone in the system. Translation devices like this little blob on a clip had made communication possible between Raksamat and Gidanta. Had made peaceful agreement possible, let people talk to each other whenever they needed it. Had probably saved lives. But. "We can't be the first to notice this."

The Sovereign set the groundcar moving again. "Noticing something and realizing it's important aren't the same thing. And maybe lots of people have noticed, but they don't say anything because it suits them to have things as they are. We need to tell the Terraforming Council. We need to tell the Assembly. We need to tell everybody, and we need to retranslate the treaty. We need more people to actually learn both languages instead of only using that thing." She gestured toward the translator clipped to Ashiban's collar.

"We need the translator to be better, Sovereign. Not everyone can easily learn another language." More people learning the two languages ought to help with that. More people with firsthand experience to correct the data. "But we need the translator to know more than what my mother learned." Had the translations been unchanged since her mother's time? Ashiban didn't think that was likely. But the girl's guess that it suited at least some of the powers that be to leave problems – perhaps certain problems – uncorrected struck Ashiban as sadly possible. "Sovereign, who's going to listen to us?"

"I am the Sovereign of Iss!" the girl declared. "And you are the daughter of Ciwril Xidyla! They had better listen to us."

* * *

Shortly after the sky began to lighten, they came to a real, honest-to-goodness road. The Sovereign pulled the groundcar up to its edge and then stopped. The road curved away on either side, so that they could see only the brief stretch in front of them, and trees all around. "Right or left?" asked the Sovereign. There was no signpost, no indication which way town was, or even any evidence beyond the existence of the road itself that there was a town anywhere nearby.

When Ashiban didn't answer, the Sovereign slid out of the driver's seat and walked out to the center of the road. Stood looking one way, and then the other.

"I think the town is to the right," she said, when she'd gotten back in. "And I don't think we have time to get away."

"I don't understand," Ashiban protested. But then she saw lights through the trees, to the right. "Maybe they'll drive on by." But she remembered the young woman's story of how a Raksamat settler had been received in the town yesterday. And she was here to begin with because of rising tensions between Gidanta and Raksamat, and whoever had shot their flier down, days ago, had fairly obviously wanted to increase those tensions, not defuse them.

And they were sitting right in the middle of the path to the nearest Raksamat farmstead. Which had no defenses beyond a few hunting guns and maybe a lock on the front door.

A half dozen groundcars came around the bend in the road. Three of them the sort made to carry loads, but the wide, flat cargo areas held people instead of cargo. Several of those people were carrying guns.

The first car in the procession slowed as it approached the path where Ashiban and the Sovereign sat. Began to turn, and stopped when its lights brushed their stolen groundcar. Nothing more happened for the next few minutes, except that the people in the backs of the cargo cars leaned and craned to see what was going on.

"Expletive," said the Sovereign. "I'm getting out to talk to them. You should stay here."

"What could you possibly say to them, child?" But there wasn't much good doing anything else, either.

"I don't know," replied the girl. "But you should stay here."

Slowly the Sovereign opened the groundcar door, slid out again. Closed the door, pulled her cloth up over her face, and walked out into the pool of light at the edge of the road.

Getting out of the passenger seat would be slow and painful, and Ashiban really didn't want to. But the Sovereign looked so small standing by the side of the road, facing the other groundcar. She opened her own door and clambered awkwardly down. Just as she came up behind the Sovereign, the passenger door of the groundcar facing them opened, and a woman stepped out onto the road.

"I am the Sovereign of Iss," announced the Sovereign. Murmured the translator clipped to Ashiban's shirt. "Just what do you think you're doing here?" Attempting more or less credibly to sound imperious even despite the one hand holding the cloth over her face, but the girl's voice shook a little.

"Glad to see you safe, Sovereign," said the woman, "but I am constable of this precinct and you are blocking my path. Town's that way." She pointed back along the way the procession of groundcars had come.

"And where are you going, Constable," asked the Sovereign, "with six groundcars and dozens of people behind you, some of them with guns? There's nothing behind us but trees."

"There are three weevil farmsteads in those woods," cried someone from the back of a groundcar. "And we've had it with the weevils thinking they own our planet. Get out of the way, girl!"

"We know the Raksamat tried to kill you," put in the constable. "We know they shot down your flier. It wasn't on the news, but people talk. Do they want a war? An excuse to try to kill us all? We won't be pushed any farther. The weevils are here illegally, and they will get off this planet and back to their ships. Today if I have anything to say about it."

"This is Ciwril Xidyla's daughter next to me," said the Sovereign. "She came here to work things out, not to try to kill anyone."

"That would be the Ciwril Xidyla who translated the treaty so the weevils could read it to suit them, would it?" asked the constable. There was a murmur of agreement from behind her. "And wave it in our faces like we agreed to something we didn't?"

Somewhere overhead, the sound of a flier engine. Ashiban's first impulse was to run into the trees. Instead, she said, "Constable, the Sovereign is right. I came here to try to help work out these difficulties. Whoever tried to kill us, they failed, and the sooner we get back to work, the better."

"We don't mean you any harm, old woman," said the constable. "But you'd best get out of our way, because we are coming through here, whether you move or not."

"To do what?" asked Ashiban. "To kill the people on those farmsteads behind us?"

"We're not going to kill anybody," said the constable, plainly angry at the suggestion. "We just want them to know we mean business. If you won't move, we'll move you." And when neither Ashiban nor the Sovereign replied, the constable turned to the people on the back of the vehicle behind her and gestured them forward.

A moment of hesitation, and then one of them jumped off the groundcar, and another few followed.

Beside Ashiban the Sovereign took a shaking breath and cried, "I am the Sovereign of Iss! You will go back to the town." The advancing people froze, staring at her.

"You're a little girl in a minor priesthood, who ought to be home minding her studies," said the constable. "It's not your fault your grandmother made the mistake of negotiating with the weevils, and it's not your fault your aunt quit and left you in the middle of this, but don't be thinking you've got any authority here." The people who had leaped off the groundcar still hesitated.

The Sovereign, visibly shaking now, pointed at the constable with her free hand. "I am the voice of the planet! You can't tell the planet to get out of your way."

"Constable!" said one of the people who had come off the groundcar. "A moment." And went over to say something quiet in the constable's ear.

The Sovereign said, low enough so only Ashiban could hear it, "*Tell the planet to get out of the way?* How could I say something so stupid?"

And then lights came sweeping around the lefthand bend of the road, and seven or eight groundcars came into view, and stopped short of where the constable stood in the road.

A voice called out, "This is Delegate Garas of the Terraforming Council Enforcement Commission." Ashiban knew that name. Everyone in the system knew that name. Delegate Garas was the highest-ranking agent of the Gidantan Enforcement Commission, and answered directly to the

Terraforming Council. "Constable, you have overstepped your authority." A man stepped out from behind the glare of the lights. "This area is being monitored." The sound of a flier above, louder. "Anyone who doesn't turn around and go home this moment will be officially censured."

The person who had been talking to the constable said, "We were just about to leave, Delegate."

"Good," said the delegate. "Don't delay on my account, please. And, Constable, I'll meet with you when I get into town this afternoon."

THE COMMISSION AGENTS settled Ashiban and the Sovereign into the back of a groundcar, and poured them hot barley tea from a flask. The tea hardly had time to cool before Delegate Garas slid into the passenger seat in front and turned to speak to them. "Sovereign. Elder." With little bows of his head. "I apologize for not arriving sooner."

"We had everything under control," said the Sovereign, loftily, cloth still held over her face. Though, sitting close next to her as Ashiban was, she could feel the Sovereign was still shaking.

"Did you now. Well. We only were able to start tracking you when we found the crash site. Which took much longer than it should have. The surveillance in the High Mires and the surrounding areas wasn't functioning properly."

"That's a coincidence," Ashiban remarked, drily.

"Not a coincidence at all," the delegate replied. "It was sabotage. An inside job."

The Sovereign made a small, surprised noise. "It wasn't the weev... the Raksamat?"

"Oh, they were involved, too." Delegate Garas found a cup somewhere in the seat beside him, poured himself some barley tea. "There's a faction of Raksamat – I'm sure this won't surprise you, Elder – who resent the illegal settlers for grabbing land unauthorized, but who also feel that the Assembly will prefer certain families once Raksamat can legally come down to the planet, and between the two all the best land and opportunities will be gone. There is also – Sovereign, I don't know if you follow this sort of thing – a faction of Gidanta who believe that the Terraforming Council is, in their turn, arranging things to profit themselves and their friends, and leaving everyone else out. Their accusations may in fact be entirely accurate and just, but that is of course no reason to conspire with aggrieved Raksamat to somehow be rid of both Council and Assembly and divide the spoils between themselves."

"That's a big somehow," Ashiban observed.

"It is," Delegate Garas acknowledged. "And they appear not to have had much talent for that sort of undertaking. We have most of them under arrest." The quiet, calm voice of a handheld murmured, too low for Ashiban's translator clip to pick up. "Ah," said Delegate Garas. "That's all of them now. The trials should be interesting. Fortunately, they're not my department. It's Judicial's problem now. So, as I said, we were only able to even begin tracking you sometime yesterday. And we were already in the area looking for you when we got a call from a concerned citizen who had overheard plans for the constable's little outing, so it was simple enough to show up. We were pleasantly surprised to find you both here, and relatively well." He took a drink of his tea. "We've let the team tracking you know they can go home now. As the both of you can, once we've interviewed you so we know what happened to you."

"Home!" The Sovereign was indignant. "But what about the talks?"

"The talks are suspended, Sovereign. And your interpreter is dead. The Council will have to appoint a new one. And let's be honest – both of you were involved mainly for appearance's sake. In fact, I've wondered over the last day or two if you weren't brought into this just so you could die and provide a cause for trouble."

This did not mollify the Sovereign. "Appearance's sake! I am the Sovereign of Iss!"

"Yes, yes," Delegate Garas agreed, "so you told everyone just a short while ago."

"And it worked, too," observed Ashiban. Out the window, over the delegate's shoulder, the sun shone on the once again deserted road. She shivered, remembering the cracked flier windshield, the pilot slumped over the controls.

"You can't have these talks without me," the Sovereign insisted. "I'm the voice of the planet." She looked at Ashiban. "I am going to learn Raksamat. And Ashiban Xidyla can learn Gidantan. We won't need any expletive interpreter. And we can fix the handheld translators."

"That might take a while, Sovereign," Ashiban observed.

The Sovereign lifted the cloth covering her mouth just enough to show her frown to Ashiban. "We already talked about this, Ashiban Xidyla. And I am the Voice of Iss. I will learn quickly."

"Sovereign," said Delegate Garas, "those handheld translators are a good thing. Can you imagine what the past hundred years would have been like without them? People can learn Raksamat, or Gidantan, but as Ashiban Xidyla points out, that takes time, and in the meanwhile people still have to talk to each other. Those handheld translators have prevented all sorts of problems."

"We know, Delegate," Ashiban said. "We were just talking about it, before the townspeople got here. But they could be better."

"Well," said Delegate Garas. "You may be right, at that. And if any of this were my concern in the least, I'd be getting a headache about now. Fortunately, it's not my problem. I'll see you ladies on your way home and..."

"Translation unavailable," exclaimed the Sovereign, before he could finish. Got out of the groundcar, set her empty cup on the roof with a smack, opened the driver's door, and slid in. Closed the door behind her.

"Young lady," Delegate Garas began.

"I am the Voice of Iss!" the Sovereign declared. She did something with the controls and the groundcar started up with a low hum. Delegate Garas frowned, looked back at Ashiban.

Ashiban wanted to go home. She wanted to rest, and go back to her regular, everyday life, doing nothing much.

There had never been much point to doing anything much, not with a mother like Ciwril Xidyla. Anyone's wildest ambitions would pale into nothing beside Ashiban's mother's accomplishments. And Ashiban had never been a terribly ambitious person. Had always wished for an ordinary life. Had mostly had it, at least the past few decades. Until now.

Those Raksamat farmers wanted an ordinary life, too, and the Gidanta townspeople. The Sovereign herself had been taken from an ordinary girlhood – or as ordinary as your life could be when your grandmother and your aunt were the voice of the planet – and thrown into the middle of this.

Delegate Garas was still watching her, still frowning. Ashiban sighed. "I don't recommend arguing, Delegate. Assassins and a flier crash in the High Mires couldn't stop us. I doubt you can do more than slow us down, and it's really better if you don't. Sovereign, I think first we should have a bath and clean clothes and something to eat. And get checked out by a doctor. And maybe get some sleep."

The Sovereign was silent for a few seconds, and then said, "All right. I agree to that. But we should start on the language lessons as soon as possible."

"Yes, child," said Ashiban, closing her eyes. "But not this very moment."

Delegate Garas laughed at that, short and sharp. But he made no protest at all as the Sovereign started the groundcar moving toward town.

COPYRIGHT

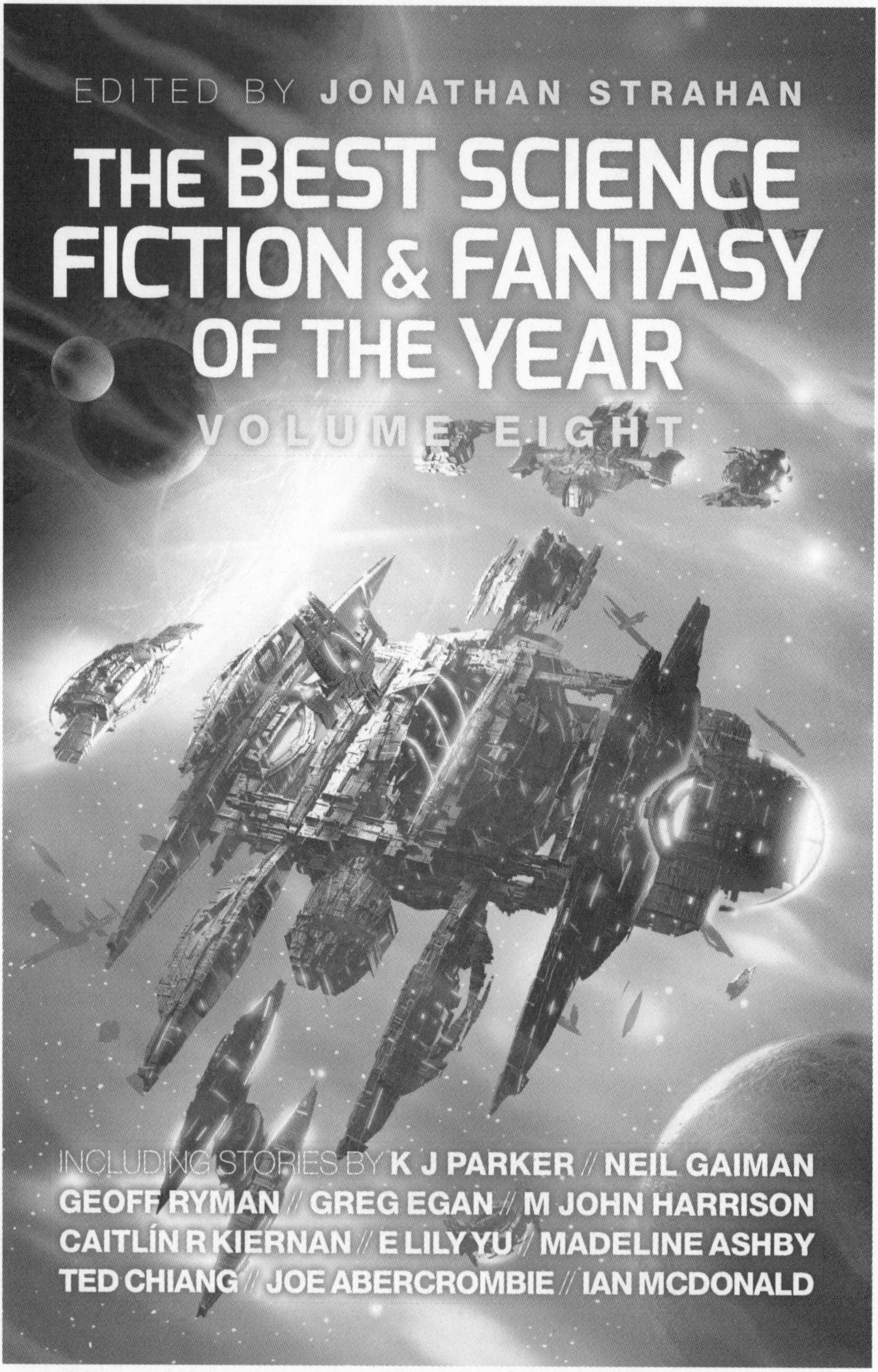
EDITED BY JONATHAN STRAHAN
THE BEST SCIENCE FICTION & FANTASY OF THE YEAR
VOLUME EIGHT
INCLUDING STORIES BY K J PARKER // NEIL GAIMAN
GEOFF RYMAN // GREG EGAN // M JOHN HARRISON
CAITLÍN R KIERNAN // E LILY YU // MADELINE ASHBY
TED CHIANG // JOE ABERCROMBIE // IAN MCDONALD

THE BEST SCIENCE FICTION & FANTASY OF THE YEAR

VOLUME EIGHT

From the inner realms of humanity to the far reaches of space, these are the science fiction and fantasy tales that are shaping the genre and the way we think about the future. Multi-award winning editor Jonathan Strahan continues to shine a light on the very best writing, featuring both established authors and exciting new talents.

Within you will find twenty-eight incredible tales, showing the ever growing depth and diversity that science fiction and fantasy continues to enjoy. These are the brightest stars in our firmament, lighting the way to a future filled with astonishing stories about the way we are, and the way we could be.

FEATURING:

GREG EGAN • YOON HA LEE • NEIL GAIMAN • E LILY YU
K J PARKER • GEOFF RYMAN • M BENNARDO • RAMEZ NAAM
TED CHIANG • PRIYA SHARMA • RICHARD PARKS • LAVIE TIDHAR
M JOHN HARRISON • JOE ABERCROMBIE • JAMES PATRICK KELLY
CHARLIE JANE ANDERS • THOMAS OLDE HEUVELT
BENJANUN SRIDUANGKAEW • ELEANOR ARNASON
IAN R MACLEOD • SOFIA SAMATAR • AN OWOMOYELA
KARIN TIDBECK • MADELINE ASHBY • CAITLÍN R KIERNAN
ROBERT REED • IAN MCDONALD • VAL NOLAN

UK ISBN: 978-1-78108-215-7 // US ISBN: 978-1-78108-216-4

EDITED BY JONATHAN STRAHAN
THE BEST SCIENCE FICTION & FANTASY OF THE YEAR
VOLUME NINE
FEATURING STORIES BY
LAUREN BEUKES
PAOLO BACIGALUPI
JOE ABERCROMBIE
K. J. PARKER
KEN LIU
GARTH NIX
ELIZABETH BEAR
KAI ASHANTE WILSON
RACHEL SWIRSKY
CAITLÍN R. KIERNAN
GENEVIEVE VALENTINE
AND MANY MORE

THE BEST SCIENCE FICTION & FANTASY OF THE YEAR

VOLUME NINE

Science fiction and fantasy has never been more diverse or vibrant, and 2014 has provided a bountiful crop of extraordinary stories. These stories are about the future, worlds beyond our own, the realms of our imaginations and dreams but, more importantly, they are the stories of ourselves. Featuring best-selling writers and emerging talents, here are some of the most exciting genre writers working today.

Multi-award winning editor Jonathan Strahan once again brings you the best stories from the past year. Within you will find twenty-eight amazing tales from authors across the globe, displaying why science fiction and fantasy are genres increasingly relevant to our turbulent world.

FEATURING:

KELLY LINK • HOLLY BLACK • KEN LIU • USMAN T. MALIK
LAUREN BEUKES • PAOLO BACIGALUPI • JOE ABERCROMBIE
GENEVIEVE VALENTINE • NICOLA GRIFFITH • CAITLÍN R. KIERNAN
GREG EGAN • K. J. PARKER • RACHEL SWIRSKY • ALICE SOLA KIM
GARTH NIX • KARL SCHROEDER • ELLEN KLAGES • PETER WATTS
KAI ASHANTE WILSON • MICHAEL SWANWICK • ELEANOR ARNASON
JAMES PATRICK KELLY • IAN MCDONALD • AMAL EL-MOHTAR
TIM MAUGHAN • ELIZABETH BEAR • THEODORA GOSS

UK ISBN: 978-1-78108-308-6 // US ISBN: 978-1-78108-309-3

FEATURING STORIES BY KEN MACLEOD • PAT CADIGAN • ELLEN KLAGES
ALASTAIR REYNOLDS • KAREN LORD • GREG EGAN • LINDA NAGATA
ADAM ROBERTS • HANNU RAJANIEMI • ALIETTE DE BODARD AND MORE
REACH FOR INFINITY
EDITED BY JONATHAN STRAHAN
"One of the most respected editors in the genre."
New York Times best-selling author Sean Williams

HUMANITY AMONG THE STARS

What happens when we reach out into the vastness of space? What hope for us amongst the stars?

Multi-award winning editor Jonathan Strahan brings us fourteen new tales of the future, from some of the finest science fiction writers in the field.

"A strong collection of stories that readers of science fiction will certainly enjoy." Locus Magazine on Engineering Infinity

"**Stands as a solid and at times striking contribution to 'the ongoing discussion about what science fiction is in the 21st century.'"** The Speculative Scotsman

"If you want science fiction, rather than space opera, this is for you." Total SciFi Online

FEATURING:

GREG EGAN • ALIETTE DE BODARD • IAN MCDONALD
KARL SCHROEDER • PAT CADIGAN • KAREN LORD
ELLEN KLAGES • ADAM ROBERTS • LINDA NAGATA
HANNU RAJANIEMI • KATHLEEN ANN GOONAN • KEN MACLEOD
ALASTAIR REYNOLDS • PETER WATTS

UK ISBN: 978-1-78108-202-7 // US ISBN: 978-1-78108-203-4

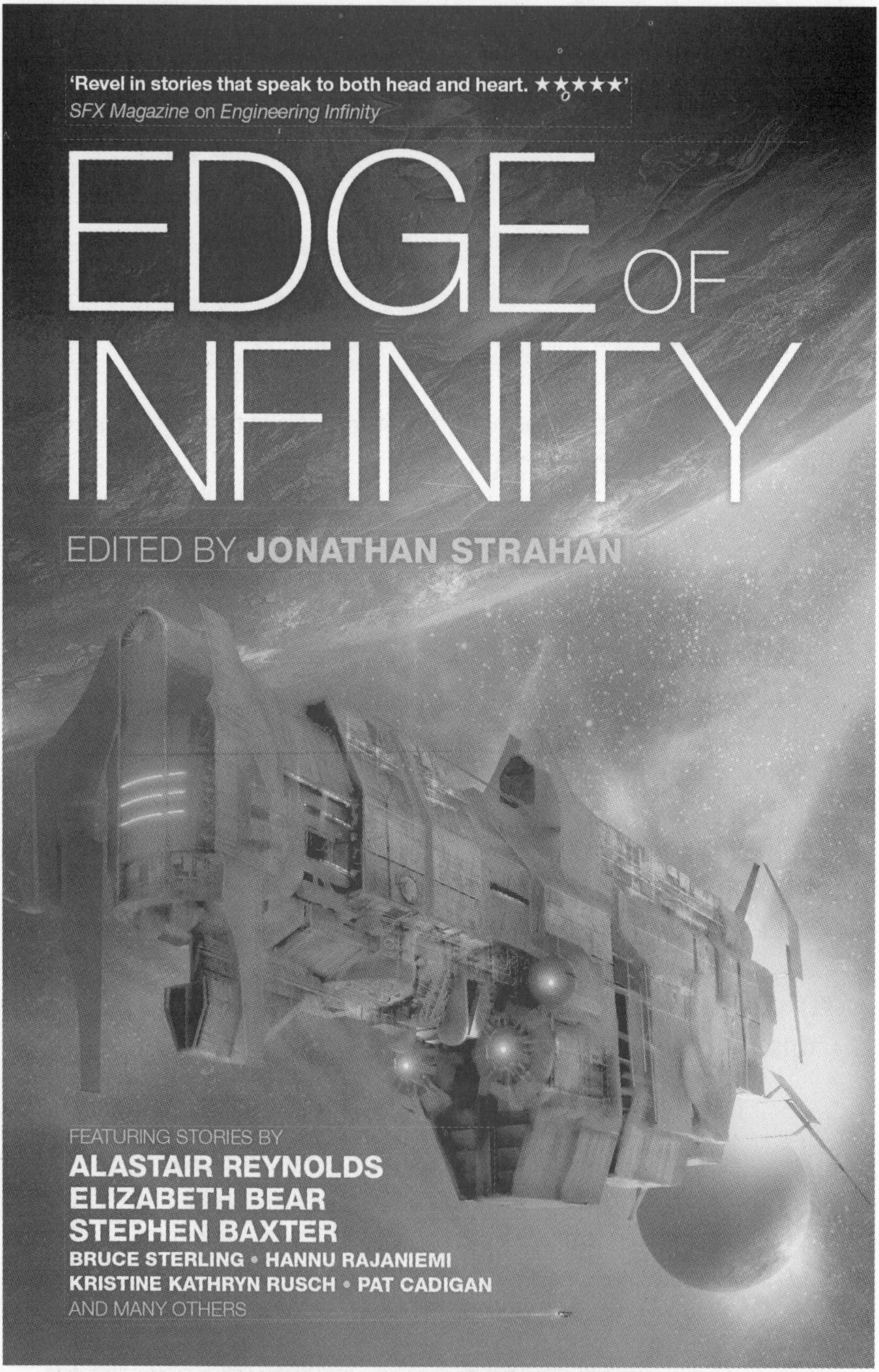

'Revel in stories that speak to both head and heart. ★★★★★'
SFX Magazine on Engineering Infinity
EDGE OF INFINITY
EDITED BY JONATHAN STRAHAN
FEATURING STORIES BY
ALASTAIR REYNOLDS
ELIZABETH BEAR
STEPHEN BAXTER
BRUCE STERLING • HANNU RAJANIEMI
KRISTINE KATHRYN RUSCH • PAT CADIGAN
AND MANY OTHERS

ONE GIANT LEAP FOR MANKIND

Those were Neil Armstrong's immortal words when he became the first human being to step onto another world. All at once, the horizon expanded; the human race was no longer Earthbound.

Edge of Infinity is an exhilarating new SF anthology that looks at the next giant leap for humankind: the leap from our home world out into the Solar System. From the eerie transformations in Pat Cadigan's "The Girl-Thing Who Went Out for Sushi" to the frontier spirit of Sandra McDonald and Stephen D. Covey's "The Road to NPS," and from the grandiose vision of Alastair Reynolds' "Vainglory" to the workaday familiarity of Kristine Kathryn Rusch's "Safety Tests," the thirteen stories in this anthology span the whole of the human condition in their race to colonise Earth's nearest neighbours.

"One of the year's most exciting anthologies." io9

FEATURING:

HANNU RAJANIEMI • ALASTAIR REYNOLDS • JAMES S. A. COREY
JOHN BARNES • STEPHEN BAXTER • KRISTINE KATHRYN RUSCH
ELIZABETH BEAR • PAT CADIGAN • GWYNETH JONES
PAUL MCAULEY • SANDRA MCDONALD • STEPHEN D. COVEY
AN OWOMOYELA • BRUCE STERLING

UK ISBN: 978-1-78108-055-9 // US ISBN: 978-1-78108-056-6